Praise For
LINDA BARLOW'S
Leaves of Fortune

"More excitement than a year of soap operas. . . .
Hard-to-put-down romantic adventure."
—*Boston Herald*

"Something for everyone . . . money, lots of it, as
well as power plays, revenge, death . . ."
—*New York Times Book Review*

"Two strong, dynamic women, a forbidden love, a
tea-importing empire started in colonial New England
by an alleged witch, a family curse—these are but
some of the elements in Linda Barlow's enthralling
contemporary saga."
—*Rave Reviews*

"From India's Himalayas to Boston's Beacon Hill,
Linda Barlow's novel of love, lust, greed, incest, and
ambition whirls at a rapid clip. . . . Imaginative twists
and shocking revelations keep the reader riveted."
—*New York City Tribune*

"A big, lush . . . thoroughly satisfying novel."
—*Chicago Tribune*

"A FAST-MOVING PAGE-TURNER."
— *News*

LINDA BARLOW

HER SISTER'S KEEPER

WARNER BOOKS

A Time Warner Company

WARNER BOOKS EDITION

Cover design by Diane Luger
Cover illustration by Jim Griffin
Hand lettering by Carl Dellacroce

Warner Books, Inc.
1271 Avenue of the Americas
New York, NY 10020

W A Time Warner Company

Printed in the United States of America

First Printing: April, 1993

10 9 8 7 6 5 4 3 2 1

For Tom Huff, aka Jennifer Wilde,
mentor, colleague, and beloved friend,
in memoriam. I miss you, Tom.

Prologue

Cornwall, 1918

The war was nearly over, and Verity Trevor Marrick was in love.

She stood alone atop the windy slope outside the corrugated tin building that served as the main office for Cadmon Clay and Porcelain, surveying the dusky green moors of her native Cornwall. The hills and the sea were changeless, but everything else, especially her own fortunes, shifted, readjusted.

This love, she knew, could ruin her. For several years she'd sought to stand alone, a free woman, capable and independent. All would have been well had it not been for the unpredictable ravages of war, the inexorability of death, and the mysteries of the human heart.

Verity gathered the folds of her somber cloak around her. She was in mourning for her father, Henry Trevor, inventor, engineer, and aviator, who had been killed two days before in the crash of one of his aeroplanes. Verity hated aeroplanes. Over and over she had pleaded with her father to give up his obsession with the things of the air, but he had never listened.

From where she stood high in the hills overlooking the moors, she had an excellent view of the gravel track that wound up toward the claypits. She watched the road for some sign of her sister Bret's approach, but all she could see was a lorry loaded with pale blocks of finished china clay picking its way carefully down the road, trailing a white cloud of claydust at it chugged along.

She tried to focus on the landscape, which was dominated by white mounds of earth—the Mountains of the Moon, as Bret had always called them—thrusting up from the ground. Known here in the St. Austell vicinity as skytips, the chalky mounds were composed of the sand and gravel that remained after the extraction of china clay, the main ingredient in fine British porcelain. Nowhere else in England were amber moors and sun-drenched meadows punctuated by ice-white mountains and tropical pools. The effect was strange, almost mystical.

But the beauty of her surroundings did not stop Verity's stomach from tightening. Was Bret as nervous about their reunion as she? Surely not. Bret had never known fear, shyness, loneliness, deprivation. As far back into childhood as Verity could remember, her sister had dwelled in the light.

As the wind shifted, the racket from the claypits struck her with increasing force. Cadmon Clay and Porcelain was a ferocious, chaotic place, but over the years she had grown accustomed to the smells, the noise, and the thick accents and rough language of the claypit workers. She reveled in the lively confusion.

The nearest claypit was just behind her, and the old beam engine screeched and clattered as it pumped the water necessary to wash the china clay out of the granite and raise it from the ever-deepening pit. More racket was caused by the squeak of tram wheels and cables, which trundled out the waste material and deposited it on the skytips.

Shading her eyes, she looked down the moors toward the port village of Charlestown, the site of the china factory that was her greatest achievement. During the war years she had revivified the part of the family business that had always fascinated her, the manufacture of English bone china. She was proud of what she had accomplished. Her only regret was that Papa had seemed never to notice. She had never been able to please him.

"What are 'ee staring at? Waiting for Bret?"

Verity jumped at the sound of Daniel's deep voice. He had an annoying habit of sneaking up on her; his ability to move his tall, big-boned body so silently never failed to surprise her. Daniel Carne, her father's enemy.

She turned, managing a raw-nerved smile. She fingered her dark hair where it was pinned at the back of her neck, searching for loose strands, hoping there were none. Were her lips and cheeks still pink where she had rouged them this morning, or had grief and apprehension brought out her pallor again? Was the arch she had penciled in her thin eyebrows still evident, or had she rubbed it off while bending over the china company accounts? She wanted to look her best for him, especially now that Bret was coming home.

"If she arrives today, she'll ring me first from Cadmon Hall."

Daniel shaded his eyes and looked down the road. She noticed his hands—large, thick-fingered, strong. She always noticed his hands, and fantasized about their pressure on her skin. "I thought ye told me she'd be here last night."

"She telephoned from London and said so. But then she's never been dependable." Verity regretted this last remark as soon as it was out. It was her blasted defensiveness speaking. Her insecurity. Her inability to believe that Daniel loved her. Her fear that he might return to Bret.

He shifted his gaze to her, his blue eyes far too guarded to reveal his feelings. Verity sensed that he too was apprehensive. "Have ye told her yet?"

"No. We spoke so briefly. And with Papa's death to deal with, it didn't seem the appropriate time."

"She'll hear it quick enough from the local gossips if not direct from 'ee."

"I'll tell her as soon as she arrives."

"Good."

There was a note of satisfaction in his voice. He wanted Bret to know. There was a fierce necessity in his tone. He needed, on some level, to hurt her. He had never let her go.

Will he ever feel that strongly toward me?

"I'd like to greet her when she comes. I'm off now for Carne Clay, but ye can ring me there anytime."

She nodded, and Daniel strode away, the wind ruffling his

black hair. She loved his sleek stride, the easy swing of his muscled arms, the proud elevation of his chin. *Behold, thou art fair, my love; comfort me with apples, for I am sick of love.*

What would happen when he saw her sister again? Would his passion rekindle? Or would Bret's return revive his oft-proclaimed determination to seek vengeance against the entire Trevor clan, herself included? Which was stronger, Daniel's hatred or his love?

Returning to her office, she sat down at the ornate Chinese desk that had once belonged to her grandfather. There was paperwork to do, accounts to reconcile. Her father's death had left a chaotic fiscal situation, the ramifications of which she had not yet determined. It was imperative that she stop dithering and concentrate.

Verity focused on her work for nearly an hour. Every account book she studied increased her unease. She'd known that Trevor Aviation had debts—her father had never been good at financial management—but she hadn't realized things were as grim as they were beginning to look. Her own business, Cadmon Clay and Porcelain, was barely surviving. The war years had been hard on British industry.

"If you're in need of funds, come to me," Daniel had whispered to her last night, the sweat still damp on his skin in the aftermath of love. "You're mine now, and I'll take care of you."

How humbling a reversal. A Trevor beholden to a Carne.

Perspiration blossomed under Verity's arms, along her spine, between her thighs. The tiny office, little more than a hut, was stuffy and hot, and the noise outside was a constant grating on her nerves. Lifting her head, she rubbed the back of her neck, then poured herself a glass of lukewarm water from the china pitcher she kept on the bookshelf. Sipping it, she gazed out her only window, a small, greasy pane of glass, which looked out over claypit 3, currently tapped out but yet to be filled.

The pit was a scar on the landscape, a ragged hole from which everything of value had been dredged. There were moments when it seemed apt that her only vista should be the gaping abyss of a claypit. Sometimes when she stared into it she felt a strange, dissociative feeling, a melding of mind and landscape almost transcendental in nature. When such moods prevailed, she couldn't distinguish between the pit she saw through her window and the pit that spiraled into the depths of her own soul.

Despite the heat of the airless office, Verity began to shiver. Her throat ached, and she thought for a moment the tears were going to fall, the tears for her father that had not come, would not come, *could* not come. She could not understand how she could be so crisp and ironed in her grief and, at the same time, so searingly insecure in her passion for her sister's former lover.

For love is strong as death; jealousy is as cruel as the grave: the coals thereof are coals of fire, which hath a most vehement flame.

It was, she knew, a love that could ruin her. The hell-cursed love of a Trevor for a Carne had been both families' legacies for centuries.

Always, or at least as long as anybody could remember, there had been the land. And on the land had been the Trevors and the Carnes.

The Carnes had been there first—a Cornish family old as the standing stones, their beginnings buried in myth. Some said they had fought the Romans and later been warriors in the armies of King Arthur. The men were drinkers, fighters, and poets. The women were mystical, sad, and wise.

The Trevors did not come to Cornwall until the sixteenth century. They were of the north, hard Yorkshire men and women from a harsher, higher country. But they were wealthy, of old aristocracy that dated back to the Norman invasion, and before that, to their patrician roots in France.

Cadmon Hall, named in tribute to the first English poet by a Trevor ancestress who loved a precise image and a metered line, had been a land grant from Elizabeth of England to the Trevors in gratitude for services rendered early in her reign. And thus the conflict began, for the grant included land the

Carnes had long claimed as their own. But they possessed no proof of ownership, and the Trevors, the interlopers, had a paper from the Queen herself.

From the start they rubbed against each other, the Carnes, the true Cornishmen, and the Trevors, widely regarded during those first few generations as foreigners. They fought over moorland, farmland, and grazing rights for sheep, and during the eighteenth century when tin and copper mining was booming, they fought over mineral rights to the earth and its treasures. Most fiercely of all, they fought over china clay. Both families wanted the hitherto barren section of the moors where Cadmon Clay spread out and developed. The Carnes claimed to have a legal deed to the land, but they could not produce it.

The men hated one another. But between the Trevor men and the Carne women, the Carne men and the Trevor women, other sentiments smoldered, emotions that simultaneously calmed and exacerbated the feuding. No one knew how many times these passions were acted upon, but there were rumors, low and close to the ground.

The first love affair sprang up in the sixteenth century, during the early years of the Trevors' tenure. Catherine, the youngest Trevor daughter, became enamored of a rough but tender lad named Michael Carne. Their romance ended when Catherine conceived a child and died during the abortion her frightened lover had arranged for her with an old Gypsy midwife. With her death, the rage of the Trevors swept down upon the Carnes. Michael died in a brawl with Catherine's brothers, and the Gypsy ended her days in prison, where, according to legend, she put a crudely rhyming curse on both families:

> *May passion's poison o-erflow each vein,*
> *May they know naught but conflict and strife,*
> *May their lads be crushed by the sin of Cain,*
> *May their lasses breed hatred in each new life.*

The curse must have been powerful, since it was fulfilled from one generation to the next. But a prophecy also dated from those days. The feuding would continue, it was whispered, until one of these hapless lads and lasses should, despite their enmity, join together in harmonious wedlock, producing a new line of children who were descendants of both the Trevors and the Carnes.

What true love has torn asunder, ran the prophecy, *only true love can heal.*

Part One

1896–99

Thou art my mother, and my sister.

The Book of Job 17:14

Chapter One

Everybody said Grandpa was dying, but Verity didn't believe it. He was arguing with Papa, just as he always did.

"If you don't get off your bloody arse and pay some attention to the business I'm leaving you," Rufus Trevor said in a voice that was feathery but firm, "you're going to ruin this family, Henry."

"Hell's bells and damnation!" Verity's father paced back and forth along the dragon's tail that curled on the Chinese carpet beside Grandpa's sickbed. "Why don't you stop worrying about your wretched china clay and get the sleep the doctor ordered."

"The doctor's a damned fool. The only sleep I'll be having now is that bloody eternal nap, and for that I can wait, goddammit, and so can you!" Grandpa plucked at the coverlet with his long, bony fingers. "How can I rest when I have a rare fine dreamer for a son?"

"Too bad you won't exert yourself to live long enough to see my dreams come true," said Verity's tall, red-bearded father. "You're still a vigorous man, so why are you so determined to die?"

Please don't shout at each other, Verity whispered inside. *Can't you ever be friends?*

"I'm a realist, not a fool, so cut that nonsense. Like it or not, somebody's got to take over Cadmon Clay and run the place. It's up to you, boy." Grandpa's voice had diminished in tone and volume but was no weaker in will. "You've got the character to make something of yourself." His voice grew resonant. "I never got the chance to start manufacturing

11

porcelain again from our fine china clay, but that's a task I expect you to take on, son.''

"I don't know the clay business. And I'm no good at dealing with the laborers. Besides, I have my own work.''

"Piffle. Give it up, boy. That tinkering you do isn't man's work. Where you got this desire to waste your time among those moldy books and strange mechanical contraptions I've never understood.''

It was exactly the sort of argument they always had, two men who looked alike, spoke alike, and responded to everything in the same stubborn, irascible way. The only difference between them was that Papa was more of a mystery. Grandpa never hesitated to proclaim what he thought about everything, but with Papa you never knew. One thing was for certain, though—Papa had no interest in Grandpa's precious china clay.

Verity was only eight, but she understood that her family owned Cadmon Clay and Porcelain, one of the largest clay-mining operations in the St. Austell region of Cornwall. The porcelain-making part of the company was now defunct, although Grandpa had dreamed of starting it up again. The china that had been produced there during its forty years of operation in the preceding century was much prized by collectors.

Verity had always loved to go to the claypits with Grandpa, who would hold her hand as she watched the workers scour the kaolin out of the granite rock where it formed. The process held a fascination for her that Papa didn't share. Grandpa couldn't fathom how he could have sired a son whose passions were not for the things of the earth but for the phantoms of the air.

Whereas Rufus had devoted his entire adult life to Cornwall's minerals—tin, copper, and, most extensively, china clay—Henry dreamed of conquering the more ethereal realms of aviation. Why should he take an interest in unlocking white powder from granite when he could be building a flying machine that would take to the air under its own power and remain aloft? "Mark my words," he'd said to his daughter many times, "in our lifetime people will fly so effortlessly that the sky will seem familiar, and these earthbound days most strange.''

"Damn bloody fairy tale, this aviation business," Grandpa said now. "The only reality's the earth beneath your feet, which is probably where I'll be before sunrise.''

"No, Grandpa," Verity whispered, speaking for the first time.

He lifted his head from the pillow to look in her direction. "Hello, pumpkin. You're so little and quiet, fading into the shadows with your dark hair and eyes, that I didn't even realize you were there. They've got you in for the bloomin' finale, ey? Well, come on over here and give your old grand-dad a kiss.''

Verity sped to his side. With all his cursing, he didn't sound as if he was losing his vital life force, despite the grim look on the doctor's face and the whispering of the servants. But his hands were frail as they closed over hers, and his cheek was papery when she touched it with her lips. His white beard, which had once been red, like her father's, was so wispy now it reminded her of one of the many paintings about the house of silk-robed Mandarin elders, old and wise and nearly hairless.

A weak heart, the doctor had decreed. Still, she didn't believe he was going to die, that he wouldn't be around to yell at the servants or tell his bawdy jokes, that he wouldn't come storming home from the claypits, complaining of the ineffectiveness of his pit bosses or the laziness of his laborers. That he would no longer take her out on the moors, wave his big hand over the land, and boast that all of it, as far as the eye could see, had belonged to the Trevors once upon a time.

"Times were better then, lass," he had said to her. "People knew their places; it was all a matter of degree—master and servant, lord and churl. There was none of this 'organize the laborers into unions' sort of talk. You wanted someone to do something and he jumped to it, anxious to please you, grateful for the work. But now the world is changing, and I don't know if I want to be around to see it.''

"Yes you do, Grandpa, if only to complain all the more loudly.''

"Cheeky baggage," her grandfather had chided her, laughing, before sweeping her slight body up into his arms and carrying her off to the claypits to watch the digging and the hauling, the refining and the drying, which were all part of the process that produced lumps and blocks and pyramids of pure white china clay.

"Don't let 'em hound you into kissing me after I'm dead, pumpkin," he said now. "Disgusting practice, in my opinion. I just want to be wrapped up and shoved into the ground, with none of this mournful tripe beforehand. I want to be remembered alive and kicking, not stiff and cold."

"Grandpa, stop saying that. You're not—"

"None of those tears now, girl. This is what we all come to sooner or later. No point fussing about it. We are all of the earth, and she takes us in the end. That's the truth of things, no matter how much your father may try to deny it. So do your best to get him to be sensible about the claypits. Damn me, if you were ten years older and a boy, I could die in peace!"

"Well, I'm not a boy, but you can count on me, Grandpa, I swear. I'll take care of the clay company if Papa doesn't want to do it. So what if I'm a girl? You always told me I could do anything!"

He smiled and touched her cheek, then he told Papa in his most scathing voice that he ought to be ashamed of having a daughter who was more devoted to the family business than he was. In response, Papa bent over him and kissed him on the forehead, then on the sunken cheeks, and then, fleetingly, right on the mouth, to which Grandpa responded with a disgusted sound. As he turned away, Verity was astonished to see tears rivering down her father's face.

That night, unable to sleep, Verity crept back into Grandpa's bedroom. Papa was still there, sitting beside him, but he had nodded off in his easy chair. Verity heard his light snoring, as well as her grandfather's labored breathing.

She tiptoed to the bed and stood beside it, looking down upon that dear old face, now so pale and hollow. Rex, Grandpa's faithful Irish setter, who had been curled on the carpet beside the bed, got up stiffly and pressed his snout against her, giving a halfhearted thump of his tail. Then he put his chin on the bed and stared hopefully at Grandpa's face.

Without warning, Grandpa's eyelids lifted. Looking directly at Verity, he said, "Get me the box. Open it. Quickly."

"What box, Grandpa?"

"From my desk. Hidden. Underneath." He coughed and gasped for breath. Verity jumped as she felt one of his hands move from his side and fiercely grasp her own. Rex's tail began to wag at the sound of his master's voice. He pressed his cold nose against the hand.

"I had a dream," Grandpa said, forcing out the words now. "Deathbed rot, maybe, but 'tis true that an injustice was done. Dammit, child, I don't believe in God, never have, but that dream—" His entire body shuddered. "Don't want to die with that sin on my soul. Be a good girl now. Get me the box."

"I'll get it, Grandpa. I'll go downstairs to the library and get it right away. Just let me wake Papa, so you won't be alone—"

"No, no." Grandpa shook his head weakly from side to side. His entire body had gone rigid and Verity noticed that his lips were a dusky blue. "China clay," he gasped. His eyes seemed to be fixed upon the face of the Buddha in the Chinese wall hanging on the wall directly opposite his bed. "In my desk. Chinese."

"Grandpa, I don't understand." She was frightened; tears were prickling in her eyes. Was the box he was referring to Chinese, or was his mind wandering? She didn't want to disappoint him. He seemed so frantic. "Papa," she said loudly. "Papa, wake up."

Her father jolted upright in his chair. "Verity?" He blinked the sleep from his eyes. "What are you doing here at this hour?"

"Grandpa wants me to fetch a box for him from his desk. He had a nightmare, and—"

"Injustice," Grandpa said clearly. He was squeezing her fingers, hard enough to hurt. Then, slowly, the emotion faded from his eyes, leaving them opaque. His fingers relaxed and fell back to the bed.

In her mind she knew what the sudden limpness meant, but her heart could not accept it. ''I'll get the box for you, Grandpa,'' she whispered and ran from the room, rushing through the shadowy hallways that would normally have frightened her. When she reached the library she frantically searched her grandfather's desk, every drawer, every cranny, and every square inch *underneath*, but she found no box. Nor anything Chinese. Grandpa's library was the one place in the house that wasn't filled with Chinese furnishings and ornaments. It was an ordinary, masculine, English gentleman's study. It contained no mystery box, or any evidence of injustice.

Verity continued her quest, which she regarded as a sacred mission. She searched until she collapsed, curled on the floor in her nightgown, her bare feet freezing, tears sticky on her cheeks.

In the morning she woke to her father's voice confirming that Grandpa was dead. Her tears spilled, hot and stinging, partly for Grandpa and partly because the way Papa was holding her opened a hole in time, dropping her into an earlier year when he had told her in the same manner and with almost the same words that her mother was dead, gone forever, and that Verity would never again know the warmth of Mummy's slender body, the reassurance of her laughter, the exotic scent of her fine Chinese herbs, or the angel touch of her soft black hair against her cheeks.

''Would you like to see him?'' Papa asked.

She had never seen her mother's body, which was lying for all time in her wrecked sailboat beneath the surface of the sea. In fact, Verity had never seen anybody dead before, and wasn't sure she wanted to, but she didn't want Papa to think she was afraid. So she followed him down the silent hallway to Grandpa's room.

She hesitated on the threshold, conscious of the great change that had come over the room since the preceding evening. It had always been a noisy place, windows thrown open to let in fresh air and birdsong, an antique clock that clicked and gonged, the scratchy sound of one of those newfangled phonographs—for Grandpa loved gadgets and collected all sorts of useless things—the dry rustle of paper as he turned the pages of his books, the blustery sound of his voice.

This morning the room was tomblike. Although it was full daylight, the twelve-foot windows were shut and draped against the sun. The ancient oaken bedstead where generations of Trevors had entered and gone out of the world was draped also, black hangings having replaced the rich maroon and gold with which she was familiar. There was no music and no one had wound the clock.

The air had a cloying, perfumed scent that reminded Verity of church. She realized it must be coming from the fat yellow tapers that formed a rectangle around the bed. The candles cast dancing shadows on the Chinese rugs that covered the floor and sent wavering smoke up to obscure the face of the Buddha, vacant and serene, who sat meditating in the misty portrait that hung on the wall.

She stopped near the foot of the bed, wrapping her arms around her in a self-protective gesture. All she could think of was how gentle Grandpa had been with her since Mummy's death. He'd bought her a pony—her beloved Ginger—and taught her to ride, and in the autumn he had taken her grouse hunting with him and promised her that when she was ten years old he would give her her very own shotgun and teach her to shoot.

"Looks like I'll never have myself a grandson," he had said. "But no matter; the Trevor women have always been the backbone of the family anyhow. Most of the men have been a worthless lot. And that goes for your father as well, blast the lad, despite his nonsense talk of being made for greater things."

Verity couldn't imagine many things greater and more exciting than making the mountains of white clay slag that rose so high they towered over the moorland and brushed the glassy surface of the sky. Only a king or a god could make mountains, and to her Grandpa was both of these.

But even a king could die.

He lay in the middle of the bed, his head propped on two thin pillows, his body covered from toe to throat with a stiff sheet. His face was empty of expression, rigid as stone. She had heard it said that the dead appeared peaceful, as if relieved that their suffering had come to an end, but Grandpa just looked blank. All the emotion that life had written on his face had been erased, swept away as if it had never been. Knowing Grandpa, she'd expected him to be enraged and incredulous that death had presumed to challenge and defeat him. She'd believed it would still be possible to glimpse some remnants of his personality. Instead, his life force had utterly withdrawn from his flesh. What remained had nothing more to do with Grandpa than a teapot had to do with the rich hot liquid inside.

Gingerly, she reached out a hand and touched him. He was cold. She jerked her hand away. She couldn't believe human flesh could ever feel so cold. It seemed a violation of nature, somehow, and it frightened her. This must be how her mother's body had felt after she drowned. Cold and rubbery.

We are all of the earth, and she takes us in the end. Grandpa had seemed so resigned to it, but Verity's heart rebelled. "Come back," she whispered. Her throat was tight and her eyes were swollen and burning. "I love you, Grandpa. I don't want the earth to take you. Oh, please. Don't leave me all alone."

A vast and empty silence answered her. She would never hear his booming voice again. Never again would he toss her over his shoulders. Never again would he praise her or tease her or even yell at her. He wouldn't be here to protect her from Miss Lynchpole, her new governess, who forced her to spend every single hour of every single day indoors at her books. Miss Lynchpole believed that young ladies should be angels of silence and propriety, industrious as ants, straight-shouldered and dainty as princesses. Never again would Grandpa laugh at the governess behind her back, calling her Miss Lunchpail or Miss Lynchmob, and telling Verity not to worry, she wouldn't last long.

With Grandpa dead and Papa so obsessed with his flying machines that he had no time to spend with his daughter, who was left to play with her? To make her laugh? To love her?

Over the whimpers issuing from her throat, Verity heard a slight whining behind her. Rex was there, his tail between his legs, his huge dark eyes staring at his master's body with what appeared to be an ancient and sorrowful comprehension.

Verity knelt and put her arm around the dog, who nuzzled her and licked her fingers. "You miss him, too, don't you, Rex?"

The dog's thick silky coat absorbed her tears.

The following day the body of Rufus Trevor was moved to the Great Hall and the broad oak doors were flung open so the local farmers, villagers, and clay laborers could come, if they wished, to pay their respects. Verity wanted to protest that Grandpa had requested that there be no elaborate ceremony, but she knew Papa and Aunt Dorothy and Miss Lynchpole wouldn't listen to her. They never did. Anyway, these formal obsequies had been the Trevor custom for generations.

People came. Verity was astonished at how many filed through the hallway, under the high wooden beams of the most ancient section of Cadmon Hall, perhaps to reflect upon the incontrovertible evidence that even the wealthy and the powerful will be laid low in the end.

It was toward the end of the viewing hours that the Piper appeared. He was a fair-haired young man, sinuous and curiously light on his feet, with the most angelic face Verity had ever seen, at least until she looked into his eyes, which were dancing with mad blue fire.

He came alone, as the sun was failing. Rex growled and shifted fretfully, and Verity was forced to seize his collar and hold on tight.

The fair-haired man approached the catafalque from the opposite side of the spot where Verity and her family stood. He was clad in the white-stained jacket, cap, and trousers of a clay worker. Close up she could see he was not so young at all. His face, which had seemed so beautiful from a distance, was marred with lines and ruddy with the perpetual flush of strong drink. His golden hair was turning birchen at the temples, and the body which moved with such grace was slack-muscled and thickened around the middle.

He reached into his pocket and removed a small wooden shepherd's flute. Poising it against his lips, he began to pipe a sprightly air that would have been far more appropriate at a wedding or a festival than at a wake. As he played, he gazed into the death mask of Rufus Trevor, his eyes as merry as a gypsy's on a midsummer's eve.

Verity heard the harsh drawing in of her father's breath, but nobody moved, nobody stopped him, perhaps because the tune was a brief one, and they were all so startled. When it was done, the fair-haired man removed the pipe from his lips and smirked at the body.

"May that sing 'ee straight to hell, ye thievin', cheatin' bastard," he said loudly, then spat into Grandpa's face, his saliva tracking down the rock-cold cheeks like freezing tears.

There was an outcry then, but the golden-haired man danced out of the way of those who tried to seize him. He turned and ran laughing from the Great Hall, while Miss Lynchpole, who had been standing solemnly next to Papa, patting his arm every time his eyes misted over, said, "I wasn't aware that Trenwythan boasted a village madman."

"That wasn't a madman," Verity's father said. "That was Jory Carne. He's sane enough, except when his wits are muddied by gin. The Carnes and the Trevors have been enemies for generations."

"Indeed?" Miss Lynchpole's tone was very dry. "Why?"

"All the usual reasons. A love affair gone wrong, a mysterious death, some disputed land, and the bottle."

That night in her dreams, Verity's grandfather's shrouded body floated down a sluggish river toward the dead-dark sea, rocking to the breathy rhythms of mad-eyed Piper, who reached out to take her hand.

Chapter Two

It was wicked, she knew, but Verity hated her new stepmother. Not only had Miss Lynchpole taken over the household and stolen her father's affection, but she was also determined to exile her stepdaughter from the only home she had ever known, Cadmon Hall. She was to be sent to boarding school.

"Oh no, please," Verity said when told. "I wouldn't be happy away from home."

"Nonsense," said the former Miss Lynchpole. "You'll receive an excellent education and you'll make new friends."

I won't, Verity thought. Although she was comfortable enough with people she knew well, she'd never found it easy to talk to strangers, and she couldn't imagine herself marooned for an entire school term in a dormitory full of strange girls.

Papa had married Miss Lynchpole two months after Grandpa's death. Verity knew now that she ought to have suspected it would happen: Miss Lynchpole was pretty. Her figure was petite and she had hair the color of yellow leaves. Her blue eyes always looked mildly surprised, which her father seemed to find charming, but Verity knew better. She had seen those wide eyes harden and those dainty hands clench into the fists that held the switch she used to enforce discipline, a tactic to which none of Verity's former governesses had ever found it necessary to resort.

After the wedding, which was a quiet affair befitting a house in mourning, Miss Lynchpole had informed Verity that from now on she was to call her Mummy. Verity declined on the grounds that she had a mother, even if she was dead.

"You barely remember your mother."

"I do so. I remember her very well."

It was true. Although Alison Trevor had died three years ago, she remained a vivid presence for her daughter. Verity's memories were composed of loving words and whispers, warm touches, lingering scents. At least once a day she went to the picture gallery on the second floor where Alison's smiling portrait had been added to the dusty portraits of the Trevor dead.

Mummy's hair was purest black while Verity's was brown, her roses-and-cream face a perfect oval while Verity's, with her too-sharp chin and her too-thin lips, was angular and pale. But the likeness was there. Aunt Dorothy had once remarked that God had taken Alison's flawless visage and reproduced it in her only child, but just before sending Verity into the world, He'd passed His hand over her features, blurring them slightly, dulling the vibrant colors, removing all possibility of beauty with a flick of His wrist.

Verity also felt her mother's presence in the many lovely things scattered through Cadmon Hall that had belonged to her, relics from her life in China, where her father had been a missionary. There were Chinese rugs and wall hangings, hooked and embroidered of the most delicate silk. There were lacquered tables, chests, and desks, many of them exquisitely gilded. There were bronze statues of horses, dragons, birds, and meditating Buddhas. There were paintings, both pastoral and mercantile—scenes of quiet family life under willows and ginkgo trees, images of shipping and harbors and busy Chinese scurrying about the business of the China Trade. There were delicate folding fans and bolts of silk and Chinese robes and tiny ladies' slippers that no Englishwoman could ever hope to wear. Best of all there was porcelain—creamy, translucent china of every shape and size. Teacups with and without handles, plates and dishes and serving platters and tea services in varying designs; large jars and jardinieres; bowls of every shape and color; teapots, inkwells, mustard pots, saltcellars, and spice holders; flasks, tea strainers, spoon holders, and thimbles—every item that could possibly be made out of porcelain, from the most mundane to the most remarkable.

Verity's mother had loved these pieces and had invented a history for each, which she passed on to her daughter, regaling her during stormy evenings with her childhood memories of the exotic land where the willows brushed the silent waters, the mountains embraced the sleepy earth, and the rising sun was a huge red globe so close you could almost touch it.

Oh yes, Verity remembered her mother. Alison was there in the house, a gentle, laughing spirit, and Verity was not going to let Papa's new wife intrude upon that . . . or send her away.

"Why can't you simply engage another governess?" she asked.

"That is out of the question. You are too old to start with another governess. Besides, the social intercourse that a proper school will provide is vital to your development as a well-rounded young lady."

Verity didn't care about social intercourse, whatever that was. All she wanted was to remain in the house where she had once been loved and happy. "I won't go."

Miss Lynchpole's dainty mouth hardened into a frown. All her governesses—Miss Lynchpole in particular—had taught her that a young lady doesn't question or argue with her elders, but Grandpa had never forbidden it. On the contrary: "Don't be such a meek brown wren," he used to say to her.

"This is my home and you can't just send me away."

Those wide blue eyes iced over. "Can't I?" she said in a manner that meant she knew she could. She was Papa's wife now and could do absolutely anything she pleased.

Verity hated her. Deep inside her something was boiling, just like the Fiery Furnace, which was the most fearsome image she encountered while studying the Bible every Sunday after church. She'd never been able to forget the way the Babylonian tyrant Nebuchadnezzar had ordered Shadrach, Meshach, and Abednego bound and thrown into the Fiery Furnace, and the vivid image of them walking around inside the glowing fire had always terrified her, even though God had delivered them from harm.

In Verity's mind the biblical Fiery Furnace was synonymous with the great wrought-iron boiler Grandpa had installed in the deepest, darkest basement of Cadmon Hall, a mammoth, many-armed monster that provided hot water not only in the pipes that led to the kitchens but in the baths throughout the houses. Convenient though it made the washing up and the bathing, the boiler heaved and shook so much when coal was loaded in that the servants refused to go near it, so petrified were they that it would explode, spewing flames, hot gasses, and molten metal throughout the house.

Grandpa had been proud of his boiler, but since Miss Lynchpole had married Papa, Verity had begun to feel that there was a Fiery Furnace deep inside herself, glowing like the molten core that Grandpa had told her was at the center of the earth. It was inside her, but at the same time she was inside it, and like Shadrach, Meshach, and Abednego, she was stumbling around in an inferno.

Oh, Grandpa, she thought miserably. *Why did you have to die?*

"Give me back my doll," Verity said.

She was in the yard of the village school in Trenwythan, surrounded by hostile children, many of them the sons and daughters of the clay laborers who worked for her father. When Papa and Miss Lynchpole had gone away on holiday in Newquay three days before, Verity had been seized with an idea so splendid it terrified her. She would enroll in the local grammar school, where she would be able to study hard and make friends with children her own age without leaving home. Her dream was to settle in so well there that Papa and Miss Lynchpole would relinquish their plans to send her away to boarding school.

But from the moment she'd greeted her new classmates with a shy smile and the words, "I'm Verity Trevor and I've come to join you this year," her dream had been in trouble.

To her great surprise, the village children seemed to know exactly who she was and, more important, who her father was. "Ye don't belong here," the eldest pupil in the school, a beautiful girl with shining corn-colored hair, silk-lashed eyes, and rose-petal skin, had said. Verity had heard the other children call her Tamara. "Go on back to yer fine house and leave us poor folk alone."

But Verity had stayed and now, at recess, the children seemed determined to make her regret it. They'd stolen her schoolbag and tossed it from one to another while Verity chased them, snatching futilely. They'd removed her books, which were precious to her, and mocked their fine leather covers and gilt-edged pages. They'd laughed at the writing in her copybook. Worst of all, they'd poked about in the bottom of the bag until they found Guinivere, the Chinese lady with the delicate porcelain face that had been her mother's very own doll.

Verity had taken Guinivere to bed with her every night

since Grandpa's death. When she held her close, she was able to go to sleep easily, no matter how wild the wind or how brooding the shadows. Even during the day sometimes, when nobody was looking, she would cuddle the doll and whisper to her, imagining they both were fairy princesses to whom nothing bad could ever happen.

"Please give her back," she begged the thieves.

"Looka this—the big baby's got a little baby!"

"Don't hurt her!"

"Crybaby, cry, hold yer dolly tight!" they taunted, tossing her precious doll high above their heads. Several of them spat on her as they arced Guinivere from child to child.

"Please don't be so rough with her! If you drop her, you'll smash her face."

Her anguish only incited them to further violence. They pulled Guinivere's silky hair, which Verity had lovingly combed this morning, tore her crimson Chinese robes with their grubby hands, and when one little girl didn't catch it in time, the doll landed in the mud. Verity lunged and slipped and fell in a puddle, her skirts flying up behind her, which made her tormentors laugh all the louder. One of the boys in the class scornfully scooped up the doll and held it to his nose. "Ugh! It smells like dirty nappies."

Crouching in the mud, stunned and humiliated and wishing herself and Guinivere far, far away, Verity was dimly aware of someone pulling at her skirts to reveal—and to mock—her lacy underthings.

"Do 'ee wear nappies, too, Miss Posh Lady Trevor, or do 'ee wet the straw at night whilst cuddling to yer dolly?"

I mustn't cry, Verity thought. *No matter what they do to me, they will not make me cry.*

She pushed to her feet and faced them. It was a scruffy young boy who had pulled up her skirts, but standing right behind him, holding Guinivere, was the beautiful Tamara, whose hair was done up in ribbons and whose frock was unmussed despite all the activity. Once again it occurred to Verity that Tamara was the loveliest creature she'd ever seen. If she'd lived in an earlier age, a knight of the Round Table would surely have fallen in love with her and pleaded to wear her token on his sleeve as he thundered into battle.

"Why are you doing this to me?" she demanded, looking straight into Tamara's eyes. "You owe me an answer."

"Because ye're a Trevor, that's why."

"Why should it matter who my father is? Please." Verity put her hand out as graciously as she could. "I'd like to be friends."

Tamara's eyes blossomed as she heard these words, and she looked with scorn upon Verity's dainty, uncallused hand. "Ye're not my friend and can't ever be, not after what yer family did to us Carnes."

Carne? The Trevors' ancient adversaries? Verity blinked at Tamara's golden hair, her dawn-sky eyes: Was she the daughter of the malevolent Piper who had spat on Grandpa's corpse? "We don't want 'ee in our village," Tamara added, "and we don't want 'ee in our school." Swinging back her arm, she tossed Guinivere several yards away into a drainage ditch.

Between her fingers Verity could feel a handful of mud that she'd unconsciously clawed; without hesitation she flung it at Tamara, hitting her squarely in the throat.

Tamara did not flinch or cry out, but as the mud soaked into that pristine gray fabric, spreading an ugly brown stain over Tamara's breasts, her beautiful face turned pale. For Verity it was the first moment of triumph she'd known all day.

Several of Tamara's friends were exclaiming over the damage to her frock. Verity heard the scruffy boy who had mocked her underthings say, "Pa'll skin 'ee, Tam, for gettin' yer frock dirty."

He must be Tamara's brother. Verity had heard there were two children in that awful family.

"No, Daniel, somehow I'll clean it before he sees it," Tamara said, but her face remained white, and Verity wondered at the power of a father whose possible anger could induce so much fear in this seemingly self-assured girl.

"There's a water bucket inside," someone offered. "Come on, don't fret, yer dad'll never know. Men don't notice things about frocks, anyway."

"Mine does," Tamara said miserably. "He'll thrash me."

As she left the fray, Daniel, the brother, cried, "So, ye're so rich ye don't mind gettin' the poor girls dirty? Don't suppose it's occurred to 'ee it might be her only frock?"

Verity knew a moment of shame because it hadn't occurred to her. On the other hand, the children hadn't cared about ruining Guinivere's delicate clothing. She regarded the Carne boy, who looked about her own age or a little younger. He had a fringe of black hair hanging into his face, hiding his forehead and partially obscuring his eyes, which were a startling shade of blue. She had seen him running in the wind and she knew he let his hair hang in the front to hide a long ugly scar that ran diagonally from his scalp to the corner of his right eye. It looked as if someone—most likely his father—had taken a knife to him.

"I s'pose ye figured ye could come to our school and treat us any which way you liked all because Henry Trevor's the big boss? Well, my pa says yers is a thief and a liar, and everyone round here knows it!"

"Why should I care what your father says?" Verity retorted. "He's a drunkard and a madman."

"He is not!" Although the boy was no taller than Verity, there was an intensity about him that made him seem older. His blue eyes were huge and thick-lashed and the shock of staring into their depths almost unnerved her. But his nose was running, and every couple of seconds he cleared his throat as if it was hurting, which made him seem less threatening. "It's yer pa who's a thief and a cheat who stole my father's land," said he. "Ye're all thieves and cheats! All o 'ee Trevors deserve to rot in hell!"

"You little wretch!" The Fiery Furnace inside Verity was churning. She swung her arm and slapped his face, the way she'd often seen Miss Lynchpole cuff a lazy housemaid. Even as she did it, a part of her mind was observing, appalled. She had never struck anybody before.

Daniel Carne lowered his head and rammed her, knocking her to the ground. They rolled over and over, flailing at each other while the other children screamed in excitement at the spectacle. At one point she managed to gain her feet and run, but she got no more than a few yards away before Daniel tackled her and brought her down again, resulting in bangs, bruises, and a good deal more dirt and damage to her frock than his sister had sustained.

"What in the name of God is going on here?" a deep voice roared.

"Uh-oh, Brockelsley," somebody hissed, and the children scattered. A moment later, Verity felt herself being dragged up from the ground by a rough hand jerking at the back of her collar.

"At it again, are you, Master Carne, you spawn of Satan," Schoolmaster Brockelsley said to Daniel, whose collar he had gripped in his other hand. He shook the boy, then turned his attention to her. "And you, Miss Trevor? I am shocked and disappointed to find you engaging in such deviltry. Not that I have any doubt who started this ruckus. You, Carne, know the penalty for brawling. Inside, both of you."

"Where's Guinivere?" Verity whispered. "I must find Guinivere."

But no one listened, no one cared.

Verity and Daniel Carne were ordered to stand on the elevated platform at the front of the classroom while the schoolmaster removed a supple willow switch from the tray under the blackboard and flicked it idly through the air. "I presume, Master Carne, that you struck the first blow? Hold out your palm, then, for you shall be punished first, and most severely." Mr. Brockelsley's voice conveyed an unpleasant edge of anticipation that chilled Verity, particularly since her conscience was reminding her that she had hit Daniel first.

The boy received half a dozen heavy blows on the tender flesh of his palm. The color washed from his face and his nose ran more than ever, but he didn't cry out, and even managed a wan grin for his classmates when his chastisement ended.

"Now you, Miss Trevor. I shall be more lenient with you. Three stripes only. Hold out your hand."

Verity took a deep breath. "That wouldn't be fair," she said in a barely audible voice.

"What? Speak up, girl."

"It wouldn't be fair for me to have less of a punishment

than he did," she said, trembling. "I was the one who struck the first blow."

There was a moment of silence as everyone in the classroom stared at her. Clearly they had not expected such an extraordinary admission of guilt. More loudly she said, "I slapped him and I threw mud at his sister as well."

Mr. Brockelsley puffed out his chest, as if highly insulted. "Indeed? I am most seriously displeased to hear it. In that case, you shall receive three more stripes instead of three less. I do not tolerate such disgraceful behavior in my school. Present your hand at once."

Nine. She didn't think she could bear it. If God had struck her dead right then and there, she would have sunk gratefully into the earth.

Her fingers were stiff and her palm was sweating, but somehow she managed to obey. With the first blistering blow she passed beyond shame, beyond fright. Everything turned dreamlike, unreal. The only reason her legs didn't collapse was that they weren't her legs anymore, just as her body wasn't her body. She endured the nine cuts in silence by allowing herself to float out of the classroom, above and beyond them all. Going to school was the first independent thing she'd ever done, and this was how it had ended up.

When Verity fled the schoolhouse that afternoon, her palm so raw she couldn't close her fingers, she was surprised to find Tamara Carne waiting for her outside, her corn-colored hair tousled by the wind.

"Are ye all right?" Tamara asked.

Verity blinked, confused by her tone, which seemed to contain within it a tentative note of friendship. Impossible, she thought, especially from a Carne.

"My brother and me're used to beatings from our pa, but ye're not, I reckon. I try to remember something my mum told me afore she died: 'He can't touch 'ee inside, where it counts. Inside ye're beautiful.' "

Tiny stinging tears sprang to Verity's eyes. *Inside ye're beautiful.* But it was the inside of her that nobody, save Mummy and Grandpa, had ever seen or acknowledged.

"Daniel shouldn't have fought with 'ee. The truth is, he's

cranky today. He's got a sore throat and won't admit he's sick.'' She sighed. ''When Ma was alive, she didn't allow fighting. I try to be like a mother to him, but he doesna mind me.''

''My mother's dead, too.''

''I know. Here.'' Awkwardly, Tamara Carne held something out to Verity. Guinivere. She was battered and besmirched, but her porcelain face was intact. ''She's beautiful, too. I reckon we were all jealous of 'ee for having such a pretty doll that's all yer own.''

Verity did something then that she would never have anticipated and could not account for. Hesitating for only a moment, she handed Guinivere back to Tamara. ''Would you like to have her?''

''Don't ye want her?'' Tamara fingered the doll's molded features in fascination, her fingers seeming to have a natural affinity for the translucent china.

''I—I want you to have her.''

Tamara raised her head and looked into her eyes. Verity felt her soul stripped bare, her deepest impulses exposed. The Piper's daughter smiled. ''No, you don't.'' She returned Guinivere to Verity's arms. ''I can't take her, but I thank 'ee. And I won't forget.''

''Neither will I,'' Verity swore.

Chapter Three

Her enemy was going to have a baby.

Verity wasn't sure how married people got babies, but she suspected it had something to do with the way Miss Lynchpole giggled and flirted with Papa, particularly in the evenings after she'd had a glass or two of claret. On such nights the two of them would disappear early into their bedroom, while the servants smirked at one another, and nobody came to kiss her good-night.

Such a simpering hypocrite! Why couldn't Papa see that she was false as fog?

Verity had been spared boarding school by an attack of scarlet fever that had nearly killed her. It had struck shortly after her adventure in the village school, from which Papa and Miss Lynchpole had angrily withdrawn her as soon as they'd returned from their holiday trip. Several of the village children to whom she'd been exposed, including the Carne boy, had gone down with the fever, and its aftermath had left Verity far too weak to be sent away from home.

Miss Lynchpole had made no secret of her displeasure, but now that she was in the family way, she'd adopted a policy of leaving Verity to her own devices. She had summoned her own old nursemaid from years ago, Nanny Winter, to move into Cadmon Hall and help her prepare for the birth of her son.

" 'Twill be a different world for 'ee," Nanny Winter told Verity. She was a stout woman with a full head of brassy hair who kept a gin bottle hidden in her bedroom. "Yer father's desperate for a son, and if he gets his wish, ye willna' be the center of his universe anymore. 'Tes a good thing, too, or ye'll be spoilt past saving."

Since Verity had never felt herself to be the center of his universe, the threat lacked sting. She was fascinated by the unborn child, this half-sibling whom her stepmother was so certain would be a son, this mysterious being who grew fat and active in his mother's belly, causing her to smile at inappropriate moments, and to seize her husband's hand and place it on her distended stomach so he could feel the baby move around.

"Would you like to feel it?" Henry asked Verity one afternoon at tea time in the drawing room when the child was active. "This is your little brother, and soon we'll be holding him."

Verity allowed her father to take her hand and place it on Miss Lynchpole's belly, which was hard and tight like the skin of a drum. Then the most extraordinary thing happened:

she felt a vigorous rolling beneath her palm. She made a sound of surprise and delight.

"You were like that once," her father said, voice faraway and dreamy. "You were very active. I used to lie for hours in front of the fire, watching Alison's belly undulate like ripples on the surface of the sea."

Miss Lynchpole drew back sharply, her expression black. "Really, Henry, you might try to remember that you're addressing a nine-year-old child."

An imp took control of Verity's tongue. "You loved my mother, didn't you, Papa?"

His expression turned mournful. "I loved her very much."

"Then how could you marry *her*?"

Miss Lynchpole reached across the tea trolley and slapped Verity across the face. Papa began yelling at her—at his own daughter—and deep inside her, the Fiery Furnace shuddered and shook. A huge red swell of emotion swept her, and Verity picked up the teacup from which she'd been drinking and heaved it at the wall. A syrupy brown stain of sugared tea formed on the elegant ivory wallpaper and the china splintered into flinty chips of turquoise, white, and gold.

"You selfish, wicked girl," Miss Lynchpole said. "That was one of our finest pieces of Cadmon porcelain, part of an ancient tea service that was complete and undamaged until this moment. You have committed an act of desecration. It is high time you learned the value of the items you so casually abuse."

Papa had risen, his handsome face flushed with a rare show of anger. "I won't tolerate this sort of behavior, Verity. You're long overdue for a beating. Get up from there at once and come with me."

"Beat me, then, I don't care! You can't hurt me any more than you already have!"

"Please, Henry, I'll handle this." Miss Lynchpole stooped down and collected the chunks herself, no easy task with her belly sticking out.

"You're not well, Caroline, so I must insist—"

"I'm quite well enough to deal with a rebellious child. Let me punish her. My way will be far more effective, I assure you."

Every day for the next fortnight Verity was locked in her old schoolroom on the top floor of Cadmon Hall from dawn till dusk with nothing more than hard bread and weak tea—served in a tin cup that gave it the most awful metallic taste—to sustain her as she labored over the task Miss Lynchpole had set her, which was to memorize everything there was to know about the history, composition, and relative value of hundreds of varieties of porcelain.

At first Verity was determined to be stubborn and thick-headed, impossible to teach, but her intellectual curiosity quickly scuttled that approach. If nothing else, she decided, she could learn to appreciate the lovely pieces of china that had belonged to her mother.

Soon Verity knew that the special white clay used in making porcelain was to be found only in China until the eighteenth century, when a man named William Cookworthy discovered china clay in Cornwall, giving rise to a new British industry.

"To make porcelain," Miss Lynchpole lectured, "you combine china clay with china stone, which fuse to create a hard, translucent substance. The china clay is sometimes referred to as the bones of the china, and the china stone the flesh. To extend the metaphor, the glaze may be regarded as the skin."

Verity liked this image. It made her feel as if the lovely porcelain pieces in Cadmon Hall were alive.

It wasn't long, though, before she began to hate the word *glaze*, for it was at this point that her studies grew difficult. One could tell a great deal about the date and quality of porcelain from its glaze, but in order to do so, Verity had to memorize the dynasties of China—their years and their rules—as well as the colors and types of glazes prevalent during each period. She had a devilish time with the emperors of the Ming and the Ch'ing dynasties, whose names and dates she tended to confuse. They had interchangeable, unpronounceable monikers like T'ien Shun and Ch'ien Lung, T'ai Chang, and Tao Kuang.

"You lazy, worthless, good-for-nothing!" Miss Lynchpole stormed at her after a fortnight of hard labor when she wrongly identified a precious blue and white bowl cast during the fifteenth century in early Ming period as an inferior piece of eighteenth-century Chinese Lowestoft. "Have you learned nothing? Can you honestly stand there and pretend that you can't tell the difference?"

"I'm doing my best," Verity said, stung.

"It's a good thing you didn't attend boarding school, after all, for you would have disgraced us all with your wretched slow-wittedness. Clearly you take after your mother, who was a hopeless dolt of a student."

"Don't insult my mother," Verity said in a barely audible voice.

"What did you say?"

Verity pointed her chin at a map of China that Miss Lynchpole had pinned to the schoolroom wall. "What I said was, don't insult my mother. It's wrong to speak ill of the dead."

"How dare you presume to instruct me in what is right and what is wrong? Besides, I am your mother now."

"You're not and you never will be! My mother was beautiful and good. My father and I loved her. You're nothing compared to her, nothing!"

"How dare you?" Raising the pointer with which she had been indicating china-producing regions on the map, Miss Lynchpole brought it down viciously across the backs of Verity's hands. She was about to lash out again when Verity leaped from her stool, grabbed the pointer, and broke it into pieces across her knee.

"If you ever strike me again, you will regret it."

Miss Lynchpole took a step back. It was as if her face had cracked open, revealing a glimpse of a different person behind it, someone with weaknesses, someone not quite so self-confident. She clutched at her swollen belly as if for reassurance. "You wicked, wicked child," she sputtered. "I'll have you removed from this household. You'll never see your father again. And don't fancy that he'll try to stop me. He doesn't love you. How could he, vicious little demon that you are? It won't be until my son arrives that Henry will have a child he can truly pour his affection upon, a child who's truly deserving of the Trevor heritage."

Shaken, Verity retreated to the threshold of the schoolroom, pausing there to say, "I hope he never has a son. I hope you and your miserable, puling infant die. That's what you deserve for your lies and your cruelty."

She ran down the stairs and pushed blindly through the massive oaken doors to the gardens and vast moorlands beyond.

Verity sped north, toward the highest ground in the area, Cadmon Tor, a wild place, undulating with ancient burial mounds. The spot commanded a panoramic view of the moors and fields dotted with sheep, the woodland valleys rich with beeches, oaks, and sycamores, the hawthorn brakes rustling with small birds and animals, the old tin and copper engine houses with their stone chimneys stabbing at the sky, the farmland cottages, sun-drenched white with roofs of graying thatch, the great carpet of green that sloped down to the granite cliffs, Gribben Head and Black Head—the proud sentinels of St. Austell Bay.

At one time, it was said, Cadmon Tor had been a watch hill, posted with a guard who would make a signal fire should enemies be sighted invading from land or sea. If there were any justice in the world, Verity thought, the beacon would have smoked a warning when Miss Lynchpole had arrived at Cadmon Hall.

Verity wandered on, climbing north over the moors, not stopping until she reached the abandoned tin mine beside a rushing brook at the northern border of the Trevor lands. She hid herself in the crumbling stone engine house, piling straw in a corner and curling up against the early-evening chill. She was never going home again.

It was nearly dark when her resolution began to falter. She'd already beaten away numerous bugs and spiders when she heard a scurrying that sounded suspiciously like a rat. An odd rumbling in the earth beneath her put her in mind of every whispered tale she had ever heard of the knackers, the wicked gnomelike creatures who were said to inhabit the mines throughout Cornwall.

As she scrambled out of the engine house, the breeze was blowing from the north, carrying with it the low murmur of voices. " 'Tes here, right here on the ground we're standing on," a man said. "Thur's clay, the finest, whitest, most powdery in the region. And there's tin, too, that's nowhere near tapped out. The earth's riches, all here, waiting to be mined. Waiting for us to mine 'em."

"But thes be Trevor land," a child's voice replied.

"Thes be *disputed* land, lad, according to them thievin', cheatin' bastards. According to us, it's our'n, fair and simple. Always had been, until they stole it from our ancestors."

"Back in the time of Good Queen Bess," the boy said. His voice had the singsong quality of someone who has heard the details many times before.

"That's it, lad. But 'twas our'n again, this bit, along with all the land that's now called Cadmon Clay. My ancestor Jason Carne ate his pride and bought it from the Trevors a hundred and fifty years ago. Signed a paper to prove it, too, but the fool didna' get himself a copy. He thought a handshake from a gentleman were enough. Old Amos Trevor kept the paper."

"Or destroyed it, most like."

"Aye, lad, so that when old Amos Trevor's descendants wanted to open his claypits, he insisted the land was his, had always been his, and that his family'd been letting Jason Carne mine the tin and keep the profits out o' the sheer goodness of his heart. They built up Cadmon Clay on the land that were our'n and now they're all the richer for it."

"There's no honor or goodness in the heart of any Trevor," said the boy in a singsong voice, as if it was a sentiment he'd parroted many times before.

"A Trevor heart's a heart that's rotten to the core."

A half moon broke free of the clouds that were cloaking it, and its light gave Verity, crouching at the side of the engine house, confirmation of what she had already guessed—the fair-haired man doing most of the talking was her grandfather's old enemy, Jory Carne, and the boy listening, enrapt, to the lecture was his son, Daniel, her enemy of the schoolyard.

They were moving away from her, their voices fading as the breeze died down. But she clearly heard Jory say, "We'll get it back one day, boy. I swore that to Rufus, that old blackguard, and I've sworn it to his son. The land's for 'ee, Daniel, d'ye hear me, boy? 'Tes yers to own, yers to work.

One day ye'll make 'em acknowledge the truth o' that. One day ye'll defeat 'em. Ye'll take back all our land. Swear it to me, boy."

"I'll take it back, I swear," said Daniel Carne.

Cadmon Hall was in an uproar when Verity reached it some twenty minutes later. Light poured from the tall windows, and she heard the clatter of a carriage arriving in the front drive as she slipped through the formal garden and into the west side of the house. She concluded that her father had dispatched searchers to look for her, and shuddered to imagine what sort of punishment Miss Lynchpole would devise for her this time.

She crept through the kitchen door, hoping to escape notice that way. She had nearly reached the top of the back stairs when she encountered Nanny Winter, all in a bustle, lugging a bucket of hot water. She barely noticed Verity, except to say, "There now, you wicked child, get out from underfoot. 'Tis your last night of having any importance in this house, you can count on that."

"What's happening?"

"The mistress has gone and started her labor a month before her time, that's what's happening. No doubt because she was upset about something, or someone," she added darkly. "If anything goes wrong there'll be the devil to pay, you mark my words."

Verity remembered the way Miss Lynchpole had clutched at her belly during their confrontation. "I'm sure nothing'll go wrong," she whispered, mostly to herself, as she retreated to her bedroom.

It wasn't long before she began to hear moans and, later, screams from the master suite. They got louder and louder until Verity had to block her ears with her palms. Not even then could she entirely shut them out.

When the afternoon stretched on without any news, Verity became increasingly anxious. "*I hope you and your miserable puling infant son die! It's what you deserve for your lies and your cruelty!*" Verity had said to her.

What if Miss Lynchpole's baby did die? What if in her

innermost heart Verity was just as jealous of her new brother as Miss Lynchpole was of Papa's first wife? More than once she'd wished he would vanish from her stepmother's belly. If he died, would it be her fault?

Verity slipped to her knees on the bare floor and whispered the Lord's Prayer, following it with a special request that her brother be born safely. She promised to love him with all her heart and with all her soul and with all her might. She promised to hold him and rock him and sing lullabyes to him just the way her mother had sung to her. She would be so good to him that both her father and Miss Lynchpole—Mother, she resolved to call her—would be proud of her and no one would ever say cruel things or yell at her again.

She fell asleep that night clutching Guinivere. Early the following morning Nanny Winter came to fetch her. "It's a girl. She's to be named Elizabeth Caroline."

A sister! Verity was delighted. Miss Lynchpole had been so certain that the baby was a boy that she'd never even considered what it would be like to have a sister. "May I see her?"

"You'd better see your stepmum first. For the last time."

Verity blinked, not understanding.

"She's finished, poor thing. Your father told me to bring you to say goodbye. Poor motherless child! 'Tisn't right she should have to grow up without her mum." Nanny's voice cracked as she continued, "Oh lordy, 'tis a cruel world we live in. I warned her not to come to this godforsaken part of the country, not to make me come with her." Nanny broke into loud wailing sobs. "Now she's finished and I don't know what's to become of me."

Nanny Winter's tears shocked Verity even more than the unbelievable words she had just said. Miss Lynchpole was dying? How was that possible? She had always seemed as healthy as one of the plump calico cats that lived in the stableyards and gorged regularly on baby birds and mice.

"Come along then, girl, look sharp. Your father said you were to come straightaway."

Verity hopped out of bed, carefully putting on her slippers and her night robe because she knew Miss Lynchpole wouldn't approve of her walking about the cold house without them. As she followed Nanny down the hall toward the master bedroom suite, she continued to press Guinivere to her chest.

Her father was present, and Dr. Cowan, and a strange woman whom Verity supposed to be a nurse. "Go on in, child," Nanny said, pushing her from behind.

Slowly Verity crossed the red, blue, and gold oriental carpet and stopped near the foot of the bed where her stepmother lay motionless. Her head was propped up and she was covered by several quilts and blankets. Her face was the color of china clay, her blond hair dull and matted on the pillows, and her eyes were shut.

Nobody spoke to Verity or paid her any attention. Papa didn't look at her; he was absorbed in studying his motionless wife. Verity could see the glint of moisture on his cheekbones and the droplets that had caught, like tiny crystal bubbles, in his beard.

"Is she going to die?" she whispered. *Is it my fault?*

Her father lifted his head. Verity was shocked at the ravages that grief was working upon him. There were bruisy pockets underneath his eyes and a pallor to his skin as if all the nutrients that gave it life had been sucked out of him. He stared at her for a moment with what Verity imagined to be an accusatory glare in his eyes, then, without answering, looked back at his wife.

"She was very weak from the protracted labor," Dr. Cowan said. "And then the hemorrhaging wouldn't stop."

She wasn't pretty anymore. Her skin had stretched taut over the bones of her face. Her stomach, vaguely outlined beneath the bedcovers, was flat again, reminding Verity that somewhere about was the new baby. Nobody was paying any attention to her, either. They all just stood there, waiting. Nobody did anything, not even the doctor and the nurse. Verity wanted to scream at them to do something.

Miss Lynchpole jerked and began to breathe unevenly. Verity was frightened; there was a clicky sort of sound coming from her throat that was like nothing she had ever heard . . . or would ever forget.

"She's going," Dr. Cowan said.

"Dammit, no." Verity's father bent over and grabbed his wife's shoulders as if to shake her back to health. "Caroline, stop it! Stop it right now. You can't leave me. Not you too. You're all I have. Dammit, Caroline, stop it I say. Come back to me!''

It was more than Verity could endure. She shot up and caught at the tails of his waistcoat from behind.''She's not all you have, Papa. You still have me. Can't you see it—you have *me!*''

"Jesus!" He jerked away and whirled upon her. The emotion in his face was terrible to see, all the more so because it was something he usually kept hidden. "I ought to take a strap to you! You wouldn't even call her Mother. That's all she wanted, and you couldn't even give her that.''

Verity's world shrank down until it compressed into a single bitter, heavy point. Her father hated her.

Desperately, she turned to the woman on the bed. *Open your eyes, Miss Lynchpole*, she willed her. *Oh, please, open your eyes.*

There was one last, light breath, then the chalky-faced body shuddered. Verity waited for her to breathe again, but her chest remained fixed and still.

Like Grandpa's.

"Mother?" she whispered.

There was no movement, no sound. Even worse, there was no love or forgiveness in her father's face.

That night Verity could not sleep. She yearned for the warmth of her father's arms around her and the pleasant scents of brandy and tobacco and tweed. But all she could see was Miss Lynchpole's dead body. At first her stepmother lay prone, then suddenly she rose and walked, smiling that false smile, her fingers turning into talons that seized Verity and held her, scratching her tender skin, drawing blood. Then she began to pull Verity into her cold body, into that place from which babies are born, laughing wildly as she proved that she was indeed entitled to be called Mother.

Bathed in perspiration, Verity tossed and twisted in her sheets, uncertain if she was awake or asleep. She sat up with a jerk. Someone was crying. It was not a cry of mourning. It was too insistent and demanding.

The baby.

Verity pulled the covers over her and hugged Guinivere, waiting for Nanny to make the crying stop. Instead it grew louder. Verity rose from bed and stumbled down the darkened hallway toward the nursery, shivering as she passed the bedroom where her father was keeping vigil over her stepmother's dead body.

She pushed open the door to the nursery, which was dimly lit by a low gas jet in the corner. Nanny Winter was slouched in the chair, her heavy body heaving with her stentorious breathing, her bodice unbuttoned so Verity could see the pendulous mounds of her breasts, one of her legs propped on an ottoman, the other dangling almost girlishly over the arm of the chair. Her mouth hung open and her brassy blond wig was askew, revealing thin wisps of white hair on her crown and above her left ear. She looked like exactly what she was—a pathetically aging woman who could no longer be trusted with the responsibilities of her longtime profession.

There was an empty gin bottle on the floor beside the chair, and the smell emanating from the woman's cavernous mouth was appalling. While she snorted and slept, the baby continued to cry.

Half curious, half reluctant, Verity approached the bassinet. Her sister was tiny and loud, wrapped in the white swaddling clothes, dingy with age, that had been passed down from one generation of Trevors to the next. Her face was red and squashed-looking, but her tiny fingers, clenched in fists, were the smallest, most perfect things Verity had ever seen. Her hair was a vague fuzz of auburn.

"Hello, Elizabeth." At the sound of her voice the crying stilled, which Verity thought was remarkable. "You can hear me, can't you? Aren't you the clever one?" Instinctively she raised her voice to a higher pitch as she spoke. "Are you hungry? That nasty Nanny Winter hasn't fed you? She's been too busy nursing herself with gin."

Verity looked around for a bottle of milk, which she found on the windowsill, chilled by the air that was coming in through a crack in the casement. But she had no idea how to feed a baby. At first she simply placed the bottle into the bassinet, expecting those thrashing hands to grab it. But her baby sister only turned her head toward the rubber nipple on the bottle and made sucking motions with her mouth. When she couldn't find what she could smell, she wailed even louder until Verity bent over and picked her up.

She was squirmy and warm and wet. Her cloth napkin was soaked, as were the swaddling clothes, but her cries changed from piercing screams to gasps of anticipation that settled into moans of pleasure when Verity fitted the nipple between her sister's gums.

Verity stumbled over to Nanny Winter's bed and sank down there, the feeding baby in her arms. It took Elizabeth a long time to drink the milk, but she seemed contented. When she was finished, Verity found a fresh napkin and changed her, conscious of the acrid smell of urine and the dry feel of the talcum powder she dusted onto the soft little bottom. All the while Elizabeth looked straight at her, her blue eyes intelligent and alert. Then she began to cry again. Verity held her to her chest, patting her gently and wondering what to do next.

Despite what must have been an overwhelming need and desire to sleep, those blue eyes remained open and alert. She must be frightened, Verity thought. Her mother was dead. Elizabeth couldn't possibly understand that there was nothing to worry about. That she would be loved and taken care of. It must terrify her to search around the nursery with her intelligent little eyes, looking for Mummy and not seeing her anywhere.

"But you won't be alone," Verity said. "I promise you'll never, ever be all alone."

She felt the baby burp against her, and remembered having heard that newborns must expel gas after feeding. She patted her between her shoulder blades, holding her close and rocking her. Soon Elizabeth was sound asleep in Verity's arms.

She carried her back to the bassinet and laid her down. She thought of taking this new baby sister into her own bed, to ensure that she wouldn't wake up feeling frightened or alone, but she was concerned that she might roll on top of her and smother her. Instead, she decided, she would get a quilt and sleep here on the floor.

"You're safe now, little one." She covered her sister with

the soft wool blanket that her own mother had knitted for her when she was a baby. "I'll be right here beside you."

On an impulse she ran back down the hall to her room to get Guinivere, whom she placed in the bassinet. "That's so you'll have someone beside you to cuddle to and keep you nice and warm." She stroked the sleeping child's fair wisps of hair. "I love you, Elizabeth. Sleep, little sister, sleep."

The baby's mouth moved reflexively, her lips briefly forming a smile.

Chapter Four

"No! Hot! Hurts!" the little girl screamed.

Verity heard the cry one evening after supper as she entered the nursery bath just as Nanny Winter was putting her two-year-old sister into the huge lion-footed tub. Nanny cuffed her, saying, " 'Tesn't hot enough to get the filth off you, young lady, after you've been rolling about in the garden wi' your puppy."

But Elizabeth, whom they called Bret, an adulteration of Beth, which the child couldn't pronounce, continued to howl and jump about, and although she could be obstinate at times, Verity could tell that her cries were in earnest. She plunged her arm into the water and found it scalding. Snatching her naked sister from the tub, Verity examined Bret's legs and feet. They were tender and red.

"You've burned her. You're supposed to test the bath water with your elbow; how could you be so careless?"

"Mind your own business, you wretched girl!" Nanny grabbed at Bret with the intention of forcing the screaming child back into the water. Bret clung to Verity, her arms tight around her sister's neck, her howls escalating. " 'Tes my job to bathe your sister."

"It's not going to be your job much longer if you keep doing things like this."

"How dare you talk back to me? Go to your room!"

Verity was surprised at herself, for on top of the diffidence she had always possessed, she had, since her stepmother's death, developed a numbness about the things that once would have made her wildly angry. The moment she felt the curling tendrils of incipient rage, she would flash to an image of Miss Lynchpole's last rattling breath and subsequent stillness. Her anger was a thing of fearsome power, a serpent that must stay coiled. So she'd learned to keep it wrapped inside her, hidden in her secret depths, below her awareness, causing no more than an occasional ripple on the surface of her mind.

This was different, though. Nanny was hurting Bret.

"I won't let you injure my sister. I'm not trusting her any longer with a drunken old witch like you." She grabbed a towel from the brass rack and wrapped it around Bret, then strode out into the nursery holding her firmly in her arms.

"You come back here, Verity Trevor."

Verity ignored her. Pulling a nightgown over the still-crying Bret, she seized one of Nanny's gin bottles from the cache hidden behind Bret's storybooks and ran downstairs in search of her father, leaving a stunned Nanny Winter sputtering behind her.

Although she hadn't wanted a sibling, Verity could hardly remember what life had been like in the great collection of rooms, suites, galleries, and corridors that was Cadmon Hall without the sound of those faltering footsteps, that high-pitched giggle, those first few fumbling words and sentences. Her sister's smile, part joy, part mischief, part adoration, always had the power to banish her cloudy spirits. Just yesterday Bret had looked at her, her thumb in her mouth, and said, "How much do you love me?"

"I love you the best."

That smile—big and broad and joyful. "I love *you* the best," Bret had said.

It was the first time since her grandfather's death that anybody had loved her wholly, unconditionally, and the best.

She found Papa in the library, which had been his refuge

since his second wife's death. It was an old room, located in the most ancient part of the house. Three walls were solid with bookshelves from floor to ceiling, and even then there wasn't room for all the books, many of which were piled on their sides. The oldest of the books—some volumes were several hundred years old—were protected in glass cases, but most of the newer books were stacked haphazardly.

On the fourth wall were several portraits of Trevor ancestors. Verity's favorites were a wickedly handsome depiction of Roger, a sixteenth-century baron who had gained a position of power and trust at the court of Elizabeth Tudor, and her great-grandmother Penelope, a gifted mathematician who had cut her hair, donned a false beard, and successfully masqueraded as a tutor at Eton for several years before being discovered and dismissed.

"Nanny drinks, Papa," she said, holding the baby in one arm and the neck of Nanny's gin bottle in the other. "It's high time you did something about it."

Henry Trevor looked up from the project he was hunched over, his eyes bleary, his manner faintly surprised, as if it were a bit too much of an effort to remember that he had two daughters. In the two years since his second wife had died, Trevor had severed most of his connections to life. Verity had heard the village gossip asserting that Cadmon Clay was on the verge of ruin because Papa was too grief-stricken to care whether the clay business turned a profit.

His interest in flying machines had become an obsession. He had begun corresponding with aviation enthusiasts in England, France, and the United States, sharing information and dreams, sketches and designs. He built small, precise models out of paper and light wood and tested them on the flat south field. When they flew, he enlarged them until they were big enough for a man to crouch beneath, strapped to the underside of a set of wings. To Verity's horror, he proceeded to leap from boulders and bluffs, rising briefly with the air currents, spinning around a few times, then gliding—or, all too frequently, crashing—back to earth.

He had broken both arms, one leg, his collarbone, several ribs, and even his aristocratic nose. But he persisted, and Verity had heard the servants whispering that he was yearning to join his dead wife. The fear that she and Bret might be left orphans was enough to haunt her nights and keep her huddled in the dark long after everybody else in the house was asleep, listening to the relentless ticking and gonging of the various clocks that proclaimed the passing hours.

Papa was working on one of his aeroplane designs now. Sketches and glue and thin bits of balsa wood were scattered all over the surface of his desk. He scowled at the prospect of being interrupted, but for once Verity was too passionate to care.

"Nanny Winter put Bret into a tub of scalding hot water and burned her feet. She wasn't paying attention to the water temperature because she was drunk."

Bret had gone quiet at the sight of her father, whom she adored. Her expressive face burst into a smile and she held her chubby arms out toward him. Henry pushed back his chair and smiled as Verity brought her to him. Once in her father's arms, Bret cuddled to his shoulder, pressed her cheek against his full red beard, and laughed.

Papa put his lips to the top of her head and kissed her. He was always tender toward Bret, which pleased Verity at the same time as it stirred up feelings of jealousy inside her.

"She seems all right to me."

"Look at her feet. They're red."

He did so, and Bret whimpered a little as he touched her skin.

"Nanny's been drinking since she first came here. On the night Bret was born I found her unconscious in the nursery, stinking of gin. She drinks herself into a stupor nearly every evening. If Bret wakes up crying, I'm the only one who hears her. You've got to do something, Papa. Nanny's not fit to care for a baby."

Henry's examination of his younger daughter's feet had resulted in a crimson staining on his face and neck that far exceeded anything on Bret's toes. "By Christ! Where is the wretched woman? What does she have to say for herself, damn her?"

"Scalding her is only the latest thing she's done to Bret.

A few months ago she allowed her to roll off the dresser where she changes her nappies, *when* she changes them, which isn't nearly as often as she ought. And last week I caught her striking poor Bret's bare bottom with a ruler until there were red streaks across her skin.''

Henry was now on his feet. ''The stinking bitch! Before I'm through with her, *her* feet will be burning to get clear of here.''

''I didn't think you'd believe me,'' Verity said in a small voice.

''Why shouldn't I believe you? I haven't brought you up to lie.''

You haven't brought me up at all, Verity was thinking, but she held her tongue. ''It's not easy to talk to you, Papa.'' She moved her hands in helpless little circles. ''Since Miss— uh—Mother—died, you've been . . .'' she paused, as if not knowing how to describe what he'd been, ''so unhappy.''

''Hell's bells and damnation!'' he roared, sounding exactly like Grandpa. ''Take me to this woman. If she's drunk, so help me God, she'll be out of this house before morning.''

There was a burning sensation in Verity's throat as she led the way to the nursery. He'd listened to her. He'd believed her. No longer would she have to defend her sister all alone. ''Everything's going to be all right,'' she whispered to Bret. ''Papa's taking care of us now.''

On the night after he'd dismissed Nanny Winter with enough of a pension to keep her well supplied with gin for the rest of her days, but without the references necessary to secure her another position scalding and spanking children, Henry Trevor slipped quietly into the bedroom where his elder daughter slept.

''Verity's as thin and wraithlike as a ragamuffin from the slums of London,'' his sister Dorothy had said during her last visit to Cadmon Hall. ''It's obvious that she hasn't been taught how a young lady ought to behave. Really, Henry, when I think of the advantages you could be giving her . . . it's shameful. And as for the baby, she's a terror. A more spoiled, noisy, and mischievous child I've rarely seen. These are important years in the lives of both your children, and you're doing nothing to see to their nurturance. It's a disgrace.''

She was right, he'd realized; the Nanny Winter affair had proven it. It had also awakened him from what now seemed a self-indulgent two-year sleep.

Henry had had a talk with Mrs. Chenoweth, the busybody housekeeper who always seemed to know everybody's private business. He'd discovered the reason why Verity was always so pale and weary-looking: she didn't sleep well at night. She was too busy guarding her baby sister from the abuses of her nursemaid.

Verity's room was dark but for the flickering of the nightlight. Wasn't she getting too old for that? She was curled up on her side, breathing slowly and all too carefully. Gently he touched her ankle, and she started, drawing her knees up and making a muffled sound.

"It's all right, lovely. It's only me."

"Papa?" She rolled over, pushing herself up on one elbow. Her breath came out in a long sigh. "You frightened me."

He sat down beside her. She'd grown into such a strange creature, so grave, so silent. She'd never been a demonstrative child, but she'd had something when Alison was alive— some spirit, some verve. That had evaporated lately. She was closed off, self-contained, although he sensed a curious tension between her quiet outer bearing and the explosive emotions she held inside. Last night, indicting Nanny Winter, she had reverted to an earlier state, reminding him that ten years ago she had been a red-faced and demanding baby whom he had delightedly held in his arms shortly after her birth, marveling that she was bone of his bone, flesh of his flesh. How had she changed from that squalling infant to this tense, disquieting ten-year-old? When had the multitudinous layers of character been laid down?

He thought of all the times he'd been cross, impatient, or simply too self-absorbed to notice that she needed his attention. The days he'd sent her away when she'd come to him, her big eyes hopeful as she suggested an activity for them to do together. The nights he'd waved her off to bed without a good-night kiss. Fine father he'd turned out to be.

"Papa?" Her voice was tremulous. "What are you doing here?"

"I just wanted to make sure you and Bret were all right. Now that Nanny's gone."

He scooted closer to her, reaching out to take one of her small hands in his. For an instant she hesitated, obviously surprised, then she clutched and held on tight. From there it seemed natural to take her into his arms. She was stiff and brittle, as if she didn't understand that it was all right to relax when one was embraced. Poor child. She hadn't had many hugs from him over the years.

"Listen, lass. I want you to know that I'm proud of the way you've been taking care of your sister these last two years. And that I regret not being a proper father to you both. From now on I'm going to try to be better."

Verity made a little sniffling sound. Henry felt the warmth of her tears on his throat; they made him ashamed. He had been far too self-centered. He would change. Surely it was possible for a man to change?

"I've been missing your stepmother, you see. Before that, it was Alison I yearned for. I guess I haven't been fortunate in my marriages. But I'm extremely fortunate in my children."

Her narrow shoulders were heaving now. Odd how she could cry so quietly, be so restrained, even in dejection. He patted her awkwardly, uncertain how to comfort her, wanting comfort himself. He spoke to her gently, telling her not to worry because everything was going to be all right.

"I didn't know what to do," she whispered into his shoulder. "I didn't think you'd believe how awful Nanny was."

"Course I believe you, lass. Course I do."

"Sometimes I feel as if I have to pretend to be a grownup, but I don't know how."

Henry sighed. "Sometimes I feel that way, too."

She lifted her tear-streaked face. Her eyes were huge, underscored by dark circles that made him ache inside. "I love you, Papa," she said softly.

His arms convulsed, hugging her.

She hesitated, then added, "Do you think, maybe, if I'm good, you might be able to love me a little, too?"

"Christ, child!" Henry's throat jammed up on him. Any

second now, he'd be bawling too. "You're my sweetheart, my precious girl. I love you very much, and your sister as well."

Her breath came out in a long shudder as she snuggled more deeply into his arms.

Henry held her until she was calm again, then he lifted her out of bed—she was so light he could carry her easily—saying, "Let's go into the nursery together and check on your sister."

Leaning over the crib where Bret slept on her belly, the two fingers that she liked to suck poised only an inch from her mouth, Henry held Verity by the hand and whispered to her, "She's a lovely child, isn't she? Her hair's going to stay red, I think."

"Like yours, Papa." She sounded proud, as if red hair was something to be desired.

"I thought it would lighten to blond like her mother's. Perhaps it will one day. Her eyes are just like Caroline's, have you noticed? That same blue-green, like a tropical sea."

"She has pretty eyes."

"She has her mother's laugh as well. That bright face, so full of Caroline's passion and warmth."

Verity made a slight, fretful movement.

"I couldn't bear to think about Caroline, but seeing Bret forced me to do so. That's why I've locked myself away from you both. Can you understand that?"

"I—I think so, Papa."

"It's been two years. I've grieved enough."

Verity said nothing. She understood that he was speaking more to himself than to her.

"I swear to you it'll be different now. Bret's going to grow up secure and contented. She'll have everything she ever wants, everything she ever dreams of. I'm going to cherish her as no child has ever been cherished before. I'm going to make up for the time I've so selfishly squandered." He reached out and feathered Bret's hair. It was soft as fairy cobwebs. "Look at her, my miracle child. She'll be even prettier than Caroline, don't you think?"

Verity was very quiet. Her hand had slipped out of his.

"Will you help me? Will you help me make your sister's childhood a time of great happiness and joy?"

"Of course, Papa," Verity said. But when Henry looked from his roly-poly redheaded daughter to his slender, moody one, he was baffled by the fresh tears brimming in her grave, dark eyes.

Part Two

1907

Marriage has many pains, but celibacy has no pleasures.

—Samuel Johnson
The History of Rasselas

Chapter Five

From the time she was a little girl, Bret Trevor had longed to know what lurked hidden behind those curious low-slung clouds so common to the Cornish coast, where the sky is nearer to the ground than anywhere else in England. The cotton puffs seemed to float just overhead, casting racing shadows on the grasses and wildflowers beneath. She could have touched them, she was certain, if only she were taller. She liked to imagine herself stretching up and parting them, then flinging her spirit through to discover what lay beyond.

"Ye'd best stop dreaming of the clouds and the sky and whatnot, ye and yer father both," Mrs. Chenoweth always said. "Yer grandfather never wasted his precious time with such foolishness."

But Bret had never known her grandfather, except from Verity's stories. Her father's vision of mechanically powered flight, on the other hand, had helped to shape her young imagination. He had insisted it would happen, and he had been right. Two brothers named Wilbur and Orville Wright had made the first certified and attested engine-powered flight three and half years ago in America, and since then aviation enthusiasts all over Europe, Papa included, had been duplicating their success. He'd always said he would do it, and he had. The *Daedalus*, Papa's pride and joy, had made her maiden flight with him at the helm last summer, to the great thrill and delight of everyone at Cadmon Hall and most of the people from the area surrounding the village of Trenwythan. The flight had been a short hop into the air that had lasted for only three minutes at an altitude of less than fifty feet, but it had been a triumph.

"I could probably go higher and stay up longer," he'd told Bret, "but for your sister's fear that I might break my bloody neck."

"Your neck's important to us, Papa."

"To hell with my neck. All I care about is that I don't wreck the *Daedalus*, after all the work and money that's gone into her!"

Verity had looked so pale while watching the flight that Bret had expected her to faint dead away. She had admitted afterward that she'd been wrong to doubt Papa's vision. Of course she'd been wrong, Bret had told her indignantly. Papa was a great hero, a wizard, for he had wings and could fly, and what could be more magical than that?

"I've got a new test model," Papa said to her one Sunday morning in late June. "Would you like to come watch me fly it?"

"Of course I would, Papa." Overjoyed with the chance to do something with her father—especially on a Sunday morning that she would otherwise have to spend in church—Bret danced over the moors as they hiked out to the workshop and hangar Papa had instructed the estate carpenter to build for him on a flat, disused field that rolled on forever toward the distant silver gleam of the sea.

When they reached the south field, Bret insisted on running all the way down to the rocky bluff that jutted like a hammer over a steep descent, balancing on the narrow outcropping in the reckless sort of manner that always annoyed—and frightened—Verity. She had been staying with Aunt Dorothy in London for months and months, having a Season and trying to find a husband, but she would be coming home soon, thank goodness. Bret missed her terribly.

"Come on, Papa, let's pretend it's Land's End. We're standing on the westernmost tip of England facing the legendary land of Avalon where King Arthur was taken on the three queens' barge."

"Take care not to fall, love."

"I never fall," Bret replied with perfect confidence. "They say he'll return from Avalon one day. But he needn't, because we'll go there ourselves and find him, won't we, Papa?''

"Absolutely," Papa said, smiling. "We'll explore the western isles, and the southern deserts, the eastern mountains, and the northern wilds. We'll travel the world together, just the two of us, and confront all manner of strange things, both seen and unseen. Lands of civilization, lands of myth, we'll visit them, one and all."

"Can we go to Arizona, where Mr. Slayton is?" Mr. Zachary Slayton, an American aeroplane enthusiast who was a great friend of her father's, sometimes wrote letters to Bret, spinning wonderful tales for her of the Wild West.

"Of course. We'll ride our ponies over sagebrush and battle Apaches to your heart's content."

Bret laughed. "I wish we could go now." She spread her arms to embrace the earth, the sky, and the sea. The wind whipped her sleeves, making them flap as if she had wings. She yearned to propel herself off the heights of some windswept hill and soar with the air currents, even if it was only a few feet above the ground, feeling, for those brief moments, that she had escaped the pull of the earth.

"I feel as if I could fly there now, just leap into the sky and let the wind take me. Papa, aren't you ever going to let us go up in one of your gliders?"

"Not the gliders; they're not safe. But maybe someday, when I'm confident that I've smoothed the kinks from the mechanical aeroplanes, then we'll go up together."

"Oh I do hope so!"

When they reached the workshop, Papa withdrew an odd contraption of light wood and sailcloth. Bret knew he'd spent months on the design, consulting by letter with fellow aviators like Mr. Slayton to compare notes on wing spans, engines, and tail assemblies. The model he had constructed was large—four feet from nose to stern. His former inventions had resembled birds, but this one was boxlike, with two sets of slightly curved wings, one underneath the other, a body made of a single length of wood, and another, smaller set of double wings at the rear. A small engine was mounted on the front part of the flying machine, with a little tank for petrol strapped underneath the beam that ran down the center.

Papa explained the operation of the model to her. The elevators, he said, were set to lift when the aeroplane reached a certain velocity, which would enable it to rise slowly off the ground. When the right altitude was achieved, the tail flaps would straighten out so that the little craft could level off and go, borne by the wind, for as long as there was gasoline to drive the engine.

"It's just a prototype, but if it works—and I expect it will—I'll build a full-size model. She'll fly higher and steadier than the *Daedalus*, and I'll have more vertical as well as lateral control."

Together they moved the model outside to the landing strip of closely mown grass from which Papa had launched the *Daedalus* last summer. They were in the process of starting its miniature engine when Bret heard a soft footfall and a voice. "So you dare to probe the sky mysteries? 'Tes an arrogant thing to do."

Bret turned, startled to see a beautiful woman with long wheat-gold hair streaming over her shoulders standing a few feet away on the hill behind them. Clad in a full-skirted, heather-colored frock that the breeze was whipping around her legs, she seemed to have risen out of the moorland, as much a part of the earth as Papa was part of the sky. Indeed, she seemed rooted in the earth, a golden, fertile goddess who makes the rains come and the crops grow.

To the wheat-haired lady, Papa said, "A certain degree of arrogance is always part of the makeup of the pioneer."

"And is that what ye be, Henry Trevor, a pioneer?" the lady asked. Despite the faint mockery of her words, there was an affectionate lilt to her voice as she addressed him. Bret examined her more closely. She was beautiful, her face serene, her figure lush. She had a basket woven of moor grasses hanging from one arm; the other arm was poised on her hip. Instead of jewelry she wore a wreath of wildflowers and herbs around her neck, and bracelets coiled in the shape of serpents at her wrists.

"Either that or a fool," her father said, returning her smile with an even more charming one of his own. "Have you met my daughter?"

"I've met Verity, but not yer younger daughter," the strange lady said.

"Then let me introduce you to Elizabeth, whom we call Bret. Bret, this lovely young woman is called Tamara Carne. She comes to watch me sometimes, even though she disapproves of my flying almost as much as Verity does."

"Mebbe so, but last night I had a dream," Tamara Carne said in her honey-sweet contralto. "A giant eagle snatched me away and carried me off to his lair high in the purple mountains. I begged him to return me to my home, but he denied my pleas. I wept until he bade me look up at the sky, which was fretted with gold, and down at the land, where the grasses were alive and singing and the petals of the rose were as large as ladies' handkerchiefs. This comforted me, for 'twas beautiful, and I slowly grew to love the eagle for showing such wonders to me."

Although she was not quite ten, Bret could sense the intensity of emotion moving outward in a wave from Tamara Carne to her father, lapping around him, and returning to her magnified by a matching intensity in him. She looked curiously from one to the other. She had heard of Tamara Carne, of course. The Carnes hated the Trevors. But Papa and Tamara weren't behaving like enemies.

"Bret's helping me launch a new prototype," said Henry. "Would you like to watch?"

"I think not, not this morn." She nodded to the basket on her arm. "I'm gathering clay for my work." She smiled and added gently, "The things of the earth, not the things of the air."

"Tamara is a potter," Papa told Bret. "In her hands the things of the earth are every bit as beautiful as the things of the air."

Tamara accepted the compliment with a gracious nod. "I work with the clay," Tamara agreed, smiling at Bret. "On the weekdays I'm a bal maiden up to the Stannis claypits, scraping the blocks and making them ready for market, but my true love is clay sculpting and molding. 'Tes a talent I developed in part because of yer older sister, Verity."

"How did that come about?" Bret asked, fascinated.

"She once tried to give me a lovely doll with the face of an angel molded of creamy porcelain. 'Twas the most beautiful thing I'd ever seen, and I wanted it terribly, but she loved it and needed it more than I."

"D'you mean Guinivere? Verity still has that doll. Her mother gave it to her before she died."

"Her face was a miracle. I thought of it often after that, wondering who had made her face, and how. And so I learned. A 'course, I can't make anything half so fine, and I rarely work in porcelain since 'tes tricky and beyond my skill, but ordinary potting has become my trade, thanks to yer sister."

"I'll tell her as soon as she gets home. She'll be pleased."

"I've got something for 'ee. Look."

Bret exclaimed. In the palm of her hand Tamara held a tiny clay bluebird, lovingly shaped and beautifully painted. "Oh, it's perfect! It looks real, except for the size. How ever did you make it?"

She tipped it into Bret's outstretched hand. " 'Tes yers now."

"To keep?"

"To keep," Tamara confirmed.

"Thank you ever so much! I love it. I'll treasure it always, and—and I'll share it with Verity, since she inspired you."

Tamara smiled and nodded, then walked away, lifting her hand once in a wave as she moved into the thicker vegetation of the moor. As if it knew her, the heather parted to let her pass.

Bret's father stared after her for several seconds, then shook his head as if to clear it.

"I thought the Carnes were our enemies, Papa."

"There's an old feud, but it's foolish. It's her father, Jory, who carries it on." His voice rang with distaste as he mentioned Tamara's father's name. "Tam tries her best to have nothing to do with him. She moved out of Carne Cottage to her own small cabin as soon as she was grown."

"She's very pretty," Bret said, her owlish eyes steady on her father's face.

"Yes, she is. Well. Let's get on with it, shall we?"

They launched the little aeroplane from Cadmon Tor, the

highest point in the vicinity, pointing it south, where the land sloped toward the sea. The takeoff was perfect. Bret and her father clasped hands and watched, transmitting hope and excitement from one to the other through their linked hands, hearts, and minds.

Bret clapped in delight as the small aircraft raced across the lawn, shuddered slightly, then rose, gracefully, effortlessly, into the air, taking Bret's heart with her along with her cry of exultation. Then she was flying, really flying, climbing higher and higher with all the grace of a dove. Henry had brought his field binoculars along, and they took turns watching through the lenses until the cross shape of the wings collapsed into a featureless dot on the horizon, hanging over the pale blue of the sea.

"She's so beautiful. I can't wait to tell Verity. What a shame she had to miss it."

"Verity's not interested in flying machines," her father reminded her.

"I can't imagine why not." She was still gazing at the spot where she had last seen the prototype. "She's such a lovely little aeroplane. What will happen to her? Will she cross the Channel and fly all the way to Paris, do you think?"

Her father didn't answer. As Bret glanced up she saw tears in his eyes. It wasn't until this moment that she realized what ought to have been obvious: the little aeroplane her father had worked on so hard could fly, yes, but it was also doomed to crash. Without a pilot to sit inside and control it, there was no way to bring it down safely.

The thought of the model slowing and faltering and finally plunging into the ocean was unbearable to her, so she slipped her hand into her father's and said, "She *will* fly all the way to Paris, I know it. And what a wonder that will be!"

Her father's fingers tightened around hers, and he smiled.

It was on another Sunday that Bret next saw the wheathaired lady. She had climbed to the highest point on Cadmon Tor on a sunlit day with one of her favorite hounds for company. It was a magical spot. She could see the moorland stretching for miles on three sides.

Looking down from these lofty heights toward the south field where her father pursued his experiments, Bret saw that he was not alone. A statuesque figure was beside him, and they were apparently deep in conversation. Perhaps it was the angle, but it seemed that she was standing close to Papa, and at one point Bert had the impression that their faces were inclined toward each other's as if they were about to kiss. But before she could be certain, the sun moved out from behind a cloud and shone directly into her eyes. By the time she had shaded her face with her hands, Papa and Tamara had moved apart.

Were they in love? Bret found this possibility romantic and mysterious. Papa was a lot older than Tamara, but she knew of several couples where such was the case. Was there any chance that Papa would wed the daughter of his worst enemy? Bret was far too joyous a spirit to have much understanding of the dark passions that lead people to hate one another, but she had heard much over the years about the history of the feud between the Carnes and the Trevors. If Papa and Tamara fell in love, wouldn't that mark the end of it? The prophecy said so. *What true love has torn asunder, only true love can heal.*

How wonderful it would be if the pretty, golden-haired Tamara Carne married Papa and came to live at Cadmon Hall. Apart from the servants, there were no womenfolk in the house, and Bret had been lonely since Verity had gone away to London.

She took the tiny bird out of the deep pocket where she kept it and once again admired its beauty. How had Tamara made it? Bret traced her fingers over the kiln-hardened clay, wondering if it might be possible for her to learn to fashion something so delicate and lovely.

The bird was a thing of the earth because it was made of clay. But it was also a thing of the air, because it had wings.

Chapter Six

"Good afternoon," the stranger said as he heaved his baggage and that of his son onto the racks above their heads. Verity acknowledged his greeting with a polite nod. She hoped her new compartment mates would not bother her for conversation. She had made enough social chitchat during her ten months in London to last for the rest of her days.

"Hurry, hurry, hurry," she whispered to the swaying train. She ached to get home to Cornwall and see her father and Bret again. She longed to smell the moor grasses and the wildflowers and the sea, and most of all the chalky scent of china clay hanging over the valleys, which would be welcome after ten months in the odiferous haze and smog of the city.

As her fellow travelers settled in, she watched them surreptitiously over the pages of a book. The boy looked about Bret's age, although he was thinner and frailer. He had fair hair, brown eyes, and regular features that would probably be considered handsome someday, if he ever managed to shed his pallor. He settled into his seat with a book of poetry, which he read with a dreamy expression, his lips moving slightly as he recited the lines to himself. He was young to be so bookish; clearly he was precocious in that respect.

The father was a tall man of perhaps forty years, inclined to heaviness in a way that would not cut a fine figure in a drawing room, although in his broad shoulders Verity sensed the presence of more muscle than fat. He had large, spatulate hands. His forehead was high and his dour brown hair was already thinning at the temples. His lips were thick, his eyes narrow—an intriguing juxtaposition of the sensual with the confined.

He was neither young nor handsome, which she found vaguely comforting. She had learned the hard way that young, handsome men weren't interested in her, and she was determined never again to be interested in them. Her father had sent her to London to find a husband. She had not succeeded.

"Excuse me, miss," the father said. "Would you mind if I opened the window slightly?"

"Not at all. It's quite stuffy in here."

As he rose to open the window, he removed his greatcoat and placed it on the rack over his head. Turning, he revealed a clerical collar. Verity blinked, astonished, for his powerful, bulky form did not fit her image of a clergyman, unless one cast back to the days of the great cardinals who ruled nations.

Resuming his seat, he smiled at her, and it was in his smile that she saw the first hints of the wisdom and courtesy that she associated with clergymen. Without the smile his physiognomy suggested stern purpose and determination; with it he seemed a pleasanter man.

"Are you traveling far?" he inquired politely.

"To St. Austell in Cornwall. I live near there."

"Indeed? That's where we're going. Will you allow me to make your acquaintance? My name is Julian Marrick. I'm to be the new vicar at St. Catherine's parish in a village called Trenwythan. Do you know it?"

"It's my home parish. I'm Verity Trevor, and I'm very pleased to welcome you to our village."

They shook hands. Reverend Marrick's grip was firm and moist.

"This is my son, Simon. Unfortunately, he lost his mother some time ago, and he still feels the pain of it. I am hoping that a change of scenery will help to assuage his grief. And my own, of course."

"I am very sorry to hear it. How do you do, Master Simon?"

The boy looked up from his book. "Very well, thank you, ma'am."

"I have a sister about your age. You must allow me to introduce her to you sometime soon."

"Thank Miss Trevor for her kindness, Simon," Reverend Marrick ordered.

"Thank you, ma'am," the boy mumbled, fingering the leather binding of his volume.

Reverend Marrick asked her some questions about the area,

and soon they were chatting in a congenial manner. Since he was not only a minister but also considerably older than she, it never occurred to Verity to think of him as a man she must impress, which allowed her to feel relaxed in his company.

"How did you enjoy the Season in London?" he asked when she explained why she'd been there.

"I hated every minute of it."

"Indeed?"

Verity nodded fiercely. Her months in the city had been truly wretched. Her father had sent her to stay with his sister, Aunt Dorothy, a vain, empty-headed woman whose chief interests in life were clothes, visits, and gossip. From the moment Verity arrived, Aunt Dorothy began making remarks along the lines of: "I'm sure I don't know *what* your father expects us to be able to do for you. You have no beauty, no flair, and no conversation. To make matters worse, it's clear that you've had no proper education at all and can't distinguish between a tea gown and an evening gown and don't even care to learn the difference."

Verity didn't need to be reminded that she wasn't beautiful. Her hair had remained a dull brown, her eyes a muddy hazel, her nose a trifle long, and her chin a bit pointed. She was too small and too thin, and despite her aunt's breathless lectures on the importance of fashion, she found it difficult to develop any sense of personal style.

But all the same she had looked forward with great anticipation to her first society dance. The colors whirled around her like so many summer fruits: raspberry and peach, plum, melon and apple green, a veritable assault upon the senses combined with the thick fragrances of a full and burgeoning garden rising from the shoulders and throats and wrists of London's ripest and most marriageable young ladies.

She'd watched the waltzing from a comfortable shadow against the wall. At the beginning of the evening her feet itched in her dancing slippers, longing to lift and leap and prance with the others, but it took no longer than those first few hours in Society to understand that it was her destiny in life to be a watcher, not a participant. Soon she took to lacing her slippers tightly enough to hurt as a reminder to herself that spinning madly to the music under the radiant light of a crystal chandelier was not likely to be an activity in which she would ever find herself engaged. Not for her the pleasures of the dance, the music, the laughter. Not for her the beat of a partner's hips all too near her own, the press of a firm palm between her shoulder blades, the low pitch of a voice murmuring in her ear, the wreath of tobacco smoke around a closely leaning masculine head.

The most humiliating aspect of her failure was that she had no one to blame but herself. Plainer young women than she found partners. Because of her family and fortune, she attracted the attention of the mummies and daddies, if not the sons, but when their fascination with Cadmon Hall and its treasures came up in conversation, she could not hide her suspiciousness of the fortune hunters' motives, or bite back the sarcasm that sprang to her lips.

As a result, she acquired a reputation of being a haughty young woman. The few partners who presented themselves to her aunt at dances, asking for an introduction or the honor of a waltz, soon dropped away. "There now, you'll never make a match, you wretched girl, and I don't know what I'm supposed to tell your father," her aunt had complained.

"You needn't tell him anything. I'll inform him that I am not the sort of woman who will ever be properly courted and married, if this is the way it is done."

She did have an image of what the perfect courtship, and the perfect man, would be like. She saw him as a combination of the masculine virtue and wisdom of a Mr. Knightley with the passion and pride of a Mr. Darcy thrown in. When she tried to explain this to Aunt Dorothy, all she received was a puzzled stare. "I don't believe I've met either of those gentlemen," she said.

Sitting now in the rocking compartment of the westbound train, her thoughts distracted from Reverend Marrick and his son, she debated the merits of remaining a spinster for life. It no longer seemed such a sorry fate.

"So you didn't care for London Society?" Reverend Marrick prompted. He was looking at her with considerable interest. "What an odd thing to hear from a young lady. My impression has always been that women your age reveled in the vanity of balls, suppers, and the fawning of effete young men.''

''One thing I've learned during the past few months is that I am unlike other young women.''

''You say that ruefully, but in my opinion it's something to be proud of. Women your age do not, as a rule, impress me with their character, wit, or good sense.''

''That is probably because such attributes are not encouraged in us. We're taught by society to develop far more frivolous qualities. It makes those of us who have the wit to give some thought to our predicament feel frustrated and discontent. There doesn't seem to be anything in life for us to do.''

''What do you wish to do?''

''I'm not sure,'' she admitted. ''If I were an impoverished gentlewoman, I'd have been been forced to earn a living. I'd have been encouraged to become a teacher, perhaps, or even to attend the university and enter a profession. Instead, my father has always assumed I would marry a suitable man of equal fortune and live out my life managing his household and raising his children. Not,'' she quickly added, ''that there's anything wrong with such a life. But since I will probably never marry, I would like to have some other viable option.''

''Quite right,'' said the understanding Reverend Marrick. ''But why are you so certain you shall never marry?''

Verity made an empty gesture with her hands. ''For the simple reason that no one will have me. I'm not beautiful. I lack style. And I don't know how to talk to men.''

''I think you're beautiful,'' young Simon astonished her by saying. '' 'She walks in beauty, like the night.' ''

His father pressed the boy's hand in one of his own large ones, rather roughly, she noticed, as Simon winced. ''Please don't think him rude. The truth is, you bear a marked resemblance to my late wife.''

Blushing, and not the least bit insulted at having a line of Byron quoted to her, even if it had come from the mouth of a nine-year-old boy, Verity said, ''Oh no, I don't think him rude at all. Thank you, Simon.'' To his father she said, awkward now, "I'm sorry if my appearance causes you pain."

"On the contrary," he said, smiling.

The remainder of the journey passed rapidly, for the conversation rarely lagged. When the train pulled into St. Austell and Verity was dashing off to throw herself into the welcoming arms of Papa and Bret, Reverend Marrick asked if he might call on her sometime soon. Assuming the visit to be of a pastoral nature, Verity, without any self-consciousness, assured him that she and her family would welcome him at Cadmon Hall.

Chapter Seven

"I have a project I'd like your help on, Bret," Verity said to her sister one morning a fortnight after returning home. "We need to go through Cadmon Hall, room by room, and sort things out. We have so many lovely things tucked away in odd places. They're part of the history of our family. I want to seek them out, clean them up, and find the best way to display them."

"Like a treasure hunt?"

"Precisely."

These were magical words to the imaginative Bret, who was as eager to help as Verity was to get to work. Much as she had longed for Cornwall while she'd been away, she was chagrined to discover that she was restless and fretful at home. There was nothing to do. Although she'd been surrounded by a group of uncongenial people in London, she had enjoyed her constant activities in the huge, busy city. As her father's heir, she would one day be the mistress of Cadmon Hall. It was time, she decided, to put the place in order.

They began with the antique furniture, old bedsteads, dressers, wardrobes, and chests of drawers that were gathering dust on the upper stories of the mansion. Verity arranged to have several pieces restored, others disposed of. They moved on to the old clothing, in which Bret delighted in dressing up, and finally to the items Verity really cared about, the books, artworks, and decorative objects, including the Trevors' fine collection of china.

"I think I like the pictures better than the china," Bret said as Verity studied the styles and the glazes of various pieces of porcelain. Verity found her sister sketching a likeness of one of their ancestors. It was an astonishingly good copy of a dusty portrait. Bret had managed to capture the tone and style of the original, while imparting a certain wryness of her own to the woman's expression that hinted at a broader base of emotion than the portrait painter had been able to glean.

"Good heavens, Bret, that's excellent. I didn't know you could draw so well. You're very talented."

"That's what Miss Brenner says," Bret said, referring to her current governess. "D'you really think she's right?"

"Absolutely. In fact, I'm going to speak to Papa about it. Miss Brenner's facility for drawing and sketching isn't much better than mine, from what I've seen of it. You ought to have a special drawing master. We mustn't allow your light to be hidden under a bushel."

"That would be splendid!" She pulled out another painting of a dour male ancestor. "Look at this one. He reminds me of Reverend Marrick."

Verity felt her cheeks warm as Bret began to sketch, subtly altering her subject's features, making him look even more like the new vicar of St. Catherine's. Reverend Marrick, who had startled the congregation by turning out to be a preacher of fire and thunder, had already paid four or five visits to Cadmon Hall—enough to cause comment among the household staff. Verity had learned from her maid that they were speculating belowstairs that the new vicar was showing signs of being interested in her as a woman. Even Bret had noticed it.

"The new minister keeps staring at you," she'd whispered over tea during the second of these visits. "I think he's falling in love."

"Don't be ridiculous," Verity had said. She was so accustomed to being rejected by men that she couldn't credit the possibility.

"Just think, you'd be Simon's stepmother," Bret said, laughing.

"Don't be impertinent."

Bret and Reverend Marrick's son had taken to each other right away, even though Bret's liveliness was in direct opposition to Simon's gloom. Their first conversation, which Verity had overheard with some amusement, had cemented their friendship.

"Are you the new vicar's son?" Bret had asked. "What's your name?"

"I am one whose name is writ in water," Simon had replied, which resulted in immediate puzzlement for Bret, whose education had not yet touched upon the Romantic poets.

"Well, I'm Bret Trevor, and I personally intend to write my name in the darkest, boldest ink I can find. Do you have a holy vocation, like your father?"

"My vocation is for the secret ministry of frost."

"Do speak English?"

"That *is* English, and of the highest order. Those are lines from a poem by Samuel Taylor Coleridge. I'm going to be a poet one day, you see, and write the finest verse the world has ever known. Of course, that probably means I'll die young, like Mr. Shelley and Mr. Keats. Everybody will mourn me and recite my lovely poems with tears glistening like shattered crystal upon their pallid cheeks."

"I'd rather live a long and happy life than have people cry over my poems."

"Are you sure? Alexander the Great was given a choice between a long life and eternal fame."

Verity saw her sister's eyes glint with mischief as she said, "Really? Which one did he choose?"

"Well, obviously—" he began, then stopped. "You're teasing me."

Bret bestowed her infectious grin upon the stiff, immaculately dressed little boy. "Forgive me; I'm awful that way. Would you like to go outside and play?"

Simon had smiled uncertainly, as if playing were something he'd never tried. Undeterred, Bret seized his hand and dragged him off into the gardens, and by the time his father's visit was over, the boy didn't want to leave.

"It is thoughtful of your sister to be so kind to my son," Reverend Marrick said.

"It's her nature to be friendly."

"You are kind also, to be so hospitable to us, Miss Trevor."

"I am glad of your company," Verity had made so bold as to reply.

That evening while taking his leave of her, Reverend Marrick had requested that she call him Julian, and holding her hand in his for a far longer moment than was strictly proper between a pastor and a member of his flock, had allowed his eyes to linger briefly upon her neat, slim figure.

It would serve her father and Aunt Dorothy right, she thought now, if Reverend Marrick were to propose and she accepted. She doubted that when they'd begun angling for a husband for her, they had ever considered she might choose a poor country vicar.

"Verity?"

Verity came out of her reverie to find her sister blinking at her. She was poking through the old paintings again.

"Have you looked at these?" she asked, pulling out several of the canvases from China that had belonged to Verity's mother. Of all the many objects that her maternal grandfather had sent back to England from his sojourn in China, Verity was least interested in the paintings. Muted in color and pastoral in scene, none of them was as fine or as beautiful as the lacquered screens, silk rugs, and wall hangings, bronze sculptures, and, of course, the porcelain. But Bret examined each one carefully. "Some of these are lovely," she told her sister. "We might want to hang them somewhere."

"I doubt that."

"This one, for instance." She indicated a large painting of misty mountains rising in the background and several small groups of Chinese laborers performing various tasks. "What are they doing, do you suppose?"

"I can't imagine," Verity said, giving the picture no more than a cursory glance.

"It's a clayworks, I think," said Bret. "They're trundling down something from the mountains that looks like china clay."

Verity set aside the bronze horseman she was cleansing of dust and grime. "Let me see that."

"Each set of laborers is doing something special. See? In this corner they're making porcelain."

Indeed, the painting depicted every aspect of the china-making process in an ancient Chinese porcelain works, including the digging and refining of the clay; the throwing, decorating, and firing of the pots; and finally the shipping of the finished ware off to market. The rugged landscape of the setting struck a sharp contrast to the usual pastoral oriental scene of sinuous streams and weeping willows.

"It reminds me of Cadmon Clay," said Bret. "The mountains could almost be our Cornish moors. If you look closely you can see the workers trundling clay out of the pits and refining it for the pot makers, who are working right there on site. Did they always make the porcelain at the same place in China where they mined the kaolin? We don't do that here."

"At one time we did. We used to make china right here at Cadmon Clay."

"I never knew that."

"It's something you ought to know, Bret." Verity frowned as she remembered the lessons her stepmother had forced her to learn on the subject. If Caroline Lynchpole had lived, she would have made certain that her daughter was not so ignorant of the history of the family business. "The company was originally known as Cadmon Clay and Porcelain. You can still see the foundation of the old china works not far from the small building Papa uses as his office. The Trevors produced some very fine china a hundred years ago, and the pieces that remain are considered collectors' items. Our grandfather used to talk about starting up the china-making side of the business again someday. It was his dream. He wanted to see it all happening here, from pit to pot, as he used to say, just like it was in the old days."

"That would be wonderful!" said Bret.

Verity was staring at the painting, transfixed. *From pit to pot*. Rufus Trevor had never fulfilled his dream, but he hadn't allowed it to die with him. By telling it over and over to his young granddaughter, he had planted a seed that was belatedly beginning to sprout. She thought of the huge amounts of money spent on china engagement and wedding gifts by the young ladies she had met in London. All her acquaintances had required china at the time of their engagements, and the trend was to reject the overwrought Victorian decoration of their parents and grandparents in favor of newer, smarter designs.

If I were to start making china again, she thought, *I would make the sort of china people want to buy. Something new, something beautiful. I would restore the ancient glory of Cadmon Clay and Porcelain, and create translucent loveliness again.*

The following morning Verity rose at dawn, dressed in her most severe and serious frock, downed a light breakfast, and set off on foot before Bret and her father were out of bed. She hiked over the fragrant moors to the Cadmon claypits. As she had done so many years ago with Grandpa, she lingered on one of the slopes that looked down on the work area, observing the operations with a keener and more informed eye than she had possessed as a child.

She knew the process—the granite rock that was so plentiful in this part of Cornwall was rich in the mineral feldspar, which decomposes to form kaolin, china clay. To extract it from the rock, workers washed water into the claypits to form a thick clay slurry. Moving the slurry out of the pit was the job of the noisy beam engine and its giant pump. After the slurry was refined to remove impurities, the white china clay, thick as Cornish clotted cream, was dried and loaded into barrels or cut into blocks to be carted down the hills by horse cart to the port of Charlestown on St. Austell Bay.

As a child, Verity had loved to watch the clay making. There was something marvelous about removing white blocks of clay from the brown and stony earth. It was a magical transformation. How could one believe, simply from looking at the barren landscape, that such beauty could reside within?

Today, inspired by the Chinese painting, Verity was able

to imagine an even greater beauty. Standing on a barren hill overlooking Cadmon Clay and superimposing the Chinese images over the reality that lay before her, she envisioned both a ghost of the past and a vision of the future. Clay mined, clay refined, clay molded into china. The revival of the Trevors' greatest triumph—the re-creation of the most beautiful and delicate china Great Britain had ever known.

At last, she had a dream.

Chapter Eight

Henry Trevor gasped as the warm mouth of his lover moved down his body, following in the trail of her light, wanton fingertips. In the dark secret place where they lay, he could barely see her, for the candle she had lit in the corner had burned down to a squashed lump of wax. It was good, in a way, not to be able to see her. It added to her mystery, which was already immense.

She was like the clay, soft, pliant, and earthy, her flesh warm and malleable beneath his fingers. The gold of her hair reminded him of cornsilk; her body, when he stripped her clothing from her, was as ripe and fecund as the harvest grain. He took nurturance in her ample breasts. Dark mysteries pulsed between her thighs.

In some strange way that he could not understand, he feared her. When he dozed in her arms, he had recurring dreams of being trapped in a cave with no doorway to the outside world. Lying in the darkness, he listened to the great throbbing echoes of life as serpents twined themselves around his arms and legs and torso, softly hissing warnings into his ears. He would wake sweating, shaking, amazed that he should have such dreams while wrapped in the comforting arms of his lover.

Tamara made him cozy with straw and quilts and hanging

perfumed herbs. When he woke up frightened, she would touch him with her knowing hands and her soft, hot tongue, and soon he would feel safe, too, safer and more secure than he had ever felt before in his life.

Henry was old enough to be Tamara's father, but when he was entwined with her in the act of love, he felt like the youngest and most helpless of children. This vulnerability bewildered him; he both enjoyed and dreaded it. Often when he took his leave of her to return to his own realm—the clear sky through which he flew his beloved aeroplanes—he would vow never to return, but soon his desire would build and he would come again to worship at her altar, drink from her spring. He was careful to avoid her father, Jory Carne, the only man, she had confessed to him, of whom she was afraid.

"You're a woman, Tamara," Henry Trevor said to her after they had finished making love.

A husky giggle greeted his words.

"What I mean is, you understand other women. I don't, you see. I never have."

"As far as women're concerned, ye understand the things ye need to know."

"I'm serious, Tam. Stop that for a moment and listen to me."

"I'm hearing 'ee, my love."

"It's Verity. I feel as if I failed with her years ago. Despite my many earnest resolutions, I've never learned to be an attentive father. I'm no better with Bret, but it doesn't matter so much because she and I understand each other. She never gives me the wounded glances I get from her sister; she never makes me feel guilty." He sighed. "They both needed a mother. I ought to have married again, but I couldn't bring myself to do it after burying two wives."

" 'Tes true, children need a mother. They can do without a father, mebbe, but they need a mum to love them if they're to grow up safe and happy."

Henry kissed her gently. He had heard the sorrow in her voice. Tamara's mother, too, had died when she was a child, as had his own.

"I don't know what to do about Verity now that she's

home. She has no prospects for marriage, except maybe for that tedious Reverend Marrick, who's always hanging about. I don't think she fancies him, though.''

''I hope not. I have bad feelings about him,'' Tamara said.

''She came to me this morning and asked my permission to come and work for the clay company. She announced that as my heir, she wants to take over the business someday. She wants to manufacture porcelain again, as Cadmon Clay did in the eighteenth century. She, a woman, aspires to be an entrepreneur.''

''And what did ye say to that?''

''Naturally I told her it was impossible, and now she's in a snit.''

''Why not let her work for 'ee, if that's what she wants?''

''I can't seriously believe she does want it. What woman would? Anyway, a female running the clayworks—it's out of the question. Can you imagine the resistance I'd encounter from the clay workers if they saw a woman being placed above them? No, in my judgment Verity is casting about for something to fill the empty place inside her. What she really needs, dammit, is a man.''

''Mmm, a'course. We females jist can't get along without 'ee.''

Henry studied her face for irony. But her small moorland cottage was dark, lit only by a single candle. He couldn't see her expression.

''What will happen to Cadmon Clay when ye're gone in the earth, my love?''

''I thought I'd have a son. The Trevors always have. That's another reason why I ought to have married again. For the first time in four hundred years there's no male heir to pass along our name.''

''Ye're not too old. Ye could get yerself a son. Ye could marry again.''

Was there a wistful note in her voice? He tried to catch her eye, but she turned her head away, more mysterious, even, than usual. He wished he understood her better. Did she mean she could give him a son? Did she expect him to crown their love affair with marriage? In truth he had been considering it, imagining with a certain wry amusement the stir it would cause in Trenwythan if a Trevor were to marry a Carne.

"What're ye thinking?"

He pushed up on one elbow and smiled down into her eyes. "I was thinking how sweet it would be to be married to you."

She smiled back, but said, "Now there's a mad thought. 'Tes impossible, as ye well know." Smiling, she quoted:

> *"May passion's poison o-erflow each vein,*
> *May they know naught but conflict and strife,*
> *May their lads be crushed by the sin of Cain,*
> *May their lasses breed hatred in each new life."*

"What arrant nonsense! I thought you were too sensible to perpetuate that myth."

"The feud between yer family and mine's no myth to Jory and Daniel. They're both still scheming to reclaim the land ye've made into Cadmon Clay."

"Then they're both dreamers. I personally have had enough of this feud. But if I were to credit it at all, I'd focus on the words of the prophecy: *What true love has torn asunder, only true love can heal.*"

"Ah. But what has true love to do with marriage? I've no wish to marry, now or ever. I decided when I was but a girl never to allow what happened to my mum to happen to me."

"Not all men are like your father."

"Mebbe not. But no one knows what changes the years might bring, and once ye're wed, ye're stuck. Anyroad, there's only one joy that marriage brings a woman, and that's children of her own to raise and to love. 'Tes the only thing I miss." She paused, then added, "Course, if I decide to have a child, I'll have one. I reckon I can raise a babe on my own jist as well, if not better, than I was raised."

Was there a defiant note in her voice? She might conceive, he knew. Was she saying that even if she bore him a son, she would insist on remaining single and bringing up the child alone?

He pressed her down beneath him, challenged by her elusiveness, her independence. It occurred to him that she was the one woman he truly wanted . . . and the one he would never truly have.

Alone after her lover's departure, Tamara gathered a selection of roots and barks from her various bottles and jars. She pounded the ingredients in a mortar and pestle until the fragrant juices and oils were well mixed, then emptied the pulp into a lidded kettle and added water to brew a decoction. She steamed it long and slowly, humming to herself. She called up the Great Goddess's spirit, asking Her blessing for the moon-gathered herbs.

When the tisane was ready, she poured a measure of it into an oiled wooden chalice that had come down to her from her mother's people. She added one last ingredient—a pinch of kaolin that she had secreted in her apron during her daily work of scraping block after block of china clay. Like sugar to the finest Darjeeling tea, she stirred it in—a touch of earth to bind her love.

Ritualistically, she swallowed the potion. The herbs would strengthen her blood . . . and that of her child. This was necessary, for the destiny cards had predicted sorrow, shadows, and scandal.

She had had the destiny cards since that long-ago day when her mother had taken her to the Gypsy encampment on top of Hensbarrow. There, under a leaden sky, caressed by the sharp wind from the sea, an old woman awaited them. Tamara's mother bowed to her and kissed her hand, then put her forehead to the crone's palm in obeisance. She called her Grandmama, which may have been a title of respect or may have signified a relationship—Tamara wasn't certain which, although she knew her mother had Romany blood.

Kneeling at the feet of the crone, Tamara had looked up to see an ancient pair of eyes staring into her own. A moment later she realized that this was an illusion, for the eyes were clouded over with what seemed an opaque membrane, sealing them from the light. The old woman was blind.

But only in the way of men.

In the ways of the Goddess, she saw clearly.

She put her hands upon Tamara's head. Those brittle bones trembled for an instant before they steadied. "You are of the earth, my daughter,'' she said in a voice like dry leaves. ''You are with the hills and with the corn. You are with the grasses that undulate upon the moors. You are with the barrows and the serpents. You give life and you bring death. Your power is great.''

''Ye frighten me, Grandmama.''

''That is as it should be. You were born to one path but yearn to walk another. Such is not the road of contentment. Such is the pathway of despair.''

''I don't understand 'ee.''

''Your strengths are your weaknesses. To love is noble, but to sin in the name of love is still to sin, and sin is a debt that must be paid, one way or another. Beware your passions,'' she added, ''for they will bring much joy but also many sorrows.''

The Gypsy placed within the girl's hand a small hard packet wrapped in black silk. ''I have no more use for these. I have seen what I have seen. Use them respectfully. You have the gift.''

Wrapped within the silk was a deck of brightly colored cards. The images were fierce but beautiful. Each gave her a distinct feeling; some frightened her. ''They are destiny cards,'' Tamara's mother told her. ''Ye'll learn to interpret them as ye grow.''

The old woman had spoken correctly, for Tamara had slowly come to love and understand the cards. She laid them out now, once again studying the images that had appeared over and over again. It was as she feared: the Tower of Love had risen, but its foundation was cracked.

Chapter Nine

''Bloody hell! Why don't ye watch where ye're going!'' a male voice yelled.

Verity was out riding at dusk on the moors about a week after her argument with her father, about which she was still stewing. He utterly refused to allow her to work for the clay company. She was his heir, yes, but she was a wealthy young woman of gentle birth. Such women did not visit clay companies, much less run them. Such women collected porcelain, perhaps, but they certainly did not manufacture and design it.

Thinking of this, and of the Reverend Julian Marrick, who had been even more attentive lately, Verity rapidly crested a hill, rounded a curve, and nearly collided with three men on horseback. They were mounted on heavyset dray horses of the sort that were used to pull clay wagons, and they were all clad in the baggy pants, jacket, and cap that were the universal attire of clay workers from Bugle to the sea.

" 'Tes a woman," one of them observed.

" 'Tes Trevor's daughter, by Christ."

The men surrounded her, blocking her progress. Two of them were young, not much more than twenty, and the white kaolin dust ingrained in their hair and skin confirmed that they were clay laborers. The third man, who seemed to be in charge of the ragtag gang, was older than the other two. He was of medium height and stocky with a shock of pale hair and light blue eyes set in a hollow face. As she stared at him through the swirl of fog, she felt a jolt. He was Jory Carne, that malicious creature who so long ago had spat upon her grandfather's corpse.

"What is the meaning of this?" she cried as one of the men jumped from his mount and jerked the reins from her. In one hand he held a jug of what smelled like whiskey, which he passed to Jory Carne, who took a long pull on it as he dismounted.

"Ye out here alone, missy?" Carne said. "Unprotected by the presence of yer precious pa? Too bad. I'd have liked to have a word or two with him, by God."

Verity knew that many people in the area considered Jory Carne a colorful character, a poet and a dreamer more than a doer, a drinker more than anything else. But to her he looked rough and brutal, and there was a stink about him that suggested he and his mates had already quaffed a liberal amount from their jug.

"It's late," she said in a voice that quavered slightly. She cleared her throat, striving to regain her self-possession. "If you gentlemen have business with my father, I suggest you wait until tomorrow." Perhaps if she addressed them as gentlemen, they would begin to act that way. "If you will kindly move your horses out of my way, I wish to continue my journey before full darkness falls."

"Not so fast, Miz Trevor. Surely ye're not too busy this fine night for a little conversation."

"I'm afraid etiquette does not permit my stopping to speak with strangers in the middle of a country lane."

"Etiquette, is it?" said Carne with his mad, drunken smile. " 'Tes the hand of fortune at work this night that ye should come along. Come into the light whur I can see 'ee, and get ye down."

He put his hands around her waist and pulled. She stumbled as she landed and had to seize his arm for an instant to keep from falling. Jory Carne was not much taller than she, but there in the gathering dusk he seemed to tower over her. He put a restraining hand on her shoulder to prevent her from running away, but her legs were trembling so badly that she could not have run in any case.

"Now, now, don't get yerself all het up," Carne said. He sounded almost apologetic, as if he was trying to convince her that his wickedness was mere mischief, not to be taken seriously. The light blue eyes and the nimble quickness of his movements seemed to underscore this elfin quality. He reminded her of Puck or some equally amoral creature.

She noticed that his eyes did not have quite the same spark or energy of a few years before. He had been rumored to be ill these last several months, but he was still well enough to visit every pub in St. Austell, spending on strong, liver-rotting drink whatever money he earned with his sporadic forays into the china-clay fields.

Verity had also heard that his son Daniel endeavored to keep him out of taverns, or, failing that, to collect him when Jory was too inebriated to find his way home. But apart from the virtue of filial affection—if loving such a man as Jory Carne could be viewed as a virtue—she knew of nothing else for which to commend young Daniel. By all accounts, the boy she'd fought in the schoolyard had grown into a hellraiser who was nearly as much of a headache to the region as his father was.

"Will you please tell me what you want of me?"

He circled her, his darting eyes and jerky limbs reinforcing his Puckishness. She half-expected him to say, "Your first-born child."

"There's one thing I really want of the Trevors, and that's the deed to the land that yer ancestors stole from mine."

Verity stiffened. "You surely don't think that I have the power to grant you that."

"The power? Ye're an uppity miss, ain't 'ee? Ye sound like a bloody queen." With one hand curled around her upper arm, he dragged her into the deeper shadows at the edge of the road. "The only power ye need tonight is that of a messenger. I've got a word or two for yer pa. Ye tell him this: If he ever comes near my girl again, I'll kill him."

Verity blinked. "What do you mean? What girl?"

"My daughter. Tamara. Now mebbe ye don't know what I'm talking about, a decent young woman like yerself, all worried about etiquette and such. But he'll understand."

"Are you suggesting that your daughter and my father are—" Helplessly she sought the appropriate term.

"Sweethearts, aye. Lovers, if ye will. Though there's not much love, I reckon, on his part. I've yet to meet a Trevor wi' a warm, beating heart."

"You can't be serious. That's the most preposterous thing I've ever heard! He's much too old for her, and besides, after all the years of bad blood between us, how can you imagine that a Trevor would ever take up with a Carne?"

" 'Tesn't so unusual. 'Tes the way the bloody feud started, ye'll recall. And Tam's always been a beauty."

Verity had not seen Tamara Carne for years, but she had a flash of her during her schooldays—her soft golden hair, her lovely face, her blossoming figure. There had been rumors every now and then about Papa taking up with local women, but they were usually older, and these liaisons, if indeed they existed, had always been too discreet to cause scandal.

"Even if it is true, which I doubt, your daughter's a woman, well into her twenties, and entitled to lead her own life," Verity stated. That she was able to talk at all amazed her. She could hear herself as if from a great distance, and the voice she heard was calm. "I'm sure she doesn't require your protection."

"She's my daughter, and she'll have my protection, whether she likes it or not, until the day I die! I'll not have her consorting with any Trevor. D'ye understand what I'm saying?"

"I don't think she does, Jory," one of his friends put in. "I've a feeling this one ain't seen much o' life."

Carne laughed, then staggered. Verity thought he was going to fold up and collapse. But after swaying for a bit he straightened, and wiped his mouth on the back of his hand. "Ye seen much o'life, girlie?"

"I've seen enough to know that you and your companions are disgustingly drunk."

"Yeah, well, ye've seen more than that, I'll wager. From what I hear, the Reverend Marrick seems to think so. 'Tes true, in't, that he's been courting 'ee?"

She was silent, mortified to know that Julian's visits to Cadmon Hall had become the subject of common gossip.

"He's a fine hypocrite, our new vicar," said Carne. "Or don't ye know about his own sorry sins? Rants and raves about righteousness in the pulpit, only to go out and practice the same lechery as any other man. Ye can bet he doesn't show 'ee his true colors, missy."

"If you seriously imagine I'll listen to any more vile calumny from you, of all people—"

"Ye can damn well listen to thes: I've thrashed Tam severely to make sure she mends her wicked ways, but temptation's a nasty thing where a rich man's concerned. So you tell yer pa that the next time I catch him sniffin' around my girl, he's likely to find himself sinking into a runoff pool, his belly slit open and filled with enough china clay to weigh him down so he'll never see the light o' day again."

His expression had gone coldly serious and the elfin quality had flown. The casual viciousness of his words gave Verity a glimpse of the brutality lurking behind his glib tongue and pleasant features. She was reminded of the impression she had formed so long ago of two children—Tamara and Daniel Carne—who were terrified of their father.

"I—I have to go," Verity whispered, inching toward her horse.

One of the other men was right behind her, and as she mistakenly backed into him, his fingers closed on her shoulders with a pressure that hurt. The third man was there as well, his eyes hot as they roved up and down, admiring what he could see of her figure.

"Hey, what's yer hurry, lass? Me and Mick'd like to get to know 'ee a bit better."

Mick, laughing uproariously, said, "Jist like the vicar."

The first man was fondling Verity's arms, moving his hands up and down. "Ye know, there's somemat I always wondered about: When a lass is born in a great stone pile of a house and fed rich viands and allowed to sit about at leisure while everybody else works their fingers to the bone, does it make her softer to the touch? Does it make her sweeter and tastier, and more willin'?"

"Let go of me," Verity said, struggling.

"Behave yerself, Pete," said Carne. "Ye're drunk."

"Ye're a fine one to talk, Jory."

Carne chortled and lifted the jug again. "Richer doesna' make 'em sweeter, Pete, take it from me. Women're all the same in the dark."

"Mebbe we'd like to find that out for ourselves, Jory," Mick said. He was standing in front of her now, and while his friend held her from behind, he ran his palms down the front of Verity's frock.

"Stop it!" She fought wildly but couldn't free herself. Her teeth were chattering, and her heart was thumping, a sound that seemed to get louder and louder . . . unless . . . No. The sound was coming from somewhere outside herself.

"Ey, Jory, come on. A rider. Let's get the hell out o' here!"

"Yeah? Who? Her pa, mayhap?" Carne sounded eager.

"Too dark t' see." Pete had released his hold on her and Mick was throwing himself heavily onto his horse. "Probably someone up from the village. Come on."

Jory Carne pushed his face into hers. He was swaying again. "Right. Ye remember what I said, missy."

The anger that had stirred in her a few minutes before boiled up toward the surface, and all she could think of was the way this vile man had defiled Grandpa's body. "And you, Jory Carne, remember this!" Neglecting every iota of ladylike behavior she had ever been taught, she spat directly into his face. "That's for Rufus Trevor!"

He staggered as if her saliva packed the lethal power of a bullet.

"Filthy drunkard," she added as he heaved himself onto his horse. "You're disgusting! And as for you—" she yelled after Mick and Pete, who had made no scruple to abandon their friend, "you're bullies and cowards. The authorities shall hear about this."

She whirled in the direction of the rider who had appeared so fortuitously out of the darkness with all the power and glory of a medieval knight. She imagined him mounted on a fine destrier, sheathed in armor and brandishing a sword.

She called out, waving her arms over her head. When he came close enough to recognize her, the horseman reined in. "Miss Trevor? Verity? Good God!"

"Help me, please." Now that it was over she had begun to tremble from head to toe. "Oh God, please help me."

"Of course I'll help you. Believe me, dear Verity, there's nothing I'd rather do."

The Reverend Julian Marrick had barely dismounted when Verity ran to him. He opened his arms and she hid within them, sobbing out her fear and shame.

"What the bloody hell!"

Verity had rarely seen her father react so strongly. He reminded her of Grandpa the way he leaped out of his chair, scattering his model aeroplanes all over his desk, and stormed toward her with the wrath of Zeus.

"Precisely the way I feel," Julian Marrick was saying. He had one arm around Verity's shoulders, still holding her to his solid, reassuring form. "In the short time I've been in the area, I've heard several unsavory tales about Carne's violence and drunkenness, but this goes beyond the pale. To waylay and assault a lady—this cannot be tolerated."

Her father took her from Julian's embrace, showing the tenderness and concern that he usually reserved for Bret. He drew her close to his tall body. Verity felt the wiry fluff of his beard against her aching temples. "My poor darling. Are you really all right? What did they do to you? They, uh, didn't . . ."

As her father's voice trailed off, Verity was aware that both he and Julian were waiting intently for her answer. What would their reaction to her be, she wondered, if she'd had to confirm their fears?

"Nothing happened." Her fingers drew little patterns against her father's shoulders. Papa was outraged by the insult to her honor, and there was something wonderful about that. It almost made up for the terrors of her encounter. "They were insulting and intimidating, but nothing more than that, although—" She shuddered and pulled away. "I'm thankful that Reverend Marrick came along when he did."

"So am I, my dear, so am I." He released her. "Now repeat to me, please, exactly what that bloody bastard said about Tamara."

"You mean about slitting your belly and—"

"Not that part. I'm not interested in such swaggering nonsense. He'd thrashed his daughter, is that what he told you?"

She nodded.

"God damn him! He's been raising his bloody hands to her for most of her life, but this time, by God, I draw the line. I've put up with all I'm going to take from that vicious son of Satan, and so has she."

Verity blinked. It was true, then. It must be.

"It's time somebody dealt with the blackguard," Henry continued. "By Christ, he's thrashed her for the last time."

Verity backed away. Papa was having an affair with Tamara Carne. She felt Julian Marrick's arms come around her again. She accepted them gratefully. The walls seemed to be pressing in on her. It was *Tamara* Papa was concerned about. His unaccustomed rage had been sparked by his mistress's predicament, not her own.

"Now, Trevor, I hardly think—" Reverend Marrick began as Verity's father pushed past him and threw open the door to the hallway. "Where are you going? I wouldn't have presented this to you so bluntly if I'd thought you were going to lose your temper and go off half-cocked."

"Half-cocked! I'm fully cocked, I assure you!" Henry strode toward the front of the house, with Verity and Reverend Marrick following. "I appreciate what you've done for us tonight, Vicar, but if you think it's going to end here, without any retaliation on my part, you're sadly mistaken. On top of everything else, I've not forgotten the day Jory Carne spat through his teeth into the dead face of my father, and the time has come to ram that nasty smile of his right down his throat."

"Trevor, this is no way to solve anything. Violence begets violence and is evil in the eyes of the Lord."

Henry ignored him, consulting his pocket watch as he grabbed an overcoat from his startled manservant. "Get a stableboy to saddle my horse. I'm going to see to Tamara, then I'm going to find Jory Carne."

"Papa, perhaps you shouldn't," said Verity. With the crash of her elation came a rush of embarrassment at the spectacle of her father's acting in such an unrestrained manner in front of the controlled and rational Reverend Marrick. He, too, must understand the implications of Papa's concern for Tamara. He must know now that Jory's accusation was true. "Jory Carne had had a lot to drink, he was with friends, and—"

"Of course he'd had a lot to drink. Everybody knows he spends most of his evenings in the pubs, drinking himself silly. Once I've taken care of Tam, I'll sweep 'em all until I find the bugger."

"Trevor, I must insist that you forswear this scheme. The Lord Jesus says—"

"The Lord Jesus wasn't in love, was he?" Henry said as he slammed out the door.

In love! With Tamara? It was too ridiculous. In love at his age, and with a Carne.

"Your father hasn't been drinking, I trust?" asked Reverend Marrick.

"No, no, I don't think so. It's just his temper. It's rare that he loses it, but when he does he can be dramatic."

"I'd better go after him to be sure no violence ensues. It can be a grave mistake to take action without carefully considering the consequences."

The chandelier overhead appeared to be revolving. Verity swayed, feeling like an archetypal Victorian gentlewoman in need of her smelling salts. She clutched at him to prevent herself from falling. "Please, Reverend Marrick—Julian—don't leave me alone just yet."

The vicar of St. Catherine's lifted her off her feet and carried her to the nearest room, the winter parlor, where he deposited her gently on an ivory and gold brocade sofa. Verity could feel her heart slamming as he tucked an afghan around the lower half of her body.

"My poor injured wren," he said so softly that she wasn't certain she'd heard him correctly. "Shall I ring for your maid?"

"I—no, I—"

"My dear, it is true, isn't it, that you were not—" he paused delicately, "injured in any way? Do you understand what I'm asking you? It occurred to me that you might not have wished to disclose such a crime to your father, but I assure you, as a minister of God, there is nothing I haven't heard, nothing that could shock me, nothing that cannot be forgiven."

His words sounded compassionate, but Verity sensed that he was asking less out of compassion than out of some driving need to know. If she *had* been raped, God might have forgiven her, but would Reverend Marrick truly have been able to find that much love in his heart? Given all that had happened this evening, she would not have been surprised if he wished to end his association with her and her scandalous family forthwith.

"Nothing happened," she assured him.

"Ah, then, you were fortunate." His voice rose in volume, assuming something of the magnificent, vibrant quality that she had become accustomed to hearing from the pulpit. "Men like those, men in whom the Beast roars and evil is propagated, men who surrender themselves to the base desires that represent the gravest failings of the flesh . . . may Heaven protect the innocent from such depravity. Let us kneel and offer God a prayer of thankfulness for your deliverance.''

Verity slipped easily from the sofa to her knees, but Reverend Marrick remained standing before the ornate sofa as before an altar, looking down upon her with a benign smile and making her feel as if he were the god whom she was obliged to petition. Then he knelt at her side, their shoulders brushing and their thighs only inches apart. Despite the golden tones of his voice, she hardly heard what he was saying. Instead she allowed herself to indulge the fantasy of how pleasant and comfortable it would be to kneel every night with this man, who not only had the power to protect her from human evil but could intercede for her with God.

At first Tamara would not open the door to him, and it was not until Henry threatened to break it down that he understood why. Both her beautiful eyes were blackened, and there were bruises on her arms and shoulders. As he entered, her hands drifted to her belly, as if to protect herself down there. She moved with a stiffness that confirmed what he knew she would never admit—she had been brutally beaten.

Worst of all was the expression on her lovely but battered face. She seemed unutterably sad, and vulnerable. He'd never thought of her as vulnerable. And she wasn't—not really— for underneath it he sensed a boundless rage, the intensity of which shocked him.

Henry's anger, already at the highwater mark, surged and overbrimmed. As he lifted her in his arms and carried her to her bed, he was startled to find himself shaking. Jory Carne would pay for this. By God, he'd teach him what it meant to be thrashed.

"Henry, please. Don't ye go."

"I must."

" 'Tesn't yer battle, my love. 'Tes mine and always has been. He's my father. Leave him alone."

"It's not just what he's done to you. He threatened Verity

as well tonight. He's become a menace to women everywhere. It's time somebody taught him that he can't do this sort of thing."

"He threatened Verity?" Her expression grew even more remote.

"Waylaid her on the road with two of his mates and assaulted her with threats and curses and God only knows what else. Julian Marrick happened upon them before further mischief could be done, but I gather he arrived just in time."

Tamara whispered something under her breath. Tears stood in her eyes, but they glistened in a manner that made them look hard and crystalline instead of warm and wet.

Henry took her gently into his arms, careful not to injure her further. "I want you to consider marrying me," he whispered into her hair. "You'll never be safe from him unless you're under my protection, legally and morally."

She lay stiffly in his embrace, neither moving nor speaking. He sensed that she was far away, and that no matter how much he pleaded, she would never become his bride. Indeed, he feared that the love that had been blossoming between them had been blasted forever by the doings of this night.

By Christ. Jory Carne had a lot to answer for.

Tamara waited until her lover was gone before rising and attempting to move about the cottage. She was cramped and still bleeding, but that made no difference now. There was no reason to rest, no reason to take care. The destiny cards had been right, as always. Her womb was now as empty as her heart.

Chapter Ten

Everyone said it was an accident, but Daniel Carne knew it was murder. He had been there. He had seen.

Fog had shrouded the landscape, but Daniel had been able

to see his father, his shoulders weaving with the effects of several hours' drinking, wander out into the middle of the St. Austell road. Fingers of gray enveloped him, intermittently hiding him from sight, for it was one of those misty Cornish nights when spirits moan and the old tin knackers haunt the earth, bemoaning the demise of the industry that left them without rocky hollows to haunt and men to frighten.

And there on the verge of the road, he saw another man, a shadow man. At first Daniel thought it was a trick of the fog that sketched shapes where there were none, but when the shadow moved again, to the side and slightly behind his father, a coldness settled over Daniel and penetrated even more deeply than the autumn mists. Jory was being stalked.

"What of it?" he'd muttered to himself. "I'm stalking him myself. Following the bugger about like a bloody watchdog because Tamara says he can't take care o' himself. Though why she cares, given the way he treats her, I can't fathom."

In the distance he heard shouting and the sound of horses just as something shiny arced through the night—a tiny object that struck the road a few yards ahead of Jory. It had come from the vicinity of the shadow man, who'd disappeared into the fog.

His father stumbled. Dead drunk again, as usual. Daniel felt a familiar roiling of disgust. He'd come home from a long day at work at the Stannis claypits, laboring extra hours into the night in the drying kilns to try to make up some of the income that had been lost to the family since Pa's drinking made it impossible for him to hold down a job. Daniel had been dreaming of two things: supper, and a place to lay his weary body down, but instead here he was, combing the public houses, searching for Jory, coaxing him home.

Pa reached the spot where the shiny object had landed. Probably a coin. "Christ, that's all we need," Daniel said aloud. Jory wouldn't have left the pub if he'd still had any money. Now he'd probably turn right around and go back, and neither of them would get to bed before dawn. Damn him! Had he no self-respect?

Daniel increased his speed, no longer caring whether his father saw him. There were nights when he stayed out of sight until Jory made it home, ensuring his safety without injuring his father's pride. Why he went to so much trouble, he couldn't imagine. His father's love for him had been sporadic at best.

Hurrying forward, furious at the necessity of doing this over and over again, hating his father for the shame of it, Daniel heard another shout, followed by the sound of something rolling, booming, violently creaking. Jory, who was kneeling in the roadway, feeling for copper in the dust, must have heard it too, because he raised his head and peered toward the top of the hill.

A double team of foaming horses burst through the fog, crested the rise, and thundered down the hill. Runaways lacking a driver, they were pulling a fully loaded clay wagon at a speed that was far in excess of what was safe. Something must have spooked them as they neared the top of the long hill that cut through the outskirts of St. Austell, spooked them badly, too, or they'd never have gotten up such speed.

Jory was directly in their path. He jerked upward, trying to regain his feet, but he swayed and stumbled and fell. In desperation he began rolling toward the side of the road.

Daniel yelled for help in the direction of the shadow man, who must be closer to Pa than he was, but there was no one there now, no sign that anybody had ever been there at all. Heavily laden as it was, the wagon gained momentum as it reeled down the hill. Daniel shouted and ran, but he was too far away; there wasn't enough time. Christ Jesus, there simply wasn't enough time.

He was still yelling when the wagon dug its wheels in on one side of the road and flipped over in the area where Jory had scrambled for shelter. Daniel thought he heard someone else screaming, but it was impossible to be sure over the racket of the horses squealing in pain and terror and the wagon breaking up and the heavy blocks of china clay spilling all over the road. Heavy white dust exploded into the air, spinning with the wind, blending with the mist. Then, silence.

Daniel had no idea he was crying as he battered his way through the wreckage. He was seventeen years old and a man. All his tears had dried up a long time ago. Pa would be safe, he told himself. Everybody said he was indestructible. He'd rolled and kept rolling, and even now was probably struggling to his feet and cursing because the mound of kaolin blocks had buried the bloody coin he'd been searching for.

When he found him, unmarked and whole, lying just beyond a large chunk of splintered wood, Daniel knew a moment of thankfulness and relief. But as he fell to his knees in the dirt and smelled the strong odor of whiskey and bitters and something else as well, something thick and pestilential that hinted of open sewers and decay, he knew the truth. His father's neck was twisted at an odd angle to the rest of his body, and beside him lay the chipped block of china clay that had spun through the air and severed his spine. The block was white, pristine, and innocent; it had not even drawn blood.

Daniel laid his head on the chest of the dead man and wept. Somewhere in the distance he heard questions, exclamations, curses. Where the bloody hell was the driver . . . stopped to relieve himself . . . the horses were tired from hauling the heavy clay . . . who'd've thought they'd have the energy for so wild a run . . . something must o' spooked them . . . but what?

The shadow man. Daniel insisted to the authorities who questioned him that somebody else had been present. Somebody had thrown the coin that had fatally distracted his father. The same person might even have sneaked on ahead and spooked the horses.

"Why?" the thick-headed constable had asked him.

"Because he wanted my father dead!"

"Pretty damn inefficient way to murder somebody," the dubious fellow said. "Mebbe Jory could've avoided that wagon."

"He moves slower than treacle when he's been drinking. Anyone who knows him knows that. Anyway, 'tes there, look." Daniel had pried open his father's cold, stiffening fingers. He was clutching a battered half-crown. "Don't ye see—he must have got it from the road. If he'd had it before he'd have drunk it up."

The authorities remained unconvinced. Jory had been scraped drunk but alive out of too many ditches to surprise anybody that he'd finally turned up drunk and dead. They'd do some checking, and indeed they did, turning up what to

Daniel was the damning information that his father and Henry Trevor had engaged in a shouting match an hour before Jory's death in front of several patrons at the Lion's Paw in St. Austell. But all agreed that Trevor had been urged out of the pub by the vicar of St. Catherine's, who vouched for Trevor's presence in the vicarage until three in the morning, well past the hour of Jory's death.

"He's my father's enemy!" Daniel shouted. "The Carnes and the Trevors have been feuding for decades. Are ye crazy? Are ye blind? He fought with Pa and Pa ends up dead. Meanwhile I see someone lurking on the road and ye still don't suspect him?"

The constable informed Daniel that he had no reason to doubt the word of two such upstanding members of the community as the local lord of the manor and the local vicar.

"History's full o' bloodthirsty lords and priests. Yeah, and corrupt constables as well. What kind of bribe did they offer 'ee, I'd like to know?"

But all his ranting and raving did him not one whit of good. Pa had always held that there was no justice for the poor, and not even Tamara believed Daniel's version. "Henry Trevor would never do such a thing," she'd said, her voice shaking. " 'Twas Pa who held so stubbornly to that blasted feud, not the Trevors a'tall."

In his sleeping dreams Daniel continued to see the shadow man, sometimes more clearly than others. Sometimes he was touched by a sense of such familiarity that he could almost recognize the body, the face. In his waking dreams identification was easier. The shadow man had auburn hair and a full red beard and answered to the cursed name of Henry.

Three images were indelibly engraved upon his mind that night: the runaway horses, foaming and wild; the odd twist to his father's neck; and the broken slat from the side of the runaway clay wagon, on which was painted in huge letters CADMON CLAY.

Chapter Eleven

On the first night of her married life, Verity sat in bed in the darkened room with her arms wrapped around her knees, wishing she were a million miles away, preferably on another planet.

Her husband was in the bath, preparing for bed. He'd been in there a long time, lingering even longer than she had while she'd undressed, scrubbed her face, brushed her teeth, and, because of her nervousness, used the toilet twice. She wished he'd hurry up and join her in bed. She was anxious to get the whole business over with.

The wedding, which had taken place at two o'clock that afternoon in St. Catherine's, had been everything she could have wished. The church had been full, mostly with clay owners and their wives from Trenwythan and St. Austell, and Bret had looked lovely in her bridesmaid's gown. Simon, shy as ever, but evidently pleased that his father was getting married, had served as a rather young groomsman, and Papa had given her away. Afterward, at the reception, Bret and Simon had amused everyone present by dancing together, turning solemnly to the music until Bret got impatient and coaxed him into a lively game of hide and seek.

Thank heavens for Bret. She had accompanied Verity to her new bedroom at the vicarage to help her change. "You look smashing," Bret assured her. "I hope I'll look as pretty on my wedding day."

But Verity didn't feel comfortable in the silken night robe she had donned for the occasion. A diaphanous confection of crimson Chinese silk embroidered in gold, the garment had belonged to her mother. Its V neckline was a knife slash that reached nearly to Verity's waist. It would look lovely and sophisticated on someone with a more voluptuous figure, but

Verity's breasts were too small to do justice to the style. Instead of giving her confidence in her sensuality, it made her look like exactly what she was, an apprehensive virgin.

When Julian Marrick had proposed marriage, Verity had accepted without hesitation. His solicitous behavior on the terrible occasion of her assault and Jory Carne's death had convinced her that here at last was a man who would give her the care and attention for which she had always yearned. He was mature and intelligent, a highly rational and pragmatic man who valued such ideals as duty, responsibility, and common sense. He would make her a good friend and a worthy husband, and she imagined a union of domestic and intellectual companionship that would be far superior to the careless matches made by the young women she'd met during her Season in London.

His feelings on the matter were similar. "I am fortunate," he told her, "to have met you at a time in life when I am mature enough to appreciate the virtues that your suitors in London were blind to. With your exceptional good sense, piety, and charity, you have all the qualities necessary to make an excellent vicar's wife."

Beauty was not necessary, and her intended made no reference to it. Deep inside, a silly romantic bit of her resented this. How lovely it would be to marry a man who did find her beautiful.

As for her dream of expanding the clayworks to include china manufacture, she had given up the idea as foolish and impractical. A misty fantasy, no more. She could no longer imagine superintending a work force consisting of ruffians like Jory Carne and his two companions. Perhaps it was true, after all, that women were ill-suited to such ventures. There would be more than enough work in the parish to consume her daylight hours, and if a child were to come along, her life would be replete with all the blessings she desired.

If there was a trace of filial defiance in her decision to marry, Verity chose to push it beneath her conscious awareness. Her father did not approve of the match. But after what she'd learned about his relations with Tamara, Verity no longer approved of her father.

Once the engagement was formalized, Julian had been

eager to proceed with the ceremony as quickly as possible. "As difficult as this may be for a young woman of impeccable virtue to understand, we men of the cloth, regrettably, are not devoid of the warmer feelings that infect other men," he told her. "As St. Paul saith, it is better to marry than to burn." Thrilled at the thought that he might be burning for her, she had agreed to expedite the arrangements.

Now, on their first night in the bedroom that they would share in the vicarage of St. Catherine's, she recalled how much she had wanted to take a wedding trip; but Julian had decreed that his duties in the church made that impossible. Suppose someone were to fall ill or die while they were away? He had a sacred responsibility to be the faithful shepherd to his flock.

Verity slid down under the bedclothes when he finally finished in the bath and came to her. He was wrapped in a dressing gown, the hem of which brushed the floor. He bore in his hands a box, and smiled as he presented it to her. "This is something I hope you will do me the compliment of wearing tonight." She flinched as he drew down the covers, revealing her body clad in the Chinese night robe. "It is far more appropriate, I'm sure you'll agree, than what you have on."

With chilly fingers Verity opened the box and unfolded the tissue paper. Another gown lay within, not nearly as luxurious as her mother's. It was fashioned of pure white plain cotton with a high, buttoned neckline and wrist-length sleeves. There was a small pink rosebud in the middle of the chest. As Verity shook it out she thought it looked like a child's nightrail rather than the intimate apparel of a married woman. And yet she was oddly grateful, for she would surely feel more comfortable in it than she felt now.

"Thank you." She swung her legs out of bed. "I'll just go into the bath and put it on."

"Allow me to assist you, my dear."

Verity stiffened as her husband's hands fell upon her shoulders. He touched the silken fabric lightly, then slowly allowed his hands to drift down over the Chinese dragons that cavorted on her breasts. He did not pause, however, but continued on to the golden cord that was tied around her waist, releasing it with deft motions. Verity felt the gown loosen, then he was lifting it over her head, revealing her naked body as she knelt there before him on the bed.

She felt flushed and frightened, yet there was a part of her that was curious to see what his response would be, for although her face was plain, her maids had often complimented her on her firm breasts, her dainty waist, and her graceful, slender hips. Her body had a beauty that her face lacked, and surely Julian would take note of it. It was important to her that he should.

But if he was pleased he gave no sign. Without paying much attention at all to her shape, he removed the cotton nightgown from its box and slipped it over her head. The white cotton billowed over her as she raised first one arm and then the other into the sleeves. The elastic at the wrists was snug—a little too tight, in fact—and when he painstakingly buttoned each fabric-covered button, the elastic around her neck was too tight as well. He smoothed the folds of the gown around her body and then made her lie down and pulled it all the way down her legs until she could feel the starched cotton brushing her ankles.

How strange, she thought, that her husband was dressing, rather than undressing, her on her wedding night.

"Excellent," he said, leaning back to look at her. "Much more appropriate than this exotic garment your mother left you, which would do for the Whore of Babylon, perhaps, but not at all for an unsullied virgin." He balled up the crimson gown and tossed it contemptuously into the farthest corner of the bedchamber. "Promise me that you will never appear before me in such a disgraceful garment again."

His tone was so uncompromising that Verity assented immediately. "If that is what you wish, of course I promise. I didn't feel comfortable in it anyway."

"No. I wouldn't have married you if you had."

This remark was no doubt intended as a compliment, but it made Verity even more uneasy. If he hadn't married her, she'd have been alone—a worthless and pathetic spinster—forever.

Julian leaned over her and kissed her. His lips were dry and light and they pulled back from her mouth almost immediately. "Are you wearing scent?"

She nodded. The perfume had been a gift from Papa. He'd told her he liked the drama of it and that her husband would, too.

"Don't ever wear it again. The scent is too strong, too sophisticated. I don't care for perfume."

"I'm sorry." She felt devastated.

"It's quite all right," he said pleasantly. He took one of her hands in his and raised it to his lips. "Your palms are slick, sweetheart. Are you frightened?"

"Yes. A little." *You're making me more so*, she thought.

"It is natural. Of course you are frightened. Your innocence and inexperience make it so. For you have heard, no doubt, that men are beasts who surrender to their baser instincts, and that it is the fate of the proper young women who become their brides to accept this depravity even in the best of men."

"Yes," she whispered. "That is what I have heard." But it occurred to her that the only person she had ever heard it from was Julian himself.

He reached over and turned down the gas lamp on the table beside the bed until it was barely glowing, a tiny blue spark in the darkness. Verity heard him unfastening his dressing gown.

"It is true," he informed her, his voice sounding abstract, dreamy. "All men are sinners, and in some of us the evil sits more heavily than in others. But I will be gentle with you. That you may be assured of. I will always endeavor to be gentle with you."

Verity shivered as she felt the full weight of his body come down upon hers. Reflexively, her arms went around him, only to draw back at the feel of hard muscles tensed just below the surface of his tough, naked skin.

The starched cotton barrier between them crackled. He caressed her body through it, murmuring, "Be still, and don't be frightened, my sweet little girl. I will instruct you. Relax and do as I tell you. This will be the first of many nocturnal lessons." His mouth moved down to her constricted throat, then between her breasts, where he kissed the pink rosebud on the nightgown. "So sweet," he murmured.

Verity felt nothing but apprehension. Even her natural curiosity was deadened by her distrust at the strange way he spoke to her.

He touched her breasts and she felt his fingers shaking. "A young girl can only remain innocent so long," he said. "That is the way of the world. The lion lies down with the lamb and innocence yields to experience." He pressed her legs apart with his knees and raised her nightgown. Verity squeezed her eyes shut and tried not to resist. He had begun to breathe harshly; his intensity alarmed her, but she knew it would be terribly bad form to resist her own husband. Anyway, he had said he would be gentle, and he wasn't hurting her, not really, not yet.

"You must open to me," he said as he pressed her thighs farther apart. "That is the first lesson. You must always be open to me."

"Yes," she whispered, trembling. His hands were all over her now, stroking her breasts, her belly, her thighs, and even there, in between, in her secret place that she knew he was anxious to invade. His hands were feverish. She squirmed but she couldn't get away.

The cotton nightgown was wrapped around her hips now and he was touching the soft, bare skin of her belly, brushing the triangle of hair at the apex of her thighs. It was embarrassing, but something had kindled inside her and she felt looser now, more willing to experience whatever he had to teach her. *Yes*, she thought, *touch me there. That's good, that's lovely.*

All too soon, his hands slid away. "Be still now, little virgin," he said as he reared up over her. She glanced down, trying to see what the instrument of her defloration would be, but it was too dark; she could barely see his face.

He fastened his mouth to hers and slid between her widely spread thighs. Verity jumped as she felt his hard flesh against her there, then mewed as it invaded her, slowly, slowly, fighting the natural resistance of her tissues as well as the tension in her body.

It hurt. She told herself that she had expected it to hurt and that it would soon be over, and that, yes, it was extremely intimate and embarrassing but that all over the world, everywhere, men and women must come together to do this thing because this was the way babies got started, and the Lord knew, babies were always being born. As she lay there wincing beneath her sweating, grunting husband, a subversive thought crossed her mind: Why should this act be a pleasure for men and merely a duty for women? Particularly since women were the ones who bore the risks and the agonies of childbirth?

Julian thrust one final time within her and cried out as if in pain. Then he rolled off her body and lay silently beside her, adjusting his breathing. At length he spoke: "I am pleased, Verity. I must confess that I have been somewhat apprehensive, knowing that you had no mother or other close female relative to instruct you in your marital responsibilities, but I ought to have realized that a gentlewoman of your breeding would instinctively know how to behave. I should not have liked it at all if you had proved to have the unrestrained sexual temperament of some of those arch young ladies in London with whom you spent so much time last year."

"What do you mean?"

"Never mind." He rose to fetch a washcloth, with which he carefully washed the blood from between her thighs, looking at the stains it had left on her white nightgown with an expression that was tinged with satisfaction. "Just continue to behave as you have behaved tonight, and I shall be well pleased with you."

Julian quickly fell asleep, leaving Verity to the darkness of her thoughts. Now and forever, she and her husband were one body, one flesh. What she could not fathom was why she felt so alone.

Part Three

1913

Love to faults is always blind,
Always is to joy inclin'd,
Lawless, wing'd & unconfin'd.

—William Blake
Miscellaneous Poems and Fragments

Chapter Twelve

On the evening following the worst fight she'd ever had with her sister, Bret Trevor ran away from home. She slipped down the back stairs to the kitchens, unbolted the stout iron-banded oak door that led into Cadmon Hall's kitchen garden, and followed the path around to the stables. Peter, the sleepy young groom who was on duty, raised no objection when she asked him to help her saddle Wulf. He was accustomed to her demanding access to her horse at odd hours.

The night was glorious, the black silk of the sky spangled with stars, the air sharp with the stiff sea smells that were blowing inland from St. Austell Bay. Once free of the stableyard and the grounds, Bret let the darkness take her and sweep her clean. The magnificent animal she was riding seemed to share her desire to be lifted on the wind and race with the stars. Together they hurtled through the night without caring where they fetched up. Bret tossed her head until her hair was flowing along her cheeks and throat and shoulders. She could feel her thighs surge with the power of the steaming beast between them.

"Oh, Wulf, isn't it wonderful?" she whispered as the caress of the wind loosened her, body and soul. All her senses were alive. She smelled the mixed scents of wild grasses and flowers, coal smoke thickened with chalky kaolin dust, and the salt tang of the sea. "What a lovely night to be riding free!"

As the ground unwound beneath her stallion's hooves, she imagined she was taking to the air as a passenger in one of her father's aeroplanes, which, on rare occasions, he allowed her to do. She was flying far higher, she imagined, than her father would ever go, mounting the clouds on her magical Pegasus, leaving below the roll of the downs, the arc of the sea, the ice-tipped crags of the highest mountains; soaring ever higher until the earth beneath was nothing more than a hazy ball and the air was thin and black and the stars were close enough to snatch from the sky and hold, glowing, in the palms of her hands. How lovely the earth was from such a height. How blue and how bright and how clean.

She would be able to ride like this—flat out and flying— in Arizona. Wasn't that just about all anybody did in the American West—herd horses and rope steer? Bret had spent many pleasant hours imagining what life must be like in Arizona, reading every book on the subject she could find. Her plan was to go there. In Arizona she could be what she'd always wanted to be: an intrepid adventuress.

She had hastily packed a knapsack with a few of her most prized possessions, including the letters that Mr. Slayton had sent her from his ranch outside Phoenix. That her journey would be difficult was something Bret took for granted. Still, what sort of adventure would it be if there weren't some degree of difficulty involved? Like the dauntless heroines of the adventure novels she and her school friends had always been so fond of reading under the covers late at night, Bret was determined to overcome whatever obstacles might arise in her way. To laugh in the face of hardship. To seize control of her destiny. To triumph against all odds.

Brimming with dreams and plans, and blocking off the adult part of herself that whispered of their absurdity, Bret allowed Wulf to race over the rough terrain. Even as she urged him on to greater speeds, Bret knew that she was being reckless. But she was half-wild tonight, and Wulf was as invincible as Bucephalus.

The moorland was barren and looked unearthly, dotted with unnaturally bright green pools, streams that flowed milk-white instead of gin-clear, and pale towering skytips, which Bret had thought of since childhood as the Mountains of the Moon, for on starlit nights they seemed to glow with a cold and chalky translucence. She saw a low hillock rising before her and obeyed an impulse to drive her stallion up and over it. Although Wulf usually obeyed the slightest touch on his bit, tonight Bret had to press hard with her knees to hold him on her determined course. She laughed out loud as she felt him respond. But no sooner had they leaped onto the hillock than she fathomed her mistake. The ground seemed to give way beneath them and she recognized the mound as a low slag heap, abandoned long enough ago to be covered with the scrubby vegetation that disguised its true nature.

Wulf's legs sank in, startling him, muddying his stride. In his attempt to leap free, he reared, and Bret felt herself sliding. As he twisted out from under her, snorting and trembling, Bret came down hard on a spot of damp, soft earth.

The suddenness of the accident confused her. She lay without moving, trying to make sense of what had happened. She had landed on her stomach, her left leg bent underneath her. Gingerly she rolled over, conscious of pain in her left knee and ankle. "Hell's bells and damnation," she said loudly. She'd been forbidden by Verity to use her father's favorite oath, or indeed to curse at all. Well, to hell with Verity. "Damnation!" she repeated, rebelliously throwing the word out into the night.

She looked around for Wulf, worried that he too might have been injured, but she was relieved to see him placidly munching heath scrub some twenty yards away. She called to him and he raised his head, but did not approach. He looked at her as if to say, "Don't blame me; it wasn't my idea to go that way. I'd never have been so foolish."

"Brother," she said as she heard the growl of thunder somewhere off to the west. The sky, which had been clear and starry only a few minutes before, was clouding over.

She stumbled to her feet. To one foot, anyway. The other was hurting, badly. She tried to walk and found it nearly impossible. She whistled for Wulf, who ignored her. He was not the most cooperative of beasts in the best of circumstances, and he could be downright contrary if he was miffed about something. Losing his rider, particularly when he didn't consider it his fault, invariably brought out the worst in him.

"Come on, boy, come on, fellow. Nice boy. Lovely boy.

Yes, you're right, I was careless and stupid and you could have broken your leg. I don't blame you for mistrusting me."

Wulf eyed her sullenly, then went back to munching grass.

Bret whistled again, making it as low and seductive as possible. "Come here, you lovely beast. I need you. You're a fine animal and I'll bet that stuff you're eating tastes good, but the fog's coming in off the sea and soon we won't be able to see where we're going."

Nothing.

Bret limped in his direction. Pain ripped through her leg. With every few steps she advanced, Wulf retreated the same distance. The expression on his face told her he knew exactly what he was doing.

Thunder cracked more loudly and the wind knifed through the moor grasses. She felt a raindrop bounce off her nose. "Wulf, this isn't amusing. Come here, you wretched animal. It's *raining*. Stop dancing away like that. Can't you see I can hardly walk? Wulf, you great big hulking miserable excuse for a horse, if you don't allow me to approach you I'm going to lose my temper, and then you'll be sorry. I can be absolutely *scathing* when I lose my temper."

As she eased forward, Wulf nickered softly, his tail swishing back and forth. She noticed that the one soft, dark, intelligent eye that was turned in her direction seemed to be assessing her stumbling, uneven gait. Did he know something was wrong with her? Deliberately, she exaggerated it. People often laughed at the way she treated horses so much like humans, attributing emotions to them that they couldn't possibly have, but in her experience, it worked.

Wulf retreated once more, but only a couple of steps. As she closed in on him, Bret crooned low words of praise and encouragement. Another louder, closer crack of thunder made him skitter sideways, and she was able to grab his bridle.

Mounting him proved impossible, though, with her sore ankle, so she was forced to lead him, limping along, every step sending needles of pain along the nerves of her left leg. The thought of walking the three and a half miles to St. Austell in this condition left her a little more discouraged than she cared to admit. As the skies opened and the rains pounded down, she realized that she might have to return to Cadmon

Hall in ignominious defeat. She couldn't very well hop to America on one foot.

"Not a very good start for an intrepid heroine," she said gloomily to Wulf.

He nickered in sympathy, tame and cooperative now.

Courage, she told herself. *A literary heroine wouldn't be daunted in these circumstances. On the contrary, she'd be thrilled at the opportunity to prove her mettle.* "I'm not giving up," she informed her horse. Making a fist, she jabbed it in the direction of the sky. "So there."

For the next ten minutes, she and Wulf walked in silence. The rain was falling steadily now, further depressing Bret's spirits as it drenched her cap, flattened her thick red hair against her skull, and penetrated her clothing.

On fine days, Bret loved the moorland not only for its beauty and its fresh, grassy scents but also for its many mysteries and legends. King Arthur had been conceived here at Tintagel on the north coast. He'd had one of his strongholds at Castle-an-Dinas; and some said his court of Carlyon had been located a few miles to the west on the Fal estuary, where, according to legend, the mists hung heavy over the wooded land. Bret loved to visualize the silent river overhung with mossy branches, the ghostly barge gliding soundlessly as the three queens conveyed the dying king to Avalon.

But the moors seemed to have taken on a different aura now. Roundabout her all was desolate. The land brooded, hill upon hill, shadow upon shadow. The ground was pocked with gorse bushes, scrub grass, and stunted trees, not to mention high crags and low tors, the stern guardians of the wilderness who, Bret imagined, were glaring at her with a certain I-told-you-so superiority. Something about their stark, relentless grandeur reminded her of her quarrel with Verity.

Her sister had begun, as usual, by criticizing the way Bret had been "frittering away" her long vacation this summer. "You're a young lady now," Verity had said. "Papa and I agreed before he left for America that it's time you gave some serious thought to your future."

Papa had left a week before for the United States, where he was attending an international convention of aeroplane buffs. He would be away for several weeks, and Verity was spending part of that time at Cadmon Hall, managing the household and, Bret suspected, poking her nose into the clay-company business as well. If there was one thing her sister was good at, it was managing.

"As for the way you fraternize with the clay laborers, that has to stop. Particularly now, with all this agitation going on. There is talk of a strike, which could devastate the industry."

"Well, my goodness, they've every right to strike, considering the wretched wages the clay owners insist on paying them."

"Don't start on that again," Verity said, referring to an argument they'd had a fortnight ago. Bret had defied both her sister and her father to staunchly defend the angry clay workers, whose children she had played with for as long as she could remember.

"You must give some thought to what you will do next year when you leave school. Papa suggests a Season in London so you can meet a husband"—Bret groaned loudly—"but I had hoped you would choose to attend an art college. With formal training, you could perhaps become an artist of note."

"I'd rather fly aeroplanes."

"Don't be absurd. You'll do nothing of the sort."

"Indeed I will. There are so many wonderful things in the world to do. I'll be an artist as well as an aviator. I'd like to live in Paris or Rome or Florence and apprentice myself to a master. I'll create great and beautiful things, and instead of a husband I'll take a lover now and then."

Verity's frown had confirmed her disapproval of that scenario.

"Or maybe I'll go to Arizona to visit Mr. Slayton and paint the desert in all its harsh grandeur. He sent me a lovely piece of Indian pottery last month, boldly glazed and designed. You don't see that sort of art in England—we British are too dull and tame."

"What you will do is attend a proper college of art in London and get the sort of education that will train and refine your talents. I had hoped you would learn china sculpting and painting so we can reopen the Cadmon porcelain works someday. Have you forgotten our Chinese painting, and our dream?"

"Verity, that was your dream, not mine. Anyway, you're the vicar's wife now. You spend your days thinking about charity and good works and Christian education. You don't have time to manufacture china, and from what I know of Julian, he wouldn't permit it anyway."

"How dare you presume to make such a remark? You think I only do what Julian permits me to do?"

"But isn't that the crux of marriage? I've heard him preach on the subject. The husband is the head of the wife as Christ was the head of the church—"

"I will not brook such impertinence. Go to your room at once."

Bret wasn't entirely sure what she had done. "Why are you so angry? And why are you always ordering me about?"

Verity had drawn herself up to her full height, which nowadays was several inches less than Bret's. "While our father is away, I am responsible for you, and you will do as I say. I repeat—go to your room. I don't wish to see your face again until you can come to me with an abject and sincere apology."

"Then you'll never see me again because I don't even know what I'm supposed to be apologizing for!"

She had slipped out of the house shortly thereafter, feeling misunderstood by everybody. She missed Papa, who never yelled at her. She felt entirely alone. Nobody, she decided, had any idea what it was like to be adventuresome, artistic, and sixteen years old.

She'd always thought her sister understood her. Verity, after all, was the one who had hired her first drawing master. She had bought her brightly colored chalk and pastels, dreamy soft watercolors, her easel, and her first set of pungent-smelling oils, all neatly arrayed in their tubes in a lovely wooden box with her initials carved in the top. Verity knew how restless she was, how she dreamed of seeing everything there was to see and doing everything there was to do. How could she pretend now that she was destined for something as mundane and ordinary as art college?

Another thunderclap shook her into a renewed awareness of her beleaguered situation. Wulf shied, and she was forced to keep a tight hold on his bridle. "Dammit, Wulf. Do you suppose she knows we're gone? I wonder if she's found my note.''

"Dear Verity," she had written, "I love you but I can't apologize. I'm off to see the world, which I'm sure will provide me with far more knowledge and wisdom about life and art than I could ever attain by attending school in London, or, worse, by becoming somebody's wife. Please don't worry about me. I'll miss you."

She had signed it, "Your intrepid sister, Bret."

"Intrepid," she said with a sigh. A gust of wind whipped a veritable flood of raindrops into her face. Why was it so much easier to be intrepid in books than in real life?

Lightning struck a nearby skytip, bathing it in an eerie glow. Bret touched the crude necklace she wore—her good luck charm, made from the rattle of an Arizona viper. According to her friend Mr. Slayton, it was supposed to keep the bearer safe from all harm.

Thunder cracked, and once again Wulf danced sideways, his apprehension building with the storm. He stamped the earth with one hoof, turning his head and looking a question into her eyes.

"The only trouble is," she said aloud, "Arizona is so miserably far away."

The intelligent animal's ears pricked up. He watched her as she added, "You know what? I'm tired and my foot hurts. What do you think, boy? Should we go back?"

Wulf rubbed his head against the back of her shoulder, nervous, but trusting her. She turned around and stroked him, barely able to see him in the rising fog. "Lovely boy," she whispered. "I've been a fool, haven't I? I'd miss you terribly if I went to Arizona. And you know what? I'm not even entirely sure where Arizona is. I'm like that little plane, I guess. I'm just not ready yet."

She sighed, blowing her warm breath into his mane. "But someday I will be ready. And then, world, watch out."

Chapter Thirteen

"Damnation," Bret said to Wulf. "I feel like King Lear on the stormy heath!"

After spending another half-hour wandering about on the moors, she was beginning to wonder if Cadmon Hall might be nearly as difficult to reach as Arizona.

The fog, which at first had been just another annoyance, had now become dangerous. After creeping almost shyly over the moors, remaining low to the ground, it had decided to well up around her, obscuring her vision. If she couldn't stay on the path, heaven only knew what would happen to her. There were bogs, sink holes, and slag heaps all around. If she blundered into one of them, both she and Wulf could lose themselves in quicksand, disappearing into the indifferent ground without leaving a trace.

"Oh, don't be silly," she said out loud. "There are bogs and sink holes aplenty on Bodmin Moor, but do we actually know anybody who ever sank in quicksand, Wulf? Course not. I'll just let you take the lead, shall I?"

She loosened her hold on his bridle, hoping he'd take it as a signal that he was to lead her. Horses and dogs could always find their way home. They used their sense of smell or something.

After another fifteen minutes she wasn't so confident. Wulf was walking along at a good clip, but during the brief moments when the patches of fog lifted, Bret didn't see any landmarks she recognized. They were on high ground, at least, but it was rocky, desolate land without a house or a tree or any sign of human habitation.

Overhead, the thunder continued to growl. The wind spat rain in random directions, making it difficult to shield her face, and all around her the moor grasses danced as the crosscurrents of air flung them every which way. Bret caught her healthy foot on a stony outcrop and tripped, barely saving herself from going down.

It all comes, she thought, *of being so bloody curious about faraway places like Arizona.* Mrs. Chenoweth, the housekeeper, had always said that Bret was cursed with a monkey-demon of curiosity that would be the death of her someday.

Wulf nuzzled the back of her neck. She felt a strong desire to clasp her arms around his neck, press her face into his mane, and howl.

"We mustn't give up," she told him, feeling enormously grateful for his presence. "Intrepid adventuresses and their noble stallions never give up."

At the crest of the next hill she found that the fog had lifted slightly. A pale pathway ribboned across the dead heather, and along that pathway moved a bobbing light. "Look, Wulf! There's a traveler with a lantern. Thank goodness. Maybe we're not lost after all."

Hurrying, she made for the road, which was little more than a cart track across the moors. She didn't realize until she got there that what she thought was someone traveling on foot was really a wagon of some sort, drawn by a team of horses. The racket as the vehicle drew near was deafening—the creak of wood, the screech of ungreased metal-bound wheels, and the scraping of the heavy chain brake that was fastened to one of the wagon's wheels.

It was a china-clay wagon similar to the ones that traveled the main highways between St. Austell and the claypits, except that it was empty of any white bricks of china clay. This wagon must be returning from the Charlestown docks.

There was only one driver, and by the light of the lantern that hung from the front of the cart he looked like an apparition with his clay-whitened skin and his shock of 'ack hair blowing wild in the wind. He was thundering along much too fast for the fog and the dark, and as he bore down upon them, Bret pulled Wulf off to one side and yelled, waving her arms over her head.

She thought he was going to roar right by them, but at the last moment he drew in his reins and clucked at his team to slow down. The clay wagon rumbled to a stop a few yards beyond the spot where she and Wulf were waiting, and the driver leaped into the road. Bret stood still, leaning against her horse. The effort of getting this far had just about done her in.

"Hello," she called to the stranger. As he approached, she began to feel apprehensive. Like most clay workers, his clothes were dusted with white; perfectly normal, of course, yet the lightning flashes made the koalin glow with a spectral effulgence, lighting him up like a ghost. Maybe he *was* a ghost. A clayman killed in a pit accident, perhaps, whose spirit had winged homeward to haunt the land. Anything was possible. Old Mrs. Yellen had sworn last month that she'd seen her grandson Jack, only eighteen and drowned in a freak accident in a flooded claypit, wandering among the graves in St. Catherine's churchyard.

Remembering that horses were more tuned in to the supernatural than humans were, she cast an anxious glance at Wulf. He seemed to be regarding the stranger calmly enough.

"Who in blazes are 'ee?" the man asked, looking from her face to the horse and back again. "And what's a lass like 'ee doing out alone on a wilding sort of night like thes?"

He sounded human. Actually, he sounded annoyed.

"I'm afraid I'm lost. I was certain I knew the way home, but with the fog and all I seem to have gotten a bit confused. Does that track lead to St. Austell?"

He didn't answer for several seconds, as he continued to assess her, taking in every detail of her clothes, her hair, her mount's trappings. She returned the scrutiny. He was dark and scruffy and his work clothes were covered with the fine white china-clay dust that branded everyone who worked in the kaolin industry. His body was tall, solid, and strong, with capable shoulders and the suggestion of muscles beneath the loose-fitting work clothes. His hands, which were loosely clenched at his sides, were big and brutal, but he carried himself proudly, as if there were no one in the world whom he would ever own to be his master.

She estimated his age to be midtwenties or so. Black hair, worn unruly and too long with a cowlick at the crown. Not even the most romantic of her school friends would have called him handsome with his rough-cast features and that appalling scar slashing his cheek, but there was something vital about him that exuded energy and confidence. He certainly looked more confident than Bret felt.

"Ye're several miles from St. Austell. Why aren't ye up on that horse instead of down on the ground? Is he hurt?"

"No. It's just that I got thrown and couldn't get back on. He's big, you see, and I hurt my ankle and couldn't put my weight in the stirrup. If you could just give me a boost up and point me in the right direction, I'd appreciate it."

"Ye're wet through."

There was something about his intense appraisal that continued to unnerve her. That or the way he was looking at her, the blue brilliance of his eyes. "Yes, well, it doesn't matter. I'll get dry when I get home."

"Where be home, then?"

She decided not to tell him that she was Henry Trevor's daughter. The families of several clay owners had been harassed lately as the impetus built for a strike, and there was something about his manner that suggested to her that he might not be willing to believe that she was on *his* side in the dispute. Besides, it was silly, but he looked so odd with that white clay dust all over him, and the night was so wild and he was looking at her too intently, and he'd been driving his clay wagon as if he were Hades the Hell God up for a midnight ride. All she wanted to do was get away from him as quickly as possible. So she answered, "Not far from Trenwythan village. Do you know it?"

"Aye, a'course. 'Tes closer than St. Austell, that's sure, but still a ways off. How bad's yer ankle? Ye'll need it to ride. Walk a bit and let's have a look."

"Oh, I'll be all right, don't worry about me." She handed Wulf's reins to him and took a couple of quick steps to prove it. The pain was hellish. She stumbled and might have fallen had the clay worker's strong hands not caught her and held her.

"Ye can't ride with yer foot in that condition. Come along, I'll put 'ee in my wagon, if ye don't mind a bit o' kaolin dust."

"Thank you, but it's really not necessary—"

"I'm not going all the way to Trenwythan, but my sister's

good with wounds and sprains and illnesses and the like. She'll fix up yer ankle and mebbe give 'ee something dry of hers to put on. Ye *are* a girl underneath those wet clothes, are ye not?''

''Last time I checked I was,'' she said with a grin. ''How far is it to your sister's?''

''Just over the next couple o' rises. If ye'd walked on a little farther, ye'd have seen the place yerself.''

The thought of refuge from the storm won out over any doubts she might still have. ''Well, all right then. Thank you.''

With more gentleness than he looked capable of, the clay worker lifted her into the back of his wagon. He tied Wulf's halter rope to the back and climbed into the driver's seat. ''Hang on. Might get bumpy.''

''My name's Bret,'' she called to him as they creaked into motion. ''What's yours?''

The wind blew away his answer.

It was not until the clayman jerked the horses to a halt in front of a small moorland cottage that Bret's weary brain made sense of her surroundings. The high windswept hills, the little dell in front of the cottage, the flowers on the walk leading up to the front door, the Roman wall in the distance—it was familiar to her because sometimes, when she was feeling adventuresome, she'd come here spying on the beautiful bal maiden who was the daughter of her father's dead enemy, Jory Carne.

If Tamara, the wheat-haired lady, was this man's sister . . . Bret's heart started hammering. Just her luck to have fallen smack into the hands of Jory's son and avowed avenger, Daniel Carne.

As her rescuer jumped down and came around the back to fetch her, Bret noted the scar again, which cut the left side of his face from the corner of his mouth to well up under the thick thatch of hair at his brow. Verity had told her that Daniel Carne had had that scar since childhood.

''Put yer arms about my neck,'' he said, bending over her. ''That's it.'' He lifted her out of the wagon. ''Elfin little thing, aren't 'ee? Most girls are heavier than they look, not lighter.''

He carried her to the door of the cottage, which he opened with an unceremonious kick. The first thing she was conscious of was the quality of the light, which was bright, diffused, and warm. And the smells: such a dazzling collection of sweet, pungent, yeasty, and verdant odors that combined to make the atmosphere as exotic as an Eastern bazaar. Something delicious was cooking in the squat cast-iron stove in the corner.

The cottage was small, just two small rooms on ground level and a loft above. The room they entered was clearly the living area, cozy and comfortable, with a large fireplace on one wall in which burned a merry orange blaze. The furniture was wooden and utilitarian: tables, benches, armless chairs, a narrow bed covered with a gaily colored quilt in one corner that served as a couch during the daytime. There was no gas, much less newfangled electric. Instead, the brightness of the room came from an array of oil lanterns and candles placed on nearly all the flat surfaces. Strings of herbs and dried flowers were hanging at intervals from hooks in the ceiling. It must be these that gave the place its blend of pleasant and unusual odors.

There was a doorway draped with a curtain on the opposite side of the room from where they had entered. It was through this that a husky voice called, "Daniel? Is that 'ee?"

"Aye, Tam. And a guest as well. I' truth, a patient for 'ee. Best bring yer medicine and some food as well; this lass is looking wistful at the smell of yer cooking."

The curtains were brushed aside and a woman with a great lovely head of straw-colored hair appeared. She was as beautiful as Bret remembered, with peachy skin and delicate features. Hers was the lush sort of body that artists loved to paint. Quite the opposite, Bret thought with some chagrin, of her own flat-chested form. Clad in a swirling of crimson, gold, and sapphire, a white peasant blouse, and a shabby clay-coated smock, she moved into the room with quick, energetic steps.

She wiped her hands on her smock, streaking it with more grayish brown clay, then waved Daniel toward the quilt-draped daybed. "Set her down there. Careful now. Ye're hurt, aren't 'ee, lass?"

Looking into Tamara's face, with its smile so like a sunburst, and her eyes, which were all-seeing, wise, and somewhat sad, Bret remembered that she had once suspected her father of being in love with this woman. She must have been wrong about that, she supposed, since nothing had ever come of it.

"It's my ankle," she said as she was freed from Daniel Carne's bearlike hold. The pain in her foot was a constant throbbing now.

"And what were ye doing out, so slick and so wet on a hell-tuned night such as thes?"

Did she recognize her? Bret couldn't tell. "I was on my way to Arizona when I rode Wulf, my horse, into a slag heap and got thrown. Then the fog came in and we lost our way on the moors. I was beginning to feel quite despairing when your brother came along with his wagon and gave me a lift, for which I'm very grateful."

Bret cast a glance at Daniel, who was listening to her explanation with an amused expression on his face. "Goodness, that reminds me, I need to rub him down—Wulf, I mean—and find some shelter for him. And I really ought to do that first, before bothering about my foot."

"I'll see to him." He paused. "Arizona?"

Bret smiled at him, struck for the first time by the husky quality to his voice. Once again she noted his eyes, which were unusual—light blue irises circled at the edges by a darker ring—and the rest of his face, which was rather nice, in a rough sort of way. The scar added a touch of pathos and drama that was not unappealing. Some of her school friends would no doubt have declared him . . . well, not handsome, perhaps, but very male.

The contrast between brother and sister couldn't have been more striking. Tamara's hair was the color of finely spun gold, but Daniel's was so black it seemed to have a tinge of blue, like his eyes, as if he were surrounded by some strange and mysterious electrical field.

He was looking at her as well.

"It's in America. The West. You know—cowboys, Indians, bury me with my boots on?"

As she spoke she pulled her soggy cap off her head, spilling a profusion of wet red hair. Tamara and Daniel both stared harder at her, and Bret was certain, from the expression in Tamara's dark eyes, that Daniel's sister knew who she was. Was she going to throw her back out into the storm?

"Let's have a look at that ankle of yers. Then we'll get 'ee out of those damp clothes. Daniel, go out and tend to the horses."

As Daniel left the cottage, Tamara bent to examine Bret's ankle. Her hands were sure and gentle; the pain seemed to diminish as she touched the area. " 'Tes sprained and swollen, but not broken. Let's soak it a bit."

Tamara helped her remove her wet things, then clothed her in one of her smocks, clean but splattered with ingrained clay. She went to her shelves, where she kept stored in jars the roots, leaves, barks, and seeds she used to make her herbal remedies. Bret watched, fascinated, as Tamara mixed together the ingredients of what she promised would be a soothing balm to reduce the inflammation. She put it into a kettle and set it on the stove to brew.

"I take it ye didna' mention to Daniel who ye be?"

Bret felt some of the tension seep out of her. "He didn't ask. What do you suppose will happen if he realizes?"

"He bears a bitter grudge against yer family." As she spoke Tamara was applying a foul-smelling mixture to Bret's ankle. Its efficacy was proven within seconds, as the pain diminished.

"And you? Don't you bear the same grudge?"

Her expression grew dark. "No, lassie. Anger, violence, revenge, those are man things. Sometimes we women are infected with them, 'tes true, but when that happens, 'tes almost always a man's doing." She paused. "And his undoing."

Much struck by her intensity, Bret did not speak again until Tamara had finished bandaging her foot with clean strips of cloth. Then she said, "Daniel blames your father's death on my father, doesn't he?"

"He could never see straight where Pa was concerned." Her voice was like iron now. " 'Twould be best not to tell him who ye be. Sit down at the table, lass." As she talked she was laying out mugs and bowls for supper. They were sensuously shaped and dramatically painted, and Bret realized that Tamara must have made them herself. Her pottery was well known in the region for its beauty and durability. Bret had heard that Tamara earned nearly as good a living as a weekend potter as she did as a bal maiden in the Stannis claypits.

"Look. I want to show you something," Bret said as Tamara spooned a hearty portion of thick vegetable soup into a bowl. She pulled from her wet clothing the leather pouch in which she had put the few special things she had not wanted to leave behind. Drawing out a small item wrapped snugly in cotton, she handed it to Tamara. "I was taking it with me. I've always treasured it."

Tamara unwrapped the cotton to find the tiny clay bluebird she had given to Bret six years before. She touched it gently, smiling, then turned her radiance upon her guest. "Don't ye fret about Daniel," she said.

Bret's appetite was not in the least decreased by her injury. She ate with enthusiasm, relishing the simple food as if it were banquet fare. She had nearly finished when Daniel returned, shaking the rain off his jacket. "Feeling better?" he asked as he helped himself to a bowl of soup. There was a new note in his voice. It made her uneasy.

"Oh yes. Much."

"Then mebbe ye won't object to telling me what ye were doing mounted on one of Henry Trevor's horses."

"Don't be rude to my guest, Daniel," Tamara said.

Daniel's face had closed up like a sea oyster, those nice eyes now hard as pearls. "Ye're his daughter, aren't 'ee? Not Verity; ye're the younger one."

Bret swallowed hastily. At least she'd finished most of her supper and had her ankle tended. She felt warm and revived and it was only about a mile to Cadmon Hall, so even if he threw her back out into the storm, she supposed she'd manage.

"My name is Bret Trevor. Elizabeth really, but no one calls me that, except Verity when she's made at me."

Daniel slammed his spoon down onto the table, rocking

the soup bowls and making Bret jump. She felt as skittish as Wulf in the storm, which eroded her heroine status even further in her own eyes.

"Daniel." Tamara's voice was sharp. "Control yerself. I'll not have ye indulging yer passions here."

Daniel's chair scraped the floor as he rose. "I'm damned if I'll break bread with any Trevor. Nor do I want one in my house."

His sister's response was instant: "This is my house. And I'm damned if I'll allow any brother o' mine to betray the most ancient laws of hospitality."

Daniel Carne laughed, a hard ugly sound. "Oh that's rich, Tam. What ancient laws haven't they broken, the illustrious Trevors of Cadmon Hall?"

"I haven't broken any," Bret said in a small voice. "It isn't fair to blame me for whatever disagreements you have with my father. I don't even know the details of the Carne-Trevor feud."

"For some reason that doesn't surprise me," Daniel snapped. "Yer brain's in Arizona."

Stung, Bret could think of no clever retort.

"Ye might as well go and tell them she's safe and that she'll be staying here the night," Tamara said calmly. "There's no help for it, and they'll be worried about her if she doesn't return."

"Let them worry and be damned."

"If ye won't go, I will."

"I'll not have 'ee going near that devil, Tam! Ye stay here and take care o' yer precious guest, dammit. I'll go."

"If you're referring to my father, he's not at home," Bret put in. "He's in America, flying aeroplanes. Verity's the only one there tonight, unless she's gone back to the vicarage."

"Well now, that's different," said Daniel, sounding sarcastic now. "Verity and me are friends from way back, as Tam'll well remember."

"Ye mind yerself, Daniel," his sister said. "I don't want to have to come myself and fetch 'ee out o' gaol."

"Really, I'm feeling much better and I think I can just go home myself, without putting anybody to any more trouble,"

Bret said, rising so hastily from her chair that she forgot her injury and was rewarded with a sharp jolt of pain in her foot.

Tamara touched her arm. "Sit down, lass. 'Twill be all right. Daniel's dramatic like our father, but nowhere near so blackhearted."

"What the hell d'ye know about it, Tam?" Daniel said on his way out, slamming the door so hard that the little cottage seemed to shake on its foundation.

Chapter Fourteen

The rain had slackened by the time Daniel Carne reached the hill overlooking Cadmon Hall. The house was an imposing edifice of smooth gray stone with a gray-green slate roof and tall, large-paned windows every few feet along each of its four stories. Daniel had never seen another building with so many windows. As a child he had imagined it as a great brooding beast with eye upon eye, all of them focused on him.

Not even Tamara had any idea how often he had come here over the years, nor could she have guessed the emotions that burned in his heart. As a boy, when he'd been purer in hate and simpler in desire, he had imagined himself the all-powerful author of chaos, capable of spreading his legs far apart and flinging down thunderbolts upon the great hall and all its occupants. His rage would crack open a great fissure in the roof and a consuming fire would erupt, sweeping the hall, turning the contents to hot red coals that would, by the light of the dawning day, collapse into dust and ashes. Such would be the end of the once-noble Trevor dynasty, which according to local historians dated from medieval times and included poets and statesmen as well as barons of commerce and murderers and thieves.

His anger had grown subtler as he'd grown older. He had begun to come to this hilltop to study the house from every angle, slowly learning to appreciate the stark beauty of its ancient lines. It was no longer destruction he dreamed of, but possession, not only of the building itself but of the paintings, sculptures, antique furniture, and elegant porcelains he imagined to be inside.

"It could 'ave been us, livin' like that," his father had said to him over and over again. "The Carnes were something oncet, lad. We owned the land, all of it, as far as yer eye can see. We'd have had tin mines and china-clay pits as well if a Trevor hadn't cheated us and stole our lands, and us'd be rich today. Ye'd like to be rich, wouldn't 'ee, boy?"

"Aye, Pa, I'd like it a lot."

"We will be, don't ye fret. I got plans to make us rich."

Daniel clenched his jaw at the memory of his father's plans . . . and what had become of them. Plans, dreams, fantasies spewed out into the night and whisked away, wind over water, on a rising tide of cheap aqua vitae. Daniel had plans, too. The difference was, he knew how to implement them. He was going to make them all come true, for himself, yes, but also for Jory, wild, reckless, contradictory dreamer that he'd been. For Pa, whose life he might have been able to save, had he been quicker and a little more suspicious.

For six years Daniel had been haunted by the injustice of his father's death. He had not forgotten, nor would he.

He descended the hill to Cadmon Hall and entered the grounds, as he'd done so many times before, always on the sly, never daring to make his presence known. This time he strode up to the front door, an ancient affair of heavy, iron-studded wood, lifted the lion-maned knocker, and let its sound thunder through the house the way his vengeance one day would echo.

Verity was in her father's study, going through the clay-company accounts, when Mrs. Chenoweth rapped at the door. Not wishing to drive in the night's foul weather, she had rung the vicarage to tell Julian that she planned to spend another night at Cadmon Hall. Since her father had been away she'd spent several nights in her old bedroom at home, enjoying her unaccustomed freedom.

"There's someone here to see 'ee," the housekeeper said.

Reluctantly Verity looked up from the books. There seemed to be an inordinate amount of fiscal confusion at Cadmon Clay. Her father had not asked her to attend to it, but he wasn't around to forbid her, either. "At this hour?"

The elderly housekeeper was fidgeting on the threshold, pulling at the sash around her ample waist. " 'Tes about Bret. It seems she's run off and lost herself on the moors. This fellow happened upon her in the storm and took her to his sister's cottage." She paused, eyeing the carpet. " 'Tes the Carne lad."

"Daniel Carne?"

"That's right," said a deep male voice from the shadows behind Mrs. Chenoweth. He moved past her, into the room. Verity nodded to the housekeeper, who reluctantly withdrew.

"So, Mrs. Marrick. It's been a while, hasn't it?"

"What's happened to my sister? Is she all right?"

"Her ankle's sprained, but other than that she's well. Tamara's caring for her."

Verity hadn't seen Daniel Carne since the time of his father's death, when he'd been a youth of sixteen or seventeen, skinny, uncertain, enraged. He was a man now, tall, broadshouldered, physically powerful. His features, including the eerie blue eyes, reminded her of Jory. But his hair was black, and there were no telltale signs of weakness and dissipation about his mouth. He was wet and shabbily dressed, but this appeared not to concern him. Nor did he seem in awe of his surroundings. Verity would have expected him to be as hungry for wealth and privilege as his father had been, but he spared no glance for the fine art on the walls or precious volumes on the shelves.

"You're sure she's not badly hurt?"

"I said so, didn't I?" His expression was as dark as his coloring. For a moment the full force of his antagonism radiated outward. Verity could feel his strange blue eyes upon her, taking her in, measuring her, assessing her. His expression grew insolent and surprisingly erotic.

As this thought struck her, she felt her cheek grow warm.

"Then why didn't you bring her home to me instead of leaving her with your sister?"

"She was drenched and exhausted. Tam was putting her to bed. I reckon I've done enough tonight for any spawn of the Trevors." He spoke with deliberate rudeness. "Go and fetch her yerself in the morning. I came to tell 'ee, that's all."

"I hope you haven't done or said anything to frighten her."

"She doesn't strike me as the type who frightens easily," he said. His attention had shifted to the two portraits hanging opposite each other on the walls. One was a painting of a Trevor ancestress. Although faded in color, the picture was marked by its style and energy: a woman of perhaps forty years, her auburn hair graying, her eyes direct and challenging, her mouth curved slightly upward in tolerance and good humor. Her cheekbones suggested that she had been something of a beauty in her younger days, and she was still a woman of distinction, for the artist had somehow managed to capture her spirit.

Her name, printed on a gilt-edged nameplate on the rather ornate frame, was Alexandra Douglas Trevor. Her dates were given as 1538–1625, and underneath them was inscribed the word *matriarch*.

The other portrait was a recent one of Bret in the garden with a dog at her feet. The resemblance between the two women was uncanny, and Papa had often teased Bret about being a throwback to an earlier century.

Verity cleared her throat. "I know you bear a grudge against our family, Mr. Carne, but don't you think the time has come to put it aside? My sister and I have no quarrel with you. Surely there's no need to carry this infamous feuding into another generation."

"Ye think not?" His blue eyes were glittering now. "Ye seriously imagine that now that my father's so conveniently dead, I'm going to offer my hand to his murderer's daughters in fellowship?"

"Your father died by accident. That was confirmed at the inquest."

"Yeah, right."

"Look—"

"Henry Trevor killed him. They had a shouting match in a pub in St. Austell—plenty of witnesses testified to that. Yer father got him even drunker than usual, then lay in wait for him alongside the highway and lured him into the path of that runaway clay wagon. I can't prove it, but I know it's true, and ye're all going to regret it one day. It may take me a while, but sooner or later I'm going to dismantle Cadmon Clay and ruin the lot of 'ee."

If he hadn't sounded so icily serious Verity might have smiled. It was ludicrous that a poor son of a drunken clay worker should entertain such a fantasy.

"Ye don't believe me, do 'ee?"

"You must admit the notion is a little farfetched."

"Ye're just like the others, aren't 'ee? All o' ye clay owners're cut from the same cloth. High and mighty with no thought that ye might fall. Yer doom is coming, Mrs. Marrick. Sooner than ye think. There's a clay strike in the works, ye know that, don't 'ee?"

"I hardly think it will come to that. Lay down your tools and you'll lay down your jobs."

"Ye got no one else to quarry yer pits but us clay workers. We've more power than ye imagine. Ye can't fight us all."

"We won't have to. You may be an ardent young agitator, Mr. Carne, but you don't have a wife and a family to feed. You can clamor all you like for a work stoppage, but the older, more responsible workers won't follow you. It's easy to be a radical when you've nothing to lose."

"And ye? What, I wonder, d'ye have to lose?" He was once again studying Bret's portrait, his dark head tilted slightly to one side, his expression intent. "An unusual girl, yer younger sister. Mebbe ye're right that this feud shouldn't infect another generation. Yer father and me are hopelessly mired in it, all the more so now that there's going to be a clay strike, but I've no reason to dislike her. They say redheads are a passionate lot."

Verity rose to her feet, no longer so self-assured. "Bret is just a schoolgirl. How dare you threaten her?"

Daniel Carne advanced upon her, not stopping until he was within touching distance. "Would ye rather I threaten 'ee?"

His physical power—and magnetism—were overwhelming. As children in the schoolyard, they had been of a height, but he must be close to a foot taller now. Absurdly, she remembered how he had knocked her to the ground, how strong he had been, how much stronger he must be now. Verity shuddered with the realization that she found him attractive. More so by far than she found her husband.

"Get out of here," she whispered.

For an instant she thought he wasn't going to comply. She thought he was going to touch her, maybe even . . . She wasn't sure what. She seemed to have lost her normal poise and dignity, and she hated him for that.

He turned away, thank God. "Come and get her in the morning. Don't worry," he added, "I won't be there."

He slammed out, leaving Verity hugging herself with both arms.

Instead of heading back to Tamara's cottage, Daniel hiked north, climbing higher into the moorland. He passed the sky-tips of Cadmon Clay with its vast acreage, its modern engines to pump water over the rock face of kaolinized granite and to lift the waste material out of the clay slurry, its mammoth rows of settling tanks, its barn-sized pan kiln and adjacent linhay. The buildings were shadows in the stormy night. He left them behind. They did not concern him, not anymore, not tonight.

He tramped on to the northeast until he crossed into a strip of Carne land that shared a streamside border with Cadmon Clay. On the Trevor side of the stream were the workings of one of the area's oldest tin mines, Wheal Faith. On the Carne side there was china clay. Its quality was excellent. Daniel's dream was to quit his miserable job at the Stannis claypits and start his own company. Jory had wanted it too, talking freely about "Carne Claypits," but he'd been no more successful at this venture than at any of the other things he'd attempted in life. Daniel could still hear the voices of his tavern mates taunting him: "Ain't much point in callin' it Carne Claypits when it don't produce one speck of Carne clay."

Daniel walked to the edge of the shallow exploration pit

he had dug himself and stared down its sloping sides. Squatting, he reached down to pick up a hunk of earth. It was tinged with white minerals. Pressing the pale earth between his hands, he thought disjointedly of all the events of the night—the funny redheaded creature who had turned out to be the daughter of his enemy; Verity Marrick's pale-faced reaction to his remark about redheads and passion. He hadn't meant it, really. He wasn't interested in schoolgirls. Tense, frustrated housewives, on the other hand, had a certain appeal. Verity Marrick was not a beautiful woman by any means, but she had a contained fervor about her that intrigued him.

He, too, remembered scrapping with her in the schoolyard. Something to do with his sister and a doll. He'd been caned for it; they both had. But even worse than the caning had been Tamara's scorn: "Ye don't attack girls. Ye'd better learn that now, ye vicious little devil, or ye'll end up just like Pa."

Tam. Pa. Aye, his memories were crowding in on him again. The dark, the fog, the sensation of being whirled on the winds of a series of wild, out-of-control emotions . . . it was all too reminiscent of so many other foggy nights, filled with contradiction and confusion. As a child, he'd wanted to grow up to be like his father. At the same time, he'd been terrified that that was exactly what would happen to him.

One evening when Daniel was no more than four years old, Jory Carne came home from his job at one of the local claypits blabbering about advances and new patents and all the riches to be made from the pieces of machinery he had invented. Daniel could tell that his mother was not impressed. She'd heard it before.

After he and Tamara had gone to bed that night in the loft where they slept, Daniel heard his parents shouting at each other. His mother informed her husband that she'd had enough of his drinking and his dreaming. It was a bad example to set for the children and she wasn't going to tolerate it anymore. His father retorted that she'd tolerate whatever he damn well ordered her to tolerate and had silenced her with a resounding crack of his fist.

It was always that way. When his father was in one of his

moods, an expression would steal over him, turning his face into something as huge and glowing as the full moon. Angry, Jory grew taller, wider, deeper, and stronger. Even though Daniel knew this could not be possible, it felt real and he believed it happened.

His mother believed it, too. " 'Tes yer father's rising time," she would say, her voice lower in pitch and in volume than usual, a hum about her, a vibration that Daniel would sense and fear because it made him resonate inside, deep in his gut where the emotions arose. Rising, like the moon, so luminous and powerful, harshly over the moors, yet beautiful. Could there be beauty in his father's rage?

His mother must think so, or why would she stay? She could have taken her children and returned to her Gypsy kin. Why deliberately put herself on misery's path?

Daniel sensed that his mother was drawn by something in her husband over which she had no control. It drew Daniel, too. Jory could be vicious in his anger, but he could also be lyrical and imaginative, telling the boy the most wondrous stories about giants and dwarfs, witches and fairy princesses. His words painted visions in Daniel's head that were so convincing that Daniel would lie awake in the dark, unable to sleep, almost *seeing* the lush scenes and irrepressible characters his father had woven for him. They would shimmer there before him, as real as anything the local moors had to offer.

When Jory drank too much, lost his temper and beat his wife and children, he was always sorry afterward. Sometimes he wept. "God forgive me, I never meant to hurt 'ee," he would say. He would take Daniel's flinching body into his big arms and hug him hard. "It comes over me, this deathly dark rage, and I can't stop it. My own father had this evil in him and his father before him. It goes back in our family, for generations, perhaps. Ye'd better pray to God it doesn't get 'ee, too."

So Daniel prayed, for at that age he believed God would hear and answer his prayers. He tried to sink a mineshaft to the depths of his soul and bury his own violence there, for sometimes it would rise along his spine and flash along his nerves, radiating out to all the farthest reaches of his body. It would travel to his brain and permeate every cell, taking control of his thoughts, his dreams, his imagination. It was this that he must resist, or else his father's sickness would be upon him, too. He must be ever vigilant.

After his mother's death, Daniel's feelings for his father became a confusing mixture of love, fear, and shame. They did well together except when Jory was drunk or terrorizing Tamara. Jory talked man to man with him and joked with him and taught him everything there was to know about working the claypits. When Daniel's body shot up toward manhood and his blood boiled with the need to know more about those mysterious creatures, women, Jory explained to him about that, as well. He told him what to do with that sway-hipped widow up to Tremayne Farm, and he cheered in an outpouring of shared masculine pride when Daniel admitted he'd gone and done it.

They were partners, mates. His friends envied him for having such a loose, hearty relationship with his dad. He felt thankful for it, lucky . . . except on the days when his father was drunk. The days—and nights—when the violence erupted, and the dark place inside Daniel grew, infected by the same seed that had sprouted in Jory.

Such was the core of him. Violence, his father's violence, running back for generations in their family, all the way back into the evil mists of time.

Daniel rose to his feet, flinging the hard-packed clay from his clenched fingers. He stood over the exploration pit, his little kingdom, his paltry territory, and rubbed his hands together wearily, as if helpless to get them clean.

Chapter Fifteen

On the day after Bret's adventure with Tamara and Daniel Carne, Verity sat hunched on the commode in the WC just outside the vicarage kitchen, her belly and lower back aching with cramps as the dark blood seeped from between her legs. She was weeping silently, afraid that her husband might hear. This was her grief, her disappointment, her guilt, and she didn't want him to know.

After six years of marriage and several early miscarriages, she had believed herself once again with child. She was late, her breasts felt heavy and swollen, and she had already begun to imagine the tiny perfection of the child growing inside. Now, as always, it was leaking away, silent as a dream.

Having a child had been her last hope for something that would bring her and Julian together on a more equal footing. Childbirth was another of the passages in life that confirms a woman to be an adult, and, as usual, Verity had fallen behind other women her age. There seemed no end to her failures. She was that saddest of all God's creatures: a barren woman.

She wondered if she was being punished for the brief stirrings of lust she had felt when looking upon the young, lean, hot-eyed Daniel Carne.

She'd slept poorly after Carne had left her the preceding evening. She'd risen early and set out by horse carriage with two servants to fetch Bret from Tamara's cottage. Upon arriving there she had found her sister elbow deep in Tamara's clay, absorbed in a pot-throwing lesson. She seemed not the least bit chastened by her misadventures of the night before. Exasperated, Verity had seen her safely back to Cadmon Hall, then returned to the vicarage, where a multitude of parish tasks awaited her. Soon afterward, her flow had begun.

Wearily, Verity rose from the commode and fitted herself with one of her collection of linen pads, which she kept discreetly in the bottom corner of her bureau drawer. At Cadmon Hall her maid had fashioned these—and some for herself—from fraying bed linen, and attended to the laundering of them every month as well, but this was a task Verity had taken upon herself since her marriage and move to the more modest surroundings of the country vicarage. She no longer had a personal maid, although they did employ a parlor maid, a cook, and a scullery maid. Verity had hoped they would soon employ a nursemaid as well, but apparently the Lord in His wisdom had other plans for her. Unfortunately He had not yet made them known.

* * *

"Ah, here you are at last, my dear," Julian said when she appeared downstairs for luncheon.

Julian, she noticed, was indulging in his usual large midday meal of meat and potatoes, several crusty hunks of bread, wine, and his favorite oranges, a luxury that he had shipped in each week at an exorbitant expense. Once or twice she had ventured, tactfully, to suggest that he ought to cut down on the large meals he fancied, for she had noticed signs of thickening around his stomach, hips, and buttocks in recent months, but he had ignored the hint. Since he concentrated his efforts in the pulpit on the more carnal sins that flesh is heir to, gluttony was not something he was concerned about, at least not in himself. If she overate, though, he was quick to take note of it, urging her to take care not to lose her girlish figure.

She poured herself a cup of tea and sat down at the opposite end of the table from her husband. She felt a queasiness along with the cramping in her belly and was not inclined to eat.

"The servants were gossiping in the kitchen this morning," Julian said. He sipped his wine, then swallowed another square of crusty bread. "Normally, as you know, I don't pay attention to such frivolity, but this time the subject was your sister and her scandalous behavior of last night."

"Really." Verity became aware of a familiar pounding in her head. More and more often lately she'd been suffering from excruciating headaches. She suspected that it was because she had taken on too many things: charity and committee work, visiting parishioners, running the vicarage and the household.

"Running off in the middle of the night is hardly the sort of behavior one expects of the daughter of one of the area's leading citizens," her husband continued. "Particularly during this period of agitation among the clay workers. It sets a bad example. I hope you have berated her sufficiently."

"Berating Bret and seeing any results are two entirely different things. She's at the age where she doesn't listen to her elders' advice."

"She's also at the age where young women cannot be

trusted to guard their virtue. I shudder to think what may have happened between her and that young hell-raiser, Daniel Carne. I have heard that he has been the ruin of more than one young village maiden, and if he's anything like his father . . .'' His voice trailed off and Verity was astonished to feel a stab of guilt, as if she, somehow, had been responsible for what had almost happened to her at the hands of Jory Carne and his friends all those years ago.

"Bret does not always behave with the highest standards of propriety, it's true, but she doesn't mean any harm.''

He smiled that knowing, superior, cat's-in-the-cream smile that always made her flinch. He pointed the tines of his fork in her direction as he said, ''Don't be too sure, Verity. When it comes to wickedness and sensuality, there is nothing more undisciplined and contrary than the human heart.''

Because of the cramping she experienced that afternoon, Verity cut short her scheduled parish duties, which included several visits to parishioners and an organizational meeting for the annual church bazaar.

She felt quite guilty about this, although she rarely took time for herself. Julian kept her much too busy.

She tried to nap but was unable to fall asleep. She kept thinking about Bret, poised at the beginning of a life that was rich with the spirit and wildness of forest, moors, and sea. There was an inner radiance about her sister that was foreign and almost incomprehensible to Verity. Child of darkness, child of light, the servants at Cadmon Hall had always called them. She felt one of those lightning flashes of envy for which she always hated herself.

Verity was miserable. It was not simply her inability to carry a child. Her wretchedness ran deeper than that. She was bored with teaching Sunday school, organizing church teas and Bible study classes, interceding between the choirmaster and the members of the choir whom he routinely terrorized, visiting the sick and the sore at heart, attending weddings, christenings, and funerals, smiling graciously until her cheek muscles ached no matter how rude people were to her, and generally living up to the image that the community held of the vicar's wife. Although her responsibilities were as numerous as Julian's, she received no recognition of any kind. When it came to church policy, her opinion didn't count. Although she knew as much about the parish as her husband did, the members of the vestry, who, along with Julian, administered church affairs, never consulted her about anything.

She was powerless in the church and in her home, and her marriage had cut her off from the one venue in which she might conceivably have carved out a niche for herself—Cadmon Clay.

Before leaving for America, her father had informed her that he was putting his pit boss, Gil Parkins, in charge of the day-to-day operations at the claypits. Verity had been envious. If she had tried harder to convince her father to allow her to work at the clay company, she might have been the one he'd have trusted to manage things while he was gone.

Julian, of course, would not have approved. Bret's comment about Verity's requiring her husband's permission had rankled so much because it was true. In marriage, she had lost her right to make independent decisions about anything.

During her first year with Julian, Verity had been, if not exactly happy, at least contented in her new life. She'd enjoyed the challenges of running her own household, and she'd particularly looked forward to Saturday nights, when Julian would read his sermon to her, practicing diligently to make certain he achieved the most effective emphasis and intonation. He would solicit his wife's comments, although she soon understood that he wasn't interested in her suggestions and never followed them. What he seemed to require was her admiration. She always provided it, and when Julian finished working himself up to a passion over the evil in men's hearts and the saving grace of the Lord, he would turn to his wife and tell her to take off her clothes.

In those early months, once the shock of her wedding night was over, Verity had welcomed her husband's lovemaking, and Julian seemed satisfied with her as well. But it had gradually became apparent to her that her husband was somewhat peculiar in his sexual demands and desires. He continued to insist that she come to bed in pure white cotton nightgowns. The more childish and inexperienced her responses, the better pleased he was. He wanted her "cooperation," yes, but he had no desire to arouse her passion.

Verity was reluctant to question his preferences, lest she betray her own lamentable ignorance, but as time went on she felt increasingly frustrated and distressed. Marriage had awakened her erotic desires, which Julian did not recognize. He expected her to be eternally virginal, and perhaps even disgusted by the act that "beast in mankind" couldn't help but perform.

"I feel sometimes as though you don't really *like* making love to me," she plucked up the nerve to say to him one evening.

"Do you imagine that I enjoy feeling like a rutting animal? Such impulses are heavy with human vanity and sin."

"Surely not. Didn't the Lord create Eve to be a companion to Adam? Surely He intended them to take pleasure in each other."

"Don't speak to me of Eve." Julian's voice was harsh. "She was evil incarnate, the first temptress, the downfall of her husband, the Originator of Sin. Don't ever speak to me of Eve."

Yet the thought of this temptress seemed to inflame him and his passion rose to new heights that night, as if evil and temptation excited him. It excited her also, rousing a sweetness in her breasts and belly and thighs that she yearned to explore further. But Julian never seemed to caress her quite the way she needed him to. As always, it was over too soon and he withdrew from her, turned coldly away, not touching her again for the remainder of the night.

Lately he had not touched her much at all.

How would it be, she wondered, to make love with someone young, someone handsome, someone who treated her tenderly and cared about her feelings? Someone with the body, though not the character, of course, of Daniel Carne. She lay quite still, telling herself that she must not indulge in such immoral, indecent thoughts, but this only made them all the more vivid and exciting. She pictured what it would be like to exchange secret glances with a potential lover, stolen kisses and caresses, passionate embraces, and, finally, after a period of exquisitely erotic courting, a soul-shattering consummation.

Such thoughts evoked a deep and abiding sense of shame and she berated herself for the miserable excuse of a minister's wife she had proven to be. In this manner she was able to beat her feelings and fantasies back down into the basement with the Fiery Furnace where they belonged, and slam the iron doors upon them.

Chapter Sixteen

Two weeks after her aborted journey to Arizona, Bret lingered in the general store—cum post office run by Mrs. Bream in Trenwythan, reading over her latest letter to Mr. Zachary Slayton, checking for embarrassing mistakes. It was not that she wrote badly, only that she wrote fast, which sometimes resulted in spelling errors and grammatical oddities. And there was also the problem of her handwriting, which, instead of being clear and ladylike, tended to emerge in a bold, dramatic scrawl.

Mr. Slayton's letters were quite different: neat, deliberate, and logically organized. They weren't stuffy, though—not in the least. There was something magical about the words and images he used that suggested there were vast wells of emotion lurking underneath his friendly, courteous style.

Bret and her father shared an odd correspondence with this man from Arizona whom neither of them had ever met. It had begun several years before, when Papa was working on a revolutionary design for an aeroplane engine. He'd published his results in an aviation journal, and the first letter from Mr. Slayton had arrived some weeks later, suggesting an improvement that Papa thought was brilliant. The two men had become enthusiastic correspondents.

In the beginning Bret had participated by scribbling her name at the bottom of her father's letters. Mr. Slayton had responded by sending her a necklace made from the rattle of a snake he had shot. Bret was delighted with this gift. She spent many hours imagining the viciousness of the creature and the epic battle that must have been fought between Mr. Slayton, whom she pictured as a giant of a man with long white hair and a pointed beard like Buffalo Bill, and the hideous serpent. Her thank-you note to him was the first letter she'd ever written, and it must have amused him, since in his next letter he'd included a note addressed to "Miss Bret Trevor." They had been writing back and forth to each other ever since.

Dear Mr. Slayton,

You would have been so surprised if I'd gone through with the plan I had a fortnight ago—like the intrepid adventuress I'm determined to be, I set out to visit you! Unfortunately I didn't get very far. My horse threw me, which was entirely my fault.

My adventure wasn't a total waste, however, because in the course of it I met a most unusual family. The sister's name is Tamara Carne and she lives high on a windswept moor, making pots out of clay. She has a brother, Daniel, a sinister clay worker who bears a terrible grudge against the Trevors. According to my sister, he is a dreadful miscreant and rascal who will destroy my reputation forever if I venture near him again, but I think she's exaggerating, don't you?

Verity neglected to forbid me to associate with Daniel's sister, however, an oversight of which I've shamelessly taken advantage. Tamara's teaching me to work the clay. She says I have talent, even though the pots I've thrown so far have been vile. "Ye've got the eye for it, honestly ye do," she told me one day. "Ye're jist at a awkward age, hand-wise."

I think that was a polite way of telling me I'm clumsy.

Did you finish building your latest aeroplane? I do hope you will be careful not to take off in anything unsafe. Papa hasn't been up—or allowed me to go up—since that French friend of his was killed when his aeroplane turned upside down in flight and he fell out. I certainly hope you strap yourself in properly when you fly because falling out seems to me an extraordinarily silly way to die.

I still hope to come to Arizona someday to visit you. Maybe next summer.

> Yours very sincerely,
> Bret

It wasn't too awful, she decided, puzzling over what she thought—but wasn't positive—was a misspelling. There were some commas out of place, but Mr. Slayton wouldn't mind. He was fairly lax about punctuation himself.

"Another letter to the Wild West?" Mrs. Bream commented as Bret handed over the envelope. She was a big woman with malletlike fists and arms that were well muscled from hefting such commodities as flour, lard, raisins, and rice down from the shelves to sell to her customers. The General Merchandise, as the locals called the shop, sold everything from sweets to corn plasters, treacle to shoe black, tinned meats to tea. Because Mrs. Bream also served the function of post mistress, she was well apprised of everybody else's business.

"I'm determined to go there someday, instead of only writing."

"And get yerself murdered by outlaws or scalped by Indians? You'd best stay put, Elizabeth, and behave yerself."

Not me, Bret thought, stifling a laugh.

After leaving the shop, she plodded down the broad main street of the village, picking her way through the slurry of whitish clay mud that clogged the streets. Trenwythan was small, just one main road that ran east to St. Austell with a few lanes twisting off it. The men in the area had worked for the tin industry in its heyday during the eighteenth and first half of the nineteenth centuries. The squat stone chimney of Wheal Tremoss rose from the hillside below the village, and there were more such chimneys to the south in Polgooth, reminders of the prosperous days of tin and copper that were no more.

The weather was fine and Bret regretted that she hadn't brought along a fishing rod. She had recently discovered a clear, cold stream near Tamara's cottage that she suspected would be teeming with trout at this time of year. She decided to stop at the vicarage and borrow one from Simon.

St. Catherine's and its adjoining vicarage was located at the far end of the village. Tess, Verity's sullen young parlor maid, opened the door to Bret's knock and looked disapprovingly at her wild hair and mud-splattered boots as she let her in. "The mistress isn't home," she said ungraciously. She was the latest of a series of what Bret considered extremely rude and incompetent maids employed by her sister and her husband. Bret's father had remarked that rude though the girls might be, every one of them was pretty in a sly sort of way. "Despite all his hair-raising sermons on the wages of sin, deep down he's as randy as any man."

Bret knew all too well that this was true. Ever since she'd returned home from school, Julian had been making excuses to get her alone, ostensibly because he had some words of moral wisdom to impart. On the first of these occasions, she had cooperated, certain that it must be her own overdramatic imagination that suggested to her that her brother-in-law was standing too close, brushing her arm or her shoulder too often.

On the third occasion, just last week, he had embraced her, one of his hands sliding down to touch her thigh through her frock, and she'd realized that his intentions were not strictly brotherly. Sickened, she'd escaped by feigning a coughing fit, and since then she had taken care not to be alone with him.

"It's Simon I've come to see. Is he home?"

"He's in his room. I'll tell him you're here."

"Don't bother, I'll go right on up." Bret was already on her way to the narrow staircase that ascended to the second floor. She tiptoed through the darkened hallway—just in case

Julian was somewhere about—then continued up the narrower set of stairs to the third floor, where Simon's room was.

She rapped on the door.

"Who is it?" Simon's voice was lethargic.

"It's me. Can I come in?"

"Me who?"

Bret opened the door. "You know my voice perfectly well." She advanced into the gloomy room, arms akimbo. Simon was stretched at full length in bed, his legs covered by a brocaded counterpane. "What are you doing in here? It's almost tea time."

"I'm feeling poorly."

"As usual." She went to the window and flung open the thick velvet curtains, letting the sunlight pour into the large room with its adjoining dressing closet and bath. Over the years she and he had spent a great number of hours here, playing cards or chess, reading, talking, writing poetry, staring into the fire, and telling each other their plans and dreams for a sunny future.

As Simon closed his eyes, groaning, she said sternly, "You're wasting a lovely summer day."

"What's lovely about it?" he said, his elegant fingers plucking at the coverlet. "The world is an ashcan. Human life is pointless, wretched, and a bore. Everything dies, everything rots. What is there to get up for?"

"Honestly, Simon." She sat down beside him on the edge of the mattress. "You've got to buck up."

Simon's lower lip took on a hint of petulance. He was strikingly handsome, with liquid brown eyes, golden hair, and fine, aristocratic features. If his mouth was a trifle too sulky, his cheeks too pale, and his mannerisms too nervous, it was due, no doubt, to what her father termed galloping young manhood. At seventeen, Simon was a year older than she. Bret noted the evidence on his upper lip that confirmed that he was trying to grow a mustache.

Simon had always claimed to have a weak constitution, but Bret didn't believe a word of it. Although he often had a cold or a cough or an earache, only rarely did his symptoms progress to anything more serious. "That's because I rest at the first sign of illness," he insisted. "If I ran about the way you do, I'd catch my death."

For years Bret had felt sorry for her friend, restricted from the vigorous activities she herself so enjoyed. Staring at him now, his handsome face propped elegantly on one slim wrist, his body so languidly posed, she wondered, not for the first time, how he would ever make his way in the world. The ordinary business of living seemed to her to require a good deal more energy than Simon was willing to invest.

"I'd expect a little sympathy from you, of all people," he said. "My spirit is sensitive; I can't help my moods. Besides, all the great poets suffered from some sort of spiritual malaise. Byron, Keats, Tennyson, Shelley, Shakespeare—"

"Shakespeare certainly wouldn't have lain about all day, moaning and groaning about the human condition. He'd have been much too busy storming the boards at the Globe Theatre or getting Anne Hathaway pregnant. He'd have been *writing* at the very least. Have you written any new poems since you've been home from school?"

"Well, no, but—"

"Do get up. We're going fishing."

Simon groaned again and tried to pull the covers over his head. But Bret was ruthless. "Up. Right now."

"I'm still in my nightshirt, for heaven's sake."

"I'll turn my back while you dress."

"You'll probably peek."

"Simon, dear, I already know from all the times we've gone swimming together that you have the physique of a young Apollo, but the only bodies I'm inclined to admire today are plump, silvery, and scaly. Now hurry."

He sat up and reached for his dressing gown. "We used to bathe together in one of the quarry pools, remember?" he said with considerably more enthusiasm in his voice.

She didn't admit it, although she remembered very well.

His expression grew glum again. "Someone might come in. You'd better wait for me downstairs."

"Only if you promise to perform the Herculean task of getting ready for the day in record time—ten minutes or so."

"Blast you, Bret. I wish you *had* gone to Arizona."

* * *

Julian Marrick had just returned to the refuge of his vicarage after a difficult morning at church—the members of the altar guild were quarreling with the choir master over his choices for the autumn music—as Bret descended the staircase from the upper floor. There was, as usual, a wild, ungoverned look about her flamboyant hair. It was the color one might expect to see adorning the head of a woman who walked the midnight streets of London. Of course, her body was not as buxom as one would expect of that sort of woman. She was slender, with a neat waist, long slim legs, and tender little breasts.

"Hello, Julian," she said briskly. "Is Verity with you?"

He remembered that she had been avoiding him lately and said, "Verity is engaged in her usual parish duties. She is not, as you know, inclined to idleness."

The girl lifted her chin as she absorbed the rebuke. He doubted that she was likely to pay any attention to it, however. "What are you doing here? I should not like to think that you have been upstairs in my son's bedroom unchaperoned."

To the tilt of the chin was added a slight flush of the cheeks, which inspired more lascivious thoughts in Julian. He tried to suppress them, damning himself for the ease with which his sinful passions were activated these days. Why, after so many hours on his knees, pleading with his Maker, must he continue to wrestle with such evil and unruly forces? It was the oldest struggle in the world: the pitched battle between the body and the soul, and he was afraid he was losing. No longer was he comforted by the thought that the Almighty in His wisdom presented the greatest temptations to those who were best equipped to withstand them, since lately he had not been able to resist.

Bret was sixteen, exactly the age he found most appealing. It was the time in life when a girl was more than a girl and somewhat less than a woman. The bloom was upon her, the expectant innocence just about to burst open as life filled it. So firm, so fresh, so vital! There was no time more exciting, more rewarding in a female's life. They were open and pliant and indeed eager to listen to a man's counsel and advice; they were still willing to please.

"Simon and I are going fishing. I'm to wait for him downstairs while he gets ready."

"Come with me, Bret," he said, quite unable to control his tongue or the words that it generated. He made a gesture toward his study, which was down the hallway that stretched behind the staircase toward the rear of the house. "I have an important matter I wish to discuss with you."

She smiled pleasantly and did not move. "I'm afraid I haven't time. Simon will be right down."

Julian felt a surge of annoyance. How dare she refuse?

She moved past him toward the front door, sending a whiff of violets to his appreciative nostrils. "Please tell him I'll be waiting for him outside."

Julian stalked down the hall to his study. He sat at his desk, ordering himself to begin working on next Sunday's sermon, imagining the merciless rhetoric with which he would lash his congregation for their weakness, their baseness, their inability to keep the commandments of the Lord. He would, as usual, make them so preoccupied with the evil in their hearts that they would not seek it in their children, their spouses, their neighbors, their friends . . . much less in their pastor, whose conduct ought to be beyond reproach.

There was blackness in his soul. He feared and despised this evil and prayed fervently for it to be expunged. Each night as he prepared for bed he exhorted himself with the words of Peter: "Be sober, be watchful. Your adversary the devil prowls around like a roaring lion, seeking someone to devour. Resist him, firm in your faith." Each morning he awoke with the hope that he had been scoured of sin, and that hereafter he would verily prove the kind, selfless, charitable Christian minister he so devotedly yearned to be. When, as a venerable old clergyman, he expired upon his deathbed, he would rise up to his Father with a clean heart. He would be welcomed into Heaven, the refuge and reward of the Just, and spared the everlasting torments of the Pit.

Julian's terror of eternal damnation had been with him since his childhood when his father had punished every boyish prank with brutal floggings, describing in gruesome detail the fires that would sear him, the rats that would gnaw upon him, the vultures that would pluck out his eyes if he failed to resist the temptations of sin.

He had tried. He'd become a clergyman, devoting himself to the saving of souls, including his own. His intention had been to live a life so holy that no threat of damnation could ever frighten him.

It could not be, surely, that he was failing?

Julian was startled by a rap on his study door. Verity was away for the rest of the afternoon, and he had heard Simon and Bret go out together. He was alone in the house, except for the young servant he had hired several weeks before, Tess.

"Come," he called, pushing his chair back slightly as the crow-haired, plum-lipped, pear-breasted parlor maid entered the room. She was a little older than Bret, but still young, still tender. She was a lovely girl.

She said not a word as she came around his desk and placed herself athwart his lap. She knew when to keep silent; he had instructed her well. Pressing his shoulders against the leather-covered seat, she nestled against him and pressed a long, slow kiss to the surface of his lips. He held her close, delighting in her rosy, unlined skin, her girlish body, the freshness and cleanliness of her youth. Holding a lover of such tender years helped him to forget the aging of his body, the inevitable decay, the inexorable progress toward death, and the horror that awaited sinners after the final dissolution. When he was deep inside Tess's firm, tender flesh, Julian was no longer afraid.

The water was flowing high and clear in Bret's newly discovered trout stream when she and Simon arrived there some forty-five minutes later. He had puffed all the way, complaining about the heat, the bright sunlight, and her rapid pace over the moors.

"A little fishing'll fix you up," she said. In truth she was hoping it would fix her up. She still felt a little sick from what she had sensed of his father's feelings for her. Rather than fading for lack of encouragement, they seemed stronger than ever.

Poor Verity! How horrible to be married to such a man.

"Fishing's a stupid bloody sport," Simon groused as she sat down on the bank to take off her shoes and stockings. Bret used the sash from around her waist to ruck up the skirts of her light summer frock while Simon glared at her in disapproval. "You're not going to wade, surely? The water's freezing."

"Mr. Slayton's advice is to get right into the stream with the fish. That's how they do it in the American West."

"Well, it's considered crass and unnecessary here."

"Do shut up, you silly old thing. Fish are very sensitive to people's emotions."

"What rot. Trout brains are about the size of a cherry pit."

"Honestly. Keep it up and your clouds of gloom will send them finning upstream all the way to Scotland."

"Look," he said. "There's a rise."

"Your fish. Go get him. I'm going upstream a ways."

Once he began casting, she knew it would be a while before she heard another word of complaint from him.

Leaving him to set up his rod, Bret walked quietly up along the grassy bank, keeping away from the water so that her shadow wouldn't spook any fish that might be feeding on the stream's abundant insect life. She found a spot to wade in several hundred yards from where Simon was casting. The stream had taken at least two twists, so she could no longer see him. She was alone with the water, the rocks, and the trout.

It had been a couple of weeks since she'd gone fishing— she'd had to wait for her ankle to mend first—and she'd missed it, less for the thrill of the hunt, although that element was there, than for the peacefulness brought her by the sound of ripples flowing over stones, the brush of cool water against her bare skin, the hypnotic rhythms of her casting.

Her father had taught her to fish the summer after Verity had left to get married. In the beginning she hadn't been interested in the fishing part at all, only in the lovely feeling of being close to her father.

Right from the beginning, Bret couldn't bear to watch him kill the fish they hooked. "Can't we just catch them and let them go?"

"That's hardly my idea of fishing," Papa had said with a laugh, but he'd agreed. He had taught her how to do it: gently twisting the hook from the fishes' jaws, cradling them in the water against the rush of the current, stroking their bellies until the gills began to flicker. Now and then he would insist on keeping a particularly fat and juicy trout for the skillet, but Bret had never been tempted. She'd always released her catch, watching with pleasure as well as relief as they darted away.

Bret tied a mayfly on the end of her fine horsehair leader after threading the greased silk fly line through her rod's guides. The cool water sent a chill through her as she waded in, moving carefully over the slippery, stony bottom, looking for a place where she could cast to a rising trout. She settled into a comfortable spot and waited, not moving, her eyes alert to any dimples or ripples on the surface upstream. Her entry into the water would have spooked any nearby fish, but if they heard or saw nothing more of her, they would relax and start feeding again. Since trout have to face upstream while waiting for their supper, in order to avoid being swept away in the current, Bret had a slight advantage.

At first she saw no rises. She focused on a large wedge-shaped rock ten yards upstream. If she were a trout, she'd have hidden in the shadows just below it, waiting for whatever struggling insects the currents funneled around it. It was a perfect feeding lie.

Ha! A bubble popped the surface and a circular ripple spread out around it. Mentally marking the spot, Bret checked behind her for possible obstructions before launching her backcast. When she felt the pull of the fly line straightening out to her rear, she began her forward cast, bringing the fly gently down to the surface about four feet beyond the spot she had selected and letting the current whisk the fly toward the rock.

Nothing. She lifted her line and cast again.

About a second before her fly reached the rock on the fifth cast, Bret saw the quick ripple of a rise. A real insect disappeared from the surface of the water about a foot to the left of the spot to which she was casting.

"Well, you're a sly one, aren't you?" she whispered.

Her next cast was too short, the one after that too far over to the left. Her silk line already felt a bit waterlogged; it probably needed to be greased again, an onerous task. "Bother!"

Calm down, she ordered herself. This always happened. She got excited and the precision of her casting went straight to hell.

The trout rose again; she caught a glimpse of its golden snout. A big brown. Wise and careful. She waited, afraid of scaring it. *Learn its feeding rhythm,* she reminded herself. Her father always said that an angler's greatest strength lay in his patience. Too bad the good Lord hadn't graced her with much of that particular virtue.

When he rose again to sip in a mayfly Bret forced herself to watch and wait. And again. She examined the surface of the stream and realized that a hatch had started and that the flies the trout was rising to were slightly different in color from the one she was using. "That's what you're hungry for, hey? That's what I'll offer you, then."

She bit off her original fly and searched among her artificials to find the pattern that most closely approximated the tiny insects that were hatching just above the water. Her father had tied most of the flies she used. Bret had enjoyed watching him but hadn't quite gotten the knack of it yet. She could work clay, but securing bits of feather and fur to the shank of a tiny hook with fine silk thread was a skill that had so far defeated her.

After tying on a new mayfly she waited and watched again. The trout rose, then disappeared, rose, then disappeared. Bret prepared to cast. She had the rhythm of his hunger now.

She raised her arm and threw the fly line into its backcast. Concentrating, she brought it forward and smiled as it settled onto the surface of the water, exactly where she'd wanted it to go.

Her tiny mayfly drifted with the current—quickly, above the rock, more quickly still around the side of the rock, then slowly in the pool in the lee of the rock, only an inch, perhaps, above and to the right of her trout's lie. The fly bobbed on the surface, barely visible. "Come on, fish," she whispered. "Eat it."

The water dimpled around her mayfly. Yes! She waited a split second, then raised her rod sharply. The tension ripped along the silk of the fly line, down her rod, and into her arm. Her fish broke the surface. Golden, shining, iridescent. She had hooked a lovely brown trout.

As it leaped again, its muscular body spitting tiny diamonds of water, Bret was struck, as always, with admiration for her quarry's strength and beauty. She would battle it now, maybe losing it in the process, but that wouldn't matter. She was going to release it anyway. But it would be good to see the trout up close and hold it for a moment first.

Her reel sang as her fish tore line off it in his rush to get away. Goodness, he was strong! Bret laughed out loud as the tension threatened to pull her off balance and topple her into the stream. What a magnificent fish!

Life, she decided, was just about perfect.

Chapter Seventeen

Daniel Carne was on his way home from an exhausting day at the Stannis claypits when he noticed something that looked like a whip coiling in great lazy loops in the air just over the steep banks of the brook not far from Tamara's cottage. Because the sun was in his eyes, distorting his view, he shaded them as he moved closer. The moors were strange and wild, and as a child he'd listened, awe-filled, to his mother's tales of witchery and superstition. There were goddesses of springs, gods of the waters and of the rivers, and no one truly knew what mysteries they held.

"Bother!" he heard the goddess say.

Approaching the bank, he caught a glimpse of Bret

Trevor's red hair streaming like a flag in the wind. She held a fishing rod, and the loops in the air were being formed by the casting of her fly line, which she did with some dexterity.

Daniel had no patience with this type of fishing, which he considered affected. It was something rich people wasted their time with. If he'd had time to fish—which he did not because he was too busy working in the claypits—he'd have used a plain old branch, string, and worm.

It struck him that it was unusual to see a girl fishing, no matter what she used for tackle. He noted grudgingly that she did it with a certain grace. He had not thought her as graceful when he'd met her out on the moors. In fact, he scarcely thought of her as female. But standing there in the dappled sunlight with her hair whipping around her face and her frock sticking to her slender body, she was a curiously moving sight.

Bret was not what he usually considered pretty, but there was a certain drama to her looks. She had the wildest, reddest, most unusual hair he'd ever seen. Her nose was decidedly straight, and her lips weren't soft at all, but rather thin and severe, except when she was smiling. A'course she had plenty of things to smile about, since she'd never had to scrounge for a living in the claypits. No hardship had ever touched her life.

Bret's rod bent as she hooked a trout. As it leaped, shimmering, into the air, she let out a little whoop of delight.

Daniel watched her battle it, surprised to see her prevailing, although with much splashing, not only of the hooked trout but of the angler as she moved through the water, rod held high.

Her skirts and petticoats were rucked up around her knees to keep them dry. She must have removed her shoes and stockings, because as she moved into shallower water Daniel was able to see her bare legs, which were smooth and slim. The cold water funneled around them, creating little splashes and rivulets around about her knees. He wondered what she was doing *in* the water. Other people stayed on the banks while fishing.

The trout made another desperate lunge and Bret arched her shoulders against its weight, her small breasts rising and pressing against the bodice of her frock. Daniel's throat began to ache as he imagined how it would feel to touch her—her cheeks, her breasts, that soft skin on her legs.

She's too damn young for 'ee, his conscience insisted even as image after image assaulted him, the fantasies of teasing, touching, loving that tended to plague him when he was in the company of women. He had little control over such feelings, and they often left him tense and irritable, even after a successful seduction.

"Ye're a slave to it, ain't 'ee?" his mates at the claypits taunted him whenever they heard the gossip about his various exploits with the opposite sex. "Who's it this month and how come they never hold on to 'ee? One of these days ye'll meet yer match, Daniel. One of these beauties of yers'll haul 'ee into church and keep 'ee dipping into the same pot for a while."

"Not likely," he'd reply.

"Come on, you darling, lovely fellow," Bret was crooning to her fish, which she had managed to reel in close to her body. Her seductive voice—wasted on the trout—reminded him of the stories his mother told of the Sirens who lured seafarers to their deaths with the sweetness of their songs. The fact that she would never use that tone with a poor clayman whom she undoubtedly regarded as not nearly good enough for her made him hate her more, in that moment, than he could ever remember hating anybody in his life.

With the exception, of course, of her father.

"There now, I've almost got you," Bret whispered to her trout. Her joy was nearly complete. Her fish had fought bravely and proudly, yielding at last to his own exhaustion and the superior cunning of his two-legged predator. It wasn't fair, really. If she hadn't been armed with a nasty device of bamboo, metal, feathers, and silk, she'd have had no chance of capturing him.

As she reached into the water to unhook the brown, a loud voice addressed her: "What're ye doing down there? Poaching?"

Bret looked up, startled. The glare of the setting sun was in her eyes, but silhouetted against it she saw a man who had taken up a position high athwart the bank, his feet planted apart, his fists clenched at his side.

It was Daniel Carne. Her enemy.

Splash. Bret lost her grip on the trout, who slipped through her fingers and *dove* back into the water. "Damnation!" she cried, not caring what Carne thought of her language. The hook was still in the fish's mouth, and line whirred off her reel as he sought to escape.

"You shouldn't sneak up on people like that." She jerked up her rod and hauled on her line, muttering more curses under her breath. When Daniel jumped down to the edge of the stream, settling on a flat rock a couple of yards to her right, she gave him the withering look that Mrs. Chenoweth assured her was capable of freezing small animals in their tracks at thirty paces. Unfortunately, it didn't seem to work on trout . . . or on Daniel.

"This is Carne land." He was clad in his work clothes and thick laborer's boots, his jacket and his hair covered with white kaolin dust, as usual. He looked weary, impatient, and belligerent. "And those are Carne trout."

"You're the gamekeeper, I suppose?" She was trying to sound cocky and unconcerned, but she wasn't too confident of her success. Was it his land? She didn't think Tamara would mind her fishing here, although she hadn't actually obtained her permission. "I wasn't aware that your sister"— she put a faint stress on the words—"owned this segment of the moors."

"No, I reckon not. Folks as rich as the Trevors know the boundaries of their own land, but they're not so finicky about other people's property."

He was angry. It wasn't her fishing, of course. Clearly, he was determined to carry over whatever acrimony existed between him and her father to his intercourse with her. "You have quite a chip on your shoulder, don't you?"

Instead of answering he moved closer to her. There was something about his big, sturdy body that made her feel vulnerable. This wasn't something she cared to admit to herself—intrepid heroines weren't supposed to be frightened by sullen claymen—but there was something intimidating about Daniel Carne. It wasn't a seductive sort of thing, though. It was more as if he were barely restraining himself from leaping upon her and pummeling her.

Reaching down into the cold water, she managed to work her fingers along her taut line until she was able to catch hold of her fish again. He wriggled in her hands, living quicksilver. A beauty, she thought again, keeping him just below the surface of the water where he'd be able to survive. A tired beauty, nearly spent from the exertion of a second fight; an unnecessary struggle for which she had Daniel to blame.

With more care than usual, she twisted the hook from the brown's jaw and massaged him to help him recover his strength. He was quiet in her hands now, as if he'd sensed that he could trust her. His gills pulsed, his tail flicked, and the muscles along his sides began to quiver. He was gathering himself for another shot at freedom.

"Gently, now," she murmured. "Easy, my lovely one. It's all right; you'll be free in a moment, just as soon as I'm sure you're strong enough. Easy. What a beauty you are."

"Christ," Daniel said. "It's just a fish, and you're going to lose it."

He splashed into the water beside her, reached down, and grabbed the slippery trout right out of her hands, raising him into the air above the stream and holding him harshly around the middle so he couldn't leap away.

"What are you doing? Don't squeeze him like that! He'll die!"

"Isn't that the idea? What the hell are 'ee torturing it for?"

He proceeded to squat down and bash her fish's head against a flat rock. The trout went limp as the life drained out of him; the brightness in his round eyes faded.

"Here." Daniel held the dead trout out to her. "Have it for supper along with the other ye've poached."

Bret made an inarticulate sound and jerked backward, losing her footing on the slippery bottom of the brook and nearly falling. Daniel grabbed her forearm to steady her but she shrank back from his touch. Her mind groped with the reality of sudden, senseless death and rejected it. For a moment she couldn't believe what he'd done.

"You killed him." Blindly, she took the trout and stroked it as tenderly as if it were still alive. He'd been a brave and beautiful fish, flush with life and glory, and now he was nothing more than a cold slab of meat.

"It's kinder to do it that way. If ye're too squeamish to kill yer catch properly, you shouldn't be fishing. One blow and they're gone. You were letting it flail to death."

"I was freeing him!" She practically screamed the words.

"What for? What was wrong with it? Too small? Ye got bigger ones in yer creel?"

She shook her head, which was aching. The trout felt cold in her hands. "I don't carry a creel. I always release my catch."

"What the hell are ye angling for if ye're not going to eat the fish?"

"For the sport! For the fun of it and the thrill of it and the pure absolute joy of it. But you don't understand that, do you?"

Her stomach was churning, which was an excessive reaction, she supposed, to the death of a fish. She had killed fish before, usually through incompetence—hooking them too deeply or fighting them too long. Now and then when she released a trout it would seem fine for a second, then turn belly up. She hated it when that happened. It always made her realize that much as she loved it, fishing was not an entirely benign sport. If she was going to fish, some of these graceful creatures were going to die.

But this was different. This was deliberate, and cruel.

"I release my fish," she repeated. "I would never kill them willfully, or purposefully, or—or casually, with no respect for their pride and their courage and their beauty. I'm sure people consider me eccentric for this, but it's the way I am. And I certainly would never kill a fish just to *get* another person."

"What d'ye mean by that?"

"You killed him because you hate me." All she could see were Daniel's brutal hands, which were capable of killing, and the darkness of spirit that lurked behind his vivid blue eyes. "You hate me because my surname is Trevor, which isn't fair at all. You don't know me. You might even have liked me if you'd given me half a chance."

She stomped past him, out of the water, dismantling her

rod as she went. She bit the fly off the end of her leader with a savage little snap of her teeth. Her rage was so profound that for several seconds all she could think of was that if she'd been capable of cracking Daniel's head against the same rock, she'd have done it.

Years ago Verity had told her that a young lady mustn't show her anger, that she must bite her lip, if necessary, to keep bitter, hurtful words from spilling out into the world. There were times when Bret's lips were raw from biting things back, but in general she wasn't very good at it.

"People say harsh things about you," she continued as she climbed the bank of the brook, "but I've ignored them. I like to make up my own mind about people. Anyway, it didn't seem possible to me that Tamara could have a violent, heart-less—" she paused for an instant, seeking the right noun for the occasion, "jackass for a brother."

As Daniel followed her up the steep bank, his long shadow, cast by the crimson sun sinking into the hills behind them, overtook hers. His hand settled on her shoulder, and she was conscious of its thickness and its weight. She knew how a fish must feel when it was drawn inexorably to the giant feet of an angler; how hopeless it must seem to battle something so much bigger and stronger than itself.

Violently, she shook off his hand as images of hooked trout leaping into the air crowded her brain. She'd always thought their somersaults and flips were beautiful, but now they seemed to her little more than an anguished dance. They couldn't free themselves, and she wasn't sure that she could, either.

She couldn't see her own shadow now. His had engulfed hers. With that perception came another: Daniel Carne was going to hurt her. She knew it with pure, terrible clarity. She didn't know when, she didn't know how . . . she just knew it would happen, and that there was nothing she could do to stop it.

He touched her again, his fingers clamping around the flesh of her upper arm, and she swung around to face him, thinking of nothing but the absolute necessity of getting away. Holding the dead trout by its muscular tail, she swung her free arm and slapped the fish's head against Daniel's cheek. A fin caught him at the edge of his eye, drawing from him an involuntary grunt of pain.

I'll bet that *hurts,* she thought, torn between satisfaction and regret. She dropped her weapon at his feet and turned her back. She wanted to find Simon, return the tackle she had borrowed, and go home.

Barely an instant later she was on the ground. Daniel had tackled her from behind, throwing her to her knees. The unexpectedness of it shocked her. Neither Simon nor any of her other friends would ever have dreamed of laying violent hands on her.

Her fishing rod went flying as she rolled sideways atop the steep bank of the stream. He came with her, moving effortlessly despite the way she was flailing at him. The next thing she knew he had her facedown in the dirt, his legs straddling her back, her right arm trapped behind her in an unbreakable grip. He twisted it toward her shoulder blade, making her feel the promise, if not the actuality, of pain.

"Now." He whispered the word into the soft skin at the back of her neck. "Beg my pardon or I break yer bleedin' arm."

"Go ahead, you bully. You murderer."

He increased the pressure slightly, making her spine stiffen with combined fright, defiance, and frustration. *Fool, fool!* she screamed at herself. *You've really done it this time.*

"Let's hear 'ee, Miss Rich Britches. Beg."

"I won't." *I can't,* she was thinking. *Heroines don't beg.* "You don't know me. I'm intrepid. I never surrender." She could hear her voice shaking, not sounding very convincing. She wouldn't be able to cast too well with a broken arm.

Daniel swallowed hard, feeling her arch and twist, her body active and electric despite his weight upon her. Intrepid—Jesus. She was crazy, that's what she was. He didn't think he was hurting her, but he couldn't be sure.

You're crazy too, a voice inside him said. *Look at you. This is the sort of thing Pa would have done.* "Don't make the mistake of thinking that just because ye're a girl, I won't hurt 'ee."

"Actually I was thinking that just because I'm a Trevor, you probably will."

"Christ," he muttered, loosening his hold on her slightly. Rationality was creeping back, bringing with it tiny threads of guilt. He could see his father slapping Tamara across the face . . . her gasp of pain . . . the sight of her falling to the floor and rolling herself up into a tight ball. *I would never do that. I would never strike a woman; never actually hurt her.*

"Listen," said Bret. "I shouldn't have hit you, I admit it. For that I beg your pardon. But that doesn't mean you can bully me. You'd better apologize for that, because I'm not moving until you do."

"Ye're not moving? Have 'ee forgotten who's holding 'ee down?"

"I also expect you to apologize for killing my fish. No apology can ever restore his life, but you must at least admit that what you did was wrong." She paused, then ventured, "I don't think you'll break the arm of a helpless girl, no matter who I'm related to."

No, he thought. Her wrist was so slim and delicate, her skin so smooth, her entire body, trapped beneath his, so vulnerable. Her body. He swallowed hard as his aggression subtly altered its course. No, he couldn't hurt her.

Breathing hard, he released her arm and levered himself enough to flip her over onto her back. He remained straddling her body, and the weight of his palms on her shoulders prevented her from sitting up. "Ye're not scared of me a'tall, are 'ee?"

Eyes wide, Bret stared up at him. She squirmed a little, sending shocks of awareness racing through Daniel. She felt so soft and smelled so sweet. He'd never been this close to an enemy before, never held someone he hated between his thighs, her belly almost touching his, her hair flowing over his wrists and knuckles, her chest moving quickly up and down, her eyes softer now and alarmed for a different reason.

"Yes, I am. At least," she paused for a moment, a tiny puzzled line forming in her brow, "I'm scared of *something*."

An odd tenderness rose up in him, defying everything he'd been feeling until now. She looked so vulnerable lying there, that half-scared, half-defiant look in her eyes. When it came to the ways of men and women, she was clearly an innocent. But not unwilling? Her lips were slightly parted and there was a wash of color across her cheekbones that hinted at the possibility of warmer feelings.

He imagined what it would be like to press his mouth to hers, invading her slowly with his tongue. She'd be surprised, but she wouldn't resist, at least not for long. They didn't, usually, the girls he kissed.

She would be another conquest, and probably easier than most. But special, very special. What could be more of a triumph than luring Henry Trevor's daughter to his bed?

She raised one hand and lightly touched the scar that marred his left cheek. When he flinched, her eyes opened wider, questioningly. "Does that hurt?"

He shook his head. It was an ugly scar, and it always surprised him to discover that women didn't mind it in the least. Some even kissed it, but none had ever touched it as gently as Bret had just done.

He was ashamed. He had assaulted her and she had responded with tenderness.

"I caught a fish once who had a scar like this on his head," she said. "He'd been attacked by a bird of prey, but he'd escaped."

In the distance Daniel could hear the cawing of similar birds, and the splashing of the brook, but all he was really aware of was the absolute necessity of resolving his conflict with this girl. It wasn't just kissing he wanted from her, it was much, much more.

He touched her hair where it lay against her throat, trying to be as tender with her as she had been with him, but he was all too conscious that his hands were big and clumsy while her body was so light and delicate. "Did you release it?"

"Oh, yes."

"I'm sorry I killed yer trout."

"I'm sorry I hit you with it." As she said the words, she smiled, as if noting the ludicrousness of her action.

"I like it when ye smile."

The corners of her mouth turned impish. "I'd love to know if you *can* smile. All you've ever done is scowl at me."

Daniel made an effort and produced a crooked grin, which made her laugh with delight. The laugh in turn filled Daniel

with such a profound feeling of joy that without thinking he
did the only thing he could imagine doing, which was to press
his lips to hers.

He felt her entire body tense, but only for a moment before
her mouth, which tasted delicious, softened under his. She
shyly kissed him back. The tentative brushing of their tongues
gave him a feeling that was at once hot and urgent and lovely.
He wanted to get closer to her. He would get closer to her.
It was meant to happen. She, Bret Trevor, his enemy's daughter, would be his, now and forever. It would make up for
everything he'd yearned for, everything he'd envied, everything he'd never been permitted to have.

Chapter Eighteen

Simon Marrick had stalked several trout, glad to have forgotten for at least a little while the decline of art and the
futility of hope and the pathetic state of the world in general
and the clay-producing region in particular, when it occurred
to him that he'd been working his way upstream and should,
by this time, have encountered Bret, or at least caught sight
of her. Rounding the last bend that had separated them, he
noted that the brook flowed straight for the next several hundred yards and that there was no sign of her anywhere.

His heart—which he'd always suspected of being weak—
began to palpitate. Something had happened to her. She'd
lost her footing and fallen into the stream, sinking inexorably
with the weight of her clothing like the poor waterlogged
Ophelia. She'd hooked herself in the eye or throat with a
fouled cast and had passed out somewhere on the bank, horribly disfigured and fainting from loss of blood. She'd been
snatched at pistol point by outlaws who were even now rav-
ishing her slim, lovely body.

Oh, stop, he told himself, forcing several deep breaths into his lungs. Bret was always berating him for taking the most pessimistic view of everything.

Convincing himself that Bret was not to be found in the stream, Simon stowed his gear and walked up a rise to higher ground. Shading his eyes against the setting sun, he examined the rolling moorland that was bisected by the brook.

He saw her, then, a couple of hundred yards away, talking to some rough-looking bloke dressed in laborer's clothing.

Simon slowed his pace, having no desire to join her in conversing with a clay worker, if that's what the chap was. He'd warned Bret that she ought to stay away from such dangerous and unpredictable elements of society, but she'd pooh-poohed his concerns. She was friendly to everybody— too friendly.

Bret turned away from the clay man, who seemed to wish to continue the conversation. He laid his hands on her shoulder. She shrugged it off. When he touched her again, she swung around and struck his face with something. Moments later, the man, who was a big, hulking fellow, knocked Bret to the ground.

Simon's heart jolted. Sweat sprang up along his backbone and his blood pounded so hard in his ears that he was sure he'd faint. He tried to run to her, but his legs had turned leaden. *Beastly coward!* he yelled at himself, but he was paralyzed by his history—year upon year of envisioning the worst.

Simon knew he was a coward; he'd been one all his life. He'd grown up hating thunderstorms because he might be struck by lightning. He hesitated to go swimming with the other children because the currents might bear him off to a watery grave. He refrained from wandering away from home lest he become lost on the moors and never find his way back. Every time he caught a cold he was convinced that it would turn into pneumonia and his body would be buried in the churchyard before the week was out.

His only consolation had been that things were bound to be different when he grew up. He would prove that he had it in him to be brave, dauntless, smilingly careless about his fate. Now he was nearly eighteen; grown up by most standards. Old enough to prove his courage and virility. Was this his test?

Bret and the disgruntled clay worker who had tackled her rolled over in the high grass, her red hair coming loose in the wind. She hated the color of her hair, but Simon had always liked it. To him it was a reflection of her fiery and free spirit.

The idea that somebody was trying to crush that spirit of hers was what finally jolted him into action. Bret was everything that he was not—fearless, defiant, joyful, energetic— and Simon had loved her dearly from the moment they'd met. Coward or not, he wasn't going to let anybody hurt her.

Dropping his fishing rod, he began to hurry toward them. But he quickly realized that Bret didn't need his help. Her arms were wrapped around her assailant's shoulders and she was kissing him.

In that moment Simon had a physical sensation that was more intense than any heart palpitation. Instead of being located in any of the usual locales—his chest or his throat or his head—it slashed him in the pit of his stomach and spread down into his groin. He might have found a polite metaphor for it in one of his poems, but his brain wasn't working politely just now. The sensation was raw and wild; it left him feeling as if someone had stripped off his skin and left his nerves and blood vessels exposed to the pitiless air.

He loved Bret Trevor. All his life, she was all he'd ever wanted, the only girl he could ever imagine himself touching, stroking, kissing. He loved her, and she had betrayed him.

Simon turned and fled in the other direction.

Faint sounds from the outside world penetrated Bret's shattered awareness just as Daniel Carne was putting one of his big hands to her breasts, which were swelling and throbbing with the most incredible sensations. Her body felt loose and taut at the same time. A warmth had invaded her and she knew she wasn't behaving in a decorous, ladylike manner at all, but that knowledge was as distant and as unimportant as the farthest star.

It came as a shock when Daniel broke the kiss, rolling off her into a sitting position. The air felt cool on her lips. She ran her tongue over them, astonished at how sensitive they felt. Why had he stopped kissing her? How had he been *able* to stop? "What's the matter?"

"I thought I saw something. Or someone." He jerked his head in the direction of the brook.

Bret pushed herself up on one elbow to look, but with her head swimming the way it was, it took her several seconds to adjust to the outside world. "I don't see anybody."

"He's gone."

"It might have been Simon." She was breathless, and when Daniel looked down at her, the color rose in her cheeks.

"Simon? You mean Simon Marrick?"

"Yes. Do you know him?"

"I know he's yer sister's stepson."

"He's that, yes. He's also my friend."

"What the hell would he be doing here?"

"Well, I guess he was looking for me." If it had been Simon, she was thinking, he couldn't have turned up at a more inconvenient moment. This had been her first kiss. She'd have liked a little more time to savor it!

"Does he always follow 'ee about?"

She didn't like Daniel's tone; he sounded annoyed again. She shook her head, still trying to get her bearings. Everything had happened so fast. One moment she'd been angry, then frightened, then confused, then she'd felt the most extraordinary rush of affection for Daniel, whom she was sure hid so much hurt behind his hooded blue eyes.

"I was fishing with him. That is, he was downstream a ways. In all the—the excitement, I forgot he was there."

"Ye forgot."

"Yes." Instead of meeting his eyes, she concentrated on straightening the front of her frock, which his hands had disarranged. The thought of his touching her there made her want to kiss him again. This was lust, she supposed, trying out the word. She'd never felt it before. "Did he see you kissing me?" Goodness, what must Simon have thought?

"Probably." Daniel got to his feet and extended a hand to

her. She took it and stood, carefully shaking out her skirts, then dusting them off. She didn't know why she was paying such exaggerated attention to her clothing. To avoid meeting his eyes, perhaps. "Look, I'm sorry," he said.

"Oh, don't be, please. It's all right. It's just that I'd hate to hurt Simon's feelings. I think he's in love with me, you see. I even suspect he wants to marry me."

No sooner were the words out of her mouth than she regretted them. Daniel's body tightened and his lids curtained his all-too-vulnerable eyes. Oh dear. Any moment now he would resume his bitter attitude and they'd be right back where they'd started half an hour ago.

She touched his arm lightly. "But I'm not going to. I love Simon, you see, but not that way, and—"

He jerked away from her, and Bret knew that this was one of a seemingly infinite series of moments when she ought to have kept her mouth shut. Naturally he was angry. She could imagine her more sophisticated school friends howling with laughter at her mistake. You don't tell a man who's just knocked you down and passionately kissed you that someone else wants you as well.

"Look, I shouldn't have brought it up. I'm tactless sometimes." She called upon her most ingenuous smile, although she felt her lips trembling at the corners. "I say things I shouldn't. My friends agree that it's one of my most irritating faults."

Unappeased, Daniel ignored her. The heady emotions that had led him to grab her on the riverbank were still swirling around him and he hated it, this feeling of not being in control. Christ, what was wrong with him? He never should have touched her. He knew who Simon Marrick was. He'd seen him in Trenwythan, a posh public schooler, tall and tweedy and rich-boy handsome. Just the sort anyone with any sense would expect Miss Elizabeth Trevor to fall in love with and wed.

Fool. Fucking dreamer. She's not for 'ee.

"Daniel, I'm sorry."

She looked up at him, her green eyes large and liquid and a little bemused. He thought of the way her mouth had softened, how silky her tongue had felt under his, the sharp excitement that had gripped her untutored body and made it arch against his. Jesus! He mustn't think about it.

"Ye've nothing to be sorry for. 'Tes my fault and I apologize. Now ye'd best go make yer explanations to yer fiancé."

"He's not my fiancé. I don't intend ever to marry. I'm going to be an artist and take lovers and live in sin."

She sounded so earnest that he almost laughed at her. She was a child. She'd probably never kissed a man before, and she'd certainly never made love.

"Ye can sin all ye like, but not with me. Now take yer fishing gear and go on home before I start getting ideas about having my revenge on 'ee for yer father's crimes."

Turning his back on her, he began to walk away.

"Daniel?"

She sounded wretched, which made him feel guilty. *Blast all females*, he thought.

"I don't believe for one minute that you're as tough as you pretend to be," she called.

It took all his considerable willpower not to turn back.

Verity was descending the stairs for supper that evening when she was surprised to encounter her stepson, who stormed past her without a word—very odd behavior for Simon—and hurried down the hallway. Moments later she heard the explosive slamming of his bedroom door.

"Do you have any idea what's wrong with Simon?" she asked her husband as she joined him at the dinner table. "I just met him on the stairway. He seemed upset about something."

"All I know is he went out this afternoon. Fishing, I believe. With your sister." There seemed to be a slight strain in his voice as Julian added, "Perhaps he failed to net a trout."

"His behavior was distinctly odd."

"I can't imagine why," Julian said, even as it crossed his mind that the stupid girl might have told Simon some nonsense, totally untrue of course, about what had happened on the day when he'd embraced her in his study.

"Perhaps I ought to go up and have a talk with him," Verity said.

"Indeed, my dear, I must insist that you do not."

When his wife looked surprised at the vehemence of his tone, Julian quickly added, "I won't have the boy coddled. Neither do I expect you to be dancing attendance on him as if he were a child of six. As his father, I believe I know what's best for him."

He noticed that his wife's lips thinned significantly as she answered, "Very well, Julian. You know best."

"No doubt the smell of supper will bring him down shortly. Tess reported to me that he did not take tea this afternoon. For all his malingering, I've rarely known him to miss a meal."

Verity had turned her attention to her food.

"Speaking of Tess," Julian went on, "she came to me in considerable distress last evening, complaining that you were being short with her for no good reason. I don't know why you seem to have so much trouble keeping parlor maids, considering the size of the staff you were accustomed to dealing with at Cadmon Hall."

"Has she given notice?" Verity would have been delighted to be rid of Julian's latest experiment in disadvantaged domestic servants. Tess always had an obsequious smile ready for Julian, but her manner with her mistress was uncooperative and sullen.

"I fear she will if you cannot contrive to placate her."

"*Me* placate *her*?" The taste of her tea had grown bitter in her mouth. "I don't like that girl, Julian. She strikes me as both insolent and lazy. In future I wish you would allow me to hire the household staff. Most of the girls you've chosen have been—" she searched for a word that would not be too insulting, "difficult."

"The girls I've chosen are the objects of parish charity. I've tried to explain to you that they come from troubled backgrounds and need our help in order to get a better chance in the world. Surely you could find it in your heart to be a little more tolerant."

Verity felt the first twinges of a migraine.

"Be patient with her, Verity. She has promised to try

harder. Indeed, I shall take it upon myself to see that she does."

"Very well." It was impossible to argue with a man who could justify his every whim with protestations of Christian charity. "I will try."

That night, Verity did something unusual: she defied her husband. Simon had not appeared for dinner, and she had been fretting about him all evening. She waited until Julian was asleep, then knocked on her stepson's bedroom door. A sliver of light under the threshold told her that Simon was still wakeful.

No answer.

She knocked louder.

"Go away."

Instead she pressed down the handle and entered. She found him sitting in the alcove in front of the window, staring out over the churchyard and beyond it to the moors. He turned to look at her as she entered the room. It was obvious that he had been crying. Verity stopped, stricken at the sight and uncertain how to react.

"Simon, my dear. If there's something troubling you, perhaps talking about it will help."

A long sigh, somewhat more dramatic, Verity suspected, than it needed to be. "I just want to be left alone."

"You went fishing with Bret. Did something happen between you? A disagreement of some kind?"

"Why don't you ask her? She's your sister." The words were flung at her, as if being Bret's sister were an offense against truth, justice, and common decency.

"Are you in love with her?"

Simon's back went as rigid as a palace guard's.

Verity tried to picture it. They would complement each other's characters so nicely. Bret's cheerfulness would lighten Simon's melancholy, just as Simon's seriousness would temper Bret's frivolity. They would look well together, too, with Simon's tall, slender, almost languid beauty providing a nice contrast to Bret's healthy and energetic grace. Yes. Why not? If Bret was safely engaged to Simon, there would be no more nonsense about her flying off to see the world. "I know she cares about you as well. Very much indeed. I've always hoped the two of you might make a match of it someday.''

"Not much chance of that.'' He looked back at her, his handsome face a mask of lovelorn agony. "She doesn't want me. She never has. She never will. There's no hope.''

"Nonsense.'' Simon's tendency to exaggerate had been augmented, she decided, by the torments of love. In all probability they'd had some sort of minor argument. "Bret was telling me just the other day about her ludicrous desires to live abroad, paint, sculpt, and take lovers whose identities are as yet unknown. Schoolgirl notions, and nothing more. Don't pay any attention. She'll come round.''

Simon laughed, a caustic, bitter sound. "I doubt it very much.''

"Listen, Simon, will you allow me to give you some advice? Bret is a lively, adventuresome girl. She's also quite romantic. If you could find some way to appeal to those elements of her character, I'm sure she would begin to see you in a new light. That might be all you need. Just to have her notice you, if you understand what I mean.''

"Notice me? I'm right here in front of her eyes. That's precisely the trouble. She takes me for granted.''

"You're a handsome young man, and Bret has a woman's heart. Surely there is some gesture you could make.''

"Bret has the heart of a proud wild animal. A lioness, perhaps, or a wolf. She'll only mate with someone strong enough to hold her.'' He sighed again. "It won't be me.''

"You're too pessimistic.''

He smiled sadly. "A poet must see and see clearly, and I have observed nothing that might encourage me.''

Verity kissed him and took her leave, wondering what it must be like to feel so poignantly the pangs of unrequited love.

Chapter Nineteen

"Tamara, I need to ask you something," Bret said from the threshold of Tamara's cottage the following Sunday. Her friend's door was thrown open to the afternoon sky. Several days of gloomy weather had passed since her encounter with Daniel. She hadn't seen him since, but she'd been thinking of him constantly, reliving every word, every touch. "The world is transformed for me today," she'd written in a passionate letter to Mr. Slayton. "I have met the man I will love forever and nothing will ever be the same again."

"Come in then, lass, but leave the door ajar. The sunlight's a boon to me."

As usual on her days off from the claypits, Tamara was pounding clay. The process was similar to kneading bread, but fiercer. The heels of her hands were as purposeful as mallets, and her strength and energy were formidable. The pounding was necessary to remove any tiny pockets of air. Bret had neglected the step during her own first attempt at potting, and the squat, ugly bowl of which she had been so proud had shattered in the kiln.

"Is something amiss with 'ee?" Tamara asked as Bret came in, pulled up a stool, and settled down with her chin in her hands.

"No, not exactly, but, I was wondering . . . can you foretell my future? You're descended from Gypsies, aren't you?"

Tamara looked at her sideways, her arching gold eyebrows drawing together briefly before she turned her attention back to the clay, which her fingers continued to coax into smooth round shapes. She was wearing a white cotton smock over a crimson, orange, and peach patterned frock, the sleeves of which she had rolled up over her elbows. Bret had noticed on other occasions that even though Tamara's smocks didn't entirely cover the colorful fabric of her blouses and dresses, she seemed never to stain the latter with clay. Indeed, when she stripped the smock off at the end of the working day and shook out her thick honey-colored hair, she looked as neat and tidy as if she'd been primly embroidering all day. Bret was just the opposite. She tended to get wet clay all over her—on her clothes, under her nails, on her cheeks, behind her ears.

"I've Romany blood, yes." Tamara reached into the bucket under her feet for another handful of clay. "But why're ye fretting about yer future all of a sudden?"

"Because of my art," Bret said, avoiding her eyes. She was afraid Tamara would see right through her. Her perceptiveness was as pure and hard as Cornish stone. "It's going to take so many years of study, and I don't know if I'll ever be successful."

"Ye make success, lass, by holding the image of what ye want in yer mind and working yer tail off to get it."

Bret selected a small, wet piece of clay from the pile and worked it between her sticky palms. She enjoyed the feel of it, the smoothness, the pliability. The clay wouldn't take shape for her as easily yet as it did for Tamara, but she felt the glimmerings of power there, nevertheless.

Still, it was true that during the past few days she'd begun to question whether she wanted to study art seriously in London, Paris, or Rome. Perhaps it would be better to stay right here in Cornwall. This was her home. Her family and friends were here. Daniel was here.

Treacherously, her mind flashed a memory of that wonderful kiss—the heat of his breath, the pressure of his lips, the sweet invasion of his tongue. It had been so nice, that contrast of male to female, his hard muscles against her softer ones, his strength, her vulnerability. Would it be like that the next time he kissed her? Would she feel so breathless, so transported?

"Bret?" Tamara's voice was sharp, and Bret blushed.

"I've started to wonder whether I'm being realistic," she said in a rush. "About being an artist. It's going to be difficult, especially for a woman. No one takes women seriously.

I'll have to be twice as good as any man before anybody'll pay attention. Maybe it's arrogant to think I have that much talent. Maybe I'll just have to resign myself to leading an ordinary life. You know, with a husband, children, a happy home.''

Tamara's lips tightened, and Bret noticed the sad, haunted, regretful expression that sometimes crossed her face. It manifested most clearly in her eyes, which were usually so comforting in their kindness, reassurance, and love. But in her brief tiger moods, as Bret thought of them, those eyes would flash with an emotion that was almost sinister, and Bret would sense that something dark was stirring in her friend.

''Ye disappoint me, lass.''

''What do you mean?''

Tamara pounded the clay against her worktable, giving it a harder beating than usual, destroying any errant air bubbles that might have had the temerity to form. '' 'Tes Daniel, isn't it?''

Bret tried her best to act surprised, but Tamara nailed her with another look. ''I've seen it since the first night he brought you here. The attraction was obvious enough.''

''It was?''

Tamara nodded grimly. ''It comes like that sometimes— sudden and blinding, like the sun bursting out of the clouds. But 'tes doomed, so ye'd best forget it.''

''Don't say that!''

'' 'Tes true. Would ye have me lie jist to make 'ee feel better? Ye and he have nothing in common. Besides, 'tesn't in Daniel to love anybody unselfishly.''

''How can you say that about your own flesh and blood?''

''He's mine and I love him. But that doesn't make me blind to his faults. 'Tes passion that makes people blind. Ye'd do well to remember that. There are passions in him, strong ones . . . and in 'ee, too, I reckon. My advice is to beware yer passionate nature. 'Twill be the cause of much joy as well as many sorrows.''

''Is that a prediction about my future?''

'' 'Tes something that was told to me by a wise old woman. It has proven true on several occasions.'' Tamara selected a fresh ball of clay and centered it on her potter's wheel, then stood up and wiped her hands on her smock. "I suppose I could see yer future in the destiny cards. But 'tes better if ye try it yerself. Here, sit down."

"Why?"

"Do it and ye'll see."

They exchanged places, Bret putting her hands on the clay and her foot on the pedal. "Close yer eyes," Tamara ordered. "Feel the clay between yer palms. Truly feel it, I mean. Ye have to focus inward. Make yerself one with the clay."

"One with the clay?"

"Try it."

Bret complied, having a little difficulty managing the potter's wheel with her eyes shut. But soon she got the gist of it, and there was a certain freedom in not seeing—or caring— what shape the clay was taking as it whirled.

"Jist let yerself drift." Tamara's voice was low-pitched and sinuous. "Hear the sounds around you, then rise above them. Everybody has an inner guide, a wiser self, a spirit, if ye will, that can show 'ee the path ye've got to tread. Ye have to rise above the wheel, which spirals to infinity. Rise about the cottage, the moors, the earth, the clay."

Something about Tamara's voice made Bret's perceptions begin to run in circles. She felt Tamara's hands stroking her forehead and heard her friend's whispering unintelligible words. Then there was a sphere of light around her, enveloping them both. Round and round she turned with the clay, drawing it up her fingers, feeling its essence blend with her blood, feeling her spirit rising up through her spine and into her head, then out, gracefully, into the cone of Tamara's fingers, which were now cupping the top of her scalp.

Then she sensed a great surge of power moving down through Tamara and into her, through her and into the clay, through the clay and into the ground. There was light— pure, bright, and luminous, wrapping them in a shimmering cocoon. What freedom, what energy, what joy! Together she and Tamara formed a bridge between the heavens and the earth, and she knew that if they were to move higher into the channel, they would have the ability to see across gulfs and distances, back into the past and forward into the future. They would have the wisdom to fathom great mysteries, and the courage to seek the shape of God.

No. Please, I'm not ready. She envisioned the model aircraft her father had sent flying toward the sea, beautiful but doomed. An ominous tingle began at the base of her spine. It threatened to rise and flood her with sights and sounds and faces she could not bear to see. *No.* Someday perhaps, but not yet.

"Tamara, I'm frightened." She let up on the pedal, slowing the wheel. Daniel was there, but his face was turned away from her, and in the background she kept seeing images of fire and destruction. Cadmon Hall draped in black, and herself on the outside, looking in. A man beside her . . . two men . . . or was it three? Tall men, wearing uniforms, their weary faces as deathly white as china clay. "I can't do this." Her hands thrust at the bowl she'd unconsciously been shaping. "Oh, please, let me stop."

Bret stumbled from the wheel, knocking over the stool in her haste to escape the revelations. Tamara's arms came around her from behind, reassuring, earthbound. But as she pressed close she could feel her friend's body trembling nearly as much as her own.

"What *was* that? What happened?" she asked, opening her eyes to gaze into Tamara's pale and troubled face.

Tamara's hands stroked gently through her hair. " 'Tes all right, lassie."

"You saw something, didn't you? Something bad, something frightening? Tamara, your grandmother was a Gypsy . . . does that mean you have the Sight?"

"We all have the Sight, lassie, some more'n others. 'Tes running strong in 'ee."

"You saw something," Bret insisted. "Tell me."

Tamara hugged her harder, shaking her golden head. "Don't fret about it, lassie. 'Tes Cornish superstitiousness, nothing more."

He was there, on the path, directly in her way, as she left the cottage. She nearly ran into him; she stumbled and blushed, her confusion deepening when his hand touched her arm to steady her. Then he jerked his hand away at once, as if the contact was as electrifying to him as it was to her.

"Hello," she said brightly, recovering.

He nodded without a word.

"What are you doing here?"

"She is my sister, ye recall."

She could see the look of confused emotion in his face, revealing to her that he, too, felt something powerful, something he couldn't reconcile.

She noted that he had a book under one arm. "What are you reading?"

For a moment she thought he wasn't going to answer. His voice contained a hint of defiance as he said, "History. Economics. Some pamphlets on trade unionism, what little I can find in the St. Austell library. 'Tesn't much."

"We have an excellent library at Cadmon Hall. I could look and see if we have anything on the subject, if you like."

"Don't bother. I want nothing from Cadmon Hall."

"Of course you don't." She felt rejected and nearly walked away, but for the tiny voice inside her that told her she needn't be as rude as he. She left a pause, then said, "I agree with you that the clay workers have some legitimate grievances against the clay owners. I'm going to speak to my father about the problem as soon as he returns."

His expression turned disdainful. "We're not interested in yer pity, Miss Trevor. What we want is thicker pay envelopes."

Miss Trevor! This man had kissed her passionately and he was calling her Miss Trevor! "You think I'm just being frivolous, but I assure you, I'm not. I'm interested in the clay company. My sister is, too. She once had a dream that we would run it together, and start up the old china-producing that we used to do there as well."

"Yeah? Two women running a claypit? That's about as likely as me running one myself."

"Is that your dream?" she asked, excited at the prospect of learning something so intimate about him.

"One of them. Which of us poor clay workers wouldn't wish to be the King of Clay?"

"Do it, then," she said.

Daniel's eyes focused on her.

"If that's your dream, make it real. You can do it, I know you can."

He gave a harsh laugh. "Think what ye're saying. If I succeed, I'll be yer father's rival one day."

She gave him that same joyous, lighthearted, life-affirming smile she'd offered him on the riverbank. "That'll make life interesting, won't it?"

"Why are you being polite to me?"

"What do you mean? I'm not—"

"Mebbe polite isn't the word. We clay workers don't have the vocabulary of the gentry, do we? And 'tes a surprise when we're caught trying to better ourselves with books. Not polite, condescending. That's a word, isn't it? Meaning that ye act civil to someone who's beneath 'ee, for reasons o' yer own?"

"Maybe it's because I like you. Maybe I want to get to know you better, despite all the dire warnings from my sister and even *your* sister. They keep telling me it would be the greatest folly I could ever commit. Maybe if you weren't so bowed over with that burden of hatred and resentment you carry around with you wherever you go, you'd see that I'm not so awful after all!"

Daniel blinked at her. The sky was growing dark around them and she couldn't clearly see his face. "Oh, what's the use," she added, and turned away from him. The wind had come up; she felt it riffling her hair at the same moment as she felt a pricking at the back of her eyes. She had been caught up in her romantic reveries, but he, obviously, had been spared such torments. The kiss on the riverbank had meant nothing to him. She wasn't his love, his dream, his passion. She was still just Bret Trevor, the youngest member of a family he hated.

"Bret?"

She stopped, nearly at the end of the path to the moorland now. Tall and dark, with a silent way of walking that reminded her of everything she had ever imagined of Mr. Slayton's Indians, Daniel came up beside her. She was highly conscious of his closeness, the near-brushing of his upper arm against her shoulder. "Look at 'ee. I can tell ye've been potting with Tamara—ye've got clay on yer cheeks and yer hair's come loose.''

"Who cares?" she tossed back. "I love the feel of the clay, and as for my hair, if it weren't so hot on my neck and shoulders, I'd always wear it loose."

"I don't think ye're so awful," he said, low.

Deep inside her, something started to thaw.

"Ye've really been warned off? By Tam?"

"Absolutely. I think she's afraid you'll seduce me as a means of getting your revenge on my father."

He seemed me thoughtful than surprised at this revelation. "What do ye think?"

"I don't know what to think. But with your history and your economics and your trade unionism and all, you must have more important things to worry about than seducing me."

"That's true enough. There's a clay strike coming, make no mistake about it. 'Twill keep me busy, ye can be sure of that."

"Surely a clay strike, if it comes, would make you idle."

"Not for the activists who start it, and see it through."

"Of which you're one?"

He shrugged. With a finger he reached out and brushed a shining lock of red hair away from her forehead. "I'll tell 'ee what I think, Bret Trevor. I think I'm a clay man, and ye're the daughter of a clay owner. I'm a Carne and ye're a Trevor. I'm twenty-four years old and jaded, and ye're eight years younger and still a schoolgirl."

"Actually, I've almost finished school. One more year and I'll be done." He was so near. She was trembling.

"For yer own sake, Bret, ye'd best stay away from me."

"I can't," she whispered.

"Then I'll just have to stay away from 'ee."

But the blue fire in his eyes belied his words.

Chapter Twenty

Verity was late for a parish meeting—tea in the churchyard with several prominent women from the congregation, none of whom she liked. Sipping tea among the gravestones was not her idea of a pleasant way to spend a sultry July afternoon, but one of the women, the wife of a wealthy clay owner, was interested in parish history, and it was she who had made the arrangements and invited the guests. As the vicar's wife, Verity had no choice but to attend.

Bret was coming into the vicarage as she was going out. She was carrying a fishing rod and tackle and was disgracefully clad in trousers, cap, stout boots, and a loose-fitting shirt that Verity suspected belonged to their father.

"Hello, Verity," she said, throwing her arms, rod and all, around her sister in an exuberant embrace. "It's a lovely day. I caught three trout." She stood back. "Are you feeling all right? You don't look well."

"I'm fine," Verity said, although in fact she had a headache and had lain awake for hours the previous night suffering from an attack of insomnia. "I'm late for tea, though, and must hurry."

"Are you going out to join those old biddies in the churchyard? They look like ghosts, strolling among the tombstones in their Victorian finery. It would be hilarious if it weren't so blatantly offensive."

"What do you mean? Offensive to whom?"

Bret put down her fishing gear and took off her cap. Her long red hair had been tucked up inside, and it flew around her shoulders as she shook it out. It needed a good brushing, and Verity felt a needle of guilt. With Papa away in America, Bret was even wilder than usual, and the talking-to she'd given her after her misadventure out on the moors last month seemed not to have had any effect.

"Why, to the clay workers, of course. And their families. It's rather an insult, don't you think, to see rich women entertaining themselves in such a bizarre and frivolous fashion while the clay laborers are struggling so hard to improve their meager existence."

"If they're so eager to improve, why have they walked off their jobs?" Verity countered. Just two days previously thirty men from one of the local claypits had refused to report for work. Despite the owner's threats that they would lose their positions, they had been recalcitrant so far, and their discontent was spreading. Clay laborers from all over the region had been gathering in noisy meetings to demand a pay increase and other benefits, including union membership. The clay owners were universally opposed to any negotiation, fearing that if they met one demand, others would spring up unchecked.

"All they want is an increase in wages from eighteen to twenty-five shillings a week. That seems reasonable to me, considering how hard they work, and under what conditions. Laborers all over this country are being disgracefully exploited by the owners of businesses and factories. It's horribly unjust."

Verity's headache escalated. "Listen to yourself. You sound like a socialist. And you're too passionate about everything. Some things in life simply can't be changed."

"If something is unjust, why shouldn't it be changed?"

"Your sympathies might be with the workers, but you are the daughter of an owner, which makes you a possible target of the militants' rancor," Verity said in her most severe elder-sister tone. "Just last week someone painted an offensive slogan in shaving cream on James Stannis's motorcar when it was standing in front of the milliner's shop in St. Austell."

"What a jolly idea. I think I'll snitch a jar of Papa's shaving cream and go about painting slogans myself."

Verity frowned, which made Bret laugh and give her a hug. "Go on to your silly tea party and don't fret about me."

As it turned out, the tea party was frivolous, and Verity was much put off by the conversation, most of which revolved around the "ungrateful" behavior of the clay workers. There were three clay owners' wives among the group, and they were unanimous in their condemnation of the workers, whom they discussed as if they were troublesome animals. Although she was not particularly sympathetic to the strikers' demands, she knew many of the clay workers' wives as a result of her parish work. They were good women—honest, warm-hearted, and devoted to their families. She liked and respected them.

Her head was pounding by the time the tea was over, and at one point her hands were shaking so badly that she had difficulty holding her cup and saucer. When the women left, she retreated into the darkened church and sank to her knees in front of the altar. "Lord, in Your mercy," she whispered, "lift this shadow from my heart."

" 'Scuse me, ma'am," said Tess, the parlor maid, the following day, "but that newfangled telephone machine in the front hallway is shrilling away like a fiend from hell. What should I do? I don't know how to work it, or what I'd say into the wretched thing if I did."

"I'll take it," Verity said, exasperated with the girl. She hurried out to answer the ringing before it stopped.

The caller was Gil Parkins from Cadmon Clay. "I'm sorry to bother you, Mrs. Marrick, but we've got a problem here. I didn't know where else to turn. Do you suppose you could come up this morning and give the lads a bit of a talking-to? Now that your father's out of the country, they're demanding to speak to the next Trevor in authority. I reckon that's you."

Several seconds passed before Verity managed, "You want me to talk to them?"

"He told me before he left that I should come to you if anything happened that I couldn't handle myself."

"He did?" Amazed, she stopped speaking to clear her throat. "Of course I'll come, if you need me."

"I'm embarrassed to admit that I do," Parkins said. "Things seem to be getting out of hand here, Mrs. Marrick. A'course it's no different from what's happening all over the region these days, but working conditions aren't as bad here as they are at some of the pits, so I was hoping we'd avoid the worst of the trouble."

"So was I. Do you think our men will join the strike?"

"Unless you can talk 'em out of it."

Verity's stomach clenched up. The clay strike was spreading. Additional claypits were shutting down every day, and the clay owners' attempts to resume operations were having no effect. The strikers had formed picket lines around each company, discouraging the few laborers who wanted to work. Cadmon Clay was among a small minority of clay companies that was still fully operational. Shutting it down had become one of the main objectives of the strike organizers.

"I'll be there as soon as I can," she said to Gil.

Driving up to Cadmon Clay in an old motorcar that had been donated to the church by her father, Verity considered what to say to the clay workers. Since many of them came from families who had worked for the Trevors for generations, she might be able to appeal to their loyalty. At the same time, she must convince them that their concerns would be heard. This was not the time to take a hard line. Other owners had tried that, and their claypits were standing empty, their machinery idle. She did not want that to happen to Cadmon Clay.

She envisioned herself saving the day with her sympathetic demeanor and her stirring words. Cadmon Clay would be the one claypit in the region that would *not* be crippled by the strike. Papa would return from his trip to find that the daughter he had underestimated had acted decisively in a crisis, thereby saving his business.

Her heady dream lasted until she entered the grounds of Cadmon Clay, saw the huge gathering of angry men, and felt the surge of hostility that was directed her way.

It was evident that no work was being done. The nearest claypit was empty of workers, the beam engines were silent, and the carts that trundled refuse out of the pits were motionless on their tramways. The men were standing about, talking heatedly among themselves, and the expressions on their weather-hardened faces were mutinous.

When Verity stepped from the motorcar in front of the office building, the workers muttered and stared. Being the local vicar's wife had forced her to develop her social skills, but in tense situations she tended to lapse into her old shyness.

Her sister, to whom social intercourse came naturally, would have grinned and tossed a wave, cheering the men with her friendliness. But Verity was incapable of such an action.

She was about to retreat into the main office when Gil Parkins stepped out. "Good morning, Mrs. Marrick," he said, coming up and sticking out a hand, which Verity gratefully shook. "Thank you for coming." He ushered her inside, shutting the door on the men who were gathering in even larger groups outside. "I'm sorry to put you through this. I wouldn't have rung if it hadn't looked as though we were about to have a major rebellion on our hands."

Although his appearance was not prepossessing—he was short and stocky and his black beard always looked unkempt—Gil Parkins was an intelligent, hardworking man who had been employed at the clay company since his boyhood. Papa had recognized his worth and promoted him up through the ranks. He knew the business better than anyone, and Verity respected him. She hoped he would come to respect her in return.

"What would you like me to do?"

"Listen to them, mainly. Reassure them. Reason with them, if you can. They won't listen to me because they see me as one of them, which is true, in a way. They weren't going to be satisfied unless they could talk to the owner, and you were as close as I could get."

Damn Papa for leaving the country at such a crucial time! The labor troubles had come as no surprise; the situation had been tense for months. He didn't care about the clay company. He never had.

"Don't promise them anything," Gil warned. "If you do, they'll expect you to keep your word."

"Goodness, you're not asking much of me, are you?"

Parkins smiled. "You can do it."

Moments later Verity was standing on a slight rise to the right of the corrugated tin office building, looking down upon a wealth of discontented faces. "I understand you wish to speak with one of the Trevors." She was trying to project her voice over the warm breeze that was buffeting the area, sending fine gusts of white claydust into the eyes and noses of all present. "I'm here to listen."

No one said anything for several seconds. Then a tall gray-haired man stepped forward. "We wanted to speak wi' 'ee because there be changes coming around here."

His tone was belligerent, and his words were cheered.

"Tell me your name, please," Verity said to the gray-haired man. He looked like a leader; the others were deferring to him.

"Harry Thomas, ma'am. I'm the boss of pit number three."

"Thank you, Mr. Thomas. Now please tell me what sort of changes you and your men would like to see."

"We want the same salary increase that all the others round these parts are asking for. We can't feed our families on less than a quid a week. We work hard, ma'am, but we haven't had a pay raise for over two years. Prices have gone up in that time and we're worse off than ever before."

"I understand that," Verity said. "But you must also understand that prices have gone up for the owners as well. It's costing us far more these days for coal, machinery, and transportation. Unfortunately, the price at which we sell china clay has not gone up, which is why we haven't been able to increase your wages. Our profit margin is insufficient."

Since Verity thought her explanation was reasonable, she was surprised by the chorus of angry shouts that greeted her words:

"She's no different from the rest o' 'em!"

"All they care about is profits, and to hell wi' the workers who slave and sweat!"

"What did 'ee expect from someun who drives up in a motorcar? She never has to wonder where her next meal be comin' from!"

Verity raised her voice as she said, "I was hoping for some sort of dialogue here, but if you shout me down, we'll accomplish nothing. Please, Mr. Thomas, tell me the rest of your concerns."

"Very well, ma'am," said the spokesman, his authoritative voice rising above the babble. "We aren't working for slave wages, and we aren't enduring harsh working conditions any longer, either. Now mebbe we Cornish workers are hardy and mebbe we can take a lot of abuse, but enough's enough."

"The working conditions here are by no means harsh."

"Conditions're harsh all over the region," someone yelled.

"All over the country," someone else echoed. "The workers have been exploited by the rich for as long as anybody can remember!"

"The owners—the capitalists—don't care what happens to the men who work for 'em! Why should they—they got plenty o' meat on their tables and soft beds come nighttime. They've no care for the poor blokes who work their fingers to the bone from dawn to dusk."

"I understand your feelings. But let me ask you this: How could we keep men working for us if it were true that we treated them so inhumanly?"

"How about Jeb Methany?"

Verity had no idea who Jeb Methany was, but from the way the group took up the shout she could tell he was some sort of cause célèbre. "What happened to him?"

"Jeb was a man who, because of the strength in his arms and shoulders, was given a pick-'n'-shovel job removing overburden—ye know what that is, I trust?" said Harry Thomas.

She nodded, flushing. They had no respect for her, she realized. She was a woman, and ignorant, in their eyes.

"After near on fifteen years shoveling the stuff, one day poor Jeb hurt his back shoveling. When the doc in St. Austell told him he had to lay off the heavy work for a few months, yer father dismissed him as unfit. 'Twas his job that caused his injury, but now he has no way to support his family. He limps about in great pain, his heart bitter, his pride in shreds."

Verity turned to Gil Parkins. "Is this true?"

"Aye, I'm afraid so. It's not the first time, either."

"There ought to be some sort of compensation for injuries incurred on the job," Thomas went on. " 'Tisn't right that a man should spend his health and his strength working, only to be discarded when he's no longer fit to continue."

Verity nodded. The demand seemed reasonable to her. "It may be that some of your complaints are justified," she said as placatingly as she knew how. "I'm certainly willing to study them. In due time, we'll arrive at a compromise that will be acceptable to both sides."

"We're not interested in compromise," Thomas said. "You get word to your father that if he doesn't meet the demands of his workers within forty-eight hours, everyone at Cadmon Clay will lay down their tools and refuse to report for work."

Verity swallowed hard. Her presence seemed not to be having the desired effect. "I've shown that I'm willing to listen, and I assure you I'm willing to negotiate. If more pay can be granted you, it will be. As for the working conditions and the possibility of some sort of disability pay, I'll see what can be done. It's going to take more than forty-eight hours, though. You'll have to be patient with me."

"We've been patient wi' 'ee Trevors long enough," someone growled toward the back. The voice was familiar to her, but she couldn't see the face of the speaker. "I say we lay down our tools and join our brothers across the region. I say we stand tall and condemn the way we've been treated by the rich bosses who oppress us."

Shouts of approval greeted these remarks. Verity had to yell to be heard. "What good will it do you to join the strike? You'll lose your jobs. The claypits have to be worked. Cadmon Clay will hire other laborers to work in your places."

"What others? All the able-bodied men in the clay industry be strikin' already. There's no others."

"Not here, perhaps, but there may be jobless men in other towns, or even in other counties. What's to stop the owners from bringing workers in from other regions?"

"Ye can't train hundreds of men at once," said the familiar voice from the rear. "And even if ye could, we wouldn't let 'em cross our picket lines. Ye can't fight all of us, Mrs. Marrick. Ye'll just have to admit defeat."

Verity felt a lurch in her belly as she recognized the physique of the man who stepped out from behind several others. Tall, husky, with hair of jet and a scar running down the side of his face. Daniel Carne. Damn him. He didn't work for her father. He had no right to be here.

"That's the key to it, a'course," he continued in a loud, lilting voice. " 'Tes like the old matchstick proverb. If ye take those matchsticks one at a time, they're easy enough to break in half, but if ye hold a bundle of 'em in yer palm and try to break that in half, ye can't do it. What's more, if ye light that bundle, ye get yerself quite a fire. That's what we got goin' now, a helluva bonfire.''

A cheer greeted his words. ''You have no say in this, Mr. Carne,'' Verity said, but her words were drowned out. She had heard that Daniel had been rabble-rousing at several of the area's claypits, but she had not expected him to show his face here, in the heart of his enemy's territory.

''I say we lay down our tools today,'' he shouted. ''Right now. Why wait another forty-eight hours? Is Henry Trevor really going to listen to our demands? Not likely! The Trevors have exploited their workers for generations, lording it over us with their fine house and their elegant clothes and their motorcars and their high and mighty ways. The only reason they want to keep the claypits operating is to make them even richer, at our expense. I say we hit 'em where it hurts—right in their bloody profit margin. I say we close down the pits, and let their white gold languish in the earth without a buyer!''

''He's right, by God!''

''Join the strike!''

''Down with the capitalists!''

''To hell with all the Trevors!''

Verity cupped her hands to her mouth, pleading with them to calm down, to allow her to speak, but it was useless. The workers surged away from her. The mood had turned, and Daniel Carne was responsible. They didn't care, apparently, that he wasn't employed here. He had fanned their anger faster than Verity could extinguish it.

She remembered his words of just a fortnight ago: *I'm going to dismantle Cadmon Clay and ruin the lot of 'ee.*

She felt a light touch on her shoulder. Gil. He shrugged as she turned to him. ''You did a damn fine job of talking to them, Mrs. Marrick. I'm sorry it didn't turn out better.''

''That was Daniel Carne. He doesn't even work here.''

''He doesn't work anywhere. He and his mates were among the first to go on strike up to the Stannis claypits. Since then he's been going around to all the other companies, agitating, causing trouble. Got a natural talent for it, if you ask me.''

''He should be arrested! I'm going inside to ring the authorities.''

"Don't bother. You don't see him about, do you? He's gone."

"Damn him!"

Gil Parkins raised his eyebrows. He was shocked, no doubt, to hear the vicar's wife blaspheming. She glanced around at the empty claypits, the dwindling group of workers. They were gathering up their belongings and leaving the premises. Damn them all. They thought they had defeated her, but they were wrong. She would find other workers. She would train them herself if necessary. Cadmon Clay was not going to stand idle like all the other pits in the region.

Daniel Carne had underestimated her. Everybody had.

No Carne was *ever* going to ruin Verity Trevor.

Chapter Twenty-one

"There's another one of them clay-worker women here to see 'ee," said Tess one morning as Verity was finishing her morning cup of tea.

"Show her into the parlor, please, Tess. I'll be right in."

Two weeks had passed, and Verity had not succeeded in getting Cadmon Clay operational again. The strike had continued to spread. By the middle of August, five hundred men from all over the region had thrown down their tools, and the trade unions had achieved a foothold in the clay industry at last.

The silence from the claypits had been difficult to get used to, as was the absence of clay wagons rumbling through the village, trailing white kaolin dust. But the carnival atmosphere that had prevailed during the first few days had faded now that the men had been without pay long enough that their households were suffering.

Verity had been hearing anxious whispers from the village women about the stubbornness of their men. "Eighteen shillings a week is better than none," they said, and even some of the men, unaccustomed to so much leisure, were growing bored and apprehensive. The owners would make no concessions. They were certain the strikers would soon come crawling back, pleading for their jobs.

Each afternoon Verity found time to drive up to Cadmon Clay, cross the lines of militants posted outside to discourage scab laborers from entering the pits, and meet with Gil Parkins. She found no shortage of things to do. After attending to paperwork and correspondence that had been neglected for months due to her father's abysmal record-keeping, she'd insisted that Gil take her carefully through each phase of the clay process, teaching her what each man did and how strenuous the labor was, and how much he was paid. She demanded reports on injuries suffered by Cadmon Clay's workers over the past several years, and she made a point of visiting Jeb Methany and his family to assure them that they had not been forgotten, and to slip a much appreciated five-pound note to Jeb's wife.

Julian did not approve of her new preoccupation. "You are neglecting your work in the parish," he had objected during the first week of her visits to Cadmon Clay.

"On the contrary," she had argued. "The main concern of the parish at present is the clay strike. In doing whatever I can to help to resolve it, I am providing a more valuable service to our parishioners than I have in years."

She was convinced that this was true, especially during the last couple of days when the womenfolk had begun appealing to her for help.

Verity walked down the hallway to the parlor to greet the latest supplicant. "Good morning, Annie," she said when she saw who it was. Annie Trillian was a strong woman of about thirty with broad shoulders and a firm body that did not look as if it had borne the weight of six children. Her husband had worked for Cadmon Clay since his youth, as had his father before him, but they had never been a prosperous family. The children were all in school now, and she had begun to devote her considerable energy to various projects around the village, including the church, where she taught Sunday school.

"This strike is killing us, Miz Marrick. We need that pay envelope. 'Tes the same with all the families I know—babes are goin' hungry, ma'am. Ye're the vicar's wife. Can't ye do somemat for us?"

"Believe me, Annie, I want your men to return to work. Gus's job is safe. If you can persuade him to break with the strikers, there'll be a two-shilling bonus in his envelope this week, along with my promise to try to persuade my father to raise all the salaries as soon as he returns."

"That's very generous o 'ee, ma'am, but the men are sayin' any raise has got to be across the board at all the claypits in the region. They're talking about solidarity, or some such rot. 'All for one and one for all' sort of nonsense, like schoolboys together in the same gang o' mates. They've all gone a trifle mad, if ye ask me."

"I can't pay them if they won't come back to work."

"I know. But they're so blasted stubborn. I was sayin' to Gus myself jist thes morn that if he won't take 'ee up on yer fine offer, I'll come to work in his place. I'm strong; I've raised six children. I'm sure I could shovel clay into wheelbarrows as quick as any man."

With a smile, although she did not doubt Annie's abilities in the least, Verity said, "I'm sure you could, too."

"I mean it, ma'am. I'm willin' to work, and so are lots of other women. Someone's got to earn some copper in my family. If not him, why not me?"

Why not, indeed? Verity pictured the giant kiln house at Cadmon Clay, where blocks of china clay were dried and made ready for market. The linhay where the clay was loaded into carts and wagons for shipping had always been the domain of the the bal maidens who scraped the blocks before shipping. They were tough, hardy women who had labored all their lives. Every claypit in the region employed bal maidens, many of whom had been reluctant to join the strike.

How many of these women would be willing to come back to work? How many of them would enjoy the challenge of learning the tasks that had always been reserved for their male co-workers? Suppose she reopened Cadmon Clay with *female* labor?

She broached the subject with Gil the same afternoon. "If

the men won't come to work, why don't we hire women to do their jobs?''

Gil Parkins raised his eyebrows, looking amused.

"I'm serious."

"The work's too heavy for females, Mrs. Marrick."

"Perhaps that's true of strenuous pick-and-shovel work, but I see no reason why women can't mix and purify clay as easily as men. They could certainly be trained to operate the pumps and other mechanical equipment, to tend the settling pits and to add the bleaching agents. They could even work in the pan kiln. The bal maidens who haul those blocks around are strong and eager to work."

"It would take a considerable amount of time to train them," Gil said doubtfully. "Our male workers spend years perfecting a particular technique."

"Nonsense. They master the process quickly enough; they're just not allowed to move into the higher-paid jobs because that's the way the system works. There's always somebody ahead of them. None of the work seems to me to be particularly complicated."

"Don't let the strikers hear you saying that. They'll hate you even more."

"It's my guess that the strikers will think more seriously about returning to work if they see women mastering their jobs in short order. Their pride will demand it."

Gil shrugged. "Maybe so."

"It's the wives who are frustrated and angry. They're begging their stubborn men to bring home the pay envelopes again. They'll work gladly, and teach their men a thing or two about what's important and what isn't."

"I really don't think—"

"I want to try it, Gil," she said firmly.

"Even if you could train them, you'll never get them into the pits. Those militants manning the picket lines have intimidated many a brave man. Imagine what they'll do to women."

"They wouldn't dare use the same strongarm tactics on women as they use on men. I suggest, though, that we keep our plans as quiet as possible. They will never expect this development. They won't know how to counter the surprise."

"On that point," Gil said with a grin, "I agree with you."

"The first person to learn all the various jobs will be myself," Verity added. "If I can master them, other women can too."

"You're determined, aren't you?" Gil said quietly.

She nodded. She had accepted defeat in so many other areas of her life. The time had come for her to fight.

Within a fortnight, Verity had assembled and trained her small group of women. There were just under twenty of them, led by an enthusiastic Annie Trillian. Although just over half of them had had experience as bal maidens either at Cadmon Clay or elsewhere, the others had never done manual labor in their lives, other than the domestic variety. But all came from clay families, and they had grown up listening to their fathers, brothers, and husbands discussing the business.

Everything and—more important—everyone was ready. The women had crossed through the lines and were all safely within the confines of Cadmon Clay. Several of them had been questioned as to why they were spending several hours a day there. "I told 'em you were a neat and finicky lady who'd hired us to clean up a hundred years of male mess," Annie told Verity. "Damned if they didn't believe it!"

Verity was standing in the control house of the great beam engine that had been silent now for several weeks. The beam engine was the symbol of Cornish industry, and once it began its infernal roar, her scheme would be a secret no longer. Both the smoke from its chimney and the noise from its pumping would alert the militants, and indeed the entire countryside, to the fact that one claypit, at least, was operating in defiance of the strike.

It was five minutes to eight in the morning. The coal in the burner was hot. The reading on the steam gauges confirmed that the pressure was high enough to run the engine. Down in the claypit, several women were ready to shovel coarse sand and small rocks onto the trundle carts. Others were waiting to tend the rise at the bottom of the shaft that would siphon clay slurry down into the level—or tunnel—under the pit and convey it to the foot of the pump shaft. From there it would be pumped to the surface.

Atop the skytip, four workers armed with shovels would unload the trundle carts. At the sand and mica drags to the left of the claypit, more women would rake the slowly moving channels of slurry and release the drain plugs every couple of hours to remove any excess sand and mica. At the blueing house, a former bal maiden was waiting to add the bleach, a skill that came only with practice. Getting the color right was a small but vital part of the process since it could well determine the marketability of the clay blocks that resulted.

"Don't worry about getting it perfect," Verity had told her. "The only point we're trying to make at the moment is that we can do this, not that we can do it without flaw."

As soon as she started the beam engine, Verity would walk over to the kiln house and light the coal fires. Today they would be drying old clay that had been waiting since before the strike. It would take hours, if not days, for today's slurry to reach the final stage of the process. But since Verity wanted to make the point that women were capable of every phase of the operation, an experienced bal maiden was ready outside on the linhay with two recruits, waiting to scrape the finished blocks and stack them for market.

The only thing they were not attempting was the transport down to the Charlestown docks, which would have meant leaving the premises and encountering the strikers. This step would have to be taken eventually, but for now Verity had decided to concentrate all her energy on showing the world that a small group of angry and determined women could run a claypit as well as a larger group of stubborn men.

"It's time," said Gil as the hands of the clock reached the hour. "Give the signal and we'll start the engine."

Verity drew a deep breath. Once she gave the order, she would be set on a course that would take her into the unknown. *Be with me, Grandpa*, she said silently. *This is for you.*

"Now," she said firmly.

There was a slow squeaking and grinding as the pump

machinery began slowly to revolve. The noise grew louder by the second, filling the engine house, making it shiver under the vibrations.

Moving outside, she waved encouragement to the excited women who were about to begin their new jobs. The pump was operating. The slurry was churning. The trundle carts were inching up their tracks.

Cadmon Clay was operating once more.

Chapter Twenty-two

Three days after her sister's triumphal reopening of Cadmon Clay, Bret sat wedged in the boughs of her favorite sycamore in a little copse on the edge of the moors north of Trenwythan, reading a novel called *The Desert Flower*. It was a romantic tale of a young Englishwoman seeking her missing father, an archaeologist, in the deserts of Egypt. Bret had just reached the part where the plucky heroine falls into the hands of the ruthless but handsome Arab with the mysterious blue eyes who was the sworn enemy of her father when she was interrupted by voices below.

She peered through the thick leaves of her hideaway. Two husky men, one fair-haired, the other dark-, had stopped in the shade of her tree to munch on pasties that they unwrapped from a plaid cotton napkin. "They've got to be stopped," the dark-haired man said.

"Agreed. But how? They're women, for chrissakes. We can't beat 'em up for crossing the lines. At least, not without having their men come down on us."

Both voices were rough and unpleasant. The dark-haired man sounded like a Cornishman, although Bret didn't recognize him. The other's accent was of some other region. Bret inched more securely into the shadows. She was glad she'd taken this precaution when she heard the next remark:

"We must strike at the source. What's her name?—Mrs. Marrick. We stop her and we stop 'em all."

"There's a problem. Besides being the daughter of one of the wealthiest and most respected men in the region, Verity Marrick is the wife of the parish minister. She's untouchable."

"No one's untouchable."

"I'm telling 'ee, nobody'll interfere with her," the dark-haired man insisted. "The women in town already regard her as a folk heroine. And the clay owners're backing her because they think she's going to succeed in shaming the men back to work."

"She must have enemies. Vicar's wife or no, the wealthy always have enemies."

"Well, now that ye mention it, she does have one enemy. At least, her family does. Ye know him. Daniel Carne. The Trevors and the Carnes have been at each other's throats for generations."

"Excellent. We have our solution, then. If anybody can stop her, Carne can. We'll get him to pull a job like the one Michaels took care of last week at Wheal Chester, and that will be the end of Mrs. Verity Marrick's petticoat brigade."

" 'Tes risky. If any of the women should be hurt—"

"We'll order the operation to take place at night. Providing your man Carne agrees. He seems committed to the cause, but is he likely to have reservations about something like this?"

"When it comes to stopping the Trevors, Daniel Carne'll do jist about anything."

Their pasties finished, the men moved away, leaving Bret huddled above them with a clenched fist in her belly. There had been an explosion at Wheal Chester last week, destroying the pump house of one of the claypits there. It was believed that one of the militant strikers had planted the bomb.

Would Daniel really do anything? Was it possible that he would do *that*? He'd told her he was one of the strike organizers, but she hadn't realized he was one of the militants.

She thought back to the way he'd behaved on the night they had met out on the moors. He'd seemed pleasant enough

. . . until he'd found out her surname. As for that day by the trout stream, she'd been selective about her memories of that, focusing on his kiss and conveniently forgetting that he had also knocked her down and threatened to break her arm.

"Oh, Daniel," she said out loud. "I don't know what to make of you sometimes."

She had nothing new to go on. During none of her recent visits to Tamara had she run into him. "He's busy wi' the strike," Tamara told her every time she caught her rubbernecking around.

Busy blowing things up?

Bret was proud of her sister's success at Cadmon Clay. Despite her sympathy for the strikers' demands, the idea of a group of women banding together in defiance of the men who would never dream them capable of such a thing was irresistible, and she was delighted that Verity had found a way to help the families of the laborers who were being subjected to so much hardship during the work stoppage. She wasn't going to let anybody, particularly the man she was going to love for all time, interfere with that.

Bret waited until dark, then slipped out of Cadmon Hall as its blaze of lights was being doused. She had bathed, washed her hair, and dressed in her prettiest green frock. She'd tossed a light shawl around her shoulders and knotted it in the casual way that Tamara knotted her Gypsy shawl. It was important that Bret look her best.

There was an oak tree a few feet from the ledge outside her window, with a convenient branch that she had used many times over the years as a means of egress. She crawled out, more wary than usual of dirtying her frock, and climbed nimbly down to the ground.

It took her longer than she'd expected to hike to Carne Cottage. The moors were black, and the moon and stars were cloaked with clouds. Her way skirted the edge of the clay fields. All claypits looked forbidding at night: the white barrows of slag, cold as ancient burial mounds, the deep extraction pits, the unwieldy mechanical cranes used to pump the clay out of the pits, the corrugated tin shacks scattered here and there across the land, the shadow of Cadmon Tor in the background, brooding over the site.

When at last she reached his cottage, she had a sudden fear that he might not be at home. Perhaps he was already out planting bombs. "Dear Mr. Slayton," she said aloud. "It seems I've fallen in love with a saboteur."

Because of a ghostly gathering of the summer mists, she did not at first see any light in the small cottage on the grassy slope. Thick curtains were drawn across the windows, but someone was in there, she was sure, for the building was emitting a clattering sound that she couldn't identify.

Bret moved closer, staying in the shadows. The sound grew louder as she crouched underneath the window. Clatter-clatter-clatter-*ding* . . . clatter-clatter-clatter-*ding* . . . It was, she realized, a typewriter.

She risked a peek through the window. Through the barest sliver of space where the two halves of the curtain met, she could see some shelves, one end of a cluttered table, the right side of a chair, and half of a man's back. He was facing away from her, his fingers striking the keys rapidly, without pause.

Bret put her hand over her mouth to suppress her amusement. She had been imagining him hot in the midst of a planning meeting with his fellow militants, or, if he was alone, attaching fuses to some sticks of dynamite. Instead he was typewriting!

Now what? Here she was, on a wilding sort of night, out playing the heroine again. What would he say when she confronted him? What would he do?

Be intrepid, she reminded herself. *Fearless. You've come this far, adventuress.*

She marched around to the front of the cottage and, hesitating only an instant, knocked upon his door. The clattering stopped. After several seconds, it resumed. Maybe he thought she was the wind.

She rapped again, vigorously this time.

The door swung open. When first he saw her, she could have sworn he was glad. "Bret? What the bloody hell?"

"How *could* you, Daniel?"

"What in blazes are 'ee doing here?"

"I'm glad I've found you at home. I was afraid you'd be

out about the countryside, stirring up more trouble at the claypits, inciting what few workers are left to lay down their tools. Or worse.''

"Ye've worked up quite a head of steam, haven't 'ee? What about, I wonder?''

"I daresay you know the answer to that.''

He shrugged. His nonchalance called to mind her image of the handsome desert raider who had kidnapped the heroine of *The Desert Flower* and held her for ransom. Bret hadn't finished the book yet, but she expected the heroine and her captor to fall madly in love and live happily ever after.

"Would 'ee like to come in? Or do 'ee intend to lurk out there for the entire night?''

"I'm not lurking. I've come to confront you, and inside or outside, it's all the same to me.''

He closed the door after she entered and lounged back against it. He was clad in dark trousers and an open shirt. His feet were bare. His hair was tousled. He had a thicket of wiry black hair on his chest. She stared openly at him, startled by the strength of her reaction to his physical presence. *I do love him*, she thought helplessly. *He's so beautiful*.

She couldn't resist a quick, curious look around the cottage. She'd seen Carne Cottage from the outside many times, but this was the first time she had ever been inside. She was struck at once by how utilitarian everything was, especially when she compared it to the cozy, colorful interior of Tamara's cottage. The floor was flagstone, chilly and hard, lightly strewn with rushes that reminded her of an earlier era. The walls were bare, and there was no electricity. Several oil lamps provided the only light, and they were both set low, casting the central chamber into shadow. The fire on the hearth was nearly out, and the summer warmth had not penetrated the thick walls.

The furnishings were plain. She wasn't certain how many rooms there were, no more than three, she thought, with a loft overhead, but this must be the main living area. There was a solid oak table, a sink, some shelves stocked with provisions, and a heavy iron cooker to the right in the kitchen area, and several stubby chairs gathered around the fireplace in the middle. To the left was a large bookcase liberally stocked with books, an easy chair, and a table on which stood the typing machine. She saw no bed. He must sleep in one of the small back rooms, or in the loft above.

She returned her attention to him. He'd obviously been watching her as she surveyed his domain.

" 'Tes not as elaborate as the stable where ye keep yer horse, but I manage.''

"You just have to make that sort of remark, don't you? I think you want me to feel sorry for you.''

"I don't want 'ee to feel anything for me. Nor do I fancy having 'ee here, in the middle of the bloody night, alone and unchaperoned. Ye may be a skinny young schoolgirl, but ye're old enough to set tongues a-wagging.''

A skinny young schoolgirl? She sighed. Maybe she hadn't expected him to swoon with desire for her (although it would have been nice), but he needn't be so insulting. "I assure you''—she made sure her voice was as scathing as possible—"I didn't come here to seduce you.''

"Well, there's a mercy.'' There was a tightness to his mouth that suggested he was under more strain than he cared to admit. "Did yer sister put 'ee up to this?''

"Of course not. She has no idea I'm here. I pretended to be going to bed early, then climbed out my bedroom window and down the trunk of the old oak beside it. I can't stay long because if anyone checks on me and finds me missing, there'll be another uproar, especially considering what happened last time.''

"So no one knows ye're gone, no one knows ye're here, and no one, including yerself, it seems, has any idea of the trouble ye could be getting into?''

"You're in worse trouble than I am. I came to tell you to stay away from Cadmon Clay. I don't always agree with my sister, but I support what she's doing there. She deserves a chance. I'm not going to let her efforts be destroyed by a bunch of mindless militants. If you cause any harm there, to anyone or anything, I will go straight to the authorities and tell them everything I know.''

"Christ.'' He'd been keeping his distance, but now he exploded across the room. Bret's consciousness of him as a ruthless desert raider took another leap.

"Don't touch me." She retreated a step and backed into the wall.

He followed. "What *do* ye know?"

"I know that you've been chosen to commit an act of sabotage against Cadmon Clay. A bombing. And I'm warning you that if you agree to any such thing . . . if you even consider it—"

He took another step forward, moving his arms up casually until they were caging her. "Where the devil did ye hear that?"

She ducked her head in an attempt to scoot under his right arm, but his large hands fixed upon her shoulders. He leaned slightly, pinning her against the wall. "Stay still. Ye'd be wise not to make me angry, Bret."

His voice was nasty. She remembered his slam-damning anger on the night they had met. The way he had held her down beside the trout stream and twisted her arm. The various accounts she had heard over the years of the brutality of his father, Jory Carne. The criminal act he had been ordered to undertake. She lifted her chin. "I'm not afraid of you."

"Yeah, I know. Intrepid, right?"

She blushed, feeling like an idiot.

"Fact is, I'm bigger, stronger, and meaner than 'ee. So start talking. I want to hear exactly what ye know about a bombing and how the bloody hell ye know it."

"I heard it this morning from a couple of your strike-inciting friends. I don't know who they were. I was hiding. But I heard everything they said. They were discussing a bombing like the one at Wheal Chester. Verity's actions at Cadmon Clay are undermining the strike, but who could they get to attack the vicar's wife? Who better than Daniel Carne, who'd surely make the most of any opportunity to harm the Trevors."

"Damn 'ee, Bret. Where were ye that ye were able to overhear all this?"

"I was up in a tree. I was reading *The Desert Flower*."

"*The Desert Flower*? What the hell's that about? Arizona?"

"The Sahara, actually. It's a romantic novel." His eyes were gorgeous, she noticed. Robin's-egg blue, fringed by thick black lashes. ''Your friends stopped under my tree to eat their pasties and make their vile plans.''

''What d'ye suppose would have happened if they'd caught 'ee?''

''Well, they didn't. No point in fretting about something that didn't happen.''

He shook her. ''Ye're a fool. The radical militants are dangerous men. Ye could have been killed.''

''What I want to know is, is it true? Are you going to plant that bomb?''

He had controlled his expression so completely that she couldn't read the answer in his face. ''What if I am?''

''Then I'll stop you somehow.''

''How? I'm curious. Ye came rushing over here tonight. Ye must have had a plan. How were ye going to stop me? Ye think arguments would do it? Pleas? If I were a bomb layer and an arsonist, would a few words from 'ee be likely to change my mind?''

''Probably not,'' she admitted.

''Well then? This isn't one of yer blasted romantic novels and I'm no goddamn gallant desert hero. What the bloody hell did ye think ye were going to do?''

''Distract you,'' she whispered. She tried to relax the tension in her body, imprisoned so close to his.

Daniel's senses sparked to full awareness as he felt her loosening. He took in the diaphanous, almost floating quality of her frock. She was defiant no longer.

It struck him that when she'd entered she had brought in the light. Her red hair picked up the dim glow of his lantern and reflected it throughout the room, dispersing a radiance that had long been absent from his life.

Earlier in the evening, before he'd become so involved in planning and typing out the latest version of his dream—how he would run his Carne Clay, what he had learned so far from the strike—he had been musing about her. How it would be to touch her. To hold her in his arms. To kiss her. To introduce her to the delights of love. Such fancies had played in his mind all too often since the last time they'd met.

Now she was here. So close. So willing to distract him. It was as if he'd called her up from the depths of his imagination, cloaking his fantasy in her true physical being. How strange it was that he hadn't noticed her beauty until the afternoon of the fishing. It wasn't the sort of allure that usually drew him; it wasn't even something that other men were likely to comment upon—not yet, at least. There was something unrealized in her womanhood, as if she was waiting for someone to urge open the petals and reveal the loveliness inside.

Waiting for me.

No. She's too young.

She's old enough for love.

She's Trevor's daughter.

All the better. Show no mercy.

Ye're a heartless bastard, Carne.

"I think ye'd better leave," he forced himself to say.

Don't. Stay with me awhile.

"Daniel, listen to me. I know you hate the Trevors. But I don't believe there's malice in you. I don't believe there's evil. I think that if I reach out to you, I'll uncover something noble, something fine."

He bit back the sarcastic rejection that leaped to his lips. She sounded so earnest that he couldn't bear to mock her. His gaze kept wandering to her hair, so soft, so bright. How long had it been since he'd touched something soft?

Threads of a brief discussion he'd had with Tamara wandered through his mind. "Leave her be," Tamara had ordered. "She's a young thing who likes 'ee far more than she ought. Ye hurt her, ye'll have me to answer to."

This was not an insignificant threat. There were times when his sister's dark, intense depths truly frightened him. But if she'd intended to discourage his feelings for Bret Trevor, she'd accomplished just the opposite. He'd been pleased to learn that Bret liked him far more than she ought.

"Ye shouldn't be here," he repeated. "If there's anything noble in me it's the part that's still willing to let 'ee leave."

"I'm not leaving." She spoke more confidently now, and her smile was radiant.

Jesus. He didn't want her to be hurt, particularly at his own hands. Tamara was right about him. She knew his quick temper, his pride, his single-minded ambition. He had bigger dreams than any Bret Trevor could fulfill. All she would do is get in the way of them for a while. Which was why he ought to turn her around and shove her back out that door. A kinder man would send her out of his life forever.

He couldn't do it. But he could warn her, at least. "Come with me. I want to show 'ee something."

"All right," said Bret as he grabbed his lantern from the desk and indicated that they were going outside. As she moved past him she felt the brush of his hand against the back of her shoulder. The air was humming with the summer heaviness that precedes a storm. Somewhere in the distance she heard thunder rumbling. *Another storm,* she thought. *Why is it that whenever I'm around him, the elements throw up a storm?*

"Look at this, this barren land," he said. "Nothing grows here except thorn and scrub."

"What do you mean, nothing grows? It's lovely and green most of the year."

"But it's barren. Useless. Except for the rock under the earth. The rock and the clay."

He walked rapidly across the moors. The hand at her shoulder pressed harder, indicating the direction in which he wished her to go. It was a large hand, strong, capable, warm. "Once this area was rich, awash in copper and tin. Even the Romans came to Britain for our tin."

They hiked for ten minutes, then crossed over a small stream onto Trevor land, the same land that Daniel's father had laid claim to for so many years. He stopped by the side of a rocky outcropping that rose dramatically into the night sky. Atop this mound, some twenty feet above them, were the ruins of an old stone engine house, one of many that still dotted the hills of Cornwall.

"Ye see that cavern?" He pointed to a narrow opening in the rock. "That's the entrance to the Wheal Faith tin mine. There's tin there still. Come on."

He led her to the mine, ducked his head, and went inside. She followed, wondering at the trust—or folly—that allowed her to join this man in an abandoned mine. Since her childhood she'd been warned to stay out of them. Too many accidents had been attributed to such places.

It was black inside. Daniel reached back and took her hand. "Crouch down," he ordered as they moved along a low and narrow passage that sloped sharply into the earth. After several yards it opened into a large cavern. Several decaying beams lent support to the rock ceiling that arched overheard.

Bret shivered. The air was cool inside the earth, and it had a sharp, metallic flavor that invaded her nose and mouth.

"See that vein up there?" Daniel's lantern flashed on the tracings in the rock above them. Water dripped somewhere nearby in a slow, steady rhythm. "That's tin. I used to think Cornwall's tin days were over, but lately I've wondered about that. There are other places in the world where the labor is cheaper, but the metal's fine here, and someday the demand'll increase enough to justify reopening the mine. If it belonged to me—as it damn well ought to—I'd consider doing so. The riches of the earth oughtn't to be wasted."

If I had any say in the matter, Bret thought, *it* would *belong to him.*

"With kaolin," he continued, "the future's much more secure. There are other places in the world where ye can find it, yeah, but the best quality's right here in Cornwall.

"There's more to selling clay than just the quality and quantity. That's the thing that people like yer father and yer sister don't see. They have no imagination. They don't understand that there's far more ye can do with china clay than make porcelain. I realized because of Tam and her medicines. It was one of those things that suddenly comes into yer mind that ye can't fathom why ye never thought of before. Or why nobody else has, either."

"What do you mean? How did you realize it?"

"It was one day last year. I'd eaten tainted food and my belly was all cramped up with dysentery, so I went to my sister for a remedy. She mixed me a potion of kaolin diluted with water. It was thick and white, like chalk. I couldn't believe it when she told me to drink it—whoever heard of drinking china clay? But she told me it would stop my belly cramps and diarrhea flat. She was right, too. Damned if it didn't work."

Bret couldn't help laughing at the idea of people drinking watered-down kaolin to cure their stomach troubles. By the light of his lantern she could see that he was smiling, too. He seemed so much more approachable when he smiled.

He ducked and led her back through the tunnel to the opening of the mine. From the heights where they emerged they could dimly see the entire countryside, the undulating moors, the conical skytips, and in the distance the odd darkening of the sky where it merged with the sea. No stars were visible to the south. Clouds were moving in from St. Austell Bay, bringing with them the thick atmosphere that precedes an electical storm.

"I'm sure there are better ways to stop diarrhea, but it got me thinking about kaolin a different way. Ye see the claytips that surround us? They are numerous and high, but not as numerous nor as high as they'll be a decade from now. The demand for clay will grow, but it won't happen in a big way until we learn who to sell the stuff to. Heavy industry's going to be the way o' the twentieth century. Industrial uses for kaolin will develop. Our chief customers a few years down the line won't be luxury china and dinnerware manufacturers at all. Think about it—how much more porcelain goes into a bathtub than into a teacup?"

"A lot more."

"Right. Kaolin will be used in paper, paints, pastes, and other compounds. In construction materials and in concrete. It's the great whitener. With it I'm going to paint the entire world white."

She had a curious thought: Daniel Carne was a man of vision like her father, whose own dream was a world filled with huge aeroplanes capable of ferrying passengers from one part of Europe to another, maybe even across the oceans. How sad that they were adversaries when their minds worked in such similar ways.

"As for all the rivalry among the various clay concerns here in the St. Austell region, mebbe someday that'll change as well. I'd like to see us working together, not against one another. One huge amalgamation of claypits, producing all the kaolin the world needs."

"And who will be the one running this supercompany? You?"

He managed to look a little rueful. "In my wildest dreams, yeah, but who knows?"

It was this note of self-deprecation combined with the thrill of hearing a visionary proclaim his dream that sent Bret over the edge. How could she not love this man? With his passion and determination he could bring into reality anything he desired. He was a builder, a creator. He would not willfully cause destruction.

"You weren't going to plant that bomb, after all."

His expression closed over. "What makes ye think that?"

"You could never do it. No matter how you feel about my family or Cadmon Clay, you couldn't deliberately damage the workings of the earth you so love. I'm sure those men asked you to do it. But I'm also certain you refused."

Lightning forked into the ground not far away. She jumped. Then the sky opened. Daniel seemed not to notice the rain that began pelting both of them. He was looking into her eyes. Flashes of lightning illuminated his dark face, his broad shoulders, his restless hands. "Ye're right. Fact is, I could make a bomb if I had to—most miners can—but a man's got to draw the line somewhere. I told the bastards to go to hell." He paused, then added, "So ye see, ye needn't have come."

"I'm glad I came, Daniel."

His arms came around her and drew her close. She tilted her head to look at him. Her tongue touched the surface of her bottom lip, licking away a raindrop, an unconsciously sensual gesture that stirred something in the depths of his blue eyes. One of his hands moved into her hair, twisted, held her still as his mouth moved toward hers. Then they were kissing, faces uplifted in the falling rain.

Chapter Twenty-three

She said, "We shouldn't."

He said, "I know."

They kissed more deeply, his tongue sliding between her lips in a manner that sent thrills scurrying through the pit of her belly. *That's it,* she was thinking. *Yes. Kiss me again. Kiss me again and never stop.*

His mouth was hot, soft, and tender. He didn't hurry the kiss, nor did he proceed too slowly. He seemed to know exactly how to please her, at the same time arousing her passions and his own.

He leaned away for an instant, his lips poised over hers, close, so close, but no longer touching. His eyes had gone a smoky blue and his hands were trembling as they arrowed up under her hair until she could feel his fingers caressing her scalp, holding her still so his mouth could descend once more.

Her arms wound tightly around his shoulders. She heard herself panting as his tongue plunged deep inside her. Soon she was making strange moaning sounds in the back of her throat. Her belly was on fire and there was a tingling sensation in the peaks of both breasts. Would he touch her there? she wondered. Would he stroke his big hands down her body, touching her all over?

"We're getting wet," he whispered.

"Yes." She pulled free and lifted her arms toward the sky and threw back her head and laughed. "But it's a warm rain, and lovely. Oh, Daniel, feel how lovely it is."

The sight of her dancing, laughing, opening herself body and soul to the elements made Daniel want to laugh and do the same. "Ye're the lovely one," he said, coming up against her, slick as a seal, pasted to her by the rain and the heat and the night. Her frock seemed to have melted. The gossamer fabric stuck to her breasts and hips and thighs, creating a kind of suction between them. She felt hot, she felt naked, and he could barely restrain himself from throwing her down to the wet ground and loving her until he was lost in her and she in him.

But she was innocent and he didn't want to frighten her. Still, she felt so good that he couldn't resist moving his hand a little. Down her arm and in, just a little. Why did it feel so wonderful to touch a woman's breasts? All he knew was that he had to do it, had to feel her soft beneath his palms and fingertips, had to claim that much of her, at least.

She made another breathless little sound and moved her body almost imperceptibly, giving him access. In some other woman it would have been encouragement, even a demand, but he doubted that Bret was even conscious of her actions. The exclamation of surprised delight she made when he took her small breast into his hands and brushed his thumb over the engorged nipple told him that this was a new sensation to her, and that she wanted to savor it.

He took a step back from her. She stood there glowing, her hair plastered to her neck and shoulders from the rain, her face rapt, her eyes on his, completely trusting. Daniel's fingers were shaking as he fumbled with the tiny buttons that ran from her neckline to her waist. There were so many, and the wetness of the fabric made it difficult to pull them free. He made a rough sound of frustration and she helped him, her fingers covering his. Together they loosened enough buttons to open the frock halfway to the waist, then his hands slid in, both of them, and she was so smooth and soft, creamy, silky. Again she threw her head back, young and proud, a pagan goddess on a hilltop in the rain.

Bret looked down at the erotic sight of his dark hands against her lighter skin—pale where the sun never touched it, pale where no man's hands had ever wandered before— thinking, *There, now it's happened. So easily. Without thought, without effort.* It was like flying. When you were swept up in the currents you could only watch the earth fall away and feel yourself soar, captive to another element, helpless to do aught but relax and let the wind take you where it would. She had always expected to feel shame, or at least reluctance, but there was no trace of either. This was right. His hands *belonged* upon her. Her body was meant to be shared, and he was the one special man with whom that sharing must take place.

Reaching out, she touched his cheek, tracing one finger along the scar. "I love you, Daniel."

His eyes closed and he jerked her against him again. Not a kiss this time, not an erotic caress. He just held her, hard and tight against him, the two of them folded together like a dove's wings, one body, in the pouring rain.

He took her back to his cottage, to the back room she had not seen. There was a small blackbellied stove in one corner and a narrow wood-frame bed across from it. He lit the stove and opened its grate so they could see the orange glow of the coals from the shadows where they lay.

It was not gentle, this first loving of theirs. But it was not awkward either, as she had feared it might be. He removed her clothing first, and then his own. His body, black hair against firm, tan, muscled flesh, was more beautiful to her eyes than the most celebrated work of sculpture. When he came to her, she knew nothing beyond the pleasure of Daniel's hands, Daniel's tongue, Daniel's strong arms bearing her down into the straw, Daniel's warm flesh against her own. Instinctively, she knew what to do and did it fiercely, without qualm or inhibition, giving pleasure and receiving it without a trace of self-consciousness.

She discovered that she loved him simply for being a man, for being hard where she was soft, rough-skinned where she was smooth. She loved his callused fingers upon her tender breasts, his taut belly against her softer one, the force and power of his weight upon her. Joyfully, she parted her legs so he could come between them, tilting her hips to receive his first thrust. She did not mind the bleeding, which was a fleeting thing, or the pain, which was rather more than she'd expected. He gave her the time she needed to adjust to him, then taught her the ancient rhythms of love.

Afterward, when they were drained and spent, their smiles lazy now, their bodies languorous, he examined her, afraid he might have hurt her, sponging between her thighs with a soft, warm cloth, sliding it up her belly and across her breasts, massaging them until she quickened again, then back between her legs, more roughly now, faster and faster until she cried out and burst with pleasure. In return, Bret knelt over him and studied his smooth, firm-muscled body with considerable interest, for she had never seen a man naked before.

"Ye won't get with child," he told her, showing her the thin rubber sheaths he used to protect her. She marveled, never having heard of such a thing, but grateful to him for knowing about it. She loved him, yes, but that didn't mean that she had entirely given up her dream of studying art in Italy and Paris. Perhaps they'd go together, touring the world. One could always marry and have children later, when one was ready to settle down.

He showed her how to touch and caress him in the ways he most enjoyed, and grinned at her, half tenderly, half proud, when she exclaimed over the results. When he entered her again, she laughed out loud with the sheer joy that came from the ancient and timeless experience of surrendering to her lover, welcoming her man.

"I've got to go," she whispered sometime in the darkest, stillest hour of the night. "It'll be dawn soon. If anyone discovers I've been gone—"

"I'm not letting 'ee leave me." His mouth covered hers as he added, "I'm keeping 'ee prisoner. Right here, prone and open to me, my hostage of the bed."

She giggled. "Just like in *The Desert Flower*. That's the novel I was reading. The heroine gets captured by a desert raider."

"Yeah? And then what happens?"

"I don't know the end." She caressed the scar that marred his face. "But I'm sure they'll live happily ever after, even though they started out as enemies."

"Happily ever after's for fairy tales."

She heard the lover's teasing in his tone, but she heard something else as well, steel under silk. He shifted slightly, putting a couple of inches of distance between them, and she felt a ghost of uneasiness touch her. The full significance of what they had done was just beginning to penetrate. Every action has repercussions. When you plant a seed in the orchard, all you know is the kind of tree that will grow of it, not the quality of its fruit.

All the way home, Bret kept expecting Daniel to stop somewhere and pull her into his arms again, but he did not. What did you say to a man who had kissed you and touched you and made love to you like that? It was rare that she couldn't think of something to say. Usually she chattered on, too much, she suspected sometimes, but tonight she was as tongue-tied as an embarrassed bride.

At Cadmon Hall, he walked her around to the oak outside her window. "Need a boost up?" he asked, his voice casual.

She was miffed. "I can do it." She hoisted herself up into the branches with her usual dexterity, climbing rapidly for a few feet, then slowing down. Maybe he didn't know how much she'd enjoyed it. Maybe he thought she was angry with him for taking something that a young lady wasn't supposed to be willing to give.

She slid back down, half-falling the last few feet. He caught her, his eyes smoky, worried. "What?"

She slung her arms around his neck and pressed her lips to his. She could feel him quicken against her, the depth and the passion with which he returned her kiss.

"I love you, Daniel Carne. Don't you go doubting it now."

He touched her chin with one knuckle. "No shame? No regrets?"

"It's horribly immoral of me, I'm sure, but no, none."

"I love 'ee, Bret." He pressed her back against the wet tree trunk for one last lingering kiss. "Take care," he added as she tried the climb again. "I'm terrified ye'll fall."

She laughed. "You're of the earth, Daniel, but I'm of the sky. I never fall."

"That's crap. Ye're of the earth, like every woman. Ye just don't know it yet."

"Ha!" She leaned down and blew him a kiss from the safety of her window ledge. "Remember the words of the prophecy, Daniel. *What true love has torn asunder, only true love can heal.*"

"That's crap as well. But ye're mine, Bret." The words drifted up to her from the darkness below. "Ye're mine forever now."

The phrase echoed in her mind as she climbed into bed and lay there, exhausted, yet much too alive and excited to sleep. His kisses still felt hot on her lips. She relived it, every word, every touch, every moment. When she came to the end, she relived it all again.

In the morning, dazed from lack of sleep, yet too exhilarated to care, she rose and slipped out to the stables to saddle Wulf. The ride they took together was swift, reckless, and joyous. The feel of her horse's hot body surging between her thighs brought constant reminders of Daniel's lovemaking, and she was startled to find herself burning down there, as if she had to be with her lover, as if she could never get enough. She rode until her bottom was sore and her knees were stiff. But she couldn't ride out the passion, now that it had been unleashed.

Chapter Twenty-four

Verity sat atop the lumbering clay wagon that contained the first of the Cadmon Clay kaolin that had been mined, refined, dried, and shaped into blocks for market by the Petticoat Brigade, as everybody was now calling her female labor force. Behind her was a second wagon, driven by Annie Trillian, who'd had the most experience with horses. A freighter was due in port this evening, and there was only one thing left to do to prove that Cadmon Clay was back in business. They were going to transport the clay to the Charlestown docks.

Gil had offered to drive the wagon, but Verity had insisted on doing it herself. "We've demonstrated that women are capable of all the other tasks. This is our final challenge, the last point we have to prove."

Driving a fully loaded, four-ton clay wagon was no easy task, but Verity was less apprehensive about that than she was about the reactions of the people they were likely to meet along the way. During the week that Cadmon Clay had been back in business, there had been several threats from the militants, but nothing had come of them.

Bret was sitting beside her sister on the wagon, having insisted on coming along this morning despite Verity's efforts to dissuade her.

"In Papa's absence you and I are both his representatives," she had said. "I'm not letting you do this alone."

"But if there's trouble—"

"There won't be." As usual, Bret sounded supremely optimistic, a feeling that Verity was unable to share. "Everybody's proud of what you and the other women have done here. It'll be a triumphant march!"

Slowly, cautiously, they drove down the hill from the high country through Trenwythan and onto the main east–west highway that connected the clay region to the rest of Cornwall. Passing under the Bodmin Road viaduct—an old stone construction—they entered St. Austell. Bret was right—everybody had turned out. Young maids and housewives, scampering children, and men of all ages, townsfolk and clay laborers, were lining the sides of the road to watch as the Petticoat Brigade drove through town.

Some were silent and disapproving, but most yelled encouragement. The women were more vocal than the men.

"That's the old fight, Miz Marrick! Show these chappies what we're made of!"

"The men won't work, the women will!"

"We can do anything they can do!"

Bret beamed at all the comments. "When the women's suffrage leaders hear about this, they'll be out here signing up new converts for their campaign."

All along Fore Street and Church Street, the crowds cheered. The onlookers grew silent, though, as the two wagons reached East Hill, the final obstacle to be crossed before the smooth downhill run along Alexandra Road toward Charlestown. This was the part of the journey that Verity had been dreading. Accidents sometimes happened here. It had taken only three horses to pull the wagons to this point, but five strong horses were required to drag the clay up the long, steep grade.

They stopped and Bret jumped down. With Annie's help she unhitched two horses from the second wagon and led them to the first, crooning to them all the way. The well-trained animals cooperated, obviously knowing the procedure. She had a little trouble reconnecting the heavy harnesses, and two men from the crowd rushed forward to offer their assistance. Verity was about to wave them away, but before she could do so, Bret accepted their help with a smile and the tip of an imaginary cap. The crowd cheered her for this and Verity made a mental note to smile more often.

Bret climbed back up beside her. "We're all set. Go."

With the five horses straining against the load, they negotiated East Hill without incident. At the crest, Bret jumped down again, unhitched four of the horses, and led them back to the bottom where Annie and the second wagon were waiting. Shading her eyes, Verity watched as another man emerged from the crowd to help with the harnesses. She recognized him. Daniel Carne.

Dismay filled her. Ever since the day he had incited her men to lay down their tools, she had been dreading his next appearance. She was convinced that he would somehow manage to shatter her success.

Don't trust him, she wanted to scream at Bret. He's here to hinder, not to help us. He'll do something vicious. He'll leave the harness unfastened, or even—God forbid—make an unobtrusive cut into the leather in hopes that we'll lose a horse or two on the downgrade to Charlestown harbor and roll out of control. Don't let him near the team, for God's sake. Don't let him near the clay.

Even from a distance she could see Bret smiling. She accepted Daniel as easily and as unconditionally as she accepted everyone. She allowed him to hitch up her horses, and she didn't spare a glance at his handiwork to make sure he'd gotten it right. Nor did she protest when Daniel Carne, clay worker and militant, put his big hands around her waist and lifted her up beside Annie, to the uproarious shout of the crowd, who knew full well the bad blood that ran between the Trevors and the Carnes.

When the second wagon reached her, Verity climbed down and switched the two horses she needed to continue the journey. "How could you trust Daniel Carne?" she asked her sister. "He's going to try to stop us. I'm sure of it. He's got something nasty planned."

Bret laughed. "Don't worry. We're quite safe."

Angrily, Verity checked the harness on the second wagon. All the fastenings were buckled tightly. She could detect no sabotage. "I've warned you about him. You never learn! He told me baldly that he intends to destroy Cadmon Clay. He hates us, Bret."

"He doesn't hate *me*," Bret said blithely.

"You're a fool if you believe that."

"I'd rather be a fool than a cynic and pessimist who can never see the good in people."

"You'll be speaking out of the other side of your mouth someday if you continue to be so undiscriminating."

Bret shrugged off this prediction in her usual careless way. "Let's not argue now, Verity. Let's get this clay to market. You can lecture me about my foolishness and irresponsibility later."

Verity fully intended to do so. But her relief was so great when the Petticoat Brigade reached Charlestown without further incident, unloading their clay to the amazement of the husky stevedores who worked the docks, that she put Bret's folly entirely out of her mind.

Bret was awakened that night by the sound of gravel being flung against her bedroom window. She rose from bed, clad only in her nightgown, and threw open the casement. She leaned out. He was there, her lover, arms akimbo, gazing up at her.

"What are you doing here?" she called down in a whisper. She glanced toward the servants' wing. All the lights were out.

He swung himself into the oak tree and began to climb.

Goodness! "Be careful, Daniel, please!"

"Are 'ee suggesting ye're a better tree climber than me?" There was a stout branch from which it was possible to swing over to her windowsill, and he headed for it unerringly. He paused there, his smile schoolboy-mischievous. "I was hoping ye'd still be up."

She was embarrassed to admit to him that it was only because she'd been finding sleep elusive, so busy was her mind with her passionate reveries.

"May I come in?" He was gazing at her with an expression that was full of tenderness and affection and something hotter, something that caused a lick of pleasure deep down in her body. Those eyes had the oddest effect on her. She, who was ready with a verbal retort for every possible occasion, felt tongue-tied and awkward when he turned that liquid blue gaze upon her.

"No, you may not."

"No?" He hopped easily from the tree to the sill, swinging one leg inside. His hands flashed out and captured her, pulling her against him. He covered her face with kisses.

Bret giggled in spite of herself. "You're mad! What if someone hears us?"

"I must be mad because I don't care. I kept imagining 'ee sitting atop that wagon this morn, proud and cocky as an Amazon, yer red hair billowing in the wind. I loved 'ee dearly, even though ye and yer damn sister were ruining my fine clay strike with yer antics. If the men give in and return to work, ye'll be partly to blame."

"Daniel, I'm sorry. That's not why we're doing it. It was to prove something, don't you see? To prove that women are just as capable as men."

"No need convincing me. I love women. One in particular."

His voice was soft, enticing, and her halfhearted struggles against him quickly died. He swung his body in and lifted her into his arms. As he carried her to bed, excitement swept her, all the more intense for the way it was tempered by misgivings. Was he going to make love to her right here in her own bedroom?

As he laid her down she whispered, "My door isn't locked."

"Does it have a key?"

"Yes, but I never use it. If anybody should come by, my sister or one of the servants—"

He left her for a moment and went to the door. He turned the key in the lock. It squeaked, and Bret smothered a laugh.

"Ye'll have to oil it for silence," he whispered as he rejoined her. He sat on the side of the bed and pulled off his boots.

"Daniel—" All further protests died as he stretched out full length beside her. The mattress sank under his weight, tipping her toward him. He combed his fingers through her hair, then kissed her forehead, her cheeks, her eyelids, the end of her nose.

"I've missed 'ee," he said. "I know it's only been a couple of days, but I couldn't stop thinking about 'ee."

"Me too! It's all I seem to do these days—sit about yearning for you."

He touched her breast. Gently with the tip of his finger, a light, erotic brushing against her nipple, which pebbled in response. Then he lifted his hand until it hovered half an inch above her body. She needed the contact so much that she arched her back to push herself against that teasing hand. He grinned, his teeth a flash of white against his dark complexion. He hadn't shaved since morning, and the shadow of his whiskers made him look hard and tough and thoroughly disreputable.

"Ye want me."

"Yes."

"Say it."

"I want you, Daniel. But I'm afraid we'll get caught. Sound carries in this old place."

"Don't fret." Leaning over, he penetrated her mouth with his tongue. "There now, ye see?" he said after several impassioned moments. "That'll keep 'ee quiet."

Afterward, Bret lay spent as Daniel rose to explore her room by the light of a small electric torch. He seemed fascinated with the paintings and photographs on her walls, the old toys that still littered her shelves, the porcelain figures she'd collected for a while as a child, her globe, her calendars from every year since she'd been born, her desk stacked with books and pens and writing paper, her walk-in closet jammed with clothes and shoes for all occasions.

He picked up a china shepherdess, impractically clad in diaphanous skirts and bloomers with little pink slippers on her feet. "Ye have so many things."

"I'm sorry it's such a mess." Bret hadn't picked up her

room for a couple of days. The maid came in to dust and do the heavy cleaning, but Bret was expected to put her clothes and books away, which always seemed to her a gargantuan task. She tended to take off her frocks and toss them over a chair, and because she liked to have whatever books she was reading near at hand, a pile of them invariably ended up on the floor beside her bed.

He fingered her books in the bookcase and examined the latest watercolor on her easel. Done primarily in shades of blue, green, and violet, it depicted a woman, languorous and dreamy, washing her long hair in a moorland stream. "Did you paint this?"

"Yes."

"It's lovely. God knows I'm no judge, but ye seem to have a talent for it."

"Thanks. Your sister says I've more talent as a sculptress, but I've always wanted to paint."

He leafed through the book that lay on the center of her desk. Shelley's poetry. He noticed the inscription, written in a fluid hand. " 'For Bret,' " he read, " 'May these verses gladden your heart, enrich your mind, and pour showers of inspiration upon your artistic spirit. With love from your eternal friend and admirer, Simon.' "

"Some of those things are private," Bret said, feeling uncomfortable under his stare. "Simon's always been given to that sort of nonsensical hyperbole."

"Ye told me that afternoon by the trout stream that ye and he were engaged to be married."

"I certainly did not. I said I thought he might want to marry me. That doesn't mean I want to marry him."

"So ye're not committed to him?"

"Of course not. Simon's a dear friend of mine, who's sweet and kind and sensitive, but that doesn't mean I want to marry him and spend the rest of my life chained to his side."

"Or to his bed," said Daniel, his voice low.

She felt it again, that curling sensation in the pit of her belly. My goodness. It had been only a few minutes since he'd satisfied that craving, and here it was, back again. Was that possible? It seemed she still had a lot to learn about her body.

"I'm not going to marry him."

"They'll make 'ee."

"They can't make me. I'll marry whomever I choose."
She paused, then added, "I'll marry for love."

"The wealthy don't marry for love. 'Tes against the law."

"What d'you mean, against the the law? That's the most
ridiculous—"

"The wealthy have their own laws."

Bret didn't know how to deal with him when he was like
this. When they were naked in each other's arms, it was easy
to forget that she was rich and he was poor.

He had moved on to an elegant Chinese doll that graced
the top of her dresser. Its face was exquisitely painted porcelain with black eyes, rice-white skin, and red lips. The robes
were made of layered silk and belted with a jeweled sash.
"This must be worth what the average clay worker earns in
a month." He laughed harshly. "Back in the days when the
average clay worker was working, that is."

Suddenly she found the room and its contents embarrassing. She had all this, and what did Daniel have? The
clothes on his back, a small thatched cottage to sleep in, and
his dreams. He could count on nothing in life except to toil
in the claypits alongside all the other laborers who populated
the region, breaking their health and their hearts for low
wages and a future of unrelenting hardship.

"Daniel, look." She reached for something from the end
of her bed. "I hate that Chinese lady. I'm almost afraid to
touch her. This is my favorite." She showed him a stuffed
puppy with a raggedy body and legs that hung loose from so
many years of being well hugged.

"I was never fond of dolls, particularly, but I loved this
bedraggled hound. His name's Sloppy. I think you can see
why."

Daniel came back to the bed and sat down beside her,
taking the limp animal from her hands. "Ye love this old
thing better than that other? Ye're telling me true?"

"Far, far better, and excellently true."

In a gesture of tenderness that was very much at odds with
his mood of seconds before, he lifted Sloppy to his lips and
kissed him. Then he slid into bed with her again.

Less than a week later, the news came. The owners had agreed on a small pay increase, and the workers, eager to get back to work and ready to compromise on their demands, had accepted.

The clay strike was over.

Chapter Twenty-five

"Hell's bells and damnation! What the devil has been going on around here while I've been gone?"

"Papa!" Bret leaped up from the dining table at Cadmon Hall, where she and Verity were discussing the possibilities of reopening the china factory at Cadmon Clay, and flung herself into her father's arms.

Verity sat still and silent. Bret was delighted to see their father again, but Verity, she realized, was not. She wished he'd stayed in America a little longer and left the running of Cadmon Clay to Gil Parkins, and to her.

"There was a strike, and Verity broke it. Not single-handedly, of course, but her efforts contributed greatly. The men are back at work now, Papa, and we're selling clay again."

"So I've heard," Henry said wryly. "I understand she organized something they were calling the Petticoat Brigade."

"It worked," Verity said quietly. "The women of Trenwythan gained the respect of their menfolk, and took deserved pride in their own accomplishments."

"Sounds outlandish to me, but if it worked, I guess you're to be congratulated."

"Thank you."

Bret dragged her father to the table and sat him down. "Tell us about America, Papa. Do you have lots of plans for new aeroplane designs? Did you see Mr. Slayton? Did you ever make it out to Arizona, after all?"

"Yes to the first two questions and no to the rest," Henry said with a smile. "The United States is a huge country, and going to Arizona would have meant traveling nearly as far again as I did to get from London to New York. I did speak with Zach several times over the telephone, though. Pleasant man, and brilliant when it comes to aerodynamics. He sends you his best and promised to try to visit us next summer before attending the next aviators' convention in Paris."

"Oh good. I should have been very jealous if you had gone to Arizona and met him while I was stuck here at home. I *tried* to come, actually. Did Verity tell you? I didn't get very far."

"I wish I could have taken you with me," said Henry to Bret. "You would have loved the new aeroplanes I saw. The developments during the last couple of years have been incredible. I feel inspired, and I'm going to have to work hard, because believe me, Bret, the Americans are damn clever and creative. Their genius for the mechanical has not been overrated. If I hope to accomplish anything in this field, I'm going to have to commit myself totally, because the competition is much fiercer than I'd realized."

"Tell me about the newest aeroplanes, Papa."

Verity quietly left the room. They seemed not to notice her departure. Nothing had changed. Despite the upheaval of the strike, her father was no more interested in her—or the clay company—than he had ever been.

"I have to go back to school," Bret told her lover in late September. "My term begins next week."

He stared blankly at her. His eyes were underscored with dark smudges and his face was unshaven. Gently, Bret reached out and stroked the scar on the side of his cheek. She had come to love his scar.

"I'll have to leave you, Daniel. But I don't want to go!"

"I forgot about yer schooling," he admitted. He ran a hand through his tangled hair. They were together in his cottage in the late afternoon, lying naked on his blanket-tossed bed. "Why haven't ye mentioned it before this?"

"I wanted to forget about it, too. I wanted to pretend that

we would always be together, never have to part. It's only one more year, then I'll be done. But it's going to seem interminable.''

"Ye'll forget me.''

"Don't be silly. I love you.''

"Then quit school and stay with me, Bret.''

"I can't do that.''

"No, a'course ye can't. No Trevor's ever going to acknowledge her love for a Carne. Ye love me now, but it willna' last.''

"Don't start with that tommyrot again. You're just like my sister—you're both pessimists.''

"I've got plenty to be pessimistic about. Can't get a blasted job. I can't very well expect 'ee to plight yer troth to a man who's incapable of supporting 'ee.''

The striking clay workers had gone back to work, but Daniel was not among them. His brief career as a militant was too well known. James Stannis, owner of the claypits where Daniel used to work, had refused to take him back. Nobody else would hire him, either. Stannis had passed the word along that Daniel Carne was an insubordinate troublemaker. He was on every clay owner's blacklist.

"You'll get a job when the rancor dies down. I'm sure of it.''

"Not working for any of the local sons of bitches, I won't. Good riddance to them. I've been dreaming about opening my own claypit for years. No excuse not to do it now. I've laid some money by. I'll start small, and grow.''

"That would be wonderful!''

"It'll give me something to do while ye're at school. Something to throw myself into. Without that''—he pulled her into his arms—"I don't think I could endure it.''

"I love you so much," she whispered as he pressed her down. "Nothing can separate us. Not distance, not time. I know we'll be together again.''

" 'Tes odd,'' he said with a wry smile. "Damned if I know why, but I believe 'ee, Bret.''

"What true love has torn asunder," she whispered, "only true love can heal.''

Part Four

1914

And mistress of herself, though china fall.

—Alexander Pope
Epistle II. To a Lady

Chapter Twenty-six

"You all strapped in, lad?" Bret's father asked.

Simon nodded, unable to force words out through the tense muscles in his jaw. His bladder felt about to burst even though he had relieved himself behind the hangar a few minutes ago. Maybe he shouldn't have chugged that bottle of stout before leaving home. Without it, though, he'd never have found the courage to go through with this.

"Contact!" someone yelled as the engine roared and the propeller began to turn. Then they were moving forward along the ground. He could feel the air rush by his cheeks, faster, ever faster. *I've changed my mind*, he felt like screaming. *Let me down, let me out!*

Henry, seated at the controls just in back of him, was yelling something about thrust and velocity and the position of the elevators. Simon took refuge in Henry's calm voice. He'd flown this aeroplane dozens of times before. Hell, aviation enthusiasts all over the world were getting into these contraptions every day, executing crazy maneuvers like loops and rolls and dives. For centuries human beings had been earthbound, but now they'd grown wings.

"Open your eyes, lad," Henry screamed over the sound of the engines. "You're missing everything!"

Simon pushed back his cap and dared a look at the earth just as the flimsy flying machine rocked on its front wheels and leaped into the air. The ground tilted. His belly heaved. Good Christ, what was he doing? He didn't even like to climb trees.

They were going to crash, he knew it. Nobody could do

this. Oh, theoretically it was possible, yes. He'd been reading up on aerodynamics for the past couple of weeks, ever since this mad idea had taken possession of his brain. It was elementary physics: forward thrust of the engine, the lift provided by the airflow over the wings. It was a wonder no one had managed to do it in an earlier century. The principles were simple enough.

So his reason said, but in the more primitive regions of his brain where doubt, fear, and superstition resided, he remained convinced that flying was impossible. Even as the aeroplane rose smoothly into the air, straining forward as if rejoicing at the prospect of freedom, Simon couldn't believe the experience was real and was happening to him.

He imagined what Bret would say when she heard. She had often tried to persuade him to fly; she'd frightened him more than once, laughing and sticking her head and shoulders out as she waved to him from her father's aeroplanes, leaving him weak in the knees at the thought that she might fall out. He'd always envied her courage, her daring, her optimistic spirit that refused to take into account the possibility of anything going wrong. And she, in turn, had always laughed at him—gently—for his morbid imagination that saw disasters springing up everywhere, like warriors from dragon's teeth.

Now, though, she would be proud of him. Now that he'd finally done something brave, something adventurous, perhaps he would be able to tell her what was in his heart.

Simon had come home from his first year at Oxford to discover that his feelings for Bret were undiminished by the unexpected success he had had at college with another young woman. His good looks and gentle manner had led to his first sexual affair with a barmaid at the local pub. Daisy had been smitten with him, and he with her, until an upperclassman had lured away her affections. Simon had taken it philosophically. Daisy had a seriousness about her that had made him nostalgic for Bret's laughter, and when he returned home for the summer and saw his old friend again, she seemed to him to be lovely, vivacious, sensual, and everything he had ever desired in a woman.

He wanted to marry her. But she seemed still to regard him as "dear old Simon," her trusted but unromantic friend.

Simon had spent his first week back in Trenwythan writing love sonnets, struggling over the images and the rhyme scheme. At one time he might have shown them to Bret, but now he tore them up. They were foolish, sentimental. He would not win her love with mawkish emotion. Anyway, love poems didn't seem quite the thing now that the country was bracing for war.

Early one morning Simon had seen through his bedroom window what he initially thought was a bird wheeling against the horizon. Like most poets, he'd written odes and sonnets on the skylark, the eagle, the nightingale, the phoenix. *Inspire me, bird*, he had thought, wondering at its droning flight.

At length he had realized that the bird was Henry Trevor, putting one of his aeroplanes through its paces against the cloudless sky. And an idea for a way to take Verity's year-old advice and make Bret notice him had exploded in his brain.

"You all right back there? Still got a hold on your stomach?" Henry yelled. Simon nodded. His stomach was settling down, as was the pounding of his pulse. They soared higher, the angle of ascent steeper and the sound of the engine a passionate roar.

Tentatively, he looked down. As Henry banked, the earth rotated beneath. The trees shrank until they were barely taller than bushes. Hedgerows and woodlands darkened to greenish black, and there were pinpricks of rainbow colors where the summer flowers bloomed. The cone-shaped slag heaps were like icebergs, and the cultivated fields were checkerboards of emerald and olive green, amber and brown.

And the buildings. The whitewashed cottages were Lilliputian. The old stone engine houses at the abandoned tin and copper mines turned into children's playing blocks. As the aeroplane circled, Simon saw the green slate roof of Cadmon Hall, noting clearly for the first time the perfect E shape of its design. It wasn't possible, from the ground, to appreciate the classic perfection of the sixteenth-century building's architecture. From the air, everything was made perfect: each house, each moor, each meadow, each meandering stream.

It came as a shock to him to realize that he was actually beginning to enjoy this.

"What d'you say, lad?" Henry mouthed. "D'you like the view?"

"Go higher," Simon called. "I want to see the sea."

Henry grinned and pulled back a little farther on the stick.

"Well? You fancy it?" he asked twenty minutes later after executing a perfect landing and shutting down the throbbing engine.

Simon felt like a medieval knight who'd just had a vision of the Holy Grail. "Will you teach me to fly? I never knew it before, but this is what I want to do."

"Hell's bells and damnation, lad, I'm glad to see there's some life in you, after all!"

Bret held Zachary Slayton's latest letter in her hand and daydreamed about Arizona.

> You'd like it here, Bret. There's a stark beauty to the landscape. If I were a poetic man, maybe I could make you see the dry, rusty earth spiked with saguaro cactus, the mountains that rise red and ocher in the distance, the dust devils that shimmer in the desert heat. Sometimes I amuse myself by imagining you riding my best roan mare up the dry gulch toward the canyon, that red hair you profess to hate streaming out behind you, same color as the horse.
>
> You, young lady, owe me a mess of letters. I suspect you're spending your days writing to some more fortunate admirer. Shame on you for neglecting a poor lonesome wrangler.

Smiling at the image of the grizzled Zach Slayton as a potential admirer, Bret took up her pen. It was true she hadn't written to her American friend for ages; even this letter had gone unanswered for several weeks. Her letters to Daniel had absorbed her during the months she'd been away at boarding school, but now that she was home, finished with school at last, she was to carry on her relationship with Daniel in person instead of by post.

Dear Mr. Slayton,

I do apologize for letting such a long time go by since my last letter. I'll try not to be so reprehensibly lazy in the future.

Papa's building a grand new aeroplane, as I expect he's told you in his own letters. I missed all the test flights because I was away at school, but I'm home now. I don't think I've ever missed Cornwall as much as I yearned for it during my final term!

Isn't it dreadful about this war? Everybody says it's not going to amount to much, but still, I hate to think of young men dying and killing each other in the Balkans, for no very good reason that I can see. Who would have thought that the assassination of an Austrian archduke and his wife by a ragtag band of Serbian nationalists in some place nobody's ever heard of could cause such a ruckus? One of my friends says it's all an imperialist plot for the rich to get richer and make the poor poorer. But I suppose that's what all wars boil down to.

She laid down her pen. It was Daniel who was taking the worker's view of the Balkan conflict. Considering that he was now a claypit owner, she found it ironic that he still ran on about the evils of capitalism.

She read over what she had written. The tone seemed to lack something that her old letters had contained. Frankness, perhaps, she thought wryly. She used to feel free—too free, perhaps—to tell Zach Slayton anything, but during the past year she'd been more circumspect. In a way, she wished she had told him the whole story. He was a man, and she needed a man's insight and advice.

It had been nearly a year since she'd fallen in love with Daniel, and the time had sped by, dreamlike. The separations had been awful, but during her school holidays they had found ways and times to meet that were outrageous. Moments snatched here and there, plagued by the constant fear of getting caught. They had made love inside, outside. In Tamara's cottage one lazy afternoon when she was attending a childbed. In the shack Daniel had constructed at Carne Clay, which was now producing and selling kaolin. In his cottage. Among the grasses on the moors. By the banks of the trout stream. In the trout stream. In the Wheal Faith mine, dark and humid, where he spoke to her again of the wealth and the beauties that reside deep inside the earth.

At present, though, Daniel was being difficult. He wanted her father and Verity to know that she had fallen in love with their enemy. He wanted her to defy her family, abandon her home and her heritage, and come and live openly with him. He did not, however, offer her marriage. If he married her, he insisted, people would think that he was doing it because he was after her money, her property, her higher position on the social ladder. He would accept nothing from the Trevors. One day he would meet her father as an equal, but this would come about through his own labor, his own cleverness, his own determination. His pride was too great to ally himself through marriage with his most bitter enemies.

"I don't know about my pride," Bret had argued, "but my common sense is too great to allow me to live openly in sin with a man who continues to profess his hatred for the rest of my family and his determination to destroy everything the Trevors have ever built."

"If ye love me as much as ye claim to, ye'll trust me enough to take any risk."

"If you love me as much as you claim to, you'll marry me, Daniel!"

The upshot of this discussion had been one of an increasing number of quarrels between them.

Bret longed to write to Mr. Slayton that Daniel's masculine pride was stronger than his love. His desire for vengeance seemed more powerful than his desire for reconciliation, and his stubbornness made Bret wonder if all men were like that. She did not know how to get through to him.

For months Bret had hoped that she and Daniel would be the lovers who fulfilled the old prophecy. A Trevor and a

Carne were one day supposed to marry and produce children who would unite their blood, ending the feud forever. She wanted herself and Daniel to be those lovers. It had become her most cherished dream.

But it was a dream that seemed especially fragile on that August day in 1914. The morning newspapers had announced the shocking news that England was at war. The complex chain of events that had been brewing in the Balkans had snaked across the entire continent. Little Serbia, homeland of the assassins of the Austrian archduke, had mobilized troops against the powerful Austro-Hungarian empire. Russia, concerned that the alliance of Austria and Germany would threaten her western borders, had also begun amassing armies. France, friendly toward Russia and terrified of Germany, followed suit. England, currently a tentative ally of her traditional enemy, France, had endeavored to maintain her neutrality, but when the Germans moved to invade the nonmilitant Belgians, Britain had no choice. At midnight on August 4, 1914, war was declared.

Young men were already heeding the call to enlist. War fever had gripped the country, and the honor of Britain was declared to be at stake. The brothers of several of her school friends, including the charming and handsome Charlie Blount, her best friend Maggie's brother, were commissioned officers from Sandhurst, which ensured that they would be among the first to go. Although both Papa and Julian insisted that the conflict was nothing more than a minor eruption of hostilities that would be over and done with before the British Expeditionary Force arrived in France, Bret was worried that her friends might be called upon to serve, to fight, perhaps to die.

What if Daniel had to go?

"You're not going to enlist, are you?" she asked him.

"Not me. While the privileged classes of both sides rush out to kill each other on the battlefield, the ordinary laborers'll stay at their jobs, providing the industrial support necessary to keep their countries functioning."

"But surely if the conflict spreads, the army will want ordinary laborers to serve."

"I doubt they'll badger me. I had scarlet fever as a child; it's left me with some sort of trouble in my heart."

"What do you mean, trouble in your heart?" she asked, alarmed. "Is there something wrong with you?"

"Nothing to fret about. A slight murmur. It's a blessing. I'm free to leave the fighting to the poor fools who think there's something honorable about being blown to bits for their country."

"I hope Simon doesn't have to go," she mused aloud.

As usual, the mention of Simon—or any other potential rival—raised Daniel's hackles, and he set about to make her forget Simon, the war, her very self under the onslaught of his passion.

The August days were slow, seamless. Bret existed in a place where the outside world seemed alien and distant. Her paintbrushes went unused, her clay pots unformed. She wrote no more letters to Mr. Slayton. She caught no fish. She did little besides ride Wulf, knit socks, and wind bandages for the soldiers in France—every female in the country was doing that, it seemed—and slip out to meet Daniel. The hours when she wasn't with him were dreamed away, either in anticipation or in reminiscence of every tiny detail of the feverish lovemaking they shared.

They spoke no more of marriage or of the future. But as August 1914 drew to an end, the whispers of the outside world turned louder, shriller. Battles were being fought, troops were on the move. The British Expeditionary Force had moved out to confront the Germans on battlefields in Belgium and in France. Word began to creep back of fearsome casualties. Brave soldiers, confident of the justice of their cause and the superiority of their weapons, were astonished to find themselves pushed back, defeated, butchered. There were shrapnel wounds and fractured limbs, and far too many deaths. With every day that passed, there were fewer young men to dance and make love and seed another generation.

Sometimes on the nights when she was alone, Bret dreamed of evil things and portents. It was at those moments that Tamara's words from last summer came back to haunt her:

"Beware yer passionate nature. 'Twill be the cause of much joy as well as many sorrows."

Chapter Twenty-seven

"Come with me. I've got a surprise for you."

"Hello, Simon." Bret wiped a lock of hair out of her eyes, unknowingly smearing her forehead with dirt from the garden. Armed with a trowel and a watering can, she was tending the rosebushes, a task she'd taken over when the head gardener quit his job to enlist. A shortage of servants was bedeviling the country as young men gave up the uniforms of domestic service for the more glamorous uniforms of the British army.

Simon looked handsome in his wind-whipped trousers and leather jacket. He seemed to have filled out in the last few months, and his skin was tanned and healthy. Even as she summoned her friendliest smile and got up, leaving her trowel in the grass, she felt a shaft of guilt. She'd been avoiding him. "Where are we going?"

"You'll see."

He led her out through the hedgerows and down the path that wound through the park and out onto the moors. It was a fine September day, sunny with a light breeze blowing in off the ocean. High thin clouds were scattered in wisps across the sky. The worst heat of summer had faded, leaving the earth warm and fertile with the long slow languor of fall.

In England, at least. In France and Belgium the earth was warm with blood.

During the first ten days of September, Bret, along with everyone else in the country, had been poised in a state of fretful anticipation, hungering for the daily newspapers with their reports of the news from the front. The German army was thundering across France in the direction of Paris. If Paris fell, England would be the Huns' next objective.

When the Germans crossed the Marne, the last natural barrier keeping them from Paris, despair was universal, but the heroic performance—and the horrendous casualties—of the Allied troops at the Ypres had forestalled the advance, and shortly thereafter a new push had driven the enemy back to new lines east of the Marne.

The war had become more personal lately with the death of a former clay worker from St. Austell, a member of the British Expeditionary Force. It was as if his death had put the spurs to the men who had known him—and many who had not—for suddenly the claypits were losing workers to the army's recruitment efforts. Patriotism surged all over England. Young men responded to the call, and young women—including Bret—began rolling bandages. Everyone, it seemed, was eager to do something to aid the beleaguered armies who were fighting so bravely and dying for God, the king, and St. George.

Papa was working madly on new aeroplane designs, with the government's blessing. Flying machines were no longer a novelty but a potential weapon against the enemy. Verity had organized the women of the parish into groups working to provide some of the necessities for the boys at the front: bandages, blankets, and knitted items such as socks, scarves, and sweaters. Simon, who had initially declared that as a poet and believer in universal love he was opposed to war, had begun to talk about the virtues of fighting for a noble cause, and Julian had stressed the need for troops to have sufficient access to the pastoral care of army chaplains.

Daniel too was preoccupied with the war, although he seemed to see it less in terms of its human consequences than its commercial ones. Porcelain production at Meissen and Sèvres would suffer if hostilities continued, he explained, which would mean a larger share of the market for the British porcelain companies, and possibly a higher demand for china clay.

Clay was the last thing Bret wanted to talk about during their stolen hours together, but as the news from the battle lines grew increasingly dire, the private world of their love affair seemed less and less secure.

Simon was leading her across the south downs to the aviation field. "What are we doing?" she asked. "Did my father ask you to come watch him perform some new aerial stunt?"

"Not exactly," Simon said, sounding mysterious. "Your father's not flying today."

With her trailing behind, he crossed the field to the landing strip. The biplane stood poised at one end, her father beside it, tinkering with the engine. When they reached him, he clapped Simon across the shoulder in a familiar manner that startled Bret, who had never thought the two of them were particularly friendly.

"So," Henry said to Bret, "you've come to watch my pupil perform?"

She blinked in confusion. What pupil?

"I haven't actually told her yet," Simon said.

"Told me what?" She looked from one to the other, trying to make sense of the mischievous expression on her father's face and the exalted one on Simon's. From the pocket of his jacket Simon removed a makeshift aviator's cap, which he donned along with a pair of goggles. He leaned down and kissed her gaily on the cheek, then climbed the struts and strapped himself into the aeroplane. Her father went around to the front to heave the propeller into its first turn as the engine sprang to life.

It was the last thing Bret had expected, and her entire body flexed with apprehension. "Simon?"

He grinned at her and waved as the plane rolled down the strip away from her. Bret clutched her father's arm. "Is he out of his head? Have you both gone mad? What's he *doing*?"

"I guess you might say he's spreading his wings."

"He can't be. He's afraid of aeroplanes!"

"Not any longer," her father said cheerfully. "As a matter of fact, he's turned into a pretty damn good pilot for someone who was such a bleeding coward for most of his life."

Bret watched as the little aeroplane raced down the landing strip, gathering speed for takeoff. It was the moment that always thrilled her, but today, for the first time, she was struck by the unnaturalness of it. How could this man-made object take to the air, especially with Simon at the controls? She half-expected the gods, enraged at this invasion of their element, to fling him, like Icarus, to the ground.

The aeroplane was aloft now, climbing at a steep angle, graceful as a swallow. When he gained sufficient altitude, Simon leveled off and began a slow circle of the area, tipping his wings in salute. After making an additional circle, he executed a series of loops, rolls, and figure eights, leaving Bret weak-kneed and dizzy. She had watched many a flight from this makeshift airfield, but never had she been so astonished.

Slowly, however, her surprise turned to admiration, her admiration to pride. Knowing Simon as well as she did, she recognized the full measure of his achievement—the courage he must have unlocked within himself, the terrors he must have overcome. This was Simon, her Simon, and how splendid he had become!

As he landed and rolled toward the place where Bret was standing beside her father, Simon felt like the victor in an Olympic race hurrying to claim his laurels. When he climbed out on the struts and jumped to the ground, she was there, running to him, flinging her arms around him, and transporting him to a place that was even higher than his mechanical wings had taken him.

"Oh, Simon, that was wonderful! You darling, I'm so proud of you!"

He closed his arms around her and swung her off her feet. She laughed, arousing in him a heady combination of confidence and passion.

"How did you learn? And when?"

"I've been at it for most of the summer. Your father started teaching me shortly after I got home from Oxford."

"But why didn't you tell me?"

"I wanted it to be a surprise."

"Well, it was certainly that. I'm amazed that you were able to perform this miracle without my ever once suspecting. I'm so proud of you," she repeated. "You can't imagine how excited I am."

"Then it was worth it." He slipped his arm through hers

and added, with a confidence and hardness of purpose that he barely recognized as his own, "Let's take a walk."

"No, let's take a run! And don't tell me your asthma's acting up, you old faker." Pulling at his hand, she jogged across the landing strip. "Anyone who can breathe that fine thin air has got much healthier lungs than he's ever been willing to admit!"

And so he ran with her until they were both out of breath, panting and laughing their way up the rocky tor that looked out over St. Austell Bay. "I'm still stupefied," she teased. "It's so unlike you to take up such an adventuresome hobby."

"I did it for you."

"Rot. You did it to prove something to yourself: that you're not the coward you've always imagined yourself to be. And you've succeeded. You can do anything, dare anything, do you realize that? You're finally free."

"There's only one other thing I've any desire to dare."

"Well, do it then." She gestured toward the hills, the sky, the sea. "Papa always used to say that when you're a flyer the entire world is beneath your wings."

"All right." The next instant his hands were on her shoulders. He bent his golden head and touched her lips with his, tentatively at first, then with all the eagerness and longing that had been building inside him for so long. He felt her sweet mouth open as his tongue slid inside, and his pleasure and relief were ten times what he'd imagined they would be.

"Simon—"

"No, don't say anything yet." His exhilaration was such that he didn't notice her sudden wariness. In the weeks since he'd started flying, everything had changed. He'd proved himself capable and brave. He'd done things he would never have dreamed himself capable of doing, and nothing was beyond him now. When he was in the air, he felt dauntless, invincible, as powerful as an eagle. It was the eagle inside him that would swoop down and conquer the woman he loved.

"I want to talk to you. I want to tell you how I feel. I've wanted to tell you for ages, but I didn't feel able to until today."

"Wait a minute, Simon. I don't think—"

"Shh, let me finish." He didn't see the sadness in her eyes or hear the apprehension in her voice. "I'm not very good at this, I'm afraid. That is, I'm supposed to be clever with words, but it's a good deal easier to be eloquent in poetry than in ordinary discourse. I realize I don't have much to recommend me. I've never known how to be dashing or charming with young ladies, but with you, I feel so comfortable. Always. As if our minds are one.

"I love you, Bret. Perhaps you know it. I know I don't deserve you, but I'm trying to make myself worthy. That's why I learned to fly. I knew it wasn't possible that you could love me the way I was, but is there any hope, do you suppose, that you'll be able to love me the way I'm endeavoring to be?"

She touched him then, her hands on his hands, and for a moment his heart erupted with gladness. Then she did the most extraordinary thing—she bowed her head, the fall of her bright hair hiding her eyes from him. He raised his palms to touch her face, and there he felt her tears, wet on her silk-soft cheeks.

The melancholy that ran so deeply in him crept upward, thick and miasmic as a winter fog. If she loved him, Bret, his Bret, his child of smile and sunshine and joy, would laugh, not mourn. If she loved him, she would be bursting with light.

His mouth stumbled on, as if it chose not to believe what his senses proclaimed. "You're all I've wanted since the first day I met you. You took me out into the garden and showed me the pet toad you had stashed under the flower pot. It was an ugly brown toad, and you had made a pet out of it. You put it right up to your lips and kissed it, remember? And when I made noises about how disgusting that must be and how you'd probably get sick and who'd want to kiss an ugly, foul-smelling toad, you laughed and said that maybe if you gave it enough love, it would turn into a prince."

Her tears were rivulets now, warm and wet against his chilly hands.

"I love you, Bret. Will you marry me?"

She looked up and he saw the tears. "I can't."

Just because she said it, looked it, breathed it, was no reason why he had to believe it.

She took both his hands in hers. "Don't misunderstand me. I love you dearly. You're so important to me, and I'm so proud of you, but . . . I just can't. Please try to understand."

"I know it's sudden. Please take some time to think it over. You needn't say anything definite now. We're both young, and with the war and all—"

"Thinking it over won't make any difference. Oh, Simon, the truth is, I'm in love with someone else."

No, he thought. *No.* He felt his face whitening, then slowly turning red. "Who?"

She looked away.

"You don't even know any other young men. That is, you've been at home now for a couple of months and there's no one who's eligible hereabouts. Unless . . ." His voice trailed off. She was studiously avoiding his gaze. "Surely not that clay worker you were kissing last summer? Surely not Daniel Carne?"

"Simon—"

"Don't bother to deny it!" he shouted, even though she hadn't. Deep in his gut he felt that same grinding ache he'd experienced on the long-ago day when he'd seen them together. "I was there. I saw him throw you down, I saw him kiss you. I was rushing to defend you when I realized that you were kissing him back."

She tried to touch him, but he shook off her hand. "You've been in love with him ever since, haven't you?"

Her chin lifted. "Yes. I have."

"Are you lovers?"

Once again her eyes, usually so candid and direct, slid away. The images that rose like gorgons in Simon's imagination nearly overwhelmed him. He felt a rage he hadn't supposed himself capable of, the kind of rage that made him want to climb back into his aeroplane and fly it into the ground.

He wheeled away from her. He felt her fingers trail along his arm, but then they clutched at empty air, so fast and furious was his retreat. He fled back to the biplane where it stood in the short grass, its engines still warm. Bret's father had discreetly disappeared.

Simon slid his hand over the smooth wood of the wing and leaned his forehead against the strut. It smelled strongly of gasoline and heavy, oily smoke. Nice smells; comfortable smells. Smells that would have disgusted him as recently as two short months ago.

Couldn't she see how much he had changed? Didn't she understand that he had done these things for her, certain that, if he proved himself in this dramatic way, she'd see him, finally *see* him, and recognize that she loved him as much as he loved her? That they were perfect for each other? That they were meant to be together?

How could a dream so powerful not come true? How could a love that was so deep, so resilient, so perfect, not be returned?

Fool, the darker side of himself mocked. What could be more ordinary, more commonplace, than unrequited love? The poets had sung of its torments since the dawn of time.

She was there, beside him. He caught the scent of fresh violets in the sun. He felt her affection, her sadness, her compassion, but they were not enough. "I do love you, Simon." Her husky voice sounded puzzled, young. "Please don't think I don't. Maybe it's a truer kind of love than the other . . . I don't know. It's not as if it's perfect with Daniel. Sometimes I think that maybe we're not ready yet for this sort of thing. That we ought to grow up more but that our bodies won't let us wait."

"Just leave me alone. Go to him, why don't you? Take him into your body that's so eager it can't wait. Let him knock you down again so you can feel overwhelmed and overpowered and not the least bit responsible for the lust that makes you lie there and open your legs."

She jumped away as if he'd slapped her. The Bret he thought he knew would have retaliated against his crudeness with an equally snappish remark, but she only blinked at him for a moment, saying nothing. Then she turned and walked away.

The stinging tears that had been gathering at the back of

his eyes flooded over, mixing as they fell with wood varnish and engine grease and the faint traces on the biplane of the mists of clouds. What a strange, unfair place the world was. She, who was his dream, his love, his life, had turned her back on him forever. Despite his prowess, despite his courage, she remained elusive. Not even an eagle could take her.

Verity had the vicarage to herself for an hour that morning. She had nothing scheduled until her luncheon meeting with the group she had organized to visit and extend comfort to the many parishioners whose sons and husbands were in service abroad. After lunch she would hurry up to Cadmon Clay, as she continued to do every afternoon, to consult with Gil on the effects that the war was beginning to have on the china-clay industry. Since her father had returned from America the year before, he had resumed his cursory supervision of Cadmon Clay, but he spent more and more time at his hangar in the south field. It was Verity who did the accounts, helped Gil, observed, planned, and dreamed.

Julian's disapproval was fierce. He took every opportunity to remind his wife that her place was at his side, not in the clay-producing hills. And on the rare occasions when he turned to her in bed, he continued to treat her as an ignorant young girl whose sole purpose was to gratify his desires while experiencing none of her own.

She led a busy life. She couldn't think of any reason not to indulge her dreams for just a little while.

Verity took a box from the bottom of her chest of drawers and removed from it an object shrouded in many layers of protective cotton. Slowly, ceremoniously, she unwrapped it, revealing a lovely sculpture of two lovers embracing, executed in the finest Sèvres soft-paste porcelain. She set the piece on her dressing table.

The lovers were nude. Their skin was creamy, their curves and muscles graceful, well defined. The expressions on their faces, which radiated pleasure and delight, had been molded by a master. They held each other as if dancing, a sensual dance that promised the fulfillment that was missing in Verity's life.

What must it be like to surrender to such powerful yearnings? How did it feel to know the firmness of a virile male body against one's naked flesh, the swell of passion, the singing of the blood?

With these images came the desire, too strong to be resisted, to join in the dance. From the middle drawer of her dresser she extracted the exotic red silk nightrobe that had belonged to her mother. Stripping off the plain cotton frock she wore, she allowed the silk to slip down over her naked body. It fit her much better than it had on her wedding night; her figure had filled out agreeably during the past seven years.

Verity loosened her hair, which had grown very long, shook it out, and tossed it over one shoulder. The color might not be vibrant or beautiful, but the texture was full and thick and shining. Surely somewhere was a man who would desire to stroke it, to wrap her hair around his fingers, his wrists.

Dreamily, she took up her hairbrush and drew it through her hair. As she felt the sensual pull of the bristles against her scalp, she gazed at the porcelain lovers and imagined a man standing behind her, touching and caressing her, readying her for love. She could almost see him: his burning eyes, his tender smile, the tan flesh of his hands against her pale skin as he parted the front of her crimson robe and gently aroused her breasts.

Shutting her eyes, Verity revolved slowly around the room, dancing to a music only she could hear. Above her was a crystal chandelier, and around her danced a score of other women, all of them in brightly colored evening gowns, but none so lovely, so desired, so admired as herself. Ah, the joy of it! Faster and faster she whirled in her secret world of gaity and light. Here was beauty. Here was ecstasy. Here was love.

The slam of a door somewhere downstairs, followed by rapid footsteps on the stairs, jolted her out of her reverie. She seized a plain white cotton dressing gown and flung it around her, her flesh cold and her heart a-gallop with the fear of discovery. If her husband caught her . . . if he found her decking her body in crimson and gold . . . and dancing, actually *dancing* . . . She looked desperately around the room, at the heavy drapes drawn against the light of the fine autumn day, the porcelain lovers caressing each other . . . her own guilty eyes and flushed skin . . .

A door at the far end of the corridor slammed, and Verity sank back against the bed in relief. It was Simon, not Julian, thank God.

Ten minutes later, during which time Verity managed to get herself dressed, her bedroom tidied, and her emotions under control, she heard her stepson's footsteps again, followed by a sharp rapping on her door.

"Verity? Are you in there? Open up."

He didn't sound like her stepson, and when she let him in he didn't look like her stepson, either. His golden hair was wild, as if he'd been forcing agitated hands through it. His eyes were red and wounded, as if he had been crying.

"Simon! What on earth—"

"I'm leaving," he said abruptly. "Now, this morning. Would you like to come with me?"

She blinked. "What are you talking about?"

"My country needs me. No doubt it could use you as well. Nursing has become quite the thing among upper-crust ladies."

"Simon, what are you saying?"

He stalked about the room, never stopping, never standing still. "Are you happy with my father?" he asked.

His tone implied that he knew she was not. Her immediate instinct was to sputter an indignant reply, but instead she turned her head and stared out the window, trying to contain the tears that had unexpectedly flooded her eyes. The past few months with Julian had been hell. He found fault with everything she did. He never came near her in bed. And he disapproved so strongly of her work at the clay company that she'd taken to lying about the amount of time she spent there, pretending to be taking an afternoon constitutional on the moors when she was actually consulting with Gil.

"No one would blame you if you left him, you know."

"My God, Simon! I could never leave him. We're *married*."

"My mother left him."

"Don't be ridiculous. She died."

"She died all right. After she left him." He jerked a cigarette and a box of matches out of his trousers' pocket and lit up. Verity had never seen him smoke before. Had he asked her permission, she would have refused, but he gave her no opportunity to speak. "She died of enteric fever, contracted in one of the slums of London, after she ran away from my father and tried to survive on her own."

Verity's blood had begun to pound with a slow, hopeless rhythm, like the tolling of a churchbell. "Why?"

"Because of the way he treated her. Because he abused her. Oh, not physically; he didn't beat her, or at least I never saw him beat her. But he abused her soul."

His words thundered through her, even though they were spoken in a low, tremulous voice.

"I expect you know what I mean. Small insults, demands that seem justifiable but are actually offensive; the refusal to tolerate the slightest disagreement. Stony silence, followed by a moral lecture on the terrors of damnation that awaited her if she went too far." He sucked on the cigarette, held the smoke inside for several moments, then blew it out. "I've seen him do the same thing to you."

"Simon, don't."

He seemed not to hear her. "I was only seven when she left. I still remember what happened. He knows I remember. It's one of the reasons he hates me."

"He's your father. He doesn't—"

"Of course he does. He hates me because I'm one of the few people who knows the truth of what he is inside."

More smoke, wreathing his head. "There was an argument over supper. He was belittling her, as usual, making her out to be a village idiot in front of me, which was, I think, the thing she resented the most. 'Sons grow up thinking the worst of their mothers as it is without your adding to it,' she finally screamed at him.

"He rose from his chair like the wrath of God, jostling the supper table in such a way that it heaved into her and knocked her chair over. I don't think he meant to do it, but she fell to the floor and came up spitting, with the fire poker clutched in her fist."

"Simon . . . !"

He opened the window and tossed out his half-smoked cigarette. It made a brief, bright flare before disappearing. "The side of her face was bruised and bleeding where it had struck the hearth bricks. She swung the poker at Father, who was backing away from her. I remember thinking that he was a coward at heart, just like me.

"I thought she was going to kill him. But her blow went low and struck the bulk of his shoulder instead, then bounced out of her hand and hit me across the side of my head as it fell. I remember the heavy, numbing pain of it. And I remember her screams, her sobs, her heartrending apologies."

I mustn't allow him to speak to me of such things, Verity told herself. But she was helpless to stop him.

"The next morning she was gone, leaving a note saying she wasn't fit to be a mother. He allowed her to do it. He told me, dispassionately, that she'd abandoned us because she'd gone insane: only a crazy woman would attack her husband with a poker. It was like having my heart ripped out. I yearned to go to her, but I was afraid of him, and besides, I had no idea where she was.

"He never even looked for her. It was almost a year later that we heard from a distant cousin that she'd taken the fever and died." He lit another cigarette. "That's happened to your predecessor, Verity. Are you going to stay here and allow it to happen to you?"

Verity didn't know what to say, what to feel. In a way, she hated him for having told her this ugly thing. Why was he doing this?

It got worse: "When we met you on the train from London, I knew what would happen. You looked so young, and he's always had a fancy for young girls. 'Tis a peculiarity of his. One doesn't expect it in a clergyman, which makes things easy for him. All those girls seeking their pastor's advice during the tumultuous years when their blood is hot and they're feeling guilty about allowing the boys to fondle them in the hedgerows. They come to him for penance, and he's quick to tell them exactly what they must do in order to be absolved."

"I won't listen to another word. You're telling vile, disgusting lies about your father. No matter what happened between him and your mother, it's wrong for you to vent your spleen in such a manner.''

"Haven't you ever wondered why a man of his talents and intellect was assigned to such an insignificant little parish as Trenwythan? The bishop has his suspicions, I'm sure.''

"That's *enough*. I don't believe you. The anger you've been harboring for years has overwhelmed your reason.''

"You don't want to believe it,'' he said pitilessly. "Just as I didn't want to believe how impossible it would be to make Bret love me. None of us wants to believe the worst, particularly if it means we have to give up someone we love.''

"Is that why you're doing this? Have you had a fight with Bret?''

He tossed out his second cigarette and did not answer. Five seconds went by, ten. He stared into her eyes, but she could see that his were blind, looking inward, remembering, reliving. They began to shine with tears that seemed to poise at the rims forever before breaking free and sliding down his cheeks.

"Oh, Simon. My dear, my dear.''

His shoulders began to shake. He wrapped his arms around his middle and shuddered all over. The low sounds he made were those of a beleaguered animal. They were the echoes, she realized, of the sounds that were locked inside her own heart.

She went to him and held him, her petite form sheltering his young man's body. He clung to her as desperately as if she were the mother he had lost. *Which I ought to have tried harder to be*, Verity scolded herself.

How wretched we all are! she thought. *How easily we fail to give of ourselves to the people who need us. How dimly we perceive. How imperfectly we love.*

"I'm sorry, I'm sorry,'' he told her over and over. "I didn't mean to hurt you. Forget what I said, I made it up. It was all—every bit of it—a lie.''

Of all the words he had spoken, these were the only ones she didn't believe.

Chapter Twenty-eight

"You wanted to speak to me?" Bret asked her father, entering his office at teatime one afternoon a few days later.

"I gather you told Simon you wouldn't marry him. I suppose it's just as well, unless you were prepared to be a widow, like so many other young women your age."

"What do you mean?"

"He's joined up. He's gone and offered himself as the latest lamb in the sacrificial slaughter."

"What?"

"I know; I was surprised too. The lad keeps proving he's got more mettle than I thought. Damn fool thing to do, though, the way the casualties are multiplying."

Bret couldn't take it in. How could he do such a thing? Simon had been so happy and proud of what he had accomplished in the air. It didn't seem right to her that such a triumph of spirit should be followed by a disappointment of the heart. And now . . . "How could he pass the medical examination? He's always had so many problems with his heart . . . his lungs . . ."

"Quite normal, according to the doctors who examined him. Course, they'll take anybody now with things going as badly as they are, as long as you've got good reflexes and a sound stomach. No, Simon's healthy all right."

As an onslaught of emotion ripped through her, all she could think of was the way Simon had forced her to look inside her heart. She didn't much care for what she had discovered there—a young woman who'd been so wrapped up in her own dream of love that she'd been blind to everything else, even the hopes and desires of her oldest and dearest friend.

"I've got to stop him," she whispered.

"It's too late," her father said, but Bret barely heard him. She was running, running. He might be able to fly, but, dammit, he couldn't join the army. He was too melancholy, too sensitive, too much the poet. He'd never survive the horrors of combat.

When she reached the vicarage, however, it was indeed too late. Simon had already left for the military training that would enable him to play his own small part in the monumental tragedy that would one day be known as the Great War.

That night Bret went to bed early, low in spirits and utterly exhausted. After failing to stop Simon, she had raced Wulf wildly over the moors until she and her beloved horse were bone- and muscle-weary. As she rode, she could not help but remember the night—it seemed so long ago now—that she'd tried to run away to Arizona. She had met Daniel that night and been drawn to him, which was what had started all this trouble. How long a journey she had made since then, without stirring from Trenwythan! The real adventure in life, it seemed, was not to be found in travel or faraway places, but on the darker and more tumultuous journey to the hidden corners of the human heart.

The corners of her heart, she decided, were dark indeed.

She'd fornicated.

She'd lied.

She'd defied her father and her sister.

She'd betrayed her oldest friend.

"I should have gone to Arizona," she said to Wulf, and the horse angled its head as if in agreement. "I'd have caused a lot less trouble there!"

She had been asleep for a little more than an hour when she was awakened by a sound at her window. Daniel. *I can't,* she thought. *Not tonight; I can't, I can't.*

She rose to let him in. As he swung over the threshold, he grinned at her with the lecherous expression that usually caused a lick of pleasure deep in her belly. But all she could feel tonight was guilt.

"Daniel, I'm very tired."

"Yeah? In that case, I'll do all the hard work while ye jist lie back and enjoy."

He followed as she backed away, making her feel as if he were stalking her. "Honestly, I want to go to sleep."

"I'm here, luv, and I'm mad for 'ee. Hush now and let me stay." His voice was low, enticing, and when he cornered her against the wall and lifted her into his arms, her halfhearted struggles against him wavered and died. "The door," she whispered.

"Unlocked as usual? Well, 'tes easily mended."

He turned the key in the lock, then carried her to bed. No sooner had he laid her down and begun shedding his clothes than she felt her throat close. Tears began to sting her eyes.

"Bret? What's the trouble?"

She couldn't answer. The harder she tried to control her emotions, the more overwhelming they became. A tear escaped, tracking slowly down her cheek. She didn't want to tell him, but she couldn't hold it in. "It's Simon."

His blue eyes instantly darkened with suspicion. "Have ye been seeing him?" He came down partly on top of her, a movement that was meant to assert his dominance. "I'll kill him if he's touched 'ee."

"He asked me to marry him a few days ago."

He cursed. As his hands tightened on her, she quickly added, "I refused, of course. But I feel so guilty. I could see he wasn't taking it well, but I never dreamed he'd do what he's done now."

"Not killed himself, I'm sure. Young Mr. Marrick doesn't have the spine for that."

"He has more spine than we've been giving him credit for. He spent the summer learning how to fly. I never even guessed. I knew Papa was teaching somebody, but I've been so self-involved, or rather so involved with you, that I never thought to ask how Simon was spending his time. He did it to impress me. He thought I believed him a coward and that if I saw him fly I'd fall in love with him."

"Ye haven't, have ye?" She could feel his anger. She'd seen evidence of his quick temper before.

"No, of course not. But when I told him I couldn't marry him, it crushed him. We've been friends forever, and it's inconceivable to me that I should cause him so much pain."

Daniel found it difficult to empathize with Simon Marrick's pain. Bret was different tonight, and that worried him. She was pulling away. In the months that had passed since she'd accepted him as her lover, he had gradually allowed himself to relax, content in his belief that her love for him was real. But, Christ, he didn't like the way she was fussing over Marrick one bit.

He'd fallen hard this time. He'd thought at the start that if anyone was going to be hurt, it would be Bret. But he was in too deep now. He loved her, he *needed* her, and it frightened him.

"Do you know what Simon's done?" she was saying. "He's run off and joined the army. All because I said I wouldn't marry him. He's going to get himself killed in France, and it will be my fault."

"Christ Almighty." Lying beside her, Daniel pulled her tightly against him, breast to breast, thigh to thigh. *Good*, he was thinking. With any luck at all that pale-haired nancy boy *would* get himself killed. "Love, listen to me. If he's chosen to do something so melodramatic, 'tes his responsibility, not yers. Whatever happens to him, 'tes not yer fault."

She sniffled against his shoulder, unconvinced.

"Whatever ye had with him, 'tes in the past now. I don't want ye thinking about him, especially when ye're in bed with me. D'ye hear what I'm telling 'ee? Ye're mine, Bret. Ye belong to me."

"Oh, Daniel, I wish you wouldn't put it quite so—so intensely. I mean, I really don't belong to anybody but myself."

"No, Bret, ye've got that wrong. Ye're mine."

Against her belly she could feel his sex, huge and hard and ready to invade her. She shivered, partly in pleasure, partly in fear. No, not fear exactly. Apprehension? Anticipation? What she felt was so powerful that she couldn't put a name to it.

"I want to hear 'ee say it. I want yer promise that you'll always love me, that you'll never drop me for Marrick or any other of those rich buggers that yer father favors."

"I love you, Daniel. You know that. We belong to each other, like Tristan and Iseult, Romeo and Juliet."

"They died. Swear it." His fingers were hurting, closing on her bare shoulders and biting into her flesh.

"I love you," she repeated, more comfortable with that phrase than the one he demanded. She reached up and with her palms pulled his face down to hers. "You're the only man I think about, the only man I want."

"All right, then. Listen. I think ye should get married. But to me, not Simon Marrick."

This statement, coming after his long months of insistence that they not get married, angered her. "I didn't tell you about Simon in order to get you to compete with him. I told you because I was upset. I needed somebody to talk to. If I can't talk to my lover about the things that upset me, whom can I talk to?"

"I want to marry you. It's got nothing to do with Marrick."

"Forgive me if I find that difficult to believe. You've never wanted to marry me before."

"Which has never upset 'ee as much as 'twould have upset most women. Ye know what I think? I think ye're reluctant to stand up before God and the people of Trenwythan and declare yer love for a man who's so far beneath 'ee."

"You're the one who insisted you'd never compromise your pride by marrying a Trevor!"

"So mebbe I've changed my mind."

"Well, maybe I haven't!"

"Look, Bret, we've been together a year now. It's time to tell yer father about me. Yer sister as well. Tomorrow. It's time to stand up for me. If ye love me, dammit, that's what ye'll do."

"Prove my love, you mean? I don't think I'll ever be able to prove it to your satisfaction. You have no faith. You'll never believe in me—not totally. That's what the curse on our families really means. We can't trust each other, even when we're in love."

"To hell with the bloody curse."

"Your father infected you with it and now you can't let it go. I can't make you happy. The only thing that'll ever make you happy is beating me down, controlling me, striking at my family through me. You don't love me. What I really am to you is the instrument of your revenge."

He punched the pillow, startling her. She rolled away from him, angry and confused. Where was the joy of love, the sweetness, the adventure? Where was the tenderness?

"And if you're going to lose your temper, you can damn well save it for sometime when we have the privacy to scream and yell and throw things. I refuse to do battle with you here in my bedroom, where my father or Mrs. Chenoweth is likely to come running to my rescue. We've been making too much racket as it is."

She could feel him trying to moderate his too-rapid breathing. The mattress groaned as he turned over. "I don't want to battle with 'ee, Bret," he said. His tone was conciliatory, coaxing. Reaching out, he stroked her shoulder. "I want to love 'ee, that's all."

She still felt testy. "That makes too much noise as well."

"I know a way to solve that problem." He took one of the pillows from the headboard and removed its linen slip, then began folding it into a long strip.

"What're you doing?"

"Ye're right to be worried about the noise. Ye make a lot of it when ye thrash and moan and cry out yer pleasure."

"Don't you like it?" she asked, more miffed than ever.

"I love it. But ye're right, we don't want to get caught, at least not before ye've told yer family that we're getting married. Come here, sit up. Open yer mouth."

Mystified, she did as he asked, only to feel the cloth going into her mouth like a gag. He pulled it around to the back of her head and tied the ends together under her hair. "There now. That'll take care of the problem. Tonight ye willna' be able to cry out."

Bret was startled, scared, and then, in a flash, excited. She never knew what to expect next from Daniel. She made an experimental sound. It came out muffled.

Daniel pressed her down. His naked flesh against hers stirred her desires again, particularly when he stroked his sex against her belly, letting her know once again its hardness, its smoothness, its relentless force.

"I can't kiss your mouth, so I'll have to kiss elsewhere," he whispered, pressing his lips against her throat.

The sensation of the gag jammed between her lips and pressed against her tongue was erotic in a totally unexpected way, as was her realization that he could do anything to her and she would be unable to protest. He kept her arms pinned while he explored her throat and downward with his hungry mouth. When his lips closed over a nipple she moaned again. He raised his head and grinned at the faint sound before moving to the other breast and continuing his sensual assault. His teeth scraped her slightly, and she moaned again.

Daniel raised her hands over her head until her fingers were touching the intricately carved wooden bars of the headboard. "Hang on here. Don't let go."

She obeyed, gripping the bars as he slid down and dropped kisses all over her belly and thighs. She felt his hands parting her legs. She was slick and damp down there and his fingers slipped inside her easily. She wriggled and arched against his hand, her muffled moans coming continuously now. She almost cried when he took his hand away. *Don't stop,* she'd have yelled at him, had she been able to speak. My God, she couldn't even beg.

He forced her legs even farther apart and knelt between them, parted her with his fingers, and touched his velvety tongue to that exquisitely sensitive nodule of nerves and flesh. She let go of the headboard and reached down to caress the top of his head while he continued to nibble and stroke.

She was convulsing in her climax when he moved up, still straddling her, and pulled the gag away. His mouth came down on hers, his tongue entering her at the same moment as he thrust between her thighs. He covered her palms with his own, pinning them against the pillow as he slammed his body into hers. She felt helpless, dominated, and now that her excitement had peaked there were threads of misgiving at the edges of her mind. There was something ruthless about Daniel. Something dark.

He began to move more quickly, going deeper every time. He'd never been so rough with her before. At last he moaned and shuddered. "Christ, that was wonderful," he said as he withdrew. He rolled to one side and threw a leg over her possessively, his sweat-slick skin sticking to hers. Bret put arms around him and held him hard. She was trembling a little, her mind and body in a state of upheaval.

"Forget Marrick," Daniel said as his panting slowed. "Ye're mine, Bret Trevor, now and forever."

Bret, who *had* forgotten him, began feeling guilty all over again. "I think you'd better go."

"Not yet. I'm not through with you yet."

The anger that had been rising and falling all evening surged again. Easygoing though her temperament was, she hated to have anybody order her about, and Daniel's high-handedness tonight had crossed every imaginable line. "Daniel, this is my bedroom. What if my father heard you in here?"

"The door's locked," he reminded her.

"He's the master of Cadmon Hall! He's got a duplicate key to every door. What if he'd walked in a few moments ago?"

"I wish he had. I'd have liked him to see what I was doing to his precious daughter."

Somewhere in the region of her heart, Bret felt an icing over. "You can't mean that." She jerked away from him and sat up. "Is that all I really mean to you? Was everybody right about you, after all?"

Daniel raised his head, his expression wary. "No, a'course not. I didn't mean that the way it came out. It's just that—" He stopped, unable to explain himself.

"You meant it exactly the way it came out. That's what's behind your passion, your relentless desire to break into my bedroom and ravage me in my own house. You're attacking my father through me!"

"I wasn't trying to ravage you. I thought you liked it. You're so warm and responsive that I thought we could do anything together. I love you, Bret. Don't look at me that way."

"I did like it. But there's something violent inside you, and it scares me sometimes. This feud between you and my father torments me. I'm torn between the only two men I love. Can't you forgive him, for God's sake? Can't you try to put the past behind you?"

"I love 'ee, Bret, but that's asking too much. Sooner or later ye're going to have to choose between us."

"I won't be forced to make such a diabolical choice."

"Women choose their lovers over their fathers every day. It's what happens when ye marry. It's what happens when ye grow up."

"Keep your voice down. We could still get caught."

"To hell with that." Rising, he threw on his clothes. "It's a choice that wouldn't be so blasted difficult if I were rich like Simon Marrick. Ye wouldn't even hesitate if choosing me didn't mean ye might be flung out onto the heath and forced to live the meager existence of a clay worker's wife."

"That has nothing to do with it!"

He waved his hand around the room. "Ye'll never give this up. I can't say I blame 'ee. If I were 'ee, I sure as hell wouldn't give it up either, for the sake of a warm body and a little heat in the night."

"How dare you denigrate my feelings that way? I *love* you."

He jerked on his boots. "Through the entire history of the world, the rich have never really loved the poor."

"You're so bitter and filled with hatred for the rich that you can't recognize love when it stares you in the face."

He opened the window. "I'm leaving."

"Good. Don't ever come back!"

He whirled around, stalked back to the bed, and grabbed her wrist. "I'll come back all right. And when I do, ye'll welcome me." He inflicted a rough kiss on her mouth. "Ye'll receive me jist as eagerly as ye did tonight. So eagerly, in fact, that I'll have to tie yer gag deeper to stifle yer cries of pleasure at the things I do to 'ee."

"Get out," she said through clenched teeth.

He was a shadow against the moon as he climbed through her window and disappeared.

Chapter Twenty-nine

A little more than a week after Simon's departure, Henry Trevor summoned Verity to Cadmon Hall to announce that at the orders of the War Office he would be leaving shortly for an unknown destination to participate in a war-related activity whose details he was under orders not to divulge.

"You're going to build aeroplanes for them, aren't you?"

"I'm afraid I can't discuss with you the exact nature of my undertaking," Henry said, but Verity knew she had guessed correctly.

"Are you permitted to tell me how long you expect to be away?"

"Long enough to get some plans in place. If all goes as I expect it will, I should be back in the area soon, with a few more people to help me. It will mean dedicating myself completely to the war effort, of course, for the foreseeable future."

"If that is to be the case, who is going to run the clay company? You spend little enough time there as it is, but you do make all the major decisions."

"Not any longer," Henry said with what sounded like satisfaction.

Verity sighed. This damnable war! More than ever she felt as if the entire fabric of her life was unraveling.

Since the morning of her dreadful conversation with Simon, her nervous attacks had assailed her in full force. She was weary from nightly bouts of insomnia, and short-tempered with everyone—parishioners, servants, even her husband. Not that it made any impression on Julian. With the increasing suffering and anxiety generated by the war, demands for his holy offices had become so numerous that he was rarely at home.

"What I would really like to know is how much of this aeroplane design and building is going to be paid for by the government and how much of it will come from our own pockets," she said. "It seems to me that you've already wasted far more than you can afford on this foolish dream of conquering the air."

"Hell's bells and damnation, girl! Are you blind to what's been going on in the world of aviation these last few years? The technical developments have been vast and the hope for the future is great. I tell you the day will come when people will climb aboard my aeroplanes and fly off to another city as casually as they board a train."

"You *are* paying for it."

"If you're worried about your inheritance, don't be. Cadmon Hall and its properties are protected by a complex hierarchy of trusts."

"I'm worried about Cadmon Clay, and so should you be. How long do you suppose you can continue to run the clay business if you pour all the profits into your wretched aeroplane experiments?"

"Long enough to suit me."

Threads of pain were beginning to wrap themselves around her head. She resented her father's stubbornness, his refusal to take her seriously. If only he had been present during the clay strike, he would have seen that she was competent, and a worthy successor to him. "Cadmon Clay is a major employer of many of the men in the region. If we have problems, so will they."

"That's not going to happen. We're the world's primary source."

"It happened in the tin and copper industry right here in Cornwall half a century ago. Our ancestors survived that catastrophe because their holdings were diversified, but many other wealthy Cornishmen did not. The war, if it continues for any length of time, is certain to reduce the demand. Who's going to be able to afford fine china in the middle of a war?"

"Stop haranguing me, Verity. There's a fortune to be made in aviation someday, if making fortunes is so damnably important."

"It's not the making of fortunes I'm worried about. It's the prospect of losing the one you already have."

"Well, Verity, I'm going to rely on you to make certain that doesn't happen. I'm putting you in charge of Cadmon Clay. From now on, you manage the clay company. You will have full responsibility."

She blinked, unable to react.

"It's what you've always wanted, is it not?"

"Yes, of course. But—" She was so surprised she found herself sputtering: "I doubt that the majority of the clay workers will take orders from a woman. The women did, but I don't know about the men."

"I don't see why they shouldn't. You've proven your abilities. Everybody knows what you pulled off during the strike, and in addition you manage your own household, you manage St. Catherine's, and for all I know to the contrary, you manage the entire parish of Trenwythan."

But I don't, Verity thought. *That's precisely the problem: Where Julian is concerned, I'm silent, dependent, and I do what I'm told.*

"Your administrative abilities are excellent," her father went on, "and as for your financial abilities, they're clearly superior to mine. The men at Cadmon Clay know and respect you. Anyway, if this war continues the way it's going, women'll be running the factories all over England, and no doubt doing a damn fine job."

She wanted to do it, she realized. The idea of taking over in her father's place made her feel challenged, excited, alive. "I have my responsibilities to the parish," she told him. "It's out of the question that I should give those up. Even if I wanted to, Julian would never allow it."

"To the devil with Julian. What good is he? After seven years he hasn't even provided me with a grandchild. As for you, you're looking pale and lackluster these days, Verity. You need a change. You've always been fascinated with the clay company, starting all those years ago when your grandfather was still alive. I'm offering you the chance to pursue that interest, and you'd be a fool to pass it up. Besides—" he paused for a moment, "I need you."

Magic words. "I'll speak to my husband," she said.

* * *

"Absolutely not."

"But, Julian, I've explained to you. There's nobody else. The clay company employs dozens of workers. Somebody has to run it."

"Henry can hire a competent administrator. I've never understood why a man of his place in society should dirty his hands with that business anyway."

"The Trevors have always done it. And we haven't hired administrators; we've worked shoulder to shoulder with our employees. It's a family tradition."

"You are hardly in a position now to carry on the family traditions."

"Nevertheless, this is wartime, the circumstances are unusual, and my father has requested my help."

"Your father is no longer your lord and master, Verity. As a married woman, your duties and responsibilities lie elsewhere. If your father was so concerned about preserving family traditions, he would have remarried years ago and had himself a couple of sons."

His arrogant criticism of her father angered Verity, but she forced herself to focus on what she hoped would be the crux of her argument: "I've thought this through carefully, Julian. I need not neglect my work in the parish. Cadmon Clay won't take up all my time. My father has managed to stay at the helm these last several years despite the time he's spent designing, building, and test flying his aeroplanes. There's no indication that Cadmon Clay has suffered as a result."

This wasn't entirely true, but Verity doubted that Julian realized it. Not even during the strike had he expressed the slightest degree of interest in anything that concerned Cadmon Clay. "I will follow his model, spending most of my time on my parish activities and devoting only, say, three or four mornings per week to Cadmon Clay." She did not add that she already devoted at least this much time to the clay company. Her husband was unaware of the afternoon hours she spent there.

"It's out of the question. Tell your father that his request is unreasonable and that you cannot possibly comply."

"Julian, I want to do it."

"Then I'll speak to him myself. I will not allow my wife—the companion and helpmeet of the vicar of St. Catherine's—to participate in such an outlandish experiment. Now, that's the end of it. I'm late for a parish meeting, and I'm certain you have your own duties around the household to attend to."

"As a matter of fact, I don't. I finished my daily work, including my war work, hours ago."

His smile was nasty. "Then consider visiting the church and going humbly down on your knees before the Lord. Consider imploring Him to make you less prideful, less rebellious, less argumentative, and more accepting of your lot. Consider that you are an arrogant sinner whose soul is in dire need of cleansing and purgation. Prostrate yourself, Verity. I expect to find you reconciled to the will of God when I return later this evening."

He didn't care about the will of God. Damn him! All he cared about was that she should be reconciled to the will of Julian Marrick.

Bret stood at her window, staring out morosely at the waning moon. She searched the grounds below for any sign of a shadowy figure, any trace of her lover. But nothing stirred except an occasional creature of the night.

She had spent an entire week and three days without seeing or hearing from Daniel Carne, and she couldn't remember a time in her life when she'd been so unhappy. It served her right, she thought. This was the sort of misery one ought to expect for passionately flinging oneself into a love affair. This was what happened to intrepid adventuresses who failed to beware their passionate natures.

Sometimes she imagined herself to be an evil, immoral woman. She would wake up in the night and hear the sound of her own quick breathing and think, *My God, what would Verity think of me if she knew the whole story?* And Papa—how disappointed in her he would be. Much as she hated to admit it, her sister had been right to lecture her last summer. A few kisses, some sweet caresses, and she'd turned into a wanton woman!

Bret left the window and sat at her desk. Drawing out a piece of writing paper, she inked up her pen and began to scribble:

Dear Mr. Slayton,

I've gotten myself into the most dreadful scrape. Do you remember Daniel, my clay worker friend? The one who's such a relentless enemy of my father? Well, I've been neglecting to tell you that I fell in love with him last summer, and now he wants to marry me, which, when Papa learns of it, will probably make him crash all his aeroplanes. What's odd about it, I'm not entirely convinced I ought to marry him. We had an awful fight, and now, instead of dreaming about living with him forever and raising his children in some romantic moorland cottage somewhere, I'm back to my old fantasies about studying art in Italy and sculpting naked men.

I haven't had a letter from you for ages. I miss hearing from you because I enjoy our correspondence so much. Please write soon.

All my affection and best wishes,

Bret

She was recopying the letter when she heard a curious clunk against her windowpane. Her heart slammed once, then she jumped up and ran to the window. Daniel was standing there, still, silent, below her window in the shadow of the oak. There, in the starlight, his black hair falling into his eyes, he looked like a ghost. But the rough whisker shadow on his cheeks and the solid musculature of his stocky body were those of a man, as was the smoky expression in his eyes as they fixed upon her fragile nightgown billowing in the breeze.

He swung up into the oak and started climbing. When he reached the window ledge, she threw her arms around him so passionately that she nearly knocked him back down to the ground.

His mouth touched the corner of one eye, the bridge of her nose, the point of her chin. Her lips. Her mouth. Inside. She went limp against him. He looped one arm under her and lifted her off her feet and carried her to bed.

"You wretch," she whispered as he stretched out full length beside her. The mattress sank under his weight, tipping her toward him. He combed his fingers through her hair, then kissed her forehead, her cheeks, her eyelids, the end of her nose. "I hate you for tormenting me!"

"I hate 'ee, too," he murmured, kissing her soundly.

"I really despise you," she said as he began shedding his garments.

"Show me," he retorted as he covered her, warm and hard and oh-so-lovely. "Show me how much ye hate me and despise me."

"I've been so angry and so wretched and so sad and I hate feeling that way. Now I'm going to have my *revenge*."

"Yeah? How?"

She rolled on top of him and tried to look fierce. But she had begun to giggle, which tended to spoil the effect.

"Feel me trembling," he said, his blue eyes dancing. Gently with the tip of his finger he brushed her nipple. Then he lifted his hand until it hovered half an inch above her breast. She needed the contact so much that she arched to press herself against that teasing hand. He grinned, his teeth a flash of white against his dark complexion. He hadn't shaved and his growing whiskers made him look hard and tough and thoroughly disreputable.

"You still want me, don't 'ee?"

"Bad-tempered wretch that you are, I still want you, Daniel Carne."

That night Verity lay in her cold bedroom in the vicarage, staring into the dying coals of the fire. She had taken her husband's advice and spent an hour on her knees, praying for guidance. A course of action had come to her, whether in answer to her prayers or not, she had no idea. It had been a long time since she'd had much faith in prayer.

Marriage was a legal contract entered into by two consenting adults. She was one-half of a partnership. Her union with Julian might not be the most loving or romantic partnership in the world, but it was a fait accompli that she would have to endure until she and her husband were parted by death. This being so, there were several things about their contract that she intended to change.

He was still downstairs; she heard him moving about in his study. She must go to him. It had been months since he last came to her.

She rose. Her fingers were cold as they tied the silk lacings of her mother's crimson night robe. She would not wear one of the girlish shifts he favored, not tonight.

Pulling on a dressing gown, she went downstairs. He was there in the study, his eyes hidden behind the spectacles he used for reading and writing, dipping his pen in and out of an inkwell as he scribbled. She noticed that his fingers seemed thicker, coordinating with his waistline and the increasing bulk of his buttocks. He had become quite the gourmand, and it showed.

He was engrossed in his writing, so she tapped lightly on the panel of the half-open door. Startled, he dropped his pen. His face was mottled with patches of red that faded to pale as he met her eyes. He was breathing hard, as if from exercise—or sermonizing—and for a moment she wondered if he might be ill. With his size and his weight, he was exactly the sort of man likely to keel over from apoplexy or a heart seizure.

"What do you want at this hour? I expected you to have been asleep long ago." As he spoke Verity noticed that he slid a blank piece of paper over the one he was writing upon, then gathered a sheaf of papers together and ostentatiously shuffled them.

"I couldn't sleep." She advanced slowly into the room. "Are you working?"

He tied an imperial purple ribbon around the pile of papers he had made. "I was adding the finishing touches to my sermon."

This, she was certain, was a lie. He had been right in the middle of something, and excited about it, too. Her curiosity was aroused. What was he hiding?

"What is the subject of tomorrow's sermon?"

"I am going to discuss the fact that inside every human soul there is the Pit that is like unto the Pit of Hell, the place where every demon ever recorded in Holy Scriptures resides. This Pit is inside you, and it is inside me." His voice deepened as he spoke, and for an instant it felt to her as if he were thundering from the pulpit. "May the Lord have mercy on us all."

Verity shuddered. She could see into her own pit much more clearly than ever before. Married to Julian, she could no longer conceive of a God of mercy. There existed a wrathful God, though. She had felt His touch upon her.

"What do you want, Verity?"

She summoned a smile, tried to make it convincing. "It's cold up there, and I was wondering when you would be coming to bed." She paused. "It's Saturday night, and there was a time when we used to spend our Saturday nights more pleasantly."

His annoyance at being interrupted changed to surprise as he absorbed her meaning. Wariness warred with gratification in his face. "I was not aware that you missed our Saturday nights."

I don't. But she was his wife. It was a promise made for all time, before God, and she had to do what she could to make it a promise she could keep. So she smiled, as if in assent.

Julian followed her up to the bedroom and waited while she removed her dressing gown. When he saw what she was wearing, his expression altered. "I told you never to appear before me in that garment again."

She had expected this reaction, so she remained calm. She threw back her shoulders to demonstrate that she was not ashamed of her body. "Look at me, Julian. I am no longer the young girl you married. I am a woman with the shape of a woman. From now on I wish to be treated like an adult, both in bed and out of it."

There was a long silence that she was unable to interpret. At last her husband said, "I am not entirely sure I understand what you mean. You are my wife. I treat you as such."

"You treat me like a child."

"My dear, you are considerably younger than I."

"That doesn't matter. Maybe it bore some significance when we met, but I've changed since then. I am approaching thirty years of age. I'm tired of perpetually being treated as if I were your daughter or your servant. I'm tired of choking back every impulse I have to disagree with you. And I'm tired of wearing those childish cotton nightgowns to bed every night."

"You may believe yourself to be a mature woman, but you're whining like a child."

"You see! That's exactly what I mean. You sound so superior. What gives you the right to sit in judgment over me?"

"I am your husband: that gives me the right. The Bible ordains that a wife shall be obedient to her husband in all things. But quite apart from that, I am a man, your elder, and a minister of the Lord, who is most certainly your moral and intellectual superior."

Most people, she knew, would agree with him. How could she argue with such a widely accepted sentiment? The suffragettes had been asserting the rights and value of women for years, only to endure mockery, not only from men but from other women as well.

"It is extremely unfortunate that you have failed to produce a child," he went on. "If you'd had the normal responsibilities of motherhood and child rearing, you would have no time to fantasize about managing your father's china-clay business. As it is, perhaps you imagine yourself inferior to other women who are fulfilling the purpose for which God made them. But I assure you, my dear, that God does have a purpose for you. It is not always easy to understand the meaning of His plan, but—"

"I'm tired of hearing about God's precious plan! I don't believe there is such a plan, because if there were, I can see no reason it should so favor the males of the human race. I'm not even sure I believe in God."

"If you are having a crisis of faith, you will, of course, begin to question everything. I will pray for you to come to your senses. Come, let us pray together."

"It's not a crisis of faith, Julian. It's a crisis in our marriage. If you continue to fail to acknowledge it as such, I don't know what's going to happen.''

"What, may I ask, does that mean?" His voice was icy now. "Are you threatening me in some manner?"

"Of course not. All I want is that you should regard me as your partner and your equal, and to understand that as such I am entitled to make the important decisions that will determine the course of my life. I intend to start doing that. Immediately. My first decision is to accept my father's commission to manage Cadmon Clay. I'm sorry if you don't approve, but I really don't see how you can stop me."

"I can stop you," he said quietly, "by forbidding you to do any such thing."

"Then I must defy you, Julian."

From behind his hooded eyes something lashed at her that hinted at the snake beneath the skin. "Do you dare to question me, your lord and master?"

"I don't care for the term. It is degrading, and besides—"

"But that is what I am to you, my dear. You swore before God to love, honor, and obey. You have not been very obedient lately. I will not tolerate disobedience. I did not tolerate it in my first wife, nor do I tolerate it in my son."

"I hardly think—"

He took a step toward her. "It is in direct opposition to God's plan for you even to consider working in a claypit with common laborers, inspiring the devil knows what manner of lascivious fantasies." Moving closer, he fingered the golden dragons on her nightgown. "But perhaps you would enjoy the thought of wantonly stimulating those men? Perhaps a woman who would deliberately come to her husband clad in such a manner takes pleasure in the thought of them panting after her—common men, brutal men, animals?"

She backed away from him, frightened now.

"Take it off."

"No, Julian, I—"

He raised his palm as if to slap her. "Remove that robe of Satan before I rip it from your body."

Something crashed and heaved inside her, releasing the

first steamy tendrils of the rage she'd bottled up for years. "Rip it, then, for I shall wear what I choose."

This time the blow did fall, an open-handed slap that sent her reeling. "You leave me no choice, for you *shall* obey. For as St. Paul said to the Ephesians, 'Wives, submit yourselves unto your husbands, as unto the Lord. For the husband is the head of the wife, even as Christ is the head of the church . . . so let the wives be subject to their husbands in every thing.' "

He ripped the crimson silk from her flinching body. Before her eyes he tore it into shreds—her mother's beautiful nightgown from China—and tossed it into the hearth. It sent up an acrid odor as the flames caught and consumed the fragile material.

Verity's cry of anguish prompted another vicious slap across her mouth. "On your knees!"

She blinked at him, naked and vulnerable, dizzy and sick to her stomach. She could see nothing, suddenly, but Jory Carne and his foulmouthed friends and the way they had treated her on the night when this man—her hero—had swept on horseback to her rescue.

"On your knees to your lord and master, wife. On your knees to me as I go down upon my knees to God, for I am to you what our Maker is to me, and you shall acknowledge it or feel the full fury of my righteous wrath."

"I will divorce you," she heard herself say. "If you don't take your hands off me right now, I will divorce you and destroy your precious career."

A blow again, but this time the fist was closed. Clever—it was to the side of her head where her hair would cover the bruise and nobody would know. She reeled sideways, feeling him catch her and force her down before him until she was on her knees in the posture he desired and he was looming above her, huge with all the bulky indignation of an angry god.

"You will now apologize."

She bowed her head and remained mute. She expected another blow, but instead his hands fastened on her bare breasts and tightened, squeezing the nipples until she gasped in pain. "Like a wanton whore you expect pleasure and luxury. The joys of marriage, you say? What do you know of such lechery? You were a young girl when I married you. A virgin with an unformed body and a shy look of innocence in your eyes. Don't you understand that I loved you that way? That if God could grant me one wish, it would be that you had forever remained a sweet, fresh, compliant young girl? Instead you've become a woman and a whore."

He was mad, she thought. Not completely, of course; in most ways he was sane, but when it came to women and wives and sex, his predilection was for young girls whom he could dominate entirely, slavish creatures who could spare him the terror of confronting the fact of his own aging. The pieces of it had all been there before—the girlish nightgowns, his refusal to acknowledge her as an adult, and Simon's description of Julian's treatment of his first wife, which she had not wanted to believe. Her husband was a man with an obsession, who would never allow her to grow up.

Leaving her cowering on the floor, he crossed to her dressing table and jerked open her drawers until he found a white cotton nightgown. While his back was turned Verity stumbled to her feet, with every intention of running from the room, but he was too quick for her. His hands were harsh on her body as he grabbed her and dragged her toward the bed. She could feel the violence in him and was afraid to struggle, lest he strike her again.

He thrust the childish nightgown over her head and jerked it down over her squirming body, leaving her belly and her thighs bare. "No!" she cried, as he held her down with one iron arm over her breasts and unbuttoned his trousers with his free hand. Then he was upon her. Bile rose in her throat. Her husband was raping her and there was no law on earth or in heaven that would condemn him for it.

Chapter Thirty

From the bed she slipped quietly, quietly, to the floor. The chill of bare feet on bare wood, the iciness of a bedroom without a fire in the hearth, permeated her body, which was without a warmer covering than a white cotton nightgown.

She didn't stop for shoes, clothes. Julian was asleep. She had not stirred until he was snoring heavily, yet still she was terrified that he should wake before she made good her escape.

Sneaking out of the bedroom and into the carpeted hallway, she left the door behind her open a crack because of the squeaky latch on its handle. Many of the floorboards of the old house creaked; she tried to avoid them and failed. Every sound she made sent renewed shocks through her overstimulated nerves. If he should wake . . .

Down the staircase to the front hallway. Into the cloak room where there were overcoats for her body and Wellingtons for her feet. The door to his study was open, as she had left it when they had precipitously made their way upstairs. The gas jet in there was still burning, a lack of economy that Julian would never have been guilty of had he not been overwrought.

Verity, excellent manager and perfect housewife, mocked herself for the impulse that led her to enter the study to shut off the errant lamp. As she reached for the switch she noticed the sheaf of papers on her husband's desk. She had an image of him furiously writing, then thrusting his notes into that pile. She remembered his anger and impatience at being interrupted. His quick loss of temper. Composing his next sermon, he had told her. He was far too proud of his sermons to hide them away, even in their unperfected state.

She left the light on and moved across the room to the desk. It took her several minutes to find what she was looking for; the sheaf of papers was thick. It was mostly correspondence, some of it berating the bishop for denying him a richer and more important living than the remote St. Catherine's of Trenwythan, Cornwall.

The paper was crisp, the ink fresh. A letter. "My dearest Tess," it began, an exhortation that proved to be the least effusive part of the epistle.

> In vain have I struggled against the baser desires of my body, but there is no salvation from the yearning that infects me every time you pass me on the stairway, brush by me in the hall. My nights without you are darker and more full of torment than a sojourn in Hell. My days, which ought to be spent in prayer, and shepherding my flock, are tainted with the cruel, lascivious temptation of seeking you out and finding you alone. But you avoid me, cruel Tess, as if you had no recollection of the precious moments you have spent in my arms.
>
> You may forget them, but I cannot! My mind and senses are overflowing with memories of your sweet, youthful body, your tender breasts, more lovely than the fruit of Eden, your slim and agile hips, your cries of wonder and of pleasure when I instruct you in mysteries of love. You must remember these things, too, dear Tess, and yet you avoid me, leaving me more thirsty than a pilgrim in the harshest desert, more hungry than a tiger in pursuit of a gazelle. I cannot endure your reticence any longer. The anguish I have been enduring is far beyond anything that I have

The writing broke off in a splatter of ink. *This must have been where I interrupted him,* Verity thought, with what remnants of her wits remained.

Julian, her husband. Tess, the parlor maid. The impulse to laugh wildly was so strong in her that she would have given in to it, surely, had she not been so determined upon escape.

Her next-strongest impulse was to light a bonfire in the hearth and watch the letter curl and burn. She resisted this also. Instead she folded the evidence of her husband's infidelity and tucked it into the pocket of the overcoat she had donned.

"I love you."

"I love 'ee, too. Ye're so sweet. Yer eyes, yer hair. I want to go on looking at them forever."

"I love your nose."

"Don't be silly; 'tes a huge, ugly thing."

"Is not."

"Is too."

"I love this, too."

"Now that's definitely a huge, ugly thing."

Bret, giggling: "It's huge but it's not ugly."

"I think 'tes getting even huger."

"I know what we can do about that."

"Mmm. Ye're so— Ah, yes. Christ. Don't stop."

"I'm not going to stop," Bret whispered, "until you're done."

They were trying to be quiet. Daniel had locked the door to the corridor, insisting that they were secure, but Bret couldn't relax entirely. Although her wing of the house had been empty ever since Verity had left home to marry Julian, she could not free herself of her illogical fear of discovery.

Daniel thought her apprehensions silly, particularly since her father's suite was in the east wing and the servants slept upstairs. He couldn't imagine a safer or more comfortable place, he said, for two lovers to meet.

She sensed that there was more to it than that. There was something exciting to him, she knew, about making forbidden love within the ancient walls of Cadmon Hall. Still, she was reluctant to argue after what had happened between them last time. When things were good, they were ever so lovely, and she was determined to hold on to that loveliness for as long as she possibly could.

"I love you, Daniel," she whispered, holding his dark head to her breasts the way she imagined a mother might hold a child.

"Ye're mine forever," came the familiar refrain.

* * *

A motorcar pulled up in the circular drive at the front of the building, and a dark-clad figure stepped out and climbed the steps to the huge oaken door with its baronial coat of arms. She let herself in with a key and quieted the dogs, which were barking, by removing her gloves and allowing them to inhale her familiar scent. Tom, the footman, stumbled out into the Great Hall, awakened by the commotion, but subsided when he saw who the intruder was.

"I'm sorry, Miz Verity, I didna' know 'twas 'ee."

"That's all right, Tom. I don't want to disturb anyone. My father needn't know I'm here until the morning."

"I'll wake Mrs. Chenoweth so she can see to preparin' a room for 'ee, shall I?"

"No, don't bother her. I'll go on up to my old room. If you'll just get me a candle, I'll be fine."

"Right, ma'am. Here ye are, then."

The house was dark and huge and shadowed, she thought, as she climbed the great staircase to the second story. But it was a familiar darkness, quite unlike that which pervaded the vicarage. She felt safe here. Battered in body and spirit, yes, but safe.

She had decided that she would never pass another night under the same roof with the Reverend Julian Marrick.

As she drifted toward sleep, Verity thought of Jory Carne. His pale face and hair, his shepherd's pipe, the way he danced around Grandpa's corpse. His hands upon her; the reeking of his breath. Her terror and her hatred.

Then she was a child again, frozen in her narrow bed, haunted by the evil of her anger. She had wished her stepmother dead and twenty-four hours later it had happened. She had wished all manner of violence upon the person of Jory Carne, who had assaulted her. The same night, he, too, had died. In her dream she had great power. Like a goddess, she had within her the power to kill.

She woke to the sound of her baby sister crying. She rose from bed, disoriented, and walked through the nursery that adjoined her old bedroom to the door on the far side, which led to a private bath, and beyond, to Elizabeth's bedroom. By the time she reached the bath, she was awake enough to know where she was. Bret was no longer a child; she could not be crying for milk. Yet there was a sound disturbing the quiet of the night. A curious moaning, accompanied by a faint creaking of wood.

Someone moaned again, loudly this time, an animalistic sound that reminded Verity of all the superstitious tales the servants used to tell of the ghosts who haunted Cadmon Hall. The creaking grew louder and faster, and Verity shook her head in denial even as she recognized the significance of its rhythmic nature.

She entered the bath. The door on the connecting side lay halfway open, revealing the shadows of her sister's room. There were no lamps lit, but the moon was high tonight and its light entered through the open curtains.

The old wood of her sister's bedstead groaned and protested under the weight of two grappling lovers as Verity, appalled, clutched at the handle of the bathroom door, which emitted a high-pitched squeak.

The creaking abruptly ceased. There was silence for a moment, followed by a breathless masculine voice saying, "What is it?"

"Ssh. I thought I heard something."

" 'Tes all right. We're safe, I promise 'ee."

"I tell you, I heard something."

There was a laugh in the rough, uncultured, masculine voice that answered, "Christ, lass, ye needn't be so nervous all the time."

Verity had stopped breathing, her heart denying what her senses told her. Confusion clawed in her and she would have fled had Bret not chosen that moment to sit up. Verity saw her wild hair all tousled about her shoulders, her bare limbs flashing, her eyes catching and reflecting the moonlight as she glanced toward the spot where Verity stood, frozen. Then Bret let out a cry, which brought her lover's face around and into view.

Daniel Carne.

It was too much. After everything else that had happened this night, it was just too much. Verity began to laugh. Louder and louder still, the sound bounced off the ceiling, slammed into the walls, beat against the wooden furnishings, and shook the diamond-paned windows. Beneath the wild sound of her laughter she seemed to hear the high-pitched music of a shepherd's pipe, trilling out in proud, malicious exultation.

Jory Carne had had his revenge, after all.

For Bret, the next few minutes were the most humiliating she had ever experienced. The cold brightness of the moon; the whirl of cloth as Daniel protected her with what he could reach of the bedclothes; his anger—directed mostly at himself for failing to secure their privacy—her shame: it was awful.

And it degenerated even further. Verity's hysterical laughter alerted the servants, who alerted their master, and within the next few minutes her sister's racket had been reduced to raindrops in the deluge of Henry Trevor's wrath.

The image would remain with her forever. Her father in his dressing gown, cradling a rifle in his arms, and Daniel, stark naked, confronting him. She thought they were going to kill each other. The hatred and the accusations flew, compounded by Verity's cold declaration that what she had witnessed was clearly a rape, and Bret's protestations that she and Daniel were in love.

"Rape, is it?" Henry was shouting. "You bastard, I'll see you in jail, I'll see you hanged! Everyone knows your hatred for me, but for you to assault the sweetest and most innocent member of my family to relieve your rotten spite is an offense against nature!"

"He didn't, he'd never—"

"Ye're bloody wrong, Trevor—"

"I love him, Papa—"

"Yer daughter and me are going to be wed."

Only the last statement registered on Henry Trevor, who said, "Is that the rot you've been feeding her? Well, she may be young and romantic enough to believe it, but this girl's not for you and you know it." He had raised his rifle, the barrel pointed directly at Daniel's chest. His hands were shaking and Bret was terrified. "Prison's for you, Carne. Or, better yet, the trenches. We'll soon see how many women you can rape while pinned down under Jerry's advancing forces. Now step away from her. D'you hear? You've defiled her with your touch for the last goddamn time.''

"Oh, stop yer bluster. I'm marrying her, no matter what ye or anybody else thinks of it. Tell him, Bret.''

"I love him, Papa, and we want to be together. Now please, please put away your gun.''

"You little fool! The day you marry him will be the last day you ever set your eyes on me!''

"Papa!''

"You're honestly going to stand there and tell me that you would turn your back on your family, your friends, your home, your heritage, your dogs and your horses and your blasted rosebushes, your sunny future, your entire *life* for this greedy, slanderous bastard who, along with his hell-burnt father, has made my life and your sister's miserable? Dammit, daughter, is that what you're telling me?''

The moment would often come back to haunt her, but the question didn't seem important; she couldn't foresee the way it would resonate into the future. To her it was silly and bombastic and unworthy of an answer. The only thing that mattered was the loaded rifle that was pointed at her lover's heart. If she didn't do something to defuse the situation, Daniel would die and her father really would be the murderer of one of the Carnes.

And thus she made her crucial mistake. She hesitated, trying to figure out how to get Daniel safely out of the room.

Her lover turned his anger on her. "Why aren't ye answering him? What d'ye have to do, think it over? God damn you, Bret! Ye tell him this wasn't just some cheap and tawdry coupling. Ye tell him, blast ye, that ye and I are betrothed and that ye'll not hesitate to turn yer back on him and yer sister and everything else and come live in a bloody ditch with me if that's the way it has to be.''

Close to tears, Bret said, "I love you, Daniel, but I won't have your words put into my mouth. I've never actually promised to marry anybody, and I'm getting pretty tired of the way first Simon and now you keep putting so much pressure on me!''

Henry pounced at once. "There, you see, Carne, so much for your clever schemes. If you thought to get your filthy hands on my clay and my house and my estates by seducing this girl into wedding you, you've missed your shot, boy! The more fool you. No Trevor could ever truly love a Carne.''

Bret saw the look on Daniel's face and instinctively put her hand on his arm. ''Daniel, no, it's not true,'' she said, but it was too late. Her lover lifted his foot and kicked aside the rifle, then slammed into her father's face and body with vicious fists. Henry fell backward, striking his head against the wall, but he was a big man, and with a furious shake of his head he recovered his senses and came after Daniel with a roar.

''Stop it! Both of you stop it!'' Bret cried, throwing herself between them. Verity, meanwhile, was calling for assistance from the servants, which made everyone's humiliation worse. She managed to restrain their father, while Bret held on to Daniel, who, in his rage, lifted his hand to take a swat at her as well. Bret ducked, avoiding the blow, but it reminded her of everything she'd heard about the domestic violence of Jory Carne.

She thought of the war, with all its killing. Why was there so much violence in the members of the male sex? Did they seriously think it would accomplish anything to strike, to hit, to kill?

''Go home,'' she said to Daniel. ''And don't you ever dare lift your hand to me in anger again.''

She was about to address a similarly scathing remark to her father, but he was quicker, shouting at Daniel, ''Either you go voluntarily into the army and expend your violence where it'll do some good, fighting for your country, or you go to gaol, charged with assaulting me. If it weren't up to me to protect the good name of this family, by God, I'd have you charged with rape as well.''

''To hell with 'ee, Trevor. Charge me with whatever ye please; I don't give a damn.'' His Gypsy blue eyes burned right through into Bret's soul as he continued, ''Maybe ye're right, anyway. Maybe no Trevor could truly love a Carne. Maybe all she can do is fuck one.''

''Daniel!''

''To hell with 'ee as well, Bret,'' he said as he stalked out.

Chapter Thirty-one

They took turns at her, Verity and her father. She expected them to call in Julian as well, but, oddly enough, nobody made any mention of him.

Although it was her father who had threatened Daniel, it was Verity who was the most ruthless, the most pitiless, the most deaf to Bret's protests and explanations in the aftermath. She was transformed into an avenging goddess. Bret had transgressed, and there was to be no forgiveness, no understanding.

Verity ordered her to write a letter to Daniel telling him that it was over. That she would never see him again. That she would marry a man of her own class and breeding, a suitable match, approved by her family. That she didn't love him and never had.

Verity informed her that if she refused to write the letter, her lover would be turned over to the police. He would go to prison, or worse, to the front lines in France, where he would surely be killed, and his dreams of making his little clay company into a business of consequence would be dashed forever.

When Bret cried and begged her to relent, Verity turned her face away. "If you persist in this course, I will never forgive you," she told her sister, her voice as hard as stone.

Love cast down.

The truth trampled.

Daniel had been right—there was no justice for the poor.

Bret's misery boiled over. She was ashamed, afterward, of the angry words that poured out of her never-very-tactful mouth.

To her father, who was still storming on about magistrates and prison and forced marches to the trenches, Bret said, "It serves you right that Daniel hates you. For all I know, you *did* murder his father. You certainly acted as if you meant to murder Daniel, waving that rifle around like a madman. I wouldn't put anything past you, Father!"

"Then you won't put this past me, will you?" Henry said and cuffed her soundly across the mouth. "Now sit down as your sister ordered and write that letter, or by God I'll see that cocksure young mongrel rotting in gaol if I have to sell off every aeroplane I own to bribe every judge in Cornwall. You'll inscribe the bloody letter and then you'll go upstairs and pack your things because I'm sending you to my sister in London. I don't want to see your face again until you're decently married to someone your Dorothy deems suitable."

"Then you'll never see it again, because I'll never marry anybody except Daniel, whom I love with all my heart and soul!"

Henry muttered something about the foolishness of the young and slammed out to console himself with his aeroplanes.

To Verity, Bret said, "I hate you for the way you're behaving. You're my sister, you're supposed to understand me. But you're jealous, aren't you? You're married to that horrid hypocrite who rants and raves about lust and sin during his Sunday sermons while spending the rest of the week trying to get his hands on the young women of the parish. Yes!" she added when Verity whitened. "Including me, his own sister-in-law. Daniel Carne is worth ten Julian Marricks!"

Verity did not reprimand her for her appalling remarks, which Bret regretted the moment they were out of her mouth. Instead Verity said, quietly but with unswerving conviction, "You are going to London. You will pursue your art. You will forget Daniel Carne. You will mature into a sensible and responsible young woman, and one day, with a husband or without one, you will return to Trenwythan and work with me at the clay company, designing and molding the china that is going to make us both famous."

"That is your dream, Verity, not mine."

"You will do it, nevertheless. Now sit down and write that letter."

For Daniel's sake, she obeyed. But she left out the part about not loving him. Never, never would she tell that lie.

Verity drove fast, her head scarf blowing in the wind, the controlled rage in her body echoing the leashed violence of her father's sleek automobile as it pulled her around curves and flattened her against the back of the leather seat as she accelerated. The road to Carne Clay was a steep pitted track barely wide enough for a china-clay wagon, but the motorcar took its challenges without faltering.

Daniel Carne had established his modest china-clay outfit on a desolate hillside not far from Cadmon Tor. Verity took note of the looks of envy and curiosity she received from two young men in the clay-worker's caps when she pulled the motorcar, now generously spattered with mud, onto the grassy slope across from the corrugated tin building that Carne used as an office. The two workers—all he could afford to pay, no doubt—were loading white blocks of clay from the linhay onto a wagon for the journey to the port of Charlestown, but they stopped their work to stare as she emerged from the car.

"Where is Carne?" she asked.

"The master's within, ma'am," one of the men replied, nodding to the shack. The master. Verity was amused at the characterization. Master of what? She glanced around the tiny site with disdain, then went to the door, knocked once, and entered.

"Mr. Carne," she said.

Daniel rose from his desk chair, where he had been writing in an account book. He looked her up and down scathingly. "Mrs. Marrick," he returned in a barely civil tone.

Without invitation, she seated herself in the chair he had just vacated and looked around the tiny, dingy office with undisguised contempt. An ugly pine desk took up most of the room. It had six drawers, a large work space that was almost totally obscured by files, books, ledgers, inkwells, and pens, and a greasy black typewriter. At least he kept things neat. The piles were orderly and free of dust.

"What do ye want?"

She felt no trace of anxiety. She had been tempered and made strong. She opened her purse and handed him Bret's letter. He opened it, read it, then tossed it down.

"What the hell did ye do to make her write this? Starve her? Beat her? D'ye think me a fool to believe this?"

"She wrote the letter reluctantly, that is true. But she wrote it. She has come to realize that her future is not with you. It was her own decision." She paused. "You must have expected it. It was clear the other night that you didn't really believe she would ever marry you."

She saw from the despair that gleamed for a moment in his eyes that she was right. He had never been sure of Bret, never completely able to imagine that the things he'd dreamed of would come to him so easily.

"Ye couldn't make her tell me this in person, could ye, though? How firmly will her decision stand when I touch her, when I take her in my arms?"

"You had your chance for that. It's over, whether you want to admit it or not. Our father has taken her away from here. They left early this morning. You won't see her again."

His face whitened and Verity felt the old bite of envy. What must it be like to be loved so passionately? Nobody had ever felt that way about her.

"Cadmon Hall is Bret's home. Ye can't keep her away forever. Someday she'll come back, and I'll be waiting."

"You're wrong, Mr. Carne. I am the eldest and the heir. Cadmon Hall is my home, not Bret's. She will marry and go to live with her husband, quite possibly in some distant part of the country. You will never have her."

"Then why are 'ee here?"

He was not a fool. He knew Bret's letter need not have been hand delivered; for that matter, he knew that there need not have been any letter at all. The fact that they were acknowledging his existence testified to his power . . . and Bret's devotion.

"Ye're afraid, aren't 'ee? Ye're afraid I'll go find her and bring her back."

"She doesn't want to see you again," Verity countered. "You've had some occasion, I suspect, to see how stubborn she is. I doubt that we could have forced her to write that letter, much less dragged her from this place, if, deep down, she were not seeking a way out of this involvement with you.''

Her point. He avoided her eyes.

''I repeat, Mrs. Marrick, why are 'ee here?''

''I'm here because I love my sister and because the Carnes have always had a tendency to hold a grudge.''

''With good reason.''

''You and my sister are both young. Long lives, presumably, stretch out ahead of you. There will be times, after she is married, when she will return here to visit, and I don't want her plagued by your hatred, bitterness, and resentment the way my father, grandfather, and I were plagued by Jory's.''

''So I'm to will away such feelings, as if they didn't exist?''

''I'm prepared to admit that a variety of injustices have been done to your family.''

His eyebrows went up in mock astonishment.

''I'm prepared to make amends.''

''Ye've come to buy me off.'' The words were sharp as a whiplash. ''How much are 'ee offering? I'm curious to know what ye imagine to be my price.''

Verity threw a document down on the desk in front of him. ''I'm offering this.''

Daniel unfolded the paper. He saw at once that it was a deed transferring to him one of the pieces of disputed property, the high northwest field. It was but a small percentage of the land the Carnes had perennially claimed (which encompassed the entire site of the Cadmon claypits), but it was not insignificant. Here the finest deposits of china clay lay buried; here also the abandoned tin mine was located, the one that was by no means tapped out. Reopening that mine in this time of war could make him a tidy profit, which would increase the amount of capital he had to invest in china clay.

He knew this, but he doubted that the Trevors did. Except Bret. She knew because he'd told her.

''All it requires is your signature, and the land is yours.''

''And in return?''

''You are forever out of my sister's life.''

"Why this particular quadrant? It's no more than a fraction of the disputed lands. Toss the dog a scrap? What makes ye think I'll accept this?"

"It may be less than you yearn for, but it's all you'll ever get. And I think you'll accept it because my sister mentioned to me that this particular property had special significance for you."

It was the land he had explored with Bret on that storm-tossed night when she had come to him. On this land he had shown her tin and shown her clay and expressed to her his dream. On this land he had kissed her, and invited her to bed.

Verity was looking at him as if she knew.

It was then, more than before, that Daniel felt betrayed. They'd forced her to write the letter, of that he had no doubt. But if she loved him, really loved him, nothing they could have said or done would have kept her from his arms.

He took his pen, hesitated for only an instant, and signed his name.

Verity had one final thing to do. She returned to the vicarage. She had slept little in the past two days, but she felt no exhaustion. Indeed, as she went in to face her husband, she felt reserves of strength and determination she hadn't known she possessed.

She had not wasted a single moment fretting about her husband's deceit and hypocrisy. She was glad of it in a way, since it relieved her of any feelings of guilt. Never again would she allow him to hurt and humiliate her. She was free. Her chief regret was that her blindness and submissiveness had made victims of other women, young girls like Tess, whom she ought to have had the sense to warn and to protect. Although she had never liked the sly young Tess, she felt a curious oneness with her, with Bret, and with all women.

Her outrage was directed at the conspiracy of silence that decreed that women of their generation should know nothing of the side of life with which they, after all, were by nature most concerned—motherhood and its inception. The secrets of sensuality and lovemaking were kept from them by the men who had mistakenly concluded that women did not, or rather ought not to, enjoy sex.

There was a part of her that had wanted to cheer during that awful moment in her bedroom when Bret had refused to agree to her lover's demand that she give up everything for his sake. In her usual forthright, seize-life-by-the-horns manner, Bret seemed to be claiming her right to have the pleasures of sensuality without submitting to the chains of marriage. In that, as in so many other things, Verity envied her. From then on, she'd decided, she would not simply envy but would act.

"I'm leaving you," she told her husband.

"You must be mad."

"I am not mad. I am fully in control of my faculties, as indeed I have always been. I refuse to listen any longer to your assaults upon my character, my intellect, and my femininity. I refuse to subjugate myself any longer to your demands, your whims, and your base desires. I made a mistake in marrying you, a mistake I intend to rectify. I'm going to petition for a divorce."

"You cannot divorce the vicar of St. Catherine's. It would destroy my career in the church."

"You don't deserve a career in the church. Of that, I now have proof."

She unfolded the letter. It was slightly sticky from her sweat. "I found this the other night. I removed it from the pile of posturing sermons where you had tried to hide it. I know now why you've always been so eager to hire disadvantaged young housemaids. My only question, Mr. Saintly and Honorable Reverend Marrick, is how many virgins you've corrupted, and what the bishop will do to you when he finds out."

Julian rose from his chair and moved toward her so swiftly that Verity had no chance to defend herself. She saw his bulk looming over her, the fear in his eyes that was even stronger than his anger. It struck her that it was fear that had made him lash out the other night. Fear of aging, fear of death, fear of being revealed as something less than the godly preacher he pretended to be. The realization gave her courage. "Are you going to strike me, Julian? Rape me again, perhaps, so you can pretend you are a man?''

Like a bellows with the air gone out of it, he collapsed before her. He slipped to his knees, that humble position he assumed so readily at the altar. "You don't understand. I've tried so hard. It comes over me, it's like a trance and I lose myself, lose my very soul. That's when I think things . . . and do things . . . things I hate but can't control. I have prayed to God to relieve me of this horror, but my prayers are like leaves in the wind that whirl briefly upward before they come fluttering down." He sounded truly anguished. "Have pity on me, Verity. God cannot hear me, for if He did, He would surely have mercy upon me and take this curse from my soul!''

"So you blame God?''

"I blame myself. The evil inside me, inside all men. I fight against it. You've no idea how mightily I struggle. All you see is my failure. You have no concept of the dimensions of my pain.''

She felt no sympathy. All she felt was her anger, and her sense of having been abused. "I've been in pain too. You've chosen to ignore that, Julian, so I don't see why I ought to feel any pity for you.''

"Verity, for the love of God! Don't leave me. Don't condemn me in the eyes of the church and the community. I deserve the direst punishment, I know, and I'll do anything you wish, but don't abandon me to my despair!''

She had won. She had broken him. All that was left, she realized, was to bargain.

The November winds swept an early snow across the moors, creating a whirlwind of white that turned to gray as the afternoon faded into evening. But he could still see the lights of Cadmon Hall. He could see them coming on, slowly now, for there weren't so many servants these days to go through the great expanses of the building and switch them on; nor were many rooms required now that most of the family were gone.

Bret had been taken to an unknown destination—London,

probably, although none of the servants he'd tried to bribe had been able to confirm her address. Her father was away as well, building aeroplanes for the war. Not everyone in the Trevor family was absent, however. Verity had returned there to live when her husband resigned his position as vicar of Trenwythan to serve as an army chaplain in France. In the absence of her father and her husband, Verity was in charge of Cadmon Clay. Ludicrous, the idea of a woman—even *that* woman—managing a claypit.

It was still seductive, that house.

It had defeated him temporarily, but not forever.

One day, Daniel Carne vowed, Cadmon Hall and everything inside it would belong to him.

Part Five

1915–16

For I dipt into the future, far as human eye could see,
Saw the Vision of the world, and all the wonder that
    would be;
Saw the heavens fill with commerce, argosies of magic
    sails,
Pilots of the purple twilight, dropping down with costly
    bales;
Heard the heavens fill with shouting, and there rain'd
    a ghastly dew
From the nations' airy navies grappling in the central
    blue.

—Alfred, Lord Tennyson
Locksley Hall

Chapter Thirty-two

"Maggie, listen to this," Bret said one afternoon in May 1915. Several mornings a week she got together with her old school friend Maggie Blount to roll bandages and knit clothes for the soldiers across the Channel. "It's from this morning's newspaper:

" 'Nurses Needed: It's not only our brave lads who are being called upon to serve their country in her hour of need, but our young ladies as well. The Red Cross reports that although recruiting for Britain's Voluntary Aid Detachments has been active since August 1914, the magnitude of the casualties arriving from the front demands that more nurses be trained.' "

"Are you suggesting . . . ?" Maggie asked.

"Well, yes. I've never been very good at knitting, anyway."

Bret had spent several months in London. It was not until she had been living with her aunt Dorothy for a while that she'd realized how far away Cornwall was from the war. Here it was on every street: officers in their smart regimental uniforms, their swords hanging at their sides; enlisted men in khaki with their puttees wrapped around their calves, marching off to the front. She also saw the soldiers who were home on leave, many of them broken men who had been shattered in body and in mind by the horrors they had experienced on the Continent.

London had changed greatly from the gay, bright, frightfully civilized city Bret remembered from earlier visits. The winter had settled in with more than the usual amount of grayness and fog, dampening everyone's spirits. At pubs, palaces, and drawing rooms, the war was all that was talked about. Neither side had gained or lost much ground lately, and the reports from the front confirmed that both armies were firmly entrenched in their mud holes, fortified by concrete bunkers, mines, fences, and barbed wire.

Casualties were high. Fully ninety percent of the first hundred thousand men of the original British Expeditionary Force who had been sent to the Continent in August had been either wounded or killed. Bret's own troubles were trivial in comparison.

From the moment Bret had arrived in London, Maggie, a dramatic, dark-haired beauty of boundless energy, had set about distracting her. Nearly everyone in Maggie's set had friends, brothers, or lovers who were at the front, and they all felt great compassion for the brave men who must weather the cold, the rain, and the snow in their damp trenches, huddled around the feeble heat of their little camp stoves. The thought that the woollies they knitted with such devotion might warm a chilled soldier inspired them to work all the harder. But Bret longed to do something more.

"We're too young to be VADs," Maggie said. "You have to be twenty-one; twenty-three before they'll send you to the front lines."

"If they're so desperate for more trainees, maybe they won't be particular," Bret said. Like everybody else in London, she had heard enough about the VADs lately to know that they were an auxiliary of the Red Cross. The army had already come to rely on these women, many of whom were proving to be not only competent nurses but excellent administrators.

"Of course we can't be real nurses," said Maggie, thoughtfully twisting a strand of her blue-black hair around one of her elegant fingers. "I mean, we're not professionals. And from what I've heard about VADs, they're mostly fetch-and-carry squads."

"I've read that too, but I've also read that in the past few months the VADs have impressed the pros so much with their skills that they're being given additional duties," said Bret. "Some are even being sent to the front lines."

"It would be exciting to go to France, wouldn't it?" Maggie said. She did not say so, but Bret knew she must be thinking of her fiancé, Captain Justin Barnett, who had been posted to the Marne at about the same time as Simon had left for France. Simon, thank God, hadn't been sent into battle; his regiment had been assigned to Paris, where Simon had drawn a desk job requisitioning foodstuffs and medical supplies.

At Maggie's insistence—she was the practical one—they agreed to spend the rest of the day considering whether nursing was what they really wanted to do. Taking on such a commitment would mean that the classes Bret took at the Royal College of Art in Kensington three mornings a week would have to be postponed. That would be a shame, because the power that Tamara had discovered in her to shape and mold and create beauty in three-dimensional curves had continued to expand and develop. Her new mentor, the sculptor Marcus Gregory, had been very encouraging.

"Most craftsmen take the clay and work on it from the outside, shaping and forming it, stamping themselves upon it," he'd said. "What you do is much more rare. You get inside the clay. You stimulate it from within and allow it to grow and develop as it will, nurturing its own character and beauty. You are a mother to your creations, and therein lies the essence of true art."

"You mean you think I can actually do this?" she'd asked, amused as well as flattered, for Gregory was a stern and impatient taskmaster.

"You have the potential. But you must work hard, discipline yourself, and, of course, mature. You have not yet experienced life in all its terror and glory. You have not fathomed its deepest mysteries, thrilled to its most exquisite pleasures, or suffered its most agonizing pains."

"How do you know what I've experienced? Maybe I have felt all those things."

"When you have felt them, they will be there in your art."

She'd bristled, for she believed that her love affair with Daniel and its aftermath had exposed her to just about every human emotion, but Marcus Gregory insisted that she was young, she had not lived. One love affair, he told her baldly, was the merest of beginnings in the realm of the human heart. "Anyway, you will forget him."

"You're wrong. I'll never forget him."

But the truth was that away from Trenwythan, away from Daniel, away from the heady fever and sensual excitement of love, she was dismayed to discover that some of her fervor and intensity had diminished. Without seeing him, touching his body, hearing his voice, Daniel wasn't quite real to her anymore.

She had written to him several times. She knew he must be angry with her, and she feared that he would see her capitulation to her family as a final rejection of him. She explained that she had acted to protect him. That she still loved him. That she was faithful. That they could not keep her in London forever, and that everything would be healed between them when she returned to Trenwythan.

Her letters went unanswered. As the weeks and months went by without reply, she passed through hope to anger, anger to despair, despair to resignation. He would never forgive her. He didn't really love her. No happiness was possible between a Trevor and a Carne.

On the morning Bret and Maggie were scheduled for their interview with the matron at one of the major receiving hospitals for war wounded in the city, they worked hard to create the impression that they were indeed twenty-one. They put up each other's hair and dressed in their most prim and sophisticated frocks. But as it turned out, the question didn't arise. New wounded had arrived the night before and Matron was desperate to increase her staff. "Have you ever fainted at the sight of blood?" she asked Bret in her dingy little office on the ground floor of the busy hospital.

"No, Sister, never."

"Have you ever scrubbed a toilet?"

"I've mucked out a stable. Does that count?"

"Wielded a mop? Washed pots and pans? Done laundry? Got down on your hands and knees and scoured floors? Prepared and served food? Or have you had servants all your life doing those things, without your even noticing they were being done?"

"We had servants at home, yes, but I always noticed what they were doing, and sometimes I helped."

Matron considered her. "You appear strong and hearty. Long arms and legs, sturdy shoulders. We'll have to have a doctor take a look at you, of course, listen to your lungs." Matron was making notes on a paper in front of her. "Are you willing to take orders from superiors who may be of a lower social order than yourself?"

"I'm willing to take orders, yes. We're democratic in Cornwall. My friends have been people I like, no matter what their birth."

"You'd better mean that sincerely, because you'll be miserable as a VAD if you don't. We don't tolerate any hoity-toity missishness in the Red Cross. There is a hierarchy in nursing, but it is determined by skill and experience rather than by birth. All trainees are considered equal, no matter whether they're a Lady This or an Honorable that or simply common Miss Cockney."

"I like that. It sounds like life in Arizona. They're big on equality in America, you know."

Matron looked her up and down, then made another note on the pad in front of her. "Report back here tomorrow morning at six o'clock. Better get a good night's sleep tonight, because you're going to be worked like a dray horse tomorrow."

"You mean I'm accepted?"

"Don't be a dolt, Trevor. Would I be telling you to report if you weren't? We have no use for dolts in the Red Cross."

At the ungodly hour of six the following morning, Bret and Maggie were shown to a dormitory that was starker and uglier than anything they had ever known at boarding school and assigned beds diagonally across from each other. The bed frames were made of iron, with finger-thin mattresses and rough woolen blankets. At the foot of each was a small locker in which they were to store their possessions. There were two wardrobes, one at each end of the ward, for all the nurses to hang their uniforms and aprons. The beds were too close together to afford any privacy.

"It's like being back in school," Maggie said, with obvious dismay at the spartan conditions.

Bret flopped down on her bed to try it out. "Not nearly as comfy."

Penelope March, the VAD officer who had shown them into the dormitory, was frowning at them. "Blount, Trevor, store your things and change into your uniforms at once. The others are at breakfast. Shift begins promptly at seven. Normally there would be lectures for a week or so before beginning on the wards, but we're understaffed, so you'll have your training on the job. You'll be started on a sick ward, to help you get used to things a bit before you have to confront seriously wounded soldiers and surgical cases. Any questions?"

"What, exactly, is a sick ward?" Bret asked.

"Some of the soldiers we're nursing are not so much wounded as ill with nasty disorders such as pneumonia, dysentery, and chronic bronchitis caused by poison-gas attacks. We also have men down with various forms of neurasthenia, or shellshock. There's nothing wrong with their bodies except the stress of being subjected daily to the threat of violent death. You'll see all of these illnesses today. You have fifteen minutes to settle and change, so look sharp."

By the time they were dressed, they both felt as if they'd gone seventy years back in time to the days of Florence Nightingale's participation in the Crimean War. Nurses' uniforms hadn't changed much since then. The gown was a drab, coarsely woven cotton that fell to the ankles, which made both girls feel uncomfortable. They had become used to the shorter hemlines recommended by the government as a means of making more fabric available for soldiers' uniforms. The old-fashioned gown was covered by a voluminous apron with a large red cross in the center of the chest. The detachable collars and cuffs were stiff and tight, and the winglike caps were difficult to secure upon the head.

"We look like nuns," Maggie said, laughing.

"Something tells me we're going to require the patience of holy sisters."

"Not to mention the obedience," Maggie said dryly. "Come along, Trevor," she added, mocking the nurse's tone.

An hour later Bret was wishing she'd never heard of the Voluntary Aid Detachments. Nurse March, their superior VAD officer, separated them, sending Maggie to work in the laundry, scrubbing urine-stained bedsheets. To Bret she handed a long-handled mop and bucket of soggy tea leaves, which were said to absorb dirt.

"Begin at that end of the ward and scour every corner. Under the beds as well. We don't want any dust here. It spreads germs and makes breathing difficult for the respiratory cases. Is that clear?"

"Yes, Sister."

"And don't call me Sister. It makes the trained nurses livid. I am not a professional nurse and therefore not of the Sisterhood; I am a senior VAD. You may call me Nurse March. See that you don't forget it, or you'll make yourself some nasty enemies among the pros."

Enemies in a profession supposedly full of selfless, devoted women? Bret's illusions were crumbling.

She set to work with her mop and her bucket of tea leaves, although she saw little in the way of dust, no doubt because some hardworking VAD had done this chore yesterday morning. What she did see were beds occupied by young men in various positions, sitting up alertly with the latest newspapers in their hands, lying on their backs with several pillows propping up their shoulders and heads, curled on their sides, unconscious, in fetal positions. They were a quiet lot, except for the rustle of newspaper and the hollow sound of desperate, racking coughing. Several of the soldiers wore oxygen masks to assist in their breathing.

When Bret had worked her way about halfway down the two rows of beds, a contingent of other VADs came in with trays. Nurse March ordered Bret to put down the mop and assist with the patients who were incapable of feeding themselves.

"If we weren't shorthanded today, I'd keep you scrubbing. As it is, you'll get to do a little real nursing. Take three bowls of porridge from this tray and feed the soldiers in beds five, seven, and nine, then report back to me."

The patient in bed five looked easy. A well-fed young man, clad in the white hospital johnny that was regulation on the ward, he was sitting up in bed and staring into space. Bret soon realized that he couldn't talk, nor did he seem capable of moving his arms or hands to take the spoon. His attention was on some inner place, at least until he smelled the porridge, which brought him to expectant, if vacant, attention.

This, she realized, must be one of the shellshock cases.

As Bret fed the young soldier, he greedily licked from the spoon, making loud slurping sounds. At one point, Bret clumsily dropped the spoon, which hit the floor with a loud report. The shellshocked soldier cringed and whimpered, spat out his food, and trembled for several minutes before his hunger prompted him to eat again.

Bret felt embarrassed for the poor man, but nobody else seemed to notice or care. When the bowl was empty, he appeared agitated, as if waiting for more. His face turned red when more was not forthcoming, but after a minute or two he seemed to accept this. He fell back into his distant trance.

She moved on to the next bed, upset by the animalistic undertone of the first patient's behavior. It was as if the faculties that give a person dignity had disappeared in number five every bit as completely as his name.

The man in bed seven, although in his right mind, was too weak to eat. The metal chart at the end of his bed tagged him as a gassed lung case, and as she tried to prop his head up higher so that he could swallow, Bret saw the suppurating chemical burns on his neck and hands. His eyes were bandaged. The corrosive effects of poison gas had made him blind. From his chest rose an intermittent, gurgling cough. She knew from the newspaper accounts of the effects of gas warfare that this was how it killed. It destroyed the linings of the lungs, allowing liquid from the bloodstream to fill the lungs and eventually drown the victim in his own fluids.

As he tried valiantly to eat, food and saliva foamed up out of the corners of his mouth and dribbled down his chin. He went into a paroxysm of choking when Bret put too much porridge on the spoon, making her hand shake with the fear of killing him with her amateur ministrations.

The soldier in bed number nine would not eat at all—he was pasty-faced and unconscious.

"Some of them die of starvation and dehydration," one of

the VADs, a cheerful-looking woman not much older than Bret, whispered to her. She introduced herself as Polly Marks. "They just give up, like, and refuse to take anything."

"Can't you make them eat?"

"With feeding tubes, yeah, I guess that's what they do with the fitter ones, but this end o' the room we call the Twilight Ward. They're on their way out, these lads, so all we do is take care of 'em till they go, then we strip their beds and do the same for the one that takes their place. Usually there's only one way out o' here, and that's feet first."

When she finished the mopping, Bret was ordered to go from bed to bed with one of the senior VADs on urinal and bedpan duty. The use of the urinals was easier, since the receptacles were of an appropriate shape to fit over a man's penis, enabling him to void into the elongated neck of the jar. The use of the bedpans involved rolling the sick and feeble patients onto their sides, lifting their hospital gowns, which conveniently opened in the back, and placing the contoured bedpans against their bottoms. Carefully, then, so as to keep the bedpan in the correct position, the attendant rolled the patient onto his back again, and waited, then repeated the process to remove the bedpan.

The first time she tried it, Bret jostled the patient, who jostled the bedpan, spilling part of its stinking contents. Polly cursed good-naturedly. "Guess you'd better learn how to change a bed. Don't worry, Private Cheswick, we'll have you cleaned up in a jiffy."

"Doesn't he have to get up?"

"Can't, can he? Nope, we change it with him in it. That's what these extra-thick sideways sheets are here for. See? All's we have to change is that one—there's rubber sheets between it and the bottom—clever, eh? We just roll him sideways again, first one way, then the other, as we tuck in the new cross-sheet."

It was simple and clever, although it took so much extra time that Nurse March was soon giving her and Polly a tongue-lashing for dawdling. "I'm sorry," Bret whispered to Polly. "I don't want you to suffer for my ineptitude."

"Don't worry, I was new myself not so long ago."

The used bedpans were stacked on a wheeled cart as the

nurses went from one bed to the next. When they reached the end of the ward, the cart reeked of human urine and feces. Nurse March collared Bret, put the handle of the trolley into her hands, and pointed to the double doors at the end of the ward.

"There's a toilet through there and to the left and a small scullery just beyond it. Take the bedpans in, empty them, stack them, then carry them into the scullery and start scrubbing. You'll find a bottle of carbolic over the sink. Use good hot water and plenty of soap. And wipe that stunned expression off your face. If this bothers you, you might as well forget about nursing the wounded. Which would you rather clean up, good solid stools and urine, or pus, phleghm, and blood?"

Bret fled with the urinals and the bedpans.

Arizona, she thought, as she emptied them, one after another, into the toilet. Dry heat, sunshine, vivid pink and purple desert flowers, skies that glimmered deep blue and seemed to stretch on forever. Funny old Zach Slayton with his bowed legs and his leathery face and his long white Buffalo Bill beard and ponytail. What fun they'd have, sitting around a campfire eating steak and beans off of tin plates and philosophizing about life. "Did you know that the one thing you would probably assume to be the same from one person to another—their bodily waste—is actually quite different? Different colors, different consistencies. Even the *smells* are different."

"No surprise to me," Zach would say in his folksy way. "I always reckoned folks' piss and shit to be just as individual as everythin' else about 'em."

Break came at twelve-fifteen; the hospital served a hot lunch in the nurses' quarters. Maggie was there, her cap askew, her habitual smile strained. "I'm exhausted! They had me washing mounds of sheets and pillow slips and towels, all slimed with God only knows what. They have this huge copper tub, and the water's scalding. I've been in up to my elbows with lye and disinfectant until my skin feels as if it's been stripped off. Whose idea was this, anyway?"

"We knew it would be hard. We've got to stick it out or we'll be ashamed of ourselves. We've got to be intrepid."

"I suppose so," Maggie said gloomily.

"We've got to experience life in all its terror and glory," she added, thinking about what her sculpting instructor had told her.

"Terror, maybe. I don't think we're going to find much in the way of glory here."

"Trevor! Blount! Come along, girls; you're not here to relax!"

Groaning, they rose to follow the staff nurse.

"And clear your own plates and cutlery. There are no servants to wait on you here."

"Oh yes there are. Us," Bret muttered under her breath.

She spent the afternoon doing a variety of tasks assigned by the more experienced VADs, who were grateful to have a new girl on whom to dump the dirtiest work. She was given a brush and a bucket and told to scrub the floor of the scullery room where she'd scoured the bedpans earlier. She washed the plates, bowls, mugs, and cutlery from breakfast and luncheon. Later she was ordered onto the same ward where she'd worked in the morning to help Polly Marks sponge-bathe several patients.

"Down there, bed number nine," Polly said, handing her a kidney-shaped bowl of soapy warm water. "He's unconscious, but he spit up earlier and needs to have his upper body cleaned. Dry him immediately so he won't catch a chill."

Bret approached the soldier in bed number nine, whom she had unsuccessfully attempted to feed earlier. His age was reported on his chart as twenty, but his body was as desiccated as that of an elderly man. His eyes were closed and his facial expression was fixed. He reminded Bret of the photographs she had seen of the mummies unearthed from ancient Egyptian tombs. He smelled like them too, Bret thought miserably. She was beginning to recognize the odors of disease, death, and incipient decay.

Part of a nurse's uniform, she thought irreverently, ought to be a clothespin for the nose.

"Sergeant O'Hara?" she said, touching his shoulder. There was no response; she hadn't really expected one. Gingerly she leaned over and loosened his hospital gown. She dipped a sponge into the soapy water and began washing his face. His features seemed to be molded in stone, and there was a tinge of cyanosis around his lips. Bret dried his face, then opened the gown farther, catching sight of the unfortunate man's limp, shriveled genitals. Twenty years old. His skin was cold and dry; the feel of it made her shiver.

I hope I don't get to be like this, she was thinking, and for an instant she felt disoriented. Time seemed to melt around her. One day not so long ago, this man had been full of youthful energy, plans, hopes, and dreams. How swiftly his glory had passed. How inexorably his life had been compressed by this terrible war until, before he could hope to understand how it had happened, he had ended up here, on the Twilight Ward.

The same thing will happen to me, she realized, *no matter how long I live. The years will pass in the flicking of an eyelid, and I, too, will be at the end of my time. Then I, too, will lie upon my deathbed waiting for the shadows to envelop me. I won't understand how it happened any more than he does.*

She felt tears come into her eyes as she vigorously rubbed Sergeant O'Hara's chest, attempting to make him warm. War or no war, this was what happened to you. You were born, you laughed, you cried, you loved someone, and then you died. This was the way of all flesh.

"What are you doing there?"

Bret whirled. Nurse March was standing behind her, a scathing expression on her face.

"Polly Marks told me to bathe this soldier and then to dry him thoroughly so he wouldn't take cold."

"You needn't worry about his taking cold. Can't you see, you stupid girl? This soldier is dead."

Bret jerked her hands away. Her stomach dropped, then rose, and if it weren't for the challenge in Nurse March's disdainful expression she would have fled in search of a pail to vomit in.

"Come now, Trevor, it's only death. You'd better get used to it. You're going to see a lot of it. At least he went easily, without a whisper, without coughing up his lungs and screaming out in pain."

"But he died alone. No one even knew." For some reason this seemed more horrible to Bret than a more painful and dramatic death would have been. Going without a whisper: that wasn't the way she wanted it to be when her time came. "I could feel he was cold, but I didn't notice he wasn't breathing, and—"

"Never mind. He was breathing twenty minutes ago, so it must have just happened. He's not as cold as he'll get." Nurse March's voice had turned matter-of-fact. "You see that screen over there. Bring it here. Actually you ought to have screened him before beginning to bathe him. We owe these men some measure of dignity."

"I'm sorry; I didn't realize—"

"Yes, well, it's done now. You seem a bright girl. You'll learn. At least the eyes are closed. Sometimes we have to tape them shut. Ever laid out a body?"

Bret shook her head.

"Course not; I forgot you come from a wealthy family. If you were a poor woman, you'd know how to help out with birthing as well as dying. Ushering folks in and out of the world is the natural province of women. Right. Let's get this gown off. Lucky thing he hasn't stiffened up yet. After rigor mortis sets in it's no easy task to undress and lay out a corpse. Stay with him while I go fetch the doctor to pronounce him officially."

During the next few minutes Bret learned things she had never known, never thought about, concerning the final disposition of the dead. The remains of Sergeant O'Hara had to be washed clean and the various body cavities stuffed with cotton gauze (Bret couldn't bring herself to do this, and Nurse March didn't force her; but she did demand that she watch and pay attention so that she could do it in the future). Nurse March showed her how to set the jaw and bind a bandage under the chin and over the top of the head to keep the mouth from falling open. The corpse was then dressed in a fresh gown and laid out on his back, his arms folded over his chest and crossed.

"Putting them in this position makes it easier for the coffin maker to fit them in if they're stiff when he comes to get them," Nurse March explained. The final ministration was to cover the dead soldier with a starched sheet that was drawn up over his face and tucked in tightly. "Leave the screens," Bret was told. "The other patients know full well what they hide, but they can push the idea to the back of their minds if they don't have to see the corpse lying there."

When the task was finished, Bret glanced at the clock at the end of the ward and saw to her relief that her shift was coming to an end.

"Be here promptly at six tomorrow morning," Nurse March ordered as she dismissed her. She paused for a moment, gave Bret a haughty up-and-down, then added, "You'll do, Trevor, you'll do."

Chapter Thirty-three

Less than a fortnight later, Bret was transferred to the medical-surgical ward. On her first morning she found the other VADs scurrying to make up beds for eight new patients who were just off the boat train from France. Because their arrival had been unexpected, the wounded men were lying on stretchers or slumped between the shoulders of orderlies, who were cursing about the lack of organization.

"I need your help right here," the staff nurse said, summoning Bret to the bedside of one of the casualties. While the soldier, white-faced, leaned back on the pillow, she and another VAD were unbandaging a bloody dressing from his upper thigh. "Go to the foot of the bed and hold his leg still for me. Brace one hand on his ankle and the other on his knee and hold tightly, no matter what. We have to clean his wound, and when we do, it's going to hurt."

"How 'bout a drop of whiskey first, Sister," the soldier said. "I bear the pain a helluva lot better when I'm fortified against it."

Staff Nurse Walker didn't bother to answer, but Bret gave

the man—who had red hair like her own—her widest and most sympathetic smile. He returned a merry, jaunty grin that seemed remarkable coming from a man so thin and pale that he barely seemed substantial. *He's so young*, she thought. Somehow she still hadn't gotten used to how young they all were. This, surely, was the real tragedy of war, the mowing down of the country's tenderest shoots along with all their promise for the future.

Despite all she'd seen and heard during the past two weeks, Bret wasn't prepared for the reality of the wound that was revealed when the redheaded soldier's thigh was unwrapped. She was struck at once by two things: the sight and the smell. The man's thigh, which she had supposed to be so thick due to a mass of bandages, was thick instead with swollen, putrefying flesh. It was oozing—no, flowing—with thick greenish yellow pus, and the odor that rose from the wound enveloped the nursing staff like a hell-sent cloud. It was the smell of rotting, decaying flesh, and it was nearly as hideous as if he were already a corpse.

Bret gagged, putting the back of her hand to her mouth. *Intrepid*, she said to herself, seeking solace in the ever-more-distant fantasies of her carefree youth. She had taken on this job, and, hell's bells and damnation, she was going to prove herself worthy.

"You look a little peaked, Nurse," the soldier said, and she realized to her shame that he was watching her. "You new on the job, maybe? You'd best put your head between your knees."

"I'm all right," she said quickly, willing the contents of her stomach back down where she hoped they'd remain.

"What's your name, lass?" the soldier asked, his voice weak, but not so weak that it hid the distinct Scottish burr. Bret had the sense that he was focusing on her, in her position at the foot of his bed, as something to hang on to in the face of the coming ordeal.

"Trevor, sir."

"I'm honored to meet you, Nurse Trevor," he replied with an attempt at another grin. "Sergeant Francis MacDonald, at your service."

"This wound has to be cleaned," Sister snapped. To Bret

it seemed that there was no way to clean an injury like that. Sergeant MacDonald, the man, was still alive, but his leg was dead, and it seemed to her that the kindest thing to do would be to cut it off and bury it.

"Mess, isn't it?" said Sergeant MacDonald. "Stinks like the very devil. I apologize to you ladies for subjecting you to this sort of unpleasantness."

Staff Nurse ignored him, uncorking her bottle of hypoclorous acid while another nurse began washing away the excess of pus with a sterile gauze pad from the nearby bandaging trolley. Sergeant MacDonald's entire body reared and twisted, forcing Bret to press down hard on the lower part of his leg. She felt like a torturer's assistant in a medieval dungeon.

"We douse it in Eusol every four hours," Staff Nurse told Bret as the other VAD soaked several feet of gauze in the strong-smelling solution. "It's the best treatment we have for gas bacillus."

The tormented soldier began singing the Easter hymn "The Strife Is O'er, The Battle Done" in a thin but lovely tenor. Staff Nurse Walker frowned but made no objection. Anything was permitted, Bret supposed, if it would get him through this particular strife without going mad.

"Don't we have painkillers?" Bret whispered to her fellow VAD as Staff Nurse caused further anguish by the insertion into the wound of a drainage tube.

"Aspirin, which doesn't touch pain of this intensity. Morphine injections right after surgery, or to take you out of some of your misery as you're dying. Nothing in between."

"It's barbaric."

"It's war."

The Scot was the only soldier whose name she remembered from the horrors of her first day on the medical-surgical ward. The others were etched into her mind by the wounds they sustained and the condition in which she tended them: Shrapnel in Brain; Gunshot Wound, Pelvis; Double Amputee; Genitals Blown Off; Gunshot Wound, Chest.

When she got back to her small rectangle of sanctuary in the dormitory that evening, Bret fell into bed and wept. *You asked for this*, she reminded herself. *You wanted to see more of the real world. Serves you right if you didn't expect it would be so messy.*

She would learn to cope, she promised herself. She would learn to be intrepid.

She fell into a troubled sleep, waking at dawn still haunted by dream images of thundering bareback across the misty moorland toward Cadmon Hall with Wulf's coal-black body steaming between her thighs, glorying in the scent of the wildflowers around her that disguised the earth's faint exhalation of blood.

Two hundred and fifty miles away in Cornwall, Verity sat in front of her mirror in her old bedroom at Cadmon Hall. As usual, she didn't like what she saw. Her skin was clear and unlined, except for some minute tracings around her eyes, but her brown hair looked muddy, and recently she'd had to pluck out the first few fine strands of gray. Her figure was still good, but how much longer could she expect to keep it? She was not yet thirty, but she felt ancient in her soul.

She opened a small paper sack and removed several items, which she spread on the dressing table before her. The previous day she had made a special trip to St. Austell, where she had purchased cosmetics for the first time in her life. Julian didn't approve of cosmetics.

She set clumsily to work and was amazed at the difference created by a soupçon of rouge over her cheekbones and on her lips; the plucking of her eyebrows to form a thinner, finer curve; the thickening of her eyelashes with black, sticky mascara. She'd even purchased nail enamel, although she couldn't bring herself to apply it. Wearing nail enamel went too far, she decided, at least for now.

She rose and dressed, donning a navy blue jacket and skirt over a white silk long-sleeved blouse. The skirt was shorter than any she had worn before, striking the tops of her dainty black leather lace-up shoes. She added a cameo brooch at her throat and a broad blue fabric belt that emphasized her slender waist, and, as a final touch, small gold drops in her ears.

Standing back, she surveyed the changes she had wrought. She looked like a smart, thoroughly modern woman who was fully capable of managing her own affairs.

Verity had been on her own for six months. Bret was in London, Julian and Simon were in France, and her father was away most of the time at a military installation. She liked being alone. She was in charge of the smooth running of the household, which had presented her with no difficulties. Better than that, she was now officially in charge of Cadmon Clay. For the first time in her life she had work that was her own, work she could take pride and satisfaction in. When she was at the claypits, she was never bored or anxious. Her mind was active, busy with new ideas and plans.

She remembered how nervous she had been on her first day as official manager. It was shortly after Bret had been sent to London, and the two sisters had parted on such unpleasant terms that Verity had been sleepless for several nights fretting about it. She'd lost far less sleep over Julian's departure for the battle lines in France, where he was serving as an army chaplain. There, she hoped, her estranged husband would not have much opportunity to use his considerable talents to corrupt young girls.

"We've got a problem," Gil Parkins, pit manager of Cadmon Clay, had informed her straightaway on her first morning. "We're losing workers to the war. Everyone wants to rush over and kill a few Huns. I've seen four men quit to join up during the last week alone, and no one's been in looking for work."

"You mean there are no young men coming in to the industry? No new generation of boys to take their fathers' places?"

"It's the new generation who're getting themselves killed. I don't know how the government expects British industry to keep operating if they take all of 'em over to France and slaughter 'em."

"If we can't get men, we'll have to use women again. We know they can do it—our experience during the strike proved that. Let's replace the men who are leaving with their wives and sisters."

As he had the first time Verity had suggested this, Gil

expressed doubts. However, Verity's logic quickly won him over to her point of view. "The war is changing everything," she said. "All over the country women are taking factory jobs, driving buses and trolleys, doing farm work, even risking death at the front lines to nurse our soldiers. It's a major change in the fabric of society. If we put it to the men that they must either get accustomed to working side by side with women or risk losing their jobs altogether if our labor shortage forces us to shut down, I think they'll come around."

Gil grinned, the old admiration stirring in his eyes. "I reckon it's worth a try."

Verity had instituted the new policy without delay, and despite some initial resistance on the part of the male clay workers, the hiring of women for other jobs besides the traditional one of bal maiden had been working out well. Verity's female employees were devoted and energetic, and with the exception of one who had left to have a baby, none had resigned, an advantage that Cadmon Clay had over every other claypit in the St. Austell area. All in all, it was an experiment that could be regarded as a success.

Now, six months later, in the summer of 1915, the claypits were running smoothly, and Verity and Gil had developed an excellent working relationship. She looked forward to sitting down with him every morning and charting out their next moves.

"Got some news." Gil tugged at his bushy beard, a gesture Verity had grown to associate with his anxious moods. Because they spent several hours a day in each other's company, she had come to know him well. They were similar in certain ways: both hard workers, both high-strung. About thirty-five years old, Gil was married to a meek, sad-eyed woman named Ellen, who had miscarried seven children. Like Verity, he knew the grief of losing too many loved ones, as well as the disappointment of yearning for a child that would never be born. This was a bond between them that had remained unspoken.

"Remember that piece of land you and your father signed over to Daniel Carne a few months ago?"

She nodded. She suspected that Gil had been curious about the reason for that transaction, although he'd never questioned her. She had no idea how much he knew about her sister's involvement with Daniel; such secrets were almost impossible to keep in a village the size of Trenwythan. But Gil was discreet.

"Did you know there was a disused tin mine on that land?"

"I understood that it was tapped out a generation ago."

"Apparently not. There's still a hefty vein of tin down there. Carne has convinced the bureaucrats in London to give him the money to reopen the workings. Seems the country needs tin for the war effort."

"How enterprising of him."

"Meanwhile, as you know, he's doing well with his china clay. It's good quality, better than ours in some respects, and he's been selling it cheap and picking up additional orders that way."

"Are you suggesting that he might become a serious competitor?"

"I'm suggesting he already is. There's a lot of heavy work around here that women *can't* do, and Carne's looking for tin miners. We may be in danger of losing more of our labor pool."

"Why would anyone risk the dangers of going deep into the earth to dig for tin when they could work in the open air of a claypit?"

"Some of our boys had fathers or grandfathers who were tinners, and there's a certain mystique about it. The good old days, and all that rot. Besides, Carne's offering higher wages than we can afford."

"Let him. He's got nothing to back him up except the whims of the War Office. If he loses his financing, he's finished. The tin industry will die again with the end of the war."

"And if the war doesn't end soon?"

She shrugged. "He'll make money. It's what the Carnes have always wanted and never been any good at. Chances are, one way or another, he'll self-destruct."

That evening Verity took a walk up toward the piece of land she had signed over to Daniel. The night was fine, with clear skies and stars blinking over the serene landscape. It was hard to fathom that only a few hundred miles away, the same stars looked down upon artillery-pocked fields and blood-drenched trenches.

Coming out of nowhere, a harsh voice assailed her: "Come to spy, Mrs. Marrick?"

She whirled. Standing silhouetted against the pump house was Daniel Carne, his tall, husky body casting a long moon-shadow.

Verity blinked and swallowed. "Not exactly. I am curious, I'll admit. I thought the Wheal Faith tin mine was exhausted generations ago, yet I understand that you have reopened it."

"I've always known there was plenty of tin left."

"So that was why you accepted my offer as readily as you did."

"Ye're regretting it now, are 'ee?"

"Not at all."

"Good. I hear ye're running the clay company now, Mrs. Marrick. Just like ye did during the strike."

"That's correct. I am officially in charge, and will remain so, for the duration of the war, at least."

"Then I have a proposition for 'ee."

"What sort of proposition?"

He moved closer. Verity retreated a step. She'd been a fool to come here at this time of night. She was alone with him.

" 'Tes a satisfaction to me to own part of the land that the Carnes have always believed to be ours, but I'd be happier still if I had more of it. There's another strip of land, adjoining this one, that I'd like to buy from 'ee."

"Getting greedy, Mr. Carne?"

Ignoring her remark, he went on, "As ye've probably heard, I've been fairly successful so far. I can pay you well for the land. I want to develop it, and for that privilege I'm willing to pay."

"No. Absolutely not."

"Don't be so hasty. The price of clay's down because of the war. Ye could use the money. The land up here's worth nothing to 'ee. It's nowhere near your claypit workings, whereas it borders right alongside mine. Its only value to 'ee is as a symbol of yer family's triumph over the Carnes.''

"I don't care about that. You're the only one who has ever cared about that. You and your wretched father."

A muscle moved in his jaw. "At least listen to my offer."

"It won't make any difference. None of our land is for sale."

"I watched you during the clay strike, Mrs. Marrick. I saw what you did then, the way you fought to defend your ideals. I thought at the time ye were different. Not like yer father or yer granddad. Ye seemed at least to consider the plight of yer workers and to be willing to seek a compromise. Ye treated them more fairly than most."

Coming from him, this assessment surprised her.

"Given that," he continued, "I thought ye might have it in 'ee to be fair about this as well. The land is mine anyway. Ye'd be going partway to righting an old wrong if ye accepted my proposal."

"Is it because I'm a woman that you think me such a flimsy house of cards?"

There was a long pause. Then he said, "Maybe we've more in common, ye and me, than I ever realized. Ye're disadvantaged because ye're a woman. Me because I'm a clay worker's son."

She said nothing.

"I told yer sister that the day would come when yer father and I would be rivals. But maybe 'twill be ye and me going head to head."

"I consider that highly unlikely."

"Yeah, well, check back with me again in a year or so. I've got plans for 'ee, Verity. Ye and all the Trevors. Yer day is past."

His insolent use of her given name infuriated her. "I have no intention of standing here and listening to your threats."

"Don't mistake me. I'm stating facts, not threats. The world is changing. The strike was the first sign of what's coming for the working men and women of England. We're not going to be held down forever. We're moving into a new future, and I intend to be one of the people who'll make that future a reality."

He spoke with passion and conviction, which Verity could

not help but admire. She did not like Daniel Carne. She would never trust him. But she had little doubt that he would do everything he set out to accomplish.

Chapter Thirty-four

"I'm afraid we're going to have to cut back production soon," Gil Parkins said to Verity in July 1915. "Demand has fallen off and the price of clay is dropping. Nobody wants to buy luxury items like china with a war on."

"Damn the war," said Verity. She and Gil had spread out the clay company account books all over the surface of the antique Chinese desk that had once belonged to Rufus Trevor. No matter how they fiddled with the numbers, they did not look encouraging. "We're going to have to consider other markets for our kaolin. Industrial uses, in paints, paper, and construction materials, that will be even more necessary during wartime." Verity hated the idea even as she suggested it. She believed fine china to be the most important use for kaolin. To her, in fact, china clay and china were almost indistinguishable.

"The balance is bound to shift more to industrial uses in the years ahead, I'd agree with you on that," said Gil. "But it'll take some time to develop other markets and I'm not thinking that far in advance. It's this year and next that we need to worry about." He shrugged grimly. "A couple of claypits have already shut down. If the war continues—and there's certainly no indication that it's going to end soon—we could be facing ruin."

Verity's brain rebelled at the word. She refused even to think it. She had not realized her ambition of running Cadmon Clay only to see it destroyed by a quirky wartime economy.

"What we need right now is a new demand for porcelain so that the china companies will require more of our clay.

But I just don't see it materializing. Our lads in France aren't drinking their tea out of fine china but from battered army mugs made from Daniel Carne's tin.''

Damn Daniel Carne, thought Verity. *I could have opened that mine myself if I hadn't been so rash as to turn it over to him.*

She took a big swallow of the scalding tea she'd brewed for Gil and herself atop the blackbellied stove in the corner. It was her favorite—an American brand, Templetons—but on this occasion it failed to cheer her. With one finger she idly stroked the delicate antique porcelain from which her cup was made. Tea tasted so much better when served in a china cup. How unpleasant it must be for the troops on the Continent to have their bracing, fortifying tea ruined by the metallic flavor of tin.

Something stirred inside her as she recalled a passage from one of the letters that Julian had faithfully written home to her, pretending that their union was still intact and that nothing had happened to suggest otherwise:

> This morning the commanding officer poured me a cup of hot tea in a delicate china cup and saucer. I couldn't imagine where he'd got it; I've seen nothing but tin drinking cups since the day I joined the army. But our fortunate CO has an entire service for twelve in his quarters from which to serve the cream of the military aristocracy the British solution to everything, a hot cup of tea.
>
> To my embarrassment, I found I couldn't hold it. I'd been up all night praying with a shellshocked soldier and under bombardment for twenty-four hours straight before that. I was too weary, too weak. The cup slipped from my fingers and smashed on the ground and I remember thinking, No wonder they use tin. What good is porcelain in a war? Fine English bone china is even more vulnerable to destruction than fine English bones.

Fine china could break, of course, although not as easily as people thought. It wasn't like glass; it would never shatter.

It might chip or crack, but china was actually quite durable. No doubt there were ways, chemically, to make china that was nearly as sturdy as tin.

Tea, tin, soldiers under fire, china clay. Something fused in Verity's mind. She looked up at the painting she had had hung on the wall of her office where she could see it from her desk. It was the Chinese canvas she and Bret had unearthed so many years ago, a tribute to the ancient Chinese system of porcelain manufacture. The delicate painting, rich with shady trees and diffused light, was no less inspirational now than it had been then.

On the left of the painting, in the background, amidst mountains that brushed the clouds, small figures were depicted digging kaolin and trundling it on their backs down the slopes to an area where the clay was pounded into powder. A waterwheel twirled nearby, providing the liquid to turn the powder into malleable clay, which was then delivered to the potters in the foreground of the painting, who threw the pots and filled the molds. Beside the potters were the enamelers, who glazed and decorated the ware, and beyond them, more coolies who stacked it and trundled it up to the kilns. The final scene, in the painting's right foreground, showed the finished pots being loaded onto a barge on a dreamy Chinese river, thence to be transported to market. Executed in an idyllic tone and style, the painting suggested the great pride with which the Chinese regarded their china making.

Over the years Verity had decided that her fascination with the work stemmed from the efficient manner in which the entire process of digging the clay, throwing the pots, and shipping the chinaware off to market was conducted in one small area. She had never given up her dream of bringing back the manufacture of fine china to Trenwythan. But with the demand falling as a result of the war, it had seemed an impracticality unworthy of pursuit.

Verity's mind was racing. What if Cadmon kaolin went into producing not *fine* but heavy-duty china of a tougher, more durable quality? What if it were mass-produced for the army so that British soldiers abroad could take their tea out of real china cups? And—this was the most daring and dramatic part of her idea—what if she were to relaunch the china works, once the jewel and centerpiece of the Cadmon Clay and Porcelain Works, by manufacturing these cups herself?

She rose jerkily from her chair and began to pace.

"Mrs. Marrick? Verity? What's the matter?" Gil asked.

She hesitated. He'd probably think she was daft. "I was just thinking that there might be a way to use some of the kaolin we produce ourselves. Instead of selling it at unprofitable prices."

"Use it for what?"

"To make china. I've always wanted to reopen the china works. We used to manufacture some of the most exquisite porcelain the world has ever known."

"Surely the manufacture of fine china is as much an art as a business. We don't have the skill."

"I have no intention of manufacturing fine china. Or at least not yet." Her voice had grown stronger, surer.

"Then what?"

"I'm going to make teacups. Cheap, simple mugs molded of strong, durable china. I'm going to make lots of them and sell them to the army for the worthy purpose of upholding the morale of our brave troops in France."

"Their morale?" Gil sounded puzzled. He tugged on his beard.

"You pointed out that our boys in France were drinking their daily tea out of cups made of Daniel Carne's tin. I thought how depressing that must be, and the rest followed. It doesn't take any great financial wizardry to realize that in wartime the industries that supply the army will prosper while others falter. Daniel Carne knows this and is acting accordingly. I see no reason why we, too, should not take advantage of the wartime economy. In fact, Gil, we have to. Otherwise, as you say, we face ruin."

There was a long pause, during which she half expected him to tell her she was mad, foolish, ignorant. That's what Julian would have done. Gil would be deferential about it, of course, but the end result would be the same.

"Tell me more." His eyes were so encouraging—so different from Julian's in his warm, supportive manner—that she began, slowly, to explain. As she spoke, more ideas popped into her head, a veritable flood of them. She drew stimulation from the expression on Gil's face, which, though mildly skeptical at first, gradually came to reflect her hope and enthusiasm.

"The first thing we must do is learn more about porcelain," Verity said to Gil a few days later. "I was forced to learn the rudiments when I was a child, but I hated my teacher and I think deliberately forgot what she taught me."

"Maybe I can help," said Gil. "I'm something of a buff on the subject. My mother was a china painter in Stoke-on-Trent before she met my dad. She had a piece, given to her by the china works when she left, a lovely little shepherdess that she'd painted herself. I used to admire it when I was little, and she explained to me how it was made. Later, when I was old enough, I read books on the subject."

"Goodness, you're a treasure, Gil. Will you teach me?"

"Course I will."

Verity began her lessons by inviting Gil to examine the various porcelains at Cadmon Hall. As she showed them to him, he took them down, one piece at a time, the handleless cups, the bowls, the plates, the inkwells, the saltcellars, the flasks, the teapots, the jardinieres, handling them with such love and care that Verity was ashamed of her cavalier treatment of these pieces over the years.

She found that Miss Lynchpole's lessons on porcelain, its properties and history, came back to her far more readily than she'd expected. With Gil's assistance she soon had the basics down, and they were able to move on to the more pressing issue of exactly what the composition of their china ought to be.

"As you know, we British have for decades fused bone ash with china clay and china stone to make fine bone china," said Gil. "There are other materials that can be added as well, but we run the risk of producing a blend that is no longer considered porcelain at all. This might not be a bad idea, if durability is the quality you desire. We could begin by using earthenware or stoneware for anything we plan to sell to the army."

"No." Verity was firm about this detail. "I want to reopen Cadmon Porcelain, which means that it's china, *real* china, that I want to make. The teacups will be just the start, you see. A way to get us operating again. Eventually I want to manufacture entire dinner services of fine china."

"In that case, we'll have to experiment. It's a question of getting the right mixture of china clay, china stone, bone ash, and maybe some minute amounts of soapstone or other elements. We'll have to get ourselves a kiln and play around with the concentrations until we figure out how to develop a slip that combines the translucence of porcelain with the durability of stoneware."

"Is that possible, do you think?"

He flashed her a smile. "Anything's possible."

She believed it. If Daniel Carne could embark on a risky new venture during wartime, why couldn't she? Together, surely, she and Gil could make it work.

During the next several weeks Verity learned more than she had ever wished to know about the mixing and firing of various combinations of minerals. When she and Gil found themselves befuddled, she hired a chemist, two master potters, and a former kiln operator from the china works at Worchester who had retired to the Cornish seacoast of his birth. Even with this force working on the problem day and night, it took several months to come up with a china body that Gil felt would suit their purposes.

While this was going on, Verity arranged for a tour of one of the great china works in Britain's industrial midlands. She traveled up alone, the first long journey she had taken since her Season in London all those years ago.

The visit nearly crushed her dream. She was thoroughly intimidated by the vastness of the factory, the complexity of all its operations, the huge number of people it employed, many of them highly skilled craftsmen. She toured the design studios, where concepts for new lines of porcelain, their shapes and their decoration, were carefully created and assessed for their marketability; the potting and molding sheds, which were not sheds at all but cavernous buildings where master potters and their apprentices labored over their creations; the enameling rooms where row upon row of china painters outlined, filled in, banded, and gilded the ware; the biscuit kilns where the preliminary firings were done; the decorated-ware kilns where the final firings took place; and finally the showrooms, storerooms, warehouses, and shipping docks. All were necessary, it seemed, if you wanted to manufacture china on a grand scale.

And she saw the ware itself: every imaginable design from the most mundane to the most startling and original. *We will never,* she thought morosely, *make anything so fine.*

"Not at first," Gil said when she returned to Trenwythan and described what she'd seen. "It'll take time—decades, probably. But they started small once, too."

"Oh, Gil, maybe it's a mad idea after all. It's going to cost a fortune. Just the building of the factory alone, not to mention the equipment to furnish it . . . particularly the kilns . . . will more than exhaust my personal funds."

"Where were you thinking of building this factory?"

"Right here on the grounds of Cadmon Clay. Preferably in the same spot where it once existed. The foundations are still there, I believe, embedded in the earth."

He pulled on his beard and shook his head. "It's not the best location for a factory. Up here in the hills we're too far removed from the best sources of power and transportation. This is clay country, raw-material country. We'd be better off building the china works somewhere else."

Verity glanced up at her beloved painting, where everything was done in one small area. Yes, it depicted an earlier time—centuries ago, in fact—but this was what she'd intended, what she'd dreamed about.

"I know," Gil said without her having to put it into words. "But I've given a lot of thought to this lately. Will you come for a drive with me? There's something I want to show you."

They got into the motorcar, Gil at the wheel. He drove down out of the clay fields, through the village of Trenwythan, southeast in the direction of St. Austell, through the city with its steep narrow streets where lorries were replacing the old clay wagons in the transport of china clay, and southeast down the long slope that led to the harbor at Charlestown.

With its boxy Georgian-style architecture and its wide cobblestone central street, Charlestown was an example of the sort of efficient planning that Verity admired. Its heyday had been one hundred years ago when tin and copper mines still dotted the landscape. The economy of Cornwall had thrived in those days. Such trades as pilchard fishing, rope and sail making for the great old sailing vessels, and crate and barrel making had been practiced here in Charlestown for several hundred years.

Not a major British port by any means, Charlestown's harbor could not accommodate the mammoth steamships of today, but it was still the primary port for the export of china clay.

"There's a building for sale just a few hundred yards from the harbor," Gil explained. "It used to be a cooperage with a warehouse attached, but there's less demand for barrels nowadays, and, with the war on, less wood available to make 'em out of."

They stopped the car and walked together down the main street past the foundry, the old rope works, and the church of St. Paul's. The cooperage was on the right, just up the road from the Methodist chapel and the Rashleigh Arms. Looking down the slope toward the inner basin hollowed out of rock where ships could dock, Verity was struck by the quiet beauty of St. Austell Bay as it swung inward between the two great headlands, Black Head, the nearer, on the right, with its green slopes and checkered amber and olive fields, and in the distance, on the left, the lush and lovely Gribben Head.

The cooperage, a large stone building with a wooden-plank floor, was larger than it looked from outside. "It's going cheap," Gil told her. "There's no market for a building of this size in Charlestown any longer. But it would be perfect for us. There's power to spare, and the cost of transporting our goods to the harbor will disappear. It's also conceivable that we could use part of the warehouse out back to store our china clay that's waiting to be shipped. I've always thought Cadmon Clay should have an outlet in Charlestown. Many of the other clay companies do."

Verity walked around the decaying interior of the old building, trying to envision a smaller version of the great bustle of art and craft she had witnessed in the midlands. She could tell that Gil was waiting for some reaction, but she wasn't ready to give one yet. She surveyed. She examined. She asked questions. Then she went outside.

"I have to think," she said.

Alone, she walked down toward the sea. She skirted the edge of the inner basin where a ship was taking on china clay from a chute that sent it showering into the hold, throwing up a cloud of claydust. At the end of the outer basin a stone-work pier curved out into the bay. She walked to the end and stared out to sea. The water sucked and lapped in the harbor, those age-old sounds soothing her, focusing her, helping her evaluate and assess.

The cooperage would be a practical investment, as Gil had pointed out. But it was several miles from Cadmon Clay. She had never considered setting up her china works in Charles-town. It wasn't part of her plan.

She didn't want to reject Gil's suggestion out of hand. But if it didn't *feel* right . . .

Knowing she was being illogical, she turned to look back at the cooperage and, beyond it, at the St. Austell hills.

She stared. She shook her head. She closed her eyes for an instant, then looked again.

The view from the pier was almost identical to that of her painting. On the left, in the background, rose the skytips—the Mountains of the Moon, as Bret called them, brushing the low Cornish clouds. Standing in the foreground was a gray stone building that would become her pottery, and to the right, the loading docks from which her creations would be shipped off to market.

It seemed a miracle, or at least a sign. She was *meant* to reopen Cadmon Porcelain Works. She had found her destiny at last.

Verity ran back to Gil, who stood waiting, hands thrust into his pockets, at the shore end of the pier. In an action more rash than any she usually employed . . . and one that made him blush . . . she threw her arms around his neck and hugged him.

Chapter Thirty-five

"How should I begin it?" Bret asked Private Eddie Hastings as she sat down on the side of his bed, pen and paper ready, to help him write a letter to his wife in Northumberland. It was October 1915, and she was working the night shift, which was easier in several ways. There were no meals to serve, and the next major dressing of wounds on the ward would wait until morning.

" 'My dearest love.' Is that all right? That's what she is."

"I know, Eddie. You've told me so much about her that I feel as if I know her."

Her patient suffered a paroxysm of coughing, then continued, just as if it hadn't happened, "She's such a lovely thing, my Joan. Only twenty when I married her, with blue eyes and black hair like the night. I hope the baby'll look like her. Don't they say that first children are more likely to resemble the mother?"

"I don't know about that, but it wouldn't be so bad if the baby looked like you," Bret said in a tone that sounded a good deal more lighthearted than she felt. "You're a handsome devil."

"And you're a bloody liar, Nurse Trevor." He grinned. "But you will enclose the sketch you did of me, won't you? Much too flattering though it is, I think she'd appreciate it."

"Course I will, Eddie."

The sketch had indeed been flattering, as had all the sketches she had done to entertain her patients during the last few weeks. Bret had resorted to sketching during her short breaks from the wards as a way to relieve some of her tension, but when her patients found out about it, her services were much in demand. Although she did not consider herself as talented in drawing as she was working with three-dimensional media, her sketches had a certain fun-loving energy, and both soldiers and nursing staff admired them. Since her patients often asked for drawings to be put into the post for mothers, sisters, and sweethearts, she was careful to treat her subjects lightly and never to make them appear too terribly ill.

Eddie Hastings was an older man than most of them— nearly twenty-six. Although he wouldn't admit it, he was dying. Trapped in the trenches when a shift in the wind had unexpectedly sent a cloud of mustard gas gusting back over the British lines where it had originated, Hastings had sustained severe damage to his skin, his lungs, and his eyes. He was partially blind. His face, neck, and hands, which had not been covered at the time of the accident, were raw with suppurating lesions. Worst of all were his lungs, which, according to one of his doctors, were seventy percent dissolved.

"Dissolved?" Bret had repeated, horrified.

"The stuff's like acid—it corrodes whatever it touches."

He wasn't going to make it. Bret had been hopeful for him—for his attitude was cheerful and his one great desire was to get home to his wife—until last night, when he'd spiked the temperature that was the first sign of pneumonia. Tonight he was hot with fever and coughing in a harsh, agonized fashion that made Bret's lungs ache. She'd been giving him oxygen almost constantly, nearly as desperate to help him breathe as he was to take in air.

Eddie Hastings was a mistake for her, she knew. She'd been warned not to get emotionally involved with her patients, and the pace of her work was so relentless that there usually wasn't time for it to happen. But Eddie had been on the ward for three weeks now, and there was something so winning and sweet about him that before she knew it, he had become important to her.

" 'My dearest love,' Eddie repeated. " 'Tonight I've been dreaming of the way it'll be the next time we meet, which I pray the good Lord will be soon, for I yearn to hold you in my arms.' " He stopped dictating to cough, his thin body convulsing against the three pillows that kept his shoulders elevated. " 'I know we'll be together again. The doctors give me skeptical looks when I say that, but I know God wouldn't be so cruel as to take me from you now, just when the baby's coming and you need me the most. I know He means us to be together, laughing and loving, for many years to come. He wouldn't have given me the great and wondrous gift of your lively spirit, your fragrant hair, and the perfection of your body if He hadn't meant our love to endure for half a century, at least.' ''

He broke off, strangled for air. Bret gave him oxygen, turning her face aside as she surreptitiously brushed her sleeve across her tear-filled eyes. Eddie believed what he was writing. He must surely know how close he was to death, but for the sake of his young wife and his unborn child, he was determined to keep on fighting. His faith in God's goodness was absolute, and Bret envied him for that.

She no longer knew what to believe about God and His goodness. Her faith was something she had grown up with, accepting confidently and without question the existence of a Creator, a Comforter, a Giver of all things bright and beautiful. The joy she had always taken in breathing, laughing, running about with all her senses open had always seemed to her to prove that God was in His heaven and all was right with the world, and she'd never allowed for the existence of great suffering, sorrow, or despair.

But here in the hospital she had seen for the first time that all was not right. Hope was often futile, pain unending, and death relentless—always there, always waiting, the eternal mockery of human love and aspiration. No longer could she regard the world around her as the handiwork of a just and loving God.

"Eddie, I think you ought to rest for a bit."

He shook his head. "Just a few more sentences."

Bret wrote furiously as he dictated several lines of simple, earnest words that seemed to her more eloquent than the finest poetry. When the coughing flattened him once again, she repeated that he needed to take a break. "For an hour, at least, Eddie. I know how difficult it is for you to speak, and you're making yourself worse."

"You've got other patients to attend to, I know."

"It's not that. It's you I'm worried about, and the others

are all asleep, anyway. I want to give you some aspirin and try to get that fever down. We can finish your letter later.''

''I was nearly done anyway. Let me just sign it now, at the bottom of the page. We can leave room for a few more words.'' His unbandaged eye met hers, dark and tragic, and she saw that he understood, even better than she, how close, and how greedy, the shadows were. ''I want to sign it, just in case. I don't want her to think that I was ever, for even a moment, in despair.''

Bret put the pen into his boneless fingers and held it firmly while he scrawled his name.

''Thanks,'' he whispered, giving her a smile of perfect sweetness.

In less than an hour, he was delirious. ''Joan?'' His voice was thin and dreamy. His fever had soared despite all her efforts to control it.

Bret covered his hands with her own. His fingers, weak though they were, clutched tightly. ''You're there, aren't you, my love?''

''Eddie,'' Bret said softly. ''It's me, Bret.''

''Joan?'' He sounded anxious. His eyes opened, squinting as if the darkened ward were flooded with sunlight. He looked straight at Bret, who was concentrating on everything he had ever told her of Joan, what she looked like, how she talked. *Be here, Joan,* she thought. *Wherever you really are, whatever you are really doing, stop a moment and be here in spirit with your beloved as the darkness closes around him.*

Eddie sighed and smiled. ''Ah, dearest, it *is* you.''

Gently, Bret squeezed his hands.

''Joan, I love you. You're so pretty. You're with me now and we'll never be separated again. Will we? Joan?''

''Never,'' said Bret. She smoothed his brow with a cool rag.

''Don't leave me, dearest. It's dark and I'm afraid.''

''I won't leave you, Eddie.''

He smiled weakly. ''I knew God wouldn't part us. He couldn't be so cruel. I knew He'd send you to me.''

Bret swallowed painfully.

''Joanie?''

"I'm here," she whispered.

"Stay with me. Don't let go of my hand. Don't leave me alone in the dark."

"I won't leave you, Eddie. I promise."

Peacefully, trustingly, he hung on until the end. And when it was over and he had gone into the void alone without his beloved Joan beside him . . . when there was nothing left but the shell of his ruined body, so still, so cold, so empty of hope or love or light, Bret had to abandon the ward because not water, not tea, not brandy, not even a hug from Maggie could stop the deluge of her tears.

Bret retreated emotionally after Eddie Hastings's death. She allowed her wounded soldiers to run together in her mind for a while. Not that they didn't all have their own distinct personalities. They did, even the ones who never regained consciousness before slipping into the void. It was just that there were so many of them. So many wounds, so many cries, so many small acts of courage . . . on their part as well as on her own. And all for what? The war was senseless, as was the world.

She became an expert at her duties, and having proven herself by the fortitude of her stomach and the swiftness and gentleness of her fingers, she graduated to more skilled tasks, such as the insertion into various wounds and body orifices of everything from thermometers and drainage tubes to catheters and stomach tubing. Mistress of Rubber Tubing, she called herself, which amused Maggie, who suggested that if Bret ever grew weary of nursing she could no doubt set up a lucrative specialty trade in a high-class London whorehouse.

"How can you continue to *do* such distressing work?" Aunt Dorothy asked her on her days off, when Bret returned to her father's sister's house for a few needed hours of escape. She would take out her clay on these occasions, shaping figures furiously, then flattening them into formless lumps again. Perhaps there was a God, she thought at such moments. Perhaps He was so thoroughly dissatisfied with His creations that He was forming and destroying them in a similar manner.

"Heaven knows, the country is in dire need of nurses," said Aunt Dorothy, "but really, Elizabeth, it's such a sordid profession, most inappropriate for a girl of your tender years. I shudder to think what your father would say if he had any idea the intimacies you perform for those men. This wretched war is ruining everything and everybody. I haven't been invited to a single society wedding this Season! People are getting married, but they're rushing off to do it in registry offices—can you *imagine*?''

This was exactly the sort of wedding Maggie had had in August, when her fiancé came home on leave, still whole and unwounded. Justin's elder brother had been killed on the Somme, leaving him the heir to a large estate.

"He wants a son," Maggie confessed to Bret. "Oh, I know, it's not at all the sort of thing I ever imagined myself doing at this young age, but I love him, Bret, and he's afraid he'll die without an heir. Can you imagine marrying because one is afraid one is going to die? If I have a baby, I want my husband to be with me, to watch him grow up. I love him so much, Bret. It's just not fair."

"He'll come home safely, Maggie, I know he will. This horrible war will be over, and all our boys will come home."

But neither she nor Maggie believed it. The war that was supposed to have been finished before Christmas of 1914 was now more than a year old. Autumn had brought the horrors of the British defeat at the hands of the Turks at Gallipolli, where hundreds of thousands of troops died of wounds and dysentery. Although several of the VADs she knew had shipped out for the wretched straits at the west end of the Marmara Sea, while others were sent to France, Bret had remained in England, caring for the lads who made it home to Blighty, their term for England. But she lived in her imagination with her friends and relatives on the front lines, including Julian, who had become, by all accounts, an indefatigable chaplain to the fearful, the shellshocked, and the sick at heart, and Simon, who wrote to her every week from his post in France.

No matter how busy she was on the wards, she answered Simon's letters faithfully. She had heard from so many of her patients how important letters from home were, how they were pored over and treasured, read and reread. To some men their letters were talismans of luck that they carried into battle.

"One chap I know's alive because o' his sweetheart's letters," a surgical patient told her. "Great thick things they were, full o' all her moanings about how much she missed him, and was he wearing the woollie she knit for him, and to be sure and keep his feet dry—fat chance. Anyroad, chap was so worried about spoiling his true love's words o' love in the mud that he fashioned himself a pouch from old boot leather—chap had been a cobbler's apprentice before signing up—and stitched it up snug as a virgin's—uh, 'scuse me, Sister—stitched it up nice and tight and sewed the bloody thing to the inside o' his uniform. Course, you can probably guess what happened: Chap took a hit o' shrapnel in his shoulder, and what should the surgeons find when they go to patch him up but another piece o' metal that would o' killed him sure, lodged in the pouch right over the lad's heart."

After hearing this story, Bret wrote to Simon even more often, out of a superstitious belief that her letters would somehow keep him safe. These days her superstitions, she thought wryly, loomed much larger than her faith.

Ironically, considering how many of her patients dreaded being posted to the front lines, Simon was bored with his relative security in Paris.

> I know I shouldn't complain, hearing the horror stories coming out of the trenches. It's just that I feel useless. Tommy Chumondsley, my old friend from St. Swithin's, was killed on the Marne a fortnight ago—that makes at least half a dozen of my school-mates who've died. I have the most extraordinary feelings of guilt. Why them? Why not me? I had a dream last night in which they were all together, my dead chums, sprawled in easy chairs around a cheerily burning fire with great balloon glasses of brandy in their hands, nodding to the one empty chair and beckoning as if it were reserved for me.
>
> I know what you're thinking—good old Simon and his melancholic fancies. But sometimes I'm convinced that I was meant to die here, and if that's the case, I wish I could just go on down to the trenches and be done with it.

It was odd, but now that Simon was in danger, she thought about him more than she thought about Daniel. Her love affair seemed to have happened to another person, an innocent and adventuresome girl who had snatched at life and passion without having any concept of the consequences of her actions. It was not that she'd lost her spirit of adventure, or even her innate optimism. Despite the depressing nature of her work, there were times when she enjoyed it and felt proud of herself for being able to do it. But it had changed her. She felt herself to be sharper, tougher, more cynical, more wary of the pitfalls of life.

Daniel had not answered any of her letters. She knew from Verity that he continued to avoid military service, and that even if the general conscription order that the War Office was threatening came through, he was unlikely to be drafted. Now that Daniel was engaged in the important war-related industry of tin mining, he was too valuable at home to be sacrificed on the battlefield. Apparently the mine had been producing at an even greater rate than anyone had expected, earning Daniel substantial profits that he was plowing back into china clay. If Bret was correctly reading between the lines of her sister's letters, Verity was apprehensive about the degree of competition Wheal Faith was generating, particularly now that she was trying to make a go of her china-manufacturing business. Daniel Carne was a complication she would have preferred to do without.

Do it, then. If that's your dream, make it real.

If I succeed, I'll be yer father's rival one day.

That'll make life interesting, won't it?

Daniel might not have achieved the love and marriage he'd yearned for, but he hadn't come out badly. Nothing could ever change the fact that he had been her first love and that together they had explored the mysteries of their bodies with all the joyous abandon of the young. But she had discovered, to her initial dismay, that there were other male bodies on the face of the earth that were capable of attracting her.

Romances between nurse and patient were discouraged on the wards, but they tended to spring up all the same. Several of Bret's fellow VADs confessed their love affairs to her.

'' 'Tes silly to wait for your man to come home to your

bed when chances are he'll end up in a much colder resting place in France,'' Polly Marks declared after Bret caught her in the linen closet with her voluminous skirts around her waist and the eager hips of a one-armed lieutenant pumping between her thighs. ''Might as well enjoy ourselves while there's still some males left in the world.''

Bret's first surgical patient, Sergeant Francis MacDonald, had against all odds thrown off the infection in his thigh, kept his leg, and recovered the strength and ardor of youth. Unfortunately this meant that he would be sent back to the front, and since his last night before leaving for his new post coincided with Bret's evening off, she agreed to accompany him to supper and the theater.

She enjoyed his company, for Francis was a jovial man whose energy, now that he had recovered, was boundless. Supper, which included copious amounts of vintage claret— one of the advantages of Britain's being allied with France— proved to be such a delicious experience that they skipped the theater to linger over coffee. On the way back to the hospital, Francis stopped his borrowed motorcar on a darkened street and turned to take Bret into his arms.

Although she'd been expecting and even looking forward to this moment, Bret responded to his kisses and caresses with a heat that surprised her. She tore at his clothing every bit as ardently as he fumbled with hers, so desperate was she to feel warm, healthy male flesh beneath her palms. When he bared her breasts and kissed them, she arched toward his mouth, and when his fingers found their way through her petticoats and garters to the soft, slick petals that opened to receive him, she moaned every bit as eagerly as she ever had in Daniel's bed.

In the end it was only her fear of pregnancy, stronger now since Maggie had had to resign her nursing duty after conceiving her husband's much-desired heir, that prevented Bret from taking Francis MacDonald as her second full-fledged sexual partner. It did not prevent them from stroking each other intimately until their pleasure peaked, a substitute that he accepted cheerfully.

'' 'Twould weigh upon my mind over there, lassie, if I feared I'd left you carrying my child.''

She cried when he left, but she did not brood about his safety as much as she brooded about Simon's. Much as she had enjoyed his body, she wasn't in love with Francis. Her need for him, she sensed, had been a reaction to the despair that clouded the corridors of death where she spent her days, an acknowledgment that life and laughter still existed, and that healing was possible.

For now, she told herself, it was enough.

Chapter Thirty-six

"So how's the great experiment progressing?" Henry Trevor asked Verity one evening at supper. He was home at Cadmon Hall for a few days, a rare occurrence since the war had begun. Verity had ordered a hearty meal prepared, a challenge to the cook because of the shortages of meat, fruit, sugar, fat, and white flour. She'd also dressed carefully in one of the most attractive new frocks she'd made (using fabric from her old frocks, which seemed the only patriotic thing to do in this time of shortages). She didn't expect her father to notice that her clothes were far more stylish than they used to be, nor would he ever understand that her poise increased when she felt confident about her appearance.

"The china business will succeed, I'm sure of it. I need to find a new master potter, though." Just that morning she'd had to dismiss Claude dePierre, the temperamental Frenchman who had been designing her china and instructing her female apprentices. Scornful of women, dePierre had nonetheless attempted to seduce Annie Trillian, who had settled his hash with a well-placed knee. It was his third offense, and Verity had had enough. The Frenchman had been warned that she would not tolerate his treating her female employees disrespectfully.

"I've been ringing friends in the midlands, looking for

leads, but it seems that many of our best artisans and craftsmen have left England for the battlefield.''

"How about the Frenchman's apprentices?''

"They left with their master. I'd like to find a local potter. Preferably someone female, who won't be called to war if a general conscription is implemented. I wish Bret were home. She could have helped me in this.''

"I had a letter from her yesterday. Damn challenging, the hospital work she's doing. That girl's got more spirit than even I had realized. She makes me proud.''

Verity blushed as the old envy stirred. She hated herself for still being prey to it. Now that her life was improved in so many ways, she would have thought that she would be free of her negative feelings toward her younger sister.

"Has she described her work in any detail to you?'' her father asked.

"Not recently.'' Although Verity had written several letters to her sister, which Bret had dutifully answered, there remained a coolness between them. The cheery, newsy letters that Bret used to write her from boarding school bore little resemblance to the brief, restrained epistles that arrived sporadically for Verity now. The distance between them would not be closed, she feared, until they were once again face-to-face.

"I certainly hope that along with her war work Bret is continuing her art classes. Her talent is too great to be wasted. My fondest wish is that she will return to work with me at Cadmon Clay. If she were able to be here now, my problem would be solved. I could manage the business side of things and she could oversee the artistic side. That's the way I always dreamed it would be.''

"The little world of Trenwythan will prove too small for Bret, I imagine. She was meant for grander things.''

It was no small wonder that Verity felt jealous. She questioned whether sometimes her father said such things just to irritate her.

"As I recall, Bret learned most of what she knows about potting from Tamara Carne,'' Henry remarked.

Verity searched his face. It had been years since he'd mentioned Tamara to her. "I believe so.''

"I saw several exquisite examples of Tamara's work in a shop in St. Austell. They were earthenware, not porcelain, of course. I was told by the proprietor that the pieces are extremely popular with some of the wealthier residents of the town, although she continues to support herself selling clay bowls and pots and such to her peers."

"What are you suggesting, Papa?"

"I believe you discern my meaning, Verity."

"That I hire Tamara Carne? To replace Claude dePierre? That's impossible. She wouldn't work for me."

"Are you sure of that? She's always been remarkably independent."

"Papa, you don't still see her, surely?" It was common gossip that there was a widow in St. Austell who had an "arrangement" with her father that seemed to suit them both. Verity had believed his entanglement with Tamara to have ended many years ago.

"Only as friends," he said, sounding regretful. "She lives a lonely life, which she professes to enjoy. Still, I can't help but worry how she will get on in future years. It's no life for a woman, alone on the moors."

"If it is anybody's business to worry about her, it is her brother's, not ours."

"I do not ask for your charity on her behalf. I merely offer a solution to your current problem. You need a potter. Tam's work is both beautiful and original. Even you would have to agree that she's the finest potter in the St. Austell region."

"I have not seen any recent examples of her work, but even if you're correct in that assessment, I can't believe she would ever accept a job from one of the Trevors."

"Daniel would never do so, I agree. But what is true for Daniel has never been true for Tamara. Just because they are related does not mean they think or feel the same way. Tamara is as different from her brother as Bret is from you."

Verity took offense at this. He made it sound as if he equated Bret's character with Tamara's and her own with Daniel Carne's.

When Bret had left Verity had thought that her interaction with the Carne family would reach a welcome end. But she saw Daniel every month at the local Clay Owners Association meetings, where his wartime success had made him increasingly influential. His presence at these meetings was excruciating to her, all the more so because he seemed to take pleasure in contradicting everything she said. Worse, the other owners—all men—paid more attention to his suggestions than they did to hers. In the masculine world of business, she and Daniel were *not* equally disadvantaged. The poor clay worker received far more respect than the woman.

Her dislike for him had grown. His success both enraged and challenged her, and she took whatever small measures were available to her to frustrate him. He still wanted the strip of land adjoining the tin mine. Although the money he offered was substantial and would have been welcome as she struggled to get her china factory operating, Verity continued to refuse. To sell him the land he coveted would be to concede defeat.

And to hire his sister? To have Tamara working for her enemies?

She smiled at her father. "I'll speak to Tamara. Can I count on you to help me persuade her if she is reluctant to take the position?"

"Of course."

Tamara Carne knew who was standing on the other side of her cottage door before the knocking came. She had ways of seeing, of knowing, that must have come to her from her Gypsy mother, for in no other context could they be understood.

She did not know exactly what the other woman wanted, but she understood her visit as the latest sign of the invisible ties that bound these two families, one wealthy, one poor, to each other. Their destinies were entwined, for better, for worse.

And so she admitted Verity Trevor Marrick and listened to what she had to say. And was surprised. She had foreseen neither the proposition nor her own sudden yearning. To use her talent in a grander, larger way. To be provided with all the raw materials she needed, to have her pots fired in a modern, reliable kiln. She had never expected to have such an opportunity. Which went to show, she thought wryly, how limited the sight could be.

On the other hand . . . to leave her moorland home, to be surrounded by strangers, to be forced to work on someone else's schedule—she could not imagine such a life. "I thank 'ee for yer offer. But how can I accept? There's too much bad blood between our families."

"Tamara, we are grown women. Are we really going to let this ridiculous feud haunt us for the rest of our lives?"

" 'Tes Daniel. He's more vengeful than ever since yer sister left. He'll never understand if I come and work for 'ee."

"Who controls your life? You or your brother?"

Neither, Tamara was thinking, although she remained silent. Both her course and Daniel's had been laid down long ago by the man whose actions still reverberated, even from beyond the grave—Jory Carne.

"Tamara, I'm in desperate need of a master potter. I've seen your work. You're the finest potter in the region, and the finest is what I want."

"I am flattered, but—"

Verity drew something from underneath the folds of her cloak. A doll, with a flawless porcelain face. "Do you remember this?"

"A'course I do." Tamara smiled and took the doll. Its creamy skin had been molded and enameled by a master. " 'Twas this face that inspired me to begin working the clay. I've always been grateful to 'ee for that. What did ye call her?"

"Guinivere."

"Ah yes. I remember."

"Keep her this time. Let her inspire you again. I need you, Tamara."

"I'll do it on one condition," Tamara heard herself say. "I'll not come to Charlestown. I never leave the moors. If ye send yer girls to me, I'll train them, like I trained yer sister. But I must have my independence, my peacefulness, my solitude. I cannot work anywhere else but here in my own cottage, surrounded by my own things. 'Tes the only place where I feel safe."

Verity agreed.

When she went away, Tamara laid out her destiny cards, with Verity specifically in mind. What she saw in the fiercely colored archetypes came as a surprise. "So that's to be the way of it? 'Tesn't possible," she muttered, pushing the cards aside.

On the first day of March 1916, Bret received an alarming letter from Simon. Although he sounded cheerful, she read his words with an anxious heart.

> I've applied for, and been accepted into, the Royal
> Flying Corps. It seems they're rather low on chaps
> who've seen an aeroplane close up, much less flown
> one. They're sending me to England for a couple of
> months of training, then back here to the skies over
> France. It's dangerous, of course, but I love flying,
> and I'll finally see something of the war without
> having to rot in the trenches.

She couldn't imagine worse news. What had begun as aerial reconnaissance had turned into a new method of attacking the enemy—raining bullets and bombs down on them from the sky.

Her father was one of the primary designers of these horrific devices. He had started a new company, Trevor Aviation, to manufacture aeroplanes for the war effort. Like Daniel, he had government support for his venture, but according to Verity's letters he was also using large amounts of his own funds to finance the highly expensive operation.

How corrupt this war was making everyone! Despite everything she'd seen, every horror she'd witnessed, Bret had retained the view—foolishly naïve though it was beginning to seem—that all this evil and wasteful carnage would teach everybody that war was an obscenity that must be ended forever. But so far, it seemed that all anyone had learned was how to kill other human beings more efficiently.

All his life Bret's father had been obsessed not only with

flying but with flying for a worthy purpose: exploration and, eventually, transportation. What benefit could there be in building these new weapons of war that dealt death from the skies, like pagan gods heaving their thunderbolts? What honor could possibly be left in a world that would soon be capable of lifting armies into the air to strike from above, putting at risk entire populations of civilians, including the traditional noncombatants, women and children?

This was what had become of her father's dream. His marvelous aeroplanes which she had once so wholeheartedly believed in, had become instruments of terror. And gentle Simon, with his poet's soul, would soon be at their lethal controls.

Chapter Thirty-seven

On a partly cloudy morning in northern France in the late spring of 1916, the man they called the Phoenix climbed into his reliable de Havilland biplane and buckled his chin strap. He then wrapped a woolen scarf around his neck; the air would be bitterly cold at ten thousand feet.

Two of the excellent mechanics brought from England to provide the ground support necessary for the airmen of the Royal Flying Corps at their aerodrome in northern France grabbed a blade of the large wooden propeller and began to rotate it. The Phoenix ignited the engine, and with a cough and a roar the propeller began to turn rapidly on its own. As the mechanics moved the chocks from the wheels, the Phoenix throttled up and began his takeoff roll, swallowing the acrid engine exhaust blown back at him by the wind. The aeroplane rose, thrusting forward into the air at a steep angle.

After countless hours of flying, the Phoenix still found the moment of takeoff exciting. Other pilots reveled in loops and dives, but to him there was nothing more miraculous than feeling his bird defeating the forces of gravity as it rose gracefully into the air.

As he climbed and circled to await the others in his formation, the Phoenix waved encouragingly to the pilot of the nearest aircraft, a neophyte named Simon Marrick, just arrived from flight training in England. No doubt Marrick, like all the others, was eager to earn a name for himself as a hero and an ace. Cocksure fools. The new recruits tended to regard aerial warfare as some sort of glorious knightly jousting match in the clouds, the only noble and honorable way to fight in a war that had devolved into the horrors of mud trenches, poison gas, and long-distance artillery attacks from an enemy whose face you could never see. The Phoenix did not doubt Marrick's courage, but he was no longer moved by this sort of idealism. The kid would be lucky if he made it through his first engagement. The mortality among flyers, especially the new ones, was discouraging. In times of big pushes on the ground and corresponding fierce battles in the air, the average flying life of a British airman was something on the order of seventeen and a half hours.

After only five months in the Royal Flying Corps, the newest and by far the smallest branch of the British armed forces, the Phoenix was regarded as an old and accomplished veteran. He'd survived, while most of the men who'd started when he had were dead. He was an ace, having made the requisite five kills ages ago. There may have been a day when he'd felt proud of his prowess, but if so he was unable to recreate the feeling. The last Jerry aeroplane he had killed had crash landed and the pilot, thank God, had walked away. Finding ways to bring down aircraft without causing fire or explosion had become his most intriguing challenge, after staying alive himself. He hadn't confessed this idiosyncrasy to any of the others in his squadron. He was supposed to take out the pilots as well as the planes, in hopes that Germany would find it difficult to recruit new ones.

"Hurry it up down there," he muttered as he made another circle. There were still two machines on the ground. Now that he was airborne, he wanted to get started, get it over with him. He wanted to fly, not buzz around up there thinking. If a pilot thought, he worried, and when he worried, he risked freezing up. For all his kills and all his experience, the Phoenix had never purged himself of fear.

He wondered what the new young flyers who gazed at him with such reverence would think if he confessed that he went to bed every night praying for fog that would ground them. On the mornings when the sky was clear and patrols were unavoidable, he would skip breakfast to hunch in the camp latrine while his guts turned to water.

When he was actually flying, however, the urge to survive triumphed over the terror that he would not, and he was able to keep his head clear and his stomach under control. There weren't many men in the RFC who had flown before the war, and even fewer who had the Phoenix's almost preternatural talent for it. His long years of experience had taught him how far he could press his aeroplane in all conditions. His de Havilland was an extension of himself, and when he was totally focused, flying out of that quiet place at the center of his soul, the union between man and machine was so perfect that he was as graceful—and as deadly—as a hawk.

The formation was achieved when all eleven planes were airborne. With the Phoenix in the lead position at the point of the V, and the least experienced pilots, Marrick among them, strung out behind him, they droned toward German-occupied territory.

Today's mission was more than the usual reconnaissance to ascertain whether the enemy troops were gearing up their defenses for a British assault. That was rumored to be in the vicinity of the Somme. The Phoenix's orders were to attack the ground base of the new squadron of Boche fighters that had been devastatingly effective in their harassment of several key Allied positions.

They were to assault the base quarters with as many bombs as they could drop, wiping it out, if possible, and crippling the aircraft by depriving them of their vital ground support. Such tactics were more effective than shooting down planes, which could be replaced. But the mission was dangerous, for it meant advancing into German territory, using up fuel that was better reserved for the rigors of combat, and then high-tailing it back to the relative safety of the British lines.

The Phoenix didn't like the assignment. He and his men would have to contend with patrols seeking to intercept them before they reached their objective. If they passed that obstacle, they would then be forced to deal with defensive artillery on the ground. Even worse, given the Phoenix's new scruples about killing, they would have to attack the ground base, destroying empty planes, if there were any, hangar tents, fuel depots, supply lorries, the pilots' and the backup staff's meager living quarters, not to mention essential noncombatant ground personnel.

War was war, but such high levels of destruction made him sick.

The cloud cover thickened as they approached the trenches, faint tracings far below on the enemy's western front. The complex network of pits and tunnels, bunkers, and supply depots that made up the trenches looked strange and mechanical from the air, like the famous canals on the surface of the planet Mars. There were two sets of them, facing each other, separated by a pocked and barren no-man's-land. Boundaries. Lines of demarcation. It was strange to be able to see such lines, because one of the remarkable things about flying was the awareness that it gave you of the lack of boundaries. You grew up reading maps in your geography lessons and imagined that each country was separated from its neighbors by lines marking its borders. It wasn't until you took to the air and looked down at the earth that you realized how manmade such notions were, for the earth itself knows no boundaries; one hill, one wood, one meadow melts seamlessly into the next.

They were past the trenches now, inside enemy territory. The easy part of the mission was over. From now on they must be constantly on the lookout for the insectlike specks on the horizon that would signal the presence of enemy fighters.

It was cold. No summer at this altitude. The Phoenix liked it cold. All too often he awoke shaking from nightmares in which he was on fire, his skin shredding, his fat sizzling, his nerves screaming with pain. He'd crashed twice, the first time near the British lines without much petrol left in his plane, the second with half a tankful that had ignited on impact. He'd been lucky both times—minor broken limbs, a few superficial burns. It was after the second wreck that they'd started calling him the Phoenix and predicting that he would always rise from the flames. He wasn't so sure about this himself, remembering the saying from back home: Three strikes and you're out.

They droned on unmolested, deeper into German-occupied territory. No fighters appeared. *Probably busy bombing our ground bases*, the Phoenix thought.

The lack of interceptors might also be related to the weather, which grew worse as they flew east. When he'd first started flying combat missions, he hated the changeable weather over the Continent, fearing the blindness that resulted from the gray, disorienting mists. Now he worried less, trusting his compass and, for altitude, his instincts. Clouds provided nice cover. In clouds, no sharpshooting bastard in a Fokker could pin you down against a blazing blue sky and blast your wings to smithereens.

He glanced back along the V formation, wondering how Marrick, the rookie, was doing in the cloudy weather. He'd put him in the least exposed spot, hoping he'd keep his head and his nerve, for as squadron leader the Phoenix considered the kid his responsibility.

And then, dead ahead, the target. He couldn't believe it was going to be this easy. Half a mile to go, drop the damn bombs, do a little machine-gun strafing, then wheel around and head for home.

A dark spot at two o'clock. Just a shadow from the clouds? Goddamn, another. Didn't look like much, but his body processed the sight before his brain did and he rolled, tilting his wings in signal to the pilots behind him. The spots became winged creatures—enemy aircraft. Actually, they could be French, but it was impossible to tell at this distance.

Half a minute later he knew for certain they were Huns piloting Fokkers—vicious attack planes whose technology had been designed by the twenty-five-year-old Dutch genius Anthony Fokker. The Phoenix had corresponded with him before the war; in fact, they'd been fairly good friends. The Fokker craft was a honey of a machine, swift and maneuverable, mounted with vicious and efficient machine guns. Anthony had mastered the problem of synchronizing propeller rotation with machine-gun bursts, which meant a pilot could aim and fire straight ahead of himself without shooting off his own blades. Fucking war. Instead of fighting he would have climbed into one of those spiffy planes and put it through its paces and loved every minute of it. But now he had to be wary, for Anthony's clever engineering could easily kill him.

Fortunately, there were only six of them, to his eleven. If the Jerry squadron leader had any sense at all, he'd cut and run.

Instead, he engaged. Shit.

The Phoenix gauged the distance to the target. Hell, it wasn't far. With any luck at all they could defend against the enemy attack at the same time as they proceeded toward their objective. He had three highly experienced pilots with him today, and four who'd been in combat long enough to keep their wits about them. They split up smoothly into two prearranged groups: the first, including himself, Marrick, and the four pilots who were carrying the bombs, were to keep flying no matter what; the other five de Havillands were to engage and keep the Germans off the lead aeroplanes' tails.

The battle started almost at once, the air exploding around them as the rain of bullets began. The Phoenix's group was approaching the target when the air shook with the unmistakable sound of an aeroplane exploding. *Lots of fuel*, was his first thought: *one of theirs*. He grabbed a look backward. Still six Fokkers. *One of ours*.

A German plane soared upward, slipping past the defenders. It arced overhead, then fell into a dive, coming on at a speed that the Phoenix, flying level, couldn't hope to match. Goddamn! Target below. He signaled with his wings and let his bombardiers do what they'd been sent to do. One pretty pass would be all they'd have. . . . *Come on, come on, now! Yes, perfect* . . . The first bombs were away and exploding. Then the Fokker came on hard, straight at them, machine guns belching smoke and metal. "Evade, for chrissake, evade," he muttered as the plane behind Marrick, piloted by Jimmy Evans, a hell of a good companion and a brave man, held its course to drop its bombs. The Phoenix's de Havilland screeched in protest as he banked sharply to go to Jimmy's aid. His defenders, he saw, were scattered, at least two down, maybe three. Another Fokker had broken loose and was screaming after the lead planes.

Below, the bombs were hitting, sending more shock waves upward along with several funnels of black smoke. Then smoke erupted from a much closer source as Jimmy's machine took a direct hit in its fuel tanks and plummeted earthward.

The Phoenix reacted by banking again and climbing steeply. Marrick stayed steady on his tail, exactly as he'd been trained to do. The kid had good nerves. Personally, he felt as if he were about to throw up. It wouldn't happen until he got back to base; he'd had enough experience with his belly to know that. He'd hold together fine until he was out of the cockpit. Then his legs would shake and his back would sweat and he'd topple to his knees and vomit in the mud. No one ever laughed at him. The ground crews had seen worse. Some pilots wet their pants, and one of them, a hell of a joker in the officers' mess, grinned every time it happened to him, nodded to the wet spot, and said, "Fuckin' battle always makes me come."

Both unengaged Fokkers had locked on to him. They knew he was the squadron leader; they probably had orders to blast his ass. Now the kid was in jeopardy sticking so close, so he soared off into an upside-down loop and rolled away. Marrick followed. Jesus, the kid could fly; his loop was even more graceful than the Phoenix's. One of the Fokkers slid in on Marrick's blind side and let off a burst—a tricky shot and one that the kid didn't expect. He'd seen it before; he'd seen everything before. And yet it still felt new and raw and horrible to watch Marrick veer off, his little de Havilland wobbling.

Damn, he'd lost four, maybe five planes, and now his rookie had been hit. Marrick's machine was holding together, but it continued to lose altitude, whether from mechanical failure or from the kid freezing up on the controls, the Phoenix couldn't tell.

The Fokker that had nailed the kid was coming back around. The second one, thank God, had been engaged by another of the British de Havillands, leaving the Phoenix with some space to maneuver. He flew straight at the *scheisskopf* who was trying to finish off Marrick, his engines screaming like a jay defending its young.

He drew fire, taking a barrage of shells across his nose. Ping, ping, ping, crack. And then the pain, slight at first but building, in his right arm and shoulder.

As he struggled to maintain control he saw the kid pull out of his dive. Then Marrick was up and banking, damn him, instead of getting clear, which was what he had intended him to do. Back into the Fokker's sights—hot damn but that Jerry was good. The Phoenix gritted his teeth and pulled back on the stick with his bleeding right arm. Up, up, and over onto his side. Okay, good. He wasn't faint yet, that was a positive sign. Missed his arteries, probably.

The Hun, lured into chasing Marrick again, didn't realize what he'd picked up on his tail, poor bastard. Big mistake.

The Phoenix sighted down his powerful Lewis machine gun, aiming for the fuel tanks.

He was a damn good shot, one of the best in the RFC. That's what growing up in the Wild West does for you.

He squeezed the trigger. Seconds later the Fokker exploded.

The Phoenix flew past Marrick's plane, giving him a signal. The kid's face was pasty. He must have realized how close he'd come to dying.

The signal meant, "Let's get the fuck outta here."

"You saved my life," Marrick said.

Safe on the ground, the Phoenix clapped him on the back. "Hey, we all cover each other's asses. That's what this thing is about."

"You could have been killed yourself. Your shoulder . . ."

"Flesh wound. Bullet glanced right off. I'll probably be flying again tomorrow, sad to say."

"That flesh wound spattered your blood all over the side of your plane." The kid sounded shaky as hell, which was natural. He'd have liked him a lot less if he'd been cool and cocky. "I thought you were dead for sure."

"Not me. Why d'you suppose they call me the Phoenix? It's not just because of my hometown."

"You rise up out of the ashes and fly again?"

"So far, anyway. Truth is, I wish I'd get wounded seriously enough to rest up in England for a while, but no such luck."

"What's your real name?" Marrick asked.

"Zach Slayton," the Phoenix said. "From Arizona."

Part Six

1917

Hath not the potter power over the clay,
of the same lump to make one vessel
unto honour, and another unto dishonour?

*—The Epistle of Paul the Apostle
to the Romans 9:21*

Chapter Thirty-eight

On a cold January day, shortly after the start of 1917, Verity stood at the window of her office at Cadmon Clay and Porcelain. The dust from the clay seemed to freeze in the air, the exhaled breathings of the earth.

"No sign of him yet?" asked Gil.

Verity turned, managing a smile. "No, not yet. He's late."

Gil joined her at the window. "It's like the old watched kettle."

"Exactly." They were waiting for the postman. This was the day they were supposed to hear whether their contract with the army had been extended.

For nearly a year Cadmon Clay and Porcelain had been supplying several regiments of the British army with durable china drinking cups. General Dunfrey, an old school friend of Henry Trevor, had written personally to Verity to thank her:

> I say, old girl, our chaps are infinitely more cheery since they started taking their daily cuppa from your china. Staff likes it too because it takes the vibrations of the shelling even better than tin. The chaps here are wondering—do you do plates as well? I may be able to get you orders from the other regiments if you can furnish us with a sturdy dinner service.

Verity had written back immediately to tell the general that whatever the troops required, Cadmon would be delighted to provide. Then she'd hurried up to Tamara's cottage, which was now the scene of some of her greatest design brainstorming. With Tamara's and Verity's guidance, the potters in the clay works in Charlestown were turning out exceptionally fine finished products.

All this had cost more money than she had. Her bankers had advanced her more, with the caveat that she'd better begin earning a profit or this would be the last time they would take a risk on her. Jackson Stone, the family solicitor, had informed her that the Trevors must consider more-secure investments. "Henry's aviation company is risky enough without your exacerbating things, Mrs. Marrick."

When the china service was ready, Verity had shipped off samples to General Dunfrey. He'd written back that a new, much larger contract was in the works, an agreement that would eventually allow her to supply most of the army with china. Since then she'd been edgy with anticipation, waiting for definite word.

Business was bad in all industries that were not war related and was worse than ever in the claypits. Clay companies were closing down as workers became increasingly hard to find. Not even women wanted the jobs these days; they were off to the cities to work as factory girls or bus conductors. Employment opportunities for women had increased greatly now that the men were away, and there were many industries that paid better and required less physical labor than the china-clay companies.

War shortages also interfered with business. Because there was so little petrol available, the lorries that the clay producers had begun to use before the war were back in their garages. Horse-drawn wagons rolled through the streets of St. Austell once again. Coal for the beam engines that pumped the clay slurry to the surface of the pits was also in short supply. All the while, the juggernaut of war continued, ruthlessly grinding up men and machinery, hearts and minds.

The newspapers referred to the situation as a stalemate. Every time one side or the other mounted an offensive, the heavily entrenched and fortified lines remained virtually unchanged. One army might brave the mines, poison gases, and barbed wire of no-man's-land long enough to gain a small hill or valley, only to lose it a few days later. Hundreds of lives would be given to gain a few feet of pockmarked ground. It was a war without victories, military or moral. In the view of an increasing number of participants, trench warfare was a horror that the world must learn to do without.

Verity hated the war, but she refused to be crushed by it. Her father and Daniel Carne were both profiting from the conflict, and her dream for the future of Cadmon Clay and Porcelain depended on her doing the same. "We need that contract," she said to Gil.

"We'll get it. We've done well so far. Things'll work out."

"I don't know, Gil. I have an ominous feeling that something's about to go wrong."

"Rot. We'll get the news, and it'll be good. Don't you fret. Get some work done. I'll be down at C-five." He was referring to claypit 5, currently their largest producer. "Send someone out to get me when the post turns up."

Verity massaged her temples with her fingertips, trying to still the throbbing there. She was proud of what she had accomplished, but in order for it to continue, they must have that army contract.

She left the window and returned to her desk. "Stop wasting time," she told herself sternly. She returned to work and lost track of the time. When at last the postman turned up on his rattly old bicycle, she hurried out to greet him. It was not, she realized at a glance, the regular postman. But the War Office cablegram he put into her hand was marked "official business," so she eagerly ripped it open.

It said nothing about tea mugs. What it said was that most regrettably, her husband, the Reverend Julian Marrick, had been killed in action in France.

When the initial shock subsided, Verity was surprised at the depth and fervor of her grieving. She had not expected Julian to die. When she'd thought of the dangers of the war, it was not Julian she had worried about, but Simon. The newspapers were full of the exploits of Britain's flying knights-errant—their skill, their glory, their sangfroid. The rate at which they died was not widely discussed, although it was obvious to anyone following the progress of the battles in the air. One month's newest ace was the next month's fallen hero. It was the young men, full of promise, who succumbed to this hateful war, and Julian, she'd always thought, would tough it out and survive.

Although she no longer loved him, for seven years he had been her husband, the companion of her household, and the partner of her bed. She was surprised to find that these things counted a great deal more than she'd supposed they would.

Her adjustment to widowhood was complicated by the public nature of her husband's death. Because of the fortuitous presence of a war correspondent, the *Times* had printed the story of the noncombatant chaplain who had left the relative safety of the trenches in order to go to the aid of two injured soldiers pinned down in no-man's-land during the last gasps of an insignificant battle. He had successfully dragged the first man back to safety and returned for the second man when a new burst of shelling began. Despite the explosions all around him, Julian had attempted to resuscitate the young soldier. When that had proved useless, he had performed an impromptu form of the last rites for the dying soldier, a Roman Catholic from Ireland who was crying out for a priest.

"I'm not a priest, of course," the *Times* quoted Julian as saying before he died, "but I don't believe the good Lord differentiates. I gave him the holy sacrament of Extreme Unction of the Church of England, and he was comforted, giving up the ghost in my arms in perfect peace and tranquillity."

Refusing to leave the boy while he was dying had cost Julian his own life. A shell exploded less than a yard away from him, driving shrapnel into his large body in several places. He had managed to crawl back to the Allied trenches, dragging the dead boy to whom he'd ministered, before collapsing from loss of blood.

"Ironically," the *Times* correspondent wrote, "there was no other chaplain near enough to give the last rites to this brave and selfless man, who remained conscious for several minutes before dying of his wounds. He expressed no regret, however, saying he was proud to have been doing the Lord's work, and commending his spirit to God."

Verity was surprised and moved by the response generated

by the article, not only from the people of Trenwythan—none of whom had any idea that she and Julian had been estranged—but from strangers all over the country. During the first few weeks the post brought scores of sympathy notes. The visits to his widow were so numerous that Verity had to leave Gil in charge of their clay and china production while she remained at home to receive the mourners. Julian's body had been buried in France, but a memorial service conducted for him by Reverend Greystoke, the new vicar of St. Catherine's, was filled to overflowing with the full Anglican congregation, most of the village's Methodists, numerous curious onlookers from out of town, and members of the press. The newspaper piece had made Julian a hero and his widow a somewhat reluctant spokeswoman for his honored memory.

"How does it feel to have been married to such a saintly Good Samaritan?" was the question she was asked most often.

"My husband was not a saint," she would answer patiently. "He would have preferred to be remembered as an ordinary man."

At the beginning when the news was fresh, she tried to stave off her intense and confused feelings of grief—which seemed to grow rather than fade as the weeks passed—by reminding herself that the public image that had ballooned around Julian was largely the creation of the British press, who were hungry for an inspiring story of unusual courage or heroism to set against the horrors of the ugly war. She had to force herself to remember Julian's violence, his faithlessness, his lies, his need to remain in absolute control. But she had other memories, too, which she had tended to put out of her mind since their separation: his golden preaching voice and how it had mesmerized her; his breadth of knowledge, which had been admirable; the many good things he'd done to help the members of his congregation at St. Catherine's.

"We are all imperfect beings," he had written from the front. "But I have come to believe that with God's mercy, there is not a soul among us that is irredeemably black. Not even my own."

It was the only allusion he had ever made to what had gone wrong between them. But in his letters from the trenches she'd sensed a serenity, or at least a resignation, about his role in God's plan that was different from anything he'd expressed in the past. She hoped this meant he had conquered his deepest fears and found a measure of peace before his death, and that in freeing a doomed soldier from his terror of dying unshriven, Julian himself had atoned.

In Carne Cottage, which he was having renovated, Daniel groaned out the sounds of his pleasure, kissed his lover one final time, and rolled off her body. He'd had a long day and wanted to sleep. He knew she'd climaxed and he hoped it would shut her up. It irritated him that she seemed unable to be able to go to sleep without chatting for at least half an hour. He'd seen this with enough women to be convinced that it was the talk, not the sex, that made a woman feel loved. If you said the right things to them—if you just *listened* to them, for God's sake, they'd do anything for you.

"Ye know, I'm gettin' fed up with hearing about how Reverend Marrick died such a great hero," she said. "It never stops. They're talkin about erecting a memorial to his gallantry in the churchyard."

"Go to sleep, Tess. 'Tes bloody late and I have to be up early."

"Randy old Julian a hero. Gawd, that makes me laugh. Makes a few other girls in the village laugh as well, too."

This caught his attention. " 'Randy old Julian'?"

"How he never got caught by the bishop is more'n I can tell, but I suppose they protect their own in the church, just like everywhere else. I mean, they're human, aren't they? He certainly was."

"The vicar of St. Catherine's was a cocksman with the ladies? Ye're a proper little tart, aren't 'ee, Tess? Didn't anybody ever tell 'ee not to slander the dead?"

" 'Tes no slander, 'tes the truth. The vicar of Trenwythan liked young girls. Jeez, I thought everybody knew that. Certainly the lasses round these parts did."

Daniel recalled that Tess had been a housemaid in the vicarage for a while. "How d'ye know? Were 'ee one of them?"

She turned coy. "I'm not saying I was and I'm not saying I wasn't. I'm jist saying I knew his ways, that's all."

"If ye don't want to tell me about it, fine. I'm bloody tired."

"I' truth, he's been paying me to keep my mouth shut. But now that he's dead he'll not be paying me anymore. And I think it's a proper disgrace that he's treated like a bloody hero when he ruint the lives of several girls I know."

"Jesus, Tess! Ye mean ye've been blackmailing him?"

" 'Tweren't my idea!" she protested. " 'Twas him that came to me and told me how important it was that nothing ever get about that would sully his reputation. Not that he ever worried about the reputations of the girls he used—oh no, not him. But I liked his wife, kind of—I mean, I felt sorry for her, so I agreed to keep quiet. And every sixmonth since there's been more money from him—not a lot—just a couple o' quid, to help me get on in life."

Daniel reached over and lit the lamp. Anything to do with the Trevors and their scandals interested him. "Tell me the whole story."

"Well, I don't know—"

He slid a leg between hers and brushed one hand over her breasts. "Tell me and I'll do something extra special to please 'ee after."

So Daniel learned Julian Marrick's shameful secret, and afterward, with a certain adeptness that she certainly hadn't learned from the Reverend Julian Marrick, Tess amused him by demonstrating the pure virginal act that Marrick fancied. It accorded so poorly with her true personality that Daniel couldn't help laughing, although when she played reluctant and wouldn't open her legs to him, he was surprised to find that her unaccustomed resistance excited him to greater than usual flights of passion. Since he'd lost Bret, sex hadn't been much more than an appetite to him.

It was not until this was over that Tess made the remark that destroyed all hope of sleep: "I guess I always figured ye knew about the vicar 'cause yer father knew, and Jory was a great talker."

"What d'ye mean, my father knew?"

"Just that. My pa, God rest his soul, was the publican

down to the Lion's Paw pub in St. Austell, and I used to help out, wiping tables and such when I was just a girl. One night when I was there, there was a spot o' trouble. Henry Trevor was yelling at Jory about his daughter—Verity—the one the vicar married, and Julian came in to break it up. I didna' catch it all—there were other customers, and besides, the vicar kept telling Jory to keep his voice down. But I heard enough to know they were all accusing each other. Who was Marrick to lecture him, says yer pa, since the vicar was diddling the fourteen-year-old daughter of a mate of Jory's. 'Twas shocking for me, I can tell you, me a young lass of ten or eleven. Here was a bloomin' vicar who couldna' keep his cock inside his trousers.''

Daniel had risen from bed during this narrative and was now stalking back and forth across the room. "When, exactly, was this?"

"Yeah, well, funny ye should ask because I always wondered if the vicar felt guilty about that. 'Twas the night yer pa died. 'Twas obvious that poor Jory's head twisted around backward, and it seems to me a godly clergyman would of helped him home instead of storming out of the pub and leaving him a-drinking. Yer pa was left to stagger out alone onto the highway where he never saw that clay wagon coming until it was too late."

Tess gasped as Daniel returned to the bed, swept the blanket off her, and jerked her to her feet. "Hey, ye're hurting me!"

"Are ye absolutely certain all these things happened on the night my father was killed?"

"Course I'm certain. That's the main reason it's stayed so clear in my mind these last few years. If Jory hadn't of died, he might have told what he knew about Reverend Marrick's itch for youngish girls, and Miz Trevor wouldn't of married him, and nobody'd be thinking of him as such a war hero today."

"Christ!" The shadow man; the shadow man. What had he looked like? Had he been big and heavyset like Julian Marrick? Damn the fog that had clouded his body and obscured his shape.

Tess backed away, reaching for a blanket to shield her

nakedness. Daniel seemed not to notice, or care, that he was naked as well. "What's going on wi' 'ee, luv?" she asked.

"Didn't ye ever tell the authorities about this?"

"The coppers weren't much interested, as I recall. Anyway, why should I have told them?"

Daniel cursed violently. "Ye heard my father threaten Reverend Marrick, a clergyman, with exposure of something that would blast his reputation, and ye never told anybody?"

"I only heard bits and pieces of the argument. Besides, I was a child at the time. 'Twasn't till later, when I worked in his house and the vicar came after me, that I put it all together. Anyway, so what? I thought it was Trevor ye suspected of killing yer pa."

"It is, dammit!" Daniel's brain was whirring as he sorted through the various possibilities. "But the stumbling block to that theory has always been that Marrick claimed Trevor was with him at the vicarage for most of the night. Until now there was no reason for anybody to believe the good reverend was telling a lie. But if he was a molester of fourteen-year-old girls, and if my father knew about it . . . Christ. Didn't the possibility ever cross yer mind that maybe Marrick murdered Jory to keep him quiet?"

Tess blinked up at him. "Don't be daft. Julian wouldn't murder anybody. He was a man of God!"

Daniel barked a laugh. "A man of God who amused himself by screwing young girls. All this time I've been thinking that the only person who wanted my father dead was Henry Trevor. Now it turns out Marrick had a motive as well. Either of them could have done it. Or both."

"Come back to bed, Daniel. Don't work yerself into a sweat over this. Ye still can't prove it, and anyway, Julian Marrick's dead. It's not as if ye're ever going to get justice, or even revenge."

In his mind's eye Daniel saw the great brooding bulk of Cadmon Hall, its glowing windows mocking him, its mistress wandering among the treasures that Jory had always spoken of with so much reverence, envy, and yearning.

Julian Marrick was dead, yes, but his widow was still alive.

Chapter Thirty-nine

"I agree with Mrs. Marrick," Daniel Carne said to James Stannis, who had once been his boss and was now his peer. He cast a quick look around at the other members of the Clay Owners Association before continuing, "The work incentives she's started at Cadmon Clay have earned more profits than they've cost. Instead of accusing her of caving in to pressure, we ought to be following her lead. I, for one, am going to institute similar policies immediately."

"Hear, hear," someone said. Verity was too astonished to notice who. Daniel Carne speaking up to defend her point of view in a Clay Owners meeting? Such a wonder had never happened before.

She looked at him suspiciously, noting, not for the first time, that he had changed significantly from the poor clay worker whom she'd refused to consider as a possible suitor for Bret. He wore his black hair shorter now. The premature touch of gray at his temples made him look graver, more serious. His suits were tailored, and although his shirts still retained a touch of the rumpled, loose-collared working-class look, this fit in well with his big hands, broad shoulders . . . even his sensual mouth. Success and money were never going to change Daniel into a member of the gentry, but they had accorded him an air of power and assurance.

"I'm a clay worker's son," she had often heard him say. "That's what I was born, that's what I'll always be. But I'm going to be a goddamn *rich* clay worker's son, ye can count on that."

From everything Verity had heard about the success both of his tin mine and his clay company, he was well on his way.

"I thank you, Mr. Carne, for your support," she said,

giving him a brilliant smile. She smiled more often these days because she felt more attractive. It had recently occurred to her that she looked more youthful than the other thirty-year-old women she knew. Her failure to have children saddened her, but it had left her with a girlish figure at a time when other women were struggling with expanding waistlines and drooping breasts. She rode on the moors every morning, so she felt fit and energetic. She had mastered the subtle use of cosmetics, and from French fashion magazines she had learned to dress and accessorize herself in clothing that flattered her figure.

The effect of her increased self-confidence on the males of her acquaintance had been startling. Since shortly after Julian's death she had found herself the object of the sort of masculine admiration and courtesy that she had longed for as a girl. Unfortunately, the men she knew tended to be both elderly and married. The war had claimed an entire generation of eligible younger men.

Verity felt slightly guilty that she should be relishing the attention of other men only seven months after her husband's death, but it seemed ludicrous to pretend that she had been happy in her marriage. For the sake of decorum, she would have to keep up the forms of mourning for the traditional one-year period, but this did not mean that she could not begin to feel like a woman again.

She had every reason to be proud of her accomplishments. Business was robust. Her army contract had come through and, in addition, several retail outlets were buying her durable china. Since it was less expensive than fine porcelain, the retailers expected a boom in everyday china among the members of the population who could not afford more elegant dinnerware. Once she increased her profits, she would be able to expand the production of fine china that she had modestly begun that spring.

She was a success. Even her colleagues at the Clay Owners Association were beginning to recognize it.

Daniel Carne intercepted her as their meeting broke up. "D'ye have a moment? There's something I'd like to speak with 'ee about."

Her instinct was to refuse, but he had been so polite lately that she felt obliged to reciprocate in kind. Shortly after Julian's death Daniel Carne had begun treating her with a remarkable lack of animosity. She did not entirely trust it, for she sensed a conflict between what he revealed on the surface and what he held inside, but it was such a relief not to have to spar with him at the monthly meetings that she did not question his behavior.

"I'm listening."

"Why don't we sit down." He nodded to a table in the public room of the Rashleigh Arms, where the Clay Owners Association meeting routinely met. It was an old inn in Charlestown, bulky and comfortable, just up the road from Verity's china factory.

He conducted her to the table, held the chair for her, and pushed it in with all the courtesy and aplomb of a gentleman. His hand brushed her arm as she sat down. The brief touch had a queer, unsettling effect on her. The need to escape rose once again; she had to ridicule it in order to fight it down.

He sat opposite her. The smallness of the table brought him closer to her than she would have liked. She had an unwelcome image of him and her sister in bed together on that awful night when she'd unwittingly intruded on them. The flash of Bret's bare skin, the angry challenge of Daniel's nakedness.

"I suppose it's about the land again? You're going to offer me an even larger sum to part with it? You needn't bother. The answer is still no."

He looked at her for a long moment. "Ye're a strange one, Mrs. Marrick. I can't quite make 'ee out."

"What do you mean?"

"Ye're a businesswoman, and a good one, too, from what I've seen. As ye know, there's excellent clay on that land. Tin, maybe, as well. But with all yer outlays for yer china business, ye can't afford to develop it. The money I'm offering 'ee would come in handy. It's no secret that yer father's invested heavily in his aviation ventures. That must be putting quite a drain on the Trevor fortune."

Although this was true, Verity was annoyed that he should know it. Were her struggles with her father over his expenditures—which he justified with patriotic bluster—common gossip throughout the region?

"But ye refuse to sell, no matter what I offer 'ee. Now what kind of a business decision is that, d'ye suppose?"

"It's not a business decision. It's a matter of principle."

"What principle? That the rich have the right to steal from the poor? That old wrongs should never be righted? I liked yer principles better twenty years ago. Remember the day ye gritted yer teeth and took a flogging ye could have avoided if ye'd kept yer mouth shut? In those days, yer heart was in the right place."

She flushed at his tone. "You're mocking me." She made as if to rise. And was surprised when he stopped her, one hand on her arm. It was a large hand, a worker's hand, strong.

"I wasn't mocking 'ee. Nor did I intend to argue with 'ee, honestly." He paused, then added with as charming a smile as she had ever seen on a man, "Forget the land. If ye're going to persist till doomsday in refusing to sell it, I don't see much sense in offering 'ee more. That's not why I asked 'ee here."

She waited.

"Ye're a smart woman, Mrs. Marrick. Like me, ye've found ways to take advantage of this war—ye with yer teacups and me with my tin. All the same, if ye'll permit me, there's one area in which ye're making a critical mistake. Ye can't expect to run a fine chinaworks out of Charlestown. The days of going from raw material to finished goods all within a stone's throw of each other are long in the past. Take my advice and close yer experiment down before it ruins 'ee."

"That sounds like another of your infamous threats."

The smile again, accompanied this time by a lingering study of her lips. " 'Tes just a little free advice. Ye needn't listen to it. Although I know ye're not entirely averse to taking advice from the Carnes. Ye take Tamara's."

Verity felt heat rising in her neck and face. The rapid change of mood and subject was throwing her off kilter.

"Yeah, I know she works for 'ee, quiet though ye've both kept it. Ye needn't worry that I'm going to interfere. I'm not my sister's keeper. Tam's always made up her own mind about things. Still, she's turned into a moorland recluse, and it can't have been easy to convince her to throw pots or whatever the hell she does for 'ee. It proves what I've suspected for a long time—ye're a worthy adversary.''

"So are you," she said, then flushed again. She had no idea why she'd said that. It had come out as a compliment, and she had no desire to compliment him.

"I've always admired yer spirit," he said slowly. "From the day we met and fought with each other in the schoolyard. Ye weren't afraid of me the way all the other little girls were. I'll never forget how well ye bore yer thrashing from that ogre Brockelsley. Ye were a spoiled little rich kid, but ye endured yer punishment and earned everyone's respect."

"I almost died because of that fight. You gave me scarlet fever."

"Yeah. I had it. And many's the time I've thanked God for it since it's kept me out of the war." He paused. "I also admired 'ee on the day ye came to me, alone and resolute, to give me Bret's letter. I was angry enough then to assault 'ee, or anyone else from yer family. But ye didn't seem afraid. And I have t'admit, 'twas a good deal I struck with 'ee that day."

"Not so good for Cadmon Clay. You've proven to be a tiger of a competitor."

"I've been thinking that such worthy adversaries ought to give some consideration to not being adversaries at all."

"What do you mean?"

"We've been hating each other for no good reason. Maybe 'tes time to stop."

"I've been under the impression that you believed your reasons to be excellent."

"And I'm saying that maybe I was wrong."

Verity blinked. Daniel Carne admitting he was *wrong*? "Forgive me if I'm skeptical about your change of heart. You must want that land a good deal more than I had supposed."

Something showed, briefly, in his expression, but he quickly brought it under control. "Believe what ye like, but 'tesn't the land that's motivating me to make peace with 'ee." He reached inside his coat pocket and drew out something. It was a tiny but perfect clay bird, a dove with outstretched wings. Made of fired clay, it was exquisitely painted, and its delicacy was so great that it appeared to be actually able to fly.

He held it out to her on the palm of his hand. She took it, carefully. "Where did you get this?" she asked even as it occurred to her that it must be Tamara's work. And yet there was something flamboyant about the style that did not accord with Tamara's elegant precision. "Is it your sister's?"

" 'Tes Bret's. It came to me all wrapped and packed in cotton, just a few days ago. No letter. She used to write me lots of letters, but she gave up, finally. I guess because I never answered."

Ignoring the fact, for now, that Bret was still making gestures toward her old lover, Verity concentrated on the bird, which she set on the table between them. It was beautiful. It proved everything she had ever believed about her sister's talent. She had surpassed Tamara, her teacher. She had crossed over into the realm of true art.

"The dove's the symbol of peace," said Daniel. " 'Tes what she's always wanted between our families."

Verity tried to look into his eyes, but they were averted. Hypocrisy, she wondered, or embarrassment? It was he who had kept the feud smoldering. Could he really want to give it up? "What about Jory's death? As long as you still blame my father for that, I don't see how you can possibly—"

"I'm not offering to make things up with yer father," he cut in. His eyes were on her now, and they were the same as always—light blue flints sparking angry fire. "Nor even with Bret, who betrayed me. 'Tes ye and me I'm concerned about. We have to come together in these monthly meetings with the other owners, and there may be a time when we'll have to come together in other ways if we're going to survive."

"What do you mean?"

"The world is changing, and from what I can see, few of the other claypit owners have any notion of changing with it. Take James Stannis, for instance—that old buzzard who blackballed me after the clay strike. He thinks the war'll end and things'll go back to the way they were before. He's wrong. Maybe the strike didn't change things the way we thought it would, but the war's succeeded where the strike failed. Jack's on a par with his master, and not only in the trenches. Servants are leaving the great houses and flocking to the city to make new lives for themselves. Newspapers are all over the place, so people know what's going on in the world. Women're working in the factories, wearing shorter frocks and brassieres, painting their faces, smoking cigarettes. Some are even having children out of wedlock and thumbing their noses at anyone who disapproves. Ten years ago—hell, five—could any of these things have happened? Ten years from now, what new wonders will we see? The old forms and values are exploding. The grain thresher's rolling, cutting everything down and grinding it up. Ye want to survive, ye jump up and roll along with it. Stay in the fields and ye're dead."

The force of his personality was so strong that it seemed to spread out and fill the room. As Verity tried to think of something to say, he went on, "Since the war started, the world has found other sources of china clay. The British clay industry won't survive if it doesn't change. And from what I see looking around me, ye and I are the only ones who've taken any kind of decisive action during this war. We're the only ones with any proven adaptability. A clay worker's son and a woman. Maybe we've had more incentive to show the bastards we could do it."

"That's been part of my motivation, I'm sure," Verity admitted. "When someone tells me something's impossible, I tend to take it as a personal challenge."

"I challenge 'ee now, then: Put yer mind to the problem of how ye and I can stop feuding and work toward a new future."

"You're suggesting that we should bury the hatchet, as they say in America? Cooperate? A Trevor and a Carne?"

He grinned, and this time something danced in his blue eyes. "That's right. I'm suggesting we cut ourselves a separate peace."

"Very well, Daniel. I'm willing to give it a try."

Grinning, he picked up Bret's dove and stroked it with the tip of one callused finger. "I appreciate that, Mrs. Marrick."

He watched her as she walked composedly out of the Rashleigh Arms and into the street where she had a motorcar waiting to take her home to Cadmon Hall. From the rear, her figure was slim and neat, making her appear younger than he knew she was. She wasn't bad from the front, either, with those great dark eyes and that tight mouth that seemed to be daring him to kiss it. If what he had learned from Tess about the travesty of her marriage was true, it had been a long time since Verity Trevor Marrick had known passion, heat, and sensuality. Maybe she'd never known them.

Easy. No contest. Set 'em up and knock 'em down.

What a bastard ye're turning into, Carne.

He reminded himself that he'd told her no lies. In the long run, a truce between them would benefit his business. And he did respect her as an entrepreneur. Selling inexpensive crockery to the military had been a clever idea, although her idea of making quality porcelain here in Cornwall would never succeed. There was too much competition, and the market for fine china was unlikely to expand. If that was her dream, she would have to surrender it.

At his hands, she would surrender many things.

Daniel turned Bret's dove over in his hands. Memories that he had tried for years to squelch rose to haunt him. She was still there, in his mind, no matter how hard he tried to will her away. She was an unwelcome distraction, reminding him of a time when his heart had been larger, his conscience clearer, and his pockets empty.

He allowed the dove to slip through his fingers. When it struck the floor he ground it to dust beneath his heel.

Verity felt shaky during the ride home. She was unable to forget the look in Daniel's eyes, the feel of his hand upon her arm. She remembered looking down at it, seeing the strength in his fingers, the tan skin, the faint tracing of veins in which his blood danced.

Other images came as well: again, the sight of him in bed with her sister, the virile grace of his naked physique as he confronted her father. And even—this was silly, she knew—the memory of the fight they had had in the schoolyard when he, a schoolboy, had knocked her down. It brought her a throb of pleasure, there, right down in her vitals, to imagine herself so close to him, his hands on her flesh, his body subduing hers.

What was happening to her?

That night Verity had a dream such as she had never dreamed before. A naked young man was kneeling between her widespread thighs. He was thrusting himself into her body; she could feel him going in, sliding out, going in again, harder. She could feel herself moving in response, lifting her hips to meet him, circling and heaving them in the most wanton manner while the pleasure in her belly grew and grew.

The young man murmured to her—love words, sex words, tender urgings. He was all over her, his naked flesh rubbing against hers in every possible way. He was all around her, all inside her, lovely, lovely, young and hard.

She woke to a frantic throbbing between her thighs. At first, still half-asleep, she enjoyed the feeling; then as her reason began to function and she realized where the pleasure was coming from, she rolled on her side and clamped her legs together. Shame rushed over her as the dream images replayed on the insides of her eyelids. She opened her eyes to stop them, but the sensations in her body still reverberated.

It would have been bad enough if the young man in the dream had been some nameless, faceless stranger. But she knew him. His hair was black, his eyes were Gypsy blue, and along his cheek ran the scar that marred the face of her former enemy, Daniel Carne.

Chapter Forty

During the next few weeks Verity kept running into Daniel Carne. She saw him at clay owners' meetings. On the moors. In the village. One Sunday she even saw him in church. He always greeted her, always smiled at her. He followed her with his eyes in a manner that made her feel more attractive than she ever had before.

One day while she was taking her customary ride on horseback on the moors, Daniel came thundering over a rise behind her. Smiling, he allowed his own mount to fall into step beside hers. He said good morning to her, exchanged a few pleasantries, then rode on, leaving her vaguely disappointed. Three mornings later she ran into him again. This time he asked if he might ride along with her for a while. She could think of no objection.

Seeming perfectly natural and at ease, he chatted with her about the clay business. Once again Verity was impressed with his knowledge, his vision. It occurred to her that she had begun to like and admire him. Outside in the early dawn, with the breezes caressing the moor grasses and the early sun burning away the dew and giving the air a bright misty quality, it was easy to forget the ancient rivalry between their families.

When she met him again the following morning, Verity could no longer doubt that Daniel was doing his damnedest to keep the pact of friendship they had made in the Rashleigh Arms. At the end of their ride he said, ''Tomorrow?'' When she nodded, feeling pleased and fluttery inside, he reached out and briefly covered her gloved hand with his.

Not friendship, she realized. He was trying to seduce her.

The following morning they rode hard, giving their mounts their heads and racing over the heath, laughing as they snatched the lead from each other. In a valley formed by three slag heaps of an abandoned claypit, they dismounted and talked for a while, keeping a subtle distance between them and making no move to close it.

But when he helped her back onto her horse, the feel of his hands at her waist and the small of her back caused a tumult in her body that Verity had never experienced before. He handed her the reins and she snatched them, breathing hard. She thought she saw him smile as he turned away from her. He knew he had her. The only thing left to be resolved was when.

That day, Verity resolved never to allow herself to be alone with Daniel Carne again. No good could come of it. She would ride in the evening, not the morning. She would avoid him.

The following morning, despite her resolutions, she rode out at dawn as usual. Daniel did not appear. He left her alone for the rest of the week, never once showing his face. It was her own fault, she decided. She must have done or said something to put him off. In her agony of wondering what she had done wrong, she forgot that she didn't ever want to see him again. For her to reject him seemed the right and sensible course, but for him to reject her was unendurable.

Her nights were miserable, sleepless, and storm-tossed. She wondered whom he was with; she'd heard the rumors—everyone had—about his various amours. She hated her rivals. She wanted him. It was all she thought about. Now that this chasm of longing and unfulfillment had opened in her soul, Verity understood for the first time the power of erotic attraction. She thought of him so obsessively that it seemed to her he must be thinking of her as well.

Just less than a fortnight after their last ride together, Daniel was waiting when she rode out at dawn. She saw his horse from a distance and tried to build up enough anger to turn and ride the other way, but the pull he had on her was too strong. "I've been out of town," he said as soon as she rode up. "I've missed you."

She rode past him, giving him nothing but a brief smile because she was too nervous to speak. She was afraid she'd blurt out a wild combination of pique, frustration, and lust. Had he really been away, or was that an excuse? Whichever, in that moment she felt that she hated him. And that this madness had to stop.

That night she was awakened by erotic dreams. Her desire for Daniel had mounted until it bit and clawed in the pit of her belly. Never before had she known a desire so fierce, so hungry.

Her head was aching, for the air in her bedchamber was stuffy and hot. Getting up from bed, she went to the window and threw back the curtains to let in the night. The moon was a silvery wedge in the sky, dancing amid the clouds.

Something was going to happen. Something was coming to her that she had yearned for all her life.

She shook her head. Nonsense. She wasn't the sort of person who believed such superstitious rot.

But something stirred in the shadows of the gardens below. She jumped back from the window. She had turned down the lights in her bedroom, so she didn't think she could be seen, but her caution was instinctive.

For several minutes she perceived nothing more, and was about to conclude that it had been her imagination when a dark figure moved between the griffin and the unicorn. He stopped again, on the edge of the shadow, one arm thrown over the unicorn's neck, its single horn looking as if it spouted from a human head.

She knew his shape, his walk, the set of his shoulders.

He was looking up at her window. It was a hot night and she had opened the drapes, drawing only the inner lacy curtains against the night. With the low light coming from the gas lights, she suspected he could see in through the curtains, which, against the dim glow, were all but transparent. She felt the intensity of his emotion—desire and anger, love and hate—and it frightened her.

She didn't stir, and for a long time neither did he. He was like a nocturnal predator, prowling around her window, watching, stalking, waiting. But when he looked up at her window, his unguarded expression sent the truth ringing through her soul. He'd loved her sister, but that was over. He wanted her now.

Clad in naught but a thin nightrail, Verity huddled on the end of her bed. She envisioned him scaling the wall to get to her, and herself struggling briefly before surrendering to the forces that were driving them both. All it would take to bring him to her, she sensed, was a signal that she was willing.

Was she?

Her gaze darted nervously around the room, alighting on the porcelain sculpture of two lovers dancing that she had kept hidden in a drawer when Julian was alive. It was proudly displayed on her bureau now. The woman, rapt, her head thrown back. The man, holding her firmly, caressing her. Their mutual pleasure. Their joy.

She knew then that this was a moment that might never come again, and that if she didn't seize it she would be forever sorry.

She loosened her hair and tossed it over her shoulders, then went to the window and flung it open wide.

He came. Like a bandit he scaled her walls and entered her sanctuary, his grin flashing, his eyes alight with desire and anticipation. "Verity," he whispered, holding out his hands to her. Three strides and she was in his arms. She welcomed him wordlessly, her body opening as she felt him enfold her. He swung her around in an arc, lifting her off the floor. She clung to his shoulders as the sweet sensations swept through her, so excited and terrified that she couldn't tell one emotion from the other.

Then he was kissing her, his tongue driving into her eager mouth. She met his passion with her own. It didn't matter that he had been a clay worker, her father's enemy, and her sister's lover. Nothing mattered but the pressure of his lips on hers.

He carried her to the bed and laid her down.

"I'm frightened," she whispered. A moment later, she regretted speaking. She wanted to appear confident and knowledgeable, an experienced woman capable of satisfying him. She didn't want him to know how untutored she was in the erotic arts.

But Daniel endeared himself to her with the words, "Don't ye fret about it. I'm frightened, too."

"I can't believe this is happening."

His grin turned mischievous. "Believe it. It's going to happen a lot."

He took his time with her, exploring and nurturing her body in ways that Julian had never attempted. She was so accustomed to her husband's quick, selfish gropings that she was astonished by Daniel's careful attention to her arousal and satisfaction. By the time she came to a shuddering climax, she was lost. No man had ever made her feel that way. No man except Daniel ever would.

She went to sleep haunted by what was surely the most

bewildering of emotions: She was falling in love with Daniel Carne.

Daniel lay awake long after his new lover was still and silent by his side. He ought to have felt triumphant, but he did not. The passion that had gripped them both was far stronger than he'd expected it to be. He'd set a trap and she'd fallen into it, but he was left with the vague suspicion that he'd miscalculated somehow.

His plan had not included desiring her, at least not any more than was necessary to perform the act that would bind her to him. It hadn't included yearning for her the way he'd been doing lately. Maybe now that he'd had her, his ardor would cool. Her body was nothing special. Well . . . sweet, yeah. Surprisingly soft and curved and yielding. Electric in her movements. Ecstatic in her sounds.

If she was more passionate than he'd expected . . . he figured that was something never known until tried. The prim and proper ones were the ones to watch out for. Sharp and flinty on the surface, they caught fire under the bedclothes. Verity's heat had been intense, exciting. It was as if no one had ever put a match to her before.

He'd have to be careful. He'd have to make sure things didn't balloon out of control. His yearning for sex—and the deeper bonds between a man and a woman that he knew well were possible—had always been his weakness. But he would be damned if he'd let Verity hurt him the way her sister had.

No, it was time for a Carne's revenge. For her sister's sins, and her father's, Verity Trevor Marrick was going to pay.

Part Seven

1918

Ah, love, let us be true
To one another! for the world, which seems
To lie before us like a land of dreams,
So various, so beautiful, so new,
Hath really neither joy, nor love, nor light,
Nor certitude, nor peace, nor help for pain;
And we are here as on a darkling plain
Swept with confused alarms of struggle and flight,
Where ignorant armies clash by night.

—Matthew Arnold
Dover Beach

Chapter Forty-one

Bret was spending her night off with Maggie and her baby when the call came through from Trenwythan. The evening was stormy, with misty gray skies and a steady, winter rain. She heard the telephone, the low voice answering it. When Maggie came for her, there was something about the rigidity of her shoulders and the precision of her stride that sent fear through her.

"It's your sister calling," Maggie said, and Bret knew instantly that it was bad news. *Troubles come not singly but in battalions*. Julian's death at the beginning of last year, 1917; Charlie Blount, Maggie's handsome brother, killed in the middle of May; Francis MacDonald, cured of a life-threatening infection in his leg, dead of a bullet in his brain at the end of November.

And now Simon?

She threw down the newspaper—full of dire news about advanced German war planes and the dozens of RFC flyers they'd been knocking out of the skies lately—and flew to the telephone. "Verity?" The phone line crackled with the storm. "Are you there? It's Simon, isn't it?"

"Yes," Verity said, as Bret had known she would . . . known it from the moment the phone had begun its eerie ringing.

She heard a new sound, a whimper, rising up from deep in her belly.

"Damn aeroplanes," said Verity. "All the men who designed them—including Father—ought to be shot."

"Oh please please *please* don't tell me he's dead."

"Not dead but badly injured. They're sending him home. Well, not home but to a military hospital for officers in Sussex."

"Dammit, Verity, how badly injured? What have they told you?"

"The cable didn't provide any details, I'm afraid."

Of course not. She was a professional now. Professionally, she knew full well that field hospitals, or even the ones here at home, didn't communicate to relatives the true extent of the soldiers' injuries. It was too time-consuming to do so in every case, and the details only upset the family.

That they were sending Simon home was both good news and bad. It meant he'd survived both the initial shock of his injury and the battlefield treatment, which might have been excellent or haphazard depending on the extent of the casualties on the day he'd been hurt. It meant that someone thought he was strong enough to make the journey and that there was some hope of his survival. But it was also bad, since only the most seriously wounded were shipped back to England. Everyone else was treated with bed rest and sent back up to the lines.

"What happened? Was he shot down? Did he crash his plane?"

"I don't know. 'In the line of duty' was all the cable said."

"They always say that. If he'd been bashed in the head in a whorehouse brawl that's what they'd have said. Do you know if he's a sit-up or a stretcher case?"

"I told you, I don't know anything. I was hoping that with your Red Cross connections you'd be able to find out."

There was a weariness and an impatience in Verity's tone that annoyed Bret and reminded her that she and her sister had not seen each other for more than three years. Because of the war, they had never addressed the conflicts between them, and the emotional distance had widened until it now seemed to Bret a formidable and perhaps unbridgeable gulf. In recent months it had become worse. When they spoke on the telephone, Verity seemed distracted and evasive, and her letters, which arrived less frequently now, dwelled on the most mundane of subjects. Verity had never been as open or as candid about her feelings as Bret was, but her current reticence was striking.

"I'll find out," Bret said with a trace of defiance. "I'll go to him. I'll get compassionate leave and go."

"If you could, I'm sure he would be grateful. It must be frightening for him to be so badly injured after his father's death and the deaths of so many of his comrades at arms." She paused. "This bloody goddamned war. I *hate* it."

"Verity, how are you taking it? How awful for you, after Julian's death, to go through this again. I know Papa's never home, and I worry about you all alone in Cadmon Hall."

"I'm not alone," Verity said fiercely. "That is, it doesn't feel to me as if I'm alone. I keep busy, as you know. I have my work, and I have—" She broke off for a split second. "I'm managing. Don't worry about me."

"All right," Bret whispered. *I don't think she misses me at all*, she thought. *How did that happen? Is it all just gone, that love, those sisterly feelings? Gone like everything else in this wretched war? Oh, Verity.* Tears welled. She forced them down. Simon was injured. There was leave to ask for, travel plans to make. She didn't have time to snivel.

He looked dead. He was in a coma, and his breathing was labored. The bones of his skull seemed to be pressing up through his skin. His face was unmarked by the accident, but his head was bandaged. His legs were encased in plaster, one arm in a sling. He was broken, like so many other young men who had marched off to fight for their country. He would never be the same again.

"In some ways, he's fortunate," Major Benton, the physician in charge, was saying. "No burns. Most flyers who survive come in with burns, which are hell to treat. They last awhile, in excruciating pain, while the infections get worse and worse. Some deaths are worse than others. Give me massive internal trauma to burns anyday."

"Is that what Simon has? Massive internal trauma?"

"Actually, we've stabilized him. We're not seeing any signs of internal injury to the soft tissues at present. Except the lungs. Apparently when he crashed he landed in a cloud of mustard gas.''

"Oh God," Bret whispered.

"We're not sure yet how bad the lung scarring will be. At present he's breathing well enough, but if the lining of the lungs is significantly eroded, the problem will worsen over time. As far as other injuries go, we've got numerous trauma fractures, including two vertebrae in the lower spine. There may be some lower-limb paralysis. The extent of damage to the spinal cord is undetermined. God only knows what's happening inside the skull. No fracture there, but he's been under for ten days now without awakening. We're not sure why. Medicine is still young when it comes to the workings of the brain.''

"But you're saying he has a chance?" Bret was aware that she sounded more like a devastated relative than the well-trained nurse she was.

The doctor shrugged. "I'm not saying anything definite. Even if he does come out of it, his lungs might be so badly damaged that he'll die of the first respiratory ailment he contracts. There's also the chance, given the injuries to the spine, that he'll never walk again." Major Benton paused delicately. "Are you his fiancée?"

It was too complicated to explain, so she simply nodded.

The doctor had a kind face. He was middle-aged, and his eyes were sad. "Sit beside him, then. Talk to him. The presence of a loving friend can sometimes prevail where medicine is helpless.''

"Thank you. I'll do anything."

"Call him back. If he hears you, perhaps he'll come."

Bret talked, calling up every memory she could find of the things she and Simon had done together over the years. The hikes they had taken, the trees they had climbed, the streams they had fished, the books they had read. Every day, over and over, she told him how much she loved him and how worried she'd been about him. How proud she was of his skill, his daring, and his courage. She stressed his courage because she knew how deeply his fears had run, how certain he had always been that he would prove a coward.

"I used to think that to be brave meant never to be afraid," she said. "But one of my patients told me one day that real courage depends on what he called the dignity of fear. Fear has dignity, he said, when it is acknowledged and accepted. Once you dignify your fear, you find within yourself all the courage you need."

She spoke to him of her experiences in the hospital, deemphasizing the negative aspects. "People think it must be so depressing, but I've learned that there's always love, even in the worst circumstances. In spite of this horrible war, I think people are basically good. If they weren't, you wouldn't see the small kindnesses that you see every day in hospital—someone drawing the curtains because he can see that the fellow across the ward is squinting in the sunlight, or the wife of a dying Tommy volunteering to donate blood to save the life of a German prisoner of war. To me, that reveals something about our capacity to give, and to forgive."

She spoke to him of Cornwall and how she missed the seasonal tinting of the moors, the crashing sea, the mists, the Mountains of the Moon. She talked until her voice grew hoarse and broken. When she could speak no more she sat quietly and held his hand.

She made bargains with God. Skeptical though she felt about His existence, there was nowhere else to turn. *Please let him live. If You bring him back to me I won't ever ask for anything else.*

"You're not much use just sitting there," the ward staff nurse said to Bret after she had been at Simon's beside for six full days. "It could be weeks before he opens his eyes. Here." She handed Bret a glass beaker filled with alcohol and half a dozen thermometers. "I hear you're a VAD, and I'm short of help this morning."

"I'm on leave."

"I need you," Staff Nurse said.

And so Bret began to do again the tasks with which she was so familiar. She bathed the sick and changed their sheets. She coaxed the recovering wounded out of the bed and took their weight upon her shoulders, helping them hobble a few steps as they learned to use muscles that had grown slack from lack of exercise. She fed the men who could swallow and brought trays and forks to those who were strong enough to feed themselves. She put bottoms on bedpans and held urinals; she emptied and scrubbed out both. She joked with the other nurses about the expertise they had all developed during the war at getting food into people at one end and disposing of it when it came out the other.

The work helped. And she continued to spend as much time as possible at Simon's bedside, speaking his name, summoning him back.

He was dreaming of Bret. He knew it was she because of her red hair. None of the girls in France had red hair. He'd tried to find one, offering to pay twice the fee, which had so excited Mère Lutrice that she'd ordered one of her girls to do a dye job. He'd paid, but sent the girl away. Her body was so voluptuous that the necessary veil of illusion wouldn't fall. He wasn't much good with prostitutes, anyway. Zach was always teasing him because of the many times Simon had wished him a pleasant evening and remained in his quarters alone.

But the woman in the dream was Bret, her upturned nose, her owlish green eyes, her slender neck, her long legs, her energetic step. Her hands, cool on his steaming forehead. Her scent, not musky or exotic or sharply floral like Mère Lutrice's girls but light, fresh, fragrant. Her husky voice, far quieter and more serious than usual. A vivid dream. If he could open his eyes, he thought perhaps she would really be there beside him.

But he couldn't open his eyes, and after a while he became too weary to try. Her sweet voice talking to him—he could make no sense of her words, but the sounds comforted him—was the last thing he heard before the darkness descended again.

The next time he woke he could see. He was in a long room with high windows and the sun pouring in. Everything was white and the sun made it whiter still. The brilliance hurt his eyes and he closed them, confused. He didn't know where he was. All he could feel was the pain, which was all over, everywhere, up and down his legs, in his head, in his chest, which burned with every breath, and in his bones.

He tried to move, to call out. He heard a sort of croak and wasn't sure whether he had produced it. In the distance a man was moaning, begging for something, sobbing. He sounded desperate and Simon was sorry for him. The war made you desperate. Pain made you desperate. Life and love and sex and flying all made you desperate and then they were over and that was the end of it and you died.

He remembered the crash . . . and shied away from the memory. It was too much to contemplate; he slept.

The next time he woke the images returned and wouldn't leave him alone. He and Zach Slayton, the only two left from their old squadron. Zach the indefatigable survivor, the Phoenix from Phoenix, Arizona, who by some delicious coincidence had been writing and receiving letters from Bret for years. God, how he adored the man. Zach was tough but compassionate, ice in the air and fire on the ground. Simon looked up to him and admired him. Slayton had become the best friend he'd ever had.

The day before the crash a letter from the States had arrived from someone named Cathy, whom Zach had been engaged to marry. In a bright, bitter tone she'd informed him that she was now wed to someone else.

"No great surprise," Zach said in the voice of a man who had long ago lost all his illusions. When Simon had found him with the crumpled-up letter, he was well into a bottle of whiskey. "She was bad for me in every way, but hell, she's been under my skin since I was fifteen years old."

Which was why Zach was flying his new Sopwith Camel, a real honey of a plane, with a hangover the following day. And why Simon was more frantic about Zach than he was about the Fokkers who were zipping in to attack. They'd fouled up, both of them, all because of some faithless woman in America whom Simon had never even met.

Again he remembered the crash. Zach was hit and he'd gone blazing to the rescue. Then Zach pulled out of it the way he always did and Simon caught a Jerry shell in his tail section, spinning him out of control. He'd seen the ground coming up at him and thought, ridiculously, *At least we're over our lines and it's our ground*. As if British-held earth couldn't kill him.

Which, apparently, it hadn't.

He ought to be dead. If he wasn't dead, then—what? Burned? Paralyzed? All broken up and useless inside? Life in Death, helpless and dependent and racked with endless pain? That was for the poor buggers in the trenches, dammit, not for pilots. Pilots were either whole or dead.

He tried again to call out; to sit up; to turn his head; but all seemed impossible. It was dark again. *I'm a live spirit in a dead shell*, he thought, panicking. *I'd be better off dead*.

"Simon?"

Her voice. He'd been hearing her voice in his dreams. He'd been hearing her voice forever, it seemed.

"You opened your eyes, I saw it. Do it again." Her voice carried a command that he could not disobey. "Open your eyes."

Simon tried, but it didn't work. Were his eyelids paralyzed? Nothing felt the way it should. Eyes—in the front of the head. Head? That was no problem. Head was where the pain was. Come to think of it, the pain was pretty much everywhere. Fingers? Were those his fingers? Was he moving them? Was someone holding them, touching them? Was it she?

Concentrating on his fingers, he forgot about his eyelids. They came open by themselves, and he saw her. Red hair. Tears running down her cheeks and hitting the corners of her mouth, which were uplifted in a tremulous smile.

He made a monumental effort and heard a kind of croak, the same sound he'd heard before. *Me*, he realized, shocked.

"Don't try to talk. Don't try to do anything. You moved your fingers, did you know that? Oh, Simon, I didn't think you were *ever* going to wake up!"

He moved his fingers again. You're beautiful, was what he was trying to say. I love you. I love you for being here beside me, singing to me in my dreams, talking to me, holding my hands. I came back for you. I love you so much.

But no words came out.

She was calling for the doctor. Other faces hovered. Women in pointed white caps, men with stethoscopes around their necks. He kept his gaze on Bret. He didn't care about anybody else.

"Simon? Squeeze my hand if you understand me."

He squeezed.

"Do you know who I am?"

He squeezed again, harder.

"Do you remember what happened?"

He squeezed a little more tentatively this time.

"You saved another pilot's life, at great risk to your own. You almost made it back safely, but your aeroplane was badly damaged and you crashed. There was no fire, is why you're still alive. You have a lot of broken bones, but your body's mending. Do you understand? Now that you're awake, you're going to be all right."

"How long?" he croaked, stunned to hear the words emerge.

Bret looked stunned, too. More tears washed down her face. "How long since the accident? Six weeks. You've been in a coma for just over six weeks."

It meant nothing to him. The crash had just happened, as far as he was concerned. "Where am I? France?"

"You're in a hospital in Brighton, England. They brought you here on a hospital ship shortly after the accident. I came to visit you, and I'm in the process of transferring to this hospital so I can stay and take care of you. Simon, don't try to talk. You must rest."

"I'm not going to die?"

"No, oh no. You're going to recover, you're going to be fine."

He shut his eyes, able to work them now. He felt exhausted and oddly exhilarated at the same time. "Hold my hand," he whispered.

"I am holding it. Don't worry. I'm never going to let you go."

She was crying for him. She must care about him. Now that he was back with her, maybe she would grow to love him, after all.

* * *

Simon's convalescence was difficult, especially since there did indeed prove to be some loss of sensation in his legs. Both he and Bret cried when the doctors explained the spinal cord injury, and his penchant for melancholy ballooned when they couldn't answer his frantic questions as to how much feeling he would regain. No one knew whether he would ever walk again. Or fly a plane. Or make love.

His lungs were the other problem. He coughed constantly, plagued by chronic bronchitis. He couldn't remember breathing the poison gas. It must have happened when he'd been lying unconscious in the wreckage of his plane. Nobody seemed to know whether his lungs would ever be normal again. When he asked the medical men about it, they looked unhappy and gave him no clear answer.

"I'm useless," he said to Bret. "I'll never get better. I'd rather be dead."

"Stop that. You mustn't give up."

"I'm not giving up. I just—Christ, Bret! I don't want to spend the rest of my life being wheeled around in a chair like an old man."

"That's not the way it's going to be."

"Right," he said morosely, coughing.

"Anyway, you'll have me to push you." Bret had received her transfer from the hospital in London.

"Only because it's your bloody job!"

She'd seen too much anger, fear, and frustration among her patients to be distressed by his petulance and gloom. She listened sympathetically, doing her best to reassure and distract him. The war had done horrible things to the men it had not killed, and she passed no judgment on any of them for the way they reacted to its ravages.

She was harsher, however, on herself. Simon was alive, safe, out of the war. Her prayers had been answered. However, although it was obvious that he still loved her, still wanted to marry her, she, to her shame, still couldn't conceive of being his wife. He was her dearest friend, but she was no more passionately in love with him than she had ever been.

* * *

One of the few things that seemed to cheer Simon during those interminable weeks in hospital were his stories about the Phoenix. Bret finally realized this was a man. At first she thought it was the name of an aeroplane.

"He'll come and visit me as soon as he gets leave," he told her. "I can't wait to see your face when I introduce the two of you."

"Why?"

"That's a secret. A surprise."

Bret couldn't imagine what was so special about this chum of his. When Simon spoke of him, it was with a hero worship that made her skeptical. The Phoenix was brave. The Phoenix was brilliant. The Phoenix told the most hilarious stories that made everybody howl with laughter. The Phoenix was the best pilot ever to grace the cockpit of a plane. Rather excessive, Bret thought.

She didn't expect to meet him, anyway. Flyers had a higher mortality rate than any other military personnel in the war, and the Germans, inspired by the brilliant ace Baron Manfred von Richthofen, had been winning a number of engagements in this spring of 1918. The only leave papers the Phoenix was likely to get would come directly from God.

One day in late April, Simon looked up from a letter he had received and gave Bret an unusually wide grin.

"Good news?"

"The best." Instead of elaborating, he folded the letter in his slender fingers and slipped it back into its envelope, which he carefully tucked into the pages of the book that he was reading, signaling both the letter's importance and the fact that it was private. In someone else, she would have assumed it had come from a sweetheart.

"It's good to see you smile again, Simon."

"You'll be smiling too, after you recover from your very great amazement."

Despite her considerable curiosity, he refused to enlighten her further.

Chapter Forty-two

That evening when she came off duty Bret walked out along the Brighton pier to its farthest end and stood staring out to sea. The wind had pulled her hair loose from its chignon. The sky was faded from the angry red of the sunset. The old rhyme, red sun in morning, sailors take warning; red sun at night, sailors delight, repeated itself in her head until she wanted to scream for it to stop.

The wind closed around her, chillier now. The famous Brighton pier had once been the symbol of a gay and glittering time when the Prince Regent and his society friends had considered Brighton their favorite seaside resort. Now it was quiet and dark, bereft of the lights that might make it a bombing target for German Zeppelins or aeroplanes. Lovers still walked here, however, and the lonely who came to absorb the muffled pounding of the sea.

Bret leaned against the railing at the end of the pier and gazed down into the black water. There was a low moon, just a day past full, suspended over the harbor. The waves were leaping toward it as if yearning to swallow its radiance. It seemed to Bret that this was exactly what the war was trying to do to her.

She had received a letter from Marcus Gregory, her old sculpture instructor, inviting her to join the small group of artists he was assembling to create a monument to those who had died on the battlefield. The work would be carved in marble—a sculptor's dream. She would have loved to accept the invitation. But how could she leave Simon? And how could she abandon the commitment she had made to military nursing at a time when her services were so much in demand?

Blasted war! Out of the corner of her eyes Bret saw a tiny flicker of light. She turned. A man stood nearby, touching a match to the end of a cigarette. His face was in shadow as he cupped his hands around the cigarette and drew hard to get it going in the wind. She instinctively withdrew a step or two. He was very tall, he looked strong, and the cold depths of the sea were just below.

The man's gaze shifted to hers and she relaxed. Even in the dim light of the moon she could see that his eyes contained no threat.

"Sorry if I disturbed you, ma'am," he said, his speech a slow drawl that she tentatively identified as American. After three years of isolationism, the Americans had come in last spring to join the Allied cause. They were desperately needed, for the British and French armies had been decimated by the long siege of trench warfare. The high-spirited Yanks had proven themselves tough and determined on the battlefield, although their presence had not yet turned the tide in the Allies' favor.

The American glanced over the railing to the sea churning beneath them, then looked back at her. "I wondered if you were all right?"

She smiled in spite of herself. "I'm not about to pitch myself into the sea, if that's what you mean."

He studied the somber black of her frock. "Things are pretty bad all over, I guess. Especially here in England, for you women. And over there"—he nodded out to sea—"in France, for your men."

"Have you been there?" She wondered which branch of the service he was in. He was wearing a light leather jacket— not government issue—over the jodhpurs and high boots that were usually part of an officer's regalia. No headgear of any kind—the Americans hated hats and were forever shedding them.

He nodded. "I'm based in France, yeah."

Bret continued to examine him. He was quite young, still in his twenties, she decided; although it was hard to tell these days, for even the young ones developed gray hair and dark circles under their eyes and lines about their mouths. Worst of all was the emptiness in their eyes, which had seen too much horror, too much death.

The stranger's eyes were not empty, although they were hard. And he was whole—at least, as far as she could tell.

No splints, no crutches, no telltale wheezing of gassed lungs. It was unusual to see a healthy man of his age. An attractive one, too, she realized, lanky but firm of limb, with pleasant gray-blue eyes and a mouth made rakish by the presence of a mustache.

"Are you on leave?"

He nodded. "Officially, yeah. In truth I was making mistakes. They ordered me out for a couple weeks. I'll go back clear-headed and rested, they hope, ready to resume flying."

Her head jerked back. "You're a pilot?"

He smiled. "One of the best." There was no pride in the matter-of-fact statement.

If he'd been an Englishman instead of an American she would have asked him if he knew Simon. She'd gathered from Simon's letters that the British pilots who had survived all knew one another. The RFC was a small, elite group of men.

She almost walked away. Did she really want to chat with a flyer? In some ways, she was curious. Simon didn't like to talk about it, and the hospital in Brighton had treated no other flyboys since she'd been there.

"Tell me about it," she heard herself say.

Zach Slayton stared down into the young Englishwoman's face for a moment, searching warily for the morbid eagerness that so many women exhibited when they learned what he did in the war. They regarded him as a kind of death-dealing, thunderbolt-wielding god. They admired him, envied him, feared him, and sought to make love to him. On the occasions when he complied, he felt exhausted afterward, drained of energy, a tin idol, a fake. He had learned to avoid such women.

This one wasn't that sort, or, if she was, she was good at hiding it. He read curiosity in her eyes—Christ, they were huge eyes, too—but it was a reluctant sort of curiosity, as if she secretly dreaded hearing what he had to say. The black dress told him that she'd lost someone over there. There weren't too many English or French women who hadn't lost a husband, a lover, a brother, a childhood friend.

"It's not easy for me to talk about it. Particularly during

the times when I'm trying to glue myself back together long enough to add a few more kills to my already impressive tally.''

She winced slightly at his tone and Zach was sorry. Her face was sweet. Strained, yes, but everybody looked strained nowadays. The joi de vivre of an entire generation had been wiped away by the war. He wondered how old she was. Not more than twenty, he guessed. Her body was slim and grace-ful and she was taller than most women he knew. He liked tall women. He could kiss them without getting a crick in his neck. He liked red hair, too, especially when it was long and loose and ribboned by the wind.

He studied her garb again, wondering if she was a widow, and how long it had been since she'd been to bed with a man. Then—what the hell—he carried it one step farther and wondered if there was any chance of her going to bed with him. When he'd first approached her, before he'd noticed how close she was to the end of the pier, it had occurred to him that she might be a prostitute out soliciting, but that impression had faded as soon as she'd met his eyes and spoken. He'd learned enough now about the politics of British accents to know she was a lady, despite the lilting country flavor to her speech. The fabric of her dress was fine and there was an ivory and gold cameo brooch at her throat. No wedding ring, he noted belatedly. A virgin, perhaps? No; there was knowledge in her eyes and a sensuality in her lips that belied that possibility.

He dragged on his cigarette. She didn't seem inclined to speak, so he said, "Flying is lovely, there's nothing like it. Before the war there was no feeling that could compare."

"Yes," she said softly, as if she knew, as if she under-stood.

"There's no joy in it now, and that's what I hate most. The greatest joy in my life has been turned into a thing of darkness."

"Look, you needn't talk about it. I shouldn't have asked."

He shrugged. "Maybe if I talk I'll be able to sleep to-night."

"Do you have trouble sleeping?"

"Sometimes, yeah." Actually it was a lot more often than sometimes. He rarely slept more than an hour or two at a time before being shaken awake by nightmares.

"Me too." She smiled at him then, a huge and brilliant smile.

Wryly Zach acknowledged himself to be a sucker when it came to a woman's smile. "Come on, walk with me. It's chilly standing here. Walk with me and we'll talk each other into sleepy-eyed exhaustion."

He offered her his arm, and after a brief hesitation she took it. Her hand was small and warm against his arm. Zach's stomach clenched with a sudden hard excitement. It was stronger than anything he'd felt for a woman in a long, long time. Those eyes, that smile. The vulnerability in her sweet, sad face. It was crazy because she seemed a proper young lady; he would have no chance with her at all. But he could enjoy the fantasy, while it lasted.

They walked back along the pier toward the strand, then along the pathway that paralleled the stony shore. Bret listened, asking few questions, while he spoke of France and how it felt to be high above the battlefields, high above the poison gas, breathing the harsh, cold air, soaring through cloud formations, innocent and lighthearted for a few minutes each morning before sighting the black specks on the horizon that might be the enemy, bringing with him your death. He explained how difficult it was to tell whether the planes were friend or foe until they got close enough for strafing to begin, and that there were other times, especially if the sun was in your eyes, when they could sneak right up on you from above or below and pin you against the sky like a butterfly on a collector's board.

"Do you ever feel afraid?"

"Always. The early mornings are the worst, before I get into my plane. I wonder if this will be the day that I buy it. Some mornings the thought turns my guts to water. Others, I don't seem to care."

"That's bad, not caring."

"You're right. That's when they get you. With the young ones, the hotshots who have just come over and never flown in combat before, the most dangerous feeling is invincibility.

They don't think they *can* die. There's something about conquering gravity and soaring like a bird that makes you feel the earth can't touch you, can't take you.

"Combat destroys that illusion. If you survive the first few weeks—and a lot of the rookies don't—you learn to be wary. But after a while, when you've killed again and again and made it safely back behind the lines while some other poor bastard has gone spinning out of control, you start wondering *why* you're alive and they're dead. And you can't find any reason for that. You're not a better human being than your buddy who was blown out of the sky yesterday. Maybe you're not even as good a pilot. And the Bosch you're sending to their deaths, they're just like you. If there were no war you'd sit together over a mug of beer and talk baseball or women or fishing. You don't see the point in all this. And you feel dirty because you know what you're doing makes no sense."

He paused and reached into his jacket for another cigarette. "You think too much along those lines and it starts to make you careless. That's the other time you die—when you've lost that edge, that hatred of the other side, that desire to annihilate the enemy before he annihilates you."

The sky had clouded up and they could no longer see the moon. The air had the heavy feel to it of impending rain.

"Why go back at all? Why not get out while you're still whole?"

"Desert?" He did not sound shocked by the suggestion. "I'd like to, believe me. But they need me. I'm very good at what I do."

His bitter tone had a strange effect on her. She wanted to comfort him, make it better somehow. He reminded her vaguely of her father—his height, his lanky build, the shape of his hands.

A raindrop struck the top of her head, another her nose. She smiled at the feel of it and looked up to see him watching her. The intensity of his gaze unnerved her for a moment. *He's a stranger, I don't even know his name. Before the war I never would have walked alone with a stranger along the sea front in the dark.*

"It's raining," she said.

"And chilly. My hotel is just back there." He gestured to

the narrow street behind them. "There's a coffee bar, if you'll allow me to offer you something hot."

Something had altered in his voice; he sounded tentative, a little nervous. If he had been cocky and self-assured, she would have found it much easier to refuse. "Thank you," she said, and looked away as soon as she saw the leap of excitement in his eyes.

Her heart was beating hard as they crossed the street together. He didn't touch her, but he stayed close, and the knowledge that he could so easily touch her, brush shoulders or fingers or thighs, caused mass confusion in her brain . . . and in her body.

She'd heard stories of this happening: chance meetings between lonely men and women that escalated to defiant snatchings at pleasure without care for the moral questions involved. Perhaps men had always done it, but these days women were doing it too, respectable women, women who, before the war, would have insisted on a wedding ring before engaging in anything more intimate than a kiss.

The war had changed everything. The omnipresence of death made love seem all the more ephemeral and sex all the more poignant. But Bret didn't care to reflect too much on the reason she was approaching a public hotel with a stranger she'd met in the street. The thought of Simon and how hurt he would be if he knew almost stopped her, but then a kind of defiance entered in. She was Simon's friend, and she loved him, but she had begun once again to feel strangled by his love, his longing, his passion that she didn't share.

When they reached the entrance to the modest hotel where he was staying, she hesitated for a moment. The American's hand fell on her arm. He smiled, then shook his head slightly. "Look, I'm sorry if I seem to be taking something for granted. I'm not, really. It's just that I enjoyed talking with you and wasn't ready for it to end."

"It's all right. I don't want it to end, either." She took a deep breath. *Just do it, Bret, if you're going to. You'll lose your nerve if you agonize over it. Be intrepid.* Where was the young adventuress who had ridden so wildly across the moors, fearing nothing, trusting herself to the wind? The war had killed so many; had it killed that girl as well? "I don't really want coffee," she said. "You have a room?"

"Yes, but . . ." He let his voice trail off. He stared at her, those blue-gray eyes assessing her.

"I don't know why," she said in reply to the silent question. "Maybe because you have to go back to France. Maybe because you might die there." She paused. "Or maybe because the whole world's turned inside out and nobody's sane anymore. Including me."

"Oh, I reckon you're sane, all right." His American drawl had grown thicker, more noticeable. "It's the ones who aren't affected by the horror and pointlessness who're crazy." He touched her cheek. His fingers were firm yet gentle. "It's only human to seize whatever brief moments of splendor come into our lives."

For the splendor of it, yes. For the joy. She touched his hand, feeling lighter in spirit already. Surely there were some moments in life that could simply be taken and accepted, as a gift.

He put his arm around her shoulders and led her up the stairs. The sleepy-eyed clerk at the front desk ignored them. No doubt this sort of thing happened every night.

His room was simply furnished—a bed, a chair, a table with a washbasin and jug, an empty fireplace. The bed seemed huge to her, although in fact it was rather small.

It was not until he closed the door behind them and turned the key that she began to feel uncomfortable. She wasn't sure whether to sit down, and, if so, where. On the chair? The bed? Did one simply start removing one's clothes? How could she take off her things in front of a stranger?

"I'm a little nervous. . . . This isn't the sort of thing I've—I mean, I don't usually . . ."

"Ssh, I know." She felt him behind her, close. When his hands covered her shoulders, she felt skittish and wanted to run. This was insane. She knew nothing about this man.

He was massaging her shoulders in a manner that relaxed her. She liked the expert stroking of his fingers, the feeling he projected of being in control of himself, of the situation. With Daniel it had been all passion and impatience. Daniel would have ripped her clothes off by this time and had her naked on the bed.

He turned her around to face him. She looked into his eyes. He smiled. He stroked the back of his hand across her cheek, then curved his fingers around her neck and lifted her chin with his thumb. His face moved toward hers, slowly, giving her plenty of time to protest. When she didn't, he touched her lips with his. His mouth was firm, dry, lovely. She could feel the slight tickle of his mustache against her upper lip. She moved almost imperceptibly toward him and he kissed her again, more deeply, allowing the tip of his tongue to invade her mouth at one corner before drawing back.

Bret managed a smile, feeling trembly again but knowing that this time it was caused by desire rather than apprehension. Her breasts were burning where they had brushed his leather jacket during the second kiss and her belly felt hollow and hungry.

"I've got a flask of brandy," he said, moving away from her. He removed and tossed the jacket, revealing that he was indeed wearing an officer's uniform. "I'm going to pour us both a nip."

"That would be nice. Thank you."

She moved aimlessly around the small room, touching the windowsill, the bedposts, the curtains. Some papers had been tossed on the table against the far wall, including a passport, some military documents, and a letter in an unsealed envelope that was gaily held together with a blue ribbon. From his sweetheart back home, she thought, concluding from the tattered condition of the envelope that it had been opened many times. Such a familiar sight; all too often she had had the responsibility of returning such letters to the women who had sent them, along with the other personal effects of the dead.

She moved closer, without any real thought of prying, yet aware that there was something special about this letter. It seemed to her that the handwriting on the envelope was very well known to her . . .

The letter was addressed to Mr. Zachary Slayton in Phoenix, Arizona. Which made no sense at all. Unless . . .

She whirled to look at him. Her heart was doing somersaults, her stomach lurched, and for an instant she thought she might do what not even the bloodiest wound had caused her to do—faint.

Zach Slayton was older—closer to her father's age—and not so tall. His face was weatherbeaten from the desert wind and sun. He was dressed in blue denim and creaking leather, and he was bowlegged from spending so much time on horseback. He wore a battered cowboy Stetson. His muscles were ropy, his voice thick with the flavor of the American West.

The stranger, who couldn't possibly be Mr. Slayton, *her* Mr. Slayton, came back to her side, holding out a silver flask top full of brandy. "Here we are. You'll feel more relaxed, I promise."

Instead, she backed away, unable to stop gaping at him. The insignia of his uniform told her—belatedly—that he was a major. Not an American major. His uniform was British. He was in the RFC.

"What? Is something wrong?" He set the flask on the table right next to the letter and took a healthy swig from the cup. "Second thoughts?" He grinned in a self-deprecating manner that was very attractive. "Guess I shouldn't have quit that kiss, but I didn't want you to think I was rushing your fences."

She grabbed the flask and gulped some brandy. It burned.

"Look, nobody ever said you had to go through with it." His voice was gentle now, a compassionate, mesmerizing voice. "I think you're lovely, and there's nothing I'd rather do than make love to you, but I'm not going to insist."

Bret closed her eyes. She wanted him. It wasn't just the war or the mood or the night; it was the man: his height, his long limbs and bony wrists, the curly black hair that was cropped so short, the mustache, the cleft in his chin, that carnal mouth, that husky voice, those now-gray, now-blue eyes. It was as if his face and form had been imprinted somewhere deeply upon her mind, always there, waiting, ready to be brought out and compared to the real thing when it finally came along.

What she'd experienced with Daniel had been different. He had been attractive to her, but it was something that had grown. This was instant. The classic *coup de foudre*. Yet, he wasn't a stranger at all. Because of his letters, she knew him. She knew things that didn't jive with the tough, world-weary–flyboy image he had presented tonight. She knew his gentleness, his thoughtfulness, his folksy sense of humor, his prodigious intellect. The war might have hardened him, but all those pieces of him were still there, inside.

It struck her with startling clarity that she must have been a little in love with Zach Slayton ever since she'd been a child.

But it was all wrong. He was enjoying himself hugely at the moment, no doubt, having a romantic encounter with a mysterious woman, but when he found out who she really was, he would never forgive her. The Bret Trevor he thought he knew would not do what she had done.

"I have to go." She grabbed her cloak from the bed and moved quickly toward the door.

"Wait." He moved even faster; she felt one of his arms come around her from behind. The other hand moved under her hair, caressing the back of her neck. "Talk to me. Tell me what's wrong and let's see if we can fix it."

She was torn between the impulse to sink down into his arms and an equal need to escape. "Please let me go."

"Are you afraid? I won't hurt you."

The truth of what she felt burst out of her: "I could never be afraid of you."

Zach laughed a little rawly. "You don't know me. I coaxed you up here without giving you time to think. Any sensible woman would be afraid."

"I can't make love to you. But it has nothing to do with being afraid."

"What, then?" As he spoke his fingers were untying the ribbon that held back her hair. "You seemed willing, then something changed."

"That letter." She gestured toward the table. "Who is it from?"

He glanced at the envelope dismissively. "Not my wife, if that's what you're thinking. I'm not married. Is that it? It may be a sin, but it's not adultery."

When she shook her head, unable to answer, he said, "It's not a love letter from a sweetheart, either. It's from a young girl."

Bret made a sound in her throat. Looking at her wonderingly, he went on, "She's the fiancée of a squadron mate of mine. Another flyer. He's here in Brighton, in hospital. That's why I've come. To visit him."

My God. The British uniform . . . Simon's glee about the surprise he had in store for her . . . Arizona . . . it all came together with perfect clarity. Zach Slayton was the Phoenix.

"I've never even met her," he added. "She lives in Cornwall with her father, who's an old friend of mine. I'm going to try to get out to that part of the country this time, since I have a longer furlough than usual. That's why I brought her letter—it has her address." He paused, as if wondering why he was bothering to make an explanation for something so trivial. "Don't give it another thought. She's not much more than a schoolgirl."

Bret's face had been burning, but now it paled. A schoolgirl! Not old enough, certainly, to have already had a lover. Certainly not old enough for a battle-embittered fighter pilot like himself.

"I have to go," she repeated, jerking herself away from him. She felt a tug as her hair loosened and cascaded down her neck and shoulders. Zach was left holding her hair ribbon as she fled through the door.

Chapter Forty-three

The next morning at the hospital, Zach nearly collided with a nurse in the corridor. She was clad in a bulky uniform covered with a long white apron. On her head was one of those ludicrous winged hats that made her look as if she would take flight any second. "Excuse me, Sister," he said, most of his concentration on trying to avoid the poor bandaged bastard on a gurney who was being wheeled down the hallway beside them.

He caught a whiff of violets, which was refreshing after all the heavy hospital odors of blood and sweat and carbolic. And very like the scent he had noted on his mystery lover of the previous night.

" 'Twas my fault,'' the nurse said. "I did it on purpose.''

Zach whirled. There she was, the woman of the Brighton pier, demure and pale, looking like an escapee from a medieval convent, her lovely wild hair pinned up and hidden, her eyes huge, and her smile a trifle shaky.

"I thought I'd better speak with you before you went in to Simon. Sorry if it's a shock."

"A pleasant one," he said, meaning it sincerely. "Do you work here?"

"Yes. I'm not a professional, but I've been at it long enough now to have had plenty of practical experience. Everyone's short of nurses these days, so they're glad to have me.''

"You're a VAD?"

"Yes. Voluntary Aid Detachment. Or, as we're variously called, depending on the state of mind of our patients, Very Addled Damsels, Valiant At Dusting, Verily A Darling. Or''—she smiled—"this is my favorite: Victim Always Dies.''

He grinned. He'd never expected to see her again. Now, all it had taken was a word from her and he was eager for another chance.

Everything he'd heard about hospital nurses rushed through his head: They were angels of mercy at the same time that they, too, were victims of the war. The wives, mothers, and sweethearts of most of the men at the front had largely been spared the real horror of the conflict. The women who nursed the casualties were among the few members of the fairer sex who knew the truth.

It meant you could relax with them. You didn't have to play the gallant hero, or to try so hard to uphold the traditional women-and-children-into-the-lifeboats-first standard. Nurses knew as well as you did that there was nothing glorious or noble about this war.

He'd heard other things about them, too. That because of the intimate services their jobs required them to perform, there was nothing about men's bodies that shocked or startled them. That their constant exposure to death made them snatch at life as desperately as any front-line soldier. That they demanded nothing of their lovers in the way of future commitments because they fully expected them to die.

He thought he understood now what had happened last night. Like a man, she'd been exposed to the horrors of the war; like a man, she'd sought the obvious panacea. He smiled to himself as he noted that in one sense she'd acted like a woman. She'd changed her mind.

Maybe he could persuade her to change it back.

"I must talk with you." She put a hand on his arm and drew him toward a closed door. "Please. There's a small office here where we can have a few minutes of privacy."

He went willingly. The hospital no longer seemed such a cold and morbid place. "How did you know I was coming to see Captain Marrick?" he asked as she closed the door behind them.

"Please sit down, Major Slayton."

He frowned. "We didn't exchange names last night."

"I know who you are. That is, I didn't then, not at first—" Her voice trailed off.

Zach noted the tiny muscle that was leaping under her eye. She was nervous, more so than she ought to be. Mentally, he tried to prepare himself. "It's bad news, isn't it? Is Simon dead?"

"Oh no." She seemed appalled at the idea. "I'm terribly sorry, I didn't mean to frighten you. Simon's doing well. His spirits are not the best, but physically he's been improving." She paused, exhaling her sweet breath in the manner of a sigh. "This has nothing to do with him. It concerns you and me."

"Look, if you're afraid I'll say something about last night, get you in trouble here at the hospital somehow, let me reassure you. I would never—"

"No, Zach," she interrupted. "You don't understand. You have no idea who I am."

Hearing his name from her lips seemed as intimate as a caress. Hardly anyone called him Zach over here. It was either Phoenix or Major Slayton. He drank her in. The nurse's uniform with its wide shoulders and its narrow waist, long sleeves, and ankle-length skirts intrigued him. He wanted to strip it off her, slowly. He wanted to touch his lips to every inch of flesh his ministrations revealed.

"So who are you, then?"

"I should have told you last night. As soon as I saw the letter in your hotel room. But I couldn't. I lost my nerve." Her tone was gently self-deprecating as she added, "I guess I'm not as intrepid as I used to be."

"Look, that letter was sent to me by a young lady I've never even met. Why are you—"

"But, Zach, you have met her. And she's not as young as you seem to think."

"I've never—" he began, then stopped. As the meaning of her words penetrated, he shook his head as if to clear it. Thoughts and impressions careened around up there, memories and contradictions. *Intrepid.* "You don't mean—"

"Yes. Naturally I recognized my own letters."

"God damn. You're Bret?"

"Yes. And I'm a woman, not a schoolgirl."

His laugh was forced and awkward. "I reckon so."

Her smile contained an engaging mixture of chagrin and elation as she held out her hand to him. He accepted the handshake automatically, but as their flesh touched and clung, he felt once again the pull of what was clearly a strong animal attraction. Something stirred in the depths of her eyes and he knew she felt it too, and that she was indeed a woman, not one of the sweet uncorrupted innocents he was supposedly fighting to save the world for. Not that he believed in that claptrap. But all the same, a kind of rage swept through him and he dropped her hand.

Her smiled faded. "Zach, I'm sorry."

"Why the hell didn't you tell me last night? You saw the packet of letters. You realized who I was. Jesus, you should have said something, instead of letting me walk in here this morning unaware."

"I was ashamed." With the fingers he had rejected she was twisting a loose thread from the closely gathered material at her wrist. "Because of what happened . . . nearly happened . . . between us. I've never done anything like that before.''

''No?''

Her lips tightened. ''I can't blame you if you don't believe me.'' She met his eyes levelly as she added, ''Although we do have an expression in England about the pot not calling the kettle black.''

He nodded, acknowledging the riposte. Who the hell was he to judge her? Why should it matter, for chrissakes, if a young woman who was no relation to him, who didn't even share his nationality, should prove to be something less than his ideal of feminine virtue? It was a foolish ideal anyway; no woman could meet it. Christ, he had more than done his share over the years to make certain the women he wanted *didn't* meet it. Which made him one hell of a hypocrite.

''What about Simon? Aren't you going to marry him?''

''No. We've never been engaged. It's what he's always wanted, but I'm not in love with him.''

''Well, that's just dandy. You're all he ever talked about in France. We couldn't even drag him to the bawdy house, he was so determined to be faithful to you. He's a sweet kid who adores you, and you're out on the pier at midnight, picking up strangers.''

Her color had been heightened already; now it went positively red. ''You've no right to speak to me like that. Of all people, you ought to understand about Simon and me. I rattled on about him often enough to you in my letters. I'm not proud of myself for being unable to return his passion. God knows I've tried.''

''Actually you used to rattle on about some clay worker named Daniel. What ever happened to him?''

The color faded and she looked away.

''Was he killed in the trenches?'' Zach asked in a gentler tone.

''No.'' Her voice had gone flat. ''No, he's successfully avoided the war. I thought with conscription he might be forced in, but he's reopened an old tin mine, and the government needs the tin for armaments. So he's exempted. He's clever that way.'' She tipped her head back, chin set, eyes daring him to contradict her next words: "I'm glad for him. It's a hateful war and I'm glad for anybody who's had the sense and the wit to escape it."

"So you fell out of love with your clay worker? The man you would love for all time, as I believe you wrote in one of your letters?"

She looked away. "We were very young," she said, and he heard the sorrow lingering there.

He was beginning to feel vulnerable to her again. He sensed her emotions, following along easily with her as they fluctuated. Why was that? Because of the letters? Maybe their correspondence had forged a stronger bond than he'd realized. She'd always been candid with him, probably because she'd never expected to meet him in the flesh. She'd given him her confidences in the way other young women might have inscribed them in a diary.

"And now that Daniel's no longer in contention, you haven't been able to channel any of that passion in Simon's direction?"

"I've tried," she said earnestly. "It's curious, isn't it? Why is it that you can love someone dearly but feel no desire for them at all, whereas with somebody else, somebody you've only just met, you feel—" She stopped.

"You feel an instant and powerful attraction?"

He half-expected her to deny it, but she lifted her eyes to his and smiled. "Yes."

When she smiled, it was as if she'd swallowed the sun. Zach lifted one hand and touched a stray lock of hair that had pulled loose and fallen along the edge of her ear. He didn't mean to do it. His hand seemed to move of its own accord.

Almost imperceptibly, she angled away from him. "We can't stay here any longer. If Matron catches me she'll go on a rampage. Simon is awake and waiting for you. How long will you be in town?"

"About a week," he said, extending his visit by several days.

"Perhaps this evening, if you'd like to, we could have supper together. There's so much I want to know about you— how you got here when I thought you were in Arizona, how you happen to be so young, all that sort of thing.'' She paused. ''I hope you don't think me forward. I'm speaking as your old friend now, and not as—as—''

''I understand. And I'd like very much to see you this evening.''

''After all, we've been friends for so long.''

He nodded, even though what he was feeling at this moment had nothing to do with friendship. No, it had to do with her smile and her shape and her eyes and her hair, all of which he continued to study with hungry eyes.

''Last night was a mistake, Zach,'' she murmured.

His fingers touched the burnished curl again, caressing its silkiness for a second before tucking it neatly behind her ear. ''Was it?''

Her eyes softened. ''Yes. Of course it was. Absolutely.''

''I don't think so,'' he said.

''You've already met.'' There was disappointment in Simon's voice as Bret and Zach came together to his bedside.

''Yes,'' Bret said quickly. ''Outside.''

''I wanted to be the one to introduce you. I wanted to see your reaction.'' He sounded a trifle resentful, as if he'd been cheated. He had one of his perpetual fits of coughing, then controlled it and cleared his throat. ''I've kept this secret for all these weeks just to see your expression when you finally came face-to-face with your funny old Zachary Slayton, whom you pictured to be no less eccentric a character than someone out of Buffalo Bill's Wild West Show.''

Zach shot Bret a glance, noticed she was blushing, and got a curiously strong erotic charge out of her discomfiture. ''I can rope 'em and tie 'em, ma'am,'' he drawled, ''ride them buckin' broncs and even risk my nuts atop one o' them Brahma bulls.''

She gave him an arch glance. ''No need for that, Mr. Slayton. Since I'm sure you do that sort of thing in the sky over France every day, perhaps my estimation of you was not far wrong.''

Her point. He smiled at her. Out of the corner of his eyes he saw Simon watching them both, his eyes narrowly focused, the muscles tightening around his mouth. The charge in the atmosphere was palpable; the kid must be able to feel it.

Zach dragged his attention away from Bret and sat on the stool she'd pulled up for him. "You look like shit, Marrick," he said. "When're you going to stop lazing around and get back to work?"

"You should be so lucky. I've got beautiful women seeing to my every need. If I can manage it, I'm going to sit out the rest of the war and leave the fighting to clowns like you."

Bret moved off, leaving them alone. Zach followed her for a moment with his eyes, noting that Simon was doing the same. Guilt brushed him. Marrick loved her. They had all the elements here of one hell of an ugly mess.

They talked. Simon traded masculine insults for a while, but his real mood quickly emerged. He was depressed, Zach realized. Not to mention coughing his lungs up. Fucking poison gas.

"How much longer do you suppose you'll last out there?" Simon asked at one point. "You ought to have bought it long ago."

"I'll last till it's over," Zach said.

"No one else has escaped unscathed. Why should you?"

Unscathed? Was that what you called it when going to sleep at night was just another way of going into battle? When you lived on cigarettes and cheap wine and alternated between nursery rhymes and Latin erotica at bedtime to keep yourself awake and free of the hellish nightmares?

He tried to make light of it: "An old Navajo medicine singer predicted I'd live a long life and die in Arizona. She was a spooky old buzzard, and I like to think she knew what she was talking about."

"At least you're flying. With these legs, I'll never fly again."

"Hey, flyin's easy. It's walkin' that's gonna be tricky for you."

It ought to have made him smile. In the old days, it would have. But instead Simon retorted, "Don't start with your humorless jokes. Nobody's laughing, are they?"

Bret had joined him at Simon's bedside in time to hear the last exchange. Before Zach could apologize she said, "Stop it, Simon. Zach's come a long way to see you, and a little laughter would probably do you good.''

"Right. Laughter, the universal panacea. Superior even to a cup of tea and a digestive biscuit.''

"Some days he's impossible,'' Bret told Zach. Her voice was brisk, but not without an underlying compassion. "If his blasted legs weren't already broken, I swear I'd break them myself.''

"Bitch,'' Simon said without rancor. One more shock to add to the others Zach had experienced today. The Simon he'd known in France would never have dreamed of addressing such a term to his beloved Bret.

"I don't know about him, but I could sure use a cup of that tea you mentioned,'' said Zach. "I've developed a taste for the stuff.''

"Don't go yet,'' Simon said, his mood changing instantly.

"Hey, I'm not leaving you, Ace. I'll be around for a few days.''

When visiting hours were over, Zach and Bret left the ward together. "You were good with him,'' she said when they were out in the corridor. "He's been having a rough time. I wish he'd stop feeling so sorry for himself. It isn't helping.''

"I'd turn bearish too, if I had to lie about day after day, week after week, without any prospect of ever getting up again.''

"The doctor says now that he will be able to walk. His lungs will always be a problem, but he'd be walking already, if he weren't so damned pessimistic and stubborn. He's given up, you see. That's what enrages me. He won't even try to get better.'' The emotion in her voice intensified. "I would never do that. Give up, I mean. As long as I could breathe, I'd fight. Life's all we've got''—she waved a hand at the row upon row of cots—"to put up against this.''

"What time do you get finished here?'' He hadn't meant to say it. He'd even thought, while sitting with Simon, that the best thing, the honorable thing, would be to get out of Brighton on the next train. But there it was—his mouth ignoring his brain.

"At seven.'' She glanced at the heavy army watch on her wrist. Wristwatches were fairly newfangled, and she was the first woman he'd seen wearing one. "You'll have to excuse me. It's time to go assault my patients with the ward thermometers."

He grinned. "A fate worse than death?"

Mischief gleamed in those blue-green eyes. "I'm quite gentle."

As her slim form moved away from him, Zach tried by sheer force of will to regulate his heartbeat. What a disaster. You fly with a guy, you risk your life for him and he does the same for you, that makes you special to each other. You don't go after his woman, even if she doesn't love the guy and considers herself free.

It was a major flaw in his character, Zach knew, that so often caused him to chase the forbidden.

Chapter Forty-four

"I have something to show you," Bret said, sitting opposite him in the little restaurant Zach had found for them on the Brighton seafront. Opening her purse, she drew out something brown and desiccated, which she cradled in the palm of her hand. "Do you remember the snake-rattle necklace you sent me?"

He grinned. "You've still got that old thing?"

"I carry it with me wherever I go," she said with an arch smile. "I've kept it all these years as a good luck charm."

He remembered the rattler well because he had shot it himself, after being struck by it in the boot on a dusty afternoon when he hadn't been paying enough attention to where he was stepping. Afterward he'd been sorry. He'd cradled the still-warm body of the snake in his hands, admiring its beauty and its pride and wishing he could restore its life.

"What I don't understand," she went on, "is how you've turned out to be so young. When I started writing to you, you had already been my father's correspondent for a couple of years. I was only seven or eight; I'd barely learned how to form my letters. You were supposedly an expert aviator then, not to mention a designer and an engineer. But if you're still in your twenties now—'' she raised her eyebrows, and he mouthed his age, twenty-nine, ''that means you were a teenager at the time.''

''Yup. You've caught me fair and square. I lied. I was twelve when I first wrote to your father. He told me to address him as Henry, which I did. I didn't want him to guess I was just a boy.''

''Were you really flying aeroplanes when you were twelve?''

''Not flying them. Dreaming about them. Reading all the literature I could get on the subject. And coming up with ideas for designs. I was a clever little fraud. I convinced your father, and a couple of other guys, that I was actually experimenting in the field. And as soon as I was able, I did begin experimenting. Flying, too.''

''How did you get into the war?''

''I was on my way to the aviation conference in Paris when the hostilities began. I got caught up in the push to design war planes and train pilots. Later I went to the front with the British trainees as a flight instructor, only to watch my students die. It quickly became obvious that I was a better pilot than most of the kids we were sending up to fight.

''The brass tried to get me to join the fledgling RFC. I declined, using my American citizenship as an excuse. Americans are banned from combat in foreign armies. They insisted there were ways to get around that. The truth was, I didn't think I could kill and I sure as hell didn't want to die. But one day a buddy of mine came limping back to base with a hotshot Jerry on his tail, blasting away even as he tried to land. The kid died in my arms. His jacket was shredded where the machine-gun bullets had sliced into him, and the bastard German was still up there buzzing the field.

''I jumped into my friend's still-warm aeroplane and throttled up. I caught the son of a bitch half a mile away and blew him out of the sky. After that''—he shrugged—''well, I guess you could say I wasn't a virgin anymore. My hatred for the Germans didn't last for more than the few minutes it took to kill one—they're no different from us, for chrissake—but I was in and I've stayed in ever since." He paused. "I'm not proud of it."

Bret reached over and touched his hand. But her fingers were gone again before he could respond to the light pressure. He lit a cigarette. "Is Henry still designing planes?"

"Yes. There's a new project, a bomber, I believe, called the Zephyr. It's much larger than anything he's built before. It's expensive, though, and he'll need a hefty government contract."

"We were going to build planes together, he and I," said Zach. "The war's interfered with so much."

"You can do it still, when the war is over."

"Yeah," he agreed, not looking as if he believed it.

She changed the subject, and the conversation flowed steadily, easily. The food was delicious, the wine heady and strong. They talked without pause, one subject springing to life as another faded, and always, underneath, there was that pull.

Zach was aware, even as he chatted with her and asked her as many questions as he could think of about her current life as a VAD and her former life at Cadmon Hall, that he was on his best behavior, making a conscious effort to be charming and attentive. He wanted her to like him. He wanted her to come to bed with him, too; he couldn't seem to drive that fantasy from his mind no matter how often he interjected the thought of Simon Marrick. He couldn't suppress the delicious feelings generated by her nearness, just across from him in the subtly lit restaurant, her scent—violets again—her soft skin, her slim body, her breasts, her smile, her laughing eyes.

"Tell me about Simon," he finally said.

She fiddled with the stem of her wineglass. "I told you this morning. I love Simon. But physically, it's just not there. I don't know why. He's a handsome man."

"He can't walk. Christ, he probably can't—" He stopped. Her eyes had jerked up, warning him.

"He will walk. I intend to see that he does. And the doctors tell me there's nothing else wrong with him. Except his lungs, of course." She paused, tilting her head to one side. "Why are you harping on this? Would it make you happy if I did desire him?''

He said nothing. Hell, she knew the answer to that.

God, she was lovely: so warm, so empathetic, so vital. He wanted to reach her, touch her heart. He wanted to know her, unfold her, understand her. He wanted the intimacy of her letters without the distance that they, by virtue of the fact that they *were* letters, enforced. He wanted her to hold him and love him and take care of him in the night.

All crazy fantasies, he knew. He'd wanted those things from Cathy, too, and from one or two other women as well. But it went wrong; it always went wrong. What he yearned for from romance was simply too much, and the objects of his affection tended to disappoint him in the end.

Zach knew he had a bad habit of running away from his lovers. When they got too close, he disengaged. He wasn't sure why. He suspected it had something to do with his reluctance to trust anyone with the more vulnerable side of himself, the part that didn't mesh with his skill on horseback, his daring-do in the air, his thick dark hair and mustache, his height, his grin, his hard-edged good looks.

He'd grown up in Montana, where his father had taken his mother, the daughter of a wealthy Arizona rancher, to carve out an independent life. Montana was beautiful but hard country. The winters were long and cruel. The crops didn't always grow. The livestock hunched over in the wind, stiff-legged and starving.

Zach and his family had managed well enough until diphtheria struck. The fever killed both his younger siblings, Tommy and Grace, and left Zach in bed at age twelve with a seemingly endless convalescence. Naturally a clever, bookish child, he whiled away the hours reading novels, nature books, and everything he could find on flying machines. Lonely and sad over the loss of his brother and sister, he focused inward, reconstructing the past and dreaming of the glories to come.

When he was finally up and about again, his mother insisted that they return to Arizona. There, in the heat of the southwestern desert, Zach's life changed. His grandfather, who'd never had the son he'd longed for, lavished him with gifts, attention, and a roughshod brand of love that lashed out at anything that deviated from hard, uncompromising, shoot-'em-up-pardner masculinity. Zach became, on the surface at least, the brave, tough, competent young man his grandfather expected him to be. He grew adept at hiding, though never from himself, his gentler side.

The way he'd come to figure it, women wanted men whom they could lean on, strong men, dominant men, men without flaws or cracks. When he was all these things to them, they loved him. When he was Zach, the real Zach, not quite so rough and tumble, not quite so self-assured, they started itching to leave.

Usually, he left them first.

Cathy, the object of his first and most persistent heartache, had been warm—hell, she was hot—as long as he remained aloof and disinterested, but the moment he hinted at how important she was becoming to him, she danced away and the battles started.

After an on-again, off-again relationship that lasted for nearly ten years, she'd finally agreed to marry him in the spring of 1914. By summertime she was hedging again, postponing the wedding, flirting with other men. Injured and enraged, he'd run all the way to Europe, arriving just in time for the war.

"Do you ever crack?" Bret asked him after a long silence. "Go to pieces, I mean, splinter, fall apart?"

He shrugged, puffing on his cigarette.

"I do," she said. "Sometimes it all overwhelms me. I want to scream and scream. I take myself off then, if I can. I get alone in a room and start tearing things up."

He gestured skeptically. A spark from his cigarette arced across the table between them.

"Really." Bret raised her wineglass to drink. Beads of purple tinged her lips. "Beds, in particular. Maybe because I spend so many hours of every day making them, changing them, cleaning them, seeing men suffer and die in them. Beds make me angry. I tear the pillows off and punch them, throw them around, stomp on them. Once in a while a pillow bursts and I'm inundated with feathers. If I'm really angry, I pull the whole mattress off the bed and tear into that." She was grinning at him. "You don't believe me?"

"Sure, I believe you." She'd lightened the mood and he adjusted his tone accordingly. "I'm just trying to picture it: a redheaded Amazon nurse assaulting a mattress."

She tipped the side of her head into her palm and regarded him through half-closed lashes. "Don't you ever do such things? What happens when you're so frustrated that you can't take it anymore?"

"Hey, this is a tough guy you're talking to. Self-disciplined. We flyboys are loaded with iron-fisted control."

"Liar."

No point in pretending with her, he reminded himself. She'd read his letters. She already knew most of what he hid from other women. "I've got a temper," he admitted. "I tend to think before I act, but not always, you're right." He was remembering last night. "I guess my idea of pleasure has something to do with the rare luxury of acting without thinking. Simon used to compare me to Hamlet—cautious, imaginative, speculative, yet prone to reckless acts of passion, like stabbing Polonius or leaping into Ophelia's grave."

"Or jumping into an aeroplane to get the German who'd just killed your friend."

He nodded grimly. "No pillows or mattresses necessary. I take out my aggressions on real people."

Once again she touched him. This time his fingers closed over hers. The current ran between them, opening a channel for the floods that were demanding a deeper and more permanent linkage.

It was then that he decided. He had to have her, and damn the consequences.

"It's a lovely evening," he said as they finished their coffee. "Will you take another walk along the beach with me?"

"I'd like that, Zach."

So, like last night, they were out in the wind, smelling the sea, hand in hand this time, relishing the sensation of palm against palm, fingers entwining with fingers.

She asked him what he was going to do with the rest of his

leave, and he mentioned that he'd like to see something of the English countryside. What, he asked her, would she recommend?

"That's easy," she said promptly. "If I had a few days in the country, I'd go fishing."

"Now there's a girl after my own heart. I used to love reading the passages in your letters about fishing. I'd dream of your slow-flowing English chalk streams and all the trout I'd catch."

"I don't think I've fished once since the bloody war began."

"I have," said Zach, smiling. "I do it often. When things get grim and ghastly and unbearable, I go fishing."

"In France?"

He nodded solemnly. "Day or night, winter or summer. Shall I show you how?"

"Please."

He stopped walking and closed his eyes. He held silence for several seconds, feeling her close beside him, hearing the lapping of the water on the strand. "Okay. I'm there now, on a western trout river. The water's cold and fast and I know the fish are all around me. I can feel it. They're here. I don't see any rising, but wait . . . a hatch is starting and any minute now the water's going to begin boiling as they come up to feed. There's one—see the bubble? There's another just beyond it and lots more on either side."

"So many? Is it really like out west?"

"Yeah. Not so much around Phoenix—it's too hot there. You have to go north into the mountains. Or, better yet, to Montana, where we lived when I was a kid. Fishing's amazing in Montana. You'll have to come and try it someday. When the trout get going on a big hatch, you can hear the lunkers slurping as they gulp those mayflies down.

"I see the one I want," he went on. "She's a lovely cutthroat trout. Have you ever seen one? They're indigenous to the American West, I believe, so you probably haven't. They're distinguished by a flash of crimson at their gills." He opened his eyes to smile at her. "Not unlike the color of your hair."

"I hate the color of my hair."

"You shouldn't. In the natural world vibrant color is a great attractor. My trout, for instance. She with the crimson markings is also long and sleek, strong and graceful. I want her desperately. But I suspect she'll be a real challenge to hook. I sit down on the bank for a while to contemplate the problem. I'm going to have to watch her, probe her, feel her out before I make my move. She's a canny trout who won't be easily deceived."

He felt Bret stir beside him. She knew what he was up to, of course. "I can tell she's a joyful fish from the zest with which she rises to her mayflies. Her appetite is voracious, but discriminating. I'll have to tempt her with just the right morsel, which won't be easy. However painstakingly I tie them to resemble their counterparts in nature, my flies are artificial, and my trout is accustomed to the real thing."

Beneath the lazy hum generated by a heady combination of warm winds and rising tides, Bret was conscious of a thread of apprehension. Was he warning her? Where, exactly, was the artifice here? How deeply did art—and craft—run in this magnetic man?

"When you hook this fish, which I'm quite sure you are capable of doing, what, may I ask, do you do with her?" As she asked the question, unbidden the memory of Daniel bashing a brown trout against a flat rock leaped into her mind.

"Well, I could eat her for supper, I suppose," said Zach. "With that firm, succulent flesh, she'd be a rare treat. But I'm far more likely to release her and let her fin back to her lair to grow bigger and fatter and more of a challenge for me to hunt again one day."

Bret nodded. It was about the best answer she could expect, but it did occur to her to wonder if he was someone for whom the stalk was more important than the catch.

Even if he is, so what? What am I thinking—that I'll marry him and go live in Arizona? It's far more likely he'll die like all the other men of his generation, and I'll spend my life alone.

The walk had taken them back toward his hotel. By tacit agreement, they stopped. He touched her shoulder and she responded to the gentle signal, turning to face him, tilting back her head. When his mouth came down, hers was already open. Not a tentative kiss tonight: his tongue was right there, demanding entrance, his first penetration of her.

Her arms curled around his shoulders as she joyfully accepted him.

It was a long and complicated kiss. They both knew it was a preliminary, a way for them to learn and assess each other's desires and needs. When at last he lifted his mouth from hers and asked the question that her body had already answered: "Will you come inside with me?" she smiled and whispered, "Yes."

Last night he had referred to her as a schoolgirl. It was important to her that he know she was very far from that. It was also important that she please, even surprise this experienced, possibly jaded man. There had been other women for him, lots of them, no doubt. She could not be one of those women; but she could be wholly and completely Bret.

The Intrepid Adventuress.

When they reached his room, he turned to her, hesitant, as if concerned that she might once again change her mind and bolt. Now was the time, her time. She raised her palms to stop his tentative approach. She didn't speak, letting her eyes announce her intentions.

He stayed where he was, watching as her fingers moved to the neckline of her frock. One by one, she unfastened the buttons running down the bodice. She did it slowly. Leaving her neckline open to the waist, the edges of the fabric still so close that nothing was revealed except a hint of her underthings, she reached up to loosen her hair. She shook it down.

"What are you up to?" She could hear the leashed excitement in his voice.

"I'm testing that iron-fisted control you were bragging about in the restaurant. No, stay there. You're not allowed to touch me."

"I'm going to touch you, Bret. I'm going to touch you deep inside."

"Mmm, maybe. If I decide to let you. But first I want to see your self-discipline. Become intimate with your vaunted self-control." She tilted her head and smiled. "How much pressure will it bear, I wonder, before it shatters?"

Zach laughed nervously. He hadn't expected this. She was one surprise after another, his red-haired English lady.

He nailed her with his eyes as she undid her belt and slipped first one arm, then the other out of its sleeve, revealing a silky white chemise that barely covered her breasts. She raised her arms, which thrust her breasts outward and made his fingers itch to caress them. She drew the dress up and off and dropped it carelessly on the floor. That simple gesture—not caring what happened to her clothes because she was so involved in the feelings that were flowing between them—touched him more deeply even than the sight of her, tall and slim and lovely, in her petticoats, stockings, and chemise. A sense of unreality came over him, frightening him. How could she have come into his life now, when there was so little time left? Despite his words to Simon this morning, Zach thought it likely that he would die in France. This, their first night together, could also be their last.

Her smile was impish, her eyes desire-bright. She nodded in the direction of the bed. "Take off your boots and lie down."

"Just my boots, ma'am?"

"Mm-hmm. For now." Her full bottom lip was caught for a second in her teeth before she added, "Well, your socks too—that's permitted."

He sat down on the bed, stretching a long booted leg in her direction. "And if I need some help getting them off?"

Pertly, she put both hands on her hips. His control was slipping fast. "I've never heard of a cowboy who required a valet."

"That's because cowboys sleep with their boots on. Cowboys do everything with their boots on."

She giggled, spoiling her act for a moment. He wanted to hug her, hold her, show her that none of this was necessary, but he also wanted it to continue. Which it did. She went down on her knees before him. Then her hands were on his boots, caressing him through the leather. "Another time," she whispered. "Tonight I want all of you, even your ankles and your toes."

She removed his boots. He noted the strength in her arms, shoulders, and back, gleaned, no doubt, from hefting heavy male patients around. She caressed his feet, his legs, running her hands up under his trousers. "Lie back," she commanded, and he obeyed.

She went back to work on her own things, loosening petticoats, shedding garters, rolling down stockings, slowly, one by one. When she finished she was wearing nothing but a silky chemise that ended at the top of her thighs, offering him a tantalizing glimpse as she came to the bed, climbed upon it, and straddled his body. "Tell me about Arizona."

"*Now?*"

"Oh yes. I understand from Simon that you fighter pilots are adept at being able to do several things at one time. Such versatility intrigues me. Such control. So talk to me. Keep talking until you can't form words anymore."

"What if I'm tougher than you think? What if you can't break me down?"

She smiled and tossed her head. She slid up until she could reach his mouth. She kissed him deeply, a kiss to which he, mischievously, did not at first respond. But the delicious stimulus of her tongue brushing against his was irresistible. "Oh, I'll break you down, all right," she whispered. "Tell me about the desert."

"It's very hot in the desert."

"How hot?"

"Well, you have to take off your clothes."

"Mmm?" She started on the buttons of his uniform. When she had them open she pushed apart the edges and bent her face to his chest. He went rigid as she nibbled at him. She found his nipples and touched them, one by one, with the tip of her tongue. Then she sucked.

The desire to grab her, press her down beneath him, and get on with it was almost too powerful to resist. He closed his eyes. *Control*, he reminded himself. *Self-discipline*.

"You're not talking."

"Uh, right. Well, let's see. People think the Arizona desert's nothing but sand and rock, but that's not the way of it at all. The desert's abloom with plants and flowers all year round. There are oceans of golden poppies, spreading for miles and fluttering in the breeze. And brittlebush—that looks like daisies, I think—and desert marigolds. I don't know the names of all of them, but they bloom in the most spectacular colors ranging from vivid pinks and crimsons to the deepest purplish blacks.''

"Sounds lovely." Bret unbuckled his belt, pulled it through its loops, and dropped it to the floor.

"There's wildlife, too. Mule deer and white-tailed fawns. There are coyotes and bobcats and jackrabbits. There are prairie dogs and ringtail cats and rock squirrels.''

Her hands were on the buttons of his fly. He wished she would hurry up and get them open before they burst and sailed across the room. There. Yes. *Yes*. He lifted his buttocks so she could drag his trousers down and add them to the growing pile on the floor.

"Tell me about the birds. I understand there are some lovely and distinctive birds in the desert.''

She was kneeling over him now. Her fingers crept back up his thighs and inward. Feather-light. He rolled his hips upward, seeking a heavier touch. She laughed and took her hands away.

He was caressing her as well, now. Gently he slipped his hands under her chemise and moved his open palms upward until they reached her breasts. She made a husky sound in the depths of her throat as he rubbed his thumbs across her hardening nipples. She felt so good. Soft, sweet. He got a hand into her hair and pulled on it until she bent her head to him. He kissed her mouth. Sweeter and more fragrant than any desert flower.

"Birds," she whispered, sighing.

"There's the odd little roadrunner with the long tail." He stroked along her spine and cupped her bottom. "There's the cactus wren. There are hummingbirds that suck the nectar from the flowering cacti''—he kissed her again—"and the great horned owl that flies faster than a horse can run and swoops down to feed on rabbits.'' He nuzzled her neck and, more feverishly now, kneaded her breasts.

She was caressing his inner thighs. He spread his legs to give her access. She reached between his legs, seeking, finding, exploring, coaxing. He was breathing hard.

"You're not talking, cowboy. Tell me about the cactuses. Cacti? How big are they?''

"Well, uh, some are bigger than others, of course. Saguaro cactuses are the largest. They're like trees, some of them. Great, mammoth things, and very old. They thrust up out of the sand and bloom with a lovely yellow flower . . . Jesus, Bret!"

"Tell me about roping and riding."

"Well, I hate to destroy my reputation for modesty, but I'm pretty damn good at both."

She slowly lowered herself onto his body. He could feel her long bare legs along his own. With arms around her waist he pulled her down until they were belly to belly, heart to heart, skin to skin. "I'm quite a horsewoman myself."

"Yeah? You gonna show me?"

"Well, I settle myself comfortably in the saddle . . ."

"Like this?"

"Umm . . . yes . . . a little lower . . . yes, right there. Oh. Yes. Like that."

He made a strangled sound as he slid inside her. He waited a moment, listening to her pant, then began to move. "You trot a bit first, huh? Or is trotting too uneven a rhythm? You'd rather move right into a nice, smooth lope?"

"A canter," she said breathlessly. "In England we call it a canter."

"Whatever," said Zach. "What else d'you want to know about Arizona?"

"Shut up."

"Shut up? Does that mean I win? My self-control's a match for your seduction, after all?"

She was alternately laughing and gasping. But in spite of both she managed to lift her hips and withdraw. "You tell me. Is it?"

Zach's arms moved instantly to grab her, pulling her back down. He rolled over until he was on top. He forced her legs as far apart as they would go and jammed himself inside her, groaning as she sheathed him. "Reckon not," he admitted as he gave himself up to the storm.

Chapter Forty-five

Bret wondered why Zach didn't appear the next morning at the hospital, but so many casualties were arriving that she didn't have time to fret about it. When there was no sign of him by evening, his silence took on darker overtones. He'd told her he would be in town for a week. Was he avoiding her?

By the second day she was truly worried. She needed to see him, touch his hand, hear his voice. Slaving over bandages and bedpans, she fantasized about him, her mind continually flashing to what he had said, what he had done, how it had felt to be in his arms.

"Why are you so preoccupied?" Simon asked her. "Is there something wrong?"

"I'm annoyed with you because you refuse to try walking," she told him, but he looked at her skeptically.

"Where's Slayton, I wonder? I thought he was here for a few days."

Bret noted the way Simon linked her mood with Zach's absence. How long could they hide it? He knew them both so well.

"I've no idea where he is," she said. "Perhaps he had to return to France."

"Bet he's holed up somewhere with a girl. He believes sex is the best way to relax."

"I've got patients to feed," she said testily and left him.

During her midmorning break, Bret rang Zach's hotel, half-expecting to hear that he had checked out. He'd gone for a walk, the hall porter informed her. She rang off without leaving a message.

For a walk! He *was* avoiding her. Why? Was this what it

was like to be truly in love? She hoped not, because it was awful. She recalled Tamara's old warning: "Beware yer passionate nature. 'Twill be the cause of much joy as well as many sorrows."

Bret was aware that there were subtle gambits and strategies to the game of romance, but it had never occurred to her to use any of them. Now, though, it struck her that she had broken every rule. She'd talked too much, chattering on and on to Zach at dinner instead of inviting him to talk more about himself. Afterward, she'd been much too easy a conquest— less of a challenge than a cutthroat trout! Had her heat, her pleasure, her eager desire to make love disgusted him? Should she have waited for him to initiate instead of behaving in that outrageous manner in his bedroom? Maybe he would have preferred a submissive partner.

What people liked in bed was such a mystery. Polly Marks, who seemed to know all about these things, had told her once that the only difference between an expert lover and one who was merely adequate was the degree to which he or she could perceive and satisfy a partner's deepest needs.

"You don't have to be young; you don't have to be beautiful," she'd said. "Good sex is all playacting. If you're perceptive enough to guess the words, the actions, the caresses a man yearns for, and if you're bold enough to do whatever's necessary to make his dreams come true, he'll come back to you over and over again."

"But wouldn't that be a sort of manipulation?" Bret had asked.

"Giving a man the experience he most deeply desires? To me it's one of the most generous ways of showing your love."

What was Zach's fantasy? How did one guess such a thing? What it probably wasn't, she thought gloomily, was Bret Trevor, intrepid adventuress.

On the other hand, he'd certainly seemed to like it. He'd seemed every bit as delighted with her as she had been with him.

In that case, where the blazes was he?

Late that evening, just before she was dejectedly retiring for bed, he rang her. "I've extended my furlough for a few more days,'' he told her. ''Would you like to come to the countryside with me?''

Oh yes, she told him. She'd like it very much.

She almost missed the train. Just before their scheduled departure, Zach boarded, found their compartment, stowed his gear, then hurried back to the end of the carriage for another look.

Well, finally. She was carrying a basket over one arm, and her long red hair was streaming behind her as she dashed for the train. She was dressed in civilian clothes today—one of the new short skirts that displayed a shapely ankle and calf. The high-heeled shoes hampered her progress. The train lurched and Zach let out a shout of pure frustration. Wasn't it just like a woman to turn up late!

He jumped down to the platform, earning the curse of the conductor, who was just stepping up. Zach pointed to Bret, who was waving now and running. He ran to meet her, grabbed her around the waist, and all but heaved her aboard as the rear of the carriage chugged along beside them. The conductor was shouting as Bret held out her hand to him and dragged him on as well. They both collapsed at the top of the steps, breathing hard and laughing like a couple of Bedlam residents.

''You're mad, Zach! What if you hadn't been able to get back on?''

''Hey, you're talking to a flying ace, lady. This tired old piece of machinery we're riding doesn't even leave the ground.''

''I thought I'd missed it for sure.''

''You ought to have missed it. You're ten minutes late.''

''I considered not coming. I thought perhaps it might not be a good idea.'' Her laughter had died away and she was blushing now from something more than simple exertion.

''It's probably a rotten idea,'' he agreed as he helped her to her feet.

The truth was, she had flooded him, and it was a damn uncomfortable feeling. He'd wasted two days, staying away

418 • Linda Barlow

from her because he felt so overwhelmed. She wasn't like any other woman he'd ever known, which intrigued him at the same time as it sent up a warning flag. His natural defenses had gone up, closing him off from her.

Their lovemaking had been perfect, a rare thing with a new partner. All the same, after that first night together he'd felt an almost irresistible desire to cut and run. What could come of this but misery? Death was waiting for him in France. This was no time to be toying with the affections of one of his best and oldest friends.

"Zach?" She was watching him quizzically, as if trying to fathom his thoughts.

He reached out for her hand and felt the immediate thrill as her palm touched his. "Actually, I think it's a splendid idea," he said, grinning. "Come on, let's go sit down. We have the compartment entirely to ourselves, for now, anyway."

She came close and kissed his cheek. Her frock was sea-green, which lent an emerald tinge to her eyes; her lips and hair were red. She was his flamboyant, colorful Bret Trevor, the personification of all her youthful, zestful letters.

It was there, at that moment, in the narrow corridor of an accelerating train, that the Bret of the letters and the Bret of real life suddenly fused and became one. For the first time in years, the grip Cathy had held on his heart loosened. *I could love this woman*, he thought. *I could honestly love her*.

They had a little less than a week, but the time expanded in the mysterious way it does when love alters all perceptions. They found a small bed and breakfast somewhere on the Downs, on the outskirts of a village whose name Zach couldn't pronounce. There was a stream nearby, full of trout. Around them were freshly planted fields, meadows dotted with summer wildflowers, and, in the distance, the sparkling sea. Every lazy day they fished and hiked and sat dreamily underneath the bows of a gnarled and ancient chestnut tree that must have sheltered lovers for centuries. They were happy. Life was sweet, love was new, and the war was far, far away.

Early one morning when he reached for her in bed, the spot

beside him was empty and cold. He sat up with a jerk, still half-asleep. She was seated at the writing table on the far side of the room by the window, a blanket wrapped around her shoulders, her bare feet propped on the sill.

"What are you doing?"

She tossed him a smile. "Writing a letter."

"Are you crazy? How can you think about letter writing at a time like this?"

"Want to hear it?" She turned the chair until she was facing him and began to read aloud. A mischievous grin was playing about her mouth. " 'Dear Mr. Slayton: There are certain things I've always wondered about Americans, particularly concerning cowboys from the Wild West. For example, do they come to bed with their boots and their gunbelts on?' "

Zach was laughing. "You already know the answer to that."

" 'I rather hope they do because—and I fear this will be difficult to explain—deep in the heart of every woman is the secret desire to be snatched away by a rough, tough hombre who will toss her across his saddle and bear her away to his lair where he will do unspeakable things to her sweet, innocent body . . . while keeping his boots and his gunbelt on.' "

Not just laughing. Howling.

" 'What I would really like to know, Mr. Slayton, is this: How do men make love in Arizona?' "

"Hey," he said.

"What?"

He made a gun out of his thumb and forefinger and pointed it at her. "You wanna get outta here with your life, sister?"

Bret raised her eyebrows in mock alarm. "Yessir, I do. Don't shoot, I beg of you."

"Stand up."

"What?"

"You heard me. On your feet, sweetheart. Yeah, good, that's more like it. You don't find too many obedient women nowadays, more's the pity. Females are gettin' too rebellious and uppity, thinkin' they're the ones wearing the trousers. I reckon I know a few ways to nip that in the bud. Drop the blanket."

"Really, sir, I couldn't. I draw the line—"

"Hey, you're not plannin' to go rebellious on me now, are you?"

"I might," she said coyly.

"Yeah? Better not, sweetheart, 'cause if you do I'll have to punish you. Twelve lashes at the ol' whipping post. Now that would be a real shame. I shore would hate to mark up that soft white body o' yours. The blanket, lady. Drop it."

Slowly, gracefully, she allowed the blanket to slip to the floor. She was naked underneath it, slender, perfect, lovely. Her nipples were hard in the sharp morning air. Zach drew a careful breath, his gun hand shaking slightly. Blood was surging in his groin, and he felt a hard, edgy excitement that was incredibly intense considering he'd just made love to her a few hours before.

"Well, well. Very nice. Just the way I like a woman to look: bare-breasted and bare-assed. Now get yourself over here."

"Please, sir, I must protest—"

"Twelve lashes, sister. I mean it."

She approached the bed. Zach scooted over to make room for her, the sheet falling away from his body as he moved. "Doesn't look to me as if you *are* wearing the trousers, on this occasion at least," she commented.

"Don't you dare make me laugh."

"What's the matter, cowboy? A little humor gonna result in the premature discharge of your pistol?"

Zach broke up. He pulled her sprawling down on top of him, a lovely conjunction of naked limbs that probably would have felt even better if they hadn't both been shaking with laughter. She struggled as he tried to kiss her, and they rolled over once so he was on top. He pinned her arms and subdued her arching body until the mischievous light in her eyes softened and turned into something that was at once tender and ardent. "Bret, you are the most—"

"Ssh. Kiss me."

"The loveliest, sweetest, most exciting, funniest—"

"Funniest!"

"I want you so much. Open your legs for me, sweetheart, before I burst."

"You got your boots and your gunbelt on?"

"Yeah. And my Stetson. You forgot that critical item. Believe me, I'm dressed for the part. Just close your eyes and imagine."

"I believe I'll keep my eyes open."

"The reality tops the fantasy, huh?"

"You betcha, cowboy."

With Zach she found laughter, which was something she had never really had with Daniel. She realized how important this was to her. For all his reflectiveness and moodiness, there was a lightness of spirit at the core of Zach that corresponded with her own.

They found peace as well as passion. A safe harbor in each other's arms. It was not to be spoken of, not to be expressed. But it was there, all the same.

There was only one thing she missed. He never actually told her that he loved her.

She had the sense that words were easier for her than for Zach. He told her he didn't trust language to reach the heart of experience, the deepest wellspring of emotion. "People lie too much—to others, to themselves. You have to watch their faces, their eyes, their hands to know the truth."

He was right, she thought. The communication between them was deeper than words. It existed in the touch of a hand, the sharing of a glance, the brush of his lips against her cheek. Such simple things told her of his love. She knew she did not imagine this, even though he would not give her the words.

In Zach she recognized her soul's counterpart, and the penetration of their separate identities into each other brought about an intimacy that was at times disconcerting. To her this ability to voice the same thought and share the same feeling was the epitome of what she'd always believed love to be, but she sensed that Zach was disturbed by it, perhaps a little frightened. Much more than she, he resisted the collapse of barriers between them.

On the fifth day, as he lay atop the coverlet of their bed, idly smoking a cigarette, he said, "What a lovely dream it's been, spending this week together."

"Dream? Are you implying that soon we will awaken?"

He lowered his eyes. "I love being here with you, Bret."

She chose to reply to the subtext: "I love you, too."

He sucked in smoke, then blew it away. It dissipated slowly in the heavy air. "It's just that I have this feeling that I'm not going to make it out again."

She felt an unexpected rush of anger. "Don't say that. Don't you *ever* say that."

"And don't you make me treat you like some of the other women I've been with; the ones who didn't know what it was like over there."

"You lousy American son of a bitch. How dare you compare me with the other women you've been with! Is this what you tell them? It's been lovely, honey, but don't waste your time thinking about me because I'm going to be dead soon?"

He smiled as it occurred to him that there had been one or two ladies he'd said something similar to.

"You've lived this long, you bastard. You'll live until it's over. You'll live and come back to me."

But there was a desperate note in her voice and they both heard it. Her bottom lip quivered and two huge tears turned up, shining, in her eyes.

"Don't think about it," he whispered, reaching for her. "We're still together. We still have time."

For him, it had proved all too easy to suspend reality and pretend they had a future together. Trouble was, they didn't. He figured he'd defied the odds already by surviving as long as he had. He knew no way to explain to her that he had, in recent months, gone beyond fear into that state where he accepted death. Most of his friends were there, across the dark border, in that other place that sometimes seemed as real to him as this world did. Like them, he would never know the ordinary pleasures of life—a spouse's laughter, the squealing of babies, the comfort and security of growing old with a longtime mate. Such were the things of life, and he dealt in death. Such things belonged to healers like Bret, not destroyers like himself.

Thus, as the time drew near when he would have to go, the worm of war invaded their Eden. Zach was increasingly moody. He started to notice little things about his lover that irritated him. He was neat and orderly, whereas she tossed things around. He took to picking her clothes off the floor and hanging them up, finding it annoying to think she'd have put them on again without even noticing they were wrinkled.

"You realize that you and I would never make it as a married couple," he said as they lolled together in their bedroom on their last night together. They had made love once and were lying on the hearth rug in front of the fireplace, finishing off a bottle of claret. Bret had just opened the window, sending a draft of cool air across his sex-heated body.

"Why on earth not?" she asked lightheartedly. The fact that she didn't notice that he was halfway serious increased his vexation. How could anybody go through life—go through a war, goddammit—and remain so blasted cheerful?

"You love fresh air. I'd rather sleep in a warm, stuffy room."

"Are you cold? I'm sorry. I'll close it."

"You're much franker and more expensive than I am. And we have different tastes. You like Impressionist painting; I regard most artists who lived after Michelangelo and Leonardo as marginally talented. Same with music—you love all that romantic sort of stuff, including those godawful, melodramatic operas, whereas I'll stick with motets and madrigals and strict, rule-ordered counterpoint."

"Mmm. It's true your interests are positively medieval, Zach. I suspect you spent your last life locked up in a monastery copying manuscripts until your eyes gave out."

"I smoke cigarettes, you hate the smell," he continued, ticking their differences off on his fingers. "You drink tea, I drink coffee. You're always asking for second helpings of the same vegetables that I push to the side of my plate. You're emotional, I'm rational."

"Ha!"

"You're considerably more gregarious than I am and enjoy taking up with strangers whom you're determined to make your friends. Whereas I—" He stopped. The expression on her face had suddenly grown serious, and perhaps a little hurt. Zach felt a pang of guilt. He was aware, vaguely, of what he was doing, and he hated himself for it. But, dammit, she was so unrealistic. He didn't want to hurt her—of course not—

but it was time she opened her eyes. She believed in this goddamn fantasy they had created together. She'd be even more hurt in the end if he continued to allow her to build it.

"You what?" she asked quietly. "You're sorry I took up with a certain stranger on the Brighton pier? Even though he wasn't really a stranger at all?"

Before he could answer, she added, "I thought you were enjoying our time together."

"Dammit, Bret. Don't look at me like that. I have enjoyed our time together. I've loved it."

"Then why are you deliberately trying to spoil it?"

"I'm not—"

"Aren't you?"

"Look—"

"You've been happy here. So have I. That's a gift, Zach. You don't throw the gifts of the gods and goddesses back in their faces."

"Yeah, well, some gift. It's going to end. Am I supposed to be grateful to the so-called gods and goddesses who fling a few precious moments of happiness at me only to snatch it away again?"

"That's the sort of attitude that suffocates happiness before its time."

"Jesus. I hate it when you wax philosophical. Elizabeth Trevor's Wisdom of Life."

She threw her wine in his face. Zach leaped to his feet, nearly jerking the rug out from under her with his abrupt movement. God damn! He wanted to get his fingers around her neck and squeeze. He wanted to toss her into bed and ram himself into her without thought or care for her pleasure or satisfaction.

She saw it. She drew back, obviously startled. "I'm sorry," she said quickly. "That was an indefensible thing to do. I just felt so angry all of a sudden."

He sank back to the floor, knowing he would never hurt her. Not physically, anyway. She reached up and wiped the wine from his face with the palm of her hand. "I love you so," she whispered.

He looked at her with great dark mournful eyes. "I'm sorry. I don't know what's the matter with me."

"Come to bed, Zach."

"I don't want to come to bed. When we wake up it'll be tomorrow and we'll have to go back."

Smiling, she enclosed him in her arms. "Ssh. Tomorrow's a million years away."

Before taking the boat train back to France, Zach accompanied Bret to the hospital. She knew he would have preferred to avoid it, but he insisted that he wasn't going to leave her to face Simon alone.

Bret was dreading a scene, but Simon hardly seemed to notice the guilty look on her face. "There's something I want you both to see. I've been practicing the entire time you were gone."

Slowly, painfully, he forced himself upright. As soon as he was sitting, he began to cough, but he ignored this as he reached for the crutches by the side of his bed. He hauled himself up and got them under his armpits. "No, don't help me," he said as Bret made a move toward him.

He took seven steps across the room, turned, and hobbled back to his bed, where he collapsed, sweating, his face gray with exertion. He coughed violently, and then he smiled.

Zach whistled and clapped his hands while Bret smoothed Simon's hair back from his perspiring brow. She could see an image of him running over the moors beside her, young and proud and happy and whole, on the day when she had first watched him fly. This, she thought, had taken as much effort, as much courage, as much heart.

"You see? It's going to take time, but you were right, I *will* walk again. I'll be strong again. Hell, maybe someday I'll even fly again." He smiled again, that tender old smile of the Simon she had known before Daniel, before the war, before Zach. "With your friendship to inspire me, Bret, there's nothing I can't do."

The word reverberated. Friendship. Not love. Over Simon's head, Zach's eyes met hers.

Simon glanced from one of them to the other. A strain touched the corners of his mouth. "Did you have a pleasant holiday? Catch a lot of fish? Christ, I'm envious. I'd love to be standing on the banks of a trout stream. Oh well, maybe next summer.''

"Zach'll tell you all about it,'' Bret said. She had to get out. If she didn't find a few minutes of privacy to collect herself, she was going to break down.

He knew. But somehow he had found within him the generosity to accept what must be the worst kind of heartache.

Eyes brimming, she turned and left the ward.

Simon Marrick had learned in France that he was not a coward. There, facing death daily, he had lost the irrational fears that had haunted him since childhood and accepted the realistic terrors that everyone in war must confront. His accident, also, had changed him. There had been many times during the long weeks of his recuperation when he'd been tempted to give up and let himself sink quietly into death.

Doggedly, he'd resisted those demons. Now, though, misery had rushed toward him from an unexpected source. It had taken more courage than he'd ever expected to find within himself to come to terms with the romance between the woman he loved and his best friend.

He had sensed it from the first. It had been there, that special something that was not there between himself and Bret, for no reason that he had ever been able to understand. Love had to be reciprocal before the air crackled between two people. It crackled between her and Zach.

He'd refused to believe it. He'd closed his eyes. But when Bret had gone away so suddenly on leave at the same time as Zach was going fishing, he couldn't deny it.

First Daniel Carne, now Zach Slayton.

Why was there nothing for him?

During their absence he'd decided to stop lying about uselessly in bed. Bret's love for Daniel had jolted him into learning how to fly. Now her love for Zach would teach him to walk. He was no good to her anyway, without his legs. He couldn't do much about his blasted lungs—the doctors had admitted that the scarring was permanent, and that he'd forever be vulnerable to lung infections that could easily kill him, but he was not a coward. He would endure. He would not become the object of anybody's pity.

What's more, he would be persistent. He would be faithful. Life was uncertain, particularly in time of war.

He would not give up hope. He remembered a story he had read long ago about a man facing execution. The condemned man, whose name was Hashim, lived in some opulent Eastern empire and had a particular love for spiders. One night he was visited in a dream by a genie who proclaimed that his spiders could be taught to spin webs of gold. The genie gave him a magic incantation to whisper to his insects that would, in time, produce the desired result.

Every day Hashim, an optimistic man, spent hours chanting the words of the spell, but his spiders did not learn.

At last the spidermaster, as his neighbors called him, grew tired of being the butt of everybody's jokes. He paid a goldsmith in another village to beat gold for him into the finest, thinnest, wispiest strands, with which he decorated his small hut. Then he invited his neighbors in to see the miracle.

Gold makes people crazy, he discovered. Suddenly all his neighbors wanted his spiders, which he refused to sell. The more he refused, the higher the price went, until common spiders became the most highly regarded creatures in the kingdom.

The tale got back to the sultan's vizer, who, always on the lookout for new ways to add to the empire's coffers, ordered Hashim to be brought to the sultan's palace, along with his golden webs and his wooden box of spiders.

"Is it true that these humble insects spin webs of gold?" the sultan asked him.

Awed and frightened by the sultan, but eager to please, Hashim foolishly answered yes.

"Have them spin one for us now."

Trembling, Hashim whispered his magical incantation. But no matter how much he chanted and pleaded and begged, his insects continued to spin the same webs that spiders have spun since the dawn of time.

Hashim was convicted of fraud and sentenced to death. But since it was the beginning of Ramadan, a religious festival lasting for forty days and forty nights, all prisoners were given a stay of execution until the holidays were over.

Hashim the spidermaster refused to give up hope. "Much can happen in forty days and forty nights," he declared. "The sultan may sicken and die. Or I may sicken and die. Or my slow-witted spiders may finally begin spinning gold."

Zach may die.

Or I may die.

Or Bret may come to love me, after all.

Chapter Forty-six

Zach had promised to write, but he didn't. Bret didn't hear a word from him; not one.

When she woke in the morning, she felt his presence in her receding dreams. She had conversations with him all day long, either reliving the past or inventing the scenes that would make up their future. Until the postman came with the morning mail, she would imagine the words and phrases of the letter she would receive from him, and how she would reply. When the morning post disappointed her she would readjust the scenario slightly to allow for the possibility that his letter would come in the afternoon.

She lived every day in the fear of his death. The letters that did not come seemed to prove he was dead. But Simon remained in touch with his squadron, and if Zach had been killed, he would have heard.

Her brain told her then that he didn't love her after all. That his refusal to give her the words proved it, and that if she hadn't been so blinded by her emotions, she would have recognized his silence for what it was.

Her heart told her not to listen to her brain. As always, her tendency was to follow her heart.

So the shock was all the mightier when Martin Sommers, a squadron mate of Zach's and Simon's, came to visit, saying, in response to one of Simon's eager questions, "Never a scratch on him, as usual, the lucky devil. Don't see much of him off duty, though. Rumor has it he's got some French girl. Course there's always some filly with the Phoenix. You know what they say about him—'tisn't just his aeroplane that's always rising from the ashes ready for action again."

Sommers had a jolly good laugh over that, but he must have wondered why Simon whitened and Bret fled.

In his cramped quarters on a misty autumn morning in France, Zach read the letter that had just come for him from England.

Dear Zach,

I've tried so long and so hard to understand you. At times I truly believe I do. At other times I despair.

I know what your excuse is—death waiting to take you. No point in letting yourself live, letting yourself love, when death is so greedy and so close.

But suppose there had been no war. What then? What is the reality of you? Is it the spark, the brightness, the gentleness you so often reveal in your most tender moments, or is it some fear, some insecurity, some abiding sense of self-hatred that convinces you that no woman could truly love you . . . that if she claims to, she must be lying, and that sooner or later, when she comes to see the real you, and how unworthy you are, her supposed love will die and she will turn away?

Oh my dear, she will *not*.

If you do not recognize, or wish to acknowledge, the special unity between us, there's nothing more I can say. I cannot bind you to me;

love does not seek to bind. But love endures. I
may give up on everything else, but I'll never
give up on love.

Zach, please write to me. For the sake of our
long years of friendship and affection, don't let
this correspondence dwindle into silence.

My heart goes with you, each time you climb
into your aeroplane.

All my love,
Bret

He read the letter once, then folded it up and put it away.
He went out on a mission and shot down not one, not two,
but three German fighters. They were calling him the American von Richthofen. Great. Germany's most deadly ace was
dead, shot down in April, proving that no matter how good
you were, no matter how skilled or how clever, the earth
would take you in the end.

That night, not sleeping, as usual, he read her words over
and over again, until, like all her others, they were engraved
upon his soul.

He would answer her immediately. He would write to her
by the first light of morning and tell her that she was right,
he was afraid, he couldn't love, he couldn't believe in love.
That she'd penetrated corners of himself he'd never revealed
to anybody, and that he couldn't be so vulnerable with anybody, not even his oldest friend.

But when morning came, he put off writing. The weather
would clear in the afternoon and he would have to fly. He
didn't want her to receive an unfinished, imperfect letter if
he was killed today.

Their week together had been a dream. They weren't
suited, they were opposite in so many ways. It would all blow
apart if he married her. The more passion at the beginning,
the more rancor at the end. She had her own failed affair with
the clay worker, Daniel, to testify to that eternal truth.

Simon loved her. Why couldn't she pour all her vast stores
of sunshine and affection onto him? She and Simon would be
perfect for each other. He would write to her and tell her so.

He would do the noble thing, the honorable thing. In the long run she would be much happier living with Marrick.

He would write to her. Tomorrow.

But when tomorrow came and the weather proved fair, they sent him up to fight. He was too busy trying to stay alive to think about romance.

The day after that he had two kills—four men, poor luckless bastards. A week later, one of his buddies died when his plane exploded in midair. Then it rained for several days. Only when bad weather made Allied sorties impossible could he snatch any rest. His mood descended into melancholy. He was probably going to die the next time he flew, and he hated himself because he didn't give a damn. In a way, he wanted to get the wretched experience of dying over and done with.

But he didn't die. He remained alive on the surface and numb inside, the envy of all his mates, who saw only the Phoenix, the skilled pilot, the crack shot, the bright and nerveless exterior, and never understood the effort necessary to rise up every morning from the ashes.

Thus the days passed, blending and fading into one another. And with each day he failed to write, it became more impossible to take up his pen, for he had failed her, run away from her, just as he had always known he would.

It was almost over now, the Great War that had cost so much in terms of life, hope, and illusion. The German gains of the spring of 1918 were wiped out by the Allied counteroffensive of July and August. Once the German lines had been breached, the eastward thrust of the Allied armies had been bloody but steady, inexorably pushing the Germans out of the French and Belgian lands they had captured four years before. Rumors were bruited about that a peace treaty was in the making, although still the fighting—and the dying—went on.

Along with the wounded who kept coming in, Bret and her colleagues began to see serious cases of influenza. The flu was always a problem during the cold months, but it was beginning early this year, and it was more virulent than any-

one could remember. Patients complained of severe headaches, backaches, aches and pains throughout their bodies.
They ran high fevers. They coughed violently, sounding almost as bad as the gassed-lung cases. In far too many cases,
particularly among the weak and the wounded, the flu was
quickly complicated by pneumonia. Several patients died.

Bret began to get frightened when two nurses and a physician who often worked on Simon's ward went down with the
illness. One of the nurses, a healthy young woman who was
engaged to be married to a sergeant-major whom she had
nursed through a vicious thigh wound, had to be removed to
a civilian hospital. Two days later Bret learned that she was
dead.

She was frightened for Simon. He had made excellent
progress, and could walk with the aid of his crutches now,
but he had lost weight during his convalescence. He no longer
had the strength or the energy of youth, and his lungs were
permanently damaged. He had always been susceptible to
colds and sore throats, and the doctors had warned that if he
came down with any form of respiratory illness, he might not
survive.

One morning he caught her weeping in the laundry room.
"Bret? What's the matter?"

Hastily, she tried to cover up. "Nothing. Carbolic fumes,
that's all."

Simon was not deceived. "Are you ill? You look so tired
all the time. Maybe you should have one of the doctors here
examine you, give you some sort of tonic."

"I'm all right. Please don't fuss."

"I will fuss. You've fussed over me for months."

"I'm not ill. Anyway, there's no tonic that'll cure me."

"A letter might, I think."

She tried to pretend she didn't know what he was talking
about, but Simon knew her too well. "Excuse me, I've got
to get back to work."

His hand on her arm stopped her. "I know you love him.
And I'm sure he loves you."

"Oh, God, Simon, I can't talk about this with you."

"Yes, you can. You can start by relinquishing this perpetual desire of yours to protect me. It was fine when we were younger, but it's beginning to get on my nerves now.''

"I didn't want you to be hurt any more than you have been already."

"This time you're the one who has been hurt."

Bret could feel her bottom lip trembling.

"What went wrong?"

"I—I don't know. He won't answer my letters. I think it's because he's so certain he's going to die."

Simon touched her shoulder gently.

Bret shook her head. "Maybe I was crazy. It was like Daniel, only worse. God! Me and men. I seem to be . . . I don't know . . . incompetent in that area."

"Me too," Simon said, squeezing her hand.

"I hate this war! I hate what it's done to me, what it's done to you, what it's done to everybody. What happened to the girl I used to be? Every time I try to reclaim her, she slips away again."

"Bret, let's go home."

She blinked at him, not comprehending.

"I mean it. They're about to let me out of here, and as for you, you've more than done your bit for the war. Let's go back to Cornwall. If there's anyplace where it might be possible to reclaim our old selves, it'll be there."

He was right. She was twenty-one years old and someday soon she would have to decide what she was going to do with the rest of her life. Although she had come to enjoy the independence and the feelings of competence that went along with her job, she knew now that nursing was not her calling. She had met sisters who were totally committed to their profession, but all she could see these days was a world filled with the blood and shattered bones and the stench of rotting flesh. She loved and respected the women who could look upon this without flinching, maintaining their equanimity, their sanity, and their faith in God, but she was not one of them.

More than ever, she wanted to create. To paint, to sculpt. To bring beauty into a world that had been ravaged by the ugliest war in history. She could not do it here. Her recent artistic efforts had been disasters. She had become far too intimate with destruction.

"Let me think about it," she said to Simon. "I *would* like to go home. I miss my father. I miss my sister. I miss Wulf, my stallion, and the moors and the skytips and Cadmon Hall."

"Let's do it, then. As soon as I'm ready to travel, let's get the hell away from here."

Away from wounds, she thought, *away from influenza*. The air in the westcountry would be healthy and fresh; nobody, surely, was ill there. Cornwall would be a refuge. A place of healing.

For the first time since Zach had left, a feeling of buoyancy lifted her heart. Yes. She would see Papa and Verity. She would go home.

As for Zach, she would always love him. She would have no other. But he was a free human soul. If he was so determined to turn his back on the joy, the laughter, the unity of spirit they had found together, there was nothing she could do to change him. Anyway, love does not seek to change. *Love beareth all things, believeth all things, hopeth all things, endureth all things. Love suffereth long, and is kind.*

She had never understood the true meaning of these words until now.

Two days later Bret was distributing the morning newspapers when a headline leaped out at her: GENERAL MISSING AND BELIEVED KILLED IN CRASH OF NEW BOMBER; DESIGN FLAW SUSPECTED. The story went on to describe an accident involving the Zephyr, a revolutionary new war plane that Trevor Aviation had been developing. A high-ranking military man had been aboard for the flight. He, along with the aeroplane's designer, Henry Trevor, was presumed dead.

The newspaper fell from her nerveless hands just as she saw Matron, grim-faced, coming toward her.

Part Eight

1918–1919

See what a scourge is laid upon your hate,
That heaven finds means to kill your joys with love.

—William Shakespeare
Romeo and Juliet

Part Eight

1918–1919

Chapter Forty-seven

At the crest of a hill that seemed infinitely steeper than she remembered it, Bret Trevor dropped her carpetbag valise and scanned the undulating terrain of her beloved Cornwall. In the distance, she glimpsed the majestic gray stone walls of Cadmon Hall crowning the moorlands. Its twelve-foot windows caught the sunlight, making it shimmer like a castle of ice.

Cadmon Hall. Home.

She had pictured her homecoming as a joyous event, but that dream was smashed, like so many others. Papa would not be there to welcome her. Never again would he open his arms for her. Never again would she stand beside him, hand in hand, sneaking glances at his proud and excited face as he launched the newest of his aeroplanes.

She wanted to drop down in the dirt and sob. The girl she'd been before the war probably would have done so. The woman she had become squared her shoulders and struck out across the moors. She climbed until she came to the remnants of a Roman wall, decayed and crumbling, but still visible after so many centuries. Scrambling over it, she shaded her eyes to look into the flowered dell beyond.

It was like rediscovering a dear and lovely painting. Overlooking the misty expanse of St. Austell Bay, Tamara's whitewashed cottage stood unchanged by the rhythms of war and time. Tamara, too, would be unchanged, her strength and beauty undiminished.

Bret's footsteps quickened as she crested the gentle slope that led to the front door. As always, the path was neat and flower-lined. Tamara Carne's flowers had always seemed to her to bloom larger and more colorfully than any others, and after the horrors of a war that had turned so many things of beauty into dust and ash, she was glad to discover that this was still the case.

In retrospect, her days with Tamara seemed magical. She'd been so full of hope and vitality, brimming with such plans, such dreams, the future stretching out ahead, a golden realm of possibilities. Bret Trevor, the intrepid adventuress.

Stepping forward, she rapped on the door. The sound echoed within but brought no reply. She knocked again, listening for the whirring of the potter's wheel, but inside, all was silent.

She pushed open the door. Tamara's things were all about, and the air was redolent with the lingering smells of herbs, clay work, cooking. The potter's wheel sat in its usual corner near the window, but the clay on it was old and dry. Even here, she thought, something was different, something had changed. The war had ripped apart the ancient cloth of which England and her traditions were made, and nothing had escaped its devastation.

She heard a sound behind her. Tamara stood there on the threshold, her gold hair hanging limp and loose, the bright Gypsy clothes rejected for a gown of starkest black. The only color about her was in her arms, which were filled with flowers.

"Ah, Bret," she said in her lovely contralto. "I knew ye were coming. I've been gathering flowers to lay upon yer father's grave."

Memories rushed up from long ago of a wheat-haired lady and a china bird, and Bret understood that her impulse to come to Tamara first was less to seek comfort than to offer it.

It had been there, always, all along—a love that forms and flows and never passes. Beneath perception but no less real for that. "How long have you loved him?" she whispered.

"All my life," the wheat-haired lady replied.

"And he, you?"

The smile was sweet but sad. "For a few short years when

you were a child. I was a fool. I ended it. I thought 'twould never work because I was of the earth and he was of the sky.''

"The sky killed him," Bret said savagely.

"No. The earth took what it was owed, as the earth always does. But it cannot take the part of him that soars."

Bret went to her, and held her, and cried.

Later that morning, when she finally reached Cadmon Hall, Bret was greeted by strangers. A thin-faced woman whom she'd never seen before told her that Verity was at the china works. "Your sister will be ever so glad you're here," said Miss Porter, the new housekeeper. "It's got to be too much for Miss Verity, the poor thing, grieving alone these last thirty-six hours."

"What happened to Mrs. Chenoweth? Your predecessor?" she added when Miss Porter looked blank.

"Oh, her. She went off to care for her six grandchildren after her son was killed in the trenches. Been gone for nearly a year."

Everyone had lost someone. Everyone had suffered. How much longer could this hateful war drag on?

Few of the original household staff remained. The men and boys had either volunteered or been drafted into duty on the Continent, and the women had gone off to new jobs in the cities, the fields, the factories. "It's been devilish hard to get a decent staff together," Miss Porter complained. "No one's going into service anymore."

It showed. There was dust in the corners, weeds in the flower beds, tarnish on the silver. Bret was surprised that her sister, whom she had always thought of as so meticulous, had not insisted that such oversights be corrected. But from all accounts, Verity had been working eighteen hours a day, trying to keep her claypits and china works afloat in this time of economic trouble.

There were shortages of food, natural resources, and labor. The enormous costs, both in money and in manpower, of fighting a stalemated war had stretched the British economy to its breaking point. Food was rationed. There was little coal available for home fires, much less for industrial furnaces. So many young men had been killed or injured that the army was now conscripting fifty-year-olds. Labor strikes for higher wages were paralyzing what industry was still left. The only consolation was that Germany was in even worse shape. There the populace was starving, the factories were closed, and the Kaiser's army was composed entirely of children and old men. Their lines had finally been breached, bringing them to the brink of defeat. Once again people were saying that the war would be over by Christmas, and for the first time since 1914, Bret believed it.

After settling into her old bedroom, Bret went out to the stable, part of which had been turned into a garage, to find a motorcar. The domestic staff had been hoarding petrol, so she was able to drive up into the hills to Cadmon Clay. She couldn't wait any longer to see her sister, to hold her and mourn with her, to try to erase the past.

It seemed odd to her that the landscape was so familiar. Because she was so different inside, she expected her surroundings to have altered also. But the hills and declivities, wildflowers and moorgrasses, even the sky above with its low-veering clouds, were all as she remembered them, enduring, unchanged.

Cadmon Clay seemed as busy as ever. As she entered its gates, her senses were assailed by the booming of the beam engine and the squeaking of the cables that trundled waste out of the claypits. There was a new claypit off to the left, with the beginnings of a skytip rising beside it, but the wartime economy had precluded any extensive new development.

She stopped the motorcar a few yards from the small building that housed the company's office. As she climbed out she was conscious of a pricking behind her eyes. She would not find Papa in that office; she would never look upon his face again.

She rapped on the door.

No sooner had Verity opened it than she and Bret were in each other's arms, holding each other, clinging.

"Thank God you're here—"

"I've missed you so—"

"I can't believe he's gone."

They were both speaking at once. It didn't matter. Touch was more important than words, for it was a way to ease the long-held tension between them.

It was Verity who broke the embrace, stepping back abruptly, fingering her throat.

"I feel so guilty that I didn't spend more time with him," Bret said. "I've seen so little of him since the war began. I stayed away. I didn't even attempt to come home."

"Don't blame yourself for that. He stayed away as well. I didn't see much more of him than you did. He was obsessed. It's horrible to say, I know, but the manner of his death seems appropriate somehow. Murdered by his own dreams."

"But the newpapers are saying the plane crashed because his designs were bad. I don't believe that. It can't be true."

"What does it matter? It's done now."

"You've always hated anything to do with aviation, haven't you?"

"It took my father away from me every time I needed him most."

There was such passion and resentment in the comment that Bret moved closer and once more put her arms around her sister. She was several inches taller now, the reverse of what had been true during childhood. Verity felt petite and poker-stiff, delicate as a bird. But Verity had always been strong for her, Bret remembered; loving her, protecting her, and always seeking the best for her.

"Oh, Verity. I've missed you terribly."

Her sister's arms tightened. But again it was she who broke the embrace. "I've missed you, too. I'm so glad you're finally home."

The words did not sound wholehearted, and Bret could not help but wonder what Verity was trying to hide.

After driving Bret to the train station in St. Austell to fetch her cases, Verity proceeded to the china works. "I want to show you around," she said. "We've worked so hard."

They negotiated the hill that led to the harbor, passing between the square Georgian-style building that gave Charlestown its character. Verity found a place to leave the motorcar on a cobblestone lane to the left of the cooperage, bright with new paint, that was now her factory.

They entered the building through the workshop where the china molding was taking place. Friendly nods greeted them from the staff. Bret was surprised to find that nearly all Verity's employees were women. It was like a hospital!

She's changed, Bret thought as Verity moved among her workers, graciously accepting their words of sympathy. Although her frock was black for mourning, its hem was cut as high as the most fashionable dresses in London. Her dark hair was skillfully arranged, and her angular features had been softened by the application of fine cosmetics. She was wearing eardrops, a gold bracelet, and a small pearl ring. "You look wonderful," Bret whispered. "My goodness, Verity, being a captain of industry suits you."

Verity exuded a confidence she had previously lacked. She knew the names of all the workers and many of the details of their lives. Although some of the women were older than she, Bret noticed that they seemed to look upon her sister as a sort of maternal figure, someone they could trust, rely on, tell their problems to. With economic conditions in the country as bad as they were, the women must be glad for the work and grateful for the pay. Many of them had probably never earned wages before or conceived of themselves as capable of producing anything more substantial than the family supper. It was obvious that they were grateful to Verity for making them feel like valuable members of society.

A round-faced apprentice of about sixteen years of age with clay all over her hands shyly approached Bret and told her how sorry she was about Henry Trevor's death. Bret thanked her, noting that the girl had a smidgen of clay on the tip of her nose, which reminded her of her own clumsy days with Tamara.

Verity conducted her through the design studio, where an artist and two apprentices were working out new designs; the potting shed, where the china was molded and thrown; the decoration studio, where glazes and paints were applied; and the kilns, where the porcelain was heated to the high temperatures necessary to fuse china clay with china stone. It was a small operation, but efficient. Bret could see how proud her sister was. When Verity cradled in her hands the first small pieces of elegant porcelain that had been produced that morning, touching them wonderingly, as if she couldn't quite understand how they had come to be, Bret wanted to fling her arms around her and thank her for bringing such grace and beauty into the world.

"So far we've stuck mostly to durable items, but my dream is to expand until we're producing several different lines of fine china," Verity explained when they were back in her office. "That's what our ancestors did during the first few decades of Cadmon Clay and Porcelain. I think the demand will be there. The war has caused so much suffering, horror, and ugliness. Now that it's winding down, people are going to want to remember the softer side of life, and be reminded that we humans can create as well as destroy."

"I think you're right. In fact, that's exactly the way I feel."

"I'm not artistic, though. I love a beautiful piece once it's been brought into existence, but I don't possess the creative vision necessary to conceive it. But you, Bret, have that vision. If you were to take over the creative end of things and allow me to handle management and marketing, together we would make an unbeatable team."

"You're asking me to work for you? But I thought Tamara was your master potter."

"Tamara refuses to leave her cottage on the moors. And now that Papa's dead, she claims to have lost her inspiration. You will do a better job for me, she says."

Memories came back to Bret of herself at Tamara's potter's wheel . . . the glimmerings of power she had felt in her fingertips as she'd worked the clay, the wealth of ideas for all the beautiful objects she would make, if only she could acquire the skill. The skill had come to her in London. Perhaps Marcus Gregory had been right, after all—she had seen far more of life now, and with her experience had come a broader artistic vision.

And yet, did that vision really encompass the manufacture of china? The objects she'd imagined herself sculpting were of another order—big, bold, and colorful, sensuous shapes and luxurious designs.

"I need you," Verity said. "Together we'll make Cadmon Clay and Porcelain the finest china works in England."

This had always been Verity's dream.

"I'm proud of what you've accomplished," she said to Verity. "I'm not sure that I'll be any use to you in the long run, but for now, if there's any way I can help you, I'd be happy to try."

Her sister's arms came around her. But all too soon, she drew back, once again seeming tense, nervous, and unsure.

"Before you commit yourself to that, there's something I have to tell you," Verity said. "Some news. It might make you change your mind."

Such words uttered during this war always iced Bret's heart. It was rare that the news was ever good.

"I didn't know quite how to bring it up, so I've been putting it off, I'm afraid. I— It's difficult."

"Just tell me."

Unexpectedly, her sister's face broke out into a radiant smile. Bret began, tentatively, to smile back when she was aware of a presence behind her. And a deep, familiar voice saying, "Ye still haven't told her?"

She knew the voice. She would never forget it. It sounded just as low and intimate as it had always sounded above her, below her, beside her, in the dark.

She turned. Standing behind her on the threshold was her old lover, Daniel Carne, dark, husky, and pirate-eyed as ever.

"I was just about to," Verity said.

"Daniel!"

He nodded politely. "Bret."

She was astonished to find him there, and on speaking terms with Verity, no less. She was even more astonished when he moved right by her, without a touch, without a smile, and took up a position at her elder sister's side. Verity made a nervous gesture, twisting her pearl ring, the one Bret had noted earlier. Daniel's arm slid in a familiar manner around Verity's shoulders, then he leaned down and touched his lips delicately to the lobe of her sister's ear.

"Daniel and I are going to be married," Verity said.

Chapter Forty-eight

"Congratulations," she had said.

Alone in her bedroom at Cadmon Hall, Bret was brushing her hair with short, savage strokes. She couldn't make sense of her feelings, which were already ajumble because of Papa's death. She resented being distracted from her grief. It didn't seem right for her to be tormenting herself over Daniel and Verity when she ought to be mourning a far greater loss.

She was astonished at the depth of her anger. It was Verity who had engineered her separation from Daniel, Verity who had sent her to London, destroying all hope of reconciliation. Had she wanted Daniel herself, even then? Had she been envious of her younger sister's passion for a handsome, virile clay worker when she herself was married to a hypocritical adulterer?

"To hell with her," she said the to the mirror, which reflected back the image of a pale woman with wild red hair. "I stopped loving Daniel a long time ago. I love Zach, who doesn't love me . . . who doesn't love *life* . . . who's probably out getting himself killed right this minute." She shook her head, causing ribbons of flame to swirl in the mirror. "What a world this is."

She seized a piece of writing paper and began to scribble.

Dear Zach,

Well, I'm home and it's awful.

I always used to think of Cadmon Hall as a refuge, a place to which I could retreat if things became unbearable in the outside world, an anchor that would tug me safely back to earth if I flew too high. The war has swept everything real and

familiar away, and home doesn't seem like home
anymore.

My dear father is gone, killed by the passion
that you and he share. I can't believe it. We were
going to travel the world together, he and I. Lands
of civilization, lands of myth, we were going to
visit them, one and all, in his flying machines.

His place is empty. His spark, like so many
others, has been extinguished by this horrible war.

Oh, Zach, everything is blasted for me. Daniel,
the clay worker who once loved me, is going to
marry Verity. What I felt for him has long since
been superseded by a greater, deeper love, but I
would have liked to keep bright the memory. It's
ruined, everything's ruined. How can I continue to
confide in you, *Mr. Slayton*, when you have cast
me out of your life?

She stopped writing, stared blindly at the paper, then ripped
it to shreds. No, dammit. She was not going to feel sorry for
herself.

Tomorrow they were going to bury her father. She was still
dazed from that grief; she could cope with no other. Yet she
couldn't get out of her mind the expression on her former
lover's face. It held no love for her sister. It held only triumph.
He had achieved the thing he'd wanted most. Marriage to
Verity would make him the owner of Cadmon Clay and the
master of Cadmon Hall.

From the heights of Cadmon Tor, Daniel Carne saw Henry
Trevor's funeral cortege winding down the road that led from
Cadmon Hall to the village of Trenwythan. He would be
buried today with his ancestors in the crypt of St. Catherine's
Church. In keeping with tradition, his daughters had chosen
an old-fashioned funeral, with a horse-drawn hearse. It was
blackly ostentatious, with glass sides through which one could
see the gleaming wooden coffin. A motorcar followed with
Trevor's sister Dorothy and her family, but Bret and Verity
had chosen to ride their horses directly in back of their father's

hearse. They were mounted sidesaddle, so as not to disarrange their mourning dresses and veils, and they led between them the riderless stallion that had belonged to Henry Trevor. Behind them followed a crowd of friends, servants, and curious villagers, either in motorcars or on foot.

It was a rich man's funeral. When Daniel's father had died, there had been no hearse, no riders, and few mourners. He had shouldered the coffin along with a couple of Jory's mates from the claypits. It had been heavy, and the long walk to the churchyard, where Jory Carne had been laid in an undistinguished grave far from the Trevor family vault, had seemed interminable.

When he died, Daniel wondered, what sort of send-off would he have? A poor man's or a rich man's? A Carne's, or a Trevor's?

As the cortege disappeared around a bend Daniel descended Cadmon Tor and strode over moor and field until he was within sight of Cadmon Hall. He looked upon the stately building and its grounds as he had looked so many times before, dreaming, yearning, coveting.

Verity owned it now. And he owned Verity.

Fifty years from now the illustrious name of Trevor would be nothing more than a forgotten surname, scratched on the tombstones of long-dead men.

"Are 'ee happy now, Pa?" he said into the wind.

"*Are 'ee?*" it seemed to answer.

Standing dry-eyed in the nave of the church where her husband had once been vicar, Verity watched the progression of her father's coffin. She had not been able to cry. Beside her, Bret was quietly sobbing, but she did not turn to her older sister for comfort. Since she had heard the news about Daniel, Bret had withdrawn to a faraway place.

I'm not going to think about that. Not now. Not yet.

The church was no more than half full. Last night the family had done vigil together in the Great Hall as, according to tradition, the people of Trenwythan paid their respects. The crowds were nowhere near as large as they had been for Rufus Trevor's wake, and many faces that ought to have been familiar were strange. The mourners seemed more curious than grief-stricken. They spent as much time looking around at what they could see of the interior of Cadmon Hall as they did inspecting the coffin. Because of the war, death had lost its ability to awe. Wealth still had that ability, although it, too, was diminished.

"Them tapestries look a bit moth-eaten, don't they?" Verity overheard one housewife say to another. "They ought to hang some nice wallpaper in here. Cheer the place up a bit."

"They'll be selling it off one day soon, ye mark my words," her companion responded. "Lots of the gentry've lost their heirs—or their fortunes—in the war. Seems like everything's a-changin'. The old order's gone."

It was true, thought Verity. The last male of the Trevor line lay dead in his coffin, himself a victim of that rush toward a brave new world. What had Grandpa said so many years ago? "This is what we all come to sooner or later. No point fussing about it. We are of the earth, and she takes us in the end."

Papa had tried to escape his destiny. He had fled upward, into another realm. He had denied the clay, but in the end he was part of it after all. His bones would crumble in the earth until they were as dusty and white as the koalin he had so despised.

Verity swallowed to ease the tightness in her throat. Tears? Not quite. There would be grief, she knew, for she had loved him, despite the many disappointments over the years. She knew from her experience with Julian how relentless grief could be. It would take a clawlike grip and hold her, and months would pass, even years, before she was free. Even so, along with the emptiness she felt a sense of the wheel of life revolving and a new destiny rising up to meet her, replete with risks and challenges, promises and dreams.

No longer was she the heir to a great fortune and heritage. The crown had dropped upon her brow, the mantle upon her shoulders. She was the mistress of Cadmon Hall, the owner of Cadmon Clay, and the architect of her own life.

* * *

That night Verity donned an ivory silk nightgown. Sparingly, she applied rouge, lipstick, and mascara. She dabbed perfume on her wrists, her throat, the backs of her earlobes. She arranged her hair as best she could, then gazed at her reflection in the mirror. Her eyes looked huge. They were underscored by faint shadows. She closed them. She thought of Papa's eyes, closed forever. She thought of her lover on his way to claim her on the same night as his enemy had been laid in the earth. She wished she had the moral strength to refuse him, at least on this one night.

But that was unthinkable. *Behold, thou art fair, my love; comfort me with apples, for I am sick of love.*

What if he didn't come? What if Bret's return had destroyed his desire for her older, less attractive sister? What if he turned his back upon the child of darkness to pursue the child of light?

Watching Bret at the funeral had been excruciating for Verity. Her sister was socially adept, and she was pretty. The years had added flesh to her body, erasing the youthful angles of her face, the coltishness of her limbs. She stood straight and tall and moved with sinuous grace. Her hair had been cropped to shoulder length, drifting around her throat in wavy tendrils. If her smile was not quite as carefree as it used to be, it was still as warm, and people responded to her in the openhearted manner they always had.

And Daniel? Had seeing her again brought it all back? Had he taken one look at this young woman who was so much *more* a woman than she had been in 1914 and realized that he could not love her elder sister after all? Could she blame him if he preferred the bird of paradise to the wren?

Oh, Bret. For years I've wanted you home. But now . . . I wish you'd go away again.

A rap on her bedroom door. She jumped. "Who is it?"

"Who d'ye think?" that rough voice countered, sending frissons along her spine.

He didn't need to lurk outside her window anymore. Instead he bribed certain members of the household staff, who thought it romantic that their mistress had such a dashing lover.

She rose to open her bedroom door, closing it quickly

behind him as he entered, tall and silent. His arms around
her, strong and hard. His musky scent. The roughness of his
evening growth of whiskers as he bent down to brush his
cheek against hers. The heat of his mouth, the scrape of his
teeth, the ardent exploration of his tongue. Surely they were
all the same as ever. Surely the intensity had not decreased.
Surely nothing had changed since Bret's return.

*For love is strong as death; jealousy is as cruel as the
grave: the coals thereof are coals of fire, which hath a most
vehement flame.*

He slid one arm down her thighs to the back of her knees,
then lifted her and carried her to bed. She was light and easy
to lift, he always told her. Surely when he was holding her
like this he had no thought of anybody else.

"Ye look weary," he said as he undressed. He smoothed
back her hair and touched his lips to her forehead. "I almost
didn't come tonight. I thought it might disturb 'ee too much."

"No, no, I'm glad you came."

"I couldn't come to the funeral, a'course. I won't pretend
to feel sorry he's dead."

She repressed a flicker of resentment. When you loved
somebody, you expected them to be there for you during
times of grief and trouble, but she had received no comfort
from Daniel on this occasion.

"I've missed 'ee," he said as big hands moved over her
body. "Are 'ee managing all right?"

"Yes." She reached up to stroke his hair, feeling a familiar
stab of possession. He was hers now, not Bret's. It seemed
decidedly childish that she should take pleasure in this, but she
had given up trying to account for the passion and intensity of
her feelings for Daniel Carne.

"Ye need to get some rest. One of the reasons I came was
to make sure ye slept tonight."

"Not the only reason, I hope?"

He grinned. Those blue eyes of his danced. His hands
moved on her in a manner that was more arousing than protective. "Maybe I'll make 'ee a little more tired before I let 'ee
sleep."

"Maybe I'll make you tired," she said in a tone that was

more archly flirtatious than she would have dreamed of employing before he had barreled into her life.

"Ye're welcome to try," he said, covering her body with his own.

As always with him, her excitement seemed to spiral out of control. For the first time in her life, Verity was wildly, madly, passionately in love. Daniel had unlocked her sensual self. Finally, after so many years of rejection, domination, and loneliness, she had a lover who made her feel attractive and desired. She could look at herself in the mirror and not notice the too-long nose, the too-thin lips, the slightly crooked teeth.

One year when she was a child, Verity had watched the servants remove the Christmas tree from the Great Hall on January 6, the twelfth day of Christmas, when all the decorations were traditionally taken down. Bedecked with stray tinsel, stale popcorn wreaths, and desiccated cherries, the bushy pine had been removed to the kitchen courtyard to be burned. The flare of a single match had exploded the tinder-dry pine needles into a blaze that made the tattered decorations glow briefly with a great and wondrous light.

She had felt no sorrow for the tree. Although it had been beautiful on Christmas Day when it was fresh and green and newly decked with ornaments, during the twelve days it had grown dry and droopy. But in the burning, it regained its former beauty. It would not be so terrible, she thought, to burn like that—so hot, so fierce, so shining.

Daniel loved sexy nightgowns. He adored perfume. He didn't mind when she argued with him, nor did he question her abilities as a businesswoman or her right to do the work she loved. They got on together in every way but one—he refused to discuss the way he felt about Bret, or even to confirm that it was over forever between them. He refused to discuss any of his feelings.

She was under no illusions as to why he had asked her to marry him. As her father's heir, she, even more than her sister, could provide Daniel with everything he had always wanted.

Knowing this, why had she accepted him?

Because she loved him. And love, she had discovered, was at its deepest core a mystery.

And because he had given her something wonderful, something that Julian had never been able to give her, something she had wanted for years. Her palms drifted down until they rested protectively over her belly. She was carrying Daniel's child.

Lying beside him, Verity felt strong, proud, and unafraid. Her roots were deep in the ground and her branches open to the sunlight and the rain. Through her body would come the defeat of the Trevor-Carne curse and the fulfillment of the prophecy: What true love has torn asunder, only true love can heal.

Chapter Forty-nine

"I've asked you both here to stay in an attempt to clarify your financial situation," said Jackson Stone, the Trevors' solicitor, in his St. Austell office the following day. Bret sensed from the nervous way the distinguished old gentleman spoke that he had something unpleasant to report.

"Go ahead, please," Verity said to him. She was dressed in a somber yet smartly tailored jacketed frock with a matching hat and gloves, and she looked eminently capable of withstanding whatever bad news might be coming.

"As you know, you, Mrs. Marrick, as eldest daughter, have inherited the bulk of the estate, including all interest in the family business known as Cadmon Clay and Porcelain." He turned to Bret. "And you, Miss Trevor, in addition to the income from several trust funds that should enable you to live comfortably for the rest of your life, have inherited the family company known as Trevor Aviation. Your father considered this division of assets to be in accordance with your respective interests."

"I don't care about the aviation company," Bret said. "The war ruined all that for me. What I do care about is clearing my father's name. I don't believe there was a design flaw in the Zephyr."

"You may be right," said Stone. "I've spoken with Henry's chief engineer, a fellow named Jack Denham. He insists the accident was caused by pilot error. The aeroplane had already been tested in the most rigorous conditions. The weather was perfect. The engines were under no particular stress. As you know, your father wasn't flying. Some young army pilot was."

"What does this have to do with our finances?" Verity asked.

"I'm coming to that. You, Mrs. Marrick, have dedicated yourself to Cadmon Clay for the past four years. During the same period your father created Trevor Aviation. Neither of you paid much attention to what was happening with the other's affairs. I warned you both on several occasions that this lack of communication was foolhardy."

"Please explain what you mean."

"Your father's company has built, at great expense, six Zephyrs. As a result of this accident, and the previous one, nobody wants to buy them. No pilot will even fly them." Stone's voice was mildly contemptuous. "It seems the aeroplane is regarded as unlucky."

"I didn't realize there had been a previous accident," Bret said.

Stone's gaze shifted from Verity's to hers. "It wasn't publicized. In that case, it was clearly pilot error. The chap was raving drunk, and missed his landing in the fog."

"So Trevor Aviation is in trouble?"

"Very much so, Miss Trevor. The Zephyr was expected to bring large orders from the government, but in the wake of the accident, the contracts have fallen through. There are heavy debts. Your sister has been warning your father for years that the resources of the Trevor family weren't infinite, but Henry was never a practical man where finances were concerned. He did make some attempt to control the damage. He knew Mrs. Marrick needed capital for the china factory start-up, so he assured her he could get the money he required for the Zephyr from other sources. She presumed he meant the government. But it seems he approached a private investor."

Stone produced some papers, which he handed to Verity. "These are full of legalese, but I believe you'll be able to make them out. They detail the terms of three personal loans. The rate of interest is not exorbitant, but the amounts are substantial."

Bret jumped up to stand behind Verity and read the documents over her shoulder. She noticed that although her sister's spine remained stiff and straight, her hands were trembling.

"Without informing your sister or me," Stone told her, "Henry borrowed the money to keep the aviation company afloat. He put up three separate chunks of Cadmon Clay and Porcelain stock as collateral. He made most of his payments on schedule, but at the time of his death he still owed a considerable amount. The term of one of the loans—the smallest—has already expired. The others fall due on December 31 of this year."

"So the fortunes of Cadmon Clay are tied to the fortunes of Trevor Aviation?"

"Exactly. If Trevor Aviation goes belly up, as we fully expect it to do, the remaining loans will be called in. You don't have the resources to pay it off."

"If we are forced to forfeit," Verity said, flipping rapidly through the documents, "what percentage of the stock will we lose?"

"You have already lost thirteen percent. If you forfeit on the remaining two loans, you will lose an additional thirty percent."

"That's forty-three percent," Verity said faintly. "Are you telling me that my father has put forty-three percent of my clay company at risk?"

"Through his injudicious borrowing, yes."

"Damn him!" she burst out.

"Who provided our father with this loan?" Bret asked.

"James Stannis, the clay owner. He's always been fascinated with aeroplanes, but more than that, I believe, he wanted to help Henry. They were excellent friends."

"Aren't you friendly with him too?" Bret asked Verity. She wanted to put her arms around her and hug her, but she didn't think her sister would appreciate such a gesture in the presence of the crusty old solicitor. "Can't you sit down with him and find some way to work this out?"

It took Verity several seconds to answer. "I can try, of course. I can certainly ask for more time to meet the payments."

Stone cleared his throat. "Unless you're sure you can generate revenues in the not-too-distant future, asking for more time isn't going to help. Besides, word has gone around that Stannis is himself in financial straits. As you know, the kaolin business has faltered in recent years. Your fiancé, Daniel Carne, is the only clay owner I know who has prospered during the war." He paused. "Which brings me to another point, Mrs. Marrick. If I understand your plans correctly, by the time these loans come due, you and he will be married. Could you perhaps go to him for the money to clear the loans?"

"No!" Bret cried before her sister had an opportunity to answer. "That would be playing directly into his hands."

Verity's lips tightened. "What do you mean by that remark?"

"If you put yourself in debt to Daniel, he'll control you. My God, Verity, he'll be in a position to carry out every threat he's ever made about destroying Cadmon Clay."

"Nonsense."

"It's not nonsense!" Bret knew she wasn't handling this well, but she couldn't keep silent. "I know you love him, but isn't this just a little too *convenient*? We need money and he's got it. If you allow him to pay off the loans, he'll strip you of your decision-making power at the clay company. He'll reduce you to nothing. He'll force you out. It won't be Cadmon Clay any longer. Sooner or later it'll be Carne Clay. The business that has been in the Trevor family for generations will cease to exist."

"Perhaps I will leave you ladies alone to discuss this," Stone said, rising and moving toward the door.

"That's not necessary," Verity said, but Bret nodded to Stone, who discreetly retreated, closing the door behind him.

"You underestimate me, Bret." Verity's voice was tired, and there was pain there, beneath her words. "I'm the same woman who, through my first marriage, learned everything there is to know about the subjugation of women. I may be in love, but I am not a fool.''

Bret said nothing. Frowning, Verity reached up to jam home a loose hairpin. "In the first place, I have no intention of forfeiting the collateral on Papa's loan. Somehow or other I'll raise the money to pay off James Stannis. I'm expecting a new contract for my china. If it doesn't come through, well, I'll manage something. I'm not going to lose that forty-three percent.

"Secondly, as Jackson Stone can confirm, I have set a condition to my marriage. There is to be a prenuptial contract. It is true that as my husband, Daniel is entitled to a share of my property, just as I am entitled to a share of his. Therefore we have made an agreement. If you insist, I'll tell you its terms.''

"Please do.''

"The house, grounds, and furnishings of Cadmon Hall, as you know, are in trust for the Trevor heirs. No one ever owns the property outright. It will remain in my control throughout our marriage. At my death it will pass to the eldest of any children Daniel and I might have. If I bear no children, it will pass to you and your heirs.

"As for Cadmon Clay, Daniel does wish to have a voice in the way the clay business is managed. I see nothing sinister about this—china clay is his life. I have therefore agreed that he shall control ten percent—and no more than that—of the company's stock. In return, I will receive the identical portion—ten percent—of his company. But we've agreed to keep the two businesses separate.''

Bret was busy calculating. "What if Daniel and Stannis gang up against you sometime in the future? If you fail to pay back the loans and forfeit the collateral, they could pool their stock, ending up with fifty-three percent of the company.''

"James Stannis will never gang up with Daniel Carne. During the clay strike, Daniel closed Stannis claypits almost single-handedly, and James has never forgiven him. They can't abide each other.'' She shook her head slowly. "The truth is, in marrying me, Daniel acquires neither money nor property. The interest he'll have in my clay company is balanced by the equivalent interest I'll have in his. His children will be the Trevor heirs, but he himself has little to gain."

Nonplussed, Bret could think of nothing to say. Had she been unnecessarily suspicious of Daniel?

"You cannot find it in you to believe," Verity added, "that he might want me for reasons that have nothing to do with Cadmon Clay?"

"Verity—"

Her elder sister made a tiny gesture with her left hand. "Don't say anything more. I love him, Bret."

Bret was remembering that night—it seemed so long ago now—when her sister had caught Daniel in bed with her. The shame, the anger, the harsh accusations on both sides. Daniel's conviction that he had been betrayed, one more betrayal to add to a lifetime of insults from the Trevors to the Carnes. Was it possible that his bitterness had been erased? Could his feelings for Verity have freed him from the driving need to carry on the feud?

No. He was up to something. She was sure of it.

From the outside, Bret hardly recognized Carne Cottage. Daniel had built onto the original structure, resulting in a home that was three or four times larger than the old farm where she had become his lover. The outer walls were constructed of sturdy stone, the doors of gleaming oak. The roof was timber now instead of thatch, and the front garden had been planted with shrubs and saplings.

Her former lover, dressed in tweed trousers and a maroon smoking jacket, opened the door to her brisk knocking. As soon as he saw her, he started toward her. Bret backed away from what she feared would be an embrace. "Don't touch me," she said.

"What makes ye think I was going to?" He threw the door wide. "I didn't expect you, but come in. Ye're welcome in my house."

His ice-blue eyes and his hair had not changed. The scar on his cheek. His big hands and strong body. An image of that body, naked, thrusting between her thighs caught her unawares. She hesitated, which inspired a mocking smile. "Don't fret. Ye're perfectly safe."

Bret followed him to a freshly wallpapered parlor. There was a large oil painting on the wall executed in the manner of Claude Lorrain. Very classical—the idealized landscape, the perfect cypress trees, the pillars of the Grecian folly in the corner of the formal garden. Not an original. Daniel hadn't achieved that much wealth yet. One day, she had no doubt, his walls would be graced with the finest art, his shelves with the most graceful porcelain.

When had she fallen out of love with Daniel? In all fairness, she knew he had never made any secret of his ambition. She had accepted him, or tried to. She'd given him what she could, but he had never been satisfied.

"Ye look lovely," he told her. "Older, a bit, yeah, but it's becoming to 'ee. It seems the war's agreed with 'ee."

"It's certainly agreed with you," she said, taking a pointed look around the room.

"Are 'ee surprised? I always told 'ee what I meant to do."

"Not surprised, disappointed. I never dreamed you'd sink so low as to trade yourself, soul and body, for china clay."

She fancied she saw strong emotion in the set of his jaw, but all he said was, "Maybe we'd better sit down." He indicated the two easy chairs that faced each other on either side of the hearth. She sat, grateful for the opportunity. Her knees felt rubbery.

Daniel took a crystal decanter from the mantelpiece and poured himself a sherry. He offered the same to her but she refused. "I'd prefer to keep a clear head, if you don't mind."

He remained standing. She focused on his legs, which were nowhere near as elegant as Simon's or as long as Zach's. Simon would look much better in the smoking jacket. Daniel's powerful, broad-shouldered, all-too-masculine physique made him look exactly like what he was—a usurper.

"So I'm trading myself for clay, am I?" he said, sounding amused.

"You don't love Verity. All you want is to live in Cadmon Hall and control Cadmon Clay. Your overweening ambition has fueled your every action."

"What if it has?" He came closer, leaning one arm on the mantelpiece. "Seems to me there was a time when ye claimed to be proud of my ambition."

"Any woman is proud of her man as long as he's acting honorably. But everything that might have been admirable about you has been corrupted by your desire for vengeance. That's what rules you. How do you suppose it makes me feel to know that you never loved me for myself? That you're running the same game now with my sister? If we hadn't been Henry Trevor's daughters you'd never have wanted anything more from either of us than what all men want from all women."

He set his crystal glass down hard on the mantelpiece. Something flickered in those oh-so-blue eyes of his as he reached down, grabbed her hands, and pulled her out of her chair. "So that's what this is all about. Ye abandoned me and now ye're angry because I've taken Verity instead?"

"No, Daniel. That's *not* what this is all about." She jerked her hands away from him. "Whatever feelings I had for you faded when you refused to answer any of my letters."

"Don't try to blame that on me. Ye left me, Bret. Ye swore to love me forever, but ye let them send 'ee away."

"I was seventeen years old! But I wrote to you, telling you I loved you, asking you to be patient, to trust me, to wait for me, but you couldn't do that, could you?" She left a short silence. "I swore to love the man you used to be. But you're not *my* Daniel. Not anymore. You've turned into someone else."

She thought she read a flash of pain in his eyes. All too quickly, he suppressed it. "The fact of it is, people change. What did ye expect, that I would remain hungry and humble for the rest of my life? Forever dependent on the largesse of my betters? Was that yer idea of love—to condescend to the poor clay worker, take care of him, brighten up his life, encourage his dreams without ever expecting that he might be capable of pulling himself out of the morass of poverty and misery that seemed to be his lot?"

"Of course not. You were a poor clay worker, yes, but that never mattered to me. The only person it ever mattered to was you."

"Christ, Bret, don't ye understand? Everything I've done, I've done for 'ee."

"That's a lie! You've done it for yourself and for Jory Carne. Well, if he's looking down on you now from somewhere—or looking up, I should say—I hope he's proud of the legacy he's left. How close he is to getting what he always wanted."

If she'd expected to shame him, she was disappointed. "I've certainly come a lot farther than any of 'ee expected. Verity told me about the loans yer father so recklessly took out. Sooner or later she's going to have to turn to me for the money to save her business."

"Save it! I know you, Daniel. You'll destroy it."

He didn't answer. His eyes were hard as slate. Honest emotion would bounce right off those eyes, she thought. "You don't love her at all, do you?"

"I've been in love only once in my life, and it wasn't with yer sister."

"Don't pretend it was with me, because if you'd ever loved me, you wouldn't be capable of proceeding with this travesty of a marriage. My God, Daniel, Verity *does* love you. You must know that. Is there no heart in you at all?"

"Christ." His movements were jerky as he poured himself another sherry. "I'm not a villain. I treat her well, I make her happy. I'm no worse than the first man she married. Who would ye prefer to see her with? Her partner Gil Parkins? He's the one who's been encouraging her in this china-factory folly. If it were left to the two of them, they'd ruin Cadmon Clay with no help from me. I intend to put a stop to that."

"What do you mean? What's wrong with the china venture?"

"It's crazy and impractical. Everyone knows the porcelain center of Britain is in the industrial midlands. She doesn't have the resources here, nor the contacts, nor the talented artisans. It was a doomed venture from the start, and I don't see the point of wasting any more money on it."

"Verity loves the china factory. It's always been her dream."

"She wants to be a businesswoman, she'll have to learn that not all dreams come true."

"You haven't told her that, have you?"

He gave no answer.

"You haven't told her that you intend to close the factory and destroy her dream. Well, I'll tell her, damn you."

"She won't believe 'ee. She's not likely to believe much of what ye say on the subject of me." He tossed back what was left of the liquid in his glass and took a step toward her. "Verity's afraid of 'ee. Afraid of what might happen when ye and I are thrown into each other's company."

"Nothing's ever going to happen between us again. My feelings for you have changed."

"She's not convinced. Watch her and ye'll see her watching 'ee."

"If you're trying to drive a wedge between us, it's not going to work. She's my sister. I'm not going to allow you to hurt her. I'll fight you. Trevor Aviation hasn't failed yet. If I have to build aeroplanes myself, dammit, that's what I'll do."

He gave a slow smile. "Still intrepid? Good luck. Ye'll need a pilot with the nerve to fly jinxed planes and a top-notch engineer to figure out what went wrong with the Zephyr. When yer father died, ye lost both."

Bret bit her bottom lip. Ideas were flashing. "There are other pilots," she said slowly. "And other engineers."

"Don't take me on, Bret. I'm better at this than ye are."

Maybe, she thought. *And maybe not.*

Reaching out, he took a long lock of her hair between his thumb and first finger. "Ye betrayed me, Bret."

"That's not the way I remember it."

"Ye did. And I won't forgive 'ee. The Carnes never forgive. For the death of my father, and countless other crimes, the Trevors stand condemned."

I adored this man, she was thinking. *We knew great joy together. But there's a darkness inside him.* "Your father died by accident, Daniel."

He laughed. The wind had risen outside and his laughter merged with it. Bret pulled her hair free and backed away, thinking, *He is a destroyer, and I am afraid of him.*

* * *

Long after she'd left, Daniel stood alone in the room he had created, the life he had created. The scent of her lingered. Violets. It had always been violets, and he had never been certain whether she was wearing perfume or whether the scent emanated from her skin. The fragrance called up his memories of Bret laughing, moaning, crying out in his arms. Her wild red hair. Her slick, sweet-smelling skin. Her shining eyes.

He was in the past, a rare indulgence. The present was infinitely preferable, except in the matter of Bret Trevor.

Damn her. Soon he would have everything he had ever wanted. No one, not even the only woman he had ever loved, could be allowed to interfere.

Chapter Fifty

"I'd like to help you out if I possibly can," James Stannis said to Verity. She had come to his office at Stannis claypits—where Daniel had been working at the time of the clay strike—to ask her father's old friend for more time to meet the payments on his loans. "But the truth is, I've got troubles of my own."

"I'm developing a new line of china. I should be taking orders by the end of the year. If you could just give me a couple of more months—three, perhaps—"

"Look, Verity, I'm not going to break down your door, demanding your collateral, the moment those loan terms expire. The good Lord knows I don't want to be saddled with somebody else's claypits. I have enough to worry about. This slump is killing me. If business doesn't pick up soon, I'll be in worse shape than you."

"Damn this war," Verity said.

"I'm with you there," Stannis said bitterly. Once a mountainous man, strong and sunny-tempered, he'd lost both girth and cheerfulness when his only son had been killed in Flanders by a German shell. "It's taken the best of us, and driven everybody else to their knees." After a pause, he added, "What are the chances, realistically, that you will be able to come up with the money?"

"In the short term, not good at all. In the long term, excellent. My sister is home and will be helping me with new porcelain designs. She's a fine artist, and there's no limit to what we'll be able to accomplish together. When the war ends people are going to want fine things, things of beauty and permanence. They're going to want our china."

"You've got a fire in you, I'll say that for you, Verity."

"Somehow or other, I'm going to get through this. I'm going to survive."

"Well, I won't hinder you, unless my back's against the wall. You need a few more months, take 'em with my blessing. I won't foreclose on you, as long as my creditors don't foreclose on me."

Reaching up, she planted a kiss on her old friend's cheek. "Thank you, James."

"Give 'em hell, Verity."

When she reached the china works that morning, Verity was surprised to see Daniel's car stopped outside the former cooperage. Her instinctive delight was tempered with wariness. He rarely took time from his working day to visit her. Had he come hoping to catch a glimpse of Bret?

"Daniel?" she said as she crossed the threshold of her private office. "What are you doing here?"

He raised his head and smiled. He was seated at her desk, which rattled on its uneven legs every time he shifted. She had been planning to move the wonderful old Chinese desk from the clayworks to this office. Gil Parkins, who managed the clay-making operations almost single-handedly now, kept telling her it was too damn ornate for his tastes, but Verity liked it.

"Ah, there ye are. I was wondering when ye'd get here. Come in. I was just having a look at yer books."

She was surprised by the thread of annoyance she felt at the sight of him seated in her place, surrounded by her things.

Her office was her personal sanctuary. "I didn't think you were interested in the porcelain business."

"I'm interested in anything that makes money. Or loses it. Looks to me as if ye've been doing a lot more of the latter than the former. Course, that's to be expected, with a relatively new venture, but given the trouble over yer father's loans, ye need to find a way to get these accounts out of the red."

"I've been at James Stannis's office. He's promised to give me more time."

Something flickered in those blue, blue eyes. She wished she could read him better. She could never tell what he was thinking. "Has he, now? Then he's a damn sight more charitable to folks of his own class than he ever was to common clay workers."

She knew that Daniel hated James Stannis, who had refused to take him back to his old job after the clay strike. Stannis, like her father, would always be a target for Daniel's relentless grudge-keeping.

"So he's extending the term of the loans?"

"Not formally, but he's promised to refrain from collecting for as long as he possibly can."

"Have ye got that in writing?"

"For goodness' sake, James and I are old friends."

"Ye don't have it in writing, he can grab his shares of Cadmon Clay anytime after the end of the year."

"He'd never do that. I trust him."

"On his honor as a gentleman? Christ, woman. Ye're far too trusting of everybody."

It was his tone more than his words that irritated her. He sounded a bit like Julian. "May I have my seat back, please? The china factory is my concern."

Unexpectedly, Daniel grinned. "Come here."

"Why?"

He pushed back his chair and nodded to his lap. "Ye wanted yer seat back. Come on, then."

She recognized the tenseness in his muscles, the tightness around his mouth. Her body quickened. She approached him slowly. "If I sound snappish, I'm sorry. I've been wearier than usual, ill in the mornings, and irritable besides. The doctor says it's quite usual.''

"Take off your clothes.''

Heat roared through her. ''Daniel, not here.''

"Why not here? I want to feel 'ee in my arms.''

"I do, too. Always. But I believe you're trying to distract me. What we were talking about a moment ago was important.''

He sighed. "All right, let's talk.'' He rose and let her have the chair while he leaned against the desk. "I'll be honest with 'ee, Verity. I've had my doubts about this factory ever since ye opened it. 'Tes a risky and unprofitable business. Ye can't hope to compete with the established china companies in the midlands. Many of them are famous throughout the world.''

"Cadmon Porcelain was famous once as well.''

"In the past, yes. But the world is changing. 'Tes the future that must concern us.''

"You're not interested in china, are you, Daniel? Only china clay. And that only for its potential to make your fortune.''

He sat back, his face a mask. "Am I not to offer 'ee any advice?''

"Not with regard to my china business, no.''

"How about money? Will ye take that from me?''

"No, Daniel. I've told you before—I'm grateful for the offer, but I don't think it would be wise.''

"We're to be man and wife. Part of the ceremony says something about my endowing 'ee with all my worldly goods. Then there's the for-richer-for-poorer bit. Did ye imagine 'twould always be ye who was richer, and me poorer?''

"Don't get angry.'' Her hands moved protectively to her belly. There was a vague connection in her mind between anger and miscarriage that went back not only to her days with Julian, but further, into her childhood. Something about Miss Lynchpole and the manner of her death. She knew she couldn't count on the safe delivery of this child. Her physician had warned her that, given her history, she must be especially careful until the first trimester was successfully behind her.

"I'm not angry," Daniel said in a manner that belied his words. "I'm trying to understand 'ee, that's all."

"I expect our marriage to be an equal partnership. I didn't have that in my first marriage, and I insist upon having it in my second. Julian wouldn't acknowledge me as an individual, and he joined the army because I refused to submit to his domination."

"So ye're warning me, I take it, that ye won't submit to mine?"

"Yes. Especially with regard to my finances or my work. For almost as long as I can remember, I have dreamed of making porcelain. I'll give up the claypits before I'll give up my factory."

A pause. Daniel was looking out the window; she could not see his eyes. But his hands were clenched in fists. "It's that important to 'ee, then?"

"Yes. Do you see that painting there on the wall?" She pointed to the Chinese china works painting, which she kept hanging where she could easily look up from her work and see it.

"Yeah, I've been wondering about it. It must be valuable. Why d'ye have it here? There's barely any security. Surely it ought to be back at the house."

"Look at it, Daniel. It's an important painting for me. My inspiration, you could say."

"Why?"

"Just look at it. Tell me what you see."

He leaned back, his fingers laced behind his head. "I see a fantasy. A neat, serene oriental model of perfection."

"Come outside with me. Keep the picture in mind."

Shaking his head doubtfully, he allowed her to lead him down to the Charlestown pier. The wind was brisk and there were whitecaps on St. Austell Bay.

When they came close to the end of the stone pier, she laid a hand on his arm. "Look inland from here and tell me what you see."

Daniel raised his eyebrows as if wondering whether pregnancy might have addled her wits. "I see some scenery. Very pretty."

"Is that all?" she asked, disappointed.

"Verity, I don't have time for this."

"Don't you see any similarity between this scene and the picture in my office?"

"Not really. This is England. That's China. They look completely different to me."

Verity said nothing. Gil had seen it. Gil understood.

Daniel's big hands fell upon her shoulders. "I'll tell 'ee what I see," he said in a lighter tone. "I see a stiff little brown-haired woman whose hair loosens and whose face softens when the sea breezes blow." He touched his lips to her forehead. "Right now, that's enough for me."

She relaxed in his arms. He was so tall, so strong. His merest touch kindled her passions, and his lovemaking—which was frequent—never failed to delight and satisfy her. It had become an essential part of her life; something she could not imagine giving up. Whatever their differences, they could work them out.

But moments later, she was aware of his tensing beside her. She turned to see what had turned his eyes so glittery and covetous. A motorcar had pulled up in front of the factory. Out of it sprang the long legs and wild red hair of her sister, Bret. She was wearing old clothes, completely out of fashion and not very feminine, but this did not prevent Daniel from examining her from every angle. She was accompanied by Simon, whose train she had met that morning.

Bret looked seaward. Their eyes met. She lifted an arm and waved. Then she cupped her hands around her mouth and yelled with all the volume of a stevedore:

"Verity! Daniel! Isn't it splendid? Simon's home. Come and say hello."

Verity knew that Daniel didn't give a damn about Simon, but this didn't prevent him from moving toward his former lover with a stride she could match only by hurrying.

He still wants her, she thought as the old envy burst through her. *She will always be there between us, even after our child is born. He will never let her go.*

Chapter Fifty-one

"It's huge, isn't it?" Bret said to Simon as they stood together outside the hangar on the south field where her father's prototypes were still kept. They were looking at the largest aeroplane either of them had ever seen. It was the twin of the Zephyr that had crashed, one of six that had been built with the anticipation that the government would be soon ordering dozens more. The others were at the Trevor Aviation factory outside Plymouth, one of many aircraft assembly plants that had sprung up during the war. Aviation was now a massive industry employing 350,000 people and turning out new aeroplanes at the rate of 30,000 per year.

"It's hard to believe that a thing like that ever could get off the ground," Simon agreed. At Verity's insistence, he was staying with them at Cadmon Hall. He was walking easily now, using his cane more as a prop than as a necessity. But the rasping in his chest was worse than ever.

The Zephyr was a twin-engine biplane. The narrow fuselage, which could carry a heavy payload of bombs, was dwarfed by the enormous wingspan. It was powered by two engines mounted between the wingstruts on the right and the left of the plane. The propellers resembled the sails of windmills, and the aeroplane in its entirety looked clumsy and unwieldy.

"But it does fly. Papa made dozens of successful test flights. With the fierce offensive that's going on over there, England needs planes like this one. Bombers." She paused. "God, listen to me. I sound just like my father."

"The war'll be over before any more of Trevor Aviation's aeroplanes make it to the battlefield. The Central Powers are in retreat."

"So what's the use?" she said gloomily. "No one's going to order the Zephyr if the demand isn't there."

"Not as an offensive weapon, no. But we've taken to the air during this war, and there we'll stay. We'll ship cargo, we'll fly the post, and, someday, passengers as well. There'll be no shortgage of investors willing to gamble some of their capital on air transport. It's a glamorous field, and the war has made it more so."

"Then you don't think I'm daft?"

"I think if you could get the Zephyr back into the air, preferably with a crowd of newspaper reporters to witness and report that there's nothing unlucky about it, you could attract the investment capital necessary to go on building aeroplanes, save the company, and pay back those outstanding loans."

"Oh, Simon, it's all I can think about. Before this horrible war began, Papa was so excited about his sky-birds. They had nothing to do with killing and everything to do with science, vision, and human aspiration. I won't allow his dreams to die with him. Nor will I tolerate anyone's proclaiming him to be a careless designer. If it weren't for Henry Trevor, there might not even *be* an aviation industry."

Simon took her hand and squeezed it. "Fortunately, you've got yourself a pilot."

"You mean you'd risk flying her?"

"Assuming I still have the nerve, yes. I want to fly again."

"Simon—" she hesitated before continuing, "do you think you're strong enough to take on something like this?"

"I'm fine," he said shortly.

"Well, you're not taking up the Zephyr unless we're sure it's safe. You may be a splendid pilot, but you're not an engineer."

"No, but Slayton is. We send him the specs, plans, diagrams, and everything else we know about this monster and let him go over them. If he confirms that the Zephyr is airworthy, I'll fly her. In the meantime, we'll take a trip down to your father's factory and make sure his workers are still doing a good job on the smaller planes they've been building for years."

If she asked for his help, Bret was thinking, Zach would have to write to her, if only to decline. "What if he doesn't answer?"

"If it's anything to do with aeroplanes, he'll answer. It's only love that he's trying to duck."

"You write to him, Simon. I can't."

"You can't forget him either, can you?" Simon's voice was sad.

She touched his arm. "It's getting easier," she said.

"I know your personal priority is to save the Zephyr, but I would appreciate your help in the china factory," Verity said to Bret at supper a few days later. "There's a trade show shortly before Christmas in London, and I must have some samples ready to present there. I need your designs."

"I'm not sure if I can switch gears so easily," Bret said. "I'm concentrating on wingspans, engine rpms, and optimum rates of climb."

"I thought Simon had most of that under control."

"He does. He's been wonderful. But he's not well, Verity. His chest is worse, and there have been cases of flu at the factory. I'm so afraid for him."

"Please, Bret. It's what I've always dreamed of, you and I in business together, making china the way our family used to do a hundred and fifty years ago."

"I know it's important to you. But I'm not at all sure that it's what I want to do with my life. Besides, I've never worked with china clay. I understand it has quite a different feel to it. And I don't know anything about porcelain."

"That's easily remedied." Verity picked up the sugar bowl from the center of the table and set it beside the saltcellar Bret had been using to season her food. They were each a different pattern and style. "The first thing to learn is the difference between hard-paste and soft-paste porcelain." She put the yellow, gilt-edged saltcellar into her sister's open hand. "This was made in Meissen. It's hard paste, the so-called true porcelain, a compound of china clay and china stone. You see how severe it looks, not only in form, but also in the quality of the china itself?"

"Yes. Very German."

"Run your fingertips over it." She watched as Bret caressed the china. "How does it feel to you?"

"Hard and cold."

"Now compare it with this piece of French Sèvres." She handed Bret the sugar bowl, a delicate object of ivory and rose. "Do you see the difference?"

"Yes. The French china is much softer. The first is like milk, the second like cream."

"Exactly." Reaching behind her to the sideboard, Verity hefted a large ivory serving platter painted in a floral design. She tapped her fingernails, which were painted with scarlet enamel, against the rim of the platter. It made a ringing sound. "Now examine this Spode platter. What would you say this is?"

Bret took it and ran her palms over it. "It's more like the hard-paste china, I think."

"Actually, it's bone china, what we English are so famous for. It's durable, and graceful as well. Most of the kaolin we sell nowadays goes into the manufacture of bone china."

"What about your china? Is it hard-paste, soft-paste, or bone?"

Verity rose and removed a china bird from the corner cabinet. "This is Tamara's work, using slip from Cadmon Clay and Porcelain. Look at it, then you tell me."

Bret handled the bird lovingly; it reminded her of the tiny one Tamara had given her many years before. She made them herself now; indeed, birds were among her favorite figures. She realized that her own style had evolved in a manner that was quite different from Tamara's. She had become a more flamboyant potter than her former mentor.

She stroked the china. It wasn't as creamy as the Sèvres piece, she decided. Nor as severe as the Meissen. "I'd say it's bone china," she guessed.

"Excellent," Verity said. "You're showing promise already."

Bret smiled. "End of Lesson One?"

"Until tomorrow morning, when I hope you'll accompany me to the china factory."

"All right, Verity, you've snagged my interest, I'll admit,

but please don't count on me forever. I've discovered that I'm rather fond of aeroplanes, after all.''

Three weeks later, in the middle of October, Simon decided to end one of his private battles. If the Zephyr was to fly again, he wanted to be the one in the cockpit, but first he had to find out whether he still had the guts to pilot an aeroplane.

If he hadn't been disabled in France, his superior officers would have sent him right back into combat—a variation on remounting the horse that's thrown you. But he hadn't had that chance; instead, the fear had been allowed to build. It was a good thing, he told himself wryly, that to him fear was such a familiar emotion.

He didn't tell Bret what he intended. She was busy during the day, working with Verity to produce a new line of china. As a result, most of the responsibility for Trevor Aviation had fallen upon his shoulders.

He went alone to the south field, unlocked Henry's hangar, and pushed out one of the old biplanes. It was the same two-seater in which Henry had instructed him. He filled her with Petrol and started his careful preflight check, a routine he'd refined each morning before his sorties in France.

It felt good to be underneath the belly of an aeroplane again, tinkering about. She was a damn fine plane, the little Trevor two-seater. Maybe not quite as much of a honey as the Sopwith Camel he'd flown into the ground, but a beauty nevertheless.

A fit of coughing interrupted him as he was finishing his check of the engine. Although his legs had healed, his lungs were still a mess. He had a persistent phlegmy cough that made it difficult to breathe. The army physician in Sussex had recommended he see a London specialist about the problem, but he hadn't done so. Vestiges of his old hypochondria, perhaps—he didn't want to learn anything that might confirm his worst fears. Nor did he want to put any doubts in Bret's mind about his fitness to continue managing Trevor Aviation.

At the aeroplane factory near Plymouth, Simon had discovered within himself an ability, instilled in the Royal Flying Corps, to inspire confidence in other people. He got along superbly with Henry's workers, who considered him a war hero. They listened to him, respected him, and followed his orders. He was honest with them about the disaster threatening the company, although he insisted that it was not a foregone conclusion. They were still filling orders for smaller biplanes, and if they could get the Zephyr safely into the air again they'd have a chance, he explained, to mend their damaged image with the public.

He hadn't mentioned that it was going to take every ounce of the courage he'd so painfully acquired over the years to get him back into a cockpit again.

The crash in France ought to have killed him. He had a recurring dream in which it did kill him, although for some reason his spirit had been intercepted and returned to earth. An angel on his shoulder whispered that something remained here for him to do, if only he could figure out what it might be.

While in the hospital, totally dependent on the doctors and nurses around him, Simon had believed there was only one thing he wanted to do: love Bret and stay with her forever. But Bret, he knew, was still in love with Zach. He knew also that despite his long silence, Zach might reappear. If he had survived, he would rise up from the ashes of the worst war the world had ever known. He would want something lovely then, something joyful and life-affirming. He would remember Bret's bright eyes and fiery hair. He would long for her laughter. He would yearn for her touch. He would come for her and claim her. He would take her away.

Stop thinking about it, Simon ordered himself. *Focus on flying. That's what you're here to do.*

As he climbed up into the cockpit, he expected to be terrified. But, although his heart was beating more rapidly than normal, he was not afraid. He was excited. He'd missed this.

He roared off down the airstrip, feeling the kick, the glide, the weightlessness. As the wind moved beneath his wings, lifting him, he rose strong and happy and free. It was as good as ever. Better, in fact, since there were no Jerries to watch out for, no ordnance to deliver, no enemy to kill.

Banking, he made a lazy circle over the skytips, the claypits, the moors. He recalled his reaction to a female letter carrier who had ridden her bicycle up to him one morning at

Cadmon Hall and handed him the post. A burst of lust had assailed him at the sight of her bare legs working the pedals. She must have found him attractive, too, because she'd flirted with him. Before riding off, she'd whispered her address in St. Austell, which he'd memorized. He hadn't pursued her, but maybe he should. Invite her for a drink. Flirt a little. Dust off his seductive arts. He'd never been fully confident of his skills in that area, but there had always been willing women around. "You're good-looking, available, and disinterested," Zach told him once. "That's a combination that drives 'em crazy."

Bret was there on the ground when he landed. Her hands were propped on her hips. She did not look pleased.

"Just what do you think you're doing, Simon Marrick?" she said when he rolled to a stop and climbed out.

"I'm a pilot. It's what I do."

"You didn't tell me."

"No. It was something I had to do alone. Why are you here? Shouldn't you be at the factory with Verity?"

She pulled a face. "Verity and I had a slight disagreement. I took a walk to stop myself from screaming at her."

"What about?"

"It's not important." She looked from him to the plane and back again. "Were you frightened?"

"Not nearly as frightened as I thought I'd be."

She blew out a deep breath. "Well, I was." She put her arms around his neck and went up on tiptoe. "I'm so proud of you." She kissed him lightly on the cheek.

It was nothing more than a friendly, affectionate kiss. But it drove all thoughts of the leggy postal carrier from Simon's mind.

From high on the moors overlooking the south field, Daniel Carne lay belly down in the scrub with a collapsible spyglass in his fist. He'd chosen the right day for it. Until this morning he would have laid a large wager that Simon Marrick, who'd come back from the war hollow-chested and limping, would never fly an aeroplane again. But he was still a pilot, with Bret's kiss for his reward. What would she give him for flying the Zephyr? A full-fledged fuck? He'd probably had that from her already.

Damn her, Bret had been nothing but trouble since she had returned to Trenwythan. He suspected she'd had something to do with Verity's refusal to accept his bailout offer on her loans, and now she was trying to pull off a last-minute miracle with the aviation company.

What a pair, he thought wryly. Neither sister was naturally submissive. They both challenged him, and deep down he supposed he liked that. At least he wasn't bored.

He didn't mind a bit of a struggle; if anything, it excited him. But one thing was certain—he intended to win.

Chapter Fifty-two

"This isn't exactly what I had in mind," Verity said, holding a soup bowl that Bret had designed, molded, and painted as a sample for their new porcelain line.

Bret groaned. She was sitting with the girls in the last row of the china-decorating shop, supervising the banding process that was the final step of china painting. Verity was proud of the way she had organized the decorating shop. In the first row were the outliners—women whose job was to sketch the basic design on the ware. When this was finished, the china was passed backwards to the second row, where the enamelers would fill the outlines in with paint. In the last row, experienced artisans waited to apply the final brush strokes. Banders carefully rotated the ware on a wheel with one hand while painting lines with the other. An error at this stage could ruin the ware, so only the most experienced decorators performed the task.

"You mean you don't like it?" Bret said.

"It's too garish," Verity said. Her head ached. As was so often the case, reality and fantasy didn't mesh. She and Bret couldn't agree on what Cadmon Clay's fine china ought to look like. Verity wanted classic lines, muted colors, graceful-ness. Bret wanted bold new shapes, lush colors, broad geo-metric designs, and perhaps a little humor. Their styles were totally at odds.

"Garish? Goodness, Verity, it took me ages to get the look right. The colors are bright and true."

"The look is exceptional, but I want elegance, not drama." Verity knew her tone was sharp, and she noted several of the girls exchanging glances. "Come into my office, please," she said to Bret.

Rising, Bret wiped her clay-covered hands on the front of her smock. She shrugged elaborately, which made the entire decorating team smile and increased Verity's resentment.

"I don't agree," she said to Verity when they were alone. "I've told you that I think our designs have to be dramatic if we're to make any sort of dent in the market. Elegant's been done to death by the established china manufacturers."

"It's my responsibility to worry about marketing. I believe I have a better sense than you do of what will sell."

"I'm not so sure about that. I'm the one who's been out in the world these last four years."

"How dare you speak to me that way?"

"My God, Verity, the way I speak to you reflects the way I feel. If it sounds tactless, I'm sorry, but for the past three weeks I've been doing my best to help, and you've done nothing but find fault."

This was true, Verity knew. Several times she'd angrily raised her voice to her sister. Once or twice Bret had been so annoyed by this treatment that she'd walked out, only to return later, her good spirits restored by a brisk hike across the moors. On these occasions Verity tended to have flashbacks to the days when Miss Lynchpole had harangued her into learn-ing about china. She heard herself criticizing Bret in a manner that was similar, and probably just as insulting. Grown up now and dominant, Verity was laying into Caroline Lynchpole's daughter as if she were finally taking revenge.

She loved her sister, but their differences had never been more real. Often when they were together, Verity felt as if the old Fiery Furnace had been reborn inside her——her anger building up steam, shaking the boiler, rattling the pipes. Her insecurities about Daniel, who had been somewhat distant and evasive since Bret had returned, had ballooned.

"I don't mean to be so critical," she forced herself to say. "I do appreciate everything you're doing for me. And I'm confident you can give me what I want. Please try again."

"This time I'm going to give you colored sketches in advance so we can settle any differences of opinion before I begin decorating."

"An excellent idea."

"And I'd appreciate it if you could refrain from criticizing me in front of the staff. It makes them nervous to see us disagree. They're overworked as it is."

Verity winged her eyebrows toward the ceiling. "Don't start giving me plight-of-the-workers diatribes again, Bret. These women are exceptionally well paid, better than I can afford."

"Yes, I know. They love their work and they respect and admire you. But you're pressuring them, and it's causing resentment. They break their backs to meet your tight deadlines, and a little praise instead of so much criticism would be much appreciated."

"Dammit, Bret! Don't tell me how to manage my workers. I've been doing it for years, and quite successfully, I might add!"

"All I'm asking is that we try to ease up a bit," Bret said in a more conciliatory tone. "We all know what's at stake here. Let's not make things worse."

"Thank you," Verity said, "for your sage advice."

"I wouldn't be so angry," Bret said later that evening to Simon, "if there were any doubt about the quality of my work." They were together in the tower room in Cadmon Hall, which Bret had converted into a studio. Brushes, easels, canvases, and tins of paint were scattered about the room, and in the center was a covered bucket of clay and a potter's wheel, which she used for trying out new inspirations. She was sitting on a stool in front of it now, toying aimlessly with her clay.

"I know my designs are good. Tamara thinks so too. She says my concepts are more original, my shapes more sensuous, and my hands more skillful than they ever were before. It drives me wild that my sister can't see that. She's trying to impose her own values on me."

"You mustn't allow her to interfere with your personal artistic vision. If you and Verity can't work together, you'd better resign."

"But I want to help her, Simon. She's happy in her personal life, especially now that she's pregnant, but at work she's so frantic all the time. She's afraid of losing the business. To make matters worse, Daniel doesn't support what she's trying to do with the china works, and she doesn't even realize it."

"She loves him. She can't see the real Daniel any more than you could four years ago."

"The odd thing is that I'm beginning to think Verity and Daniel might actually be good for each other. She has much more in common with him than I ever did. They're both ambitious, hardworking, and well organized. And they're both so *serious* about everything. I don't think either one of them has ever learned how to laugh. They have a hurt and angry place inside them, and it's out of that place that all their actions arise. It's as if they both feel cheated by the world, so they're damn well going to show us all someday."

"Meaning they're both miserable."

"Maybe. But I'd like them both to be happy. Verity was a mother to me. She was always there, loving me, encouraging me, comforting me. I think she wanted to give me what she hadn't had as a child, and she succeeded. It's because of her that I've always been such a contented person. I *do* know how to laugh, you see. Verity created an atmosphere in which laughter was possible."

"That's true. She tried to do the same for me when she was married to my father."

"That's why I can't quit, even though we no longer share a vision. She deserves something back from us, Simon. Maybe not forever, not for the rest of my life, but for now I have to do my best to help her."

"Are you your sister's keeper?" Simon asked rhetorically.

"The answer to that question, I think, is supposed to be

yes. Ultimately, though—'' she paused, furrowing her brow, ''the clay company is her obsession, not mine.''

''What's yours?''

Arizona, she thought. *The harsh beauty of the desert. Navajo sand paintings. Hopi pots. Wings against the sand. Zach Slayton.*

He had not answered Simon's letter. There had been no advice on the Zephyr, no note of condolence for her father's death. Simon made excuses for him—he was wounded, perhaps, or sick with influenza. The post was bad, particularly in this time of advancing armies. Perhaps the letter had not arrived.

But in Bret's heart there was no excuse for him. Even if he didn't wish to communicate with her, he had been Henry Trevor's friend long enough to acknowledge his death in some manner. A short note of condolence, at least. Some communication. Some word. In his silence he was throwing away much more than a wartime romance. He was discarding a close, long-standing, and affectionate friendship. For this she could not—would not—forgive him.

Bret dug her hands into her barrel of the white china clay. With deft, quick motions, she shaped the figure of a tall man clad in the jacket, jodhpurs, and Sam Browne belt of an officer of the RFC. She stood the figure on the surface of her table. Because its base was improperly balanced, it promptly toppled over. It was too white, she thought. Lying there so pale and still, her figure looked dead.

''What's your obsession?'' Simon asked again. She looked up to find him watching her. Banishing her dismal thoughts, she shrugged and smiled. ''The war's almost over, thank God. Maybe I'll go study in Paris or Florence, after all. To hell with soup bowls and coffeepots. I want to sculpt naked men.''

Simon grinned. ''May I offer myself as a model?''

For an instant, the cold clay figure she'd just made of Zach seemed to merge with her image of Simon, who stood there tall and skinny, his hair a darker gold than she remembered, his eyes a deeper brown. He too had worn the uniform of an officer in the RFC. She was worried about the way he continued to cough, the difficulty he had in breathing. She'd hoped to see him gain weight now that he was eating home-cooked meals instead of hospital rations, but he remained gaunt and hollow, looking older than his years.

A fine shiver stole over her skin as she flashed back to that bizarre experience in Tamara's cottage, her hands in the clay, her foot on the pedal that made the potter's wheel of fortune spin. She did not like to remember the things she'd seen that day. Tamara had said she had the Sight, but Bret hadn't wanted to believe her.

She had envisioned the fire and destruction of the war, Cadmon Hall in mourning, and two men in uniform. One of them had worn the fixed, pasty expression of the dead.

Chapter Fifty-three

At eleven o'clock in the morning of the eleventh day of the eleventh month, a time deliberately chosen by the Allied leaders for its numerical symmetry, the guns and artillery fell silent along the Western Front. Zach Slayton and several of his fellow pilots had "liberated" a staff motorcar during the night and driven from their temporary aerodrome several miles to the rear to be on the front lines at the moment of victory. The Kaiser had abdicated and fled to Holland the previous day. The Great War, which had lasted four years and killed 10 million people, was over.

Thick fog had covered the battlefield at dawn, but as the sun rose higher it burned off, leaving a ghostly mist along the ground and a sparkling dew on the tanks, guns, barbed wire, and leafless trees.

There had been sporadic firing right up until the deadline, with several needless injuries and deaths. The silence that followed the marking of the hour was eerie. To Zach it was the sacred silence of church, the profound silence of the grave.

Then the shouting began.

Troops from both sides began pouring into the no-man's-land that separated their lines. Zach was propelled forward with the crowd. Men were laughing, dancing, slapping one another on the back. Zach found himself face-to-face with a skinny German soldier who couldn't have been much older than sixteen. His eyes were downcast, his cheeks hollow, his uniform in rags. Most of the Germans were beardless boys. Their older brothers had died months—even years—ago.

He offered his erstwhile enemy a cigarette. The kid took it gratefully. He tried to light a match, but his fingers were shaking, so Zach lit it for him.

Another boy looked pleadingly at Zach's cigarettes. He started shaking them out of the pack, passing them out, reaching into his pockets for more. The same scene was being enacted all around him as Allied and German forces exchanged cigarettes, rations, coffee, tea, chocolate, and schnapps. The mood turned jovial as both sides got down to some serious horse trading—helmets, belt buckles, Iron Crosses, St. George medallions, knives, uniform buttons, bayonets.

Zach had passable French and some fractured German, and many of the Germans had sufficient English to communicate. No one mentioned the war. They spoke of their families, their homes, their mothers, wives, and sweethearts. Battered photographs were pulled from pockets and smoothed out carefully on the palms of chilblained hands. Zach exclaimed upon the beauty of many a German fraulein and lamented that he had no photograph to display in return. He pictured Bret's laughing face, her red hair wild and unruly, her cheeks flushed in the aftermath of love. Deep inside him, something pulsed as the thought exploded into his brain: *The war is over and I am still alive*.

The first German to whom he'd given a cigarette tapped him lightly on the shoulder, then danced away, ran a few steps, then turned with a grin, daring Zach to follow him. Mystified by the exuberant blush on the boy's face, Zach looked around and discovered that all over the battlefield men were slapping each other and running while others chased them. Incredibly, they were playing tag.

This is insane, he thought, as he chased the boy and easily overtook him. The kid was coughing. Flu, probably. He'd heard in headquarters that there had been more deaths from influenza during the past couple of weeks than there had been among the wounded.

None of the troops on either side looked particularly well fed or healthy, but this didn't prevent them from cutting loose now that hostilities had ended. Shouting that his name was Friedrich, the German whirled and started after Zach, who ran several yards in the other direction before being tagged again. All over no-man's-land, exhausted, demoralized, battle-weary soldiers were dodging and laughing like children released from the classroom, free at last to play together in the sun.

Bret and Simon were together that morning, painting the Trevor Aviation logo on the Zephyr's fuselage for what they hoped would be its triumphal flight. At midmorning Bret cocked her head and looked to the east. "Listen. Can you hear the bells?"

He glanced at his wristwatch. "Eleven on the eleventh." The churches in Trenwythan were peeling out the joyful news. "The bloody war's finally over and done with."

Bret tossed aside her paintbrush. "We ought to declare today a holiday, don't you think? How shall we welcome in the armistice?"

"Let's go fishing," he said.

"In November?"

"Doesn't matter if we don't catch anything. I like to watch you fish."

She laughed. "You've changed, Simon, d'you realize? There was a time when I used to have to drag you outside. Remember? All you ever wanted to do was lie about in bed."

"Plenty of time to lie about after I'm dead."

Her face whitened, which he regretted. In the old days she

would have mocked him for his anxieties, but now they were hers as well.

Half an hour later, though, he was lying about on the riverbank while Bret waded into the water, screaming because it was so bloody cold, bemoaning the fact that there were no insects hatching or any signs of rising trout. It felt good to be with her, to watch her lithely casting her fly line, to listen to her throaty laugh.

Two days before, Simon had had a consultation with Dr. Arthur Cowan, son of the physician who had attended the Trevors and the Marricks when they'd all been children. Cowan was a gangly young man, tall and awkward, with an intellectual forehead and an empty sleeve where his left arm ought to have been. Dryly, he told Simon that the arm was buried in Belgium. "Probably right next to the lining of my lungs," Simon had replied.

The news had not been good. Cowan had showed him the X rays and explained what they meant. "Do your living while you still can," had been his advice.

"What the hell does that mean?" Simon had asked.

Cowan had shrugged, but in his eyes Simon read the truth.

"How much time have I got?" he'd managed to ask.

"There are lung chaps in London who can estimate better than I can. But I'd say a year. Maybe not so long."

A year. He hadn't absorbed it yet. How could you make sense of something like that?

One lousy year. Or less.

"Hey, I think I've got one!" yelled Bret.

Simon rose and climbed down the bank. She was near the edge of the water, her skirts rucked up, her shoulders straining as her rod bent almost double. He hadn't told her. He wasn't certain he believed it himself. "Keep your tip up."

"I'm trying, but it's a big one."

"Need some help?"

"No, I don't think so. I—" She broke off as her rod was dragged forward by the struggles of the fish. She pulled it backward even as the line whirred off her reel. "Hell's bells and damnation! Look at it, Simon. This one is really a monster."

"Be careful. Looks like he's turning. If he runs downstream you'll never bring him to your net."

"This may be the biggest fish I've ever had on. My arms are aching." The line went nearly slack. "Damn, I think I've lost him."

"Maybe he's swimming toward you."

Bret retreated a step and raised her rod. The tension returned to her line. Over her shoulder, she tossed Simon a grin. It cost her, for at that moment her fish shot off upstream again with such a spurt of energy that the rod was nearly jerked out of her hands. In trying to hang on, she lost her balance and went down in the cold water, cursing and sputtering.

He waded in after her, got his hands under her armpits, and hauled her back to her feet. She was still clutching her rod, but the tautness was gone from her fly line. "He broke off, dammit," she cried, shaking the water from her hair.

"Bad luck," he said sympathetically.

"Damn, damn, damn!" She looked like an angry goddess rising from her watery domain. He was fascinated by the tiny droplets of water sparkling on her skin. "I just wanted to see him, that's all. I wasn't going to keep him. You stupid fish," she yelled upstream. "I wasn't going to hurt you. I wanted to be friends!"

Simon smiled. She glared at him for several seconds before the corners of her mouth quirked. Then she was laughing, and hugging him, and getting him all wet, which he didn't mind in the least. Unable to stop himself, he gathered her thick red hair into his hands. It was so soft, it smelled so good. Bret's body relaxed and went loose as he caressed her. Slowly she raised her face to his.

Incredibly, she was still smiling. The expression in her eyes was encouraging. He stood motionless for a moment, digesting this. She looked as if she would welcome his kiss.

He was about to do it, to take that risk, when a spasm of coughing caught him, doubling him up, making him gasp for breath. He choked up more of the same thick yellow stuff that had been percolating in his lungs lately. He had to twist his face and his body away from her to spit it out.

"Simon . . ." Her voice was soft and worried, her hand

on his shoulder gentle. But he didn't want gentleness from her. He wanted what he thought he'd seen for a moment in her eyes—her love, her passion. For a little while, dammit. A year . . . or maybe not so long.

"Don't touch me." Dragging himself to his feet, he climbed the bank of the stream, panting for breath. Sweat had exploded along his spine and under his arms, and he felt dizzy, as if he was going to pass out. *Christ*, he thought, despairing; *Cowan was right*.

"I'm worried about you," Bret said, following him, reaching out to him, solicitous as always. Suddenly he hated her for it. For being healthy. For having hope. If she weren't so goddamn optimistic all the time, she'd have realized, she'd have known. *I am one whose name is writ in water*.

"Simon, I want you to see a doctor. A lung specialist. I'll go with you to London. There must be something they can do."

He whirled upon her. "There's nothing they can do."

"Don't be ridiculous. Of course there's—"

"For chrissake, stop pretending. My fucking lungs are full of abscesses. They can't drain them, they can't operate. The war may be over for all those poor devils on the battlefield, but it's not over for me. I'm going to die."

"Now you sound just like you used to when you were twelve years old." Her face had gone pale as bone. "Talking about dying, imagining all sorts of morbid things."

"It may be morbid, but it's not my imagination. I saw Cowan a couple of days ago. He gave me a year."

"Oh, no, Simon! That can't be true. He's not a lung specialist. Don't listen to him. He's—"

"He's a battlefield physician, who knows what the bloody mustard gas can do. I trust him more than I'd trust some Harley Street quack who's spent the entire war in London sitting on his duff." He coughed again, his intense emotion making him spasmodic. There was a pale froth of blood mixed with the phlegm on his hands when he took them away from his mouth. Defiantly, he held them out to her. "You don't believe him, look at this. You're a nurse. Look at it!"

She looked away, disgusted, no doubt, and his rage mounted. She'd been about to kiss him, maybe even to make love with him at last, and now she was revulsed. "Don't turn away from me," he shouted, grabbing her shoulder, spinning her around.

"I'm not—"

"It makes you sick, doesn't it, seeing me this way?"

"Please, Simon, don't think that." Her voice was trembling; she had wrapped her arms around herself as if she were frightened or cold.

"Right, you're a VAD, and you've got a strong stomach. You're schooled to hide your reactions. Heaven forbid that you should betray your natural revulsion for one of your hapless patients."

"Is that what you believe?" she shouted back. "That I'm put off by you? That I'm disgusted?"

"Yes, dammit, that's what I believe. The worst of it is, how can I blame you? I'm thin, I limp, I'm weak, and I cough up pus. To look at me is to look upon the face of death, and I probably stink as well. No woman in her right mind could want to kiss me, much less take my failing body into her arms."

"You are not your body, Simon. You're you, the man I've known and loved and cherished since we were children. Do you think I care if your flesh isn't as healthy as it once was? It doesn't matter."

"Of course it matters. Don't lie to me. I'm *dying*. I deserve the truth from you."

"I'm not lying. I—" She paused, and Simon sensed that she was struggling, trying to explain something that she couldn't put into words. "We're more than bodies," she whispered. "I mean, of course it's true that flesh is all we know, all we can prove exists, but there must be something more, there must be a reason for all this pain and misery, there must be a God whose actions are motivated by love and justice, surely, there must be . . ." Her voice caught; he realized she was fighting back a sob. "Oh, Simon, did Dr. Cowan really tell you there wasn't any hope?"

He nodded. She was looking at him now. He saw no revulsion. Instead her lovely eyes were wet with terror, despair, and empty aching sadness.

"Don't cry for me," he said. "You have no right to cry

for me.'' His own tears were erupting now, damn them. What a miserable wreck she must think him—weeping, coughing up his fucking lungs. ''If you can't love me, Bret, you shouldn't cry.''

Her arms wrapped around him, holding him close while he shuddered against her. ''I do love you, you silly ass. I love you very much.''

That night Bret lay in bed and howled, her sobs escalating until they became great, sharp, tearing things. In her dreams she had been lying beside the long-dead soldier Eddie Hastings, holding him like a lover. She caressed him, wondering why his flesh was so cold to the touch, not realizing until she pressed her lips to his that he was gone. She woke up knowing that Eddie's death and her reaction to it had been a preparation for this other, more terrible loss.

Later, when there were no more tears, she lay for a long while in the darkness, feeling the steady breathing of her own healthy lungs. She sensed that she would live for many years in this world. Simon had a year; less, if influenza struck.

She kept thinking of his love, his loyalty, and his endurance. He used to count himself a coward, but the last few years had laid to rest that particular ghost. He had withstood the enormous stresses of battle. After his accident he had withstood great pain. He had not collapsed into that depressed and lifeless state from which so many wounded men never emerged. He had little to hope for, yet still he hoped. He expected none of the passionate love from her that he had bestowed upon her, yet still he loved.

What was love, anyway? Was it what Daniel had given her, motivated so strongly by envy, possessiveness, and revenge? Was it what Zach had given her, a unity of hearts and minds that had been sabotaged by his fear of letting down his self-protective walls? Zach was all she wanted, but he, it seemed, did not want her. Simon did, but he would never ask, especially now that they had both confronted the bitter truth of what was coming.

He believed she felt revulsion.

She could think of only one way to convince him that she

did not . . . and to make him happy, for a little while, at least.

She rose and washed her face in the cold water from the pitcher beside her bed. She brushed out her hair. She applied two dabs of her favorite violet-scented perfume and changed into a filmy nightgown that she had bought one afternoon from an exclusive London shop. It made her look more voluptuous than she actually was.

When she was ready, she left her bedroom and moved quietly down the corridor toward the room in the east wing that Verity had assigned to Simon. Silently, she opened his door. The light of a nearly full moon gave substance to the shadows. As she approached his bed she saw that he was sleeping on his back, his head and shoulders propped up by several pillows to make it easier to breathe.

Bret sat down on the bed beside him. Despite his illness, he was still a handsome man. How would his mouth feel? Would he be quick and rough like Daniel, or slower, more subtle, more exuberant, like Zach? Simon was a sensitive man, a poet, who loved to look around him and see the world in all its infinite variety. He admired the lyrics of Coleridge, who could find a mystical experience in the workings of frost on a windowpane. How much more delightful would he find the intricate workings of a kiss?

She touched his shoulder.

Simon woke to find her leaning over him. He blinked, afraid he was dreaming. But he could touch her. She was here.

"Bret?"

"Move over," she whispered, smiling.

"But, why? Are you, are we—" He felt like an idiot for fumbling, but he couldn't believe the intention he read in her eyes.

She slid under the covers beside him. He could feel the warmth of her body beneath that thin frothy thing that seemed to be all she had on. "I love you," she said. "I want to be with you."

"Bret, you're crazy. I can't—"

She caressed him, running her hand from his shoulder

down the middle of his chest, and lower. "Yes, you can," she said several seconds later.

"But . . . what if I start coughing, or have a fit or something—"

"It doesn't matter. Whatever happens is all right."

"Jesus, Bret." He rolled over onto his side, facing her. "Are you sure? I love you. Once you've slept with me, I couldn't bear it if . . . that is, it can't be just once. Do you understand? If we make love, you're mine."

"I know. It's what I want."

"If Zach comes back—"

"We'll tell him he's too late."

God. He'd gone to bed despairing and awakened to this miracle. All he could think of was that if he was going to do it, he was going to do it right. He wanted to please her. Surprise her. Delight her. His lungs were a mess, but the rest of his body worked fine.

She reached out to touch his lips, stroking her finger over the top one first, then, more slowly, over the bottom. He sucked her fingertip into his mouth and bit down gently. She made a sound in the back of her throat. He kissed each of her fingers, letting her feel first his lips and then his tongue and then his teeeth.

"That's good," she murmured. "That's lovely, Simon." The blatant eroticism of his caresses startled her, for it was not at all what she'd expected. It helped her to relax. She wanted to feel something . . . and had feared she might not.

She had never thought of him as sensual. She'd certainly never regarded him as sophisticated, or even particularly experienced. But when his tongue darted rhythmically between her lips at the same moment as his fingers approached, but playfully avoided, a full caress of her nipples, Bret realized how wrong she had been. He knew what he was doing. He could fly planes, he could love women. He was no longer the languid old Simon, declaiming lazily about the absurdity of the universe.

Effortlessly, he made her nightgown disappear. And then his own nightshirt. She had seen his naked body so many times that the sight seemed natural to her. When she closed her eyes and heard his dear, familiar voice telling her she was beautiful and that he loved her and that he'd always known it would be like this, she smiled in the darkness and guided him inside her. If her pleasure didn't quite match the intensity of his, it was something he would never know.

When it was over Simon was terrified.

He half-expected her to roll away from him, reject him, cry.

He didn't expect her to push up on one elbow, lean over him, and blow gently on his eyelids. Nor to touch the bridge of his nose with her lips and whisper, "Well?"

"Uh, well what?"

"Ask me."

"Ask you?"

She smiled down at him, her blue-green eyes merry, her hair tossed about every which way. "Ask me the question that an honorable gentleman is supposed to ask the lady of his heart in circumstances like these."

"Will you marry me?" His voice was hoarse as he spat out the words.

"Yes."

Simon's arms slipped around her shoulders, hesitated, then tightened. "I ought to allow you to take that back. It's not fair to you. You're sentencing yourself to be more of a nurse than a wife. A nurse for a short while . . . and then a widow."

"Nothing's certain, not life, not death. If you're happy and content, you could live longer than the doctor thinks."

"That wouldn't be fair to you either."

"Listen." She sat up. "I'm going to make a condition. No more of that sort of remark. Ever. I'm not doing this because I feel sorry for you. I love you. I want to be with you, for however long we have, not only for what I can give to you, but also for what you can give to me. Your gentleness. Your kindness. Your skill as a pilot and your enormous help with Trevor Aviation. Yes, and this as well—" She stroked his body. "I want everything you have to offer."

"Christ, Bret," he said as she continued to caress him. "You won't regret it. I'll make you happy, I swear to God."

"I'm happy already," she said.

* * *

"We're getting married," she had said.

Daniel was alone in Carne Cottage, drinking cup after cup of coffee. It was a substitute, he knew, for something stronger. He'd grown to like the taste of gin, brandy, and ale a little more than he ought to. With all his self-discipline, therefore, he avoided them. He was damned if he was going to end up like his father. Not when he'd come so far.

"We're getting married," she'd said this evening at Cadmon Hall, holding the hand of that blond weakling she'd always had a fondness for. "Can you believe it's taken me all this time to say yes?"

She'd been speaking to her sister, not to him. She never spoke to him unless it was absolutely essential. Heaven forbid that she should acknowledge the past.

Verity, of course, had been beside herself with joy. Daniel didn't think she'd believed it at first. Marrick didn't look as if he believed it himself. He'd had a dazed expression on his silly patrician face, and he kept sneaking moony glances at Bret that were full of reverence, amazement, and complete devotion.

"We're getting married."

Daniel flung his coffee at the wall. He slammed out of his house and tramped across the moors, not slowing his stride until he reached Tamara's cottage half a mile away. "I need yer help," he announced to his sister when she opened her door. "Everything's coming out wrong."

Tam had become more of a recluse than ever. Since Henry Trevor's death she had worn black every day. God damn all the bloody Trevors. They caused nothing but heartbreak among the Carnes.

"If everything's coming out wrong, Daniel, 'tes yer own doing."

"To hell with that. I need ye to make me one of those herbal potions of yers. Ye know the sort of thing—it makes the person who quaffs it fall in love."

"There's no such thing, Daniel. Ye must know that. Unless . . . Have ye been drinking?"

"No, dammit."

"Who d'ye want to fall in love with 'ee?"

"Who d'ye think? Don't be such a twit, Tam. And I know ye have the means for it. I've heard ye brew up such things and sell 'em to the village girls."

"Ye've heard nonsense. But if I had such a potion, I'd give it to 'ee whilst ye were looking upon yer fiancée. Ye can't be chasing after Bret now. 'Tes too late. She's no longer in yer destiny cards."

"Then who is?" he demanded.

"Verity. See?" She showed him a layout of colorful images on the table in front of her hearth. "There she is—the Empress, or sometimes the Queen of Coins. She's of the earth, like 'ee. She'll grow even earthier as ye both get older. She's coming into her own."

"I don't love Verity. I'm using her, I know, and for that I'm sorry, but I don't feel for her what I feel for Bret."

"Ye don't know what ye feel. Ye want her because ye can't have her. Ye've always wanted what ye cannot have."

He slammed his right fist into his left palm, all the more frustrated because he sensed she was right. Without his knowing how or when it had happened, the chance for loving Bret had passed him by.

"She's out of yer element. Verity's yer true match. There were feelings between the two o' 'ee before Bret was even born."

This, he realized, was true. He still remembered Verity from the schoolyard, scared and stubborn and angry like he was, trying desperately to shape her own life.

"Ye'll never have Bret," Tamara said. "Her path lies elsewhere."

"She says she's marrying Marrick. Do yer precious destiny cards confirm that?"

Tamara shrugged. " 'Tes yer own fate I'm looking at, not Simon Marrick's. Yer path has always lain with Verity. As does yer future, for she's carrying yer child."

The child. Yes, dammit, he wanted the child. As for the lovemaking that had started it, yeah, he wanted that as well. He and Verity had always been good together in bed. "If she can keep the pregnancy. She's always miscarried before."

"She'll keep it unless ye drive it out of her."

"What the hell does that mean?"

"Ye know well enough what it means, I warrant."

Guilt washed through him. Verity was his true match, she'd said. But how could he love someone whose business he was systematically dismantling?

"If all goes well ye'll have a boy, an heir," Tamara said. "Ye'll have a son to inherit the entire Trevor estate. A Carne. Now what, I wonder, would Pa have to say about that?"

Are 'ee happy now, Pa?

Are 'ee?

Chapter Fifty-four

As he circled his Camel around his base in eastern France, Zach Slayton's stomach roiled. He felt as if he'd been drinking rattlesnake oil. His head was aching, causing pain to radiate into his shoulders and back. He was exhausted. In the week since the armistice he, along with the other men of his squadron, had been cleaning up the detritus of war. There were still missions to fly, but he'd gone from combat pilot to messenger boy, shuttling information about the Allied withdrawal back and forth from the command posts to what remained of the front lines. The men wanted to go home. He was working to facilitate their withdrawal.

This morning's mission had been to convey a pouch of communiqués to the French. He was grateful to set his machine firmly on the ground, for he seemed to be coughing now as well. There were knives in his chest. Must be the flu. Everybody had the blasted sickness. It was ravaging the troops like some hell-cursed medieval plague. Guys were dying of it.

He stumbled into his tent and hit the cot, kicking off his boots on the way. An hour later he woke up shivering. With one hand he searched the floor for a blanket, cursing weakly when he couldn't find one. He called out for someone to toss the bloody blanket on top of him, but it was lunchtime and he was alone in the tent. His head hurt too much to sit up, so he curled up his legs, turned on his side, and huddled to get warm. Despite the pain and the chill, unconsciousness swallowed him.

There were dreams. He was in the desert southeast of Phoenix in July, without water. Around him were sandgrasses and cacti, sagebrush and brittlebush and chaparral. Bret was smiling at him and saying, "Tell me about the desert." Circling him were coyotes and prairie dogs and hummingbirds and cactus wrens. "You lousy American son of a bitch," she shouted at him, which seemed too mild a rebuke. He had loved her. He had never told her. He had abandoned her.

Where was she, the woman who had loved him wholly and unselfishly, who'd made him laugh, who'd touched his heart? Did she still love him? Would she ever forgive him? Or would she always hate him for betraying the best part of himself?

There was no water on the desert. The heat seared his lungs. He could not breathe. He heard Bret say, "Tomorrow's a million years away." She was wrong. There were no tomorrows.

He heard voices, but couldn't tell if they were part of his dreams: "Hey, Slayton! Jesus. We'd better get him out of here."

"Heavy son of a bitch, isn't he?"

"Fine chap, especially for a Yank. Hope they can save him."

"Those butchers? Hah! All they're good for in that makeshift hospital tent is chopping off gangrenous limbs."

"They save a lot of chaps."

"They lose a lot more."

Zach muttered that they weren't losing him because he was damn well going to find Bret and take her home with him to Arizona, but he didn't think they heard him, whoever they were.

By day, Cadmon Hall was still a house of mourning. By night, life stirred within its walls. Since Armistice Day Bret and Simon had been sleeping in the same bed. When Verity complained that the servants were talking, Bret laughed and said she was sure they found Daniel's nocturnal visits more exciting than Simon's, who lived here anyway.

She never actually saw Daniel coming to her sister. But since her return to Cornwall, she'd taken care never to wander about the house at night. And she always locked her door. Even now that they were both betrothed to other partners, she and Daniel could not meet without embarrassment. This did not help matters with her sister, who was increasingly tight-lipped and short-tempered as the deadlines for her new line of china bore down upon them.

There was no time for creative wrangling. Since it was essential to have a line of dinnerware ready for the Christmas trade show, Bret tried harder to give Verity what she wanted. She finally settled on a design that suited them both—ethereal white doves against a powder blue background. Each of the plates had a rim scalloped with interlocking outstretched wings. Except for the molding on the rim, the ware was simple, and highly elegant. Verity was delighted.

"The trouble is, my heart's not in it," Bret said one night to Simon. "I can't pursue my own vision here. I hope she doesn't grow to depend on me too much."

Coughing, Simon observed that there were already too many people depending on her.

When she was with him, she gave herself completely. But in response to his requests that she name the day they would marry, she held back. Not quite now. Not quite yet. She was waiting. For what, she did not know.

In recent weeks she had convinced herself that love's passion, its beating of the blood, its obsessive thinking, its strange sense of time stretching into eternity, its whispering fear coming up from the darkest parts of your mind that you weren't worthy, or good enough somehow . . . that all these things had nothing to do with the firm and lasting bond that could unite two people through every kind of horror and heartbreak.

And yet . . . what about the feeling of perfect empathy, perfect unity she had known with Zach? That sense that they were two souls standing up together before God?

There was no point agonizing about it, she knew. She had made her decision. Zach might be her soulmate, but Simon was her dearest friend, and right now he needed her more.

He was dreaming of Montana, where he'd lived as a boy. The rolling grasslands under a wide sky that perversely seemed to crowd him, pressing down sharp and blue in the summer, amber with the reflection of swollen grain in autumn, harshly pale during the endless winters. A deceptive land, huge, expansive, and cruel in its promises.

He'd been ill in Montana. Diphtheria. Tommy and Grace, his brother and sister, had contracted it too.

It had been years since he'd thought about them. Chubby Tommy, five years old, blond hair that curled in ringlets around his sweet face. Always screaming with laughter, chasing butterflies. And Gracie, just the opposite—unusually mature and serious at age nine, with brown hair and chocolate eyes and creamy skin that men would ache to caress when she achieved her womanhood. He'd called her Princess. He'd teased her by kneeling at her feet, predicting that she, with her gravity and wisdom, would rule great kingdoms. Grace had adored him. Both she and Tommy had followed him everywhere. They'd wanted to do everything he could do, have everything that belonged to him.

What had he given them? The fever. He'd caught it from a girl he'd been trying—at twelve—to kiss. Later, horseplaying with his brother and sister, not realizing he was sick, he'd passed it on.

Both Zach and the girl of his youthful passion had survived. Tommy and Grace had died horribly, gasping for breath.

He ought to have died with them. Even his mother had believed that. Never would he forget the way she'd looked at him over the pathetic little corpses of her two younger children. Weeping, she'd whispered, "You're my own surviving child. But how can I ever forgive you for bringing this plague into our home?"

You lousy American son of a bitch. Did you think I wouldn't find out that you killed your sister and brother and that your own mother rejected you?

He was in a dark house with many rooms. He wandered through it, opening the doors. It was a house of the dead, his dead. His grandfather. Tommy and Grace. The young pilots he'd instructed, only to see them fall. The squadron mates he'd led into battle, only to watch their aeroplanes explode. They were all there. Room after room, each filled with those who had gone before.

At the heart of the house was an empty room. He knew as soon as he opened the door. It felt familiar. The room was his.

He stepped inside.

Simon was awakened by a piercing cry. Bret was huddled up in bed beside him. She was hugging herself, trembling. Her hair was wild, her skin slick with perspiration. The fear in her eyes was haunting enough to stand the hair in its follicles all over his body. When he reached out to touch her, she spun away.

"I can't feel him anymore," she said. Tears were sliding down her cheeks. "I could always feel him. Far away, but there, at the edges of my mind. But now that place is empty. I think he's gone."

"Bret, you were having a nightmare. Relax, it's only a dream."

"No, no. It's not a dream. Oh, Simon, I think he's dead."

I hope he's dead, Simon thought for one vicious second, before the better part of him edited the emotion.

She rose from bed and went to the window. Standing there as motionless as one of the statues in the garden below, she stared at the night sky. He wanted to hold her, comfort her, carry her back to bed, but something in her posture forbade it. When he finally asked her what she was doing, she said she was listening. Trying to hear.

But he knew it was more than that. Her lips were moving, repeating the same one-syllable word over and over again. She was calling him. She was sending out her soul.

You'd better be dead, my friend. Because if you're still alive, you've won.

"This one looks pretty far gone. How bad are his lungs?"

"Pneumonia in both, sir."

Zach was aware of something cold resting on his chest. "Still congested, poor devil. Vital signs weak. Fever?"

"Last time we checked, 104.6. It's been up there for nearly forty-eight hours. I was sure we were about to lose him a few minutes ago, but he seems to be breathing easier now."

"Well, he's a healthy-looking specimen, unlike some I've seen. Officer?"

"Yes, sir. RFC. Someone said he's a famous ace."

"One of those cocksure flyboys, 'ey? The way some of them behave, you'd think they'd won the war all by themselves. Try to force some fluids, Sister. Probably won't do any good. This flu's taking the young and healthy ones. Damnedest thing I've ever seen. Get 'em through the war only to watch 'em mown down by influenza."

"Yes, sir."

"I thought most of the RFC chaps were already dead. This one must have thought himself one lucky bastard before the sickness hit. Ah well, *sic transit gloria*."

Zach moved his mouth. "Physician, fuck thyself," he said.

A chuckle. "Check his temp again, Sister. I have a feeling it's breaking."

Something antiseptic and glassy was shoved into his mouth. He gagged. Sister wasn't sympathetic. She held it in until she was finished. "You're lucky, handsome," she told him. "Looks like you're going to live long enough to have your mouth washed out with soap."

But Zach knew it wasn't luck. He'd come back because he'd heard a woman's cry, followed by the insistent chanting of his name.

He remained ill for several days while his lungs cleared and his fever dropped. They kept him abed in the field hospital for close to a fortnight. By the end of that time he was restless and ornery, but he'd recovered with nothing worse to show for his bout with the flu than a hacking cough and the resolve to quit smoking once and for all.

He was lying on a cot in early December when an orderly brought him the mail, or the post, as the Brits called it. There was a letter from his cousin in Arizona, and a mangled envelope, its ink faded. Recognizing Simon's handwriting, he ripped it open. It was dated October 1—more than two months ago—a nasty delay occasioned, probably, by the fast-moving advance of the Allied forces as the German lines broke and the war wound down.

The letter informed him of the death of Bret's father. It went on to detail the Trevors' financial difficulties and to give engineering specifications for the Zephyr. "It still seems incredible to me that you don't love her, won't even write to her," the last paragraph read. "You've broken her heart. But she needs your help now, as do I."

"God damn!" Ignoring his weakness, Zach scrambled from bed.

"I've always loved her," Simon's letter continued. "If you have more serious and honorable intentions toward her than you have so far exhibited, please inform her at once. For my own selfish reasons, I hope you are indeed the cad that your behavior seems to indicate. But for the sake of our friendship, and Bret's peace of mind, I am offering you the chance to prove that you are not."

"You self-righteous son of a bitch, Marrick! Get out of my way," he said to the orderly who tried to restrain him. "I've had it with this germ-laden excuse for a hospital."

"Sir, come back. Where are you going? The doctors won't allow it. I won't allow it."

"Fuck you, fuck the doctors, and fuck the RFC. I've survived the war, I've survived the plague, and by God I ought to be able to survive falling in love. Get out of my way. I'm going to tell my girl I love her and ask her to be my bride."

Chapter Fifty-five

Bret was riding Wulf on the day Zach Slayton came to Trenwythan. It was late afternoon and she had ventured high on the moors to seek some wildflower berries recommended by Tamara as a plant dye. She had been experimenting at the china works with new colors in the glaze, and she didn't like the effect she was getting with the materials she had. After finding what she wanted she let Wulf have his head, and together they soared over the hoary ground, breathing the sharp air that smelled of the coming of winter.

She was on her way home when she saw a man hiking up the road toward Cadmon Hall. She was too far away to see him clearly, so she wasn't certain what it was about him that alerted her. No visitors were expected, and it was too late in the day for tradesmen.

As she cantered toward the ribbon of roadway, something began humming in her head. Fainter than a heartbeat, it was a vibration she had never thought to hear again in this life. For three weeks she had listened, hearing nothing, seeing nothing. Each day she'd dreaded the arrival of the post, by which she expected to have her worst fears confirmed. But now . . .

As she hastened toward him, the man stopped. He stood in the middle of the road and watched her coming, shading his eyes with the brim of his Western-style hat.

He was very tall. His limbs were loose and bony, his shoulders broad and strong. He wore a bushy mustache and she could swear there was a dimple in his chin.

"Well, would you look at that, Wulf. The rat is alive."

Restraining the impulse to whoop like an Indian, she cantered down slowly, drinking in the sight of him, loving him, hating him, alternately wanting to sweep him off his feet—

which were shod, she noted, in cowboy boots—and lash him with her riding crop until he belly-yelled for mercy.

"You shameless bastard, Zach Slayton." She raised her crop as, for a moment, she was angry enough to do it. But he moved in on her before she was able to. Wulf's nostrils flared before he was calmed by a murmur from the slick American cowboy, who proceeded to grab Bret around the waist and swing her down.

"God, you're lovely. Is this Wulf? He's lovely, too." He tried to kiss her. She evaded his lips. The rascal actually grinned at this, although his eyes revealed a deeper seriousness. "I know everything you're thinking. And you're right. I deserve your anger. I was a first-class bastard. I've come to make amends."

"If you think you can just come strolling back into my life, after all this time without a line, without a word—"

"I don't think that. It was rotten, I admit, but—"

"How come you're so skinny?" she interrupted. Her emotions were flying all over the place. "Have you been wounded? Ill?"

"I had the flu. Goddamn doctors gave me up for dead, but I surprised them."

"I thought you were dead. I was sure of it. One night I woke up screaming."

He brushed her cheek with his knuckles. "I heard you scream. It brought me back." Holding her face still, he gently touched her lips with his.

Bret burst out in tears. His kiss—and her instant, powerful response to it—told her that she had made a terrible mistake. She had underestimated the strength of this bond; the temptation of this body. But she was committed now to Simon. It was a promise she would never break.

"What?" he whispered.

"Oh, Zach, it's too late." She held out her left hand, showed him the betrothal ring Simon had given her. "I'm going to marry Simon."

He pulled her closer. She could feel his chin resting gently on the top of her head. "I was afraid of that."

She inhaled his smell. He was here. He was all she wanted. He was forbidden to her.

* * *

When the woman he loved slid down from the horse the Phoenix was leading, Simon felt a surge of rage such as he had never experienced before. *No*. Not this time. This time he wasn't going to be shunted aside. This time, dammit, he would fight.

It proved to be a bizarre reunion. As he walked down the steps of Cadmon Hall to greet them, Simon saw Verity and Daniel drive up in Carne's motorcar. Her face nearly as red as her hair, Bret made the introductions: "Verity, Daniel, this is Major Slayton. Zach, this is my sister and her fiancé, Daniel Carne. Simon, Zach's come. He was ill but now he's fine. Zach, Simon and I hope you'll be able to stay for the wedding."

Unsmiling, Zach nodded to Simon. His gaze moved on, curiously, to Daniel Carne. Verity glanced from Simon to Zach to Daniel. Her hands rested over her belly, and Simon could have sworn she was biting back a smile. Daniel dismissed him, the way he always did, to glare at Zach with slitted eyes. Zach picked up on this and glared right back, cold as a gunslinger at noon.

You're making a mistake, Slayton. I'm your rival, not Daniel Carne, Simon thought.

The tableau, which had lasted no more than a couple of seconds, dissolved as Zach turned to Simon and enveloped him in a bear hug. "Hey, kid, I've missed you. You look like shit."

Simon returned the hug more fervently than he would have thought possible. *I love this man*, he reminded himself. "You're no prize yourself, Slayton."

"Yeah, well, I nearly bought it, after all. How's the spine? Looks like you're walking okay."

"The spine's healed; it's the lungs that are killing me."

"Nah," Zach said, obviously not believing it. "You look pretty good, actually. Bret's done wonders for you."

"You're right. She has."

"Well, uh, congratulations. She's one helluva girl. Can't stay for the wedding, though. Got to get back to Arizona."

* * *

As soon as she met him, Verity felt a strong affection for Zach Slayton. She found him handsome, with that tall, lanky body and that impudent mustache. And she found him charming. He had the frank and easy manner that she'd always associated with Americans, a mysterious quality that always made Englishmen seem stiff in comparison. And there was something very moving about the sight of him hovering so close to Bret, clearly itching to touch her, and, however he might try to hide it, hurt and angry that he could not.

They belonged to each other. Anyone could see it. For the first time since her sister had returned to Trenwythan, Verity felt her fear and jealousy ease. Whatever passion Bret had felt for Daniel must have ended, irrevocably, when Zach had come into her life.

As my fear loosens, Verity thought sadly, *poor Simon's is increased.*

Supper that night was rife with undercurrents. The three men at the table had all been lovers of her sister. Everybody was bending over backward to pretend they didn't know this . . . or didn't care.

In spite of this—or because of it—it seemed to Verity that the conversation was inspired. Slayton gave an account of the last days of the war. He and Simon talked about the future of aviation. Daniel talked about the future of china clay. Verity talked about her plans for the china company. Only Bret had little to say.

They ate off Cadmon Clay's new line of china. "I wanted to test it," Verity told Zach. "To see how it looked on a dining table before I had the courage to show it in the Christmas trade show."

Zach held up a quarter plate and examined the new blue china with its delicate enameling and its rim of tiny interlocking doves. "Damned if I know anything about it, but it sure looks good to me. I like the wings on the rim. Seems appropriate somehow. It's an intriguing combination, aeroplanes and china. You'd never expect the same family to be involved in both."

"We won't be in aviation much longer," Verity replied.

"Nonsense," Simon said. "The Zephyr's about to make a comeback."

"I can't believe ye're actually planning to fly that deathtrap again," Daniel said.

"There's nothing wrong with her," said Bret.

"No? Ye've had two fatal crashes with that machine. 'Twould be irresponsible and reckless to put it up again."

"Not necessarily," said Zach. "If the accidents were caused by pilot error, there's no reason to blame the plane. I've had a look at the plans Simon sent me. I can't find any obvious flaw."

"And I've checked her thoroughly mechanically," said Simon. "She's a fine machine."

"The Zephyr's the way of the future," said Zach. "She's big enough to move cargo. All you need is a little favorable publicity. Get her back in the air with a few press people around to write the story and Henry's company will be taking orders again."

"Do you really think so?" Verity asked.

"Sure. Guaranteed."

"I hope you're right, because I'm running out of time. It doesn't look as if I'll be getting any significant orders for my china until after the trade show. Nobody seems to remember Cadmon Clay and Porcelain's history as a manufacturer of fine china. When you're as small a company as we are, you can't get the necessary publicity."

"We get too much publicity in aviation," said Zach. "I guess that's because of the thrills, the danger of dying. Half the time I think the spectators are secretly hoping for a crash."

"It doesn't seem fair, I must say, that the press will rush up here to record the flight of a failing aviation company but won't write a word about a potentially successful china works."

"Well now, ma'am, the curious thing about the press is that you've got to know how to manage them. They'll write just about anything if you can convince them you've got a story that people'll pay to read about."

Staring at Zach Slayton, Verity had that nerve-tingling

frisson of excitement she recognized from earlier moments of inspiration. She was thinking the Zephyr and china, the trade show and the press, air transport and publicity, and suddenly it all fused. She needed to ship her china to London for the trade exhibition. Bret and Simon needed to demonstrate that air transport was practical and, above all, safe. Both Trevor Aviation and Cadmon Clay needed a healthy dose of favorable publicity. What if all these needs could be combined?

"Can you fly cargo in the Zephyr?" she asked Simon.

"That's the plan. It was originally intended as a bomber, but now that the war's over there's no need to load her with ordnance."

"Fragile cargo?"

"Why not, as long as it's well packed."

Verity's excitement must have caught Bret's attention, because she leaned forward, her long hair brushing the surface of the table. "What cargo, Verity? What do you have in mind?"

"China. I can hardly believe I'm saying this, but I'm thinking of using one of Papa's wretched aeroplanes to fly my china to the London trade show."

Bret's smile brightened the entire room. "What a splendid idea! I'll go too. I can see the headlines now—'Inventor's daughter trusts china—and herself—to father's doomed flying machine.' "

Daniel scraped his chair back from the table. "Ye must be mad," he said to Verity. "Ye're going to destroy yer aeroplane, kill yer sister and yer stepson, and vaporize yer china, to boot."

"Only if she crashes," said Bret. "Which she won't."

"I'm glad ye're so bloody sure about that. I'm not," he said darkly and stalked out.

Verity started to rise to go after him, then thought better of it. When his temper flared, Daniel was impossible. "What if he's right?" she said. "We all want the Zephyr to fly again, but not at the risk of anybody's life. The only person who could have verified the aeroplane's airworthiness is Papa, and he's dead. Unless—" She paused, aware that she had Zach Slayton's complete attention. And Simon's, who was looking at her as if he would like to wring her neck. *Don't finish the thought*, she ordered herself. *You'll be causing unnecessary heartache to the people you love the most.*

But it was too late. Zach was with her; they all were. "I can verify it," he said slowly. "From a design point of view at least. Give me some time with her. I'll stay a couple of weeks and go over her inch by inch. If she's safe to fly, I'll take her up myself."

"I'd appreciate that," said Verity, avoiding everybody's eyes.

"I'm sure Zach wants to get back to Arizona." Bret's voice sounded shaky. "He's been away from home for more than four years."

"Hell, what's a few more weeks? I'd be happy to lend a hand."

"How could you, Verity? I don't want him to stay."

"I'm sorry. I was thinking aloud. I didn't know where it was leading."

"Simon's barely spoken a word since dinner. He's scared. I hate to see him this way."

"The truth is, Bret, we do need his help. Would you rather Simon flew the wretched machine without first knowing it was airworthy?"

"No, of course not. But this is an impossible situation. Dammit, Verity. I should have entered a convent at the age of sixteen."

Verity smiled. "You in a convent? Ha."

Bret made love to Simon that night with a passion that bordered on desperation. He was no less ardent. Any lingering doubts she may have had about his sexual sophistication were extinguished when he used his mouth on her, over and over, not allowing her to stop. She was sweaty and exhausted when he finally finished with her. And she could not help but wonder whether anyone else in the house had heard her noisy cries.

Because she thought he was asleep, she was startled, and deeply ashamed, when he leaned over an hour later and brushed the tears from her cheeks. "Bret, don't," he said heavily.

"I'm sorry. I don't know what's the matter with me."

"You love him, that's what's the matter. For chrissake, if that's the way you feel, go to him. Go to him and get out of my sight."

"Stop it. I love you. I'm not going anywhere."

"No good can come of betraying your feelings. It just isn't right."

"Stop talking that way. What's right is for us to be together."

"I don't want a woman with a divided heart."

"You can grouse all you want, but you're stuck with me. He had his chance. It's over."

"I'd give anything to believe that."

"Trust me, Simon. Please."

In the bedroom they had given him, Zach willed her to come to him. Maybe after everybody else was asleep.

He waited, shifting restlessly. An hour crawled by and nothing happened. She must be with Simon. Damn her. Damn him.

He tried to convince himself that Simon was better for her. A gentle, kind man who would never fail her, never disappoint her, never run away. Hell, he loved Simon nearly as much as he loved Bret. He wanted what was best for both of them.

Yeah, right, Slayton. Sure you do.

If she did come, he would have to send her away. Only the scroungiest louse in the universe would romance his best friend's bride.

You should have waited for me, Bret. Never mind that I gave you nothing to believe in, nothing to hope for. Love endures, you told me. You should have trusted your heart.

She would come to him, he knew it. Right or wrong, the currents running between them were that hot, that strong. She would come, and he wouldn't be able to send her away. She would come, and he would love her. She would come, and he would never leave her again.

The dawn was showing behind the trees when at last, lonely, jealous, miserable, he slept.

Chapter Fifty-six

"So which one of us is going to take her up and test her out?" Zach asked Simon a few days later.

They were standing on the south field alongside the Zephyr, which they had put through every conceivable test on the ground to determine its airworthiness. There was nothing left to do but to fly the thing.

"I'm running the company for Bret. It's my responsibility," Simon said.

"Nonetheless, I think it had better be me. You're engaged to be married. If something goes wrong, I'm the more expendable."

"That's a ridiculous thing to say. Besides, nothing's going to go wrong."

"Anything could go wrong at any time. What's more, if it does, I'm better equipped to handle it."

"How do you reach that conclusion?"

"Simple. I survived three full years flying combat missions for the RFC. You lasted less than two. I'm the better pilot. QED."

"I got shot down trying to save your bloomin' ass." But Simon knew that Zach was the better pilot. There were some things you couldn't argue with, and the Phoenix's preternatural prowess in the air was one of them. As for the other areas in which the American excelled, he chose not to think about those.

All the fondness Simon had ever felt for his former squadron leader had come flooding back. He enjoyed having him around. As a friend, as a brother, Zach was incomparable—

affable, eager to help out, quick to laugh. Even as a rival, Simon couldn't fault him. Despite the obvious tension that shot through his body whenever he was around her, Zach had been scrupulously well behaved with Bret. As far as Simon had been able to tell, he had not pursued or tempted her in any manner.

But he was here, and that was all it took to make Bret misty-eyed and distant. She smiled less frequently. She almost never laughed. She made love frantically, as if seeking a place where she could be blind to the knowledge that she was in bed with the wrong man. She never admitted this, of course, but Simon felt it daily, and it was grinding him down.

There was something between Bret and Zach that never relented, never disappeared. North pole and south, they strained toward each other, causing massive disruption in the magnetic field around them, around everybody.

No three people had ever been more polite, more civilized. No three people had ever been more miserable.

"Why don't we toss a coin," Zach said.

For an instant Simon thought he was proposing this as the way to decide Bret's future, then he realized they were still on the subject of who was going to fly the Zephyr.

They tossed, and Zach won.

Zach was strapping himself in when he heard the clunk of boots against the fuselage. Bret climbed up on the struts and leaned into the cockpit. She had a furrow between her eyes.

All he could think of was that she was closer to him than she'd been since the day he'd arrived. He could see her breasts, smell her scent. If he dragged her aboard, they could fly off together, never coming down, never touching the ground.

"I'm scared, Zach."

"Hey, don't be. I know what I'd doing."

"But what if you're wrong? Maybe my father made a mistake. Maybe he couldn't bear to admit it and flew the Zephyr defiantly, that final time."

"No. She's a lovely machine. Perfect." He touched her

worried brow with his gloved index finger. He could have sworn she arched into the contact, like a cat. "Don't worry. Your plane'll soar and your loans'll be repaid."

"It isn't the plane I'm worried about," she said, low.

"Well, don't agonize on my account. I may die in an aeroplane one day, but this isn't going to be the one that kills me."

"How do you know?"

"An old Indian woman told me I'd live to be an old man, and I figure, after surviving three years in France, that she must have known what she was talking about."

"Be careful," she whispered and did the thing she never did—kissed him on the mouth, a quick hard kiss that made him groan. "Christ, Bret. How can I concentrate on flying if all I can think about is what it would be like to get you beneath me and—"

"Stop it," she cut in. "Get your mind into the right place for this, Zach, or I'm not letting you take off."

"Don't kiss me, then. Don't even get near me. Don't come whispering in my ear, telling me you're afraid and begging me to be careful."

"I'm sorry." Her face looked stricken.

He sighed. "Just get down, okay? It looks as though the sky's clouding up a bit. I want to get this over with while the weather's still fine."

She twisted her head to gaze at the sky. "In Cornwall when the fog rolls in the visibility drops to zero in no time at all. It's dangeerous, Zach. If you see any fog, come in at once."

"Yeah, okay. Clear off, Bret. I'm taking her up."

She jumped down. Simon spun the right propeller while Zach ignited the engine. He moved over to the left side and spun that propeller as well. As Zach started his roll and throttled up, he saw Bret wave. She was mouthing words he couldn't hear over the roar of the engines. He fantasized that she was saying, "I'm yours, Mr. Slayton. How can I marry Simon when I'm still in love with you?"

The Zephyr lumbered along the ground, shaking and rattling, a monstrous object that didn't feel as if it would ever get airborne. Zach had a bad couple of seconds as he approached the speed at which the thing should start to lift. It didn't feel as if it was going anywhere but into yonder rocks, and he was going a bit too fast to abort safely. He pressed the elevator control carefully. *Bret's watching. Don't fuck up.*

She lifted off, gaining all the grace in the air that she lacked on the ground. She handled beautifully, her climb smooth, steady, perfect. *Christ, Henry, what a shining gem of a machine.*

Glancing below, he could see Simon and Bret with their arms in the air, cheering. Their hopes were airborne.

The sky had a dreamy quality about it today. The air was hazy, not entirely clear. Shapes shimmered, appearing less than real. Looking down, he saw Cadmon Hall perched on its bluff, high above the undulating moors. He banked around it and flew over the clay fields, gazing curiously at the pits and skytips, the icy domain of Daniel Carne. He'd met Carne on several occasions and liked him well enough, although he couldn't picture him with Bret. They were too different. Carne never laughed. He had no joy in him. Simon believed the clayman was still in love with Bret, but Zach disagreed. In his estimation Daniel and Verity were fine together—linked minds and kindred spirits.

Like himself and Bret. The thought enraged him. How could she be so set on marrying Simon? He had to stop her. It was all wrong.

He tested the Zephyr's maneuverability as he flew over the uninhabited moors, the rolling grasslands, dry and brown with winter, desolation stretching out on every side. He climbed. He dived. He rolled, making himself sick. With a fervor that verged on recklessness, he stalled her out and started her up again.

Sweet machine. The pilots who had crashed her must have been incompetent, or drunk.

He flew inland toward Bodmin Moor, then back out toward St. Austell Bay. As he neared the coastline he saw at once that the sea was vanishing below as the fog came rolling in. It moved insidiously, at ground level, ghostly fingers creeping over the moors.

Time to take her down.

He headed back toward Cadmon Hall, becoming slightly

alarmed when he saw that the blanket of fog was moving faster than he was. "Terrific," he muttered. "God damn."

He threw her into a landing approach. The visibility was lousy. As he came in over what he thought was the landing field, he couldn't see the ground. He could see Cadmon Hall, though, high on its hill, so he lined up the Zephyr with the picture in his mind of the airstrip's position relative to the house, thanking God he was so observant about such things.

Landing blind. He'd done it before. But someday someone was going to invent some sort of instrument that would help pilots see in bad weather. Aviation would never go anywhere as an industry if it remained so damn weather-dependent.

At one hundred feet the strip appeared below him. He was slightly off course, but there wasn't time to correct, and it was too late to take her up again. The damn plane was too big, too heavy, and too close to the ground. He set her down moments later, too roughly for his liking, but under control.

Bret was there when he shuddered to a stop. There was an elusive quality about her that he had never noticed before. Far beyond him, unreachable, part of another world that he could never enter, the world of goddesses, of women. She stood there waiting for him as he climbed out of the cockpit, straight and tall, part of the landscape almost, a crimson-headed poppy, rooted in the moorland, her face turned up to the foggy sky. She swayed as he approached. He thought she would fall, but her mooring held.

She was crying. The loveliness of her cheeks was marred by the tracks of her tears.

"What?" he whispered.

The expression she turned upon him was fierce, and for an instant he felt shy, almost afraid of the little English girl who had grown up calling him Mr. Slayton and scribbling her confidences. He feared her strength, her power, her remoteness, her femininity. He feared that she would irrevocably reject him and cast him out into the cold landscape from which he was trying to escape. Winter in Montana. The bleakness of the freezing plains, the dying buffalo.

"I hate you, Zach."

He moved closer, catching his breath when she backed away. His hands snaked out and fastened to her shoulders.

He felt her twisting in his grasp. "You were going to die. You were going to crash in the fog. I was going to have to watch you die. In my father's doomed aeroplane."

"There's nothing wrong with the plane. It was me. I wasn't paying strict enough attention to what was happening on the ground. That was stupid. I'm sorry."

"You wanted to die. You've always wanted to die. That's how it would always have been between us if we'd stayed together. I'd forever be waiting on the ground, visualizing your death."

"No, Bret. It wouldn't be that way." He allowed his palms to run down her body from her shoulders to her hips. She flinched as his loins responded with a heavy, clenching heat. "Maybe you're right that I wanted to peg out in France. But not any longer. I realized something when I was sick with pneumonia. I've been punishing myself for years. Not letting myself commit to life because something inside me believed I didn't deserve it. That my death was a debt I owed to some people who are no longer with me on this earth. But that feeling's gone now. It's been gone ever since you summoned me back." He shook her slightly. "It's because of you that I'm still here. Dammit, we're supposed to be together."

She pulled away. "I'm marrying Simon."

"I'm tired of listening to that shit. You don't love him. You love me."

"Once that was true, but now—"

Hawklike, he targeted her mouth, attacking swiftly, without mercy. When she fought it, he fastened his fingers in her hair. Thick, silken, fragrant. She smelled and tasted like flowers in the autumn desert, new life after the ravages of summer. And she opened to him, slowly, like the desert rose, clenching at first but gradually relaxing her corolla to the sun, becoming soft and sweet and willing.

When he released her she turned away, drooping. He touched her cheek, saw her tears. Christ, he hated that. He wanted her to be Bret, his Bret. He wanted her to throw back her head and laugh.

"I can't betray him. I won't disappoint him. He's been through hell already, and it's going to get so much worse."

"Look, I love him too. He's my best friend. Do you think

I want to take you away from him? Do you think I asked for this?''

''No, of course not, but—''

His hands made another pass over her body. She moved forward until they were plastered together; neither could let the other go. ''Bret. Listen to me. This is something that will not be denied.''

''It must be denied.''

''Is Simon Marrick your heart's true desire?''

''He's my oldest, dearest friend. He's been faithful to me and loyal. He's—''

''Is he your heart's desire?''

''Stop it, Zach.''

''Who is your heart's desire?''

''I don't love you. I won't marry you.''

''Who, Bret?'' He was shaking her again, not violently, but enough to send her hair ribboning in all directions. A long strand of it wound around his throat. ''Who is your fucking heart's true desire?''

''Go to hell!''

''Who, dammit? Who?''

''You are!'' She all but screamed it at him.

''Then marry me.''

''I can't.''

''Marry me.''

''No.''

''Bret, I love you.'' The words he could never bring himself to say hung in the air between them. ''Please marry me.''

Her face softened, her eyes cleared; he thought he'd won. She smiled fleetingly, that old joyous, intrepid smile. Her lips touched his cheek, just above the corner of his mouth. ''Simon's dying, Zach. He won't talk about it; he doesn't want anyone to know. His lungs are useless. He's getting worse.''

''Jesus, Bret, is that why—''

''He's given me so much over the years. He deserves something back. I'm going to stay with him, until the end.''

Stunned, he watched her walk away. Simon dying? Sure, the kid looked like hell and coughed like the very devil, but

Zach hadn't added it up. Just about everybody who'd been to the front had come back looking like a warmed-over corpse.

Jesus. Simon. Jerkily, he lit a cigarette and took a long hard pull. He'd cut down on smoking for a while after having the flu, but the tension of the last few weeks had scuttled that.

It was one thing, he decided, to try your best to lure the woman you loved—the woman who loved you—away from a rival who wasn't right for her, but it was something else entirely to steal the only comfort of a condemned man.

Damn. He was going to have to leave.

"You're sure you won't change your mind and stay for the flight?" Bret asked Zach the following morning at the St. Austell station.

"Nope." They were standing on the platform, beside his train. "It's been too long since I last saw the desert."

Tell me about the desert. Keep talking until you can't speak anymore.

"Your Zephyr'll fly like the wind. You and Verity and the china company will be the toast of London."

"I wish you could see it happen."

"Look, I can't. I've hung around for too long as it is." He shifted his duffel bag from one hand to the other. "It's no good for him—my being here. Christ, we were close friends. Skin-tight. We saved each other's lives on numerous occasions. I can't stick around and hover, like a vulture waiting to feed."

"I know. You're absolutely right. But—"

He took her face between his palms and kissed her. Their mouths met and clung; separating was torture. "Take care of him."

"I will."

The locomotive was chugging, ready to embark. Bret was remembering another train . . . running to catch it, Zach's strong arms wrapping around her and slinging her on board. Zach in the moonlight, his body damp with passion. In a river, flycasting gracefully, effortlessly, always taking trout. In the cockpit of the Zephyr, laughing in the teeth of death.

"Zach—"

Once again he jerked her close. His kiss was ferocious, tongue and teeth. "Come with me, my love."

"You're a shameless bastard, aren't you? Get on the bloody train."

"You wrote to me once that love endures. You might give up on everything else, you said, but you'd never give up on love."

She was crying. She made no attempt to stop the tears.

"It will endure," he said. He touched her hair gently. Then he kissed her one last time and climbed aboard. "Will you write to me? Like in the old days?"

She managed a soggy smile. "Yes, Mr. Slayton. Of course."

He remained in the doorway as the train pulled away from the platform. He blew her a kiss. Weeping, she watched until the train vanished into the fog.

Chapter Fifty-seven

Three days before the Zephyr's scheduled flight, Bret awakened with a vicious headache and a cough. She got up anyway, doing her best to ignore her symptoms. Just a cold, she told herself. Nothing to fuss about. But halfway through breakfast she doubled over in a fit of coughing. The pain in her head, back, and limbs was frightening in its intensity. "I'm all right," she insisted when Verity and Simon expressed alarm.

Her sister's palm felt cool upon her forehead. "You're feverish. That settles it, you're not going to fly."

"I can't be sick, and I have to fly. The press will be here. They love the brave-daughter angle."

"They'll have to do without. I've just been told that we've

got a scullery maid and a parlor maid down with the flu this morning. You probably have it, too.''

"It's not the flu, and I'll be better tomorrow," Bret said, even as she shifted her chair away from Simon. She was more afraid for him than she was for herself.

"Of course it's the flu. And you're going straight to bed."

"Damn, damn, damn!" she cried.

By evening she was worse, and Verity was worried. Dr. Cowan came from the village and diagnosed influenza. New horror stories about the epidemic were recounted every morning in the newspapers: The war widow who had nursed her six children through the illness, only to die of it herself; the impeccably dressed banker, strolling down Oxford Street, who'd collapsed in the gutter, dead; the bulging hospitals where doctors and nurses were as sick as their patients; the overflowing mortuaries that could not open graves quickly enough.

"We'll postpone the flight," Verity told Bret that evening as she spooned consommé down her sister's throat.

"You can't. You can't change the date of the trade exhibition. Much as I hate to say it, you'll probably have to go ahead without me. Where's Simon? Is he all right?"

"He's camping outside your door. Arthur Cowan forbade him to enter, but he's not too pleased about it."

"He shouldn't even be in the same house with me. You shouldn't either. You've got your baby to think about."

"I'm not worried," Verity said. She leaned over and smoothed a limp strand of hair away from her sister's fevered brow. "I had all the symptoms of this flu a couple of months ago, just before Papa died. Fortunately I was able to throw it off in a few days."

"Well, that's good. I don't think you can get it again."

"As for Simon, there's nowhere safe to go. Dr. Cowan says it's spread throughout the village now."

"Then I'm thankful he'll be flying out of here. Maybe by the time you and he return from London the worst will be over. I can't believe I'm going to miss the flight. What rotten luck!"

"Simon's saying he doesn't want to leave you, Bret. You've always been so healthy. It frightens him to see you ill."

"I'm not that sick, for heaven's sake. It's just a mild case."

To Verity's great relief, this turned out to be true. Bret marshaled her strength and vitality, and by the eve of the Zephyr's flight she was on the mend. Although not down to normal, her fever was lower than it had been the preceding night, and she reported to Verity that the awful muscle pains had relaxed to dull aches. She continued to cough, but Dr. Cowan found no pneumonia in her lungs.

"I think I'll be able to fly tomorrow, after all," she announced when Verity brought in her tea.

"No, Bret, absolutely not."

"Then you'll simply have to take my place in the Zephyr. That way the press will still have their story. It'll be even better, in fact. 'Inventor's daughter fears aeroplanes, but trusts her life to her father's doomed plane.' "

"I'm not getting into an aeroplane. Not now, not ever."

"Think what an adventure it'll be. And how much publicity we'll get. You'll be a heroine. A pioneer. You'll rise up from the ashes of the nineteenth century and soar into a splendid new future."

"The fever hasn't affected your imagination, I see," Verity said.

On the inky, moonless night before the scheduled flight of the Zephyr, Daniel Carne moved silently across the moors to the workings of Wheal Faith, where he descended into the earth. The dynamite was kept in a disused section of the mine, where it would do the least damage should it accidentally ignite. Six sticks ought to be ample to do the job. He unearthed them from a metal trunk and folded them in a square of oilcloth.

Carrying the explosives home, he closed and locked his doors. While he worked, binding the sticks together, attaching the fuse, he permitted himself to think of nothing else but the task ahead of him. No envisioning what would actually happen. No fretting about the unlikely possibility that somebody might be hurt. Stupid to think too much. 'Twas action, not thought, that mattered in the world.

From his vantage point overlooking the south field, Daniel had witnessed the test flight of the Zephyr. He'd felt a reluctant admiration for Bret, whose determination he'd underestimated. Together with Marrick and Slayton—both of whom were obviously besotted with her—she'd brought her father's company back to the point where its survival was a definite possibility. If they were successful in their flight to London, the investments would come pouring in. Verity's debt to James Stannis would be paid in full . . . a denouement that would scuttle all his carefully laid plans.

The survival of Trevor Aviation was something Daniel couldn't allow to happen. *Sorry, Bret, but you have to be stopped*, he thought.

Out of nowhere came an image of her standing beside him on the night they had become lovers, her eyes shining, her long hair streaming fire into the wind.

You weren't going to plant that bomb, after all.

What makes ye think that?

You could never do it. No matter how you feel about my family or Cadmon Clay, you couldn't deliberately damage the workings of the earth you so love.

"Ah, Bret. Looks like ye were wrong about that. Anyway, the Zephyr was not of the earth. 'Twas of the sky, and fair game," he whispered to himself.

Verity was unable to sleep that night. She missed Daniel, whom she'd banished from the house for the duration of Bret's illness. "Don't be daft, I never get sick," he'd objected, but she'd explained that she would be sitting up nights with Bret.

Despite the sensuality that continued to smolder between them, Daniel had been short-tempered and impatient with her ever since she had thrown her support behind the plan to fly the Zephyr. The wedding was only two weeks away, but he could still change his mind. He could disappoint her, the way Papa always had.

She punched her pillow. Damn him. And damn Papa as well.

Rolling over, she tried to settle into a more comfortable position. Soon she was tossing again. Her agitation was natural, she told herself. She was in love. She was pregnant. She was worried about her sister and her stepson. She'd been working too hard.

So much had had to be done to get ready for the trade exhibition, at which buyers from all over the country—and the world—would be present. Her china had had to be finished, crated, and loaded. Brochures and advertisements printed. Salesmen consulted. A demonstration of china decoration by several of her girls was scheduled to take place inside Harrods, in hopes of piquing shoppers' interest. Bret was supposed to have presided, but Annie Trillian would have to take her place.

In addition, there were the aviation people to contact. If the flight of the Zephyr succeeded, would anyone be willing to invest? Or would their dramatic gesture go for naught? Would Trevor Aviation fail anyway, and Cadmon Clay and Porcelain be pulled down with it?

So much to worry about. No wonder she couldn't sleep.

Ten minutes later, she rose, exasperated, and got dressed. She needed Daniel. Since he could not come to her, she would go to him.

"Fuck," Daniel muttered as he nicked himself with the blade he was using to trim the fuse. It had been a while since he'd handled explosives. The union agitator who had taught him during the clay strike had been killed on the Somme.

Tying off the last wire, he set the crude bomb on the desk in front of him. It was compact, ugly, and lethal. He envisioned the explosion it would cause tonight in the deserted hangar. A blast, an uprush of flame, and the crumpling of the flying machine that Bret and Verity had pinned their hopes upon. Included in the inferno would be Verity's china, which had already been loaded into the cargo section of the Zephyr in anticipation of the early-morning flight.

Shit. Maybe this wasn't such a good idea, after all. Destroying Verity's china bothered him even more than destroying the Zephyr. She had worked so hard.

Stop it. No guilt. Only action counts.

He rose, brushing his hands on his trousers. Pulling out his pocket watch, he squinted at it in the dim light of a single oil lamp. Nearly midnight. Time to move.

The sharp rap on his front door sent a wave of sweat down Daniel's backbone. Somebody knew. Somebody had guessed.

Christ, man, get a grip on yerself.

He opened a drawer and placed the explosives—carefully—inside. Then he took a couple of deep breaths to steady himself. As he went to the door, he was seized with the conviction that he would find Bret on his threshold. Just like that wondrous night five years ago when she had come to accuse him of a crime he'd declined to commit.

Another knock, more tentative this time. Instead of going to the door, Daniel moved to a window that looked out over the front steps. Careful to keep his body in the shadows, he peered through the thin curtain. There was a woman standing there. Not Bret, of course. Verity.

Damn. He stood in the darkness, silent, unmoving. He hadn't been with her for several nights. A surge in his groin testified to how much he'd missed that. Bloody sex. It was one of the few things in his life he couldn't control.

If he let her in, he would take her to bed and love her. They would give each other the pleasure they both craved and delighted in. In the process, he would lose the opportunity to destroy her father's wretched aeroplane.

If he didn't let her in, he would spend another night alone.

It was ridiculous, considering all his careful planning, to find himself hesitating, weighing the woman against the aeroplane, lovemaking against a bomb.

Ye're out of yer mind, Carne. What, are 'ee going soft?

She knocked again. From his vantage point at the window he focused on her slim body, her dainty hands, the curve of her throat. It struck him that he'd grown attached to Verity. He admired her firmness, her courage, her determination. He liked her small bones, her lovely breasts. He delighted in the transformation that occurred when they were in bed together. Under his hands, his mouth, his muscles, her primness and rigidity vanished. She turned soft and sensuous. She made frantic little sounds. She reached eagerly for pleasure. She returned it just as avidly. He savored her swelling belly and the knowledge that she was nurturing his child.

Slowly, Daniel stepped away from the window. Fuck the Zephyr. Even if it flew all the way to London, revitalizing Trevor Aviation and saving Cadmon Clay, the final outcome would be the same. Once they were married, he had her. There was no escape.

"Fly, then, damn 'ee," he said softly into the darkness. " 'Tesn't my fate to bring 'ee down."

He opened the door.

Chapter Fifty-eight

"They're here, Miz Marrick, look at 'em," said Annie Trillian, grinning at the news photographers who had come to document the flight of the Zephyr and its cargo of fine china from Cadmon Clay and Porcelain. "Ye'll have yer picture in the newspaper and everybody in England'll know who ye be."

"They'll know your work as well, Annie. They'll know that we're primarily a bunch of women, and that we're as skilled and as clever as any man."

"A damn sight cleverer than most," said Gil Parkins, who would be supervising things at the clay company while Verity was in London. "We've already had calls for orders. Even before pulling this stunt, the word's gotten about."

"One of my first projects for the new year will be to start an advertising and publicity department," Verity said. "It obviously works."

It was a fine day for flying—bright and clear with good weather predicted for the rest of the week. And it was mild for late December, well above freezing. At the request of the reporters, Verity held up samples of her china for the cameras.

The sunlight shining through from behind accented their translucency and delicacy.

Fragile, she thought. *Like human life*. She glanced toward the Zephyr, its huge winged body poised at the end of the airstrip. It was made of light wood and canvas, with metal for the engine parts, and it seemed too flimsy a contraption to fly all the way to London. Papa had gone to his death in an identical plane. Last night after making passionate love to her, Daniel had called her a fool for trusting her future to a strange mechanical device that was not of the earth.

"I have no choice," she'd told him. "I'm up against the wall."

"Ye're a woman, Verity. Soon ye'll be a wife and a mother. Don't ye think 'tes time to give up this obsession?"

"What are you talking about?"

"The bloody clay company. The china factory. All of it."

She'd pushed herself up in bed, troubled to the heart. "I'm not like other women. I thought you understood that. I love you and I will love our child. But I love Cadmon Clay and Porcelain as well. I will never give it up."

Coldly, he'd turned his back and gone to sleep, leaving her to fret about the possibility that marriage to Daniel Carne might prove to be as stifling and inhibiting as marriage to Julian Marrick.

"Where's the daughter?" one of the reporters shouted. "We want to know her feelings as she prepares to risk her life."

Several others in the crowd took up the cry, shouting down Gil as he tried to explain that the daughter who had intended to fly was down with the flu and that the other daughter was going up to London by train.

"The daughter!" they all yelled. "We're here for the daughter, to see her fly."

Verity raised both arms to get their attention. "I'm Verity Trevor Marrick," she told them. "I'm the owner of Cadmon Clay and Porcelain, and it's my china that has been loaded upon the Zephyr. It's a precious shipment—my entire investment in the future of my china company. But I'm fully confident that it will arrive in London without so much as a chip."

Her words elicited a cheer from the crowd. "That's the spirit!" several people cried.

"Still, I expect you're more concerned about your neck than you are about your china," one of the reporters said. "I know I would be. You're a brave woman, Mrs. Marrick. Now let's get a shot of you climbing into the flying machine."

"Actually, it was my sister Bret who—"

"Aren't you the same Mrs. Marrick who broke a clay strike here a few years ago?" somebody else shouted. "You marched in there with a bunch of women and got the claypits operating again." He tipped his hat to her. "You're quite a lady, if you don't mind my saying so."

"Come on, ma'am. Get into the aeroplane."

"Our readers'll love you for this, ma'am! You'll be the toast of London when you land."

The shouting, milling crowd took Verity back to her first day at Cadmon Clay. The gauntlet that the strikers—including Daniel Carne—had tossed at her feet. The boldness and verve with which she had defeated them.

You'll be a heroine . . . a pioneer. You'll rise up from the ashes of the nineteenth century and soar into a splendid new future.

What would it be like to lift from the earth and skim above the trees? To pierce the clouds and enter a realm where the sun always shines? Papa, Bret, and Simon had all experienced it. Even her china was going to be airborne, while she remained on the ground.

It was mad and reckless, but suddenly Verity wanted to soar.

"I'm coming with you," she said to Simon, who was making one final check of the engines. "Where do you want me?"

"Good God, Verity, are you sure?"

"Yes." She was already climbing up onto the wingstrut, and the journalists were gathering around, their pencils poised over their notepads. "I must be mad, but I'm sure."

"Get your cameras ready, everyone! The daughter's ready to fly."

"Good luck, Mrs. Marrick. Happy landings!"

"Any final words before you take off?"

"When I was a little girl," she told them, "my grandfather railed at my father, insisting that his dreams of air travel were nothing more than fairy tales. 'Mark my words,' Papa answered. 'In our lifetime people will fly so effortlessly that the sky will seem familiar, and these earthbound days most strange.' Henry Trevor was right, gentlemen. I trust my father, and I trust his aeroplane. I'll see you in London."

The crowd roared.

I hate *aeroplanes*, Verity was thinking as she settled into the small, cramped spot where Simon had told her to sit.

And yet my future depends on them.

You'd be laughing at me, Papa, if you could see me now.

From the old schoolroom window on the top floor of Cadmon Hall, Bret stared in disbelief through her father's old field binoculars as Verity climbed into the Zephyr. My goodness, she'd suggested it, but she'd never dreamed her sister would actually *do* it.

"Oh, Verity, you darling," she cried, clapping delightedly as the Zephyr lumbered down the airstrip, then lifted smoothly into the air and climbed toward the heavens. Amazing that after all these years, her sister could still surprise her. And make her proud.

Bret followed the Zephyr's progress for as long as it was visible, remembering all the other times when she had done the same with her father's flying machines.

"She's such a lovely aeroplane," she said aloud. "What will happen to her? Will she fly all the way to London?" In her imagination Bret raised a toast to Papa, wishing he were here to see the wonder his creativity had wrought. "She *will* fly all the way to London. And what a wonder that will be!"

It was London, the scene of Verity's mortifying social failure during her nineteenth year, that was now the scene of her greatest triumph. The newspapers had already made her famous. From the moment Simon landed and rolled the Zephyr to a stop, she was besieged with people who recognized and applauded her for her determination and pluck.

After so many years of war, the country needed a heroine, and so she was anointed. It was a role, she thought wryly, that would have been better suited to Bret.

She and her china—which survived the trip intact—were taken by limousine to the trade exhibition, which was crowded with curious spectators. Not only Cadmon Clay but the entire china industry was showered with more publicity than it had ever received before. The next day's morning edition of the *Times* carried a story about the history and manufacture of china, and an historical piece on Cadmon Clay's eighteenth-century porcelain works was featured in the evening edition. As for the decorating demonstration at Harrods, so many spectators turned out to observe the banders and enamelers perform their magic that the exclusive emporium was forced to hire extra security guards to prevent a riot.

On the third day the newspapers unearthed the old story of Julian's heroic sacrifice and retold it, presenting Verity as the brave widow struggling with the additional tragedy of her beloved father's death. This was followed by articles about Bret, the selfless VAD, and Simon, the dashing RFC officer. But no matter how much she protested that she herself had played a small to nonexistent role in the resurrection of the Zephyr, Verity remained the focus of public adulation.

Once a shy and awkward spinster who couldn't find a partner at a society ball, Verity was now everybody's darling. Handsome men paid her extravagant compliments. Wealthy investors offered to pour money into Trevor Aviation and/or Cadmon Clay. Women hurried to the shops to place orders for her china. "Verity Trevor Marrick is the Symbol," the suffragettes trumpeted, "of the magnificent achievement to which all women may finally aspire."

But the moment that amused her the most came at the end of three glorious days in London when she arrived at her aunt Dorothy's home for the obligatory family visit. To the team of reporters who were still following Verity about, Dorothy shamelessly declared:

"I'm sure you'll want to include in your newspaper accounts that *I* was the one who introduced my talented niece to Society. I *knew* she would amount to something one day.

She had such poise, such presence. I used to tell her then how much *potential* she possessed. Oh my goodness, yes. I always predicted she would be a *splendid* success."

Chapter Fifty-nine

As soon as she was up and about again, Bret went to see James Stannis. "We're not going to make your original deadline of December 31, but we'll have the money soon," she explained to him. "Verity rang last night from London to confirm that both the Zephyr and her china are doing smashing business."

"I've seen the newspapers," Stannis said. "You've my most sincere congratulations. Still, fact is, I'm not the one to talk to anymore. I'm out of it."

"What on earth do you mean?"

"Stannis Clay is finished. The war killed us; we can't go on."

"I'm sorry, I had no idea—"

"I thought we'd last a few months longer, but I can't fight him anymore. I'm old and the world is changing. I lost my only son in the war. There's no one to carry on after me, and truth to tell, I don't much care anymore. He's the last person I thought I'd ever get mixed up with, given his deplorable conduct during the clay strike, but there's no denying that he's the best player in the game."

"He, who?" Bret felt the beginnings of a headache. "Are you referring to Daniel Carne?"

"Damn right I am. He's been at me ever since the strike when I wouldn't take him back. The man can certainly hold a grudge."

"I don't understand. What's Daniel got to do with your company's failing?"

"He's been my primary competition, and to put it simply, he's done a better job than I have selling clay. But that aside, he foxed me. Guess he didn't want to take the chance that I'd survive."

"How? What do you mean?"

"Like your father, I took out some loans a year or so ago. I never met the largest of my creditors—it was all done through my bankers. He wanted to remain anonymous. I should have been suspicious, but, hell, I needed the cash. Your father owed me money, and so did several other people, and I've never been much good at twisting people's arms."

"Your anonymous benefactor turned out to be Daniel Carne?"

"Correct. And he's not so reluctant about demanding his due. When he heard that I couldn't meet my payroll, he instructed my bank to call in his loan. It finished me."

Bret was speechless, awed by the extent of her old lover's treachery.

"I'm selling out and he's the only clay owner in the region who's in a position to buy. This much I'll say for him, at least—he's offering me a fair price. As for your father's loan, Carne'll be taking over the note. Technically, it's still due on December 31, but that shouldn't be a problem since your debt's all in the family now. Instead of my having claim to forty-three percent of Cadmon Clay, Daniel Carne'll have it."

"Actually," said Bret, "combining your forty-three with the ten Verity has guaranteed him in their marriage settlement, he'll have fifty-three percent. And full control."

"I have to talk to you," Bret said to her sister as soon as she and Simon returned from London.

"Do you like this frock?" Verity held up a liquidy gray silk dress. "I bought it off the rack at Harrods—the first time I've ever done such a thing. I thought I might wear it for the wedding. It's difficult to know how to dress for a second wedding, especially at a time like this, with our house still in mourning for Papa—"

"Please, Verity, this is difficult." An understatement, Bret thought. She'd been dreading this moment. "While you were gone, I went to see James Stannis to assure him that he would be getting his money, after all."

Holding the new frock up against her, Verity stepped in front of her dressing table mirror. "He must have been relieved."

"No, actually. His clay business is in the process of folding. He's selling everything, including the note to Papa's loan."

"What do you mean? To whom?"

"To Daniel. He, not James Stannis, is your new partner. He owns you, Verity. Marry him under the terms you've agreed to and you'll lose Cadmon Clay."

Looking away from the mirror, Verity shook her head. "No," she said. "I don't believe you."

Bret related the details of the conversation she'd had with James Stannis. As she spoke she watched her sister clutch the new gray frock closer and closer to herself, leaving wrinkles in the fabric.

"Once he gains a majority of the stockholdings," she finished, "he'll be able to do whatever he wants with the company, including shutting down the china works, which he regards as unprofitable. Verity, this is the man you love. He intends to destroy your dream."

There was a long silence. Bret moved to take her sister into her arms, but Verity backed away. The frock she had bought for her wedding slipped from her hands and fell to the floor. "Thank you for telling me," was all she said.

"What are you going to do?"

"I don't know." Verity turned to stare out the window. She felt numb. She noticed, as if from a great distance, that winter was settling onto the moors. The faintest tinges of hoarfrost tipped the grass. She felt an affinity for the cold.

"You have to break him, Verity."

"What do you mean?" Her voice came out in a whisper.

"You have to slice him open and find whatever remnants are left of his heart. I know him. He's not evil. He's your lover and the father of your child. He'll change for you, if you force him to.''

Break him. Two images were assailing Verity. The first was the Fiery Furnace, steaming, churning, ready to explode. The second was a gold-haired man with an evil smile on his face and a shepherd's pipe to his lips. Jory Carne. ''He'll break me first.''

''No. Nothing'll ever break you, Verity.'' More lightly, she added, ''You're a heroine, remember. That's what it says in all the newspapers, so it must be true.''

''I'm no heroine.'' Verity was shaking her head. ''But no one, not even Daniel, is going to destroy my dream.''

In her cottage on the lonely moors, Tamara felt something gathering. She tried to calm herself by separating anxiety from precognition. But something gathered still.

She laid out the destiny cards. Cups and coins as well, crossing each other. The world of the emotions being assailed by the practical world of money, business, financial affairs. The Fool, dancing on the edge of a precipice. The Devil, deep in his cave, holding man and woman in thrall. Worst of all, the Tower, blown apart by lightning, with tiny human figures tumbling to earth.

She tried to concentrate, to understand. What were the images trying to tell her?

But she could find no answer. Her mind insisted on replaying the words to the old curse upon the Trevors and the Carnes:

May passion's poison o-erflow each vein,
May they know naught but conflict and strife,
May their lads be crushed by the sin of Cain,
May their lasses breed hatred in each new life.

Frustrated, she spread the cards again, several times. The same images came up. Cups, coins. The Fool. And the Tower. *La Maison de Dieu.* Catastrophe. Destruction.

Chapter Sixty

Daniel was drinking. It was not a vice that he indulged in often, and when he did take a nip, he was always careful to limit himself to a single glass. But tonight he had broken that personal rule. Tonight he didn't give a damn.

Verity was back from London. She was famous. A bloody heroine. Just like during the clay strike, but on a much grander scale. She was triumphant, this woman who was carrying his child.

He wasn't drinking because of that. No, it was something subtler. Something to do with his own soul.

Investors or no investors, Verity would never get the money before the last day of the year. He had her. In a few days, they would be married. He'd have everything he'd ever wanted. Then what?

No one had ever told him that when ye got everything ye'd ever wanted, ye'd better set yourself another goal. All the heat, all the excitement, all the passion was in the striving. The actual *having* wasn't so wonderful after all.

Anyway, there was one thing he'd never thought to desire, but without it his victory simply wasn't enough. He'd never thought to desire a good opinion of himself.

Treacherously, he had outwitted a couple of women. But they, not knowing they were beaten, had taken to the sky.

What was the difference between Verity Trevor Marrick and Cadmon Clay and Porcelain? Had they become one and the same? If he destroyed her business, would he do irreparable harm to the woman? Would she never forgive him, this stiff-spined yet all-too-vulnerable woman who had, without his noticing it, brought warmth, trust, and companionship into his lonely life? Would she continue to love him? And why, dammit, did it suddenly matter so much?

Any woman is proud of her man as long as he is acting honorably.

Daniel Carne was not particularly proud of himself.

He was well into his third glass of gin when he heard a knocking on his cottage door. He rose, surprised at the dizziness he felt. Unlike Pa, he wasn't accustomed to the effects of too much booze.

Once again there was a woman on his doorstep. Verity.

England's high-flying heroine was haggard and pale. The night was wild . . . a blast of frigid air accompanied her inside. His arms went around her automatically, wanting to warm her, shield her from the wind, the cold. She brought out strong protective feelings in him, especially since he'd found out about the child.

" 'Tes hardly the sort of night for 'ee to be out and about, lass. Why didn't ye ring? I'd have come over and saved 'ee the trip.''

She shrugged off his arm and put a distance between their bodies. She rounded the table where he'd been drinking and faced him from the opposite side. "I came here because I did not wish to receive you in my house. Not tonight, or ever again.''

"What the hell does that mean?"

"The worst of it is that I dug this hole for myself. I knew what you were and I chose to ignore it.''

"Verity, what is this?"

"I know about James Stannis. Bret went to him while I was in London to explain that the money we owe him would be available soon and to beg him for a little more time.''

He blew out a deep breath. "So that's it.''

"Yes, Daniel, that's it.''

"And Stannis told her that she'd better come and do her begging to me. Which, a'course, she would not do.''

"Is that what you wanted? Bret on her knees?"

"Of course not.''

"There, at least, you're probably telling the truth. If Bret— or me—on her knees was what you'd wanted, you wouldn't have been so devious. No, what you wanted was a marriage settlement that gave you ten percent of my company combined with a bad loan that gave you an additional forty-three percent. What you wanted was to snake Cadmon Clay right out from under my nose.''

''Verity, for God's sake.''

''You've had this planned for months, haven't you? You systematically ruined James Stannis. I saw that coming; what I failed to understand was why. I thought it was because of your old grudge against him, but it was more than that. You knew that once you had him where you wanted him, you also had me.''

''I had 'ee anyway. Don't be such a fool.''

''You didn't have me. Not in any way that counts. In bed, yes, there I've been a fool for you. But where the real power in a marriage is concerned I learned my lesson from Julian. I refused to turn myself over to you as slavishly as I did to him. I insisted on a prenuptial agreement. Actually, I thought I was being generous. I could have refused to give you any of the company. But ten percent wasn't enough, was it? You wanted more. You've always wanted more.''

She paused, feeling a twinge in her abdomen. *Calm down,* she ordered herself. *For the baby's sake, you must not get overwrought.*

''You know how much I loved you,'' she went on. ''I think you could have loved me, too. We are alike in so many ways. We could have shared a dream.''

''What d'ye mean, we could have? We do share a dream. And as for love, I'm trying. It doesn't come easily to me.''

''You loved my sister.''

''Yeah, well, I don't anymore. What happened between her and me is dead and gone.''

''As far as I'm concerned, what happened between you and me is dead and gone as well. The marriage is off. You can take the shares you've secured from Stannis and be damned. You'll never have more.''

He had been listening to her words through a fog of gin. She didn't seem to realize that he had been drinking. Why should she? He'd tucked the gin bottle into his jacket before letting her inside. She'd never seen him drunk before. It was a temptation he had always resisted—the hot, clear-colored evil that had destroyed his father.

''You can't call off the wedding. You're pregnant.''

"Do you honestly think that will stop me? I've been weathering gossip ever since the clay strike when I organized the Petticoat Brigade. I've never been overly concerned about the opinions of others. I don't need a husband to have a child. If I could survive without a mother, my child can damn well manage without a father."

"Yer child has a father, by God!" He was on his feet now. "Ye're not taking my son or daughter away from me."

"And you're not taking Cadmon Clay and Porcelain away from me, Daniel Carne!"

He moved suddenly, kicking aside the table between them. Things smashed onto the floor, some of them rolling, others, more brittle, breaking. Like everything in his life. Some rolled, some cracked, some shattered.

Verity backed away from him. Her hands had come up defensively. She reminded him of something. Someone. His mother, fending off his father. Tamara, doing the same.

"Daniel? Don't you dare lose your temper with me."

He grabbed her and jammed her into a chair. The suddenness of it made her bite her lip. She snatched the inkwell from the nearby desk and heaved it at his head. He ducked, but black liquid splattered on his hair, running down his face and neck to stain his shirt.

He raised his hand as if to strike her, but she bounced to her feet and scuttled away from him. He followed her, breathing hard.

It had always been there. Inside. Waiting. His father had warned him of it years ago. Back, back into former generations of Carnes it went. *My own father had this evil in him and his father before him. It goes back in our family, for generations, perhaps. Ye'd better pray to God it doesn't get 'ee, too.*

He knew how to do it. How to hurt her. He'd seen it many times. Jory with Mum. With Tamara. His body knew what to do. So did his hands. His palm would leave an angry imprint on the side of her face. She would cringe. Try, maybe, to run away. She wouldn't get far.

It was best to use the flat of the hand. Or the strap. Pa had used the strap, and most effective it was, too. He'd felt its lashing on his own body often enough to know its power as a destroyer of defiance, of will. Fists were too dangerous. You didn't do it to damage or cause pain—you did it to control her. She couldn't leave you then. She couldn't argue or deny you. She would hesitate to match her wits with yours if she was physically afraid.

That was how you broke her. With your hands. How else could you deal with a woman like Verity, so small, so fragile, so strong-willed?

"Keep away from me, Daniel." She had raised her chin—a gesture he used to see in Bret as well. The Trevor stubbornness, the Trevor defiance. He would beat it out of her the same way Pa used to do. Jory's rage was burning inside him along with Jory's gin.

"You will not do this to me," she was saying. "I will not tolerate it. Not again. It will not stand."

He continued to stalk her. She couldn't go much farther. Soon her shoulders would come up hard against the wall. He would have her. The Carnes and the Trevors had always hated and loved and destroyed one another. It was as inevitable as the wind, the snow.

"Julian attacked me once. In my rage and humiliation, I swore it would never happen again. Do you hear me? I sent him to France. I sent him to his death. Touch me and by God I'll do no less to you."

He stopped advancing to absorb what she had said. It reminded him of something else. He was not so drunk that he did not remember.

"And my father?" he asked.

She seemed confused. "What do you mean? I'm telling you about Julian, not your father."

"But he attacked 'ee too, didn't he? He and a couple of his mates? I heard they attacked 'ee on the same night Jory was killed."

"That's true, they did, but—"

"And ye would not tolerate it. It would not stand. So yer father, and Julian, yer lover, and maybe ye as well, sweet Verity, ye all got together and murdered him?"

She was pressing her hands to her belly. *The child*, he thought. He couldn't hurt her. She was carrying his child.

"Ye sent Jory to his death, didn't 'ee, Verity?"

"Certainly not."

"I've never wanted to think 'ee capable of such a thing, but hell, ye're a Trevor. The life of a Carne is nothing to 'ee."

Verity shook her head. Behind her she felt a solid wall. A cramp gripped her belly, frightening her. The baby. She and the baby were both cornered. *Break him*, Bret had said. Just as she'd feared, it was going the other way.

"Ye're right to cringe away from me. I was going to savage 'ee." His arms pressed the wall on either side of her, forming bars; his body was a scant few inches from hers. She had to tip her head back to see his face. "Rape 'ee maybe, too. He used to do that to her as well. That's how love was in our family—always a struggle. He used to wallop my jaw and say, 'I love 'ee, son,' while he was doing it. I got used to being smacked or kicked along with hearing I was loved."

"Daniel—"

"I was going to beat 'ee, but that's finished. It's time for a more absolute accounting. We'll go to the law, ye and me. We'll tell them the truth. Pa'll have justice at last."

"Your father had all the justice deserved on the night he died. But if you're implying that I killed him, or indeed that anybody did, you're crazier and more obsessed than I've ever realized."

One of his hands moved into her hair. He pulled, forcing her face up. "If ye didna' kill him, who did? Yer precious father? Yer saintly husband? They both had reasons for wanting him dead. But ye, my china queen, so hard and cold and brittle, ye had yer reason, too. Heaven forbid that any man should ever raise his hand to 'ee."

"Let go of me, you bastard."

"I suppose it could have been a woman that night. I've always called him the shadow man, but 'twas too dark to distinguish his sex."

"You couldn't identify him because he wasn't there!"

He shook her. She felt the jar of it throughout her body. "I want the truth, dammit. By God, I'll have it at last. He was a son of a bitch, there's no denying it. Maybe he did deserve to die. But he didn't deserve to be murdered. No one does."

Verity felt a piercing pain in her abdomen. Just this morning she had felt the child quicken within her. It had been a flutter, hardly noticeable, like a butterfly's wings. So tiny, her daughter or son. So much in need of her protection. Even more than the clay company or the china works, her baby was becoming the focus of her existence. There was nothing she wouldn't do to protect her child.

The pain came again, harder.

"You're the murderer," she gasped. Without thinking, she grabbed at him for support, clinging to his shoulders, so solid and so strong. "You're killing your child."

His face changed, looking confused, then uncertain as Verity keened in anguish. She felt a wetness there between her thighs. "Help me," she whispered, reaching out for him again. As Daniel lifted her she thrust her own hand under her skirts, in between her thighs. It came away wet with her blood.

A scream was wrenched from her, rising up from the deepest levels of her being. All her images were confused—the Fiery Furnace was finally exploding, but instead of flames it was spewing blood.

Chapter Sixty-one

"Dear God," Daniel whispered. He thought he was going crazy. An image burst into his mind as clearly as a nightmare—he was standing on a windswept moor watching as the Zephyr—with Verity aboard her—lumbered down the field. It was barely airborne when it exploded, raining debris everywhere.

Christ, what had he done? She was bleeding. She was going to die.

Still holding her small body in his arms, Daniel rushed to the telephone. It took him several minutes to discover that there was no doctor to be had. They were all out, attending patients in St. Austell and Trenwythan who were gravely ill with the blasted flu.

He snapped at the operator to connect him with Cadmon Hall. While waiting he came face-to-face with the man he had become. A wrecker. A destroyer. Not even Jory had stooped so low.

He looked down at her, not daring to meet her eyes. Her light-boned, slender body. Her soft, prim lips. The way the bottom of her knot of brown hair just brushed the soft place on the nape of her neck. Verity. Jesus God.

In a moment of perfect clarity Daniel knew his own heart: Tamara had been right. It was Verity he loved after all.

"Sweetheart, hang on," he whispered, folding his arms more tightly around her. He was shaking; he could barely breathe. He hated the way he was feeling—weak and panicky, at the mercy of his emotions, he who prided himself on his control.

When Bret came on the line, the sound of her voice struck not even the faintest chord of nostalgia in him. "Bret? Thank God. I need 'ee. And a doctor if ye can find one. If not, ye and yer nursing skills. 'Tes Verity. Come to Tam's. I'm taking her there. No. 'Tes the baby. She's losing it, I fear."

Outside, it was snowing. The whiteness was cold, blinding. The wind howled. White, white snow. Red, red blood. And the longest half-mile in England.

"Don't fret, love," he said to her over and over. "Ye'll make it, both of 'ee. Ye'll be fine. Ye'll be all right. Ah, God, lassie, don't turn yer face from me."

She made no answer. All she did was breathe too hard, and whimper now and then, softly as a ghost.

"Ye bastard! Ye're jist like Pa!" screamed Tamara.

"Shut up. Ye've been saying that all my life."

" 'Test true. More than ever now. Ye're drunk. Ye're violent. And ye've got a woman holding her pregnant belly and keening because ye've beaten her and killed her child."

"I didn't beat her, dammit. I never— Christ, Tam, tell me the child isn't dead. I'd never hurt her or the child."

Tamara had Verity flat on her back in bed now, with her knees up. She raised her skirts, stripped off her underthings. "Ye're scum, Daniel. All my life I've tried to prevent this. But ye're exactly like him. He killed his grandchild this way. My child. He knew I was in the family way, and he wasn't having it. Oh no, not his daughter. Not with his worst enemy. He'd rather have seen me dead."

"What the hell? What are 'ee saying, Tam?"

"Hold that cotton between her legs. That's it. Don't let go." His sister was throwing herbs and barks into a kettle as she spoke. She put it on the stove, then filled a mug with several foul-smelling herbal tinctures from her shelves. "Drink this," she said to Verity, holding it to her lips. "I know, 'tes vile, but drink it down."

"What're ye giving her?"

"Shut up, Daniel. Ye never knew it, did 'ee? Oh, ye knew he was thrashing me—ye'd seen that all yer life. And ye went on loving him, in spite of it. Ye chose not to see what was before yer eyes." She put her ear against Verity's belly, manipulating her gently.

"I was in love," she went on. "I was carrying my lover's babe. Wait, I'll hold the cloth. Stir the kettle. It's got to boil."

Daniel did as he was told. "I never knew ye lost a child, Tam."

"Ye never knew anything, ye great blind fool. 'Twas Henry's. Ye'd no idea in those days that I was yer famous enemy's lover, did 'ee? But Pa knew, and so did Verity. Even Bret knew, child though she was at the time. But not 'ee. Ye could never see the good in Henry, any more than ye could see the evil in Pa."

"Of course I saw the evil in him. I've tried to fight it in myself. But sometimes it just seems to rise up and take me over."

"That's no excuse. Ye're yerself, not Jory. Ye've the will to act, or not to act, on yer own."

He made an anguished sound.

"I acted." Tamara's voice was cold. "I acted and I've never regretted it. He brutalized me most of my life. He killed my child. He deserved to die."

"Oh, God, Tamara. What are ye saying?"

"I told 'ee over and over again that Henry Trevor had naught to do with Pa's death. No, nor Reverend Marrick, either. 'Twas me ye saw that night."

Verity cried out and raised her head. "Hush now," Tamara ordered. "Relax. The bleeding's letting up, I think, but ye've got to keep quiet."

"It's letting up?" said Daniel. "Ye mean the child's all right?"

"Don't start celebrating yet. 'Tes touch-and-go."

"Tamara, ye're not telling me ye had anything to do with Pa's death?"

"I'm telling 'ee I killed him. As good as, anyway."

Daniel and Verity both groaned.

" 'Twas me who threw that half-crown in the road. 'Twas his own hell-cursed money. He'd flung it at me an hour before when he'd burst into my cottage and found me in my bath. He saw my belly. I'd been hiding it from him. Hiding it from everybody. Not even Henry knew.

"He dragged me out of the tub and beat me brutally. He wanted me to lose the child. No daughter of his, he swore, was going to give birth to a Trevor bastard."

"Jesus!"

"He left me bleeding on the floor. He threw the half-crown at my feet. He shouted at me that I was a whore and the coin was my payment. A half-crown, say he, was all I was worth. Not even a Trevor would give me more.

"Afterwards, when it was over and my child was dead, I went after him. I took a carving knife, hiding it under my cloak. I was going to find him and kill him. I was going to stab him through that empty place in his chest where every other human being has a heart."

"Jesus Christ, Tamara."

"I took the coin. I don't know why. I found him in a pub. I waited in the shadows till he emerged, drunken, sick with it. I followed him up the road. Where it was darkest, I was going to do it. But then I heard the shouts, I heard the wagons. I threw the coin at him. I didn't know how it would happen until he stooped for it. Then I saw it, the way I see with the destiny cards. He was going to die, right there, that night, drunken on the highway. 'Twas was his fate.

"I swear he was glad to see the money. Now he could go back to the pub and drink it up. He didn't even hear the wagon till it was too late. He died scrambling in the dirt for silver, much more of a whore than I could ever be.

"There's the truth o' it at last. Here's yer murderer, Daniel. Ye still want revenge, ye'll have to direct yer hatred toward me."

Verity was weeping. Tamara fetched the hot herbal brew from the stove and poured it into her mug. "Drink this. 'Twill stop the contractions. It didn't work for me, but it'll work for 'ee."

"Are ye sure it'll work?" Daniel asked in a strangled voice.

"I've seen it in the cards. I've taken one life, but I've saved another. Does that satisfy yer yen for revenge?"

"Why didn't ye ever tell me, Tam? How could ye let this fester in silence?"

"Ye loved him. I was afraid ye'd turn on me." For the first time, her voice broke. "Ye're all the family I had left."

"Sweet God in heaven," Daniel said wearily. "I'm not yer judge. I've hounded the Trevors for years over this. I've based my actions on a lie, a failure of vision, a mistake."

"That was yer choice. No one asked 'ee to seek vengeance for Jory Carne."

Daniel leaned over and kissed Verity on the brow. Weeping still, she turned her face away. "Forgive me," he whispered. "I know ye can't, but I want 'ee to know I asked it, all the same."

He stepped away. "Daniel?" said Verity. Somewhere in the distance she heard a door slam. "Where is he, Tamara?"

"Lie back, Verity. He's gone."

The herbs must have had the power to make her sleep, because when Verity next opened her eyes, Bret was holding her hand. Simon was standing beside her. They both looked chilled and flushed from their late-night rush across the moors, and Simon, as usual, was coughing.

"My baby? Have I lost my baby?"

"No, Verity," Bret whispered. "Your baby's safe."

"And Daniel?"

Tamara placed something in her arms. Glancing down, she saw it was Guinivere, sweet as ever with her lovely porcelain face. She clutched her tight. "Where's Daniel?" she repeated.

Tamara shook her head. "Nobody knows."

Daniel wandered like a blasted soul across the moors, blind to his surroundings, impervious to the wind and the snow. *Verity*, he kept thinking. He wanted to howl her name aloud. *Verity*.

He saw her in the schoolyard, a frightened child, but honorable, and willing to fight for what she thought was right. What had he done to her then? Beaten her and thrown her to the ground.

He saw her as Julian Marrick's wife, hurrying about the village, comforting the sick and visiting the lonely. And later, as Marrick's widow, toiling in the clay-company office, her brow creased with worry as she calculated the accounts. How had he treated her during those years? Rudely and disrespectfully, losing no opportunity to mock and criticize her.

He saw her as his lover, rising to fling her arms around him whenever he came to her, her prim mouth made lovely by her welcoming smile, her eyes excited, her body eager. In bed she was always passionate and sweet, her love undampened by his stubborn refusal to show tenderness or affection. He'd used her as the receptacle of his lust, yet never had she berated him for his selfishness.

He saw her as the reluctant heroine of the Zephyr's successful flight, gamely climbing into a contraption that terrified her. He'd never stopped to think about the courage that must have demanded. Instead, he'd seen her triumph as a threat to his own rotten plans.

He saw her as the mother of his unborn child—her hope and delight when the conception was confirmed, her dreamy satisfaction as the life within her quickened and grew. She loved the child; she loved the father. How had he returned her love? With coldness, with deceit, and, finally this evening, with a viciousness that had nearly ripped their baby from her womb.

Yet, even so, she'd reached out to him. In pain, in terror, she'd turned to him for help, clinging to him, her nemesis, her tormentor. She had loved him, even then. For a little while, she'd loved him.

"Christ in heaven," Daniel whispered. His voice rose with the wind. "Verity!" he cried.

Until he reached the churchyard of St. Catherine's, Daniel had no idea where he was bound. Yet his destination had a certain logic. There, in the far corner, was the final resting place of his father.

He stumbled over to it. He stared at the mammoth headstone, a more elaborate monument than had ever before graced a Carne's grave. Daniel had erected it himself when he'd become a wealthy man.

He squatted down. From his jacket he took what was left of the bottle of gin. Uncorking it, he raised it in a mock salute. "Here's to 'ee, Jory Carne. May ye burn in hell."

Instead of drinking, he poured the liquor into the ground, blinking snowflakes from his eyelids as he watched it sink into the hungry earth of his father's grave.

Chapter Sixty-two

Verity woke the following night when the sky was still dark. She had been dreaming of Daniel. He came to her on the wind. She could not see him, but she knew him by his scent, the rhythms of his breathing, the spider touch of his fingertips upon her face. He spoke to her in whispers, no more distinct than the hissing of the wind through the moor grasses outside.

For he was the wind, as he had always been—he the wind and she the fire, his elemental nature fanning hers, expanding her, making her burn more intensely, making her hot all over, choking heat, stifling, stealing the air from her lungs and consuming it, making it impossible to breathe.

She arched to wakefulness, finding herself alone in the dark, trapped in a woollen blanket that had cocooned around her while she thrashed in sleep. Part of it was covering her face, creating the sensation of breathlessness. She freed herself and sat up, feeling the chill of perspiration that blossomed along her hands, her throat, her thighs, her spine.

Her stomach lurched, cramping up, and she thought, *Oh no, it's happening again*. Weak and dizzy, she crept from bed and stumbled to the toilet. She expected another violent eruption from her womb, but, thank God, she passed no blood. After shivering for several minutes in the dark she rose and tried to gather herself together. She wet a sponge and pressed it to her face and neck. She felt shaky, weak, and very close to tears.

Conscious of her need to protect the baby, to stay off her feet, she returned to bed and lay down. As she tried to draw a calming breath, a pain arrowed through her chest. Her heart fluttered and flexed, her pulse hammered in her ears. The ache went deep, so deep. It wasn't a pain, exactly. It was an emptiness.

Ah, Daniel. He was broken, all right. As was she.

Forgive me. I know ye can't, but I want 'ee to know I asked it, all the same.

She could, perhaps, forgive him. But how could she ever marry a man who was capable of doing to her what Julian had done?

"I loved you so," she whispered into the darkness. "With my body, I thee worship . . . ah, Daniel, you were everything to me."

Verity began to cry. Great, loud, racking sobs that escalated in their violence. For far too long, her tears had been contained.

She was drained of emotion and limp with weariness when Bret came to her and stroked her forehead. When Verity made no resistance, she lay down beside her. "I heard you from my bedroom," she said gently, smoothing Verity's wet hair away from her face. "I would have come in sooner, but I thought perhaps you needed the release."

Verity reached for a handkerchief to wipe her face. "You were right. I feel a little better now."

"Let me stay with you awhile."

"Thanks." Verity sniffled back the last of her tears. "It reminds me of the way I used to come to you when you woke up crying in the night. I used to rock you and cuddle you until you fell asleep."

"I think I remember. I used to love having you with me."

"Do you remember our baby bird?"

Bret shook her head. "I don't think so."

"You were very young. No more than three or four. You discovered a blue jay that had fallen from its nest and demanded that we care for it until it was ready to fly."

"Really? What made you think of that?"

"I'm not sure," Verity said, lost in the memory. "It wasn't a very attractive bird—more gray than blue, with a stubby tail and little wings that were more quill than feather. You suggested that we make a nest for it. I didn't think the two adult jays who were perched overhead would care for a nestling that had been touched by human hands, but you insisted that the bird parents would continue to love their child. I wasn't as sanguine about that as you were. I had very little evidence in those days, you see, that my own father loved me."

Bret rubbed her shoulders soothingly.

"But you turned out to be right. We made a nest out of a basket and put it up as high as we could reach, and the adult jays began flying in with food in their beaks.

"One morning Papa came into the garden, asking what the bloody hell we were doing haunting the place. You ran to the nest to show him . . . and started screaming."

"Was it dead?" Bret asked.

"Not quite. It was lying on its side. The light had gone from its eye, and when I desperately tried to stand it upright, it was too weak even to flinch from my touch."

"What went wrong?"

"I never knew. There were no signs of wounds or injury.

It had been hopping about, trying to learn to fly. I've no idea what went wrong," she said, her voice cracking.

"Verity—"

"I'm all right. Let me finish. The nestling had always regarded me with fear and suspicion, no matter how hard I tried to show my love. Now, though, it stared straight at me, unafraid. There was something ancient and timeless in that look of resignation, an odd sort of meeting of spirits between a witless bird and young human, in the face of death. A few moments later the tiny quilled body swelled once more, and shuddered, and went still.

"You were sobbing, but all I could feel was the swift, fierce anger that I usually reserved for larger, more important events. I was scanning the branches above for the two parent jays, but they were gone. Once they'd determined that their child was dying, they'd abandoned it. You and I were more that bird's parents than they were.

"I hated them, and when Papa went blithely off to his aeroplanes, unaffected by this insignificant little death, I hated him as well."

"Verity—"

"He was never there when I needed him. He tried harder with you. I used to be wretchedly jealous of the things he did with you, the way you laughed together, your interest in his wretched aeroplanes. I railed against the injustice that dictated that I should grow up with a father who didn't care that I existed, while you had all his love."

"But, Verity, that's not true. Of course he loved you. How can you think that he—"

"He rarely showed it, which is almost as bad as not feeling it," she cut in. "He was different with you. This is horrible to say, but if he had neglected you, you and I would have had so much more in common, and I wouldn't have continued to feel so alone."

Wordlessly, Bret stretched out her arms. Verity moved closer, unable to resist her sister's natural warmth and sympathy. She herself had never been so quick to embrace people. A vestige of her old shyness, she supposed.

"I wasn't even very nice to him toward the end. The clay company meant so much to me—it's the only thing I've ever felt competent doing—and he was wrecking it the same way he'd wrecked everything else. I let him know, by the way I treated him, that I held him responsible for everything that had gone wrong with my life.''

"But he wasn't responsible," Bret said. "Not entirely, anyway. He made mistakes. But he tried his best.''

"I know," Verity said reluctantly. "I realized that in London when I saw how crazy everybody went over the flight of the Zephyr. He had a rare and original talent, one for which the human race will, someday, be grateful. I never understood that before. I was too wrapped up in my selfish concerns.''

Bret hugged her harder.

"I would like to have been reconciled with him before his death. Now it's too late.'' Verity's voice trembled as she added, "The thing is, he was very important to me. I wanted so much to please him, to make him proud of me. But I—I never told him that I loved him. There was silence between us at the end." She was sobbing again. "I never cried for him, you see. When he died, I couldn't cry.''

"Ah, Verity." She felt cool lips brush her forehead, along with a tiny drop of moisture from her sister's eyes. "He knew you loved him. He loved you, too.''

Verity shook her head. "I don't think so. Nothing ever comes out right for me. I feel so empty, so cut off from love." She shuddered as long-forgotten images from her childhood came back to her—Mum and Grandpa, who had died; Miss Lynchpole, who had hated her. "Sometimes I think God's punishing me.''

"Well, I don't know if I believe in God anymore, but I do know this—no one is ever cut off from love. It's around us, everywhere. There's always enough love.''

"I wish I could believe that. But all I see is darkness, everywhere. It was in Papa and Julian; it's in Daniel, and sometimes I think it's blackest right here in my own heart.''

Bret pressed her palms to her sister's belly. "Even here, Verity? There's no darkness here. What's here is life. Hope. Regeneration.''

"Maybe not. Maybe my child will grow up like his father. Bitter, angry, and hungry for revenge.''

"Daniel wants to see you, Verity. He was here today, asking for you. He seems different. Changed."

Verity was shaking her head. "I won't see him. I can't."

"He's done some terrible things, but he's not beyond redemption. No one is. He loves you, Verity. Don't give up on him."

"It's not just me. I have a child to protect."

"He didn't actually hurt you, right? He didn't do what his father did?"

"No. But it's in him. How can I ever feel safe with him again?"

"Maybe love has nothing to do with feeling safe."

Verity sighed. "Last night at Tamara's it all seemed so fragile. Life, I mean. People do the vilest things to one another. There's so much rage and violence. There's never enough love."

"Oh no." Bret's voice was strong, earnest. "There's always enough love. All you need do is strip your flesh and bare your bones and offer your beating heart to the gods."

Verity smiled and hugged her. "I love you, Bret."

"I love you the best," her little sister said.

Chapter Sixty-three

As soon as he felt the pain radiating from the back of his head down into his shoulders, Simon knew it was the flu. There were chills and sharp, random pains in his muscles. There was weakness, and an alarming increase in the mucus in his throat.

He didn't tell Bret. She had not wanted him to accompany her the other night when she'd rushed to Tamara's. "It's bone-chilling outside; you'll get sick," she'd warned him, but he'd insisted on going along, and now he felt like a guilty child whose mother's direct warnings had proved right.

As his headache escalated, he ordered himself not to panic. The sickness couldn't be as bad as everybody was saying. According to the newspaper, its effects were idiosyncratic—it had killed a substantial number of strong, healthy people, yet spared some of the weakest and oldest. Maybe he'd be one of the lucky ones.

On the other hand . . . *A year. Or maybe not so long.* Lately he'd been hoping for better. He'd felt so much healthier since he and Bret had been together. He'd half-convinced himself that Arthur Cowan must have been wrong. He wasn't a lung specialist, and anyway, no one really knew the long-term effects of mustard gas on the respiratory system. No one could say, definitively, what his fate would be. In spite of the cough that continued to plague him, especially at night when the fluids tended to accumulate in his lungs, he had succeeded in pushing death back to the edges of his consciousness again . . . something to be faced one day, but not now, not soon.

He wasn't ready, dammit, for this perception to change.

But at bedtime, aching and feverish, he held back from taking his lover into his arms. "I have a bit of a cold," he confessed. He coughed. The spasm went on and on, exhausting him.

"Your cough sounds different," Bret said, placing her hand on his forehead. "Simon, you're hot."

He pulled away from her. "I'm all right."

"Please, get into bed. If it's the flu—"

"It's not the flu," he insisted. "I'm just a bit tired. I'll be fine in the morning."

But he woke the next day, groggy and hot, to the sensation of Bret's sticking a thermometer into his mouth. He tried to spit it out, grousing that just because she'd been a VAD didn't mean she was going to start doctoring to him like some bloody quack know-it-all.

"Keep it under your tongue and stop trying to convince me you're not sick." Her voice was shaking, and when he shot a look at her, she averted her eyes.

More coughing. It arched him off the bed and brought a nauseating rolling to his belly. "At least it's a change from the days when I used to try to convince you I *was* sick," he said when she removed the glassy instrument from his mouth. "Well?" he said as she squinted at the mercury. Her eyebrows had drawn together, etching a furrow in her brow. "How high is it?"

"Not too high." Without showing it to him, she shook the thermometer down. "Close your eyes and rest."

Because he was able to read every mood, interpret every expression that moved across her lovely face, Simon knew she was lying. And that she was scared. He was tempted to challenge her, to insist on knowing what his temperature was, but instead he subsided, turning his face into the pillow so she wouldn't see the tears that had sprung into his eyes.

I will recover, he said to himself, over and over. *I will recover. I will.*

"It's 104," she whispered to Verity, who met her in the hallway outside the bedroom she had been sharing with Simon. She had in her hands a washcloth and a bowl of tepid water to bathe his body in an attempt to reduce the fever. She had given him aspirin, but so far it hadn't had any effect. "Oh, Verity, I've seen this before. I'm sure it's the flu. Have you rung Arthur Cowan?"

"Yes. He'll be here as soon as he can."

"I'm so frightened. What if he dies?"

Bret felt her sister's hands on her shoulders, gently massaging the tight muscles there. She reached out a hand to touch her. *I love you, Verity. Please take care of me.*

"We could send for Tamara as well," Verity suggested. "She saved my baby. Maybe she can save Simon."

"Oh yes, please, let's have her in."

By the time Arthur Cowan arrived and confirmed that Simon had influenza, Bret's anger had outpaced her fear. "I'm so bloody tired of this!" she exploded to the young physician. "Will it never end, these bedside whispers, this vigilance, this matching wits with Death? How can each successive year be darker and more morbid than the last?"

"If we can get the fever down and keep his lungs relatively clear, he might have a chance," Cowan said. "But—" He shook his head morosely. "I wouldn't hold out too much hope if I were you."

"Don't tell me not to hope. I've worked in hospitals. I've seen plenty of doctors make mistakes. You're not infallible, goddammit!"

Cowan said nothing, and within moments Bret was ashamed. "I'm sorry, Arthur." She ran her sweat-slickened fingers through her hair, leaving it wild. "I'm not myself. As for you, you look tired. Would you like a cup of tea?"

"Can't. I've got more than a dozen other calls to make. I lost two patients yesterday to this wretched sickness, a husband and wife, dying within minutes of each other. It's like a plague, a modern Black Death."

Bret shuddered. "It's not that bad, surely."

"No," he admitted. "Most people do recover. But most of my patients start out with healthy lungs."

"I'm not letting him die. I'm trained as a nurse. I'll use all my knowledge, all my experience to wrestle the Grim Reaper back into the shadows where he belongs."

Cowan smiled. "I'd back you against death any day, Nurse Trevor."

With the help of Tamara and Verity, Bret launched a massive assault on Simon's influenza. She never left his bedside, tirelessly sponging his body and forcing him to sip water every few minutes, which both Arthur Cowan and Tamara agreed was a necessary treatment for high fever. When he coughed, which was frequently, she boosted him up in her arms to help dislodge the phlegm. She gave him oxygen to aid in his breathing, aspirin to reduce the pain and inflammation. Tamara was treating him with herbal teas that she said would loosen his mucus and allow him to cough it out. It seemed to be helping, but it also seemed that there was no end to the heavy, viscous matter that coated the inside of his bronchial tubes and lungs.

"Let's try an onion plaster," Tamara ordered that evening when the color of the phlegm had changed to the evil-smelling greenish yellow that confirmed that pneumonia had set in. " 'Twill reduce the congestion and draw out the fluids. Tell your cook to slice 'em thin and heat 'em in butter, then bring the mess here to me."

Verity hurried to assemble the ingredients while Bret remained at her lover's side. Tamara's expression, she noted, was grim, and she was afraid to ask her what she might have seen in the destiny cards. "Keep giving him drops from those tinctures I brought. Try to get them well under his tongue."

Bret complied, asking, "What's in the tinctures?"

"Various things. Some of the herbs are to make him sweat and others specifically for treating respiratory troubles—lungwort, comfrey, mullein, lobelia, goldenseal, slippery elm, coltsfoot. There's some valerian, too, to quiet his spasms and make him more comfortable."

"Will they work?"

"He's pretty bad, lass."

"Dammit, Tamara! I *won't* let him die."

" 'Tesn't up to 'ee. 'Tes up to the Goddess, and Simon himself."

Simon did everything he could to pilot himself through the illness. Feeling the fever burning him, he focused inward, imagining cool streams, spring rains, wet falls of snow. He resisted the coughing, knowing how badly the spasms weakened him, trying to expend as little energy as possible, to keep something in reserve. The worst thing was the constant feeling of suffocation—he could never get enough air, and it was that more than anything that brought him to the edge of panic.

Courage, he told himself. Using every pleasant memory he could dredge up from his life—most of them concerning himself and Bret—he blacked out his fear. He let it thunder over him. *The panic will dissipate*, he told himself. *Don't hold on to it. Let it pass through me. It will be gone and I will remain.*

For three days he managed his emotions far better than he would have expected, concentrating on fighting, floating, and hanging on. But on the fourth day, something changed. He dreamed he was reaching out toward a shimmering spider's web of the palest, purest gold. As he touched it, the gossamer filaments faded to gray, then dissolved into empty air. He felt tears sliding down his cheeks. He heard whispers—persistent high fever, pneumonia, pulmonary insufficiency, edema. Tamara Carne shaking her head, Arthur Cowan averting his eyes from Bret's, Bret weeping.

He knew he was finished. Used up. Done. The door to nowhere that had opened briefly in the aftermath of his plane crash was opening again, and this time there was no alternative but to walk through.

Dreaming still, he could see himself, as if from above— the tears shining on his hollow cheekbones, the wreck of his body, the fragility of his bones. His arms and legs had swollen as his lungs' ability to clear the waste products from his body had failed. He didn't look like himself anymore. He looked like an elderly man in the twilight of his life.

But I'm only twenty-two years old!

Courage. *If it be now, 'tis not to come; if it be not to come, it will be now; if it be not now, yet it will come. The readiness is all.*

"I love you," Bret whispered. She was clutching his hand. The room echoed with the sound of his ragged breathing. The uneven nature of it frightened her—its very loudness made her aware of how silent the room would seem when the breathing stopped.

He groaned softly. Bret squeezed his hand. Over the years there had been so many occasions when his fingers had gripped hers; now he was incapable of exerting even the slightest pressure.

She had seen the coming of death too often not to recognize the signs. She told herself that she ought to be able to endure the impending loss with serenity because she, like so many others of her generation, had been forced at a young age to confront the ending and dissolution of life. And yet, this wasn't some stranger, some soldier, some baby blue jay. This was Simon. Her friend. Her lover. The man who was to have been her husband, the father of her children.

Her mind was a garden of flowers, each of them representing a special memory. Sitting there beside him, listening to him labor for breath, she found herself running among the blossoms again, snatching at memories, trying to gather and hold them all in her hands, feeling frantic as they slipped, too early wilted, to the ground.

"Oh, Simon," she whispered, unable to contain her tears. "Don't leave me. Stay, and we'll have a lovely long life together, my darling. Please don't go."

But his breathing was uneven, his heartbeat thin, his swollen extremities already cold. They had no future. And as she clung to him, a terror came over her that she was about to lose their past as well. When the people you loved died, they were truly gone. Without their voices in your ear and their touch upon your skin, they faded, no matter how desperately you tried to preserve them. They moved farther and farther away from you, vanishing like rainbows, fading until there was only the barest trace of color in the sky.

She thought of Francis MacDonald, who had almost been her lover, gone as if he had never existed. Her own mother, Caroline, who had died at her birth. Her father, who had ridden the rainbows, punched holes in the clouds. From their flesh her own flesh had been created; now they were ashes and dust. With Simon as her husband, she would have seeded the earth with the next generation, brought forth new life. But even that was denied to him.

He stirred.

"There's a change coming," Bret heard Tamara say.

"What do you mean? A change for the better?" Even as she said it, she knew it was impossible. "He's dying, isn't he?" It was odd how she'd abrogated her own medical knowledge to Tamara's. Where Simon was concerned she could not be objective.

"I fear so, lass."

He stirred again. "Bret?" The sound was barely a whisper. He could no longer get enough air to animate his voice.

"I'm here." She clutched his fingers, which returned a faint pressure. His lips moved again, but Bret couldn't make out what he was saying. "I can't hear you." She bent over, her ear to his lips. "I'm listening, my darling. Please try and get well."

"Love you," he whispered.

"Oh, Simon, I love you too."

He coughed, but his whisper emerged from the spasm, articulate and clear. "When I was up there, in the cockpit, alone in the cold rush of the wind, I used to hold the image of your face, your eyes, your bright hair in front of me. I used to feel you with me, my guardian angel.''

Her throat was burning. She was haunted by the guilt of knowing that she hadn't given him the full measure of what he had deserved from her. Always between them had been the shadow of another man.

''Other pilots didn't make it. They exploded or crashed in flames. But you were there, with me, keeping me safe. Always.'' More coughing. ''You were there.''

I wasn't there, she thought miserably. *I was with Daniel, or Zach.* ''I'm here now,'' she managed. ''I'm here.''

''I thought—'' coughing, then the dry whisper again, ''flying would change me somehow. Make me braver, more gallant, more romantic. Make you love me.''

She leaned over and kissed his throat. ''I do love you. Please hang on.''

''I had to fly the Zephyr for you. It was what I had to do. That, and make love to you. That was for me.''

''No, darling. That was for both of us.''

He was quiet for several seconds. She could sense him moving away from her. She squeezed his fingers harder, as if to hold him back.

''Bret? When I'm dead, I want you to go to him.''

Hot tears spilled down her cheeks. ''Oh, Simon, I'm so sorry. For every moment I've made you unhappy, for every second I've caused you to doubt—''

''No, hush, don't apologize. It was perfect. You were perfect. The best days of my life have been the last few weeks. There's nothing to feel sorry for, nothing to regret.''

''You've always been more generous to me than I deserve.''

He smiled. ''I love you. But you and Zach were meant for each other. I've always known that. It's right that I should pass out of this world, and that you and he should be together.''

''Oh no, Simon, don't say that!''

''Kiss me again. I'm very tired, my love. Kiss me goodnight.''

Weeping, she touched her lips to his, feeling the warmth that lingered there, the sweetness. Smoothing his blond hair back from his brow, she allowed her fingers to linger on his forehead, caressing him. Despite the ravages of his injuries, his face was still handsome. There ought to have been many women in love with him. Yet he had dedicated himself to her. *How lucky I've been*, she thought, smiling through her tears, *to have known so fine a gift*.

"Bret?" His voice was paper-thin; his eyes were closing. "Are you there?"

"Yes. I'm here, beside you. Always."

"Hold my hand."

"I am. I will. No matter what happens, I'll never let you go."

With what little remained of his strength, Simon squeezed her fingers. She was still his joy. If he had done nothing else in his life at least he had loved this sunny, funny, lovely woman. Who mustn't be left alone.

She wouldn't be. She would go to Arizona, as she had always longed to do. Love and death—the ageless circle. The love that is like dying, the death that drives lovers into each other's arms.

He could see her, and strangely he could also see her path stretching out before her. They were side by side, he and Bret. Looking back, he saw two trails extending behind them, close together. Her path stretched on ahead, as far as the eye could see. It arched over water, meandered through woodlands, wandered through arid lands where the earth was as fiercely red as the setting sun. It went on and on, and other paths branched off from it.

His own path ended here.

The iron pain inside him mounted, spreading throughout his body, crushing him, beating him down into the earth, which was open, waiting to receive him. The earth would not be denied.

"Please," Bret was imploring Tamara. "Isn't there anything more we can do?"

"I'm tryin', lass."

Simon tried too. He focused his will upon his body. But that once-familiar mass of bone and flesh and tissue felt foreign to him. He didn't want to slip back into his fleshly envelope, which was as hot and suffocating as the interior of a smithy's stall.

"It's not fair," she was saying. "I don't understand the purpose of this. I don't know what lesson I'm meant to learn."

Oh, Bret. You do understand. I was meant to love you; I was meant to release you.

He could see his body now, pale and bony and breathing with such pathetic difficulty. His eyes were shut, his face a mask. His sweetheart was leaning over him, watching closely for the slightest sign of consciousness, unaware that he was here, beside her.

There was no time left for sorrow, or even for fear. There was time only to say goodbye. He reached out and touched a lock of her soft auburn hair. Silk. How strange that something that looked so rich and vibrant should be so baby-soft. He remembered caressing that softness, stroking it with his fingers, kissing it with his lips.

I loved you, Bret Trevor. You brought me great joy.

He was going. He didn't know where. Into the earth, he supposed. He gave Bret a jaunty wave, wishing she could see it, wishing she could know that he wasn't afraid, that in giving her up, in setting her free, he felt like a hero at last.

They tried to get her out of the room, but she would not leave him. They didn't seem to understand that it was not madness that inspired her to stay beside him, holding his hand. "I promised," she said. "No matter what happens, I told him, I wouldn't let go."

"Bret." Her sister's voice was gentle. "Bret, he's dead."

"I know." Of course she knew that. Stupid, stupid, that they should think she didn't know death when she touched it, looked upon it. She was a VAD. She had been intimate with death.

"Do you want to sit with him awhile?"

"Yes. Leave us alone. Please. I'm all right."

They left her. They shut the door. The room was silent but for the beating of one heart, the breathing of one pair of lungs.

She was sitting beside him on the wide bed. They had been lovers here. Tenderly, with infinite care, he had wooed her, come inside her. Their joining had truly been an act of love.

Soon they would put him in the ground.

As she had performed the actions of a nurse for him while yet he lived, she was resolved to perform the last necessities as well. She would not have some stranger touching him.

She closed his eyes. She bathed his body. She arranged him in a serene and dignified position and folded his arms across his chest. Around the topmost wrist she wound a bright lock of her hair, clipped from the right side, near her ear, the place he'd loved to stroke and caress. Then she wrapped him, gently, in his winding sheet.

Before covering his face, she kissed him. Through the shroud she touched his wrist, her hair. Now and forever, melded to his bone.

Hold my hand.

I am. I will. No matter what happens, I'll never let you go.

Chapter Sixty-four

In late April 1919, Verity was sorting out some old file cabinets in the clay-company office, trying to decide what to move to Charlestown and what to leave behind. She went through the entire room, emptying drawers and shelves, throwing into the rubbish bin vast numbers of papers that no longer had any significance.

She was shifting the official center of her operations from the claypits to the china factory. In reality she had made this shift months ago, but it hadn't been formalized until now. It was something she needed to do before the baby arrived. Part of the nesting instinct, perhaps—she had to make a secure place for herself.

The china works was booming. The fine porcelain she

had presented at the London trade show in December had proved extremely popular, and, with the help of Bret, Gil, Tamara, and Annie, she was manufacturing several new lines as well. Her china was selling so briskly that she could envision a day when all the clay produced by Cadmon Clay would go straight into Cadmon Porcelain, freeing her of the necessity to sell kaolin to anyone but herself. *From pit to pot.* Such had been her grandfather's dream, and she had accomplished it.

Verity stretched, rubbing her aching back. Her baby would be born in less than two months. After that one horrible scare, the child had hung on firmly, growing, kicking, getting fat.

She left the cleaning of the old Chinese desk until last. The movers were coming tomorrow to transport it down to her office in Charlestown, where she had long needed a larger desk.

One by one she emptied out the drawers, scouring away decades of dust and grime. She'd come to the last drawer on the right, and was scrubbing the inside of it, when she scraped her hand on a tiny protrusion of metal somewhere toward the rear. Imagining it to be a loose nail, she attempted to pry it out. As she tugged, the metal moved stiffly, causing a creaking on the other side of the desk. A dark oblong opened underneath the desktop to the left of her legs.

A secret compartment. Verity felt a child's excitement as she reached inside. What would she find? Money? Old love letters from an earlier generation?

At first she felt nothing but cobwebs and dust. Reaching farther back, her fingers encountered the corner of a box. It was jammed well in. Not until she used a screwdriver was she able to remove it.

The box was not locked. Whoever had put it there must have believed that the secret compartment was security enough. Opening it, she found a collection of crackling yellow papers, dating from several decades ago.

They proved to be business papers of various sorts, pertaining to the tin mining her family had been involved in before the crash of the metals markets in the middle of the last century. Dry, boring stuff. Tenant leases. A bill of sale for a beam engine. A deed of ownership for one of the mines.

A bill of sale for a portion of land. Several of the papers were in a handwriting she recognized as belonging to her grandfather Rufus Trevor.

She was about to put them all back into the box and add it to the glut of historical papers that she supposed some future family historian might be interested in reviewing when something jogged her brain. She was a child again, standing helplessly by the bedside of her dying grandfather. "*Get me the box,*" he'd said.

"*What box, Grandpa?*"

"*From my desk. Hidden. Underneath.*"

"*I'll get it, Grandpa. I'll go downstairs to the library and—*"

"*No, no. Cadmon Clay. In my desk. Chinese.*"

Goose bumps were chasing along the surface of Verity's skin. Rufus Trevor hadn't been talking about his desk in the library at Cadmon Hall, but his desk in the office of Cadmon Clay. His Chinese desk.

She picked up the last document she had glanced at. Unfolding it, she read more carefully. Handwritten, it dated from well before the age of typewriters. The script was ornate and difficult to read, and the ink was faded. But she was able to decipher it:

> I, Amos Trevor, in the year of our Lord 1747, do accept from my partner Mr. Jason Carne, the sum of £300 in payment for the stretch of land on the north side of the estate boundaries extending from the beacon hill down along the stream to the west, which shall be the new border of the Cadmon estates, to the limestone quarry inclusive on the east, which marks the present boundary. All grazing, mineral, and water rights thereupon shall henceforth belong to Mr. Jason Carne and his heirs in perpetuity.

It was signed by Amos Trevor, one of her ancestors, as well as by the said Jason Carne, an ancestor of Daniel's.

Verity envisioned the land involved. It covered the entire area that had been developed by the Trevors for Cadmon Clay.

Injustice.

"Oh my God," she whispered.

From this had come endless heartbreak.

From this, ambition, hatred, resentment, envy, and wrath.

She had not seen Daniel since that dreadful winter's night four months ago. He had tried to reach her, dropping by and ringing, but she had not trusted herself to speak to him. She had expected the bitterness—and the fear—to remain with her forever.

So she was surprised to discover, as she stared at the brittle piece of paper, that it took her no time at all to decide, irrevocably, what she was going to do.

The following day, Verity rose, dressed carefully, and drove to Carne Clay. She asked to see Daniel and was admitted to his office. He started when she entered; color washing into his cheeks, then fading, leaving his face pale and drawn. "Verity? What're ye doing here? Are ye all right? Is all well with the child?"

"Yes. But I've found something that belongs to you."

She handed him the document, and had the satisfaction, if such it was, of seeing him nonplussed. He read it through, shook his head, and read it again. Then he lifted his head and searched her face. "Where did you get this?"

She explained how it had come into her hands.

"Why didn't ye destroy it?"

"An injustice was clearly done. I could not compound it."

"So he was right. Jesus, Jory was right all along."

"Yes. But my father knew nothing of it. The box I found it in was encased in dust and hadn't been disturbed for decades."

"Someone knew about it. Someone—a Trevor—hid it in a deliberate attempt to defraud the Carnes."

Someone, yes. Grandpa. Who had boasted to her that all the land in the area, as far as the eye could see, had once belonged to the Trevors. Rufus, who could have been well contented living in an earlier age, a great feudal landlord. The Clay King, mighty and strong, whom Verity had so adored. He'd known about the paper. He'd colluded with some earlier Trevor to keep it hidden. In the end, he'd tried to put things right, but it had been too late.

"Ye thievin', cheatin' bastard," Jory Carne had said, as he'd spat into her grandfather's dead face.

She told Daniel what had happened. How Rufus had implored her not to allow him to die with this sin upon his soul. "I was a child. I tried my best to do what he'd asked. I felt I'd failed him, and in a way, I was right." She paused, drawing a deep breath. "I'm not going to fail him again. Cadmon Clay is yours. All I ask is that you leave me the china factory, which does not lie upon this land. If other documents need to be signed between us to verify this transaction, bring them to me and I will gladly so do."

"Jesus, Verity. Is that all ye can say?"

"What else is there? You were right to hate us. I'm trying to make amends."

He looked at her for a long time. At last he said, "Why? You love Cadmon Clay. Why this gift?"

"I've told you—"

"This will ruin 'ee. Not only Cadmon Clay, but yer china company as well. Ye need the clay to produce the china."

I must leave, she thought. *I must escape before I break down*. "Ruin me was exactly what you always said you would do. For the forbearance you've shown so far, I'm grateful. You gave me the time to pay back Papa's loan. You refused to take the collateral. Your generosity is now to be repaid."

He got up and came around the desk. She backed away, but there was nowhere to go. The office was too small. "Verity. It wasn't generosity. 'Tes true that for a long time, Cadmon Clay, aye, Cadmon Hall, was all I wanted. But no more. Stop backing away from me. I'm not going to hurt 'ee. Dear God, woman, what I'd give to see ye look at me without that fear shining in yer eyes."

"Daniel, I'd better go."

"Wait. I'll tell 'ee what I want now. What I dream about all day, and torment myself with at night." He stopped a scant few inches from her. "I want 'ee back, Verity."

The child rolled in her womb. "You must be out of your mind."

"Ye've no reason to trust me, I know that. I'm sure ye hate me; I know ye're afraid of me. The worst of it is, ye're completely justified. I wish I could argue that the evil ye see in me isn't really there. But we both know it is. Still, I swear on all that's holy that I'm doing my damnedest to root it out.''

''My first husband regretted his evil, too. He prayed on his knees for God to lift its oppression from his soul. But my life with him was hell.''

''I'm no good with theology, but I'm prepared to do more than just pray. I'm prepared to love 'ee, Verity. And to love the child we created together.''

''But maybe love *isn't* enough,'' she said, thinking of Bret.

''It's something,'' he said, a half-smile on his face. ''Listen to me. I used to think the earth was all that was solid, all that could be relied upon. It was here before we humans were created, and it'll remain when our line is less substantial than dust. Ye couldn't trust people, I believed. All ye could trust was the land.

''But the truth is, I've always been able to trust 'ee, Verity. Ever since ye stood up in a hostile classroom and took more of a beating than ye truly deserved. Why? As a matter of principle. Ye showed those same principles when ye paid the women of the strikers' families to do the work they needed to keep their families eating. In business, yer dealings have always been honest and fair. And today, giving me this document, when ye had every reason to destroy it, ye've proved yer mettle again. It was my father who taught me that people couldn't be trusted. Well, fuck him, he was wrong.''

''Maybe I can believe that you trust me, Daniel. But what reason can you give me for trusting you? You could be saying these things to seduce me again, as you so skillfully did once before. You could still be desperate to get your hands on my home and my wealth and my property. Or to ensure legitimacy for your child.''

He shook his head slowly. ''I can't blame ye for thinking that. But ye know what I remember most? That night when I was stalking 'ee, shouting at 'ee, terrorizing 'ee, yer pains started coming and ye *held on to me*. I was out of my head with drink and with rage, and ye knew it. Ye clung to me anyway. 'Help me,' ye said. Ye knew, better than I did, that I wouldn't hurt 'ee. Deep inside, ye trusted me.''

She wanted to turn away. She wished she could laugh derisively, fling his words back in his face. But there was something in his eyes she had never seen before—a trace of moisture. As she watched, transfixed, a tear pulled loose and trickled down his cheek.

He held up the document. "Look, I've got the thing I wanted most, don't I? Cadmon Clay."

She nodded.

"Well, here's how the new Daniel views that triumph." He ripped the paper in half. He balled up the pieces and crushed them in his big hand. Opening the grate of the cast-iron stove in the corner, he thrust what was left of the ancient document inside. They both heard the puff as the flames engulfed it.

"To the devil with Cadmon Clay."

Verity sat down weakly, her arms crossed over her stomach. Beneath the drumskin tightness of her skin, a joyous wave broke. At its heart, love was a mystery. *Behold, thou art fair, my love; comfort me with apples, for I am sick of love.*

"Give me a chance. I swear I'll change."

"I'm not sure people can change."

"I'm not sure they can either. But I've always fancied a challenge. I'm still young and I'm bloody determined. If anybody can change, by Christ, 'twill be me."

Tentatively, she reached to him her hand. He brought it to his lips. A moment later, she was in his arms.

What true love has torn asunder, only true love can heal.

The night was glorious, the black silk of the sky spangled with stars and the air sharp with the stiff sea smells that were blowing inland from St. Austell Bay. Once free of the stableyard and the grounds, Bret let the darkness take her and sweep her clean. The magnificent animal she was riding seemed to share her desire to be lifted on the wind and race with the stars. Together they hurtled through the night without caring where they fetched up. Bret tossed her head until her hair was flowing along her cheeks and throat and shoulders. She could feel her thighs surge with the power of the steaming beast between them.

"Oh, Wulf, isn't it wonderful?" she whispered as the ca-

ress of the wind loosened her, body and soul. All her senses were alive. She could smell the mixed scents of wild grasses and flowers, coal smoke thickened with chalky kaolin dust, the salt tang of the sea. "What a lovely night to be riding free!"

The moors and the skytips were but a memory.

The beast she was riding tonight was the sea.

Bret leaned against the rail, inhaling the warm night air and marveling at the similarity between the gently rolling seas and undulating slopes of her homeland. The stars were spangles of light tossed against a black silk background, and the sky stretched out as far as she could see.

"Dear Mr. Slayton," she said aloud. "You said I shouldn't give up on love. You said it would endure. I have to trust to that. I *am* trusting to it. I know you'll be there and that you'll welcome me.

"I don't come alone, my darling. Another man might balk at what I bring you. But you loved him, too. You'll love his son or daughter, I'm sure."

She touched her swollen belly as she had so often seen her sister do. "Look, my heart. Toward the west. That's where we're headed. That's where my lover is. My future. My art. In Arizona.

"Here we come, world. *Watch out.*"

Author's Note

Many people have helped me during the course of the writing of this novel, and I wish to express my appreciation toward them all.

In England, I owe special thanks to the many people of St. Austell, Cornwall, who welcomed me during my visit there and helped me with my research. In particular I wish to thank the staff of the St. Austell Library, who patiently answered my questions and directed me to the necessary books and papers; the Wheal Martyn clayworks and museum, and the people at English China Clays. I hope you will all pardon the occasional license I have taken with history and geography for the sake of my fiction. For example, to my knowledge, there was no china manufacturing factory in the area during World War I, nor was there an ancestral manor house on the grand scale of Cadmon Hall. The village of Trenwythan does not and never did exist, although its features represent an amalgam of several real villages in the St. Austell area.

In this country my enduring gratitude goes to Jeanne Bracken and the rest of the staff at the Acton Memorial Library in Acton, Massachusetts, who are always willing to assist in my research.

I owe a special debt to the following friends who read the manuscript in its various incarnations and offered me their wit and wisdom:

Susan Elizabeth Phillips—for getting me started and keeping me on course.

Carla Neggers—for always being there when I needed support, whether literary, professional, or moral.

William G. Tapply—for his patience, his discerning eye, and his many excellent suggestions.

Mark Roegner—for his interest and his enduring friendship.

Steven Axelrod—for proving in countless ways that he is a very special and remarkable agent.

Thanks also to my editor, Jeanne Tiedge, for her enthusiasm, her hard work, and her helpful recommendations.

And finally, my love and gratitude to my family, especially my husband Haluk and our daughter Dilek, for their tolerance and love; my parents, Babs and Bob Barlow, for their support; and my sister, Heather Sheldon, whose courage in recent years has been such an inspiration to me.

I love you all.